DEAD

Laurell K. Hamilton is the b_____ __ita Blake, Vampire Hunter, Novels, as w_____ __es near St Louis with her husband, her dau_____, ___ ____ and an ever-fluctuating number of fish. She invites you to visit her website at www.laurellkhamilton.org.

Reviews for the Anita Blake, Vampire Hunter, Novels

'What *The Da Vinci Code* did for the religious thriller, the Anita Blake series has done for the vampire novel'   *USA Today*

'Wildly popular'   *Entertainment Weekly*

'Hamilton's complex, enthralling world is utterly absorbing'   *Booklist*

'A hardcore guilty pleasure'   *The Times*

'Laurell K. Hamilton is the reigning queen of the urban fantasy world'
                                                  Midwest Book Review

'Always very, very sexy and exciting'   *Dreamwatch*

'This fast-paced, tough-edged supernatural thriller is mesmerizing reading indeed'   *Locus*

'The action never stops'   *New York Review of Science Fiction*

'Supernatural bad guys beware, night-prowling Anita Blake is savvy, sassy and tough'   P N Elrod

'I was enth_____ ___ire ale . . .'
                                                  Andre Norton

'A real rush . . . a heady mix of romance and horror'   Jayne Ann Krentz

Anita Blake, Vampire Hunter, Novels available from Headline

GUILTY PLEASURES

THE LAUGHING CORPSE

CIRCUS OF THE DAMNED

THE LUNATIC CAFE

BLOODY BONES

THE KILLING DANCE

BURNT OFFERINGS

BLUE MOON

OBSIDIAN BUTTERFLY

NARCISSUS IN CHAINS

CERULEAN SINS

INCUBUS DREAMS

MICAH and STRANGE CANDY

DANSE MACABRE

THE HARLEQUIN

BLOOD NOIR

SKIN TRADE

FLIRT

BULLET

HIT LIST

KISS THE DEAD

AFFLICTION

JASON

DEAD ICE

eSpecials

BEAUTY

DANCING

LAURELL K. HAMILTON

DEAD ICE

An Anita Blake,
Vampire Hunter, Novel

headline

First published in the United States of America in 2015 by
BERKLEY
An imprint of Penguin Random House LLC

First published in Great Britain in 2015 by
HEADLINE PUBLISHING GROUP

First published in paperback in 2015 by
HEADLINE PUBLISHING GROUP

1

Cataloguing in Publication Data is available from the British Library

ISBN 978 0 7553 8908 7

Printed and bound in Great Britain by
Clays Ltd, St Ives plc

HEADLINE PUBLISHING GROUP
An Hachette UK Company
Carmelite House
50 Victoria Embankment
London EC4Y 0DZ

www.headline.co.uk
www.hachette.co.uk

*I could not be with someone who did not understand my darkness
as deeply as they understand my light,
for one without the other is only half of me,
and if you love me, love all of me, or love me not at all.*

*To Jonathon, my husband,
who loves all of me, as I love all of him.*

*To Genevieve, our lady love, and her husband, Spike,
two other walkers in the darkness of the light,
who have joined us on this journey
to find ourselves and each other.*

Acknowledgments

To Shawn, who has been a constant in my life, as I have been in his—friendship forged in fire, loss, and laughter. To Jessica, who taught me competency is a superpower! Will, who helps with research, and answers odd questions without thinking them odd. They saw a book from inception to completion for the first time. Welcome to the literary salt mines. Sherry who feels she has allies at last in the battle to organize a house full of artists. Mary, my mother-in-law, whom we love. To the Word Posse—my writers group's new venture. I hope it makes all your dreams come true! And last, but not least, to Sasquatch, who sits by my side as I write, and has sat with me through many a long night for fourteen years. To Keiko and Mordor, who have been sitting at my side for only a couple of years, new furry muses to help me write.

Thanks to Peter Orca for the title *Dead Ice*, and to Isis Maria Hess for naming the jewelry store creating Anita and Jean-Claude's rings: Étoile du Soir, or "Evening Star."

And for Susan Allison, my editor for over a decade. She was able to retire early and I'm happy for her, but sad that this is the last book she will be ferrying through for me. Enjoy the horses, dog(s), your husband, and yourself, as you embark on the next great adventure.

1

"SO, YOU'RE ENGAGED," Special Agent Brenda Manning said. She wore a black pantsuit with a heavy belt that could wrap around her waist and hold the gun at her side. She was FBI and didn't have to worry about concealed carry, so the fact that her gun flashed when her suit jacket flared out, which was every time she moved, wasn't an issue. The gun looked very stark against her white button-down shirt.

"Yep," I said. My own gun was at the small of my back, underneath a suit jacket made to hide the gun from the clients at my other job. I'd also started getting belt loops added to my skirts so I could wear a belt that could stand up to the weight of a gun and holster. I'd come straight from Animators Inc., where the motto was "Where the Living Raise the Dead for a Killing." Bert, our business manager, didn't believe in hiding the fact that raising the dead was a rare talent, and you paid for talent. But lately my job as a U.S. Marshal for the Preternatural Branch had been taking more and more of my time. Like today.

The other very special agent, Mark Brent, tall, thin, and looking barely old enough to be out of college, was bent over the portable computer they'd brought with them, which was sitting on the room's only desk. He was dressed in a suit almost identical to Manning's except his was brown to match his holster, but his gun was still a black bump, stark against his white shirt. We were in the office of our head honcho, Lieutenant Rudolph Storr. Dolph was currently somewhere else, which left me alone with the FBI and Sergeant Zerbrowski. I wasn't sure which was more dangerous to my peace of mind, but I knew Zerbrowski would mouth off more. He was my partner, my friend; he was entitled. I'd just met Special Agent Manning, and I didn't owe her my life story.

"The article I read made the proposal sound amazing, like something out of a fairy tale," Manning said. She smoothed her shoulder-length hair back behind one ear and it stayed put, because it was straight as a board. My own curls would never have behaved that well.

I fought the urge to sigh. If you're a cop and a woman, never date a celebrity; it ruins your reputation for being a hardass. I was a U.S. Marshal, but ever since we'd gone public with our engagement I'd become Jean-Claude's fiancée, not Marshal Blake, to most of the women I met, and a lot of the men. I'd really had hopes that the FBI would be above such things in the middle of crime-fighting, but apparently not.

The real problem for me was that the story we told publicly was both true and a lie. Jean-Claude had done the big gesture, but only after he'd proposed in the middle of shower sex. It had been spontaneous and wonderful and messy, and very real. I'd said yes, which had surprised him, and me. I'd figured I just wasn't the marrying kind of girl. He'd told me then that we'd need to do something to live up to his reputation for the media and the other vampires. They expected their king/president to have a certain flair, and the real proposal was too mundane. I hadn't understood that flair would include a horse-drawn carriage—yeah, you heard me; he'd actually picked me up in a freaking horse-drawn carriage. If I hadn't already said yes, and loved him to pieces, I'd have told him not only no, but hell no. Only true love had gotten me to play along with a proposal so grand that trying to imagine a wedding that topped it sort of scared me.

"Oh, yeah, Anita is all into that princess stuff, aren't you, Anita?" Zerbrowski called from the chair he was half-tipping against the wall. He looked like he'd slept in his suit, complete with a stain on his crooked tie. I knew he'd left his home freshly washed and tidy, but he was like Pig-Pen from the *Peanuts* comic: Dirt and mess just seemed to be attracted to him within minutes of his walking out of his house. His salt-and-pepper hair was getting more salt and less pepper, and had grown out enough to be all messy curls, which he kept running his hands through. Only his silver-framed glasses were clean, square and gleaming around his brown eyes.

"Yeah, I'm all about that princess shit, Zerbrowski," I said.

Agent Manning frowned at both of us. "I'm getting the idea that I stepped in something. I was just trying to be friendly."

"No, you were wanting the princess to talk about how wonderful the prince is, and how he swept her off her feet," Zerbrowski said, "but Anita is going to disappoint you like she's disappointed the last dozen women to ask questions about the big romantic gesture."

I wanted to say, it wasn't a big romantic gesture, it was a freaking epic romantic gesture and I had hated it. Jean-Claude had loved being able to finally pull out all the stops and just do what, apparently, he'd wanted to do for years while we dated—the whole princely sweep-you-off-your-feet shit. I liked to keep my feet firmly on the ground unless sex was involved, and you can't really have sex in a horse-drawn carriage; it scares the horses. No, we didn't try, because we were on freaking camera the whole time. Apparently, there are now engagement coordinators just like there are wedding coordinators, so of course we had a videographer. It had been all I could do to keep from scowling through all of it, so I'd smiled for the camera so I wouldn't hurt Jean-Claude's feelings, but it's not my real smile, and my eyes in a few frames have that "wait until we're alone, mister, we are so talking about this" look.

I decided to appeal to Manning's sisterhood of the badge and said, "Sorry, Agent Manning, but ever since the story went live I'm getting treated more like Jean-Claude's girlfriend than a marshal, and it's really beginning to bug me."

Her face went serious. "I'm sorry, I hadn't thought about it like that. Years of being one of the guys and building your rep, and I ask you about your engagement first thing."

"I've never seen my partner be so girly about anything as meeting you today, Marshal Blake," Brent said as he unbent from hunching over the computer. He smiled and it made him look even younger. He seemed fresh-faced and less jaded than the rest of us. Ah, to be bright and shiny again, when you thought you could actually win the fight against evil.

Manning looked embarrassed, which isn't something you see often in FBI agents, especially not when you've just met them.

"Knock it off, Brent," she said.

He grinned at all of us. "It's just that we've worked together for two years, and I've never seen you squee over anything."

"It's the horse-drawn carriage," Zerbrowski said. "Chicks dig that kind of shit."

"Not this chick," I said, quietly under my breath.

"What did you say?" Manning asked.

"Nothing. Is the video ready, Agent Brent?" I asked, hopeful we could actually do our jobs and leave my personal life out of it.

"Yes," he said, but then his smile faded around the edges, and I saw the beginnings of the bright and shiny rubbing off. "Though after you see it we may all be game to talk about carriages and pretty, pretty princesses."

It was another first, an FBI agent admitting that something bothered him. For them to admit it out loud, it had to be bad. I suddenly didn't want to see it. I didn't want to add another nightmare to the visuals I had in my head. I was a legal vampire executioner and raised zombies as my psychic talent; I had plenty of scary shit in my head and I so didn't need more, but I stayed in my chair. If Manning and Brent were tough enough to watch it multiple times, I could sit through it once. I couldn't let the other badges think that getting proposed to by the vampire of my dreams made me one bit less tough. I couldn't let myself believe it, either, though a part of me did. How could someone who let a man lead her into a Cinderella carriage carry a gun and execute bad guys? It made even my head hurt, thinking about it.

Zerbrowski said what I was thinking. "I thought the Feds never admitted anything bothered them."

Agent Brent shook his head and looked tired. Lines showed around his eyes that I hadn't seen before and made me add between three to five years onto his age. "I've worked in law enforcement for six years. I'd thought I'd seen it all, until this."

I did the math in my head and realized he had to be around thirty, the same as me, but I'd used up my shininess years ago.

"I thought this was just another big bad preternatural citizen gone wrong," I said.

"Not exactly," he said.

"I don't like mysteries, Agent Brent. I'm only here on this little information out of courtesy to the FBI, and because Lieutenant Storr requested it."

"We appreciate that, Marshal, and we wouldn't have had you walk into this blind if we didn't feel that the fewer people who know the details, the better off we're going to be," Brent said.

"Awesome," I said, "but the foreplay is getting a little tiresome; there's no one in the room but the four of us, so what is on the video?"

"Are you always this cranky?" Manning asked.

Zerbrowski laughed out loud and didn't even try to hold it in. "Oh, Agent Manning, this isn't even close to cranky for my partner."

"We heard that about her, and you're right, Blake. I did come in here expecting the proposal to have softened that reputation. I didn't think I had that much girl left in me, and if I'm assuming that it softened you up, then your male colleagues must be making your life . . . difficult."

It was my turn to laugh. "That's one way of putting it, but honestly it's the whole engaged-to-a-vampire thing that's making some of my fellow officers doubt whose side I'm on."

"Vampires are legal citizens now, with all the rights that entails," she said.

"Legally, yeah, but prejudice doesn't go away just because a law changes."

"You're right about that," she said. "In fact, some at the bureau thought we shouldn't include you in this case because of your proclivity to date the preternatural."

"Proclivity, that's polite; so what made you decide to trust me?"

"You still have the highest kill count of any vampire executioner in the United States, and only Denis-Luc St. John has more rogue lycanthrope kills than you."

"He raises Troll-Hounds; they're the only breed of dog ever raised specifically to hunt supernatural prey. It makes him the king of tracking through wilderness areas, after shapeshifters."

"Are you implying that the dogs make him better at the job, or that he's somehow cheating by using them?" she asked.

I shrugged. "Neither, just a statement of fact."

"Now that Anita has passed muster, and I'm included because I'm her friend, show us some skin, agents, or stop teasing," Zerbrowski said.

"Oh, you'll see skin," Brent said, and he looked older again, as if this case in particular were rubbing the shine away.

"What the hell is on the video, Agent Brent?" I asked.

"Zombie porn," Brent said, and hit the arrow in the middle of the screen.

2

"SORRY, AGENTS, BUT that's not new. It's sick, but it's not new."

Brent hit the screen and froze the dark cemetery scene in midmotion. It was shaky and dark, and there were no zombies or anyone else in sight yet. The two agents looked at me as if I'd said something bad.

"Did we pick the wrong animator?" Manning asked her partner.

"Maybe," he said.

"I've been approached for years to help people make sex tapes with zombies. Dead celebrities bring out the creeps the most." I shivered, because the whole thought of it was just so wrong.

"My favorite of your sickos like that are the ones who want you to raise their high school crush," Zerbrowski said.

"Yeah, now that they have money and success they want one more go at the girl who rejected them in high school, or college." I shook my head.

"That's sick, as in seek-a-therapist sick," Manning said.

"Agreed, and I honestly think they don't really believe it's going to be a zombie. Somewhere in their minds they think she'll rise from the grave and they'll be able to prove they're worthy and live happily ever after."

"Wow, Anita, that's a romantic take on the sick bastards that just want to boff the girl that rejected them in high school." Zerbrowski actually looked surprised.

I shrugged, fought off a scowl, and finally said, "Yeah, yeah, one epic proposal and I go all girly on you."

"Boff," Agent Brent said. "I didn't know people used that word anymore."

"You young whippersnappers just don't know a good piece of slang when you hear it," Zerbrowski said.

"Don't listen to him, he's not that old. His hair just went all salt-and-pepper early."

"It's the last couple of cases, they scared me so bad my hair went white." He delivered it without a grin, deadpan, which he never did. If they'd known him, they would have understood he was lying, but they didn't know him.

"Hair doesn't actually do that from fear," Brent said, but not like he completely believed it.

Manning looked at me and raised an eyebrow.

I waved her back to Zerbrowski. "It's his story, not mine."

Zerbrowski grinned at me, and then at the agents. "Just trying to lighten the mood. That's part of my charm."

"It is actually," I said, smiling back at him.

"The sergeant is here because he's your partner when you work with the Regional Preternatural Investigation Squad. Everybody calls it the Regional Preternatural Investigation Team, but officially it's not," Manning said.

"It's the nickname," I said. "They call us RIPIT, both for the Rest in Peace, and because most of the crimes are violent, things get ripped apart. Other cops and even the media have used RIPIT for so long that people want the *T* in the actual name of the squad."

"Are we letting ourselves get sidetracked on purpose?" Brent asked.

Manning nodded and sipped her coffee. "I think we are, so back on target. One of the reasons that we're talking to you is that you have more official complaints turned in to the police than any other anima-tor about illegal or morally questionable zombie-raising requests. Once you had a badge of your own and were officially an officer, too, the complaints went down. I'm assuming that people didn't want to bring their illegal activities to a U.S. Marshal."

"You'd be surprised how many people think that just because I raise the dead I have to be evil, with a capital *E*, but yeah, the requests for zombie one-nighters and zombie sex slaves went down once I could do my own arresting."

"Disturbance of a corpse was a misdemeanor for years," Manning said.

"That's one of the reasons that there are tapes of this shit out there, because even if they were caught it was a slap on the wrist. The money they could make from the tape, because it was a tape back when it started, was worth the risk even if they were caught," I said.

"The penalties are stiffer now, but still not the same as if a real human was involved," she said.

I shrugged. "I don't make the laws, just help enforce them."

"You have done your best to enforce the laws as written, and suggested changes in the laws based on your experience, which is one of the reasons we picked you to bring into our little problem," Manning said.

"We all know it's out there, Agent, so what's the big secret? All the other zombie porn has been either people in good makeup, with no real zombies involved, or one of the zombies that's been raised for fieldwork in California or in other countries. The zombies in those films are little better than actual corpses."

"These are different," Manning said.

"Show us," I said, and tacked on, "please." I added the "please" because what I really wanted to say was either *You're being all wimpy for FBI,* or something more sarcastic. I'd been a little grumpy lately, even for me, so I was trying to monitor myself and only aim the grumpiness at bad guys.

Brent hit the screen again and the shaky camerawork continued to be shaky so that you could see it was a cemetery at night, but that was about it. It was like the opening to an amateur horror flick where someone had gotten a new camera for Christmas, and then it steadied.

I wondered if someone new was holding the camera, or if the holder had just gotten a handle on it. The answer to that question was the difference between one bad guy or two.

There was a very abrupt jump in the film from empty cemetery to a blond-haired woman clawing her way out of the grave. At first I thought it was an actress who had been buried in soft earth up to about her armpits, but then the camera got a close-up of the eyes, and I knew dead when I saw it. The zombie crawled out of the grave the way I'd seen thousands do before. It had some issues with the skirt of the dress it had been buried in, and the clinging grave dirt, which happened sometimes, and then it stumbled free, standing crooked because one high heel had apparently gotten left in the grave.

The body was tall, statuesque, with blond hair to her shoulders. Cleavage showed at the plunging neckline of the white dress, which meant the breasts had probably been implants; real breast tissue wasn't going to be that perky without a woman fluffing them back in place, and the zombie didn't know enough to do that. The small spotlight or whatever was attached to the handheld camera showed us the hair was blond, the eyes a pale gray that might have been bluer when she was alive. Blue mingled with any color from gray to green or even hazel tended to shift with a person's moods more than most eye colors. Alive, she'd probably been beautiful, but there wasn't enough home for that now. So much of a person's attractiveness is their spirit, their personality. Zombies didn't have much of that.

The next scene, if that's what you wanted to call it, was of the zombie in a standard bedroom except there were no visible windows in the room, and there was just something off about it. I wasn't sure why I didn't like the room, but I didn't. The zombie was wearing the same clothes as in the cemetery; they hadn't cleaned her up at all, so that she looked horror-movie wrong in the bedroom with its flowered bedspread and tile floor. That was part of the wrong; no one put tile in their bedroom. They did another zooming close-up of the zombie's eyes, and this time they weren't empty. This time they were terrified.

"Fuck," I said softly, but with real feeling.

"You see it, too, then," Manning said.

"Yeah, I see it."

Zerbrowski said, "Why do the eyes look scared? Zombies don't feel fear, right?"

"Normally, no," I said.

Zerbrowski got up from his chair and moved over closer to where the rest of us were sitting. "Why do the eyes look like that, then?"

"We don't know," Manning said. "What you're about to see is impossible, according to our own experts."

My skin was already running cold, my stomach tight, because I was very afraid that I knew exactly what the "impossible" was going to be.

A man in one of those all-leather masks where only the eyes and mouth showed walked into sight. The zombie's eyes followed the movement, but the rest of her stood immobile, probably because she'd been told to stand there, and until told otherwise she had to stand just there, but they hadn't told her not to move her eyes, so she followed the man's movements like a human victim who had been tied up. She was tied up, tighter than any rope or chain could ever make her. Fuck, I did not want this little film to go where it was headed. I prayed silently, *please, God, don't let them be able to do this to her*. God answers all prayers, but sometimes the answer is no.

The man slipped his hand inside her dress and began to fondle her breast. The camera caught the flinching in her eyes—she so didn't want him to do it, but nothing except her eyes was able to say no.

"Did they give her a sedative that keeps her immobile?" Zerbrowski asked.

"They didn't need to," Manning said. "There's no doubt that she's a zombie, so she follows their orders. Notice she never breathes. A live human being needs to breathe, and she never does in this one."

"Does she breathe in later films?" I asked.

"She talks, and you have to take air in to do that, but other than that, no."

The man was wearing a pair of silk boxers with hearts on them, like a parody of dressing up for a romantic evening, except for the mask, which didn't match the almost silly-looking shorts. Yes, I was concentrating on details that might help me find any clue to finding out who or where this was, but I was already trying to concentrate on the details that wouldn't haunt me as much. The silly heart shorts were almost a kindness, a break in the horror, like whoever was picking out the costumes had goofed.

I missed the heart-covered shorts when he stripped them off, because then I had to concentrate on his body, looking for birthmarks, or tattoos, or anything that made him not generic guy in a mask. I didn't want to look at his body, didn't want to search every inch of it for identifying marks. I wanted to look away, but if the woman in the film had to endure it, because that's what the eyes meant, then I wouldn't look away. I would not flinch and miss some visual that might lead us to these bastards—though part of me knew that if just watching the films would lead anywhere, the FBI would have found it by now. But I watched it anyway, because most cops believe that they will see something that everyone else has missed; it's the hope that keeps us all putting on the badge and gun every morning. When that hope runs out we find different jobs.

A man off camera told her to lie on the bed and she did it instantly, even while her eyes showed just how much she didn't want to do it. The naked man in front of the camera slid her panties down those long legs that were still covered in grave dirt, the one high heel still on. Someone had painted her toenails a soft pink, as if it still mattered with closed-toe shoes and a corpse. I expected more of her clothes to come off, but the naked man just climbed on top of her with no preliminaries, except to move her dress a little out of the way.

Zerbrowski breathed out, "Jesus," behind me.

I didn't look at him, I didn't look at anybody, and none of us looked at each other, because when watching this kind of shit, no one wants eye contact. You don't want the other officers to know you're afraid, or too emotional, and if anything this awful excites you, don't share that either. None of the other cops want to know.

The only plus was that the camera had moved back enough to catch the sex, so we couldn't see her eyes. She just lay there like the corpse she almost was, and that was the only tiny saving grace. He ended by taking his dick out of her body and doing the obligatory porn movie end to show that he'd actually gone.

The film ended there, and I felt my gut loosen a little. I'd watched it all; bully for me. Bully for us all.

"The production value goes up as the films progress," Brent said.

I turned and looked at him. "What do you mean?"

"The almost joke-worthy boxers go away, the camerawork gets better, and they put more personal touches around the bedroom to make it look less like a set and more real," he said.

"Is it always the same guy onstage?" Zerbrowski asked.

"For most of the films, but there's a second, younger-looking guy featured in the last two," Brent said.

"How many films are there?" I asked.

"More than I want to sit through again," Manning said.

I looked at her and saw a terrible tiredness in her eyes, as if just watching the one film had aged her. She shook her head. "Play the next one, Brent; let's just get this over with."

I didn't tell her she didn't have to watch them again; I let her handle her own shit. To do anything else would have been a breach of the "guy code" that all police work revolved around. The sex of the police officer didn't change the code. I only broke it with friends, or when I couldn't help myself, like Manning had when she asked about my engagement. That seemed like a long time ago, and Brent was right; pretty, pretty princess talk was looking a whole lot better.

3

THE FILMS WERE relentless. They eventually got her out of her burial clothes. We saw the zombie naked, in lingerie inexpertly put on her, so that I was pretty sure there was no woman on their crew. It was the fourth film where the zombie looked more rotted, which is something that happens to zombies eventually, no matter how good they look at the beginning. Zombies rot; it's one of the things that set them apart from ghouls, or vampires. Not all corpses are created equal.

I waited for the rot to spread, but it didn't. It just stayed with one eye filmy white, while the other was still clear and grayish-blue. Her skin had taken on a bluish tinge, and the cheeks had begun to collapse inward; the breasts were only perky because the implants held them up, but her body looked different naked now, more skeletal, but that was it. There were no other changes; the rot just stopped in midprocess, and her eyes were still full of terror. Sometimes they let her talk and she begged them not to make her do this, or that, but she seemed unable to disobey that male voice just off camera. I was betting it was the animator who had raised her from the grave. At first I'd thought the animator had raised her, taken his money, and fled, but now I knew he had to be nearby, because the rot had started and then stopped; for that you needed voodoo of the blackest kind.

"Well," Zerbrowski said, "I'll give the sleazebag props for stamina, but it's a shame that abuse of a corpse isn't a capital crime."

Brent paused the images; I think any excuse at this point to take a breather sounded good to all of us. "We thought they were just changing clothes on her to make it look like time was passing, too, at first," Brent said, "but notice the calendar on the wall."

"It's not just there to make it look more homey?" Zerbrowski asked. He made little air quotes around *homey*.

"Nobody puts a calendar in their bedroom unless it's the only space they have to live in," I said.

"Exactly," Manning said. "Did you notice?"

I thought for a second. "The month changed."

"Zombies rot, always; that's the rule that Anita taught me. It can't be a month later."

She nodded. "It's not proof that much time actually passed, but we think it may be their way of showing clients that they've done something unique."

"Her soul is back in her eyes, that wasn't unique enough?" I asked, and my voice didn't sound neutral the way I tried to sound this early in an investigation. I wasn't sure I was going to be able to pull off neutral with this case; sometimes you can't.

"You saw it," Manning said.

"We both saw it," Zerbrowski said.

"Would you have said her soul was back in her eyes, Sergeant?"

"I'm not that poetic."

Manning looked at me. "I don't think Marshal Blake was being poetic."

Zerbrowski looked from her to me. "I think I'm missing something."

"Don't feel bad," Brent said. "It took us weeks to figure it out."

"Figure out what?" he asked.

"Were you being poetic, Marshal Blake?" Manning asked.

"No."

"Enlighten us," she said, and there was something in the way she said it that I didn't like. It was just an undercurrent, but if I had to bet, I think something I'd said, or done, while we watched the films had made her suspicious of me. I wondered, if it hadn't been a male voice ordering the zombie around, would they have looked at me as a suspect from the beginning? I hoped not, but a lot of people still saw my psychic ability as evil. Hell, the Catholic Church had excommunicated us all unless we gave up raising the dead, because only Jesus was allowed to do that. Biblical scholars had pointed out that four of his disciples had done it, too, but the Pope, at the time, had found comparing zombie-raising pagans to the disciples of Jesus Christ less than amusing.

"Her soul, her personality, whatever you want to call it, seems to be in the body, except you can't raise a zombie from the grave if the soul is still in residence," I said.

"So how do you explain it?" she asked.

"She was just a walking corpse in the first film. Her eyes were empty, she was an it, but between that and the first sex tape, that changed."

"How?" Manning asked.

"You've got witches and psychics on the payroll at the FBI now. You even have at least one animator. What'd they come up with?"

"Nothing," she said.

Brent added, "They all saw what you see, that she was in there somehow, but no one had a clue how it was accomplished."

"Do you know how it was done?" Manning asked.

I nodded. "I've seen it done once."

"Give us a name and we may have our guy," Brent said, all eager for a clue.

"It was a woman, and she's dead." I added, "I believe she's dead."

"Give us a name, we're good at finding people," Manning said.

"Dominga Salvador; she was the most powerful vaudun priestess in the Midwest."

"She went missing just after she challenged you."

I raised eyebrows at Manning. "Challenged me? You mean sent killer zombies into my apartment to kill me? If that's your definition of *challenge*, then okay."

"Some of the local law enforcement officers thought you'd killed her in self-defense."

"The local LEOs didn't trust me as much before I had a badge."

"I trusted you," Zerbrowski said.

I smiled at him. "You liked me; I don't know if you trusted me."

He grinned and seemed to think about it. "I can't remember for sure, but I know that long before you got your own badge you proved anything you needed to prove to me."

"Aw shucks, Zerbrowski, you're going to make a girl blush."

He grinned wider and offered me his fist. I bumped it gently.

"Nice distraction there, Sergeant," Manning said.

"I don't know what you mean, Agent," he said.

Her lips curled down in a face that said, clearly, she knew that he knew exactly what he'd done. "It's going to take more than that to distract me."

"And that's the truth," Brent said. His partner gave him an unfriendly look and he held his hands out empty, as if to say he didn't mean any harm.

"Why do you think Dominga Salvador is dead?" Manning asked.

"Because I'm alive, and once a person like the Señora wants you dead she doesn't give up."

"How do you think she died?"

I tried to appear nonchalant and was glad that I did better blank cop face than I had years ago when I'd known Dominga Salvador, because I was about to tell a very big lie to the FBI. "I have no idea." I could feel my pulse speed in my throat; if I'd been on a polygraph I'd have failed.

Manning studied my face like she'd memorize the number of eyelashes I had. I stayed blank and slightly smiling, and felt my eyes dead and empty as last year's New Year's resolutions. I wanted to look away from her so badly it almost hurt, but I didn't. I knew exactly how Dominga Salvador had died, because I had killed her.

4

I DIDN'T FEEL bad about the death, because she'd been trying to force me to murder someone else as a human sacrifice at the time, but it was still technically murder. She'd also been the first person I ever killed with zombies that I'd raised from the grave, which was still an automatic death sentence. It fell under the magical malfeasance laws; any practitioner of psychic or supernatural gifts who used such as a method of murder, or violence outside self-defense parameters, was subject to the strictest enforcement of the laws therein. Strictest enforcement was execution, which is pretty damned strict.

It helped me meet Manning's eyes and control everything but my pulse. I even got a handle on that by thinking about quieting my breathing for shooting accuracy. Calm your breathing, and your heartbeat has to follow, eventually, and with that, your pulse will slow, eventually.

"My grandmother would have said butter wouldn't melt in your mouth, Marshal."

"I've never understood that saying; I mean, I know it implies you think I'm lying, but why would butter not melt in someone's mouth, and what has that got to do with being truthful?"

Manning frowned at me.

"I think it implies you're cold-blooded, or something," Brent said.

We all looked at him.

He had the grace to look embarrassed. "Blake asked, and my gran used to say it, too."

"Just stop talking," Manning said.

He made the little push-away gesture again. "I'm done talking, except we're here to get Blake's help, and accusing her of murder probably isn't the way to get her to share information with us."

"Why are you still talking?"

"Because I'm your partner, and I would do damn near anything to catch these bastards. I thought you felt the same."

Manning looked away first. "Would you really let a murder go?"

"I read up on Dominga Salvador, and she had the idea to turn zombies into sex slaves first. She just didn't live long enough to do it."

"We only have Blake's word for the Señora's plans," Manning said.

"Are you really accusing Marshal Blake of murder after coming to us for help?" Zerbrowski asked, and there was no joking in his tone now.

Manning rubbed her temples and shook her head. "I don't know, yes, no, not really. Do I think that Blake killed her? Probably, but if someone sent a pack of killer zombies into my home to attack me . . . we're allowed to defend ourselves from the monsters."

She looked at me and her eyes weren't just tired; they were haunted. "You haven't seen all the videos. They raise two other women and they let them rot more than this before they put their souls back into their bodies. There's a video of the moment that the second woman sees herself in the mirror. Half her face is rotted away, but she can still scream." She covered her own face with her hands and made a sound that was half exasperated sound, half muffled words.

"Sorry, Agent Manning, didn't quite catch that," Zerbrowski said.

She lowered her hands and looked at him. "I said I've heard a lot of bad screams. An amazing number of these . . . evil bastards make video or audio of their victims. I thought I'd heard the worst screams, but that one was one of the worst things I've ever heard." She turned to me. "If I thought you had done this I'd put the needle in you myself, but I'm just groping in the dark, Blake."

"What do you want from me, Manning?"

"The report you gave when you helped get a warrant to search Salvador's house talked about human sacrifice and mentioned her scheme to use zombies as sex slaves, but I feel like you left out things, because if you overexplain the magic theory too much most judges won't sign off on things. What did you leave out? How are they doing this? One of the last zombies seems to rot, then stop, and then rot worse; why?"

"You think I know all this because I reported Salvador for abuse and malfeasance years ago?"

"That and our new agent Larry Kirkland says that if anyone knows how this is being done, it would be you. He says you're the most powerful animator he's ever met, and that you may know more about the undead than anyone alive today."

"I bet that's not how he said the last part," I said.

She fidgeted in her chair. "I'm trying to keep it friendly after I had my little meltdown, Marshal Blake."

"What did Agent Kirkland actually say?"

"Anita," Zerbrowski said.

I looked at him.

"Let it go; Larry complimented your abilities, just let it go."

I didn't want to, because I was betting Larry had said something that implied my expertise came from being way more friendly with the undead than his God-fearing faith would allow him to be. Once Larry and I had been friends, hell, I'd trained him to raise the dead, but we'd stopped being friends when I stopped taking the morgue kills he felt morally bad about. Morgue executions were vampires chained to reinforced metal gurneys, holy objects all around, and the only legally accepted method of execution was a stake through the heart, then decapitation in most states. Have you ever tried to pound a hardened wooden stake through a piece of bone-in ham? Try it sometime; it's not easy. Now imagine the "pig" is still alive and begging for its life. I'd had far too many morgue kills where they pressured me into killing the vamp after dark when it was awake, so that they didn't have to risk it breaking free before dawn and hurting more people. Ah, for the idealism of youth when you believe every piece of crap someone tells you. I'd requested permission to use a shotgun at close range as a more humane method of execution, but had been refused, because silver-coated ammo is expensive and I could damage the very expensive reinforced gurneys that the vampires were chained to. Finally, I'd stopped doing morgue kills altogether when I realized most of the vampires chained to the tables for staking hadn't ever hurt anyone. "Three strikes and you're out" for vampires used to mean if you were convicted of three crimes of any kind, you got executed. Larry and I had been involved in the case that had helped give vampires a chance to go to jail for misdemeanors instead of just being killed. Good outcome, but that case had been a turning point in our friendship. After that he was like a born-again vegan who saw all meat as murder, and I was the carnivore.

"Okay, Zerbrowski, okay."

He smiled and patted my hand. "Thanks."

"What did you thank her for?" Brent asked.

"Listening to me," Zerbrowski said.

"Blake does have a reputation for not listening to people," Manning said.

I gave her a not entirely friendly look. "I've mellowed."

She gave a little smile and shook her head. "Haven't we all."

I nodded. "You either mellow or find a new career."

"Isn't that the truth?"

Three of us nodded; Brent hadn't been on the job long enough to understand. I felt all veteran-y.

"I can tell you how Dominga Salvador said she was doing it, but I never saw it done personally. She had two zombies like the ones in your videos; one was almost perfect and could have passed for human, but the other one was like you're describing, more decayed. Both of them looked out of their eyes. They were in there just like this one is."

"Our experts say it's theoretically possible for someone trained in voodoo to capture the soul at death and keep it in a jar or other magical container, but they don't know anyone who's actually done it. It's all 'my great-great-grandfather's uncle's brother did it,' or knew someone who had done it. We've followed up every rumor of a bad-ass voodoo priest or priestess, and they were either fake for the tourists, or law-abiding citizens who were horrified that their religion had been corrupted."

"What did they say about putting the soul back in the body after death?" I asked.

"There are ways to steal a piece of someone's soul and get some control over them, though it's a bad idea. It's some kind of karma balance thing; just because you can do a thing doesn't mean you should," Manning said.

"There are repercussions to dabbling too far in the blacker side of the arts of any magical path," I said.

She gave me those hard, straight cop eyes. I was betting she was hell in an interrogation room as the bad cop. "Some witches say that blood sacrifice of any kind is pretty black, and that you must have racked up some serious negative karma yourself, Blake."

"Yeah, I've talked to some of the witches who believe that. They're either the Christian witches who are okay with being second-class citizens in their own religion as long as they play by very strict Church rules, or fluffy-bunny Wiccans, or another more New Age flavor of witches."

"I know Wiccan is a modern word for witchcraft as a religion, but what's a fluffy-bunny Wiccan?" Brent asked.

"Fluffy-bunny neopagans seem to believe that there's no such thing as bad energy or evil magic; as long as they don't mess with it, it won't mess with them. It's the equivalent of civilians who think that nothing bad will happen to them as long as they don't go into the wrong neighborhood or hang out with dangerous people. Neither group wants to believe that evil lurks in good neighborhoods, too, and predators of all kinds hunt the good with the bad folk sometimes."

"Most civilians need to believe that to feel safe," Brent said.

"Yeah, but believing it too completely gets them hurt, or worse," I said.

"So you're saying the fluffy-bunny witches believe the blood sacrifice opens you up to the bad stuff, and as long as they don't do it, they're safe?" Brent asked.

I nodded.

"Safe from what?" he asked.

"It's the metaphysical equivalent of bad guys. I've seen some of the fluffy bunnies do major magic without enough magical protection and just believe that the innate goodness of the universe will protect them."

"I don't understand," Brent said.

"It's like a couple wearing mink and diamonds driving their brand-new Jaguar through the ghetto and thinking that nothing bad will happen to them, because they're good people."

"In a perfect world they'd be right," Manning said.

"We don't live in a perfect world," I said.

"Ain't that the truth," Zerbrowski said.

"One voodoo priest who was in his eighties said that there were no spells to accomplish what had been done to the poor women."

"I'm not a follower of vaudun, which is what a lot of their faith prefer to call it instead of voodoo, but I'd say the priest is right. My knowledge of their faith is limited, but Dominga Salvador said she'd invented this method, or whatever you want to call it."

"Well, either someone else figured it out, or she shared the secret before she vanished," Manning said.

"Apparently," I said.

"Can I ask a question that isn't directly on topic?" Brent asked.

Manning gave him a sideways look and sighed. "If you have to, and I know you have to."

Brent smiled at her, then looked at me. "I thought you used voodoo, or vaudun, to raise the zombies?"

"Sort of," I said. "People without any psychic ability with the dead should be able to raise zombies using just the ritual and accompanying paraphernalia, but I haven't met anyone who could do it who wasn't psychically gifted."

"So you're saying it's just another psychic ability, like telekinesis?"

I nodded and shrugged at the same time. "Yes and no. It's a magical ability, rather than a straight natural one, for most people. By that I mean that there's no ritual to enable an empath to sense emotions, but some magical abilities need ritual to prepare and open the mind to it."

"Meditation helps most psychics do better at the tests, so maybe it's all about the same thing," Brent said.

"Maybe," I said.

"You do use voodoo to raise the dead." Manning said it like it was just true.

"I was taught to do it that way."

"You sound like you're not sure you need the ritual."

I shrugged. "I've whittled down the ceremony a lot on occasion, but I know other animators who can't raise anything without all the bells and whistles. It's been my experience that the lower their psychic ability, the more magical ritual they need."

"The priest that we trusted enough to show some of the films to, he said the same thing you did, that the souls have been put into the body, trapped somehow. He said he wasn't sure if the bodies would rot with the soul inside them, or not."

"Again, I can tell you what I was told by the Señora. She found a way to put the soul back in the zombie, and once she did, it didn't decay."

"So why are these zombies rotting?"

"Because she could take the soul back out at will, apparently, and when she did the zombie rotted like normal."

"But some of the rotted zombies have their soul"—she made little air quotes—"in their eyes. Why are they rotting?"

"Dominga would take the soul out, let the body rot a little, then put the soul back in, until the zombie got to a point that she wanted. She also seemed to use it as torture, or punishment for the zombies. She called the one zombie that was most rotted, but still intact, a good warning, like a scare tactic. Do what I say, or this could happen to you, that kind of thing."

"But the zombies seem perfectly obedient; why would she need to threaten them?" Manning asked.

"It was a horror preview for the other zombies. I think the Señora enjoyed the sadism of it, but the threat was for her frenemies, like me.

It was supposed to make me too afraid of her to refuse what she wanted, and apparently it had worked on other people."

"But not on you?" Manning made it a question.

"You've only seen the fear in the women's eyes on video. I looked into eyes like that in person." I shuddered, and couldn't help it. "It was one of the most disturbing things I'd ever seen at that point in my life, and still ranks up there. I wanted Dominga dead in that moment not to protect myself, but to free those two zombies. It was just so wrong, so truly evil, that it needed to be stopped."

"Your face when you talk about it . . . you look like it stayed with you," Manning said.

I realized I'd been staring off into the room, remembering that basement and those two poor, trapped souls. Their eyes had been so afraid and pleading for help, and I'd had to leave them so that I could save myself, but there had been other days, other chances, and eventually I got to do what needed doing. Dominga Salvador would never torture anyone like that again.

I looked up at the frozen image on the computer. But now there was a new player in town and he had figured it out on his own. Fuck.

"What did Salvador want from you, Blake?"

"She wanted me to help her raise more zombies faster for her burgeoning sex slave business."

"Like what we're watching now?"

"Maybe, but if you're powerful enough your zombies can be pretty human-looking and they don't smell if they're not rotting, which they wouldn't with souls intact. You'd have a perfectly obedient sex slave that didn't need to eat, or sleep, or do anything but obey its master."

"But the animator has to be there to give the orders," Manning said.

"I don't think that was Dominga's idea. I believe she meant to do what I do for clients sometimes: You put them inside the circle and bind the zombie to them so it'll do what they say, and I go on to my next client. We'll make an appointment for them to bring the zombie back and I'll lay it to rest then, but I can't babysit every zombie I raise in a night."

"How many can you raise in a night?" Brent asked.

"It depends on the age of the zombie. The longer it's been dead, the more energy it takes to raise it from the grave. If it's a really old one then maybe only that zombie gets raised in a night, but if it's the newly dead, five or six in a night, maybe more if the travel time works out, but that's rare."

"Why is it rare?" Manning asked.

"I don't raise zombies without a good reason, and it's not cheap. The times when I've had more than five or six clients in one night in one geographic area are really rare. Sometimes I'll travel and do multiple zombies in a distant area, because I'm going to be in town, but most out-of-town trips are just one client who's willing to pay for me to come to them."

"So why is this animator in the room ordering the zombie around?" she asked.

"Maybe he doesn't know how to give control of a zombie over to someone else. It wasn't how I was taught. You stayed at the graveside and put the zombie back after the questions had been asked, or the last good-byes said. Even now it's rare for me to let anyone take a zombie off-site."

"Why?" Manning asked.

"One, some clients won't bring them back. Remember, it looks like their loved one, and I'm powerful enough that my zombies look and act alive, or enough so that if you want to believe Mom or Dad is back for good, you could. Well, for a while."

"Define *a while*."

"Until the body starts to rot. Eventually all zombies decay, Agent Manning, even mine."

"The Catholic Church claims that all animators are trampling on Jesus' territory by raising the dead."

"Yeah, that's what got us all excommunicated unless we agreed to stop doing it. What the Church doesn't understand is that for some of us it's a psychic gift, which means if we don't use it on purpose it comes out in other ways."

"Like untrained telepaths who go crazy because they can't block everyone else's thoughts," Brent said.

"Yeah, except for me it was roadkill following me home, or my first dog that died and came back."

Zerbrowski gave me wide eyes; apparently I'd never shared that with him.

"That sounds pretty awful," Manning said.

"It was, and my dad and stepmom were not amused."

"I bet," Brent said.

"Would you need a human sacrifice to do this?" Manning asked.

"You mean to capture the soul, or put the soul back in the zombies?"

"Either, both."

"The priest would be able to answer the question about the soul-capture thing better than I could, but I don't believe so, and if the zombies are the recently dead then you wouldn't need a death that big."

"Define *big*," she said.

"Most of us use chickens as the blood sacrifice for a normal zombie raising, but if it's an older body we move up to goats, sometimes sheep, but mostly goats. After that you get into cows."

"So it's literally physically larger, not smarter?" Manning said.

That was a good question, maybe a great question. "You know, I've never thought about it like that. Traditionally, I was taught that bigger sacrifice meant literally bigger, so theoretically an elephant could raise more, but we jump from cow to human sacrifice, and people are smaller than most full-grown cattle." I thought about it. "I guess there's just not a reasonable way to kill something bigger than a cow, or maybe horse, though I don't know anyone in this country who uses horses for sacrifice. I know some people use doves or pigeons instead of chickens, but the jump to human is considered the biggest sacrifice possible."

"Pigs are smarter than goats or cows; would their death be bigger?" Brent asked.

"I've never known anyone who used a pig; maybe a baby pig, but not a grown one."

"Why?" Manning asked.

"Honestly, I don't know, but I was raised in farm country, and pigs will eat people; cows and chickens, even goats, won't."

"Pigs don't really eat people unless a serial killer feeds them the pieces," Brent said.

"Feral hogs used to drag off babies left at the edge of fields and eat them."

"That's just an old wives' tale," Brent said.

"No, it's not," I said, "and if you're hurt enough that you can't get back out of the pigpen some breeds will fucking eat you."

"I don't believe that."

"My dad is a veterinarian. He used to take me on his rounds sometimes; trust me, some pigs will eat you."

"But would killing a chimpanzee or a dolphin be a bigger death than a cow, but less than a human?" he asked.

I thought about it, and finally said, "Maybe, but an adult male chimpanzee can tear a normal human being's arm out of its socket, and I can't even wrap my head around trying to get a dolphin alive to a grave site just to slit its throat to raise a zombie."

"So looking for missing persons being used as human sacrifices won't help us find these creeps?" Manning asked.

"I don't think so; in fact, I'm pretty sure not."

"How do we catch them, then?"

"Dominga's plan was to give the zombies in as fresh a condition as possible to her buyers as perpetual sex slaves, but she didn't see the possibility of porn online. I'm assuming that there must be customers paying for this stuff."

"Technically it's not illegal in most states, because the necrophilia laws have been modified so that if the corpse is moving and capable of giving consent it's consensual sex, not necrophilia, and that's a misdemeanor anyway," Manning said.

"I know some states had to change their laws once vampires were considered legal citizens, because the way the law was written, sex with them was still an arrestable offense," I said.

"Some police in certain areas made a hobby of arresting the spouses of vampires in their communities," Manning said.

I nodded. "Yeah, the early days just after the law changed were interesting."

"You can say that again," Zerbrowski said.

I looked at him.

"Hey, I was a cop when it changed. One day we could kill a vampire on sight and the next day they were legal citizens with all the protection the law offered. It was a very weird moment in law enforcement."

"It was my senior year of college when it changed. I guess I hadn't thought what I'd missed," I said.

He rolled his eyes. "I keep forgetting you're just a baby."

"You're only ten years older than me."

"Thirteen years older, thank you very much."

I grinned at him. "Oh, yeah, three years is so much more."

"You seem to think so, sometimes."

I gave him narrow eyes, because my attitude about some of my younger lovers was personal and we'd left personal behind.

Zerbrowski covered. "I'm just the old man to your young pup."

"Don't feel bad, Sergeant; you're not the oldest person in the room, though it is by less than three years." She smiled when she said it.

He offered her a fist bump and after a bemused moment, she took it.

I glanced at Brent, who was being unusually quiet, for him. "When you're the youngest person in a room of detectives or agents, you just learn to keep your mouth shut about it."

I smiled at him. "Been there, done that."

"I'll bet; you don't look anywhere near thirty."

I shrugged. "Good genetics." It was, but there was the possibility that being Jean-Claude's human servant, as well as fiancée, meant that I wasn't aging, that I might stay just like this forever. I looked at Zerbrowski's hair, grayer than when we'd met. Was I going to have to watch him age while I didn't? I didn't know, but the thought made me sad. On the heels of that thought was another one, that if he were a vampire he wouldn't age. I'd never looked at one of my friends and thought that before. I wasn't sure how I felt about thinking it now. It wasn't a good feeling, whatever it was.

"You okay, Anita?" Zerbrowski asked.

I nodded. "Sure, just thinking too hard."

He grinned. "Thinking about your tall, pale, and handsome fiancé?"

"No, why would you even ask that?"

"Because you only overthink your personal life; crime busting makes you kind of peaceful."

I let my face show exactly how unpeaceful I felt about this case. "This case isn't going to make me feel peaceful, Zerbrowski."

"I'm sorry, you're right. This one's going to hurt."

"What do you mean by that?" Manning asked.

He looked at her, and his brown eyes showed that there was a shrewd thinker behind all the messy clothes and teasing. "Some cases leave a mark on your soul even after you solve it."

She studied his face and nodded. "As long as we solve it."

"You're afraid we won't," I said.

"We're here because our own resident animator Kirkland, and the most revered voodoo, vaudun, priest in the country, plus all the witches and psychics working with and for the FBI couldn't help us find these guys."

"What do your computer techs say?" Zerbrowski asked.

She nodded again. "They say that whoever is doing the tech for these creeps is really, really good."

Brent added, "They are still working on tracing to a location, but the ability to hide the computer trail is always just a little ahead of our ability to trace it, until we catch up."

"And then the bad techies figure out a new way to pull ahead of the good guys," I said.

"Exactly," he said.

"Our tech people will crack this, or trace it, eventually," Manning said, "but I don't understand their part of the investigation enough to help, so I'm here trying an angle that I can understand more. I can look at you, talk to you, ask you questions. I don't speak enough computer to do the same for that part of the investigation."

"I just recently learned how to change the ring tones on my smart phone, so I hear you on the whole mysterious-computer thing," I said.

She gave me a weak smile. "Thank you for that, but there's usually an age line about such things. You're young to be on the wrong side of it."

"Hey, I love my smart phone," Zerbrowski said. "The wife and kids send me pics and texts all day. Helps me keep in touch when the hours are long."

"And you're over the age line, of course." Manning looked from one to the other of us. "The two of you balance each other somehow like good partners do."

We looked at each other, then both shrugged almost in unison and said, "We try."

She narrowed her eyes at us. Brent laughed.

If civilians could have seen us laughing and smiling with that horror still frozen on the computer behind us, they'd have thought we were cold-blooded, or worse. But if you couldn't keep your sense of humor in the midst of the nightmares you went crazy, or changed jobs, or ate your gun. We were all career cops, in it for the long haul, and that meant we whistled in the dark, sang on the way to our execution, joked at the door to hell—pick your metaphor. We did it. We survived. We didn't go too crazy. We did our jobs. We caught the bad guys. I glanced behind at the frozen image on the screen. The zombie, person, whatever she was with her soul trapped in there, was staring out at the screen in a mute plea. We had to find her first, but when we did I'd find a way to free her soul and lay her to final rest. This would stop. We would make it stop. The people who'd raised the zombie and were abusing her hadn't done anything to earn a warrant of execution, not legally, so I couldn't just go in there with guns blazing like normal when I was chasing monsters. They hadn't killed anyone, hell, I wasn't even sure what laws they'd broken, but morally—they needed to suffer. Was that judgmental of me? Hell yes, but sometimes you just gotta go with that part of yourself that says, *This is morally wrong and I will stop you.* Judge not, lest ye be judged, but in this case I was pretty sure God would be on my side.

5

I HAD ONE person I trusted who had known Dominga Salvador well, but I couldn't take Zerbrowski or the FBI with me, because my friend had done some really bad things when he'd been part of Dominga's crew. I needed an excuse to ditch the other badges, without seeming like I was ditching them. My text tone went off on my phone and I had the perfect excuse.

Out loud I said, "Crap."

"What's wrong?" Manning asked.

Zerbrowski was watching me a little too closely, as if something about that "crap" hadn't fooled him at all. Maybe I should have said "shit"?

"I have another appointment. Normally I'd ignore it, but do we actually have any leads to follow?"

"What appointment?" Zerbrowski asked, smiling, but his eyes let me know I wasn't fooling him much.

I held the text up so he could read it. "Remember 8:00PM meeting with jeweler. *Je t'aime, ma petite*." It had a tiny picture of Jean-Claude beside it.

"Jeweler, ooh, ooh, you're trying on rings tonight." He grinned, because he'd said too much out loud, and I was pretty sure why he'd done it. He wanted to see what Manning would do.

The grim-faced agent suddenly smiled at me. It was a good smile that seemed to erase the lines and years that the horrors on the screen had added. She was suddenly attractive, eyes all a-sparkle. Earlier I would have gotten grumpy again, but now I understood why she might have gone all girly about my engagement; she needed something to distract her from the job. As a police officer, or a first responder of any kind, you need things outside work that put the smile back on your face, because if you don't have something you'll either crawl into a bottle, burn out early, or decide to be too up close and friendly with your gun one dark night. Did Manning follow romances in the news? Did she enjoy tabloid relationship gossip? Read romance novels in her spare time? And here I was right in the middle of a public romance that seemed to fall right out of one of those books—how could she resist, and why would she want to?

She didn't say anything, just sat there holding it all in, because I'd been grumpy about it earlier, but now I understood more. I smiled at her. "Just say it, or you're going to hurt yourself holding it in."

She smiled even more brilliantly. It filled her whole face with something close to laughter, and it helped chase away some of the sadness I was feeling after seeing the video, too. Happiness is as contagious as sorrow.

"I thought you had that fabulous engagement ring that was on the news."

"Jean-Claude knows me, and he knew I'd want to help pick out a ring I'm expected to wear for the rest of my life. The ring on the video was a loaner with a possibility to buy."

Brent raised his hand, as if he needed permission to join the conversation. "I saw the ring on the news; what woman wouldn't keep that hunk of ice?"

I grinned, and let myself try to explain, not because I had to, but because I liked the atmosphere in the room better. I didn't want to be the one who brought the mood down again; this was better. "I asked him if he actually wanted me to wear the ring every day, and he said, preferably. I can't wear that hunk of ice to this job, or to raise zombies. The diamond on the top alone would poke holes through any crime scene gloves, if the ring would even fit into most gloves."

Manning's smile had faded a little. "Sad, but true."

I wanted her to smile again, so I said the truth. "Jean-Claude said, 'I would prefer that you wear the symbol of my love every day.'" I left off the "*ma petite*" that went at the end of almost every sentence he said to me. It was French for "my little one," or literally, "my little."

Manning's smile brightened again.

Zerbrowski said, "Aww, ain't that romantic."

"So we're having rings made that I can wear every day." I didn't add that we were also negotiating on a set of rings that were the bright, shiny, audacious equivalent of the ring he'd given me in the videoed engagement. He wanted us to have rings for dressy occasions that showed off his wealth. Most master vampires come from nobility, or at least centuries when nobility flaunted it if they had it; not to drench yourself in jewels and rich clothes meant you were poor. Jean-Claude had to be the king, and that meant we needed something worthy of a king and his queen. I was incredibly uncomfortable with some of the rings we'd looked at in this category, but he'd finally convinced me that it was a necessary thing. I could never envision wearing a ring like that without being terrified I'd lose a stone, or damage it in some way. I felt like a small dog dressed up in clothes; they walk very stiffly, because they just don't feel like themselves anymore. It may look good, but a dog would still rather be chasing squirrels. You can't do that in little doggie booties and a tutu.

"You are a very lucky woman," she said, and she meant it. It made me wonder if there was a Mr. Manning back home. A lot of cops don't wear wedding bands to work, so the fact that her finger was empty didn't prove anything.

"Thank you. I'm still a little amazed that Jean-Claude is my fiancé."

"Why?" she asked.

"I'd sort of given up on the idea of marrying anyone, and he's just so gorgeous. On the attractive scale I feel like a three who somehow landed a twenty bazillion." I grinned as I said it, but I meant it.

Manning narrowed her eyes at me. "Every beautiful woman knows just how beautiful she is, and you are not a three."

"Try standing next to Jean-Claude and see how high up the pretty scale you feel."

She laughed then. "Okay, I'll give you that one. He just seems perfect."

I nodded. "He's close, and I so don't feel perfect."

"You're only human, and he's not."

I nodded again. "Well, there is that," I said.

I got to leave with everyone still smiling, though Zerbrowski was watching me a little too closely. He knew I'd told the truth about the jeweler, but he was also pretty certain that I'd thought of something about the case I hadn't shared. He trusted me enough to let me get away with it tonight, but by tomorrow he'd ask. So after the jeweler appointment and the zombie I had to raise later tonight at my other job, I'd need to call Manny Rodriguez, friend and coworker at Animators Inc., and remind him of a time in his life when he'd been one of the bad guys.

6

THE CIRCUS OF the Damned had revitalized an older warehouse district, because one wildly successful business will attract more new businesses and customers. I sometimes wondered what would have happened to this section of St. Louis if Jean-Claude hadn't opened the Circus here. It would probably be like some other sections of the old warehouse district, the kind of place where the police will only come in groups. The huge building towered over the area like a big brother that kept all the bullies away. The three dancing clowns on top were frozen in the fading light. If you looked closely you'd notice the clowns all had fangs, and their multicolored outfits seemed more garish without darkness to soften them, so maybe it was a weird older brother, but it still kept the neighborhood safe and had brought the whole area more upscale.

I had no trouble finding parking right out front because it was hours from opening. An hour before dusk and I'd have had to park in the employees' parking lot out back. I walked past the big carnival posters that covered the front of the building. Posters twenty feet high proclaimed, *The Lamia, half snake, half woman!*, showing a garish but accurate image of Melanie, her long black hair swept discreetly over her very human breasts. The image didn't do justice to the multicolored scales of her tail, or how dangerous her venom was; I'd have deported her back to Greece, but Jean-Claude knew a moneymaker when he saw it, and he'd been right. Melanie had behaved herself since I'd freed her of the big bad vampire that had been her master. *See the Skinless, Formless Monster!* was a florid drawing of a Nuckelavee, which wasn't some kind of Lovecraftian horror, but a fairy from the British Isles that wasn't fit for much other work than a sideshow. I mean, if you're a skinless, near formless creature, what job can you possibly have? "Do you want fries with that" shouldn't be followed by uncontrolled screaming from the customers. *Zombies Rise from the Grave!* I had gotten Jean-Claude to stop the nightly zombie raising in the small makeshift cemetery in the carnival midway, but so many customers had complained that he'd overridden me and started it again. We had agreed to stay out of the business side of each other's life as much as possible. The poster on the left-hand side of the door showed a male figure dressed somewhere between the Phantom of the Opera and a sexy circus ringmaster: *Asher, Master Vampire and Ring Master!* Then I was at the doors, and other posters marched down the other side of the entrance showing some of the other acts and delights that awaited the customers inside. I debated on whether to knock, in case someone was close enough to open it, or use my key. I had keys to the front door and to the back door, the employee entrance, which is what I usually used. I tried to remember the last time I'd come in the front and couldn't. I usually was here after dark, which meant the crowds were so massive I didn't want to deal with it.

Now, the street out front was completely empty except for me. I knew that someone inside had seen me from the very top floor, because the guards kept watch over all entrances. There was even a sniper lookout, though we were short a sniper lately, because we'd lost one of our own. Ares had been a good guy, and for a werehyena he'd been excellent. We still had a few people who could use a sniper rifle, but no one as good as Ares. I wished I hadn't had to kill him.

If the building had been less massive they could have had someone
at the front doors to let me in by now, but I didn't have to wait forever
and a day for someone to open the door anymore. I put my key in the
lock and felt that satisfying *click*. I liked having a key. I stepped through
and made sure the door locked behind me, though honestly a lot of our
potential bad guys wouldn't have much trouble breaking the door
down, or tearing a new one in the wall somewhere. We'd hear them,
and we had enough guards with enough muscle and firepower to kill
them dead before they got very far, but locked doors were more for
the casual passerby who was curious to see the Circus during the daylight when all the vampires were in their coffins. If they only knew how
many vampires could walk around inside here without waiting for sun-
down, they'd either be thrilled or never sleep well again. It depended
on which side of the preternatural citizen movement they were on.
Whether vampires should have been declared "alive" and full citizens
of the United States of America was one of the big debates ranking
right up there with gun rights and abortion. In a way all of them are
about life and death—defining what life is, and what it isn't, and how
far we'll go to protect, or take, it.

I stood there in the huge, echoing dimness of the empty Circus and
just enjoyed the quiet of the place. The first time I'd come here during
this time of day when everything was closed had been when Nikolaos
was still Master of the City and Jean-Claude had just been one of her
flunkies. I'd come to kill her and all the bad little vampires and henchmen who had threatened me and my friends. I'd done a good job of it,
too. Now I stood there listening, almost feeling the silence of the closed
carnival midway that stretched the length of the building. The booths
where you could win giant toy bats, or vampire and werewolf dolls and
other themed toys, were all shuttered or draped with canvas. It really
was a midway complete with rides, but there was no smell of dust and
heat. It was cleaner, neater than any real traveling carnival could ever
be, but that was very Jean-Claude. He liked to take things that were
messy and make them prettier, run smoother, the illusion of perfection
so close to perfect that most people couldn't tell the difference. Only
his romantic relationships were big, messy, brawling things, because

he only fell in love with difficult people, and yes, I was so counting myself on that list of difficult lovers. Truth was truth.

I walked between the closed food stalls, where the faint smell of corn dogs, popcorn, funnel cakes, and cotton candy seemed to linger like aromatic ghosts. There was one tent in the middle of the midway— once it would have been called the freak show, but now it was the hallway of oddities, though even that some had complained about. They wanted to see the half-man, half-whatever, but they wanted it to be politically correct, because if you were all PC about it then looking didn't make you a bad person. Lately, people seemed to think that morality was the same thing as being politically correct, and it wasn't. Some of the most deeply moral people I knew were least politically correct, because they actually worried about good and evil, not just what they were told was good or bad.

Some well-meaning citizens had gotten freak shows closed down, but all the people who had protested and felt morally superior about it had other jobs. They could go out in the world and be "normal"; the "freaks" that they'd put out of work didn't always have that option. Sometimes the freak show is your only option, and sometimes it's the only place where you feel safe and okay. I really wish the "normal" people would leave us freaks alone and stop trying to save us. We get by, we take care of each other, and the people who cost the freaks their jobs didn't give them employment, or a place to stay, or a family to be a part of; they just destroyed their world and felt morally superior for doing it.

I'd seen my first ghost at age ten; by age fourteen I'd accidentally raised dead animals, including my childhood dog, Jenny. My dad had contacted my grandmother Flores and she'd trained me just enough not to have roadkill follow me home, or my dead pet crawl into bed with me. She'd worried I would grow up to become not just an animator, as in to give life, but a necromancer, which usually meant you'd gone evil. Vampires used to kill necromancers when they found them, because we have the potential to have power over all the dead, including them. I'd slipped through the cracks because I was Jean-Claude's human servant and because there hadn't been a full-fledged necromancer in a thousand years. I was one of the freaks; I just hadn't embraced it the first time I walked into the Circus of the Damned.

I turned to the left and the biggest tent, which took up nearly a quarter of this part of the warehouse interior. The tent was white-and-red striped and gave the illusion that it had just been put up that day by some roustabouts, but it was permanent, only coming down when the tent material needed to be made fresh and bright again. The ticket booth at the entrance was empty like everything else, but even if it hadn't been I'd have gotten in for free. I was engaged to the owner.

The tent flap was down over the doorway so I couldn't see inside, but I saw the canvas twitch a second before it started moving up. I drew my gun in an automatic motion; it was held two-handed and pointed at the ground before I had time to talk myself out of it. I had it pointed at the ground because I couldn't see on the other side of the canvas. You don't point at anything unless you know what or who you're pointing at, because once you point, then you aim, and then you shoot. Shooting means killing it. For all I knew it could be Jean-Claude on the other side—unlikely, but still, everyone in here was either a lover, a friend, or at least that guy I don't hate.

The hand that moved the canvas was a lot darker than Jean-Claude's, and I wasn't surprised when Socrates looked through the opening. He was tall, but not too broad; he didn't like doing the serious weight lifting some of the guards did. He'd recently cut his hair so short that my own would have had no curl left, which meant almost shaved, but his hair still had curl to it. He glanced down at the gun in my hands and smiled. "I like that you're that cautious."

I relaxed my shoulders a little and gave him the ultimate praise; I took my eyes off him while I moved my suit jacket out of the way and holstered my gun. "Some people call it paranoid."

"They've never been a cop," he said.

"How's your bid to be reinstated as a detective?" I asked.

"The two officers who got to keep their badges after catching lycanthropy on the job are both part of the U.S. Marshals Preternatural Branch. I was just an ordinary plainclothes detective on the gang and drugs squad."

"You might have more luck joining the Marshals Service and playing on my team," I said.

He grinned, teeth a bright flash in his dark face. "I was a regular cop; we save people, or at least keep the peace, or something like that. Nothing personal, but your duty description is mostly hunting down and killing people. It's closer to a soldier than a cop."

I shrugged. "True."

"I just want to be a detective again, Anita. I loved my job, and I was good at it. I've got testimonials from most of the people I worked with back in Los Angeles. I think they still feel guilty that I got cut up by the werehyenas saving some of their asses."

"Guilt can be a great motivator," I said, as I walked in beside him, and he let the canvas fall back into place. The tent opening was part of the illusion that this was a very solid, very permanent structure. The inside was a one-ring circus in a tradition old enough that I didn't actually remember it except from pictures, but the bleachers that rose up on every side were very solid and cemented in, as solid as a modern sports arena. We were able to walk side by side between the first row of steps and the rail that kept the crowd from walking out on the now-empty sand.

"Yeah, it can," he said, and he looked sad, as he ran one hand over his nearly shaved head.

I didn't want sad today for some reason, so I changed the topic. "I can't believe your hair is still curly with it cut that short. Even my curls are gone when it's that close to my head."

He half-laughed. "Mexican and German genetics aren't going to be enough; you have to go all the way to Africa somewhere in your family tree to get curls like mine."

I laughed with him. "Fine, genetically you've got a curl advantage."

He turned up the main stairs, which were wider and led not just to higher seats, but to the draped glass booth at the very top. It looked like a media booth where someone would do a play-by-play, but it was actually the office for the manager of the Circus of the Damned, whoever that happened to be, and there was a small apartment behind it.

Socrates didn't shorten his stride for me, but I managed to keep pace. The first time I'd walked the stairs my knees had hurt, and that was before I hit twenty-five. Now at thirty-one my knees didn't bother me on the stairs. I moved up them easily, just below and a little to one side of Socrates' longer stride. Yes, I was hitting the gym more now, but I didn't think that was all of it. I'd gotten cut up by shapeshifters on my job, too, but one of the first ones that contaminated me had been the one and only panwere I'd ever seen. He'd had several different forms, and apparently I'd inherited that first, so every wereanimal that bled me after that had shared their beast with me. It was supposed to be medically impossible, and the fact that I didn't change shape into any animal form was even more impossible. We all thought that was because I'd been Jean-Claude's human servant before I caught lycan-thropy, and his vampire marks somehow prevented me from shape-shifting. But we were so far out into theoretical metaphysics that we honestly didn't know. I'd learned a few months ago that some of the less public parts of the military were interested in seeing if they could cre-ate soldiers that had my combination of the best of being a shapeshifter without turning into an animal form. I'd let people know that it was the vampire marks that prevented the shifting, and they couldn't duplicate that part in a lab. So far no one had come knocking on my door about it and I was good with that.

It was awesome that I could keep pace with Socrates, who was a werehyena, and none of the old aches and pains hurt, but I wondered what else had changed. What else had changed about my body that I hadn't realized? Which led to the thought, what if all the lycanthropy and vampire marks had affected more than just my physicality?

"What's wrong, Anita? You look too serious for a woman about to see a jeweler about rings."

I smiled at him, because I knew he was teasing me. I'd never been much for jewelry. I told him about my knees not hurting.

"That's a good thing, not a bad thing," he said.

I nodded. "But what else has changed that I didn't notice?"

He sighed. "You don't mean just the physical stuff."

"Nope."

We were outside the door now. "Someday we should sit down and

I'll tell you everything I know about what I've noticed before and after I became a werehyena."

"I'd like that."

"You may not like it after you hear it all."

I shrugged. "That's okay, too. I'd rather know the truth than have to guess."

"Most people wouldn't," he said.

"I'm not most people."

"Well, now that is the truth." He smiled again.

I smiled back, because that's what you're supposed to do, but I didn't really feel all that smiley.

Socrates knocked on the door, then put his hand against the slight crack at the edge of the door. I could hear something sniffing on the other side. It was a new thing, but the wereanimal guards were using scent as their "password." You could find out passwords or secret knocks, but you couldn't change the scent of your body. Even if everyone was in human form it was still effective, though their sense of smell was heightened the closer to their animal shape they shifted.

Lisandro, tall, darkly Hispanic, and handsome, opened the door for us and ushered us into the front office. It held a desk and two chairs, and it was a nice, ordinary office, except for the vintage circus posters framed on the walls, which was really the only sign that this wasn't the office of any normal administrative assistant at any upper-crusty business in the United States. There really would be an admin after full dark tonight, when she finally woke for the day. Betty Lou wasn't a very powerful vampire, but she was a hell of an office assistant. He said, "That new hair product smells too sweet, how can you wear it?" Which meant he'd smelled it through the door; I hadn't smelled it much standing next to Socrates.

"Like I was telling Anita, neither of you has my fabulous curls, so you wouldn't understand."

Lisandro used one hand to flip his shoulder-length ponytail. "My hair is about as straight as it gets, so I don't have to worry about it."

"It's just that wererat nose of yours," Socrates said. "It means everything smells funny to you."

Lisandro grinned. "You're just jealous because rats have a better scenting capability than hyenas."

Socrates did a little head shake. "But we can eat through the side of a Buick with one bite, and you can't."

I rolled eyes at both of them. "Enough interspecies one-upmanship; take me to Jean-Claude."

"I would say you know the way, but we're being all formal because of the jeweler," Lisandro said.

I shook my head. "The daytime jeweler is the nighttime jeweler's human servant, and ancient vampires are all about the formalities," I said.

"Yeah, it's not every day you get to meet a human who can tell you that Helen of Troy had black hair," Lisandro said.

"She did not say that," Socrates said.

"Yes, she did."

"She said, these rings would be worthy of Helen of Troy, another raven-haired beauty."

"Raven-haired means black hair," Lisandro said.

"Are you saying she compared me to Helen of Troy?"

The two men stopped bickering long enough to look at me. Then they looked at each other, and back to me. Lisandro said, "Any other woman I've ever met would be flattered, but you're going to get all weird about it, aren't you?"

I frowned at him. "I am not going to get all weird."

"But you won't take the compliment either," Socrates said.

I sighed, shrugged, touched my gun and shifted the holster just a little on its belt, and thought about it. "When you're spending this much money on rings, they flatter you, it's just part of the whole thing, but no, I don't believe she's sincere when she compares me to one of the great beauties of the ages. Sorry, but I just don't buy it."

They gave each other another look, which irritated me, because it meant they were being careful around my mood, or my issue, and I hated that. I hated being difficult about my appearance. Thanks to a lot of things from my childhood, and a very ex-fiancé, I had trouble seeing myself as beautiful. People reacted to me as if I were beautiful, so I had to accept it, but I had trouble seeing it myself, so the jeweler's flattery, insincere or not, wasn't going to win points with me.

"Besides, rings don't go near the face, so what does hair color have to do with anything, it's just skin tone that counts," I said, and I sounded grumpy, but I'd managed not to criticize myself, and that was an improvement.

"Let's not keep the boss waiting," Socrates said.

It took me a second to realize he meant Jean-Claude, and then Lisandro was opening the door and ushering me inside to the larger and more richly furnished office that screamed upper-level executive, from the rich wood paneling to the desk big enough to slaughter an ox on; there was no hint that it was the manager's office for the Circus of the Damned. Nothing as garish as circus posters in here. I had a moment of wanting to ask one of the guards to stay with me, but they were bodyguards. They couldn't guard me from my sudden case of nerves, as I glanced at the jewels laid out on velvet cloths and samples of different metal wedding bands. The huge desk was covered in them as if a very proper pirate's treasure had been given over to the accountants to catalog. A tiny, dark-haired woman stood beside it, thin hands clasped in front of her; she could have passed for an accountant, or a servant in an old movie, but the eagerness in her face was another issue. The jeweler was way too excited about all of this. I must have made an involuntary movement for the door, because Jean-Claude said, "*Ma petite.*" Just that, nothing more, but it made me look at him.

Jean-Claude sat behind that huge desk and that gleaming display of matrimonial treasure, but none of it was as pretty as him. His black hair curled softly past his shoulders, mingling so perfectly with the velvet of his jacket that it was hard to tell where one ended and the other began. The shirt that peeked from the jacket was scarlet, a red that looked fabulous with the hair and that unearthly white skin of his, a perfect whiteness that no living skin could rival. He was very pale tonight, no blush of color to his face at all, which meant he hadn't fed yet. There was a time I couldn't have told, but I'd been studying his face and moods for years. Once I had refused to be food for any vampire, even him. Now the thought that he hadn't fed, and that it could be part of our foreplay, tightened things low in my body so hard and suddenly that I had to reach for the edge of the desk to steady myself, and I hadn't even gotten to his face.

I raised my head to finally look into that face, that near perfect curve of cheek, the kissable lips, and finally the coup de grace of eyes. They looked almost black in the overhead lights, but some gleam always seemed to show that swimming blue, like deep seawater where the monsters swim and there are wonders to behold. His dark eyelashes were actually double-rowed on top so they looked like he'd used mascara, but he never had to, and then the perfect arch of black eyebrow . . . He looked too beautiful, too perfect, like a work of art instead of a person. How did this man love me? But the smile on his face, the light in his eyes, said plainly that he saw something wonderful when he looked at me, too. I didn't know whether to be flattered, amazed, or ask, *Why me?* Why not a thousand more traditionally beautiful women out there? He could have had movie stars, or models, but he'd chosen me. Me, too short, curvy even with my gym workout, and scarred from my job, still struggling to heal all the issues life had saddled me with, and yet he smiled at me, held his hand out to me. I went around the desk to take his hand, but I didn't feel like the princess to his prince; I felt like a clumsy peasant to his very regal king.

"I might as well not exist when you first enter a room for each other," the jeweler said with a voice that still held the first echoes of her homeland. It had been somewhere in what would be the Middle East today, but I think had been Mesopotamia then, yeah, as in the cradle of civilization. She gave her name as Irene; I doubted it had been her birth name, but I'd learned that it was rude to ask a vampire or human servant's original name. Whatever name they came with was their name. I guess you can't go through centuries being mud-dabble-wat-wat, so Irene it was.

I blushed, but Jean-Claude continued to pull me close, and said, "But isn't our very absorption with each other part of what fascinates you?"

"Yes, my lord king."

I wanted to say, *Please stop calling him that*, but Jean-Claude had made me stop correcting her or her master. First, if someone wants to call you a king, or queen, let them. Second, when I suggested *president*, Irene had called him, "My lord president," which sounded totally wrong.

He stayed seated, so for once I was the one who had to lean down to kiss him. In all the thousands of kisses we'd shared, I couldn't remember if I'd ever been the one who had to bend to him. Sitting down, he couldn't even go up on tiptoes like I did most of the time. I put one hand on the side of his face to steady me as I touched my lips to his, because even now sometimes just a kiss could leave me unsteady. It was a light kiss by our standard "hello," but we had company, and business company at that. One thing I had learned over the last few weeks was that everything about a big wedding had some sort of business attached to it.

Irene's thin, long-fingered hands were clasped in front of her, where she usually held them, unless she was touching something. It was as if she held on to herself to keep her from touching everything. She was shorter than me, barely five feet tall, with hair as black as ours, but coarser and intermingled with gray. Her face was thin and angular, her body bird-thin, not in the way that models who diet forever are, but as if there had just never been enough food. Her skin was brown both in color and from the sun, and her eyes were the black that both Jean-Claude's blue and my own brown promised, but never quite delivered.

"My master has given me an impossibly long life, and I can say with long observation that it is rare for a couple to still be so taken with each other."

Jean-Claude smiled at her, his arm pulling me down into his lap. I might have protested, but first I wanted to be as close to him as possible, and second there was nothing wrong with what we were doing. It was just a little far for modern American affection outside a club or party atmosphere. "We are searching for the perfect wedding bands; surely that is early enough, Irene."

"But you have been dating for six years, isn't it, my lord?"

"Yes," he said.

"Something like that," I said. It had been more off-again, on-again than most of the vampire community seemed to think, and definitely more than the human media did. I'd been a legal vampire executioner when Jean-Claude and I first met, and he'd been a vampire, so romance hadn't been the first thought on either of our minds. I'd believed that all vampires were just walking corpses, and that killing them had been ridding the world of monsters. Then I'd met a few vampires who seemed nicer than the people I was dealing with, and I began to wonder just who the monsters were. Dominga Salvador had been one of the human beings who helped convince me that evil could have a heartbeat. Now, we had someone who was doing the most evil thing the Señora had imagined. She was dead, I knew that, I'd killed her, but if the animator talking offscreen had been female I might have wondered if someone had raised her from the grave and gotten some secrets. Of course, since I'd technically murdered her, self-defense or not, her zombie should have tried to come after me first. Murder victims crawl from the grave with only one thing on their minds—vengeance. They will tear through anyone in their way in an attempt to hunt down and kill their murderer. It was the reason you couldn't just raise the victim of a homicide and ask them who killed them. It had been tried and the death count was always higher than just the one murder they'd been trying to solve.

Jean-Claude stroked his hand down my arm. "You are suddenly very somber, *ma petite*."

"Sorry, work was . . . hard today."

I felt his energy stroke at the side of my thoughts, almost the way his hand had touched my arm. I tightened my shielding down just a little more, and he didn't press. The images from the zombie videos were not what I wanted to share with him as we talked about wedding rings. I was pretty sure it would be a mood killer.

"I do not understand why you do a job that steals the light from your face, Anita," Irene said.

I looked at her, and there must have been something in the look, because she gave a small bow. "I meant no offense."

"As long as you weren't going to join the vampires who think I should give up my job once I marry Jean-Claude, no offense taken."

Irene rose from her bow laughing. "I would never say that; I have had the same job for a very long time and I still find new things to learn. Why, the new technologies and metals are a constant amazement to me."

I smiled at her. "Sorry that I jumped to conclusions."

"Anyone who has asked you to give up your job is probably a vampire who hasn't led a very productive afterlife. I find that the vampires who have no business or occupation grow bored, and bored immortals find ways to amuse themselves that are most unpleasant." She shivered a little, and her face lost some of its eager glow.

Jean-Claude hugged me where his one arm lay around my waist. "Do you think that boredom is the cause of evil among vampires?"

"Forever is a very long time to do nothing, my lord."

He smiled and nodded. "Yes, yes it is."

"If I may be so bold, my lord."

"You may," he said, though I wasn't sure what she was asking, exactly.

"Many think that one of the reasons you are so reasonable and just is that you have been running businesses for hundreds of years. The fact that you perform at some of your clubs is another example of how you occupy yourself in a positive manner."

"Some of the older vampires see it as unseemly that their king is a performer."

"I have heard the gossip, but those who say it are old-fashioned and trapped in the past. They still believe that rulers are to concern themselves only with power, but your joy in performing onstage radiates from you, my lord."

Jean-Claude did the head tilt as we both looked at Irene. I asked the question. "When did you see Jean-Claude onstage?"

She blushed and cast her eyes down. "My master feels that the more we know about the people we design our rings for, the better we will please them."

"Were you there on a night when I was introducing the acts?" he asked.

She kept her eyes down, hands clasped tight, as she said, "You did introduce most of the acts."

"But I did not introduce myself."

"No, my lord, one of your charming young men did the honor of introducing you." She stared studiously at the floor.

"I have only been onstage at Guilty Pleasures once since the engagement was announced. I did not see you in the audience."

"I stayed near the back, my lord. I was there to observe, not to participate by being one of the audience you interacted with." She finally gave a quick look up, and then back down.

Jean-Claude had caused a near riot stripping onstage after the engagement hit the media. He'd put together a new act that had more romance at the beginning, but the end was romantic only if you considered "sexy as hell" romantic. I tended to think of it that way, but the human media had been split between headlines stating I was jealous and angry at him for going onstage again, to wondering how long until I might join him onstage. I had done it a few times as the pretend "lady victim" from the audience for some of my lovers, but not lately. One, the customers didn't like the idea of a plant in the audience who had already had the pleasure of, um, meeting the men for real, and two, the U.S. Marshals Service didn't think much of one of their officers going onstage at a strip club. Technically I wasn't stripping, but just helping out the show with a "victim" who wouldn't make a fuss or pressure the dancers for real sex, but somehow helping out a friend didn't cover getting up onstage at a strip club. The vampire community thought their king shouldn't be shaking his booty onstage for a bunch of humans.

"I am an exhibitionist; do you know what that means, Irene?"

She blushed again. We took that as a yes.

"Did you enjoy the show, Irene?" and he added just a touch of power to her name. I felt it thrill down my skin and tug at things low in my body. I watched Irene to see if it affected her that way. She stood very still, and then, very slowly, raised her eyes to stare into his face the way that mice must stare at cats when they are too tired to run anymore and begin to realize just how beautiful the cat is, and how it wouldn't be a bad way to die.

My voice was very firm as I said, "Stop it."

"You don't mind, do you, Irene?" Every word was thick with power. Irene's eyes were huge, her face slack, as she nodded.

"It's what you've wanted since you saw me onstage, isn't it?"

"Since before that, my lord; how can any of us stand near the flame of your beauty and not want to be closer to the heat of it?"

"But I am cold, Irene, not hot. There is no flame here, no light, only the chill of the grave and darkness."

"She is your heat, my lord, and the shapeshifters, they burn very hot indeed." Her voice was eager now, and when she said *heat*, I felt the temperature rise, and burn; it almost made me flinch, hot, holding the press of high summer.

"Do you feel it, *ma petite*?"

"Yeah," I said, and got off his lap to stand at his side, just our fingers intertwined. "Cut the mind tricks, Irene, that shit don't fly here."

The next words from her lips were someone else's; the inflection was wrong, as if a stranger were borrowing her voice. "You tried to take over my servant. I am merely demonstrating that we are not helpless against you." Irene's hands were at her side, feet apart, shoulders more straight, and just something about the way she stood said *male*.

"My apologies, Melchior, but her desire to be seduced is very strong. It pushes at my determination to behave myself." I always pronounced his name like Mel-Core, but when Irene said it, it sounded like Mill-Key-Or, and much more exotic. Jean-Claude's pronunciation was closer to hers than my middle American blandness.

"A good king shows restraint."

"A good master does not leave his servant wanting."

"I do not have your inclinations, my lord. My love is for our shared art, not the art of flesh."

"How sad for your servant," Jean-Claude said.

"Perhaps, but more sorrow if her art had been destroyed for pursuit of fleshly pleasures."

"It's not one or the other," I said. "There's middle ground."

"Irene is free to find a lover, if it does not interfere with our work."

"What would you do if her lover did interfere with the work?" I asked, watching the stranger make Irene's face look thoughtful. He stroked a hand along a beard she didn't have.

"Nothing is allowed to interfere with our art."

"Would you kill him after she had fallen in love?"

Irene's face looked at Jean-Claude. "You do allow your servant to speak out of turn, my lord. We old ones puzzle over that."

"Don't look at him when I'm the one talking to you, Melchior." I would have pulled away from Jean-Claude's hand, but he tightened his grip on my hand and I didn't fight him. I wouldn't do anything else to make him appear weak to the ancient vampire who was staring at us from Irene's face.

"This is why we do not marry our servants, Jean-Claude; it gives them ideas above their station."

"You arrogant son of a bitch."

"And she curses like a stevedore," he said, folding Irene's thin arms across her chest in a way that was again more like a man would do it than a woman; he controlled Irene's body, but he couldn't feel everything the way she did. She'd have moved her arms slightly over her breasts, not the way he had them. Interesting; he could move the body, but how much could he feel?

"Insulting my bride-to-be is arrogant, though I cannot speak of the status of your parents."

I glanced back to see if Jean-Claude was joking, but his face was empty of expression, like a beautiful statue that just happened to move. It meant he was hiding very hard, which meant this was more serious than I understood. I hated dealing with the really old vampires; they were usually arrogant, and some of them were just . . . alien, as if the huge gap of centuries made them more other. Was it time, or were those long-ago cultures more alien than history understood?

"If I insulted you indirectly, my deepest apologies, my lord." He made a bow with Irene's body that just looked like it needed a taller, beefier body to go with it. It was like a bad puppeteer. I'd seen the Traveller, one of the ex–vampire council members, take over bodies, but he was better at it, smoother, more complete. This one seemed reluctant to move Irene's feet much, as if he wasn't certain of everything around her body, or couldn't feel her feet.

I squeezed Jean-Claude's hand and then let go of it slowly, wondering if touching each other was helping us "combat" the other vampire's mind games. I could feel the power rolling off Irene more, but other than sensing the power more, it wasn't bad.

"There are other jewelers, Jean-Claude. I don't want to wear a ring made by someone who sees me as less than a person." I moved slowly toward Irene.

"As you wish, *ma petite*," Jean-Claude said, making a sweeping gesture at the sparkling treasures on their velvet cloth. "Pack these up, Melchior, and take them away."

I moved closer to Irene, but she didn't even look at me. All her attention was on Jean-Claude, as his face showed that this was unexpected. "My lord king, we are close to finishing the design for the rings."

"We will begin again with another jeweler. They may not be the great artists that you and Irene are, but I'm sure they will be able to help us create something of lasting beauty. Though finding a living jeweler who has a true flair for crowns and diadems will be difficult. It's almost a lost art among the living, don't you think, Melchior?"

Irene's face looked pained, and her hand pressed to her chest. "Crowns, diadems, this is the first you mentioned such things."

"We had been discussing having something to hold Anita's veil in place. I know your work of old, Melchior; you would have done a masterful job of it, but we will make do with someone else. Perhaps Carlo will be interested in having a chance to create the first crown for vampirekind in centuries."

"That charlatan! No, my lord, my king, Jean-Claude, please do not turn to Carlo. He has no eye, no feel for the metal."

"You are a master of metalwork, Melchior, that is true, but it has been said that Carlo has a better eye for jewels. I prefer the jewels to the metalwork, so perhaps it's just as well."

"My lord, you must be teasing me."

I was right up next to Irene now. Her feet were at odd angles. The vampire ignored me as if I weren't standing right next to his servant's body. He discounted me completely. I wasn't sure if it was my being human, being female, or both, but either way I'd had enough. I moved a little behind Irene's body and foot-swept her legs out from under her. She fell so suddenly that if I hadn't been more than human-fast I couldn't have caught her in time. I held her in my arms and stared into her eyes and could finally see that they weren't as black as her hair, but a deep, rich brown. I smiled into those startled brown eyes and said, "You can't feel her feet. If I hadn't caught her she could have been hurt."

"What is your servant doing?" He turned Irene's face to look at Jean-Claude again, rather than me, though my face was inches from his.

"If you can't feel her body perfectly, it makes me wonder how tight your bond is with your human servant. It makes me wonder how hard it would be to give Irene a choice." I whispered that last against her cheek, their cheek.

Either he felt my breath or the whisper had gotten his attention, because he turned her face to look at me. "What are you talking about, woman?"

I smiled, and knew it was my unpleasant smile, the one that said I could do really awful things and never stop smiling. It wasn't voluntary, and it always unnerved people for some reason. "Look into my eyes, Melchior."

He gave a little chuckle. "That's our line, surely."

I felt my necromancy open like a fist too long closed. The power marched across my skin in a wave of goose bumps and hit Irene's skin where we touched.

"What is that?" He looked again at Jean-Claude. "Is that you, my lord?"

Jean-Claude shook his head and smiled.

Those brown eyes turned back to me. I was still holding Irene's body in my arms as if she weighed nothing, and she couldn't have been much over a hundred pounds. Her body was fragile, as if too many of her bones were too close to the surface, and again I thought she'd spent too much of her human life near starvation. It left its mark on you, and that thought wasn't mine, nor were the memories that went with it. Jean-Claude had been born poor, and he had memories of going to bed hungry, of listening to his sister's cry from lack of food.

"It is you, my lord, I see your eyes in her face," and the voice was happy again, satisfied.

I closed my eyes and called my power, chasing back Jean-Claude's memories. When I opened my eyes again, Irene was afraid of whatever she saw there. "Your eyes . . . they are cognac diamonds in the sun, so bright . . ." I knew it was my eyes as if I'd been my own vampire. I'd seen it happen before by accident, but lately I'd been able to do it when I wanted to do it.

"Go away, Melchior; leave Irene free to answer a question for me."

"What question?" He still sounded arrogant, even with fear in the edges of her eyes.

"I will ask her if she wishes to be free of you. Free to find a lover that you won't kill if he interferes with her work. Free to have a life outside your workrooms."

"She is my human servant; only death will free us of each other."

"Irene has met our Black Jade; her master is still alive, but his tiger to call now answers to me." I whispered it into her face from inches away, as if I meant to kiss her.

She swallowed hard, and I could see her pulse beating against the side of her thin neck like a trapped bird in a net. One of them was afraid of me.

"Only the Mother of All Darkness was able to break such bonds." But his voice didn't sound so sure of itself now.

"And who killed her, Melchior?"

"Jean-Claude did."

I smiled a little wider, and it was still unpleasant. I held Irene a little closer to me, straightening up, so I wasn't having to bend my back at quite the odd angle. "And what weapon did he use to kill the night herself?"

He stared at me, the fear spilling through more of those brown eyes. "You," he whispered.

"If Irene wishes to be free of you, we can make that happen."

"It is forbidden," he said.

"I don't like slavery. I think it's so 1800. If I think that Irene is just a slave for you, then I'll see that as breaking the law, Melchior."

"Breaking what law?" he asked, and started trying to push Irene's thin hands against my chest. He couldn't use her hands right, as if even now he couldn't really feel her body. When Jean-Claude and I shared like this we got every sensation, but then we never did the whole puppet thing; maybe that's what made the difference. We shared emotions, and physical sensations, not this possession.

"Slavery has been illegal here since 1865," I said.

"That is human law, not vampire law."

"But we are now subject to human law, Melchior," Jean-Claude said.

The vampire pushed at me clumsily with Irene's hands. "This is not what the new laws mean. It is one of our greatest taboos to interfere with another master's human servant."

"I had not thought of servants as slaves before, but you see, that is one of Anita's gifts, to see things from the point of an officer of the law. If she says that you are treating Irene as a slave, and it's illegal, then I'm sure a case could be made for it."

"You would not dare," he said, pushing at me like some girl in a horror movie who'd been told to struggle, but not too much.

"Do you love Irene?" Jean-Claude asked.

"What?"

"You heard him; do you love her?"

"I . . . I love her art. I love her creations."

"Do you love her?" Jean-Claude and I asked at the same time.

Those brown eyes stared up into my brown eyes, but mine burned brighter. Her face went a little slack. "I love the way her eyes glitter as she looks at the jewels and metal, and begins to create in her head. I love her long, thin fingers, so delicate when she sets the jewels in my metal. I love that I can begin engraving a line and she can finish it with a flourish or two that I didn't see. I love that she adds to my vision, and she still loves watching me work in metal, even as she aids me."

"You love her," I said, softly.

He looked puzzled, and then slowly, as if each word were drawn against his will, he said, "I think I . . . I think . . . I do. I don't know what I would do without her at my side. I would be lost without her quick fingers and her bright eyes. Her smile is the first to greet me at night and the last I see as dawn comes. I did not realize that she was so important to me."

"You love Irene," Jean-Claude said.

Irene's face didn't turn toward him this time, but continued to stare up into mine. "I love her, don't I?"

"Yes," I said, "you love Irene."

"I love Irene," he said.

"You love Irene."

"I love Irene," he repeated.

"Put her back on her feet, *ma petite*."

I put Irene's body solidly upright, hands still steadying her. The face turned to Jean-Claude. "You have bewitched me, Jean-Claude."

"*Non, mon ami*, we have shown you the truth."

"Are you saying I loved Irene before this?"

"I suspect it was love that made you want to make her your human servant in the first place, *mon ami*."

He shook Irene's head as if a fly were buzzing in his ear. "I am not certain that is true."

"We felt her need, and we looked into your heart, Melchior, and found an answering need."

"I didn't need to love her."

"No, you already did," I said.

"I am not certain . . . I mean . . ." He turned and looked at me with Irene's face. He looked confused.

"You love Irene, and you can't wait to tell her that," I said.

He frowned at me. "I . . . tell her that."

"Some of the most glorious art in the world has been created because of love, Melchior; think what you and Irene may create with your love and art intertwined," Jean-Claude said.

"Yes," he said, "yes, we will craft you such rings, and a crown worthy of our first queen in centuries."

I wanted to argue that whole queen part, but we were winning, so I kept my mouth shut. "Let Irene be present, Melchior, and we will talk of your creations," Jean-Claude said.

"No, no, we must begin again. I did not understand love before; my designs are too cold. You need something warmer, hotter, more . . . loved."

"As you think best, Melchior."

"My king." He bowed to Jean-Claude, and then he turned to me. "My queen." He had never addressed me like that, let alone included me in the bowing.

"Go now, let Irene back," Jean-Claude said.

"As you wish, my king." And from one blink to the next Irene was there. It was the weirdest thing, because it was the same body, but you just knew it was her again. The expression, the body language, all of it went back to just Irene.

She smiled at us. "Now, where were we?"

I studied her face, and so did Jean-Claude, and then we looked at each other. I raised an eyebrow. "Do you remember anything from the last few minutes, Irene?"

She smiled at both of us, raising her eyebrows, and gave a little shrug. "I'm assuming my master has been present. I am but his vessel to fill as he sees fit."

"And that doesn't bother you?" I asked.

"He has allowed me to live for centuries beyond my mortal span, and to learn more of metal and jewels than I ever dreamt possible. He is my master not just as servant and vampire, but master jeweler. We have traveled the world and the centuries in search of art and beauty, and raw stuff of our craft drawn from the earth itself, or sometimes wicked people."

"It sounds very adventurous," Jean-Claude said.

She nodded, happily. "It is, my lord."

"If he loved you as much as he loves your art, would that not be a glorious thing?"

She lowered her eyes and blushed. "Oh, my lord, you tease me."

"I think you underestimate your worth to your master, Irene."

She shook her head.

"Should we tell her?" I asked.

"Tell me what?" she asked, looking up.

"Your master has some new ideas to discuss with you," Jean-Claude said.

"But I thought we were almost done with the design."

"He said that he has some new ideas," I said.

"Something about wanting to capture love in the rings, or something like that," Jean-Claude said, waving a hand vaguely in the air. He looked harmless and almost foppish, the way he'd hidden his power for centuries among the other vampires. He was just handsome and seductive, nothing else to see, move along, move along.

"Well, I'm sure my master knows best; he is the greatest metalsmith in the world." She smiled happily and simply began to repack all the jewelry. She never questioned our word, or that her master might simply use her like a puppet and change all their plans. It probably happened often enough, because Melchior had been an "artist" for a few thousand years. It gave you an attitude. I wondered how Irene would feel about his new inspiration.

We waited while she packed and the guards let her out. They'd make sure that her personal guards who had been made to wait in the back were at her side before she took that much bright and shiny outside the Circus. It would suck to have her mugged on the way back to her master now that he loved her.

When we were alone in the room, I turned to Jean-Claude. "Did he really love her all along?"

"I believe so."

"But you don't know so."

"No."

"Did you make him fall in love with her?"

He gave that Gallic gesture that was almost a shrug, but not quite. "We lifted the veil and allowed him to see the brightest jewel in his collection, that is all."

"You mean Irene."

"*Oui.*"

"And we're both tired of people discounting me because I'm your human servant."

"And that," he said.

"Are you really going to make me wear a tiara for the wedding?"

He smiled like some fallen angel trying to sell you ice cubes in hell. "Well, *ma petite*, it would be churlish of us to strip him bare enough to fall in love and then insult his art."

I looked at the ceiling, took in a deep breath, let it out, and said, "Fuck, you didn't tell me we had to wear crowns."

"You will look lovely, *ma petite*."

I gave him a narrow look. "If I have to wear one, you have to wear one."

He gave that almost-shrug again. "Very well."

I frowned at him, and then a thought made me try to fight not to smile at him, but I finally gave up. "Why do I think the thought of wearing a crown has been a goal of yours for a few centuries?"

He smiled, and then finally grinned wide enough to flash the edge of dainty fangs. "It has been my experience that if you have the responsibility of leadership, you might as well have the jewelry to go with it."

I laughed and went to him. "I love you, you know that?"

"I do."

"Are we actually going to say *I do* as part of the vows?"

"Come sit in my lap again and we will discuss it."

"I think if I sit in your lap again without witnesses, we'll get distracted." But I smiled when I said it.

"This meeting has run surprisingly short, and we are left with a hole in our schedule; whatever shall we do with the extra time?" he said, holding his hand out to me.

"Hmm . . . let me think," I said, walking closer.

He pulled me onto his lap, and my arms were just suddenly around him, as if they were made to fit that way. *"Je t'aime, ma petite."*

"I love you, too, Jean-Claude," I said, just before I kissed him.

7

WE LOVED OURSELVES out of some of our clothes, but not all. Our jackets had gone first, and then my belt had to go so we could put my gun carefully in a drawer. It was the only thing that couldn't just be thrown off to land wherever. I'd had a few moments where my gun had gone missing in a pile of clothes, and I had to dig for it when I needed it to protect us—so the gun was carefully placed. Our shirts were in a pile on the floor with the jackets. We only had about an hour until I had to be at a cemetery raising the dead for clients, and Jean-Claude would need to be at Guilty Pleasures lending his voice to the acts onstage. Besides, the leather pants he was wearing were one of those pairs that you had to peel down his body with lots of straps in the way. I'd learned that some clothing was better admired than stripped out of, just as some clothes that looked just as complex had a trick that made them fall off onstage at the appropriate moment. I unfastened the front of those pettable pants, and was fighting to slide my hands inside them, but Jean-Claude caught my hands in his and shook his head.

"What's wrong?" I asked.

"*Ma petite*, I have not fed tonight."

"I know."

He smiled. "I know your penchant for going down on men when they are small, and I would stay small for you until you allow me to take blood, but I do not have the patience for it tonight. Our time is too short for that much foreplay."

I sighed, and looked down at our hands sort of bunched at the top of his pants. "Okay, but I need some foreplay. I'm not really in the mood for a quick-quickie."

"I would not dream of it," he said, lifting my hands up, so that I wasn't trying to fish inside his pants. He laid a light kiss on each of my hands and then a firmer kiss on my mouth. His lips were already scarlet with my lipstick. It was a great color on him, actually.

He slid just the very tips of his fingers inside the edge of my blue satin bra. "This is a new color for you, *ma petite*; I approve."

"It matched the shirt," I said, and it did, but I also knew that it was a push-up bra that mounded my breasts up like an offering. The feel of his fingertips lightly brushing back and forth just inside the bra was distracting, but not too much, not yet.

He was looking at my breasts as he said, "Such bounty deserves attention."

"The bra matches the underwear," I said, enjoying the almost mesmerized look on his face as he stared at my breasts; he'd only recently confessed to being a breast man. It had prompted me to buy some bras I might have avoided just so I could see this look on his face.

His eyes came up to meet mine, and his smile was almost a grin, but he worked hard to not flash fangs when he smiled, so it stayed a little less happy than he seemed to be. "Oh, then I must see them together."

"I was hoping you would."

He dropped, gracefully, to his knees. I'd have just knelt, but he made it almost a dancing movement, as if there should have been a soundtrack to every movement he made. He slid his hands up along each of my thighs, working the material of my skirt upward as he did it, so that he revealed the matching underwear slowly, as if there were an audience to tease. He'd be helping some of the acts onstage tonight and his mind had already settled into that more theatrical theme. I didn't mind; it just seemed a shame to waste the show without an audience. If I'd been half the exhibitionist that Jean-Claude was, I could have made more money on stage than as a U.S. Marshal.

He worked my skirt up until it was bunched around my waist and the blue underwear gleamed in the office lights. He looked up at my breasts and back down at parts that were much closer to his face now. "They match perfectly," he said, and his voice was a little lower, a little softer.

"I've learned from the master," I said. "My master." I said the last part with a lift of my eyebrow and couldn't quite keep the sarcasm out of my voice.

He leaned in toward my thigh. "Some see the fact that you will never say that and mean it as a weakness on my part." He laid his cheek against my leg, those drowning deep blue eyes staring up at me, down the length of my body.

"Do I apologize for that?" I asked; my pulse had already sped up and he'd barely touched me.

"No, *ma petite*, I did not want a slave. I wanted a partner, and that you have given me in so many ways."

He traced one fingertip along the edge of my panties, such a light touch, but I knew what those long, gifted fingers could do, so even that touch made me catch my breath. He played his finger along the very edge of the panties in that hollow inside my thigh, so that he was tantalizingly close to other things. He moved his fingers to the front of my thigh and slipped them just inside the blue satin, so that he traced the edge of my thigh as he'd traced my breasts just moments ago. He laid a gentle kiss on the mound of me inside my panties, then reached up and began to slowly pull them down.

My eyes were already soft focused, my breath and pulse faster, and he'd barely done anything, but it was the memory of all the other times that got him the reaction. Good sex was like money in the bank; if you made regular and sizable deposits, you earned more interest. Jean-Claude had earned a lot of interest over the years.

He pulled my panties down to my ankles, so they rode just above my high heels. I would have asked him to take them the rest of the way off, but he kissed the bare skin of me, just above the places I most wanted him to touch, and it stole my words, and damn near stole my breath. The skin really was bare now. I'd fought shaving completely for years, but it had been a request to just try it, and if I didn't like it, it would grow back. It was as if everything was more heightened to touch and especially to oral without the hair to interfere, or maybe you could just lick and suck better with nothing between the mouth and the body. Besides, I didn't like picking pubic hair out from between my teeth either.

He licked the edge just above that spill into even more intimate parts. He teased back and forth, tracing the edge of me without ever going deeper, until I whispered, "Please."

He rolled those midnight-blue eyes up at me, and then rose back just enough to say, "Please, what, *ma petite?*" But he slid his fingers across the parts of me I'd been wanting him to kiss, and that stole my words away. I couldn't think; all I could do was feel what he was doing between my legs. I fought my way back to being verbal, opened my mouth, and he plunged one finger inside me. I managed to gasp out, "Not fair."

"Oh, I think it is very fair," he said, smiling, his eyes full of that dark light that has nothing to do with vampire powers and everything to do with being male. He used his free hand to lean me so hard against the desk I was almost sitting on it. He moved his finger back to playing with the intimate bits that weren't inside, and lowered his mouth back to me, so that he was licking just in front of where his fingers caressed. That delicious pressure began to build where he was licking and touching. I breathed his name like a prayer. He started licking faster, over and over on that one sweet spot, while his fingers played lower, and I was suddenly over the edge and screaming my orgasm before I'd had time to think about whether I wanted to be quiet here in the office.

He kept licking, drawing out the orgasm, and slipped his finger inside me, making it go in and out of me fast, reaching for that spot just inside, so that while I was still writhing from the first orgasm he brought me with the second kind, and I stopped screaming, because I was too lost to sensations. It was almost as if my body couldn't decide which orgasm to follow. As if he understood that, he stopped licking and just used his fingers, driving them in and out of me fast and solid until I screamed a new orgasm for him. I felt his lips on the inside of my thigh, his free hand gripping the outside of it, but his other hand kept going in and out of me, like juggling multiple balls. I stared down my body at his dark hair, his face buried against me. I felt his hand on my thigh tense, a moment of hesitation from his other hand, and then he bit me, and a second later I felt the fangs pierce me, but it was lost in the orgasm so that the feel of his teeth, his mouth locking on my skin and sucking hard and tight was just part of the pleasure until I wasn't sure which was making me orgasm: his fingers, or his bite. Then he was standing, pushing me back onto the desk with my legs dangling over the side. My panties were lost on the floor somewhere as he pulled himself free of the leather pants, so I had a moment of seeing him long and hard and ready, before he pushed himself inside me. His voice came out strained. "So wet, so tight, so sweet, *ma petite.*"

I rose up just enough, like a version of an ab crunch, so I could watch him slide in and out of me, but as his rhythm sped I had to spill back along the desk and just let my body ride the sensations of him inside me. I looked up into that face, and he stared down at me so that we were drowning in each other's eyes as he fucked me on the desk, my body moving with the push and pull of him, his hands tight on my hips to keep me on the edge of the desk. That deeper pleasure began to build like a weight of anticipation in a part of my body that he couldn't actually touch, but it felt as if every deep thrust, every pull-out over that one spot just inside, touched things that no light would ever see, no hand could ever touch, but he could; Jean-Claude could find all the dark happy places inside me.

His eyes bled to vampire glow, as if a night sky could blaze with its own light and let you know that even in the darkest hour the sky is still blue. The press of pleasure built and built as he conjured it closer and closer to the surface, and then from one moment to the next, one stroke of his body to the next, he brought me screaming, my hands scrambling across the smooth empty surface of the desk.

He held on to his rhythm until he'd brought me multiple times and I was almost boneless on the desk, my body half-conscious from the pleasure of it all. Only then did he let himself speed his thrusts for himself without aiming at the sweet spots inside me, and finally let go of all that control. I watched his face through half-closed eyes as his head came forward, all that hair spilling around him, hiding his face, and then his spine bowed backward, taking his head with it so that he was curved above me, face slack with his own pleasure.

His breathing was ragged, and I could see his pulse against the side of his neck. The sex brought him to "life" more than almost anything else. I loved watching his body react like any man's with a light dew of sweat on that pale, muscled chest. There was a faint pink shine to the dew of sweat on his chest from the blood he'd drunk from me. He might not be able to wear a white shirt to work tonight. I was okay with that, and I was pretty sure so was he.

8

JEAN-CLAUDE AND I cleaned up in the half bath that was in the back of the office. Ever the gentleman, he let me clean up first, but also because he'd take longer in the bathroom than I would, and he knew patience wasn't my greatest virtue. The compromise was that I came out of the bathroom in my bra and undies and would dress out in the office, so he could fuss in the bathroom longer. I checked my phone before I put on anything else, but there was no message from Manny, no missed call. Screw it. I called Manny again. My first phone message had been simply, "Call me." This one needed more details.

It went straight to voice mail, so he was on the phone. Damn it. "Manny, this is Anita again. I really need to talk to you about a case. I need your input." I stopped short of mentioning Dominga Salvador for two reasons. One, I tried not to share any information about ongoing federal investigations that I didn't have to, and two, his wife, Rosita, checked his phone regularly. She knew he and Dominga had been lovers once. She'd never forgiven him for sleeping with any women besides herself, even those who were years before she and Manny met. I didn't really understand jealousy to that degree, but I didn't want to make his life hard if I could avoid it. But if he didn't call me back soon, I was going to have to mention the name, because I knew that would make him call. She was dead, but it was like talking too much about the devil; you always wondered if they heard you. In Dominga's case, hearing us from hell seemed totally reasonable. Yes, she had been that kind of evil scary.

I sat there staring at the phone and thought about texting him, but Manny was like a lot of people over fifty. He had a smart phone, but he treated it like it was still just a portable phone. He never returned texts. I wasn't even sure he read them.

My phone rang, but I knew it wasn't Manny, because it was Micah Callahan's ring tone: "Lovefool" by the Cardigans. "Hey, short, dark, and handsome," I said, and was smiling as I said it.

"Hey, beautiful." And I could hear the smile in his voice, too. "I heard that the jewelry appointment was cut short."

"Wow, that's fast gossip."

"I told Lisandro I needed to talk to Jean-Claude and you if there was a free moment, so he told me."

"Okay, but I will have to leave in about forty-five minutes. I can't leave clients waiting for long."

He laughed. "They get nervous if you leave them alone in graveyards, I know."

"Cemeteries are actually damned peaceful. They just spook themselves," I said.

"I know that, too."

"Do you want us to come to you?"

"I just came up all those damned stairs, so no. I'll come to you. I love you, Anita."

"I love you more."

"I love you most."

"I love you mostest."

We hung up and I turned to find Jean-Claude out of the bathroom shirtless, but with his leather pants fastened. He was as dressed as he could get until he was sure it was safe to put the white shirt back on or he got a second, darker shirt.

"I really do like you in the blue; thank you for not getting dressed yet. Which of our cats was on the phone, for that is your endearment only to the two of them," he said.

I ignored the compliment, because saying that it had been accidental rather than undressing for him on purpose seemed the wrong thing to say, so I said, "Glad you like it, and it was Micah; apparently he told Lisandro to alert him if we had any free time to talk."

"Talk?" Jean-Claude said. "About what?"

"He didn't say, but he's already up the like bajillion steps from the underground apartments, so he'll be here in minutes and you can ask him."

"The steps were designed to discourage intruders, *ma petite*."

I laughed. "Seriously, how many steps are there, has anyone ever counted?"

I would say he sat down on the couch, but that doesn't really cover it. He draped himself artfully on the couch, long pale arms stretched along the back of it, so that the leather of the couch acted like a frame for his body. He rested one booted ankle on his opposite knee so that he managed to look both like a tough from some Old West movie and suggestive.

"Do you do that on purpose or are you just naturally that decorative?" I asked, leaning my butt against the desk.

"I did have a natural flair for being, as you say, decorative, but centuries of practice do, indeed, make perfect." He smiled, obviously pleased with himself, and it made me smile, because once he'd hidden from me just how much he liked himself. I didn't blame him, because I had so many issues with my own physicality that I'd been uncomfortable with how very comfortable he was in his own skin and with his own beauty.

He held one hand out toward me, and I went to him, because when someone you love holds out their hand to you, that's what you're supposed to do. I curled up beside him in my new blue undies and he drew me in against his body, holding me close with one arm.

"You may distract our leopard king dressed like this."

"I don't have time to talk and distract him," I said, laughing, and started to get up, but he pulled me back down, and then there was a knock on the door.

"Just a minute," I called out.

Lisandro said through the door, "It's Micah."

"I'm not exactly dressed," I said, "so him, but not you."

Lisandro laughed. "I'm going home to my wife at the end of shift, I won't peek." The door opened with a glimpse of Lisandro's dark figure turned away so he couldn't see into the room and Micah could walk past him.

Micah came through the door like he came through every door, as if the room were his room, or at the very least he was thinking of purchasing it. It was a surety and security in himself that he'd had since I'd met him. He was wearing blue jeans and a deep green T-shirt fitted to his lean runner's body, because he was exactly my height, and when a man is that short he needs fitted clothes, or he always looks like he's borrowing someone else's. His dark brown hair was back in a braid, or something so tight that you could barely tell that it curled. Loose, it fell past his shoulders. He almost always kept it back, and if I hadn't threatened to cut my hair short if he cut his, he'd have cut it boy-short, but I loved his hair, and he loved me.

He smiled when he saw us, his delicate triangular face alight with some inner joy; the sunglasses that hid his eyes stopped us from seeing that happy thought fill his eyes, but as if he heard my thought he took them off and let us see his chartreuse eyes. They were more green than gold because of the shirt he was wearing, but you could still see the yellow in them like sunlight shining through some jungle canopy. They were leopard eyes trapped in his human face; he'd had brown eyes in human form once, but that was before I met him. To me, Micah's eyes were always this amazing color, in whatever form he took, human or leopard.

"Well, don't you look pretty as a picture," he said, his voice full of that happiness that showed in his face.

"Join us and it will be prettier," I said.

He shook his head but kept walking toward us. "A man's got to know his limitations, and since I'm third prettiest in the room, I won't add to the beauty factor."

I frowned. "You are beautiful," I said.

"You are beautiful in your own right, *mon ami*."

He grinned, standing just at the edge of the couch looking down at us. "I know I'm attractive, I'll give you pretty, though when I was younger I hated being told I was pretty."

"Not manly enough," I said, and held my hand out to him.

He took my hand but didn't sit down. "No, maybe if I'd been taller it wouldn't have bothered me as much. It certainly doesn't bother Jean-Claude."

"Oh, *mon chat*, when I was your age men wore elaborate wigs and clothes more elaborate than women's fashion today. A pretty man was prized, and if he could ride, hunt, and use a sword, then he was the height of everything that was best in a man."

"I can't imagine a world where I didn't get grief for looking the way I do as a man."

"It was a man who taught me how to wear high heels, because that's what noblemen wore."

"Nice."

I pulled on Micah's hand. "Cuddle with us."

He grinned and shook his head. "If I cuddle with you wearing that I'll get distracted, and we need to talk."

My smile faded around the edges. "That sounds ominous."

Jean-Claude held me a little tighter. "In all the centuries I have been alive, no conversation that began with the equivalent of 'we need to talk' has ever gone well."

"I don't mean it like that, but I've been trying to talk to just the two of you for a few days now and the scheduling hasn't worked out. I know Anita has to be on the road in a little less than forty-five minutes, and Jean-Claude has at least two hours before he can leave the building safely for Guilty Pleasures."

"You checked our schedules," I said.

"I know your schedules, or at least Jean-Claude's. Yours is too flexible to memorize."

"Okay, sit down and talk instead of cuddle."

He gave me a look that took in every inch of me in the nice bra and panties. "I'll try, but you in more clothes might help me focus on talking."

I blushed and hated it.

He grinned and leaned down to lay a careful kiss on my mouth. "I love that you still blush."

I frowned at him. "Well, I don't."

"It is very endearing," Jean-Claude said.

"Don't you start."

"What is it you need to speak about?" he said, looking up at Micah.

Micah sat down on the couch, holding my hand, but perching on the edge of the couch as if touching me at all would make him forget what he wanted to say. "You know that I don't have a problem with Jean-Claude and you getting married. You can only legally wed one person and that's got to be our master, which is him."

"Yeah," I said.

"You have been most gracious," Jean-Claude said.

"You know that Nathaniel and I have been talking about having a handfasting ceremony with Anita for the three of us."

Jean-Claude nodded.

"We've been talking about getting rings to go on the right-hand ring finger for our threesome."

"I wish you better luck getting her to approve designs than I am having."

"You want such elaborate rings, Jean-Claude. Either they won't fly at my work, or they're just so expensive the thought of wearing them every day makes me nervous. It's like wearing Fort Knox on my hand."

"We do have different tastes in this area."

"We're going for something simpler," Micah said.

Jean-Claude looked at me. "Are you saying your taste matches theirs more than mine?"

"You know it does," I said.

He sighed and settled back on the couch a little more, which seemed a little less cuddling to me.

"Are you upset?" I asked.

Some thought passed over his face too fast or too faint for me to decipher. "No, but in a way I suppose I am. You and I have been debating for weeks on designs for our rings. I think the only reason we were moving ahead with the more elaborate set to be used in the ceremony and state events afterward is that you gave up and let me have my way."

I shrugged. "It's important to you, and I don't have to wear them every day."

"But we are no closer to a design for the set we will wear every day," he said.

"True."

"But with Micah and Nathaniel you almost have an everyday design, do you not?"

I glanced at Micah. He was studying the other man's face.

Micah said, "Not quite, but we're close."

"It seems childish, but I believe it will bother me if you have your rings designed before ours."

"I'm sorry, Jean-Claude, I had no idea," Micah said.

"Nor did I; it is strange what will and will not bother you in this complicated domestic arrangement of ours."

"Remember how upset the rest of our domestic arrangement was when they thought the four of us were planning a commitment ceremony?"

"Yes, but once they realized the wedding is just *ma petite* and myself, they quieted."

"Until they found out that the three of us were still looking at having a commitment ceremony."

"I take it they found out about the rings," I said.

He nodded.

I just hid my face against Jean-Claude's chest. I did not want to deal with the fights and recriminations from some of the other lovers in our lives about this again.

"They want to be included, or rather not feel excluded," Micah said.

"We cannot marry everyone we are sleeping with," Jean-Claude said.

"No, and I think all of us would be willing to include one other person; unfortunately it wouldn't be the same person."

"You put it well, *mon ami*."

"Jean-Claude has been in love with Asher for centuries, but none of the rest of us is willing to tie ourselves to his moods."

"I love Asher," I said. "I might even be a little in love with him, but no, I won't tie myself to him."

"Anita and Nathaniel would marry Nicky, but I won't," Micah said.

"Nor will I," Jean-Claude said.

"Nathaniel would include more people than any of us, but it doesn't include the ones the rest of us would include."

"So what, either we include everybody, or we can't have a commitment ceremony?" I asked.

"How big a fight do you want on your hands?" Micah asked.

"I will not be forced to marry someone I don't love, even if it isn't legally binding," I said.

"If we don't have our ceremony, then the problem goes away," Micah said.

"Are you willing to just give up on that?" I asked.

"Are you?" he asked.

"No; if I could figure out a way to marry all three of you for legal real, I would."

"I got the clan tigers to agree that if we included one of them in our commitment ceremony, the others would back off," Micah said.

It was our turn to look at him.

"You did what?" I asked.

"And did you have a weretiger in mind?" Jean-Claude asked.

"My first choice is Cynric."

"No," I said, and it was very final.

"He lives with us, Anita. He helps Nathaniel with the domestic stuff. When I'm out of town on business he sleeps in the bed with you and Nathaniel at the house in Jefferson County."

"Nicky sleeps with us, too," I said, and it sounded churlish even to me.

"And sometimes all four of you bunk together when I'm not there, but when I am there Cynric is the only one I'm willing to wake up and see on the other side of you, or Nathaniel. Besides, Nicky is a werelion, and that won't help us get the tigers off our back about this."

"Cynric is nineteen years old; he should be out playing the field, not settling for just hanging on to the fringes of my love life."

"How is he on the fringe? We wake up most mornings with him helping Nathaniel and Nicky cook breakfast. We go to bed at least half the time with him in the bed with us, no matter who else is included. We can all talk for hours."

"When he's done doing his homework," I said.

"He's graduating soon and already lined up for college, Anita."

"I just have problems saying I'm dating a high school student."

"He's a senior."

"A high school senior," I said.

"What difference does it make if he's in high school or college? That doesn't change what he means to all of us."

"What difference does it make? What difference does it make?" I stood up and knew I was yelling and didn't care. "He was only sixteen when the Mother of All Darkness mind-fucked us and he and I had sex. I don't even remember it, but he does. For me it was like some date-rape drug, so I know I did it, but I didn't choose to do it, and I resent like hell that it happened like that."

"It wasn't just you and Cynric that night, Anita. The Mother of All Darkness rolled about a half dozen of you."

"But only Cynric followed me home and stayed!"

"Crispin and Domino were there that night, and they live here now," Micah said.

He was right, and I knew it, but somehow it felt wrong. "It's not the same. Crispin and Domino are grown men. They came to stay in St. Louis, but when I didn't have time for them in my life they found lives of their own. They have jobs and Crispin dates other people, and Domino is beginning to, but Cynric is always there. I thought he'd go away next year to college and stay in the dorms, but now he's planning to commute."

"You are his master, *ma petite*; you could have ordered him to live in the dorms."

I glared at him. "I don't want to order people how to live their lives, I just want them to live their lives and leave me the fuck alone!"

"You mean you want Cynric to live his life somewhere else and leave you alone," Micah said.

I thought about it, and then nodded. My voice was calm when I said, "Yes, yes."

"Why?" he asked.

"Because he's only nineteen and I'm thirty-one. Because he and I raped each other when he was only sixteen. Because he was a virgin and no one should lose their virginity in a metaphysical orgy orchestrated by one of the most evil powers I've ever felt. Because every time I see Cynric I think about Her, about that evil bastard who raped us both!"

I stood there in the strangely loud silence with my own words echoing inside my head.

Micah and Jean-Claude looked at me. Jean-Claude's expression was as empty and perfect as any I'd ever seen on his face; hiding his emotions in an instant, a trick that had helped him survive in the seat of vampire power for centuries. Micah's face showed pain, compassion, and finally as many emotions as Jean-Claude showed none.

"Well, fuck," I said, softly.

Micah stood up and started to hug me, but I put my hand out and backed up.

I wanted him to hold me, but I knew if he did I might break down and I didn't want that. I wanted to think, or try to think. But of course, I couldn't think; all I could do was resonate with the clue-by-four that had fallen out of my mouth. I was like a bell that had been struck and the sound was still vibrating through me. I felt the shock of it down to my fingertips, as if I'd been physically struck and I couldn't catch my breath.

Micah reached out to me, then let his hands fall back to his sides. "Anita, what can we do?"

I opened my mouth, closed it, and then shook my head. There was nothing they could do, nothing that anyone could do; it was done. We couldn't fix it, because we couldn't change it; all we could do was move forward from here. I just wasn't as sure where "here" was anymore.

"Fuck," I said softly.

Micah approached me again, slower this time, no sudden movements, the way you act around a spooked horse. They are very large, powerful animals and you don't want them scared enough to lash out and hurt you, or themselves. I half expected Micah to start saying, *Easy, easy.*

When I didn't tell him to stop he kept approaching me, until he could lay a hand on my shoulder. I didn't push him away this time. I just sort of stood there and let him come closer. I was staring somewhere in the middle distance as if I were seeing another room, one in Las Vegas, three years ago.

Did I feel like a victim? No, but . . . but . . . something.

Micah hugged me gently, carefully, and I let him hold me. I didn't hug him back, but I didn't stay stiff; my body relaxed against him, but my arms just hung there while I thought my way through it all.

My voice sounded hoarse and not quite like me when I said, "I haven't let any of the men from Vegas get too close to me. I've kept Crispin and Domino out of the main part of my life. I've pushed them as far as they could go without sending them back to Vegas."

"Yes," Micah said, softly.

I put my arms around him slowly, almost reluctantly, and then I held him tight. "Except Cynric," I said.

"Yes," he said, and started rubbing my back in those slow, useless circles that you do.

"I blame them all for what happened, don't I?"

"I don't think you blame them, but I think it's exactly what you said, they remind you of it. Looking at them every day means you can never forget what happened."

"I don't even remember most of the sex. Why would it bother me if I don't remember?"

Jean-Claude was at our side. He laid his hand very carefully on my hair, as if afraid I'd tell him to stop touching me, and when I didn't he started stroking my hair. "Somewhere in this wonderful mind of yours you remember what happened, and if your mind does not, your body does. It's as if the very cells of the skin itself absorb some memories too painful to carry in the brain."

I turned my head, and he had to move his hand so I could look at his face. "That sounds like experience talking."

"You have shared some of my memories, *ma petite*; you know that I have my own share of horrors to overcome."

"Is this a horror?" I asked.

He cupped the side of my face and studied me for a moment. Micah just kept holding me. "*Ma petite*, one person's pleasure is another's horror, and one person's 'no big deal'"—he shrugged and made one-handed air quotes—"can be another's trauma."

"I've been through worse . . . horrors," I said.

"Perhaps, or perhaps this bothered you more than the things that you see as more horrifying?"

"Why? Why this? I've waded through blood and body parts, and just kept moving. This was nothing in the grand scheme of things. No one died but the bad guys."

Micah spoke with his face against my hair, so I could feel the warmth of his breath against my ear. "Anita, you were drugged and possessed by what amounted to a demon; that's pretty traumatic."

I pulled back enough to look at his face. "They were big bad vampires, the Mother of All Darkness, and Vittorio, the Father of the Day, but they weren't demons. If you'd ever been around real demons you wouldn't use the word for anything else."

He smiled, sort of sad. "I keep forgetting how much you've seen. I'm sorry, you're very right, I shouldn't use the word if I don't understand what it means."

I pulled away from him, from both of them, and then reached out to them and took their hands in mine. I held on to their hands, but I didn't want to be held so close. I wanted to think and I couldn't always do that in their arms; they tended to distract me in so many ways.

"They were battling each other; I was just a tool to be used, or discarded. We were all just tools like you'd pick up a gun to shoot your enemy, but you don't worry about the gun having feelings, or being able to love. It's just a piece of metal. You pull the trigger and it does its job, sort of like being a vampire executioner. I get a warrant of execution and they aim me at the rogue preternatural citizen; I hunt them down and execute my warrant. I'm just a weapon. You aim me at something, and I kill it; it's what I do, it's who I am."

Micah squeezed my hand and pulled me enough to get me to look at him. "That is not all you are, Anita. When I met you, you were already more than that."

Jean-Claude raised my hand and laid a gentle kiss across the knuckles.

"I don't remember the last time you kissed my hand."

He rose and said, "Perhaps when I was not allowed to kiss your lips. There was a time when you were a weapon to be aimed and used, but that was years ago, *ma petite*. You have forged yourself a family, friends, a life, and it is a good one, one that makes us all so very happy."

I nodded, and knew they were both right. "They tried to make me just a thing, something to be used and thrown away, or possessed so completely that I would have disappeared. Marmee Noir wanted to take over my body, and I would have ceased to be me."

"But you slew her, *ma petite*."

I kept nodding. "Yes."

"And from the stories that everyone told when you got back, if you hadn't had Domino at the end, the Mother of All Darkness might have won instead," Micah said.

I blinked and looked at him. I remembered reaching out in the fight, when I was drowning in the darkness that was her, and finding Domino's hand to hold, his power of white and black tiger completely the power I needed.

"She meant to use you both like pawns, but you turned yourself into a queen, and made Domino your knight, and destroyed her."

The Mother of All Darkness had been the night given form, and she had done her best to take me over and make me into a meat puppet for her spirit to inhabit. When that hadn't worked, she'd tried to get me pregnant by one of the cat lycanthropes that she could control. She'd been willing to wait until the baby grew old enough and then she'd have moved in, but none of it had worked out. Hired assassins had blown up her last body with modern bombs and fire, and that cleanses everything, even her, but her spirit escaped and left her shell behind. How do you kill something that is untouchable, just floating from body to body? By making it stay in one place long enough, inside one person long enough, to kill it. I hadn't done it on purpose, but she had wanted me so badly that I'd been bait enough to make her linger.

She had tried to pour thousands of years of darkness into me, and in the end I had used the vampire powers I'd gained, partly through her meddling, to drink her down. It was like drowning in a night-black sea, but instead of fighting to breathe the air I'd let myself sink and bet that I could drink the ocean faster than it could drown me. I was losing when Domino's hand had reached into that darkness and grabbed me, given me his energy to help tip the balance. Domino and Ethan, who had been the newest weretiger of all, had carried every genetic line that had belonged to the tiger clans, and it had been enough to save me and help destroy the Mother of All Darkness.

"Domino without Ethan wouldn't have been enough; it took both of them with their mixed heritage to save me," I said.

"*Oui*, if Ethan had not held the bloodlines of red, gold, and blue tiger clans, then the white and black of Domino would not have been enough, but the point stands, *ma petite*. You had the power of the tiger clans at that moment, that singular moment that the tigers had been prophesying about for over two thousand years."

"Yeah, yeah, I'm supposed to save everybody from the great bad thing, because I'm the Queen of Tigers."

"But it worked exactly as the prophecy predicted, *ma petite*; without the weretigers you could not have prevailed, and without you to harness their power they could not have killed their dark nemesis."

I'd have argued with the term *dark nemesis*, but it was too damned accurate. If the Mother of All Darkness and Vittorio hadn't forced us together, I'd be worse than dead now. I'd be trapped inside my own body, watching her use it to do terrible things. She had been a necromancer like me, but a thousand times more powerful. She could have raised an army of the walking dead to do her bidding. I wondered if she could have done what I had seen on the FBI tapes. Could Marmee Noir have put someone's soul back in their zombie corpse? I didn't think so; I was almost certain that required voodoo, which she hadn't known, but I wouldn't have put anything past her. Thinking about the case steadied me, helped me remember who I was, what I was, and that I was no one's victim. I had survived, and they were dead; if anyone was anyone's victim, they were mine.

"Fuck them," I said, forcefully.

Micah smiled at me. "That's our girl."

"Indeed she is," Jean-Claude said. He leaned in and laid a gentle kiss against my hair.

I nodded, but this time it was just a nod, not that endless, helpless gesture. I wrapped my arms around their waists, which made them wrap their own arms around each other so they could both hold me together. I pressed my face into Jean-Claude's chest and Micah's shoulder. Jean-Claude was still bare-chested, his smooth skin soft against my face. Micah's T-shirt was soft, but not as soft and warm as his skin would be. I almost told him to take off the shirt so I could touch more of his skin, and just thinking it helped me feel more like myself again. I wasn't gone, or changed, by the evil that had touched me. I was still in here, still me, and that meant sex was good, not bad. I felt bad that I'd pushed Domino and Crispin away for something that wasn't their fault. I wasn't sure I would ever feel closer to them, but I could at least acknowledge what I'd been doing and maybe why.

I'd thought I had too many people in my life, but maybe I had too much trauma attached to too many people. It sounded like almost the same thing, but it didn't feel the same. Leaving people out because you didn't feel that spark was one thing, but doing it because you blamed them for being with you when you all got mind-raped just seemed like punishing the victims. I tried really hard not to do that.

"Do I owe them an apology, or do I just keep moving?" I asked.

One of the men smoothed my hair, but it was Micah who asked, "Who?"

"Domino and Crispin."

"I do not believe so," Jean-Claude said.

I rose back enough from them to look up into his face. "Why not?"

"Because there is not enough of you to go around now, *ma petite*. I would not be willing to cut more of your time away to offer to them."

"I asked if I should apologize, not sleep with them more."

He smiled. "*Ma petite*, it is you; sex often goes with an apology."

Micah gave a half shrug, and his expression showed he agreed.

I frowned at them both.

"Truth is truth, *ma petite*."

"But you're encouraging me to put more time into Cynric."

"No," Micah said, "we're not, just acknowledging what's already happening, that's all."

"I don't understand what that means."

He glanced at Jean-Claude.

"What? What's that look?" I pulled away from them both. The anger flared immediately, hot and ready. I felt better, more myself, because anger had been one of my primary emotions for years. Sometimes when you're under stress you revert back to old habits, even the ones that you broke, because they weren't good for you, or your life.

"Did you notice that you talked about apologizing to Domino and Crispin, but not Cynric?" Micah asked.

I stood there furious with him, hands in fists at my side, my shoulders tensed and ready to fight, but I forced myself to think back over what I'd said. My shoulders loosened first, and then my fingers, so that I wasn't standing there as if the next thing I wanted was to hit someone.

"Well, shit," I said softly.

They just waited for me to think it all the way through.

I sighed, and wrapped my arms around myself, because I was suddenly cold standing there in my blue bra and panties. "Why didn't I talk about apologizing to Cynric?"

"That might be a therapy question," Micah said.

"Yeah, I guess it is. Shit." I hugged myself, starting to shiver.

Micah came to hug me, wrapping his warmth around me, but I stayed tight in his arms holding myself. "I need to get dressed and head in to work."

He rose back and looked at me. "You're shaking from emotional shock, and you're just going to dress and drive to your appointment?"

"Yes, I have a job to do."

"Throwing yourself into your work won't make this go away."

I pulled away from him. "I'm not avoiding the issue, I really have to go to work, or I'm going to be late."

"The zombie you're raising tonight is a few hundred years old; I think it'll wait a few extra minutes."

I shook my head. "I'm going to work, because it's mine. If I'm still me then I keep moving forward. I go to work, I keep my appointments, and I do my regular stuff."

"And if you give yourself a few extra minutes to process, what happens?" Micah asked.

"If I let this change anything, if I hesitate, then it gets me," I said.

"What gets you?" he asked.

"This, this issue, this thing, this emotional shit."

"So run fast enough and it won't catch you," he said, voice low.

I shrugged, still hugging myself, and shivering harder.

"*Ma petite*, would you do two things for us?"

"What?" And I snapped it at them. I took in a deep breath, let it out slow, and said in a more normal tone, "What?"

"Kiss us good-bye so we know that you will not take this revelation and punish us with it."

I wanted to argue, but as he'd said, truth was truth, and I'd run away from all the relationships in my life for months at a time for far less trauma than this.

I nodded. "Okay, what's the second thing?"

"Let one of the guards drive you to your first appointment."

"I don't want them tagging along all night."

"As I understand it, Nicky and Dino are meeting you at the cemetery with a truck big enough to tow a trailer containing a cow."

"Yeah."

"Then surely they will have room for the extra guard to drive off with them after you have raised your first zombie of the night."

His logic was great; it made perfect sense, so why did I want to argue? Answer: Because I had had a nasty shock and was all emotionally vulnerable; that usually made me want to either run for the hills or get angry and stay angry. In the end I agreed to a driver, because of how badly I didn't want one. The more I didn't want to be logical, the worse

I was hurt; once it would have led to a full-blown fight about something peripherally connected to the thing that was actually upsetting me. Now, the urge to throw logic and caution to the wind was a way of lashing out without starting an actual fight. I knew this; I actually had a therapist now, because somewhere in demanding that other people in my life work their issues, it started to seem hypocritical not to do the same. I wondered if she would be surprised by my revelation about Cynric, or have one of those "I've been waiting for you to realize that" moments.

I got dressed, and wanted to give them each a quick kiss, but that was me trying to pull away and blame everyone for the parts that were bothering me. I didn't do shit like that anymore, damn it, so I forced myself to stop and look at them both. I took their hands in mine, took in a deep breath, and let it out slowly.

"I will do my best not to fuck up all the great things in our lives because I've hit some kind of personal issue." I looked at Jean-Claude. "I won't run away like I did before, I promise. I know now that I can't run far enough, or fast enough, because most of the issues are inside me, and that travels with me."

"You have grown wise, *ma petite*."

I smiled, but wasn't sure how happy it was; it didn't feel happy. "Smarter, I'll give you; I'm working on wise."

"As you please, *ma petite*; I will not argue semantics with you."

I smiled for real then, and shook his hand a little. "That's good, because I'd probably lose right now, and I hate to lose."

That made them both laugh, which was good. I turned to Micah and had a second of getting lost in those extraordinary eyes. "You never saw me at my worst, but I'll tell you, before you ask, that I will do my best to work my shit and not let it rain down all over us."

"It's not us I'm worried about," he said.

I frowned at him. "I don't understand."

"You and I are solid; you, I, and Nathaniel are solid. I trust that. I'm going to ask you something that's much harder."

"What?" And that one word held a world of suspicion.

He gave a small smile, holding my hand a little tighter. "First, cut yourself some slack. You've just had a shock and you're barreling forward like it didn't happen, but it did, and we both know that ignoring it doesn't unmake it, so please, take care of yourself tonight." He put his free hand against my cheek and kissed me softly.

I drew back from the kiss with a smile. "I'll do my best, and Nicky will be there to help."

"He will. You are my highest priority, you know that," he said.

"Yes, but once you say it that way I know you're thinking of someone else, too."

"Don't blow up at Cynric when you see him next. He doesn't know what's going on inside your head, and he loves you."

I closed my eyes and counted a very slow ten. "Why did you have to say that? I was regrouping, and now I feel raw again."

"Because I love you and I know you; if you lose it and lash out at him you'll feel good for a few minutes while the rage finds a target, and then you'll feel worse. You'll beat yourself up, because you're taking your anger out on the other victim."

"Why aren't Crispin and Domino victims, too?" I asked.

"Because they don't see themselves as victims, and you don't see them that way either."

"That makes no sense; either you're a victim or you're not."

"Not true," Micah said. "You can experience trauma without getting stuck as the victim forever. You can choose to work the shit and rebuild yourself, or you can sit in the ruins and mourn forever. You and I both chose to rebuild."

I remembered then that he'd had his own share of trauma, first surviving a wereleopard attack that made him one, and then years of being abused by Chimera, the man who took over Micah's leopard pard. Chimera had been a sadistic bastard who had worked his personal issues out by torturing and killing those under his power. He'd been the one who had forced Micah into animal form so long that his eyes had stuck in leopard form and never went back to human. He could have been trapped in animal form forever, and never been able to regain human shape again, but he'd been powerful enough to survive intact, except for his eyes. Sometimes there isn't enough therapy in the world to fix a person, and that's when you have to find another cure. In Chimera's case dead was the cure, and I'd helped him find it. I never felt bad about that, but then he'd been trying to kill me at the time, and self-defense assuages guilt like a son of a bitch.

Jean-Claude stepped closer to us. "We all build upon our ruins."

I looked up into that almost unreal face, because no one was that beautiful, and remembered that he had endured hundreds of years of abuse at the hands of more powerful vampires before he'd been able to break free and be his own master. I'd met his last master, Nikolaos. She'd looked like a twelve-year-old girl but had been the first vampire I ever met who was over a thousand years old. She'd also been a sadist, and completely careless about the harm she did to those around her. She'd murdered a friend of mine, Phillip. He'd been everyone's victim, and was just starting to try to change that when Nikolaos had made him the ultimate victim and taken the last thing anyone can take from you: your life. I didn't feel guilty about killing her, but I still felt guilty about getting Phillip killed. Maybe she would have done it anyway, but he helped me solve some murders and she didn't like him tattling to me. I'd known he was weak, and scared, and everyone's victim, and I'd used him just like everyone else. Maybe it was for a good cause to save other lives, but in the end I doubted it mattered to Phillip. I'd told him I'd be back. I'd told him I'd keep him safe. They'd torn his throat out.

Jean-Claude touched my face. "What has put such a solemn look in your eyes, *ma petite*?"

"Do you remember Phillip?"

Something moved through his eyes, and then he blinked and gave me bland, empty, pleasant face. "Of course I do; he worked at Guilty Pleasures, and I could not protect him."

"You feel guilty about his death, too?"

"Oh, yes, *ma petite*, I feel guilty, because I was one of the vampires who took blood from him. I ran the club where he worked. I got him off street drugs, because I won't allow such things in my club, or on my stage, but he became addicted to being bitten, addicted to giving up his blood to us all. I thought I had saved him from an early death as a drug addict, but I only took him from one addiction to another, and it killed him."

"I didn't know that you got Phillip off drugs."

"We needed a handsome victim for one of our vampire dancers to feed onstage. He was brought to me as that. He cleaned up well, but it was because he had replaced one addiction with another, not because I cured him."

"Nikolaos killed him, because he was helping me solve the vampire murders."

Jean-Claude nodded. "That was her excuse. Phillip should have been mine to protect, but I was not powerful enough to help him. I was not powerful enough to help myself, until you came into my life and helped me break free of those who tormented us all."

I went to him, and Micah let me go so I could wrap my arms around the other man in my life. "I didn't realize you'd been that close to Phillip," I said.

"I wasn't close in the way that most humans mean, but he was my responsibility and I could not keep him from the monsters."

I nodded. "Me, either."

"But you killed the monsters that hurt him, and I could not even do that."

"Revenge is cold comfort when the person you're avenging is already dead," I said.

"That is true, *ma petite*, but it is still comfort, no matter how cold, or how late it is served."

I went up on tiptoe and put my arms around his neck. "Fuck revenge, here's to getting there in the nick of time."

He smiled and leaned down to whisper above my lips, "Yes, very yes."

We kissed and it was soft, and long, and full of as many shared tears as smiles, but that didn't lessen it; that made it more.

9

I DIDN'T LIKE having someone else drive my SUV, ever, but having them drive it because I was too emotionally overwrought about something that had happened several years ago just pissed me off. It felt weak, and I hated that. I wanted to aim all that self-loathing and pissiness at someone, and Nathaniel was sitting right there behind the wheel of MY car, driving me to MY job, because I was having some sort of internal crisis that I couldn't fucking handle. But it was Nathaniel and I loved him too much to take it out on him, which was probably why the other men in my life had picked him to chauffeur me. I hated being managed like this, but it was working, so I sat in the dark in the passenger seat and watched the headlights from the other cars, my arms crossed, and sort of huddling on my anger. I'd moved my gun from the small of the back to my right side, so it didn't dig in while I sat in the car. I was loving my new innerpants holster, though if I kept moving it around too much the leather wouldn't conform to my body the way it was designed to. It would be dark enough at the cemetery that I wouldn't accidentally flash the clients, but even that made me grumpy. Why should I have to hide my gun from clients when they knew I was a marshal? I so wanted to pick a fight with someone, but not with Nathaniel, and that was what Jean-Claude, or more likely Micah, had counted on. Damn it.

I glanced at Nathaniel as he drove, hands precise and careful. He didn't really like driving at night, and I knew that, so I'd be even less likely to pick at him. Nathaniel was also one third of my ménage à trois with Micah, and one of the last few that we all agreed should get a ring in whatever ceremony we finally decided on, and on the heels of that thought was that the weretigers were pushing us to include one of them in the commitment ceremony. The anger flared over my skin in a shiver of power, and distant as a dream I "saw" all the colors of tiger that I held inside me—white, red, black, blue, and gold—stare up at me.

Nathaniel shivered as he got the bleed-off from the burst of power, my beasts peeking out. He tried to rub one hand down his arm, but that moved the wheel too much and the car did a slight swerve. He put both hands back on the wheel, but I couldn't afford to distract him like that. He was my leopard to call, which made us so much more intimate metaphysically than just being in love ever could. I had to be the big, tough dominant personality and swallow the rage. It was an indulgence I couldn't afford right now. Yeah, the men in my life had managed me nicely, putting me with the other love of my life tonight.

I worked at letting go of the anger, and made myself look at him and remember how much I loved him, and how much I wanted to protect him. Me shoving my energy all over him and making us wreck was just stupid, and I tried not to do stupid. Nathaniel was dimmed in the darkness of the car, so that his thick braid looked brown, his skin almost gray-white; only an occasional streetlight flashing over showed the hair's rich auburn, the skin's clear, bright, almost luminous undertone that most people on the redhead spectrum seem to have. He glanced at me once, and a stray bit of light turned the grayed eyes to their true pale purple, like spring lilacs.

"At least you're looking at me, that's a start," he said, and went back to watching the road.

"I'm sorry, but my mood was bad enough that saying nothing was the best I had."

"I know," he said, softly, as he hit the turn signal before changing lanes with the dark line of cars, their headlights like glowing beads on a string, as the last of rush hour trickled away.

"I love that you understood that, and hate it at the same time, which doesn't make any sense at all, does it?"

"It makes sense for you," he said.

"What kind of answer is that?" I said, and it sounded grumpy. There was another whisper of energy, and I took a deep breath in slow, and let it out slow, trying to ease the tension in my shoulders. I forced myself to sit up straighter and not hunch around my anger.

He gave me a sideways glance, frowning, and he was less handsome that way than when he smiled, but not by much. There wasn't much Nathaniel could do to spoil his beauty, and he worked hard at making the most of his assets by hitting the gym regularly, watching what he ate, and keeping his hair at near ankle length. He'd finally had to trim a few dead ends so that the braid curled around him didn't actually touch his ankles anymore. I'd have strangled myself to death by accident if my hair had ever been that long, but he wore the hair like he did most things, gracefully; but then cats are known for that kind of thing and he was a wereleopard like Micah. I wondered if he'd always been this graceful, and because I could, I asked.

"Were you always this graceful, or is it the whole wereleopard thing?"

He looked at me and smiled. "I don't know about graceful, but I got spotted at the YMCA as a toddler and recruited into gymnastics, so I must have been more coordinated, or something."

"I didn't know you took gymnastics."

"I did until my mom got cancer. My aunt took me for a while, but then Mom died and my stepfather didn't think it was manly enough. He kept taking Nicholas to baseball, and he tried to get me into that, but I was never good at anything that involved hitting a ball. I could catch, but I couldn't throw, so I was shoved off into far left field where the coach probably prayed nothing too complicated would come my way." He laughed softly.

It sounded so ordinary, like a lot of people's childhoods, but I knew that at seven he'd witnessed his stepfather beat his older brother, Nicholas, to death. I had even shared the memory of that other little boy yelling, "Run, Nathaniel, run!" and Nathaniel had run. He'd run away, and been on the streets as a child prostitute by age ten. I'd never asked what happened between ages seven and ten.

This was the first time he'd offered anything positive about his stepfather, and I had a hard time reconciling a dad who would take the kids to Little League practice with the monster I'd seen swinging a baseball bat at those same boys. How could you be both? How could you do both?

"That's the most positive thing I've ever heard you say about him."

"Years of therapy and I can finally say that my stepdad wasn't always a monster. I don't remember much of him before Mom got sick, but that's when he started drinking. He was different when he drank; it was as if he became his rage like I become a leopard. When you first change shape you don't always have much control, and you don't remember what you did when you wake up the next morning. It's not that different from getting blind drunk, except as a wereanimal you have weapons instantly that can tear and claw, and rip people up."

"You were with the local wereleopards here when it happened the first time, though, right? Gabriel, your old leader, may not have been as powerful a dominant as Micah, but he was strong enough to make sure his cats didn't go out killing people when they shifted. Or do you mean he used the new leopards in some of their snuff films?"

"No, even Gabriel saw his duty as head of our pard better than that. That would have been a betrayal that we could have taken to other wereleopard groups and used as an excuse to ask for sanctuary. One of the few rules all animal groups hold to is that you take care of the fresh meat, so they don't have anything to regret when they first change shape."

"Okay, good. Gabriel was a sexual sadist and a lot of bad things, but you told me he got you off drugs before he'd change you into a wereleopard. That made me assume he'd been more careful of you when you first shapeshifted."

"I know you hated him, and I know you killed him because he was trying to kill you, but he wasn't all bad. Almost no one is all bad; that's part of what makes it so hard in therapy. There are so few true villains, just other screwed-up people who pass the damage on. He took care of me, better than anyone had for a long time. Gabriel got me off the streets, cleaned me up, and trained me how to act at fancy hotels, nice restaurants, the kind of places where people take escorts, not whores. Jean-Claude helped him tutor me on the social graces, did you know that?"

"No, I didn't."

He grinned suddenly, as he merged into a long line of cars waiting to exit. "When Gabriel first introduced me to Jean-Claude I thought I was there to sleep with him, and instead I was there to audition for going onstage at Guilty Pleasures. I thought I knew how to take my clothes off onstage, but Jean-Claude showed me the difference between shaking the moneymaker to the music and getting naked onstage, as opposed to a true striptease. I can still hear him: 'One is an art, and the other is cheap and tawdry, and nothing cheap dances on my stage.' God, Jean-Claude was so elegant in everything he did. I'd never seen anyone like him."

"He is pretty unique," I said.

Nathaniel laughed. "He was always a perfect gentleman with all the dancers. He said he couldn't be a good manager if he played favorites, so first he taught me how to be elegantly sexy onstage and then he taught me which fork to use, and not to tuck my napkin into my shirt collar."

I laughed. "I never knew that Jean-Claude took that much interest in Gabriel's wereleopards."

"He didn't usually, but I wasn't just one of Gabriel's wereleopards, I was one of Jean-Claude's dancers, and he always looked after his people, as much as he could. The power structure limited him while Raina and Gabriel were alive."

Raina had been the old Lupa, head lady werewolf of the local pack. Technically I still had the job, but only because the Ulfric, or wolf king, Richard Zeeman, hadn't chosen a new mate who was a real werewolf. I was still the pack's Bolverk, doer of evil deeds, and would kill pack members if it had to be done for the safety of others. When a were-animal went rogue, the body count could add up quick; really all I didn't do as Bolverk that I did do as a legal executioner was wait for the rogue to kill people. I could do a preventive strike out of the sight of the other cops. I hadn't actually had to kill anyone who wasn't trying to kill me or someone else yet, and hoped the trend continued.

Nathaniel took the exit, and the darkness was more complete as we went on smaller streets and there were fewer cars. "One of my regular customers was rich, really rich, and it was old money, which meant he couldn't afford to have people find out I was a hooker. He wanted to take me places besides a hotel room and to the kind of dinners where you have more silverware than you ever imagined anyone needing at one place setting. It wasn't just using the right spoon, or fork, either, but a whole different way of acting and interacting with the people while you're at that kind of dinner. Gabriel's background wasn't that different from mine, just a street kid who fought his way to management, so he asked Jean-Claude's advice, and I got etiquette lessons."

I tried to picture Jean-Claude giving a teenage Nathaniel Miss Manners lessons, and I could picture it. He'd taken me through the confusing silverware lesson so I could eat the kind of meals he'd have eaten if he'd been able to consume solid food. I carried three of his vampire marks, which meant he could taste food through me if he concentrated. We'd had dates where he watched me eat, just so he could taste the food along with me. I guess if I hadn't been able to eat a steak in over six hundred years I'd be pretty excited, too.

My phone rang that old-fashioned *brrriiinngg*; I jumped and gave a little squeak. Shit, I was really going to have to find a new main ring tone; this one always made me jump. Nathaniel wisely turned his laugh into a cough. He and Jean-Claude both thought it was cute. Micah thought I should change my ring tone.

I got the phone off its charger in the center console and said, "Blake here, what's up?" I sounded angry, which was what I usually sounded like when I was scared.

"Did I call at a bad time?" It was Manny.

"No, no, it's great. I need to talk to you."

"I've known you too long, Anita, what's wrong?" Manny had been the one who took me on my first vampire hunt, taught me how to stake them and cut off a human head. He had held my hand while I lost pieces of myself learning the ropes of our shared job. He'd helped me refine my zombie-raising ritual, because he raised the dead, too.

"Personal stuff."

"Jean-Claude treating you badly?" He asked it in that way that older men do, when they feel protective and fatherly toward you.

"No, he's great, but sometimes the bad parts of my job make the good parts of my life hard to deal with, you know?" That was the truth, and so obscure that it was almost a lie. But Manny took it for what it was: all the truth he was getting.

"I hated it when Rosita made me give up hunting vampires, but my life works better without it. You could just raise the dead, Anita. I know that neither one of us can give that up."

"Not without raising the dead by accident," I said. We'd shared stories of our powers affecting the dead by accident. My first had been my dog. His had been a toddler cousin. What did they both have in common? A lot of emotion from us, and for me, I wanted my dog back, so she came back. The college prof who committed suicide and showed up at my dorm room had been harder for me to understand, but good little Catholic that I had once been, I hadn't wanted him to spend eternity in hell, so . . . another chance to repent.

"Yes, the power will come out one way or another, but hunting monsters isn't your magic. You could give that up."

Manny didn't know anything about the Mother of All Darkness, or the Father of the Dawn, or . . . so much. Rosita had asked me to swear that I wouldn't involve her husband in any more vampire hunts after he'd nearly died in the last one we'd done together. He still did some of the morgue executions where the vampire was dead to the world and chained down with holy items, but even that made Rosita nervous. He'd been over fifty on that last hunt, and Rosita had said, "He's too old for this now. Leave my old man alone, and let him live to see his grandchildren."

What could I say? I did what she asked, and I lost my mentor, my teacher, and my partner in the undead business. Some of my worst injuries had been after I lost Manny at my back. He'd been older, not an old man, but he was currently planning his oldest daughter's wedding and if he'd stayed at my side he might have missed it.

"Anita, are you okay?"

"I'm sorry, Manny, did you say something?"

"It's not like you to lose track. Something has shaken you bad."

"Yeah, it has, and that's why I called." I glanced at Nathaniel. It was an ongoing police investigation, but what was I supposed to do, ask him to put his hands over his ears and go *la, la, la*? Of course, come to that Manny wasn't a marshal either. When he took himself out of the vampire-hunting business he missed his chance to be grandfathered into the preternatural marshal program. I loved Nathaniel, but I wasn't supposed to talk about ongoing police investigations with him, and certainly the FBI wouldn't appreciate me oversharing with my lover.

"If I can help, you know I will."

"I know that, Manny, I'm just debating how much I can share with you since you don't have a badge." I realized it was too blunt even as I said it, but I had used up a lot of my control already tonight. It didn't bode well for raising the dead later.

"Is it just me that doesn't have a badge, or are you with Jean-Claude?"

"I left him back in town to go to his job. We're a working couple; we can't spend every waking minute together." Again it sounded grumpy, but I didn't care; I was tired of Manny's issues with Jean-Claude. It wasn't personal exactly, but Manny didn't like my dating a vampire. He'd been the one who taught me that they weren't just people with fangs; they were monsters. The trouble was that I'd learned that wasn't true and Manny still believed it. It was ironic that he'd stopped killing vampires but still hated them in that racist sort of way, while I'd gone on to execute dozens more and I thought of them as people.

Nathaniel glanced over at me and cocked his head to one side. It meant a question, like *what?*

"Then if you can't talk to me about the case, why call me at all?" Manny asked.

"True." I sighed, and then tried to snake my way through what I needed to share, and what I felt I should hold back. I also didn't want to give away Manny's secrets, not even to Nathaniel, not because I didn't trust my sweetie, but because it wasn't my secret, and if the police ever found out Manny's secrets he could go to jail, or if he got the wrong judge he could be executed within a matter of weeks, or days. Some of the things he'd done when he was with Dominga Salvador fell under the magical malfeasance laws, which meant any death caused was grounds for automatic execution, none of that years-on-death-row shit.

The laws had been designed to keep the human public safe from beings with so much power there was no way to keep them in jail without risking more death. Manny wasn't that dangerous, but the law is enforced the way the law is written; it's not about true justice, it's about interpretation of the law and who has the best lawyer. Cynical, yes, but the longer I was in law enforcement the more I knew that cynical was often just the truth.

"Remember Dominga Salvador?"

"You know I do." His voice was suddenly much more serious.

"I've run across a case that's using powers I thought only she had."

"What kind of powers?" he asked.

"Remember the scheme she wanted my magical help for?"

"Work question, I'll be right back," he said, and I heard his footsteps over the phone. Was he at home with his family? Was I interrupting some warm domestic scene with this scary shit?

The next thing he said let me know he was alone. "You mean her wanting you to help her raise zombies to be sold as sex slaves?"

"Yeah, that," I said.

"There are zombies sold as sex slaves all the time, Anita. The people don't keep them after they rot, but there's a niche market for it. You and I both get requests for it."

"And we both say no."

"Of course, we say no, but other practitioners of our art are not so choosy."

"But it's not that kind of zombie, Manny. It's one like she raised at the end, the one with scared eyes."

"Zombies don't feel fear, Anita."

"No, they don't," I said.

"Then what are you talking about?"

"Think it through, Manny."

"She raised very good, lifelike zombies, but others do that, as well. Yours are almost alive now."

"Souls, Manny, souls."

"I don't . . ." Then he stopped and I heard his breathing speed up.

"Are you saying someone else has figured out how to capture a person's soul and put it back in their rotting corpse so the zombie doesn't rot?"

"And her trick of removing it, then putting it back, so it's a little bit rotted, yes."

He swore in Spanish. I caught that he asked for the Virgin Mary's help, though I think it was the Virgin of Guadalupe specifically. When he finally spoke English again, his accent was still thicker than normal.

"It can't be her, Anita. She is dead; even she could not come back after being torn apart by zombies and eaten." Manny was one of the few people I'd told about Dominga's real death. She'd been trying to force me to use an innocent victim as a human sacrifice to raise a very old zombie at the time, and only luck had put her henchmen in the circle so I could kill them, and raise a hell of a lot more than just one zombie with the rush of power those deaths gave me. He'd feared for his safety and that of his family from her, so I'd told him the truth. To my knowledge he'd never repeated it.

"I don't think it's her come back from the grave, Manny, but could it be someone who knew her? When I turned her down, did she recruit anyone else?"

"I don't know; the day I took you to see her was the first and last time I'd seen her in years."

"Who would know if she'd recruited someone else?" I asked.

"I don't know."

"Think, Manny, think; these women are being tortured in a way that no one should have to endure outside of a lower circle of hell."

"I will think on it, Anita, but I don't know who would be willing to talk to me now. They know I brought the police to the Señora's door, and only fear of my own power kept them from trying to retaliate."

"I'm sorry, Manny; I didn't mean to endanger you by asking for your help."

"A good man must help stop evil when he is called, Anita; do not apologize for that."

"I'm just tired of endangering people. I mean, it's dangerous just to be around me sometimes."

"That is not true," he said.

"Isn't it?"

"Anita, I don't know what part of your past you are fighting, but fight harder, because you are a good person, you fight the good fight."

"Thanks, Manny."

"*De nada.*"

I smiled. "If you think of anyone to ask, or anywhere to look for this bastard, let me know."

"I will."

"Now go enjoy whatever family thing you're doing."

"I'm coming, Rosita," he called out. I heard more voices, and then the voice on the phone was a woman's. "Anita, congratulations on your engagement; I am so happy you are finally getting married."

"Thank you, Rosita; now you don't have to keep worrying I'll be an old maid."

"A woman should be married, Anita, that's all."

"You know I don't agree with that."

"But you are getting married anyway," she said, as if that proved her point.

I sighed, and laughed a little. "We'll agree to disagree, but yes, I am getting married once we work out all the details."

"If you want help with anything, just call."

"You're planning Connie's wedding, isn't that enough?"

"Consuela's wedding is almost done."

"Congratulations to you and her."

"*Gracias*, but I have been to every wedding shop, caterer, everything. I would be happy to give you a list of the places we found most helpful."

"Okay, that might actually be useful, thank you." I'd pass the list on to Jean-Claude.

"I will have Manny email it to you."

"Thank you, Rosita." It was probably the longest conversation I'd ever had with Manny's wife.

"I hope you do let me help; I'd forgotten how much I love weddings." She laughed, one of the best and happiest laughs I'd ever heard from her. She was usually pretty stern and uncompromising. I tried to picture that girlish laugh from the Rosita I knew, who was five-eight and last I'd seen her well over three hundred pounds. Manny was still lean and shorter than her, so that they looked like the Jack Sprat nursery rhyme. The laugh belonged to that young slip of a girl that Manny had met in Mexico long ago.

"So no issues with me marrying a vampire?" I asked, because I couldn't leave it alone.

She made a harsh sound. "I am a devout Catholic, you know that."

"I do, and since the Church declared all vampires soulless and damned, I thought you might have an issue with my fiancé."

"They also declared all who raise the dead excommunicated, but our priest still gives Manny communion, even though he would get in trouble if they knew, so perhaps your man is a good one, too, even though the Church says otherwise."

This was so open-minded for Rosita that I didn't know whether to applaud or ask her what self-help group she'd been going to. Wisely, I did neither.

"Besides, it is not just any vampire, it is Jean-Claude, and he is . . ." She seemed to search for words, and finally settled for, "*hermoso.*"

I laughed, because it didn't mean just "beautiful" here in America, but someone who was amazing in some way that went beyond beauty. "I'll tell him you said so."

"Oh, do not do that, Anita." She sounded flustered; I couldn't quite picture Rosita flustered.

"Okay, I won't, but I will tell him you're happy for us."

"Yes, do, I cannot wait to see the wedding that will match such a proposal."

"Me, either," I said, and again the tight knot in my stomach wasn't about crime-fighting. The proposal had raised the bar too high, and now everyone would be looking for the wedding to top it, and nothing was going to top Jean-Claude in full prince-sweeping-you-off-your-feet mode, not even Jean-Claude.

We said our good-byes, and then I was in the car with Nathaniel and the sound of the wheels on the night-black road. "Manny's wife can't wait to see the wedding that matches such a proposal, she said."

"It was something," Nathaniel said, and his voice was very careful. It made me look at him and study that so-serious profile.

"What did that mean?" I asked.

"What did what mean?"

"That tone of voice and the bland phrase?"

He sighed and rolled his eyes. "Are we close to the cemetery yet?"

"Another four, five miles, and then slow down, the entrance is easy to miss in the dark. But you're not changing the subject."

"You're already upset tonight, and I'm being silly."

"Silly about what?" I asked.

"I'd have been thrilled if someone had tried to sweep me off my feet for a proposal the way Jean-Claude did for you, but men never get the big gesture aimed at them. They always have to do the big gesture."

I studied the side of his face. "Are you saying that you want a big, fancy proposal?"

"I'm saying it would be nice to be the girl once in a while."

"You already do most of the domestic stuff, and you're the one who wants a baby. I think you're better at a lot of the traditional girl things than I am."

"Then if I'm the girl, why don't I get a big, fancy proposal?"

"Are you serious?"

He gave me a look that said, with no uncertainty, that he was. Shit.

"Just me making the gesture, or me and Micah?"

"Either Micah, or you, or both of you, I don't care as long as you mean it."

"Micah proposed to both of us at the same time. I would marry you both if I could, I've said that."

"I know, and I told you it was silly."

"So if Jean-Claude had pulled up in front of you in a horse-drawn carriage with the huge-ass ring, you'd have loved it?"

He nodded. "Yeah, well if it were you and/or Micah, yes."

"Well, fuck."

"That is not quite the romantic sentiment I was hoping for, Anita."

"I'm sorry, really, but you just caught me off guard."

"You said yourself, I do most of the cooking and cleaning, grocery shopping, and you won't get pregnant for me, so is it too much to ask for a little romance?"

"I am a U.S. Marshal with the Preternatural Branch; I can't do my job pregnant, and I don't want to be pregnant. I can't see my life working with a baby in it."

"We could adopt."

"You're only twenty-three; why do you want a child now?"

"But you're thirty, and I want to have a child with you."

"I've got a few good years left in me," I said, and didn't try to keep the sarcasm out of my voice.

"Thirty isn't old, Anita, I know that, but for a woman to have babies, early thirties is decision time."

"Women have babies into their forties, or even fifties," I said.

"That's with medical technology helping out."

"My aunt had her last baby at fifty and it was a total surprise, no medical miracles involved."

He glanced at me. "Really?"

I nodded. "Really, her doctor told her she was past having babies so she didn't have to take precautions, and he was wrong."

"Okay, I take it back, maybe we do have more time. Fifty, really, wow, that is good genetics."

"Only if you want to keep popping out babies into your fifties," I said.

"I'd settle for one a little sooner," he said.

"Let it go tonight, Nathaniel; I'm feeling pressured enough from the weretigers wanting to be involved with the commitment ceremony."

"I ask for a big proposal and now it's all about you feeling pressured to add more people to the ceremony? You realize that it's not just you being pressured. They want to put a ring on Micah and me, too."

I thought about it for a second or two. "Micah didn't make it sound that way back at the Circus."

"He wouldn't, would he?"

"What's that mean?"

"I'm bisexual; Micah isn't except for me, and so if another man 'marries' us it won't matter to him as much as it does to me."

"Well, crap, I'm sorry, Nathaniel, you're absolutely right. This could be another lover for you, and Micah won't look at another man that way. So really it's your virtue and mine on the line, in a manner of speaking."

"Virtue isn't what's on the line, Anita, it's our domestic happiness on the line, and that's way more important to me."

I took a deep breath and let it out slowly, counting to ten. When that didn't do it, I tried twenty, but the fluttery feeling in my stomach didn't get any better, so I just said it. "Micah told me his choice for the tiger to marry us. What's yours?"

He glanced at me, then back at the road. "Thank you for asking. I know you didn't want to."

"Your point about the sex is fair. Who do you want in our bed?"

"It depends on how you mean 'in our bed,'" he said.

"Don't be coy, after you made me ask, Nathaniel."

He smiled then. "That's fair. Okay, Cynric shares you with me and Micah better than anyone except Nicky, and Micah doesn't share the bed with Nicky at all, but I don't have sex with either of them. They're more like brother-husbands, or something."

"So if you were picking for romance, who would it be?"

"Domestic bliss is either Cynric or Nicky; they live with us already."

"But Nicky isn't a weretiger, so it doesn't help us," I said.

"That's true."

"Come on, you have someone in mind, I can tell."

"Two someones in mind, sort of."

"Spill it," I said.

"Dev, he's truly bisexual and he's a golden tiger."

"But he's all domestic-blissed-out with Asher and Kane."

"Kane is starting to be bitchy about sharing Asher with so many people, and Dev doesn't meet any of Asher's BDSM needs. He's just another male lover when Kane is that, too."

"So you think Dev will be up for grabs soon?"

"Not exactly, but he's fun and he's as bi as I am."

"You said two people, who's the second?"

"No specific person, but the only female weretiger you've tried to sleep with is Jade, and we all agree that she's got too many issues, but what's wrong with looking at some of the other female weretigers as a possible addition? It would be another lover for all three of us, not just two of us."

I frowned at him. "Jade has been a disaster."

"But it's not because she's a woman."

"Maybe not, but I like men, Nathaniel, sorry."

"You and I have a really good time when J.J. comes to visit Jason, and she is very much a girl."

J.J. had been a lesbian most of her adult life until she and Jason found each other again. They'd dated in high school until she felt she had to pick one sex to date, and he'd respected her choice and gone on to date other women. But he was the one man she never forgot, and she was THE woman for him, though they'd both agreed that they didn't want to be monogamous. Polyamory is about honesty and loving more, and they'd started with Nathaniel, me, and Jade.

J.J. was tall, slender, her body honed down to a work of art by years of being a professional ballerina. She was with one of the most prestigious dance companies in the country, which happened to be all the way in New York. Jason, Nathaniel's best friend and my werewolf to call, had started spending more and more time with her there; he was there this week, visiting. There was serious talk about him getting a tryout with her dance company someday. If he made it, then he would be the first shapeshifter to ever become a member of a human company. There were all-shapeshifter dance troupes, all-vampire ones, and even mixed ones that were just all preternaturals, but humans didn't like trying to compete with people who were faster, stronger, and just physically better by virtue of a disease they'd caught like lycanthropy, that no amount of human practice or gym work could compete with. Jean-Claude and I weren't sure we could do without him since he was the assistant manager at Guilty Pleasures and one of the headline dancers, but we both wanted him to be happy. He and J.J. were stupid happy with each other. She was also my second-ever female lover, and I liked her better than the one who was pushing me to put a ring on her finger.

"I can't argue that, and if J.J. were a weretiger I'd consider it, but she's human; awesome, but it doesn't help us find a tiger that we all like well enough to commit to."

"We all like Cynric enough."

Unless Micah had told him, Nathaniel didn't know about my revelation about my feelings for Cynric, so I wasn't sure what to say. Either he knew and was pushing, or he didn't know and it was just an honest remark. I couldn't ask without having to share the trauma, and I wasn't ready to talk about it, not so soon, not even with Nathaniel. I agreed to look at more tigers, because it would stop him from asking about Cynric; probably not one of my smarter ideas, but sometimes you do the stupid thing to avoid the traumatic one.

I said, "True, but you said it yourself: neither you nor Micah has sex with him, it's just another lover for me. You're right; I should at least look at some of the other weretigers."

"You mean the female weretigers?"

"And some of the male ones; who knows, maybe one of them will work better than Dev or Cynric, but yes, I'll look at some of the women, too."

"Really?" he asked, and he suddenly looked and seemed even younger than he was.

"Yes, really, and you just drove past the cemetery entrance."

He slammed on the brakes and only my seat belt kept me from hitting the dashboard. "Sorry, really sorry," he said.

I swallowed past my heart as it tried to climb out my mouth. My mother had died in a car accident; it made me less than thrilled about moments like this. "Maybe I'll drive home," I said, in a breathy voice.

"At least it's a country road and there's no traffic," he said, the car still skewed across most of the road, headlights aimed at the low stone wall, but not at an entrance.

"Yeah, there's that; now just back up slowly, carefully, and go like five miles an hour once we get into the cemetery. The roads are gravel and very narrow."

"I'm really sorry, Anita."

"Nathaniel, get us out of the middle of a dark road at night before someone comes over the hill and hits us."

He stopped arguing and just backed up, slowly, carefully, and eased the nose of my SUV gingerly through the narrow opening in the wall. I wondered how Nicky and Dino had gotten a truck and the trailer complete with cow through the opening. It must have been a damn narrow fit, but they'd made it or Nicky would have called me by now. I trusted Nicky, and he was the only other man I was actually in love with, but that didn't help any of the men in my life feel the same about him. Why did we have to have a weretiger? Because I'd killed the Father of Tigers, also known as the Father of the Dawn, and I'd killed the Mother of All Darkness, just like the weretigers' prophecy had said the next vampire that could control all the tigers would do. Funny thing about prophecy: After a few thousand years, if it seems to come true it gains strength, belief, power. The fact that Jean-Claude's human servant (me), his queen (again me), had killed two such powers didn't mean I had killed them; the vampires counted both kills as belonging to my master, to Jean-Claude, so we had to include a weretiger in our ceremony, because the rest of the prophecy was all confusing about marrying the tiger to the king and queen. The metaphysical community had decided that meant that if we married one weretiger, the prophecy would be fulfilled and that would put the final nail in the coffin of the Mother of All Darkness, but if we didn't marry a weretiger there was a loophole in the prophecy that allowed her to come back from the grave. Funny how there's always a loophole when it comes to the really scary shit. I'd swallowed her essence while she tried to take over my body; the immovable object met the unstoppable force and I won, but all the good little vampires and wereanimals believed that for the victory to be complete, Jean-Claude and I had to "marry" one of the tigers who'd helped us kill Mommie Darkest. It wasn't the hurt feelings of our lovers, current or ex, that made us agree to add a weretiger; it was the belief of an entire country that wanted Jean-Claude to be their triumphant king. Even being the one who had slain the metaphorical dragon, I was still relegated to queen. I was still the one who got picked up in the carriage and swept off my feet by the prince, even if it was me holding the bloody sword in one hand and the head of the Gorgon in the other. To the vampires, especially the really old ones, I was the princess, and the princess didn't get to rescue herself, let alone rescue everyone else. They so had me confused with someone else.

"I'm not the princess they're looking for," I said, and didn't realize I'd said it out loud until Nathaniel asked, "What did you say?"

"Nothing. There are the cars. Park and it's time for me to work some magic and earn a really obscene amount of money."

"More for you to spend to sweep me off my feet," he said, as he eased the car forward, trying to park without hitting one of the old graves that huddled near the road.

"You're really not going to let that go, are you?"

"Nope," he said, and parked.

10

I WAS SITTING half inside the dark open back of the SUV, changing out of the heels and into hiking boots. I'd changed the automatic car lights so that they needed to be switched on, because the light framed you like a target at night. It also spoiled your night vision, but it was mainly the "target" issue that had bothered me.

Nathaniel stood next to the open hatch, leaning one shoulder against the side of it. He'd already texted Micah the news that I was willing to look at more tigers as prospective lovers and more.

"You didn't have to text Micah. It could have waited until we got home," I said.

"You gave me your word that you'd look at more tigers, including females; did you mean it?"

"Yes, I meant it," I grumped at him.

He smiled. "Then why not tell Micah?"

I couldn't think of a response that didn't include me whining that now that Micah knew, I couldn't back out of my newfound willingness to shop for more tigers, but to say that would have meant admitting I hadn't meant it, and I did mean it. If I really wanted Cynric to go off somewhere and have a life without us, then I needed another tiger to take his place, or join our domestic arrangement as well as he had. Either way, I needed more tigers.

"Nicky is walking this way," Nathaniel said.

"He's probably coming for a covert kiss; we made an agreement, no kissing and stuff in front of the clients."

"No kissing and stuff, really, and here I am and here he comes, and you can't kiss either one of us." He grinned suddenly, far beyond his usual come-hither smile.

"You are not going to tease from a distance and mess with my concentration."

"I'm not," he said, but he made it a question with uplift in his voice at the end of it, so that the statement was all question. His eyes might look gray by moonlight, but the shine of humor was clear enough.

I frowned at him. "You've been hanging around Jason too much. He's usually the one who can't leave well enough alone."

"He's my best friend, we're supposed to hang out, but he would never be able to distract you from a distance as well as I can." He crossed his arms over his chest, flexing just a little, so that I wondered for a second if the fitted T-shirt would hold. It did, of course, but he'd had to stop lifting so much in the gym, because genetically he bulked more than his dancer's body needed. He'd started to lose some of his flexibility, and he had enough muscles for dancing onstage without trading away some of that amazing mobility. He was double-jointed, among other things.

He gave a small and very masculine laugh, and I realized I'd just been staring at him with the one hiking boot in my hand. Crap, he hadn't even begun to try to distract me, not really. I went back to con-

centrating on putting on my boot, but by that time Nicky came around
the corner of the car, and I was suddenly sitting with one of them on
either side of me. That shouldn't have been a problem, but Nicky bent
his nearly six feet of muscled hunkitude toward me. His shoulders almost didn't fit inside the open hatch area, because he was just that big.
His blond hair was cut short except for the triangular fall that covered
most of the left side of his face. I put a hand on his chest as he leaned in;
he wrapped one arm around me, drawing me in tight to all that hard,
muscled upper body. If I'd thought Nathaniel was a threat to his shirt
seams, it was always miraculous to me that Nicky didn't split his shirts
every time he tried to pick up a bottle. I had taller men in my bed, but
no one was as massive as Nicky. He was flexible where he needed to
be for sex, and hand-to-hand fighting, but the rest was just muscle.
He lifted to be stronger, he lifted because he liked it, and genetics made
him bulk, but he didn't have a job where he needed to avoid it, so he
didn't. All that muscle made him seem bigger than men who were actually taller, but height isn't everything when it comes to size. Men, and
some women, seem to think it is, but just as obsession about length
in other areas doesn't take into account what width can do for you, the
same could be said for Nicky's upper body, and his thighs. He had to
buy bigger jeans and then have them tailored through the narrowness
of his waist, or he had to wear shorts and split the legs wider.

He kissed me firmly, but not with a lot of lip movement, because he
knew I'd be mad if he sent me to the clients with my lipstick smeared
like clown makeup. That one long fall of hair brushed the side of my
face as we kissed. His mouth stayed firm but almost chaste against
mine, but he breathed out against my skin, opening his lips just enough
to let a long, low growl slide out against my mouth. I opened for it as
if I could drink in the sound of him. It made me shiver in his arms, and
I dropped the hiking boot and just wrapped my arms around his neck.

He put an arm under my ass and lifted me up, crawling into the back
of the car with me half in his arms. I fought free of the kiss, and said,
"Work, work, work, I'm at work, damn it."

He spoke with his face just above mine, the weight of him half pin-
ning me. "It's dark and they're human, they can't see what we're doing."

I felt the car rock slightly as Nathaniel crawled into the back with us. He was on all fours on the other side of me, and I had a moment of staring up at both of them in the small, dark space of the car. The possibilities of the three of us together caught my breath in my throat and tightened things low in my body. They'd smell that I wanted them, but I couldn't help that. I pushed my way to sitting and said, "No, absolutely no."

"Absolutely no, what?" Nathaniel said, his smile faint in the darkness of the car.

I rolled my eyes at him and then began to crawl out of the car. It was actually a little hard to crawl past Nicky's shoulders. He fixed that by lifting me up and sitting me gently on the edge of the open hatch area, where I'd started. He even got out and picked up the boot I'd dropped.

I took it from him, frowning, and not looking at his face much. I was going to ignore him as much as possible. I was going to ignore them both, damn it. "Work," I repeated, and yes, I did know it was a case of the lady protesting too much. Throwing caution to the wind and having fun in the car like a flashback to high school sounded a lot more fun than raising the dead right now, but then if the men in my life weren't more fun than work, I guess they wouldn't be in my life.

"Don't the coveralls need to go on before the hiking boots?" Nicky asked.

"I was going to walk over and make sure they'd read the handouts I sent home with them, or give them a refresher on what to expect. People never listen in the office and then sometimes they freak out during the zombie-raising, and I hate that. The coveralls are hot, even in spring, so I'll talk to the clients and then get changed."

"And the boots are so you can walk on the gravel," he said.

"Yeah."

"Good plan, because I came to tell you that your clients did read the literature you sent home with them, and one of them is having an attack of conscience."

I frowned at him. "An attack of conscience, what about, disturbing the dead?"

"No," he said, with a slight smile.

"Are they upset about the whole voodoo angle? If they read the handouts they know it's not black magic."

"Not that either."

"Then what is it?"

He grinned, shook his head, and said, "It's the cow."

11

TWENTY MINUTES LATER I still didn't have the coveralls on, because I hadn't been able to convince our reluctant client that killing the cow was a necessary part of raising the zombie for them. I finally had some-one to aim my anger at, except that I wasn't angry anymore thanks to Nicky and Nathaniel. Some nights you just can't hold on to the mad long enough to use it.

"Yes, Mrs. Willis, the cow does have to die so I can raise the zombie for you," I said.

She peered up at me, which wasn't something that most people had to do. She was tiny, less than five feet, but somehow didn't seem that small; attitude can make up for inches. Her eyes swam behind some of the thickest prescription glasses I'd seen in years. Her eyes glinted be-hind them in the moonlight. The moon was only two days past full, so there was plenty of light for my night vision. Nathaniel, Nicky, and Dino probably didn't even think it was dark, because wereanimals had a heck of a lot better night vision than I did, even in human form. We hadn't advertised the fact that the only full humans here tonight were the clients. They seemed nervous enough without that. One of the younger men with them kept gazing around the cemetery as if he ex-pected something to jump out and eat him. Some people just weren't comfortable in cemeteries after dark; go figure.

"I was fine in theory, but now that the animal is standing in front of me, it seems wrong to slaughter it because we want to do historical research."

"Do you want the zombie raised, or not?" I asked.

"Of course we do." Mr. Owen MacDougal came up behind her, much taller, much broader, not fat, but solid like an old-time linebacker gone a little heavy around the middle. He looked like an older version of my other bodyguard, Dino, except Dino was darkly Hispanic and MacDougal was Middle America white bread. I knew Dino was six-two, so MacDougal was at least that tall, maybe an inch or so more. Neither of them was as broad through the shoulders as Nicky, but then I knew Dino didn't go for bulk as much as he did, and MacDougal obviously hadn't been keeping up with the gym, but he was still a big, solid guy.

"Of course we do," he repeated. "Ethel, it's a cow. You eat steak."

"I eat meat out of the grocery store," she said. "I don't watch the poor animals slaughtered in front of me." She motioned at the brown-and-white Guernsey tied to a nearby tree. It was munching the fresh grass and chewing whatever cows chew contentedly. If it knew why it was here tonight it seemed calm about it, but it was a cow. They puzzle me. I've never looked at one and thought, *I know what it's thinking*. Cows aren't like dogs, or cats, or even certain birds. Cows are mysterious things when it comes to motives, and this one was no different as she grazed among the weathered tombstones.

Nathaniel had surprised me by being nervous of the cow. All he would say was, he'd had a bad experience with a cow once. He was standing well away from it by the clients' cars, while we talked business.

I tried to think my way past the PETA-esque attack of conscience, and finally said, "Mrs. Willis, I have other appointments tonight"—which was a lie, because raising something this old would exhaust any animator powerful enough to do it, but Ethel Willis didn't know that—"so you need to decide if we're raising this zombie within the next fifteen minutes or I'm calling it, and you can figure out what to do with the live cow."

"What?" she asked, and MacDougal echoed her.

"I mean I've made arrangements with a disposal company to come get the cow carcass. It'll be made into pet food since humans aren't allowed to eat anything killed in a religious ritual, but the disposal company does not deal in live animals, so if we leave here and the cow is still alive, then it's your problem."

I heard Dino chuckle behind me, and try to turn it into a cough.

"But I don't know anything about cows," Mrs. Willis said. "Whatever would I do with it?"

"Don't know, don't care. You paid for the animal to be sacrificed when you agreed to the price for the zombie, so in effect it's your cow. If you don't want me to kill it and raise the zombie, fine, but it's still your cow dead or alive. I'll dispose of its corpse, but if it's still alive when I leave here tonight it's no longer my problem, it's yours." I glanced behind me at the narrow road that ran through the graveyard. "The biggest car I see over there is a Cadillac. It's a big car. You could probably get a goat in the backseat, but I don't know about a cow, especially not a full-grown Guernsey. They're a big animal. I don't think it'll fit, and this municipality doesn't let you keep cows except as short term for blood sacrifices or other religious observances, so no just letting the cow loose, because that would be breaking the law and when the police contact Animators Inc. asking why a cow that we purchased is roaming loose, I'll tell them it's your cow."

"How would they know whose cow it was?" Willis asked.

"They have serial numbers like license plates. The number tells you the cow's entire history including that it's now your cow, and unless I kill it here and now, you have a very big, very not-house-trained pet." The cow chose that moment to lift its tail and prove just how not-house-trained it was. I think that was the selling point for Mrs. Willis. The nice animal had done something messy and disgusting, and very real. I think it was all a little too real for the older lady. She went to sit in the Cadillac and left the rest of us to get all messy and real.

"Once I come back from the car we'll get started, but first, which of you is going to stand by the grave so the zombie will answer the questions you want to ask it?"

MacDougal and the young guy, whose name seemed to be Patrick, though I wasn't sure if it was his first or his last, looked at each other. "You mean we'd have control of the zombie and you wouldn't?" Patrick asked.

I sighed; if only they'd read the literature we give them, they wouldn't ask stupid questions, because they'd know already, but I didn't say that out loud. "No, the animator who raises a zombie controls it. It will always answer to me before it answers to anyone else, but this way it will answer your questions without me being present, so which of you wants to hold the leash, so to speak?"

They looked at each other again. Patrick took a step forward. I added, "Just so we're clear, and don't have any more misunderstandings, I will have to put some of the cow's blood on the face and body of the person who controls the zombie."

Patrick's eyes got a little bigger, and he shook his head. "Not me, sorry, but I don't want to do that."

MacDougal stepped up. "I guess it has to be me. Where do you want me to stand?"

"Behind the tombstone, so you're not on the grave, will be dandy, but I have to get the rest of my equipment ready, so just relax for a few minutes, and then we'll get started."

He nodded. "Just tell me what to do."

I turned for the cars, because what I wanted to say was, *Read the damned handouts!*

12

IT'S HARDER TO kill a cow than a goat or a chicken. First, it's a much bigger animal, which is both more difficult to kill when the only acceptable method is a blade, and a hell of a lot more dangerous. Normally, Nicky, Dino, and the other guards kept us safe from bad guys, but tonight I'd want them to help me with the sacrifice. I hadn't lied to Mrs. Willis; a Guernsey is a big cow.

When I'd asked the guards if any of them knew about handling big livestock, only Dino and Nicky had stepped up. Turns out that Dino had started life on a cattle ranch in Mexico. His grandfather had owned it and he'd grown up around cows. I'd had no idea, but I'd also had no idea that Nicky had grown up on a ranch out West in this country.

"Really, I had you pegged for a city boy," I'd said.

"I like cities, but I can lay fence, do carpentry if something breaks and I have the right tools. About the only thing I never got very good at was wiring, and I can do some of that, but I'm not an electrician."

I'd stared up at him and realized just how little I knew about his past. Of all the men in my life, Nicky had come to me with the least "getting to know you" period, because we met when he helped kidnap me. His original lion pride had been mercenaries, oh sorry, private contractors. They'd done everything from assassinations to information gathering, and probably things I didn't even know to ask about. They'd been paid a lot of money to kidnap me so I could raise a zombie that I'd already refused to raise. They'd threatened to kill Micah, or Nathaniel, or Jason. Nicky thought of Nathaniel as family now, but in the beginning Nicky would have killed the other love of my life without a second thought. Nicky was a sociopath, made not born, but the effect was the same. Weaponless, with a witch having closed off my metaphysical powers so I couldn't contact anyone for help, I'd turned to the powers of the vampire marks that were a permanent part of me now, and to my own necromancy. Thanks to Jean-Claude I fed off sex the way other vampires fed off blood. The *ardeur* was originally supposed to keep a vampire fed on a long sea voyage or in a small group where taking blood would be noticed; fucking around was more sociably acceptable. Some vampire lines could feed off fear and pain, and they would cause that so they could "drink" it down. I'd learned to feed on rage, too, but it had side effects on the victims that I hadn't learned to control yet. The *ardeur* had side effects, too. I'd addicted people to me by accident, but by the time I'd met Nicky I could stop that from happening, most of the time, but Nicky, him I mind-fucked on purpose. To save the men I loved I'd taken everything I could from him, including his free will, and turned him into my Bride, as in Bride of Dracula. It's always that term in vampireland, brides, not grooms, regardless of their gender—so sexist. Nicky had turned against his lion pride, been willing to kill his friends and what had been the closest thing to a family he'd ever known, because he was mine in a way that *slave* doesn't even cover. If I was sad, it made Nicky anxious, and he was driven to make me happy again. We'd worked hard to give him as much of his autonomy back as he had, but he could never be free of me. He would adore me forever, while I hadn't given a damn for him at first. Brides are walking, talking batteries for their creators, which can be drained of life when the vampire needs it, though most of the time they are just the ultimate servants, read "slaves." That old saying about love meaning that another person's happiness is more important to you than your own was true for Nicky. The fact that I had fallen in love with him, too, was either irony or God being kind.

Nicky led the cow to the foot of the grave. He rubbed its forehead and it seemed to respond to him the way dogs do to other people. Well, as much as a cow can behave like a dog; I think this was one animal I just was never going to understand, but since the only interaction I had with them was killing them to raise the dead, it was probably just as well. Theoretically it didn't have to be livestock. I knew some animators who used cats instead of chickens, but I just couldn't do it. I liked cats.

Dino came to the other side of the cow but didn't touch it. He was only there in case the cow complained. If I was fast enough the cow wouldn't have time to be scared or feel pain; it would be over in seconds. If I hit the jugular right. If I didn't, then it could get messy and dangerous, and it would frighten the cow. She'd been headed to the slaughterhouse because she'd stopped producing enough milk, or butterfat, or whatever, which they'd had to disclose when they sold it to us. I'd been doing pretty good at thinking of the cow as *it*, until Nicky started scratching its head and it—she—liked it. Now she seemed more real, and I was still going to have to kill her. The historical society had paid for me to raise over two hundred years' worth of corpse. I was about the only animator in the country who could guarantee a zombie this old that could remember its past and answer questions without a human sacrifice. There were definitely worse things that could be dying on this grave than a walking milk machine. Human sacrifice was illegal, but you heard rumors, there were always rumors; in fact, some of them were about me. But anyone who had died on one of my graves had been trying to kill me at the time. You should never attack a necromancer in a cemetery; it's like chasing Rambo into a building full of loaded guns. Some people seem to help you kill them.

If it's a chicken, you behead it. A goat, you slit its throat ear to ear. A cow is too big for either if I wanted a clean kill. I stroked my hand down the side of its neck while Nicky continued to scratch its head. Its neck was surprisingly soft to the touch, or the hair was. I found the big pulse, thudding thick and sure against my fingers. A bigger animal seems to have a bigger pulse; maybe it's just because the heart is bigger, but this was sure and certain. I had a moment to think, *I could do this without killing the cow*. I could cut my own flesh, use my own blood, but the zombie wouldn't be as solid. Over a hundred years was too old to be brought back by just a few drops of my own blood and guarantee it could answer questions. The historical society had questions and they were paying for answers. I could have cut Nicky's arm and had him walk the circle with me. It would work, and the zombie would be very, very alive, or that had been what happened the only time I'd used Micah's blood to walk a circle. The zombie had been too alive. It had almost killed me trying to break the circle of my power. Of course, with Micah by my side the whole cemetery had been more alive. He was my Nimir-Raj, my leopard king, and our bond was more intimate than Nicky being my Bride. But that zombie had only been weeks dead, so probably even Micah wouldn't be able to help me this time with just a cut to drip blood on the grave.

Even if I took the cow back, they'd simply kill her there. It wasn't a choice of the cow living; it was a choice of how she died. Here she would die to raise the dead and help clear up historical inaccuracies. At the slaughterhouse she'd die just to be animal food. There, I'd called her *she* again. It wasn't like me to be sentimental about the sacrifices. But the pulse under my hand was so certain of itself. She might be past milk production, but this was a healthy animal and she'd live for years if someone gave her the chance. I shook my head, hard. *Stop it, Anita, just stop it.* But I was beginning to remember why I preferred chickens. I never seemed to feel as sympathetic to them.

"You all right?" Nicky asked.

I glanced up at him and nodded. "Fine," I said, and wasn't sure if it was the truth, but whatever my feelings I knew my job. "Shield her eyes on this side so she doesn't see the blade flash in the moonlight."

I didn't have to ask him twice; he handed the halter rope to Dino and put his free hand near her eye, cupping it so her vision was obscured. He kept scratching her forehead the whole time, and she lowered her head so he could reach more spots. For a cow, there are worse ways to go.

I knelt by my leather satchel. It was a leather overnight bag, vaguely in the shape of a gym bag. Once a real gym bag had been what I'd carried my zombie-raising equipment in, but for last Christmas Jean-Claude had gotten me this. It was a nice bag, a really nice bag, too nice a bag for all the blood and death it was surrounded with. I'd taken it graciously and used it religiously, but I didn't like it. The things you do when you're in a committed relationship. Sigh. It was a really nice bag.

The leather smelled rich and warm in the summer night as I opened it up. I realized it was the final product of another cow. I wasn't sure if that was ironic or disturbing. I got two things out of the satchel: a bowl and a blade. The bowl was smooth ceramic, handmade by an artist here in Missouri. The color was shades of blue from pale to almost black. The finish made it gleam in the moonlight. I could have caught the blood in anything, but it seemed respectful to use something special. The bowl was bigger than my normal one but was just a nicely made bowl. There was no magic to it. My machete was wrapped in its newly made sheath, so that the blade didn't slide around and damage the nice cloth and leather interior of the new satchel. I thought about having Dino hold the bowl for me, but I wanted his hands free in case the cow got frisky. I placed the bowl on the grass at the edge of the grave.

I unfastened the blade catch and drew the machete out. It was as long as my forearm, dull silver gleaming in the light of the moon. The moment it was bare there was a pulse of power from it, as if it had its own heartbeat. It didn't keep beating, though, just that one pulse. It had never done that when it was loose in my bag. Something about sheathing it and unsheathing it made it happen. I'd talked to my spiritual mentor, Marianne, who among other things was a practicing witch, as well as Wiccan. You can be a witch and not be Wiccan, but you can't be Wiccan and not be a witch, sort of like all poodles are dogs, but not all dogs are poodles, or something like that. Marianne wasn't sure why the machete was reacting to being sheathed. She'd asked me to bring it with me next time I visited her in Tennessee, so she could look at it in person.

I found that thick pulse again with my free hand. I didn't need to test the point or edge of the machete; I sharpened it myself and knew it was razor ready. I picked up the bowl and balanced it in the flat of my hand, holding it where the blood would pour into it. I said a brief prayer, thanking the animal for giving food all its life and for this moment, for being a sacrifice and helping us raise the long dead. With the prayer came a sense of calmness for me, and I drew back the machete, eyed the point that was my target on the thick neck, and plunged the blade in fast, hard, and deep. Hesitation was disastrous for the sacrifice's sake. The magic didn't care how the animal died; slow death raised the dead just as easily as quick.

I drew the blade up and out, so the cut was wide. Blood poured out of the wound, splashing and dripping into and around the bowl, and over my hand and arm. It was very warm, hot even, because a cow's temperature is hotter than a human's. It makes most fresh animal blood hot to the touch at least for those few seconds before it hits the air and begins to cool, but there was so much blood that it just stayed hot.

The cow went down without a sound, its knees buckling. The front of it sank to the ground first. Dino kept the halter rope tight and Nicky continued to shield its eye, so it wouldn't see the blood. Dino was a huge shape on the other side of the animal, waiting to see if he was needed for more. I knelt with the wound, catching as much blood as I could in the bowl. We didn't need this much to draw the circle, but blood is always precious and if you take something's life you should treat the blood with respect. The cow's back end just seemed to collapse all at once, and I had to move backward on the balls of my feet as the big animal slid to one side toward me. Blood splashed over the edge of the already bloody bowl, soaking the front of my coveralls. That was why I wore them.

I got to my feet, bloody machete in one hand and the blood-drenched bowl in the other. The front of me was black with blood, and there had been enough of it that it felt like it was trying to seep through the coveralls and onto my clothes. I hoped it didn't soak through, but there was nothing I could do about it until the ceremony was complete.

"Well done," Dino said.

"I do my best," I said, but my voice was already growing distant. I was only half paying attention, because I was about to lower my metaphysical shields so I could raise the dead, and I wanted to do it. My necromancy was like a horse that had been in its stall too long. It needed to run. It needed to use all that muscle and sinew and run! I was one of only three animators in the country who could have raised something this old without a human sacrifice, which was illegal in almost every country in the world. It was a seller's market and I was the seller.

13

NOW THAT THE cow was safely dead and not going to trample anyone, I had Dino get MacDougal and stand him behind the tombstone, so he'd be in the circle but out of the way while we cast it. The tombstone wasn't much to look at, just a weathered white chunk of marble, softened by the centuries until it looked like a piece of candy spit out of a giant's mouth with the lettering worn away. I'd seen all the paperwork assuring me this was the right grave, but if I'd had to rely on the stone for name and information I'd have been out of luck; all the readable info had been sucked away by time and weather. Normally I just take the much smaller bowl of blood, or even the whole beheaded chicken, and walk the circle by myself, but I was going to need help to carry this big a bowl. I could have brought the much smaller bowl that I used when I killed a goat, and that would have been plenty to sprinkle for casting the circle, but it had seemed wrong to waste that much of the cow's lifeblood on the ground. If I needed a bigger death to raise the older dead, then wasn't part of that using more blood? I wasn't sure of the metaphysical logic, but I was stuck with the huge bowl now and I couldn't carry it in one hand with the machete in the other, so I had needed a lovely assistant, or in this case a handsome assistant.

We'd lost another two history lovers, apparently overcome by the sight of more blood than they'd ever seen before, or maybe it was seeing something slaughtered in front of them. People will eat meat, like Mrs. Willis said, but that's nice, safe meat in plastic wrap at the grocery store, or behind the butcher's window. It's not real, not a dead thing, just meat, just food. One of them had run off into the gravestones and was throwing up rather noisily. At least they'd moved far enough away and downwind so the rest of us couldn't smell it. I really appreciated that. The rest of the huddled group had exclaimed everything from "Cool" to "Oh, my God," but they didn't argue when I had Dino and Nathaniel move them back to the gravel road. I didn't want anyone drawn into the circle by accident. I'd given the orders distractedly, already staring down at the grave. My necromancy pushed at the boundaries I'd set around it like it wanted to expand to fill all available space. Usually it was like opening a tightly closed fist, a relief to let go, but it didn't push at me like this. I hadn't been raising as many zombies as in years past, because Bert, our business manager, could get more money for my time than anyone else at the firm, which meant I didn't always raise the dead every night. I spent a lot of time doing police work now, so that worked out, but it meant that my necromancy wasn't getting as much use as normal. Like Manny and I had discussed, if you don't use it on purpose it finds other ways to leak out. Raising the dead wasn't a choice for me. The only choice was how and when I'd do it.

The bowl didn't look so big in Nicky's hands. He carried it easily; now all I had to decide was, did he walk backward or beside me as I dipped the machete in the blood and sprinkled the circle into being. I chose beside me, because walking backward carrying a big bowl of blood seemed to be asking for a mess.

I was used to using a beheaded chicken to walk the circle—that sprinkled blood along my blade—but when I dipped my machete in the bowl it came out black, coated like some kind of evil candy apple. The last time I'd tried dipping into a bowl half this size I'd ended up sprinkling myself as much as the ground, so I was cautious as I dripped the blood onto the grass.

"Hmm," Nicky said, more an involuntary sound.

"What?" I asked, glancing up at him.

"You usually use more flourish."

"If I do my usual body English we'll both be wearing cow blood. Trust me, when there's this much blood on the machete you have to be careful swinging it."

"Yeah, you can get really messy when you use a machete," he said.

I studied his face for a second. "You're not talking about using a machete for casting a circle, are you?"

"No," he said.

We looked at each other for a few seconds. He gave great blank face, but then most sociopaths do. I debated whether to ask, or how, and finally said, "Animal, or person?"

"Person," he said.

"Defending your life?"

"No," he said.

"Mine was."

"You bothered that mine wasn't?"

"Maybe, maybe not. Either way, this isn't the time or place to discuss it."

"No, it's not."

"Okay then," I said.

"Okay then," he said.

"Is anything wrong, Ms. Blake?" It was Mr. MacDougal, patiently standing behind the worn tombstone.

I shook my head. "No, nothing wrong, just filling in my assistant on a detail or two. I usually walk the circle alone."

"It's a big bowl," he said.

"It is that, Mr. MacDougal, it is that." I dipped the blade back in the cooling blood and started walking the circle like I had a purpose.

14

WE WALKED THE circle together, Nicky finding just the right height to hold the bowl so that I could dip the machete in without spattering us, or even hesitating as we moved. He anticipated me in this as he did when we had sex, so that we fell into a rhythm that was almost a dance. It made it more of a ritual, some sort of liturgical dance, but with more blood than I assume the monks use during theirs. It was so smooth, so . . . something I had no word for that I was shocked when I looked down and saw blood on the grass ahead of us. One more sprinkle of blood and we'd close the circle. It didn't seem like we'd walked that far. Nicky offered the bowl to me one more time; I dipped the long blade in, pulled it slowly out, and let the thickening drops fall to touch the blood already on the grass. The moment the fresh blood hit the first drop we had cast down, the circle closed. It closed with a rush and a roar of power that left every hair on my body dancing. It pulled a gasp from my throat.

"Oh, my God," Nicky whispered. I looked into his face and found his eyes wide and his own skin reacting to the power.

It was hard to breathe through the power. My chest was tight with it. What the fuck?

Nicky whispered, "That's more power than I've ever felt when you've put up a circle."

I nodded, swallowing hard to be able to whisper back, "I haven't used a death as big as a cow in a while. I think it was more battery power than I needed."

"What does that mean?"

"It means this is going to be a really kickass zombie."

"What?"

I shook my head and it wasn't until a sound came from inside the circle with us that I turned and saw MacDougal. He was standing behind the tombstone where we'd told him to stand. He looked a little pale in the moonlight, mouth open and gasping as if he'd been running. I hadn't thought to ask if he was psychically gifted. He couldn't be very gifted, or I would have sensed it, but his reaction said clearly he wasn't a null. They felt nothing when you did magic around them. MacDougal sure felt something.

I started walking toward him, and Nicky stayed at my side as if we'd planned it. "You okay, MacDougal?" I asked.

He nodded, but he was still pale, eyes too wide.

"I have to smear blood on you, remember?"

He nodded again, but he wasn't looking at me.

"MacDougal." I said his name sharply, almost a yell. He jumped, then looked at me. "Oh, my God," he said, and it was almost a yell, too.

"Mr. MacDougal, can you hear me?"

He nodded, and then coughed sharply, as if he were having trouble breathing. "I hear you, Blake."

"Do you remember what I said I had to do with the cow blood?"

"You smear it on my face, heart, hands, correct?"

"Yes, very good. How psychically gifted are you, MacDougal?"

"I'm not, I mean . . . I can feel ghosts, but I can't see them. They're what made me want to study history, so I could hear what they were trying to tell me."

I had to take a deep breath and let it out slow, or I would have yelled at him. "You can sense ghosts? But you can't see them?"

"No, just feel them. Gettysburg was so thick with them it was hard to breathe."

"For future reference, MacDougal, if you're around necromancy and you have a touch of it yourself, you need to say something up front, and not make it a surprise."

"Is that why it feels like my skin is jumping?"

"Yeah, that would be why."

Jesus, people just didn't think the logic through, did they? I didn't want to put the blood on him. I didn't want to give him a zombie to control; would it make his own abilities with the dead stronger, so that next time the ghosts could talk directly to him? Or was it just a quirk of fate, the universe laughing up its sleeve, and this would be the closest he'd ever come to the kind of power he might have had? If he'd been in his teens, or even twenties, I'd have called it, and opened the circle and tried for another historian, but he was late forties, early fifties. It was too late for some huge jump in psychic abilities—usually. I was 99.9 percent sure it wouldn't cause a problem. I stood there debating on that fraction of a percent.

"Do you need to use someone else?" Nicky asked.

"Debating that now."

"Why can't you use me?" MacDougal asked.

"Not sure."

"Not sure of what?" he asked.

"A lot of things, but right now how it might affect your psychic abilities to give you a zombie."

"What could it do?"

I shook my head. "I don't want to say."

"Why, is it something bad?"

"People are suggestible, Mr. MacDougal; you might talk yourself into things that aren't true later."

"I don't understand."

I shook my head again. "It's okay, don't worry about it."

I turned to Nicky. "I don't like this."

"Can you open the circle and put him out, put someone else back in?"

Just that he'd asked that question meant that Nicky had watched me do this a lot lately. It also meant that he thought about my job as logically as possible, the way he did most things. "If I open it, the power gets out sometimes, too. I won't have as much control of it once the circle is open."

"Then that's out," he said.

"Yeah, and we don't have another cow. I open the circle and I may be able to raise the zombie, but weird things happen when I raise the dead without a circle of protection up."

"Like the night we met," he said.

I realized that he was right. His mercenary group's witch had put a circle of power around the whole graveyard to keep me from being able to contact Jean-Claude and my other people. They'd thought that would be enough of a circle of power for me to raise the dead, and they'd been right. I'd raised the whole graveyard for them, and used the zombies as weapons against them. It had worked, but there had been a moment when I felt that mass of zombies fight me for control. They hadn't wanted to go back to their graves that night. They had turned hungry eyes to me, Nicky, and his old Rex. It had worked out, but I wasn't eager to repeat it.

"Yeah, like that."

"So you have more power than you need for one zombie; just raise it."

Logically I knew I couldn't give MacDougal more power permanently, but it's not always about logic. "I don't know."

"You're the boss," he said, which sometimes meant he would follow me to the ends of the earth, and sometimes meant that I was being silly, usually overly sentimental. Sociopaths are so fun to work with.

"If I were really the boss I'd have sensed his ability, but my necromancy was too loud in my head, like a tune you hum without realizing you do it. It drowned out his smaller sound."

"Has this ever happened before?" he asked.

"No."

"Then odds are you were overdue to hit someone like this."

I studied his so-serious face. I couldn't argue with his logic, though I wanted to, because it just seemed like I should have felt MacDougal's abilities, but even standing this close I felt nothing from him. It was only his own reactions that had let me know anything was wrong with him. Shouldn't I have felt more from him now that I knew? All I could feel was my own power filling the circle, pushing at me to use it. God, I wasn't raising enough dead, or it wouldn't have felt like some kind of flood waiting to crash down on us, or out of me and into the ground. The power needed to be used. I looked down at the grave.

I wanted to touch it. I wanted to pull out the corpse inside that hard ground. It felt good to use my magic; that wasn't new.

I dipped the machete back into the bowl of rapidly cooling blood. "I have to smear blood on you, Mr. MacDougal."

"I remember," he said, in a strained voice.

I used my other hand to take blood off the machete and have him bend down so I could smear it on his forehead, then open his shirt so I could touch over his heart, and lastly his hands. He didn't argue, or flinch at the blood. It made me wonder what our historian did in his spare time, or maybe the magic had him, too.

"I'm going to raise the zombie now. Don't leave the circle, because if you do then you won't be able to control the zombie and I don't have time to hand-hold it for you."

"I'll stay right here."

"Good," I said.

Nicky set the bowl of blood carefully on the ground and straightened with his hands flexing at his sides. "I want my hands free, just in case."

"You think you're going to wrestle the zombie?"

"I'd shoot it first, but I'll do what's needed."

I frowned at him, but I knelt and placed the machete across the bowl. I wanted my hands free, too, but for a different reason. I looked down at the grave. It was as if the last drop of blood had been one drop too many, and it was a moment of critical mass where the death and the magic met and imploded into something bigger. It was like doing a physics experiment that I'd done a thousand times before, but the same data, the same actions, and I suddenly had a brand-new result. Chaos theory is never a good thing when it meets magic.

I went to the grave and put my hands just above the soft dip in the earth where the coffin had broken down and a pocket of decay had risen underground and then deflated like a badly made cake so that the ground was hollowed out above it. I could feel the bits and pieces of the body under the dirt, like puzzle pieces stirred about. I put my hands on the dirt, and the moment my hands touched earth, it was like a spark leapt from the remains to my hands, up my arms, across my shoulders, and over my scalp like the way scientists say lightning truly is, from ground to air, but it never looks that way. This felt that way.

I concentrated on the earth against my hands. It was dry and hard packed, the spring grass the only softness. I made myself concentrate on the physical sensation so it would help anchor me against the magic that was spilling over my skin. This was an old cemetery; it didn't have sprinklers, and nothing got watered unless it was paid for with the caretakers, so I dug my fingers into the hard earth and the coolness of the new grass, and fought to control my own necromancy. It was just so much power tonight.

I plunged that power into the hard dirt and I called, "Thomas Warrington, Thomas James Warrington, I call thee from the grave. I call you to my hand, and the hand of the man behind your gravestone. Come to us, Thomas, rise and walk with us." I was cutting the ceremony to pieces, because I didn't need words of the ritual to build power. How did I know that I didn't need all the steps to raise this zombie? I just knew, knew with capital letters, I KNEW I could pull this zombie from the grave. It would take more energy doing it this way, but I needed to burn off the extra kick of the cow's death, and MacDougal's baby psychic powers. This was my only zombie raising of the night, and the magic had to go somewhere, because I didn't want it to go home with me to Jean-Claude and the other vampires in the underground. Necromancy was supposed to be good for all kinds of undead, including vamps. I so didn't need that tonight.

I used the dead man's name, because I wasn't certain that without it he would be himself and able to answer questions, but part of me was almost certain that I needed nothing but my own hands, my own power, to pull him out of the grave.

The earth moved against my hands like water, but thicker, as if mud could move like water and not be wet. The earth separated, remade itself, and I felt the pieces collect and begin to rebuild themselves. There were pieces missing, but it was all right, I didn't need the small pieces. I gathered him up and felt him begin to be.

I plunged my hands into that moving, writhing earth, and hands met mine, hands that laced their fingers around mine, and felt as real. It was like dragging a drowning victim up out of solid water. He clutched at my hands and the ground pushed, and I pulled, and he came out of the earth to his thighs, dressed in the black suit he'd been buried in. I got to my feet and pulled him with me, and the ground spilled him up like some kind of escalator. That was new; usually even the best zombies had to climb the last few feet from the ground as if the grave was reluctant to let them out. This grave gave him up like a flower opening and pushing out a seed.

He blinked huge, pale eyes at me, gray or blue. It was hard to tell by moonlight. He looked at me, at our hands, and said, "Who are you?"

Zombies didn't ask that first thing; like all true undead they needed blood to speak, to be real, to be "alive," even for a little while. I looked up into that young face and he was in there, aware, awake, and he was perfect. Even I was impressed.

15

WE LEFT THOMAS the Zombie with MacDougal. He and Mrs. Willis were very, very pleased with the zombie. "He seems alive," Mrs. Willis whispered to me, because once we'd explained to him what he was, and how much time had passed, it had scared him. I'd seen zombies react like that before, when they didn't know they were dead. I always hated that part, explaining to them that they were dead, and there was no way to change that permanently. Not even my necromancy could resurrect the dead. Thomas the Zombie looked fabulously alive, but he wasn't, and if we left him walking aboveground long enough his body would begin to rot and the miracle would turn into the nightmare of every shambling zombie movie you'd ever seen.

I used to have a hard-and-fast rule that I never let clients take their zombies away from the graveside. I put the rule in place after a few families took their loved ones home and kept them until they were rotted nightmares, and even then some didn't want to let them go. The worst was when they tried to bathe them. Water made them rot faster and did nothing to help the smell. My zombies didn't rot initially, even back in the day when they'd looked like partially rotted corpses, but the "magic" would eventually begin to fade, and the first sign of that was that the decay process started back up, and rotting meat stinks; it just does.

But technology and enough profit to buy the technology had given us options. I had an electronic ankle cuff waiting to put on the zombie. I'd use it to track him just like the police do with someone on house arrest. This model of cuff would also alarm if it was tampered with, so if they tried to take it off I'd know and they could be charged with disturbance of a corpse, among other things.

Our business manager at Animators Inc., Bert Vaughn, had approved the expense after he lost me for entire nights while I stayed with my zombies listening to them being questioned about everything from court cases to historical events. We billed per zombie raised, not by the hour, so that much revenue loss had finally convinced even Bert that we needed a different way to keep track of our zombies. But first we needed someone to give the zombie to, which was MacDougal.

Once the zombie was aboveground, the power was fine. I pulled the circle down and the spring night was just normal. Only the zombie was extraordinary, so lifelike that it was a little disturbing. I raised the dead; I did not do resurrection—no one did outside of Bible stories—but Thomas Warrington might have made a believer out of people. Not me; I knew in a few days he'd start to rot, and being this "alive" only meant that he'd be more horrified when it started, like the poor victims in the videos that the FBI had shown me. It was the same principle, except I didn't have Thomas Warrington's soul in a magical reinforced jar somewhere, so I could put it back in, or take it out, at my customers' whim.

To raise a zombie, even a recently dead one, that looked as alive as the women in the videos, the animator had to be damned powerful. There weren't many of us who had the juice to do something like this, and fewer still who could capture souls. Hell, I didn't even know how to do that. Dominga Salvador had offered to teach me, but I'd told her I didn't want anyone's soul. I hadn't then, and I didn't now, but watching Thomas laugh and joke with everyone made me wonder, if it wasn't his soul in there, what was it? Was it just body memory? The last flickers of personality, caught in the flesh like the traumatic events that get caught in the walls and floors of a house, so they play over and over again—not a true ghost, but the echoes of emotions so strong they leave images behind? Was that all I was seeing in the tall young "man"? I didn't know and Manny hadn't known either, because I'd asked him. My grandmother Flores, who taught me how to control my power, hadn't known either. As far as I knew, no one knew the answer; maybe there wasn't one.

We made plans for them to bring him back tomorrow night to be put back down. We made the plans quietly while MacDougal asked questions and the zombie answered them, and one of the young guys, whose name I couldn't quite remember, recorded it with his phone. Ah, technology. The zombie had protested the ankle bracelet, but when I gave him a direct order to let me put it on, he'd complied like he had no will of his own. It sort of comforted me that he reacted like any other zombie, because he was almost unnervingly alive, even to me. His skin was still unnaturally cool to the touch, but other than being a little pale, he looked great; for being dead over two hundred years, he looked amazing.

Nicky, Dino, and I were using the aloe baby wipes I kept in the car to clean my hands. The wipes did well on everything except the blood that always seemed to embed itself at the roots of your fingernails. That needed soap, water, and scrubbing, sometimes with a bristle brush, but for everything else we'd be presentable. Nathaniel held a fresh trash bag so we could throw the used wipes in. Tonight it wasn't very full, but on some nights the kitchen-sized bag filled up.

"Killing dinosaurs to no purpose," I said.

"What?" Dino asked.

Nathaniel explained, "A lot of plastics used to be made from petroleum products, just like gasoline, so it's all prehistoric dead plants and animals."

"Dead dinosaurs," Nicky said.

Dino looked at both of us. "That was Anita's explanation out of your mouth, right?"

Nathaniel nodded. "Yes."

"Yeah," Nicky said.

"It's that couple thing again," he said.

"What couple thing?" I asked.

"Couples start using each other's sayings, speech patterns, jokes, and specialized information after a while, because you hear it repeated over and over."

"Coworkers and military units do it, too," Nicky said.

"Yeah, but that's usually more narrowly centered. Couples can go all over the board. I'd like to know someone that well someday."

"Are you saying you've never been part of a couple?" I asked.

"I've dated, but no, not really."

"This is my first real couple," Nicky said.

"What do you mean, real?" I asked.

"I was told to seduce people for work sometimes, or go undercover. People are less suspicious of you if you have a romantic partner. They thought we were dating, and I went along with what they thought that should be, but it was all pretend for maintaining my cover or gaining information from them."

"How long was the longest you dated someone like that?" I asked.

"Almost six months."

"That's a long time," Nathaniel said. "And you didn't care about her at all?"

"The sex was good."

I looked up at one of the men I was in love with and couldn't wrap my head around it. "And if the sex hadn't been good?" I asked.

"She was cover, so I'd have found someone who was better in bed."

"What happened to her?" Nathaniel asked.

Nicky looked at him as if he'd asked a dumb question or one that he'd never thought of before. "I don't know."

"Did anything you do bring her into harm's way?" I asked.

He thought about it for a second and then made a little waffling motion with his head. "I don't know."

"How can you not know?" I asked.

"I completed my assignment and then I ditched the cell phone and walked away. It was the only number she had for me, so if anything happened, she had no way to contact me. She didn't know my real name, background, nothing. The person she dated for six months didn't exist."

"Not once you left," I said.

He shook his head. "No, Anita, that person never existed. I was undercover as a social, charming extrovert with lots of friends, with a new party, or show, or something almost every night."

"You hate going to parties and shit," I said.

"Yeah, but socializing was the best way to gather information and to move around without arousing suspicion. The more friends I made, the closer I got to the inner circle I wanted to break into, so I could get close to my target."

"So you didn't just lie to the girl, you lied to every friend you made," Nathaniel said.

"If you want to call it that, yeah."

"What else do you call it?" he asked.

"Work."

"You scare me sometimes," Dino said, "just so you know."

"I know," Nicky said.

We all looked at him and he gave perfect blank face back.

"But you also give me hope," Dino said.

Nicky narrowed his eyes at him then. "I give you hope?"

"Yeah."

"How?"

"If you can fall in love and make a family for yourself, then I have to have a shot at it, because I'm way more charming than you are."

Nicky grinned. "You haven't seen me try to be charming."

"Yeah, I have," Dino said.

"No, you haven't," Nicky said with a smile.

"Yeah, I have."

"No, you really haven't."

Dino frowned at him.

"Anita knew what I was from the moment she met me; so did Nathaniel and Micah, Jean-Claude, all of them. I never had to pretend that I was someone else, something else. I didn't even have to pretend I was this big, tough crazy guy who would do anything, so don't mess with me."

"So even that was pretend," I said.

"People don't fuck with you as much when they think you're crazy. It scares them more than calm."

"When I met you, I thought you enjoyed the violence, or the threat of it," I said.

"Only in the bedroom. When I'm working, I'm working. It's not personal."

"Oh, come on, sometimes it feels good to hit someone as hard as you want, no holding back," Dino said.

Nicky grinned suddenly, but it was more a baring of teeth, closer to a snarl as if his lion were peeking out. "Okay, yeah, just the physicality of it, yeah."

"Yeah," Dino said, and gave a low, very male chuckle.

Nicky joined him with his own version of it.

Nathaniel and I looked at each other. "You understand this moment of male bonding?" I asked him.

He shook his head. "Nope, I've spent most of my life not understanding the 'hit 'em as hard as you can' kind of guy. Whatever it means to be a man, I'm not that kind."

"But you don't have a problem with me being that kind of man," Nicky said.

"No," Nathaniel said.

"I make a lot of guys nervous."

"And me being bisexual makes a lot of guys nervous."

Nicky grinned. "I'm secure."

Nathaniel grinned back. "Me, too."

Nicky raised his fist and Nathaniel bumped it softly.

Dino shook his head. "You guys are just fun to see and I like it, but I don't think I'm that secure."

"What do you mean?" I asked.

"I'm not as pretty as either of these two. Nicky beats me in the gym, and from what I hear the two of them are both great in bed. They both cook, and we won't even get into Jean-Claude and Micah. One is the prettiest man I've ever seen, and the other one is, well, Micah. He's this tiny guy, but he walks into a room like he owns it, and like everyone should know that."

"Anita does the same thing," Nicky said.

"Yeah, she makes us all feel a little less like 'the man.'"

"Not me," Nicky said.

"Me, either," Nathaniel said.

"We're all pretty secure," I said.

Nathaniel's phone rang, and it was his ring tone for Micah. "Hey, baby," he said, and then something Micah said made his face go serious, and he walked a little away from us.

"What's wrong?" I asked.

He shook his head and spoke to Micah. "Okay, but I'm not sure how it's going to go on our end."

"Nathaniel, what's wrong?" I asked.

He turned with a face as serious as any I'd seen, which sort of scared me. "Is Micah all right, is everyone all right?"

"There's a . . . mixer set up for you to meet the weretigers."

"A mixer, what the hell does that mean?"

"It means there wasn't time to plan a formal dinner, or a cocktail party, but they're putting something together so that all the weretigers

Jean-Claude and Micah like for us, and who are interested in the position, can be in one place at one time, and we can interact with them."

"Is this the tigers bitching about not being included in the commitment ceremony?" Nicky asked.

"Yeah," I said.

"Anita agreed to look at more weretigers, including female."

Nicky looked at me.

Dino whistled softly, grinning.

I pointed a finger at Dino. "You stay out of this."

He pressed his lips tight together but couldn't quite stop looking like he was about to laugh.

To Nicky I said, "Say something."

"When did you agree to do all this?"

"On the drive here," Nathaniel said.

Nicky looked at him, not even trying to keep the surprise off his face. "What the hell did you say to her to get her to agree to date more women?"

"I just brought it up, I swear."

Nicky turned and gave me a very narrow eye, nearly suspicious. "It's not like you to agree that easy, Anita."

"Can't I just be reasonable for once?"

"No," he said, and Dino had to walk away from us all because he burst out laughing and didn't want me to yell at him for it.

"We have time to get to the Circus and change before it starts," Nathaniel said.

"You and Anita, you mean."

"You live with us, too," Nathaniel said.

"He's right; whoever we bring in will change our domestic arrangement, so you should at least be there to wave off anyone you hate."

"What does it matter? I won't be sleeping with any of them."

"Probably not," I said, "but you're an important part of our household and you should be there to give your opinion."

He looked back and forth between us. "So if you love one of the tigers and I veto them, you'll just agree with me?"

I shrugged. "I don't know for sure, but I certainly wouldn't want to add someone to our poly that you really clashed with, because right now we all like each other a lot. I don't want that to change."

"I'm just your Bride, Anita."

I wrapped my arms around his waist and gazed up at him. "I love you, Nicky; you're a hell of a lot more to me than just Dracula's Bride."

He studied my face, then smiled a little, wrapping his arms around me, so that I was surrounded by all that muscle. Just feeling the potential of all that strength made me shiver a little in his arms.

He grinned then. "That reaction just from hugging you?"

I nodded.

"I don't think Jean-Claude and Micah will allow me to veto anyone that they like, but I appreciate that you and Nathaniel would."

Nathaniel came in from the side and hugged us both. "I love you like a brother, you know that."

"You know that most brothers don't share women, right?" Nicky said.

Nathaniel drew back enough to shrug. "It works for us."

"And for Cynric, too," Nicky said. "I really thought you'd just put a ring on his finger."

I shook my head. "If we can add someone that everyone will sleep with, including Micah, it would just work better."

"Cynric is going to be hurt," Nicky said.

"You're a sociopath—why should you care?" I asked.

"I'm a made sociopath, not a born one, which means I have some emotion, and I like the kid. He's the closest I've gotten to a little brother since I lost my own."

"He'll be at the mixer tonight," Nathaniel said.

I sighed and stepped back so that Nicky just let me go. "I can't help that."

"Are you angry with Sin?" Nathaniel asked.

"No!" I snapped, and then had to take a few deep breaths before I could say, "Let's get home and change for this party thing."

The men exchanged a look.

"What?" I demanded.

Nicky shook his head. Nathaniel said, "You are mad at Sin."

"If you want me to go to this party at all, we leave now."

We left. Dino drove the truck that he and Nicky had brought the cow in, but Nicky rode with us. They both tried to get me to talk, but I finally convinced them to leave it the fuck alone and be grateful I was looking at other women at all. I sounded angry even to myself. I really wasn't in a party mood.

16

SOMEWHERE ON THE drive some horrible tension in me eased. The anger began to slip away on the sound of Nathaniel and Nicky discussing food for the week, and if there were enough ingredients at both the Circus and the house in Jefferson County to make the meals as planned. I liked listening to them plan our domestic stuff. I loved that Nathaniel truly enjoyed that part of living together. I loved that Nicky and he worked so well together both in the kitchen and in the bedroom. Our core group worked so well together and I knew that every time we tried adding a new person even to the edges of the group, we ran the risk of upsetting all of it. Cynric was already in our life and he worked for all of us, some better than others, but he didn't make anyone unhappy. Now I knew some of the issues that made me not want to commit to him, and I hated the issues. It was like victim-blaming him for being another victim of the same trauma. Even in my own head it sounded convoluted and wrong.

"Anita, you missed the exit."

I glanced at Nathaniel. "What?"

"You drove past the exit to the Circus."

"Sorry, I'll hit the next one and backtrack."

"Are you upset about having to meet the tigers this soon?"

I took the exit carefully, forcing myself to pay attention. "Yeah," I lied. Normally he'd be right, I'd be all resistant about having to meet people to be not only a new lover, but potentially someone we'd have a commitment ceremony with, but tonight all I could think about was Cynric and how I'd thought the issue was his age, when it was just an excuse not to look at the truth. I hated that I'd been that blind about myself. I could go have hors d'oeuvres and drinks or whatever with the weretigers and chat, be charming and vague. They could parade tigers all damn night in front of me; I didn't have to pick anyone, and the moment I thought that, I realized that I was lying to Nathaniel, and Micah, and every important person in my life. Damn it, our relationships weren't based on lies.

"What's making you feel so unhappy?" Nicky said.

I didn't want to explain, but I realized that the one person I really owed an explanation to was Cynric. "Cynric, I should have called him to let him know about tonight. He's living with us and I didn't even call him to give him a heads-up about tonight and the other weretigers."

Nathaniel touched the side of my face, and my thoughts were too close to the surface. He got some of them direct, but the sharing made me swerve the car. "Jesus, Nathaniel," I said, over the thudding of my heart in my throat.

He'd jerked back. "You usually shield better than this, Anita. You're worried about Sin, but not just about calling him. I called him and he was pretty stoked at the idea that you'd be willing to look at another woman being added to our inner group."

"Really, then why won't he date anyone but me? I know some of the girls at school have been heartbroken about him being all poly-monogamous."

"He sees it as adding to our family, and the woman would be your lover, too. She'd also be a clan tiger, so she wouldn't expect her relationship with him to supersede yours."

I glanced at him. "You and he have talked about it, haven't you?"

Nathaniel nodded.

"We have to do something when you're off raising the dead and chasing bad guys," Nicky said.

I glanced behind at him, then forced myself to pay attention to the road again. I wanted to get angry about the fact that the men in my life had conspired against me to add another woman to our merry little band, but they all shared me with multiple men, and as Nathaniel had pointed out, most of them didn't even get sexual contact from the rest of my lovers. They really were very good sports about it all, so it would just be churlish to complain, but . . . I so wanted to.

"Now you're mad," Nicky said.

I shook my head. "I'm not."

"I can feel it."

"I'm trying not to be mad, because it's not logical or fair."

"Feelings aren't fair, Anita," Nathaniel said. "They're just how we feel."

"True, but I'm trying to be less bitchy about mine."

He smiled. "You're grumpy, not bitchy."

I gave him a raised eyebrow. "And the difference between the two is?"

He laughed. "If you were bitchy you wouldn't be trying to do better."

I smiled, then laughed just a little. "Fine, okay, but I am trying."

"We appreciate that."

"We love you," Nicky said.

"We do," Nathaniel said.

"But you'd like a chance to love a few more people," I said.

"If more of the other men were bisexual it wouldn't be an issue for me."

"Another woman would be nice, but she's not going to enjoy sex the way I like it," Nicky said.

"You don't do super-rough all the time," I said.

"No, but even my mild is too much for most women."

"You had to have vanilla sex with some of the women you pretended to date when you were undercover," Nathaniel said.

"Yeah, and it's better than masturbating, but it's still holding back."

"When sex is supposed to be about letting go," I said.

"Yeah."

"So, you don't think another woman will do you any good."

"Not really, but that's okay."

"Is it really okay?" I asked, as I turned into the back entrance to the employee parking lot at the Circus of the Damned. I had a reserved spot near the door, because after dark the lot filled up with all the people it took to run the permanent carnival midway, the one-ring circus in its tent, the freak show, and all the things that made it into the Circus of the Damned. Here you could have that summertime traveling carnival experience under one roof, regardless of the weather, if you were willing to wait until nightfall. But then all carnivals are at their best after dark.

Nicky leaned on the back of my seat, his face resting against my hair. "Yeah, it's really okay."

"Why is it okay? Why are you content with only me?"

"I'm not content, I'm happy, and sociopaths don't get to say that very often."

That made me smile. I reached up and touched the side of his face. He rubbed his face between my hand and my hair and said, "Your touching me like this means more to me than more sex with anyone else."

I kept touching him, but I was puzzled and said so.

"I get it," Nathaniel said.

I moved my head so I could look at him, my hand sliding further around Nicky's face, so I could curl my fingers in his hair. "Explain it to me, then."

"That small touch says love, not just lust. We've both had a lot of lust aimed at us, but not so much love."

"Yeah," Nicky said, tracing his fingers down my arm.

"The fact that you worried about Sin and his feelings, even though I know you've got this weird conflict about his age, says just how caring you are. Nicky and I haven't had a lot of people in our life that cared for us, not in the way you do, or the way Micah does."

"Micah doesn't really like me," Nicky said.

"That's not true," I said.

"Do you really like him?" Nathaniel asked.

"I think he's a good leader. He's a better Nimir-Raj for the were-leopards than I am a Rex for the lions."

"That didn't answer the question."

"No, not really. I mean I like him as a leader and a person, but he and I have less of a connection in the poly group."

"You and Jean-Claude don't have much connection either," Nathaniel said.

"No, but I could donate blood to him, if I wanted to, and that would make me more important to him in the poly group. Micah and I don't have anything to bargain with, or offer each other, that will deepen our relationship. He doesn't even like rough sex or bondage much, so we can't even play."

"We should be working on the group we have, not adding to it," I said.

"Don't back out now," Nathaniel said.

"Another girl would be nice for the other guys."

I turned in the circle of his arm and looked at Nicky. "But not for you?"

"I told you my reasoning, Anita."

"There are women in town who like sex as rough as or rougher than Anita does," Nathaniel said.

Nicky gave him a look like, *Prove it.*

Nathaniel looked at me. "If you really wanted another play partner for Nicky, I could find him someone."

I looked at Nicky. "Do you want another woman to dominate?"

"It depends on how much work it is. I like to do rough sex; I don't want to do the whole dominant with you all day twenty-four seven. Once we leave the bedroom, or the dungeon, I don't want to be in charge of your ass, or any other part of you."

I smiled. "Good to know."

Nathaniel frowned. "I know some women you could play with for a night, but you couldn't do a relationship with them because they would want more domination than just rough sex."

"And that is why I'm happy with Anita; she bottoms hard, but once we're done she doesn't need the upkeep. True submissives are fucking exhausting."

"To the right dominant they're energizing," Nathaniel said.

"I'm not the dominant they're looking for."

"Me, either," I said.

Nathaniel grinned at me. "That's right, Nicky missed all that time I was trying to get you to be my dominant in every way."

"It was exhausting," I said.

"See?" Nicky said.

Nathaniel laughed. "And I found out that I'm not that kind of submissive, I'd just been trained up that way."

"Let's take our happy dominant, submissive, and switches asses inside and shop for weretigers," I said.

"Girl weretigers?" Nathaniel said.

I smiled at the look on his face; I couldn't help it. "Yes, some girl weretigers, too. Who knows, maybe we'll meet the woman of all our dreams."

"Not possible," Nicky said.

"Why not?" I asked.

He leaned over and kissed me. "Because we've already found her."

It took me a minute to realize he meant me, and then I wanted to protest, but in the end I just took the compliment like I was supposed to. I wasn't sure I'd ever believe I was the woman of anyone's dreams. I was good, and I tried, but dream women/men were perfect and I would never be that.

17

DINO HAD PARKED the truck and trailer, then waited near the back door for us, far enough away to give us some privacy, but not so far away he couldn't still do his job as bodyguard, so the four of us walked through the back door into what had been a storage room. Now it was more like a mini–guard post complete with a coffeemaker and a mini-fridge. There were almost always two guards in the room to keep track of the back door, the door that led out into the public area of the Circus, and the door to the underground that had the living quarters.

It was usually newer guards here, so we did a quick greeting and kept moving. If they'd been slacking on duty then it would have taken longer, but since it was either Claudia or Fredo who interviewed people for the job we didn't get a lot of that. We went through the far door and were on the stairs leading down. There was no elevator to the underground; you had to physically take a half-mile of stone steps leading up and down. It was like the best glute workout ever, and it meant that if you were bad guys you had to come down a very long expanse of steps, which took time, and only had one turn the whole way, so we could sit at the angle and shoot up at you, and at the door and shoot down at you. Guards at top and bottom could take turns firing volleys into anyone we didn't want coming down the stairs. It was the first defense for the Master of St. Louis's lair, and a damned fine one.

Nicky, Nathaniel, and I walked three abreast with Dino bringing up the rear. He said in a voice that was a little winded, because cardio was never his strong suit, "What's with these stairs?"

I glanced back at him, forcing Nathaniel to pause as we stepped down. Nicky and I weren't holding hands on the stairs, because our height difference or maybe inseam difference made the stairs harder.

He took the opportunity to stop walking, which may have been why he said something at all. "I thought at first the steps were carved by someone who was taller, had a really long stride, you know."

We all nodded at him.

"But it's not that, is it?"

"No," I said.

"It's like the stairs weren't made to fit anyone's stride."

"I think maybe that's part of the point," Nathaniel said.

"What do you mean?" Dino asked, leaning against the wall just a little.

"It's more of a challenge to go up and down them, because there's no natural rhythm to the steps."

"So it's even more of a deterrent to try to break into the underground," I said.

He nodded.

"Have you tried coming down the steps in leopard form?" Nicky asked.

Nathaniel shook his head.

"I've done it in lion form and the steps work better."

"What does that mean?" Dino asked.

"I think whoever made the steps didn't make them for anything bipedal."

"Bipedal," Dino said. "Bipedal? Who uses that as a word?"

"It means exactly what I wanted to say," Nicky said.

Dino was looking at him with a puzzled frown.

"Or did you just think I wasn't smart enough to know the word?"

"No, that, no, I mean . . . it's just a little, I don't know, college professor for . . ."

"Me," Nicky said.

"No, just no." Dino was shaking his head as he pushed away from the wall.

"Does everyone think I'm not that bright?"

"I did not say that." Dino was nervous.

"You worried that Nicky will hold a grudge next time on the practice mat?" I asked.

"Maybe."

Nicky grinned and started walking again. "Let's do double time down the rest of the steps."

"Aww, don't be like that," Dino said.

Nathaniel and I grinned and followed Nicky down the steps like we were in the gym. There'd been a reason I kept my hiking shoes on and had the high heels in my bag along with the plastic-wrapped coveralls. There was always laundry to do after a zombie raising.

Dino called after us, "Come on, don't do this."

"Catch up, Dino," Nicky called back.

He muttered something, but he started down the last long steps. The three of us were all waiting beside the last big door by the time he lumbered/ran down to us. "Hate you all," he panted as he leaned against the wall.

"You really do need to hit the cardio harder, Dino," Nicky said.

"I know."

Nathaniel's text tone went off and he checked it. "It's Sin, he wants me to help him dress for the party tonight."

I wondered if that was really what the message said, or if it was more like "Why is Anita looking at other tigers when I'm already here," but I didn't press. I'd have to deal with Cynric soon enough; I wasn't jumping the gun early, and besides I had other things to worry about.

Watching one of our bodyguards pant that hard after coming down stairs that hadn't winded the three of us, I decided that maybe I should talk to Claudia about Dino's fitness level. He was great in a fight, but if he had to dash for cover or keep up with the other guards at a run, could he? Being in good shape wasn't just for fitting into skinny jeans, if your job depended on you being in fighting shape. On a heavy bag Dino was one of the hardest-hitting we had, but I was going to need to have him sparring with the other guards, because speed counted when you were almost always fighting shapeshifters and vampires.

I looked at Nicky trying to decide if he'd teased Dino just to tease, or if he'd wanted me to see the problem. Dino was half bent over, still breathing hard. Was this a problem that affected Dino's job? Nicky made eye contact with me and that was enough; he'd wanted me to see it, because a demonstration like this spoke louder than just bringing it up to me. I gave a small nod; Nicky gave one back and moved to the big dungeon-worthy door. He knocked hard twice. Short of serious explosives the door was proof against almost anything, so we'd taken to locking it and using it as the barrier it was supposed to be. But locked meant that there had to be guards always posted on the other side to let you in. We had the manpower for it, but I didn't like the new security measure. It slowed things down, and that usually made me antsy.

There were already two guards at the head of the stairs, and more in a sort of hidden crow's nest in the top of the warehouse building with a sniper rifle, and more up above circling through the permanent Circus tent, freak show, and carnival midway that was the public business of the Circus of the Damned. We had one or two bodyguards assigned to all our principals, and now we had two more guards tied up on the other side of the big door. Yes, we had the manpower, but when Fredo had come to me with the suggestion that we lock the door and put guards on it, I just hadn't realized how much it would irritate me to be on the other side of the door so often.

There was an answering knock. Nicky stood closer to the door, putting his bare hand against the big lock with its huge keyhole, so the guard on the other side would catch his scent. It was clever as hell, but I was getting really tired of it, as the door finally pushed open, and Kelly Reeder held the door open for us. She was five-five to my five-three, but I'd seen what those extra inches of leg and arm could do on the practice mat when we all worked out. If everyone is equally trained, reach matters in hand-to-hand combat.

She'd put her long blond hair back in a high, tight braid, so that her face looked pale and unadorned, as if she were waiting to put on makeup. The black shoulder rig with its gun and extra ammo was almost invisible against the black-on-black T-shirt and jeans. She was wearing black boots like I wore to crime scenes. The unrelieved black that was the guards' regular uniform was always severe against her pale yellow hair and paler blue eyes, but today her cheeks looked almost hollow; the muscles in her arms stood out, not like she'd done it on purpose, but as if she'd lost too much weight for her health.

Nathaniel gave me a quick kiss. "I'll go help Sin get ready."

I squeezed his hand and let him go, because there was something wrong with Kelly. I'd take care of the person in front of me, and save the rest for later.

"You okay, Kelly?" I asked, because somehow in the division of labor I'd ended up in charge of the emotional well-being of our guards. I wasn't always good at it, but I was girl enough to ask if something was wrong, when most of the men wouldn't ask unless invited. It was a girl/guy difference that had saddled me with the emotional caretaking, but I just couldn't walk past Kelly looking like that and not ask. Maybe I was better socialized than I liked to admit.

"I'm fine," she said, but it was automatic and totally not believable. She held the door for us, but when she'd shut and locked it behind us, she went down on one knee in front of us, head slightly down, but eyes rolled upward so she could still see us.

I started to say *What are you doing?* but she said, "I kneel before my king, my Rex, and offer all that I am for him to do with as he sees fit."

I just stared at her and I knew my surprise showed on my face, but I couldn't hide it in time. This was brand-new to me. What the hell was going on?

Nicky held his left hand out to her, as if he had a ring for her to kiss or something.

Kelly's head drooped a little and then she reached out and touched fingertips to his hand. He said, "I accept this tribute from my lioness, for she is faithful and strong."

I looked at Nicky, feeling even more like I'd missed something, maybe something important. I wanted to say *What the hell?* and I might have except that there was one more person in the room and she was giving me enough grief without me admitting that I, the queen of all I surveyed, didn't know what the hell was going on.

Lita was five-eight and managed to be slender, curvy, and muscular. She wasn't as muscled as I was, because she didn't like lifting weights. She did it because we insisted all our guards do it, but she did the minimum; but then she was a wererat and I was still mostly human. I had to work harder to play with the big dogs, because I wasn't one.

I was stronger than human-normal, but so were most of the people who gave me grief, both on my job as a U.S. Marshal for the Preternatural Branch and here at home.

Lita was beautiful and both knew it and was insecure about it, which made her issues all over the board. Her skin was the color of that first nice brown that a good tan can give you, but her "tan" was with her year-round, though she'd probably tan darker if she ever went out into the sun enough. Her dark brown eyes were edged with thick lashes and a little too much eye makeup for my taste, but she could carry it off, and we were both wearing lipstick so red it looked like blood, so who was I to bitch? Her wavy black hair fell to her waist, held back only by a slender headband that was a black so close to her hair color that I only knew it was there because I knew hair like hers didn't stay away from your face without something forcing it back. The black T-shirt tucked into black jeans, waist made tinier with a black belt with a silver buckle, and knee-high boots that were more club wear than military made her look like the gun at her hip and the AR on its shoulder strap were props for some kind of cosplay at a science fiction convention rather than the real deal. She was barely twenty-one but looked older in that lush, I-blossomed-early sort of way.

Her red lips quirked in that smile that some of the men thought was sexy, but if you looked at her eyes when she did it, they were always cold, even cruel. No, that smile wasn't about sex; it was about power. Claudia, who was one of our guard leaders, and I had decided it'd be nice to have more female guards. I'd forgotten what that might mean for the wererats. Lita and two others had come from L.A.; they were all members of a street gang there. The last new guard we'd brought in who'd had a gangster background had been Haven. He'd ended up shooting Claudia and Nathaniel and killing one of our werelions, Noel. I still blamed myself, because I had been wishy-washy with Haven. I believed that if I'd been hard enough, clear enough, from the beginning that Noel would still be alive and have his master's in English lit by now, maybe even his doctorate. He'd died trying to keep Nathaniel alive, so I owed Noel. It's hard to pay a debt to the dead, so I'd decided to pay it forward and never let another person with a certain background doubt who was in charge. I wasn't sure how to make that clear to Lita yet, but I was pretty sure she'd give me an opportunity.

Kelly started to stand, but winced hard enough that Nicky had to catch her arm, or she might have fallen. That was it; I had to say something.

"What's going on, guys? Why is Kelly hurt?"

"You smelled surprised when they did the formal greeting, Anita," Lita said with that cruel little smile on her face.

Rats actually have some of the best scenting noses in the animal kingdom. How do you hide your reaction from someone who can smell it? Answer: You don't. But you can ignore her, and that's what I did.

"Answer me, Nicky," I said, and because he was Bride he had to do exactly what I said. He had more independence and could fight me, but a direct order, or question, was still very hard for him to refuse.

"I don't know why she has fresh wounds hidden under her clothes, but I can guess."

"Then guess, and tell me why the formal greeting. That sort of shit is usually reserved for when we have company, or when someone needs to assert dominance."

Nicky's shoulders flexed before he turned more squarely toward the drapes. Dino moved apart from us, so he was closer to the drapes than we were; so nice that everyone knew their jobs. Kelly and Lita were both paying attention, too, when the drapes parted and Meng Die walked through.

She was one of our vampires, which made her on our side, and she was, but in the end Meng Die was always on her own side. She was shorter than Kelly, slender and altogether delicate with straight black hair caressing her shoulders as she walked. Her up-tilted eyes were a paler brown than Lita's, or mine come to that. She was wearing a black vinyl catsuit that screamed *sex*, and *dominatrix*. The first was true, the second not, at least not in a fetish or professional way. She wanted to be everyone's mistress if it meant being the boss, the queen, the big cheese, but the outfit meant she was working upstairs in the Circus of the Damned tonight. She made great scenery for some of the acts. Trouble was that the burning intelligence and ambition in her eyes weren't happy with being set dressing. She wanted more, a lot more. She wanted to go back home to San Francisco, but her old master wouldn't have her back. She'd probably been days away from staging a palace coup, and he knew it. Jean-Claude had refused her permission to go back and take over the territory by force. We were looking for a territory that needed a new master vampire but didn't dare send her in as anyone's second-in-command, because she wouldn't be second for long.

She gave a disdainful look at Dino as he towered over her, and walked past him as if he wasn't almost broader through the shoulders than she was tall. "Anita, did you really think you could just dump that many high-level lycanthropes and vampires into our little pool and not have repercussions?" Meng Die asked.

I didn't understand what she meant, and tried to decide if I wanted to admit I was that lost.

"Of course you did. You're so powerful that you think you can handle anything, but the rest of us only get the dregs of your power. We struggle more when you make these sweeping changes without telling us first."

"I don't know what you're talking about," I said, finally. I was too lost to bluff and I was technically the boss of her, so I could admit weakness. She wouldn't think less of me for it, because she thought so little of me already.

"The Harlequin, Anita, the Harlequin; you killed their dark mistress, the queen of us all, and they went from being her spies-assassins-bodyguards to belonging to Jean-Claude and you. You dumped over twenty of the finest warriors ever to grace vampirekind into our territory, but the real insult was that you dumped in their animals to call, as well. They'd lived hundreds, or thousands, of years because their masters and mistresses were undying."

"Yeah, they're powerful and they're a pain in the ass sometimes, there's always a learning curve," I said.

She laughed, high and brittle. "You call it a learning curve; have the werelion show you her wounds. Ask her how she likes being behind the curve."

I looked at Kelly, and in looking I saw Lita's face, too. Lita didn't look any happier with Meng Die than I did. I'd have thought they might bond over their mutual disdain for me, but apparently not. I filed that away for later, and looked at Kelly.

She was even paler, as if what little color she had had drained away. If it had been someone else I might have asked if she was going to faint, but she was a guard, she was a lion, and she was a warrior. She wouldn't admit it until she fell down. Since I was almost as stubborn, I let it go.

"Kelly." I said it softly, not angry with her, because somehow I was pretty sure whatever had gone wrong was at least partially my fault. I'd killed the Mother of All Darkness, before she could kill . . . everyone, and by vampire or lycanthrope rules that meant that what was hers was now ours, including her bodyguards, her spies, her assassins, her executioners: the Harlequin. They'd been the closest thing the vampires had to policemen. If a vampire got out of hand and was attracting too much unwanted attention, the Harlequin could be dispatched and the problem would be solved, and it would stay solved, because true death is the ultimate solution.

"How bad are you hurt?" Nicky asked.

"Not bad," she said, and I didn't have to be able to "smell" the change in her body chemistry to know she was lying. She wouldn't look at either of us, and she was fighting not to hunch from the pain, or maybe some muscle, or ligament, was trying to pull her off center. Lycanthropes could heal almost anything, but they could also heal crookedly without medical attention.

"One of you tell me what's going on," I said.

"You gave us two lions from the Harlequin."

"Giacomo and Magda, I remember, what about them?"

"Giacomo and I came to an understanding early."

"You beat the crap out of him," I said.

Nicky nodded.

"Did you know that Giacomo didn't start the fight?" Meng Die said.

I looked at Nicky and raised an eyebrow.

He shrugged as much as he could with all the muscle, and said, "She's right on one thing, Anita. These guys are supposed to be the best fighters on the planet. We're lions, we fight. We cooperate from a position of strength; if the pride is safer with you on our side, then you can stay, but if you're more danger than help, you don't get to stay."

"I know you killed two of the male werelions when you took over the local pride."

"Did you approve their deaths, Anita?" Meng Die asked.

I just looked at Nicky and Kelly, who was trying not to sway in place.

"He asked your forgiveness, but not your permission, didn't he? And Nicky is your Bride, your tame lion; if he could go against your so-careful conscience, then what do you think the rest of the animals have been doing?"

"Don't call them animals," I said.

"Oh, that's right; you're progressive and so very American. You want to make the shapeshifters equal with the vampires."

"You said it, I'm American, and we like this whole equality thing."

"The great experiment," she said, and made it sound like an insult.

"Yeah," I said.

"Once I made it clear that if Giacomo ever tried to fight me again, I'd kill him, he settled in fine. But Magda is a lioness; male lions only fight them if attacked, or for some breach of pride law."

"She's the one hurting Kelly," I said.

He nodded.

I looked at Kelly's pale face, and knew here was another dangerous person I'd brought into our happy little family who was cutting up my people. Fuck. "Isn't Magda breaking pride law?" I asked.

"No," Kelly said in a strained voice, "she's within her rights to try to move up the dominance hierarchy. I'm the only lioness still standing in her way."

"She won the fight; I'm sorry, Kelly, but she did, right?"

Kelly shook her head, stopped in midmovement, licked her lips, and said, "Not yet."

"It's only a fight to the death for Rex or Regina of the pride, and Kelly isn't my Regina."

"Technically, I'm your Regina even though I don't shift form?"

He nodded again. "The Regina is usually the mate of the Rex, or vice versa."

"Wait, I thought the lionesses didn't fight for dominance. If there's a fight, then the males take care of the heavy lifting in werelion society, just like they do in most weretiger clans."

"Modern werelions, yes," Nicky said.

"What does that mean, modern werelions?"

"It means that Magda isn't modern anything. She invoked a really old law among us. If Kelly were my lover, then she'd be safe from challenges, but she's a guard just like any of the men. She's earned her place in the pride and in Jean-Claude's guard, which makes her a warrior first and a girl second. I told Magda that if she killed Kelly I'd kill her, but short of keeping it from being a death match, there's nothing I can do."

"Well, I can," I said.

"No," Kelly almost yelled, "Anita, you can't intercede. If you protect me from her, then it means I'm not fighter enough to protect myself. I've fought too hard and too long to be a lioness who gets respect like a lion; I won't lose that. I'd rather die than lose that."

"Rosamond isn't a warrior and she's okay with her place in the pride," I said.

"Rosamond is my friend, and she'll help fight if someone attacks the pride, but they treat her like she's soft, like a girl. I don't want that."

"We are girls, Kelly," I said. I touched the hem of my short skirt. "It's not all bad." I smiled and tried to lighten the mood, but her eyes were anguished. That was the only word I had for it.

"But everyone respects you as if you were a guy, Anita. It's not fair that men get more respect, but in a world where how hard you can hit and how much damage you can do in a fight matters, men rule. I was doing good with being one of the boys and mating with some of them, and then Magda comes and goes all old-school on me."

"The fact that you've fought her to a draw is impressive," Meng Die said, and there was no mockery in the sentence, just truth.

"Three times," Nicky said.

"What?" Meng Die asked.

"They'd fought twice and if these are fresh wounds from Magda, then Kelly fought her to a draw three times."

Meng Die looked at Kelly and then gave a bow, from the waist, not like she was joking. "That is most impressive."

"Thanks, but we all know she's wearing me down. I get more hurt each time; eventually I'm going to lose." One lone tear trailed down her cheek.

"What happens if you lose?"

Nicky answered, "Magda moves up as top lioness."

"What does that gain her?" I asked.

"Since I've already turned her down for sex, nothing," Nicky said.

"You didn't mention that," I said.

He gave me a look. "If I want to sleep with one of the women, then I'll mention it."

"Damn it," Lita said, softly.

We all looked at her. "You have something to share with the rest of the class?" I asked.

She actually blushed; so she could be embarrassed, good to know. "I thought all your men came running to you if another woman propositioned them, but you didn't even know."

I looked at Nicky. "I take it that Lita offered."

"She wanted to fuck, yeah."

My face must have shown what I thought of his wording. "That was pretty much what she said, actually."

I looked at Lita. She almost squirmed and then fought it off. "What, I'm supposed to be all romantic and shit? I like big handsome men, and I like sleeping with the biggest, baddest man I can find."

"I'm bigger than Nicky, and I'm a wererat like you; why you going outside the rodere for lovers?" Dino asked.

"I don't have time for lovers, I just want fuck buddies," she said.

"Okay," Dino said, "question still stands. Why you looking outside the wererats for the biggest, baddest fuck buddies?"

Lita shook her head. "You're bigger, because you started out bigger, but Nicky's got the muscles, and that's what I like."

"So if I hit the weights more, I'd qualify as a fuck buddy?"

She looked at him then, really looked at him. He might not be her cup of tea, but he was another wererat and he had the trust of a lot of important people, including their king, Rafael.

"Sorry, Dino, but muscles won't make you as bad as Nicky."

Dino looked behind him at the other man. "I think I'm insulted."

Nicky grinned, and rolled his one eye. When I could see his whole face, the eye that wasn't there would try to roll along with the other eye. It was like muscle memory.

"Not by me," he said.

Dino turned back to Lita. "So you like the really bad boys?"

She nodded, smiling.

"If your lovers are the biggest and baddest, then you're safer," Kelly said.

"I can take care of myself," Lita said.

Kelly swallowed hard and said, "No you can't; neither can I. We can kill them, but if it's just fight after fight, size matters, upper body strength matters. I hate it, I fucking hate it, but Magda is teaching me all over again that I'm not that big, not even for a woman. She's got those long arms, and she's just getting in my guard, before I can get inside hers." She was starting to sway, ever so slightly.

"How bad are you hurt?" Nicky asked.

"I hide my weakness. I am lion. I am strong. I am . . ." She fell slowly to her knees, catching herself with one hand.

I went to help her, but she said, "NO!"

I knelt back from her, not sure what to do. "Kelly, I'm sorry, you should have said something."

"There's nothing you can do, Anita. I'm weak, you can't change that."

"You aren't weak," I said.

"Yeah, I am."

"No," I said, "you're strong, Kelly."

"Not strong enough," she said, and her eyes were shiny with the tears she was trying not to cry.

I reached out but didn't touch her. I wanted to hold her, tell her I was sorry and that it would be all right, but she didn't need false comfort, and that's what it was, because unless there was a loophole in lion culture, she was going to lose to Magda unless the other lioness was hurt enough to give up the fighting.

Kelly started to shiver. I was pretty sure it was more shock than the cooler temperature of the underground, but I took off my suit jacket anyway. She protested, but I put it around her shoulders. "Just take the jacket, at least let me do that."

She looked up at me, eyes lingering on my arms. "How can you wear so many dresses and shirts that show all your scars? It shows that you've lost fights, that you're weak. No lion would ever do that," Kelly said.

I looked down at my bare arms as if I hadn't really looked at them before, and in a way I hadn't. I'd long ago given up on covering the scars I'd acquired on the job. I looked down at my arms. There was a mass of scar tissue at the bend of my left arm where a vampire had tried to eat his way through it, through me, not because he could eat solid food, because he couldn't, but just to hurt. The cross-shaped burn scar below that on my forearm was a little crooked now because the claws of a shapeshifted witch had cut me. Her little mini-coven had killed lycanthropes in full animal form and used black magic to make enchanted belts so they could turn into those animals at will, without being cursed to follow the moon. I had friends who were witches, Wiccan, and they were nice, moral people, but every religious group has people who make you want to say, *I'm not with them*, or even, *They're evil*. There was a shiny scar higher up on my arm where a bullet had grazed me before I got enough of Jean-Claude's power to heal a non-silver bullet. The blouse actually did hide the scrape scar on my back where a vampire's human servant had tried to stab me with my own shattered wooden stake. That was back in the day when I still staked vampires outside a morgue kill; shotguns were so much less work. There was a delicate trace of scars across my ass where a wereleopard had cut me up while he tried to rape me and put it in a snuff film. I looked down at the muscled, scarred landscape of my body.

"I didn't lose any of these fights; I won them all. Everyone who hurt me is dead; I killed them. I think of the scars as an advertisement for just what a bad-ass I am." I smiled at her, and she gave me a weak one in return.

It was Lita who said, "You dress like you don't care about the scars at all."

I shrugged. "I guess I don't."

"It would bother me," she said.

"You get used to it," I said.

"So you weren't okay with it when you were my age?"

My age? I thought. I was thirty-one, and she was only twenty-one, so I guess it was accurate. I thought about it. "Actually, no, it never did bother me, if you mean cosmetically. I was worried that I might lose the full use of my arm from this." I touched the mound of scars on the inside of my elbow bend.

Lita looked at me, head slightly to one side. "You didn't worry that it'd make men not want you?"

"No," I said.

"You didn't worry that it made you look like a victim?" Kelly asked.

I frowned at her. "No, every time I look at my scars I think that I lived, and I killed what hurt me. These are victory marks, not victim," I said.

Nicky offered me his hand, and I took it, a little puzzled. He pulled me back in against the front of his body, and he hugged me one-armed so we could both keep our gun arms free. I leaned into the solid strength of him, knowing that he'd be fast enough and deadly enough to give me those few extra seconds.

"What if Nicky fucked Kelly?" Lita asked.

Whatever look Nicky and I gave her made her hold her one hand up, as if she were unarmed. The other hand staying on the strap of her AR made it sort of a halfhearted gesture, but it was better than her usual. "Hey, I thought somewhere in all that, you said if she'd been the Rex's lover there wouldn't be a challenge."

I looked up along the line of Nicky's chest, my hands folding over the rock-hardness of his forearm. "Is Lita right?"

"Kelly is one of my fighters, not a piece of ass, and she's worked hard to earn that."

"So if you and she had sex, then Magda would back off?"

"Technically, yes."

"No," Kelly said, "no, nothing personal, Nicky, but if I hide behind you like that she still wins."

"You can't keep being cut up like this," I said.

"I'll heal," she said.

"Would you really let Nicky sleep with her?" Meng Die asked.

I shrugged, still wrapped in the warmth of Nicky's hug, and then said, "To stop this from happening, yeah, if he and Kelly were okay with it, yeah."

"So you do let him fuck other people?" Lita asked.

"Not yet, I mean . . . it hasn't come up as a topic."

Lita looked at him as if he were crazy. "You could have permission to fuck other people and you don't even ask."

"I'm happy with what I've got," he said.

"But it's extra pussy and you wouldn't even get in trouble." Lita looked completely dumbfounded, as if she couldn't believe he was passing up the opportunity.

"I love Anita, and she loves me." He bent over and laid a gentle kiss on the side of my face. I turned my face so we could kiss for real. It was as tender as any kiss I'd ever had.

"But she loves the Master of the City, and the leopard king, and . . . hell, Rafael, our king, fucks her. You could fuck other women and you don't . . . why not?"

Nicky rose up from the kiss and said, "I'm happier than I've ever been. I don't want to fuck that up, literally. It's just not worth it."

"You mean I'm not worth it," Lita said.

He hugged me a little tighter in against his body. "You said it, I didn't."

"Anita likes girls, too, now," Meng Die said. "You could proposition her if you just wanted power, Lita. I mean, if all you want is to be closer to the center of things, why not go straight to the source?"

"I didn't hit on Nicky for power. I like bad boys, and big, physical guys; he's like a two-fer for me."

"And I lose out, because I'm too nice a guy," Dino said in a fake mournful voice. I knew that gleam in his eye well enough to know he was starting to tease her. Lita didn't know him that well.

"Look, you're just not my type, sorry."

He laughed a rumble of sound with that big barrel chest of his to make it echo. "You're not really mine, either."

She frowned. "Then why do you keep harping on it?"

"Because I can," he said.

She frowned harder, creating lines between her eyes that were already starting to carve their way in; if she wasn't careful she'd bloom early and age early the way that some women did who looked lush and finished at twenty-one. Those of us who bloomed later lasted longer sometimes; it all came down to genetics, if you smoked, or tanned too much. I wondered if Lita smoked; she didn't smell like she smoked.

"You'd turn me down?" she asked.

He gave that deep chuckle again. "Ask and find out."

I was no longer sure if he was teasing or had maneuvered Lita into propositioning him so he could say yes. If it was what he'd just done, then Dino was way more devious than I'd given him credit for.

Nicky hugged me, and I felt his body go still; he was watching the show, too. We were both wondering if Dino was doing it on purpose.

Lita was one of those young women who feel they can have any man they want, at least once, and Dino had hinted he'd turn her down. It was her ego that said, "So you want to do it?"

"Do what?"

She gave him a disgusted look. "Fuck, do you want to fuck after we get off shift?"

He grinned wide and bright in his dark face. "Sure, why not?" Even his answer had been calculated to make her try harder when they fucked. He was already playing her to get a second try at sex, which meant that Dino was much brighter about social stuff and women than I had ever dreamt.

"Wow," I whispered.

"Yeah," Nicky whispered into the top of my hair, which meant he hadn't known this about Dino either. He'd fooled us both, which meant we'd both watch him more closely now and not take his friendliness for granted. If you're good at playing people for one thing, you can be equally good at playing them for another. Hmm . . . I didn't like suddenly wondering if Dino's friendship was really real.

"What about you, lioness?" Meng Die asked.

Kelly was sitting on the floor now, not even pretending to be about to get up. She had pulled my jacket around her and was still shivering slightly. It all meant she wasn't fit for duty, but we'd cross that bridge in a few minutes; if bad guys jumped me now, I felt pretty secure with the guards I had.

"What about me?" she asked.

"You could sleep with Anita; no one in St. Louis picks fights with her lovers."

Kelly glanced up at me. "Nothing personal, Anita, but I'm just not into girls."

I smiled. "That's okay, it's sort of a new thing for me, too, and I think of you as just a friend."

Kelly laughed a little, but any laughter was good at this point.

"What about me?" Meng Die asked.

"I don't want to sleep with you either," Kelly said.

"I meant Anita. I even look like Jade; why pick her and not me?"

I stared at the vampire for a second or two, hoping she was joking, but she looked utterly serious. I rubbed my hands against Nicky's arm. I was nervous, because just as Dino had surprised me with Lita, this offer from Meng Die was completely out of left field. "I thought we sort of hated each other; kind of hard to date, if that's the case," I said.

"Date, date"—she threw her hands up—"fucking is all I'm talking about, Anita. I know how to please a woman."

"And that's a big reason we could never be a couple. I'm not good at just fucking."

"That's not what I heard," Lita said.

I gave her an unfriendly look.

"Be careful, Lita," Kelly said.

"Why, are you going to step in and defend Anita?"

She shook her head. "No, but you may wish I had."

"What does that mean?"

"No," Meng Die said, "this is my argument. You're late to the party, little Spanish."

"I've told you, I'm not Spanish, I'm Mexican."

"You were born here," Meng Die said. "That makes you American."

"My people came from Mexico."

"Fine, I was born in China, but I don't go around saying I'm Chinese, and I could."

I wondered if Meng Die really didn't like Lita, or if she was picking on her because picking on me didn't get her anywhere. She turned back to me and said, "Answer my question, Anita. Wasn't I pretty enough for you?"

"You're beautiful."

The compliment seemed to surprise her.

"But the only reason I'm with Jade is that she's my black tiger to call; we're metaphysically tied to each other. We didn't exactly choose each other. I'm all full up on vampires."

"You fuck Jason's girlfriend when she comes into town," Lita said.

Kelly laughed again, but this was more nervous.

I stepped away from Nicky and he moved his arm so I could do it. "First, I don't fuck J.J.; we have sex with our shared boyfriends. Second, why the hell do you care who I fuck and who I don't? Or are you like Meng Die here and want to be my new piece of ass?"

Lita blushed hard. Her pretty face scrunched down into angry lines. "I told you, I don't do girls."

"Good, because neither do I. I do women; little girls need time to grow the fuck up."

She called me something bad in Spanish.

"*Puta*, really, that's the best insult you got? I've been called the Whore of Babylon on national TV; *puta* just doesn't quite cut it."

"Who called you that on TV?" she asked.

"Malcolm, the head of the Church of Eternal Life, before we came to an understanding."

"Before you and Jean-Claude fucked him and rolled him, you mean," Lita said.

"You really don't know when to stop, do you?" I asked.

"Don't hurt her until tomorrow," Dino said, "as a favor to me."

I turned and looked back at the big man and tried to read his face. He looked pleasant, like he usually did, but I knew now that there was a hell of a lot more going on behind that smiling face than I'd known. Insight into your friends is good; insight that makes you wonder if they're really your friend or just a really well-socialized sociopath, not so good.

"Just for you, and if she stops saying insulting things, I'll let it go until after you've fucked her," I said.

"Hey," Lita said, and she sounded genuinely insulted.

Dino grinned. "Thanks, Anita, you're a good friend."

I shrugged. "I try."

My phone text sound played, and it was Jean-Claude. He was almost here, which meant he'd cut his night at work short to make the tiger reception.

"I need to get ready for the party, so first, Kelly, you're not fit for guard duty. Dino, Nicky, we need a replacement partner for Lita; who would you suggest?"

"Claudia isn't working tonight, and all the other female guards are either too new or too unstable to pair up with Little Miss Thing," Nicky said.

"What did you call me?"

He turned a very cold face to her. Nicky didn't try to hide his sociopathy; he wore it proudly. "The only reason you're partnered with Kelly is that you spend too much time flirting, or trying to fuck all the men. You're a distraction, Lita, and that's not impressing Claudia, or Fredo, or me."

"I don't care if you're impressed; you're just Anita's pet, you don't count."

"How about you don't impress me?" I said.

"You're just Jean-Claude's blood whore; I don't have to impress you either."

"Here, I was going to pick a fight, but you're doing so much better than I am at it, that I'll just let you have it," Meng Die said.

"Have what?" Lita said.

"The fight," Meng Die said.

"Fight with who?"

Meng Die laughed, shaking her head. "I knew you were young, Lita, but I'm beginning to suspect you're stupid, too."

"Who you calling stupid, little China whore!"

Meng Die just kept laughing softly and walked toward the door. "Everyone have fun, I've got to go to work."

I walked over to Lita, and she let me get close. Either she didn't see me as dangerous, or she was that arrogant about her own abilities; either way it was a mistake.

"How much of the gear you're wearing is yours?"

"What gear?"

"The weapons; is the AR yours, or did someone give it to you when you arrived?"

She almost caressed the gun. "I got it here. No way could it come on the plane."

"Then hand it over," I said.

"What are you talking about?"

"I'm firing you, so all the company equipment stays with us."

"You can't fire me."

"I can fire you and send you back to L.A."

"You can't send me back. You're not my king, and you're not Claudia or Fredo, they're my bosses."

"I'm their boss," I said. I was close enough to take any weapon she was wearing or to keep her from using them. She still didn't see the danger. She really wasn't good enough to be one of our guards. It had been Claudia and I who decided we needed more female guards, but this wasn't what we'd had in mind.

"Jean-Claude is their boss," Lita said.

"No," Kelly said, "Jean-Claude is in charge of the business side of things, but Anita is the one who makes decisions on the guards." She looked up at the other woman, sort of satisfied, which meant that Lita hadn't been all that pleasant before we got here. Sending her home just kept sounding better.

"Technically, I can't send you back to L.A."

Lita looked justified, smug even.

"But I can fire you from our security detail, and I can recommend to Rafael that you be sent back to L.A., that I can do."

She finally looked uncertain.

"You said it yourself; he is my lover. Most men give more weight to a woman's opinion if she's sharing his bed."

"You're not sharing a bed; you're just fuck buddies."

Dino said, "You know that Rafael fucks Anita, but you haven't been in town, been one of us, when it happens yet."

"So?" she asked.

He gave that deep chuckle and shook his head. "It's quite a show." I knew Dino meant that when I had sex with their king, Rafael, and fed the *ardeur* on him that I took energy from all the wererats in the area. It was a power rush of near epic proportions.

"You mean we watch them fuck?"

"I'll explain after we fuck tonight," Dino said.

I might have added to the conversation, but I felt Jean-Claude. He was almost here, and I was tired of Lita. I just reached out and had her AR in my hand, using the strap across her body to pull her off balance. She fought to keep control of the AR, not go for her handgun; again, a mistake. I used her own momentum to drive her to the floor and took the nine-millimeter out of her holster as she went down. I trapped the AR behind her back with the knee I drove into her. She tried to fight then, but it was far too late. I put the business end of her own pistol against the side of her head. My finger was on the trigger; there was no safety on this model of gun.

"Don't . . . just don't," I said low, almost caressing. I felt very calm, very still inside; it was the place I went when I pulled the trigger. It was a quiet, strangely peaceful place where I went when I killed. Once it had been white and static filled, but lately it was just quiet. I wasn't afraid. I wasn't excited. I didn't feel bad about the woman I was about to shoot. I didn't want to shoot her, but the main thing that made me not want to shoot her was that Dino liked her enough to fuck her, and I liked Dino. When I realized that was my emotional math, I tried to feel bad about it, but I didn't. I didn't feel anything much in that moment, except that sense of waiting where the world slows down and you have forever to decide, will you pull the trigger or not?

Lita was very still underneath me, her head motionless against the gun. Her hands were still pressed to the floor in the middle of her effort to get up, but she'd frozen in an almost push-up. She was part of a street gang in L.A., which meant she'd been around violence all her life, and I'd finally done something she understood.

"Anita," Dino said, very quietly, "please."

I wasn't going to kill her, but that he bothered to say please meant he liked her. I didn't understand why, but . . . I eased the gun back from her head and pointed it ceilingward, finger off the trigger. I unhooked the strap on the AR and moved it to one side. I took the hide gun that was at the small of her back and put it by the AR. I took the knife that was in a sheath at her neck, hidden by all that long hair. I had a back sheath, too; a lot of people forgot to search there.

I heard the knock on the door but knew it was Jean-Claude just by the feel of his energy, so I didn't look up, or away from the woman underneath my knee and hand. He didn't interrupt when he came through the door. He'd wait and trust that I'd explain later.

"Have I made my point, Lita?" I asked, voice still low and careful.

She licked her lips and swallowed hard enough that it sounded painful. "You're the boss, I get it."

"Do you really, or are you just saying that because I pointed a gun at your head?"

"I pushed, you pushed back. You took me. You took me without trying hard and you aren't even a shapeshifter, or a vampire. How did you do that?"

"If you stop being a pain in my ass, I might show you on the practice mat."

"You won't send me to L.A.?"

"One more chance, but you do this shit again, and you get either a plane ticket home or dead, is that abundantly clear?"

"Yeah, it's clear."

"Kelly, you feel well enough to be in charge of her weapons?"

"Yes, ma'am." She got to her feet and came and took the weapons on the ground.

"Lita, I'm going to stand up now, and you are going to stay very still until I tell you to move, is that clear?"

"Yes . . . yes, ma'am."

I stood up carefully. As a marshal I'd have cuffed someone before a search; you had to be careful, because sometimes you eased up as you got up, and that was enough to let the bad guy, or girl, fight back.

"Very good," I said. I handed the gun to Kelly to add to the rest. "If you think she deserves them, give the handgun and knife back to her. The AR will have to be earned back; right now she doesn't get to carry anything bigger than a handgun."

"I'll tell Claudia and Fredo."

"Okay, you can get up now, Lita."

She did, slowly, carefully, as if she still didn't feel safe. Good. She licked her lips, and I noticed her red lipstick was smeared on one side, as if I'd forced her face into the floor at least once when I took her down. She looked at me; her eyes flicked behind me and I was pretty sure she was looking at Jean-Claude, but then her gaze came back to me. Better; before she'd have kept looking at the hot guy, and Jean-Claude was one of the hottest around.

"You're fast, really fast," she said, and her voice was still uncertain, almost afraid.

"And I'm trained, really trained," I said.

She nodded. "And you'll teach me?"

"If you start trying to be part of the team and not just a piece of ass with a gun, sure."

"I'm not a piece of ass," she said with a flare of her old sullenness.

I fought not to smile. "No, you're not, but you gotta stop flirting with all your male partners when you're on guard duty. It's a job and if you can't treat it that way, then we don't want you here."

"I'll try not to flirt, but it's . . . it's sort of what I do."

"Work on doing something else," I said.

"I'll try, I mean that, but I can't guarantee I won't forget sometimes.

I'm not making an excuse, I'm just saying tell me to stop fucking around and I'll listen from now on, don't just kill me."

I looked into her face and saw the first real sincerity I'd seen in her. "Okay, but make sure that me just saying something is enough; don't ever make me have to put a gun to your head again, Lita."

"I won't, Anita, I swear."

"Good." I wanted to turn and see Jean-Claude, not just feel the presence of him, but there was something on the face of the younger woman that made me keep looking at her.

"The wererats call you Gatito Negro. I thought they were making fun of you, like you were a kitten they had to take care of, but that's not what it means at all, is it?"

"No," I said, "it isn't."

Dino said, "She's small, but she eats rats, our Gatito Negro."

Lita nodded. "Yeah, and I don't want to be eaten."

"Do your job, stop trying to fuck everyone, hit the gym harder, and I'll see you in practice."

"*Gracias*, Anita."

"*De nada*," I said.

"*Ma petite*, you are having an interesting night."

"You have no idea," I said, and turned around to find that he'd changed clothes for the banquet already, and I was going to have to work hard if I was going to hold my own on his arm tonight.

18

HE WAS STANDING next to Nicky and I was almost startled to realize that Jean-Claude was inches taller. I knew that Nicky wasn't six feet tall, so Jean-Claude's six feet, one inch had to be taller, but Nicky was just so much bulkier that he seemed bigger when I stood next to him.

Jean-Claude never made me feel small when I was near him; he was just tall. Seeing them side by side, I realized some of why Jean-Claude was well built; he even lifted enough weights to give definition to his muscles, but he lifted to be beautiful onstage, not to bulk, so that he looked almost willowy next to the other man.

He'd replaced the white shirt we'd stained earlier with one so red it was scarlet. It looked fabulous with the short black velvet jacket, leather pants, and boots. I loved him in red, maybe because he wore it so seldom. It made his skin seem translucently pale, like alabaster if it could blush with life, and his black curls gleam, and it strangely brought out the blue in his eyes so they were less midnight sky and more cobalt.

I wrapped my arms around his waist and found that the red shirt was silk, cool and caressing against my hands. The cloth was mounded as if it were one of his more typical white shirts with the mounded lace and collar, but silk was softer than any lace. I pressed my chin into it and found that he was wearing a platinum stickpin through the cloth to hold it in place. A diamond almost as big as the engagement ring he'd given me on the video rode in the tip of it with a circle of rubies as red as the silk, which meant they were probably antique. Pigeon-blood red was the old name for rubies that color and they were damned rare now, or they stayed in countries that weren't exporting to America. He hadn't put that on to get onstage at Guilty Pleasures. Apparently the meet and greet with the weretigers was going to be more formal than I'd thought. I'd have been less worried about what I'd have to wear if he hadn't looked so spiffy in his clothes.

I went up on tiptoes to meet his kiss. It was soft, but thorough; he knew how to kiss without smearing my lipstick over both of us, and I knew how to kiss a vampire without cutting my mouth. French kissing was harder, but we could manage that, too.

"Shit," Lita said.

It made me turn and look at her, and I was pretty sure it wasn't a friendly look.

"I didn't mean to get that look from you again, Anita, it's just"—she motioned at us—"you guys are like some romance movie. It's just not real, it can't be real."

"Oh, it's real, all right," Kelly said. "Now let's call for our replacements, before you say something else stupid."

"I'm not stupid." She snapped it, and the words seemed to hold a lifetime of maybe being told exactly that. Lita wasn't stupid; emotionally she seemed stunted, but I thought that was environmental and she was capable of more.

Jean-Claude looked at her, and I had a moment to see a considering expression before his face was its more typical smiling, pleasant, unreadable beauty. He glided over to Kelly and Lita. They both lowered their eyes so they wouldn't accidentally make eye contact with him. It had been so long since I couldn't meet a vampire's gaze safely that it almost startled me when others did it, especially when they did it around Jean-Claude.

Kelly moved back from Lita when she realized that was who he was standing in front of, as if the werelion were abandoning the wererat to her fate. Kelly looked . . . scared. It made me wonder if I'd missed something else besides Magda being a shit. I'd ask Kelly later, or maybe I'd figure it out just watching Jean-Claude with the other women.

"I assure you, *ma souris*, that I am very real."

Lita stared at the floor. "I know you're real." She tried to sound tough, but it's hard when you're staring at someone's feet.

"But you just said we are not." His French accent was a little thicker, which usually meant he was fighting some emotion, though sometimes onstage he did it on purpose. American women really dug the accent.

She shook her head hard enough that her hair fanned around her face, but with the headband her hair couldn't spill forward enough to hide her face completely.

He touched his fingertips to her chin and raised her face upward. She had her eyes closed as he raised her face, and she looked scared.

"Please," she whispered, but I was close enough to hear it.

"Please, what?" he asked in that accented, teasing voice. Once he'd aimed that voice at me. I had a moment to wonder if Jean-Claude just liked women with long, curly, dark hair. I had a moment of jealousy, which I hadn't felt in a long time. I looked at the feeling and tried to figure out where it was coming from. I'd watched him have sex with other people and not been jealous, so why did this hit that button?

"Please," she repeated. He was still only touching the edge of her chin with the barest tips of his fingers, but she began to open her eyes as if she couldn't help herself. I remembered when I'd wanted to see what face went with that voice but been too afraid to look.

I realized that was it; it was the first time I'd seen him interact with another woman where it reminded me so strongly of what he'd done with me years ago. I'd seen him with other sexual partners, but he treated them all differently, unique to them, and nothing like he treated me. I was special to him, as he was to me, but as Lita opened her eyes like a bird staring at a snake, I wondered if I'd ever looked at him in just that way when I was still fighting to stay free of him.

"Your talk is rough, *ma souris*, but you are not."

I watched her try to fight at that, the struggle to break his gaze plain on her face, her hands that tried to rise up and then just hung in midair as if she didn't remember that she'd moved them.

Nicky came up beside me and I reached out for his hand to hold, because I'd never seen Jean-Claude like this with one of our guards before. I didn't like it much and Nicky had picked up on that.

Jean-Claude stepped back from her, but she stayed frozen, staring at where his face had been, her face slack and empty as if waiting for orders.

"It is as I feared," he said in his normal voice.

"What is as you feared?" I asked.

"I did not try to bespell her, *ma petite*. I used no powers, and she is a type of wereanimal that I should have no special hold over, but she stands there enchanted and waiting for whatever I would do."

"So this was a test?" I asked, and squeezed Nicky's hand.

"*Oui.*"

I must have frowned, because he put his head to one side, studying me. "You are upset. I come through the door to find that you have a gun to her head and are threatening to kill her, but my bespelling her upsets you; why?"

"It's almost the exact same thing you used to do to me at the beginning, when you were trying to seduce me and I was trying not to be seduced."

"This is play to me, *ma petite*, or was once. When you and I began this dance I never dreamt that you would be in my life, be my love, my queen." He walked toward me, leaving Lita standing frozen and waiting for what came next. It was like she didn't matter at all to him.

"You were going to blow her brains out, Anita," Nicky said.

"Maybe," I said, and it sounded pissy even to me.

"What is wrong, *ma petite*?" Jean-Claude asked.

"It's like you don't care about Lita, at all, and you just did the big vamp thing with her."

"You know that this is not my 'big vamp thing,' this is play, and I needed to see if my powers had grown; a woman that you would threaten to kill seemed a safe choice, but I see it was not."

"Were you just playing with me at the beginning?" I asked.

"You know you began as a challenging seduction, as I began as just a handsome irritant to you." He was standing directly in front of me now, and since I still had Nicky's hand he was standing in front of both of us. "Your strength of character intrigued me, and then your power called to me"—he reached for my hand and I let him take it, but I didn't exactly hold on—"and the rest of you quite overwhelmed me, eventually." He lifted my hand up and laid a kiss against my knuckles.

I think I glared at him.

He rose up, still holding my hand loosely. "*Ma petite*, this jealousy is unlike you, especially over something so small."

I nodded. "You're right; it's just that I hadn't realized that the early part of our seduction really was just a game to you. I mean, I knew it, but I didn't, if that makes sense."

"But wasn't it a game on both our parts, the old game of the man pursuing and the woman escaping his attentions?"

I thought about it, then shook my head. "I didn't know it was a game, at the time."

"Perhaps modern people do not speak of it so bluntly, but it is the age-old game of chase and capture. There is always someone in a relationship who begins the hunt for someone's heart, and the pursued must decide whether she wishes to be easily caught, or to be a long and difficult hunt." He smiled when he said it.

I frowned at him. "Have you ever not gotten to sleep with someone you set your sights on?"

He raised the dark, graceful curve of one eyebrow. "You led me on the merriest chase of anyone I had ever met, *ma petite*."

"What does *ma souris* mean?" I asked.

"Mouse, because she is too weak to be a rat." He frowned and said, "Is that it, the French nickname? I can refrain from using that with any other woman if you like, *ma petite*."

I squeezed their hands, the impossibly beautiful vampire and the handsome solidness of the werelion. They squeezed back, Jean-Claude smiling at me, and Nicky just waiting to see what was going to happen. Jean-Claude and I were shielding hard not to feel every emotion in both of us, but with Nicky as my Bride he could always feel what I was feeling. In that moment he knew more about the tangle of emotions I'd just waded through. It seemed weird that Jean-Claude didn't understand that I was close to angry with him, but Nicky did. I could lower my metaphysical shields and let Jean-Claude know how deep the relationship crap had gotten, but I didn't. One, we'd fought too long to have emotional privacy, and two, I was mad and didn't want to make it easier for him. The moment I thought it, I knew I'd have to do better than that, but . . .

"So you tested your powers on Lita, because why?"

"You had a gun to her head; I thought you didn't care for her."

I made myself think before I spoke. "I don't really."

He smiled a little, carefully. "Then that is good."

"What I mean is, why did you test your abilities on any of the female guards?"

"I've begun to fear that my powers to bespell have grown stronger, and before I go onstage at Guilty Pleasures again I want to know just how strong they have grown. I do not want to accidentally mind-roll some human audience member."

"Did something happen at the club tonight?" I asked.

"Yes, and no, as in it went according to plan. My voice bespelled the audience, but it was the manner in which the women reacted to me when I walked among them as host. It just seemed . . . different."

"So did you do that to Lita on purpose?" I asked, looking at the woman who was still motionless behind him.

"I meant to see what my touch and gaze could do without any added power, *oui*. She is a wereanimal, which should give her more immunity than a pure human, and she is an animal that I have no tie to, which should have helped her resist me, but as you see . . ." He used our clasped hands to motion at her.

"Have you actually mind-fucked her?" I asked.

"It would appear so." He didn't sound happy about it, though.

"If you've rolled her past a certain point, then you can't undo it," I said.

He sighed, which he didn't always do, since he didn't always breathe. "I will have to be most cautious at the clubs."

"Cautious?" Kelly said. "You barely touched her, and look at her. I've seen you onstage, Jean-Claude; you touch the audience more than that." She motioned at Lita with the hand that wasn't holding a gun. She'd put the AR on her own shoulder like an awkward purse.

As if she'd heard her name, Lita took a long shuddering breath, and blinked. She looked confused, and then she saw Jean-Claude. "You son of a bitch, you fucking son of a bitch, you rolled me like some kind of human tourist!"

Jean-Claude smiled. "She remembers what I did, that's good."

Lita's hands were in fists at her side. "You bastard, how is that good?"

"It means he didn't mind-fuck you," I said.

"The hell he didn't!"

"If he had, you wouldn't remember that he'd done anything to you. You'd have just woken up and remembered whatever happened just before he touched your face, or maybe not even remember that he'd even spoken to you."

"So you mean the fact that Lita remembers what Jean-Claude did means he didn't actually roll her?" Kelly asked.

"*Oui.*"

Lita shook her head. "No, no, I was helpless, fucking helpless, and you're saying that wasn't mind-fucking me?"

"No," I said, "it wasn't."

Lita began to curse, first in English and then in Spanish in a long nervous torrent. She turned to Kelly. "Get me out of here, away from them both."

"I'll take you to Claudia," Kelly said, and led the other woman toward the long curtain. Dino raised it for them. "Ladies."

Kelly turned just before going through the curtains. "I'd noticed that I'm having a harder time ignoring you, and you aren't supposed to have the ability to call lions either. You might want to ask some of the other wereanimals and see if they've noticed it, too."

"I will do that, and thank you for telling me."

She nodded. "Now that I know you weren't doing it on purpose, I figure you needed to know."

Dino let the drapes fall back in place.

"You may go with them, Dino," Jean-Claude said.

Dino glanced at me.

"Go on, Lita may need someone to comfort her," I said.

He grinned at me. "You are the best wingman ever, Anita." He let the drapes fall shut behind him, whistling softly under his breath.

"I feel I have missed much today," Jean-Claude said.

"Dino and Lita have a fuck-buddy date after work tonight," I said.

"*Fuck buddy*, I dislike the term," Jean-Claude said.

"Me, too, but *fuck date* sounds worse," I said.

Nicky chuckled.

We both looked at him. "What?" I asked.

"You two, the great incubus and succubus eating the souls of little vampires and wereanimals out through their dicks, and you both think the term *fuck buddy* is crass."

We both frowned at him.

"Oh, come on, that's funny."

Jean-Claude started laughing first and eventually so did I. It was funny, but the fact that Jean-Claude's powers of seduction were growing wasn't. How was that going to work with the weretigers tonight? Hell, how would it work with the rest of us? That thought was so not funny I stopped laughing. Jean-Claude even sexier than before? We were all so screwed, maybe literally.

19

LEFT TO HIS own devices Jean-Claude would have made the small get-together with the weretigers something formal, with more jewelry; left to my own devices it probably would have been a backyard barbecue. So we compromised. We didn't dress up, or add jewelry, unless we wanted to, and most of us were in our work clothes. Everyone at the mixer tonight had met everyone else, so we'd seen each other in work clothes, fancy clothes, and a lot of us had worked out in the gym together; some of us had even had sex together, so it wasn't your typical matchmaking scenario. Most of the clan tigers and all the Harlequin vampires and their animals to call worked for us as guards, which meant most of the people in the room were armed and on our side. The only extra guards were the ones who routinely went with Jean-Claude, Micah, and me. Nathaniel was mingling with the tigers he didn't know as well, with Nicky just following along behind him both as a guard and to help scout prospective housemates.

I wasn't sure if that made things more awkward or less, because it was all so casual; maybe it just made it different. By the time we all settled around the living room on the two couches, the love seat, and the two big comfy chairs, I was regretting agreeing to it. I'd fought through some of my earlier panic when I realized that I was blaming Cynric for things that weren't his fault. Now I just felt stupid for running from the truth into a supernatural dating game. I needed to call Marianne, my magical mentor and accidental therapist. She was a witch and the wise woman for her werewolf pack in Tennessee. She'd helped me learn control of a lot of my metaphysical abilities, and turned into my counselor in a lot of other areas. But I'd agreed to this, whatever this was, and now I felt like I had to at least pretend to go through with it. Besides, Nathaniel's point about trying to add someone who could date people besides me in our poly group was logical. I just forgot for a moment that sex and romance aren't about logic; they're about feelings, and that is one of the least logical things of all.

What I needed to be doing was finding out how many other animal groups were having trouble with the ancient wereanimals I'd casually forced into their groups when we brought the Harlequin vampires and their animals to St. Louis. Or trying to figure out anything that would help us find and set free the zombies being used online for those horrible films, though honestly the biggest hope for locating them was the FBI cyber division. Once they narrowed the location I might be able to locate them if I was close enough to them geographically, but an entire country and possibly countries away was beyond even my necromancy.

"Ma petite . . ."

I startled and turned to Jean-Claude, who was draped artfully beside me on the couch. I was curled up on the couch beside him; I didn't really sit artfully on couches, my legs were usually too short for the graceful slouch he could manage.

"I'm sorry, I wasn't . . . I'm sorry, what were you saying?"

The woman sitting beside me raised an eyebrow that went perfectly with the cynical expression in her blue-gray eyes. "I don't think you really care what I was saying."

I turned more fully toward her, my back resting in the crook of Jean-Claude's arm. "I really am sorry, but I was thinking about a case at work. Sometimes I have trouble leaving it at the office."

She pushed a strand of her short, pale blue hair back behind her ear and studied my face, as if she didn't believe me. Her hair was very short, just barely below her ears, but with strands of it tracing the strong oval of her jawline. The pale blue color was natural, not dyed, and the blue-gray eyes were tiger eyes in her human face. Fortune was the last female of the blue tiger clan left on earth as far as we knew. She was five-ten, which meant when she first hit her height as a young adult she must have been a giant among the men, let alone the women. People just hadn't been that tall over a few thousand years ago. Okay, I didn't know for certain how old she was, but necromancy let me know how old her master was, and if her master was over two thousand, then she had to be pushing the same.

"You really don't want to be doing this, so why did you agree to it?" she asked.

I didn't owe her the truth, so . . . "According to the prophecy that the clan tigers have been keeping, if I don't marry one of you, then the Mother of All Darkness could come back to life. I don't really want that to happen, do you?"

Her eyes narrowed, and I realized that even her eyelashes were a pale powder blue. Cynric's eyelashes were black, weren't they? Could they possibly be a dark navy blue so that I'd only assumed they were black? It made me want to get him and make him stand with the light behind so I could double-check.

"Do you believe that part of the prophecy?"

"A lot of it has come true recently; don't you believe in it?"

She smiled and it was an age-weary smile, as if she'd seen everything and been impressed by none of it. "Answering the question with a question means I can't smell if you're lying."

I shrugged, and smiled back at her. "I really was thinking about work."

"Zombies or police work?"

"Both, actually; the police came to me for my expertise."

"In what capacity?"

I shook my head. "Sorry, but it's an ongoing investigation. I can't discuss details."

"I can't tell if you're lying; your heart rate doesn't change, even your scent stayed the same. It takes a very experienced wereanimal to lie with the smell of their skin."

"Since I'm technically not a wereanimal, maybe I'm just telling the truth?"

A brunette vampire who was only a couple of inches taller than me, five-six at best, came to stand in front of us. Her smile was cynical, too, but there was a shine of humor in the rich blue of her cornflower eyes. "Fortune and I think you just agreed to meet with female tigers to stop your men from complaining when you add another male to your harem."

I laughed and glanced at the woman beside me, then back to her vampire master. "Really, so why did you both agree to come if you thought it was pointless?"

Jean-Claude stroked my shoulder with the hand across my shoulders. I wasn't sure if he was trying to soothe me or himself. I hadn't even done anything that rude yet.

"When the king requests your presence, you don't disappoint him," she said.

"Even if you think it's a waste of time," I said.

She grinned wide enough to flash one delicate fang and show that she had a dimple in one cheek. Her blond hair was wavy enough that it was like big, loose curls to her shoulders. "Most things that kings want are a waste of time." She did a low sweeping bow to Jean-Claude, but the dimpled grin never wavered.

"I do not believe that I have known as many kings as you have, Echo, but I cannot disagree with your statement. I swear to you that I believed *ma petite* was in earnest or I would not have called you in from your tasks."

"May I sit down?"

"You do not need to ask for permission to sit next to your own tiger, and lover."

She flopped down on the other side of Fortune hard enough that the couch bounced a little. "You are very even-handed for your age and your sex."

"I understand that older vampires are often set in their ways, but what does my being male have to do with it?"

"Jean-Claude, do not play games; you know what men have thought of women through most of the centuries you've lived. We have been second class at best, evil temptresses, or little better than breeding animals to many very learned and powerful men."

"Do you hate men, then?"

"I don't hate sex with them, but relationships with them, yes." She went up on one knee so she could put an arm across the other woman's shoulders. Fortune entwined her fingers with hers. Echo said, "I prefer to give my heart to more reliable hands than a man's."

Jean-Claude laughed and pulled me in closer to his body. "And I have found that men and women are equally heartbreaking."

"I would ask Anita, but she's only been with two women; that hardly counts."

Fortune said, "Most American women do that much in college when they experiment. Is Jade your experiment?"

"No, not that that's any of your business."

Jean-Claude hugged me to him and let me know I'd tensed up.

"Don't be naïve," Echo said. "Jade shares you with men, because they're men, but another woman will bother her more, unless you plan to always include her in the bed with the new woman. Is that it? Are you building an all-girl ménage à trois?"

My opinion of that must have shown on my face.

Echo laughed again. "Oh, you don't like that at all, so at least one man at all times, is that it?"

"I prefer men to women, if that's what you mean."

"There's preferring men to women and then there's not wanting to be alone in a bed with just a woman, that's a different issue."

"I hadn't thought about it," I said.

"Really?" Echo said, and that cynical look was back, and those so-blue eyes seemed to try to study me all the way through, but I gave her blank cop face. She was the one who looked away first. "You really are immune to vampire gaze."

"You weren't really trying that hard, but yes, pretty much."

"You are far away in your head, Anita Blake, and haven't really looked at anyone in this room seriously. You aren't shopping for a new lover."

I sighed. "I'm sorry, you all deserve better than this. I really am working on a case that's bad. Even by my standards it's . . . haunting."

"We're intrigued," Echo said.

Fortune nodded. "If half the things they say about you are true, you don't haunt easily."

I had an idea. "Can you sense my power, my necromancy?"

They exchanged a look, then nodded.

"We all can, *ma petite*. I told you long ago that the dead respond to your power."

"But I mean if you're around someone with my powers, would you know it, even if they weren't raising the dead?"

"Sometimes," Fortune said.

"It depends on how powerful they are, but you . . . you shine like dark flame and we are moths drawn to that burning darkness."

"Even when I'm not doing anything with my necromancy, I mean like now, right now, can you sense me?"

Fortune frowned, and Echo studied my face again. "You're hunting another necromancer of some power, aren't you?"

"I didn't say that."

"*Ma petite* is very careful not to share ongoing police investigations with us."

"If you were hunting another like yourself, then some of us might be able to give you a hint where to look, if that's what you're asking," Echo said.

I nodded. "Have you touched any other power like mine?"

"You outshine the stars, Anita, so if there is another in this area you make them invisible to us, but outside your locus of control then yes, there are others."

"Where?"

"In Los Angeles," Fortune said, "but you know them all. They raise the dead for a very public living."

"I'm looking for someone who isn't well known."

"*Ma petite*, I could contact the masters across the country and ask them. They would know if there was anyone to rival you in their lands."

"Oh, no one to rival Anita," Echo said. "We'd all know if there was another dark mistress on the rise, or is this a dark master?"

I debated on whether to share that I thought he was male, but what if he wasn't? What if it was another woman who had just given the zombie's control over to the man in the films, the same way I'd given over the zombie tonight? "I'm not sure and I don't want to guess; I don't want to miss this person because I narrowed the choices."

Jean-Claude wrapped his arm tighter around me, drawing me very close. "If you desire this information, *ma petite*, I can simply tell the Masters of the City across our lands that we are interested in any new animators."

"They will think that Anita is hunting them as the Mother of All Darkness did," Echo said.

"She killed anyone who had her powers," I said.

"Yes," Echo said, "but she missed you until it was too late."

"She was right to fear other necromancers," Fortune said.

It was hard to argue that, so I didn't try. "I'm looking for someone powerful, really powerful, so powerful that if they'd been around long I think I'd have heard about them."

"So they're young in years," Echo said.

I nodded. "I think so."

She wrapped both arms around Fortune's shoulders, though she had to go up on her knees to do it. My stepmother, Judith, would have told her to get her boots off the couch, but I didn't care, not if this idea worked. I wouldn't even have to tell the FBI that I'd overshared unless the vampires found something; until the idea worked, what the Feds didn't know wouldn't hurt anyone.

20

Micah came in with Mephistopheles—Devil was his nickname, but he went by Dev—and most of the other male golden tigers, plus Good Angel, Dev's twin sister, were with them. All the golden clan were tall, between five-ten and six-four with varying shades of blond hair and a golden cast to their skin, as if they had a pale, permanent tan. They were all handsome, or beautiful. The men tended toward broad shoulders and gathered muscle easily if they worked at it, though most of them didn't like the weight room that much. The women were all model tall but ranged from model thin to curvy; the thinner girls had trouble gaining muscle, and the curvy ones muscled up like Valkyries, which had prompted some of them to stop lifting. Angel was the only one who had dark hair. She'd dyed it black, as dark as she could get it. Her eyes were still blue with a circle of pale brown around the iris just like her brother's hazel-blue tiger eyes, but the black hair made hers look a little bluer, the brown darker. I bet if she went to the right dance club they'd think they were contacts and she was going for Goth. When someone had asked her about the black hair, she'd said, "My legal name is Good Angel; maybe it gave me a complex?" She didn't hit the gym as much as I would have preferred, and she didn't train enough to be one of the guards, but I appreciated the bad attitude.

Except for Angel and one of the other males, all of them were dressed as guards, because that was their day job. They'd spent their lives being trained to keep up with whatever vampire master they ended up serving, so they could fight and do whatever their master might need.

"I need to talk business with Micah; excuse me for a minute." I got up, planting a quick kiss on Jean-Claude's lips.

"Police or zombie business?" Fortune asked.

I stopped and blinked at her. "Furry business," I said.

Echo laughed. "Furry business, I like that."

"Coalition business, you mean?" Fortune asked.

"Yeah, that's what I mean."

"We like how hands-on you are with the local wereanimals," she said.

"Thanks, I'll be right back."

"I doubt that," Echo said, "but if I had all that waiting for me I might take my time, too."

I glanced back at the golden tigers and Micah, then back at her. "They aren't all mine."

"They could be," she said.

"Yeah, but think about the emotional upkeep."

She laughed again. "Well, if you leave out Thorn and Angel, it wouldn't be that much upkeep."

I couldn't argue that, so I didn't try, just smiled vaguely at her and went for Micah. The fact that he was surrounded by the golden tigers meant I'd have to talk to them, too, but I was willing to brave the tall, gold crowd of them to talk to my other third.

He smiled that smile that was only for me and Nathaniel, and then I was in his arms and we kissed as if we hadn't seen each other just a couple of hours before.

"She never kisses me like that."

I broke from the kiss to look up at Dev, who was a foot taller than us. He was grinning to take the sting out of his words, but part of him meant it. He'd thought he was God's gift to women, and men, before he came to St. Louis, and then I hadn't been overwhelmed with his charms, and the man who was the first love of his life wasn't bowled over either. It had given Dev his first-ever blows to his ego. It can be hard when a big, handsome man gets blown out of the water seriously for the first time, but he didn't hold a grudge; he was just puzzled by it.

"I thought you'd sworn off girls for Asher," I said.

A shadow passed over his very handsome face, and the one look was enough; there was more trouble in paradise. Nathaniel had said that Kane, Asher's other main guy, was jealous of Dev; maybe that was the shadow. I didn't envy Dev giving his heart to Asher; the vampire gave a whole new definition to moody lover.

I glanced at Micah to see if he knew what was up, but he shrugged. He was clueless, too. I didn't ask *What now?*, not in front of everyone, but was betting I'd hear about it in private later, either from Dev or Asher.

"He told me that if you wanted to put a ring on my finger, he wouldn't stand in our way."

I touched his hand, my other arm still around Micah. "I'm sorry, Dev."

He squeezed my hand and said, "He has Kane, so Kane thinks I should have someone else, too."

"So you won't take so much of Asher's time away from Kane," I said.

"You are so much handsomer than that werehyena," Angel said.

I knew she was defending her brother, but . . . "And comments like that are part of what make Kane insecure," I said.

"But it's true," she said, motioning at her brother. "Kane isn't horrible-looking, but he isn't in the same league as Dev, or Asher for that matter. Honestly, I don't know what Asher sees in him."

And that was one of the reasons I didn't like Angel; even when she was trying to be kind, she managed to be mean about someone else. She was as moody as Dev was easy to get along with, which was why he could date Asher, and she wouldn't have put up with it. I wouldn't have put up with everything that Dev had taken from Asher either, so who was I to complain, but . . . "Kane is handsome, he's just more Marlboro Man than Brad Pitt."

"What does that mean?" she asked.

"It means he's ruggedly handsome."

"If that's a nice way of saying he's not pretty, then I'll agree with you."

"Kane is handsome in his own way, Angel," Dev said.

"Why do you defend him?"

I studied Dev's face, watched the discomfort cross his face, and wondered if he was attracted to Kane, too. If so, then Kane's jealousy would be a double blow to him. There was such pain in his blue-hazel eyes. He let us see it raw and unfiltered for a heartbeat and then he closed his eyes, smiled, and hid behind that joking surfer-dude charm that was as fake as my cop face. Micah reached out to him, too, so that we were both holding his hands, and the moment we both touched him power flared across our skin. It raised the hairs on our arms, danced down our spines, and woke our beasts. I could feel Micah's leopard, and I could see mine, staring up at me down that long tunnel where my mind showed me my inner beasts. I knew there was no tunnel, no landscape for the leopard to pad through, but it was part of what my human mind did to make sense of the impossible. Now, because I was touching Dev, another shape looked up at me. My golden tigress started trotting after the black shadow of my leopard, but if my human body couldn't give release to one shape, it certainly couldn't do it for two. It had been a while since my multiple beasts had tried to come forward together, and it never worked well. Cats don't like to share.

It was as if the thought wanted to prove I was lying, because gold was joined by black, blue, white, and red so that the full rainbow of tigers stood gazing up at me, and the moment they were all there, the gold stopped moving. The tigers just stood there looking up, waiting. My leopard rose up, not as some mind game inside where you see dreams, but as power, rising as Micah's beast rose in a spilling wave of power and magic, as if invisible velvet fur could flow as easily as air not just across our skins, but through the centers of our bodies. Our beasts could swim through both our bodies like great furred leviathans, but they didn't take the logical route where Micah and I were touching each other; they flowed down our hands and into Dev. His tiger should have fought them off, but it didn't. The great golden cat rolled onto its side and rolled in the power as if it were being petted.

It had happened once before, when we first met Dev, but never again. I'd thought it was just some metaphysical hiccup, but Dev's face showed the same shocked pleasure now that it had that first time. The power flowed through the three of us in a continuous velvet rub of magic. I felt something deep in my body begin to build, and knew if we didn't stop there might be more than just metaphysical pleasure.

"Let's tone it down," I said in a voice already gone breathy.

"God, let's not," Dev said, and dropped to his knees, hands holding tight to ours. His eyes were fluttering as if he were having trouble focusing on anything but the sensations flowing through his body.

"It isn't that kind of party," Micah said, trying to make a joke of it, but his voice was almost as breathy as mine.

I'd known the gold tigers were spread out like a fan around us, but it wasn't until Fortune said, "That shouldn't be possible," that I realized there were others standing around us, so that we stood in a circle of weretigers.

"She smells like all of us at once," Angel said.

"They both do," Fortune said, and moved in closer to Micah, sniffing near his hair. That I hadn't known.

"What would happen if we touched them?" Angel asked.

"No," I said.

"No one touches us," Micah said.

Thorn reached out toward us. His short curls were so dark a blond that I would have called it brown, but the day I said so he'd been deeply insulted.

"Don't," I said.

But it was Thorn; he didn't like being told no. His hand touched my arm and the power flowed over his hand, but not into him. It was like he could brush the electricity of it, but the power didn't make him part of the circuit.

"Touch them both," Angel said.

"No!" Micah and I yelled together.

Thorn put his other hand on Micah's arm, and the power spilled over and through him, but Micah growled, "We said no!" The warm, comforting power suddenly grew claws and slashed out. Thorn staggered back from us, and blood blossomed on the front of his shirt.

The power went back to being warm and sensuous, but we could break the circuit now, as if Thorn had interfered with something and freed us.

Thorn was pulling his T-shirt up, showing that there were claw marks on his stomach, when Dev slammed into him so hard that he didn't just go down; he slid across the floor. Dev was on him before he could recover, lifting him to a sitting position with the handle of the bloody shirt around his neck. Dev growled so close to his face it looked like he was going to take a bite out of it. "Mine," Dev growled, "mine!"

Thorn blinked at him as if he couldn't hear him yet, but I saw one of his hands come up and caught a silver flash.

"No!" I yelled, but there was no time to do more. The men were across the room and whatever was going to happen would be over before anyone else could get to them.

21

I SAW DEV'S body react to the blade a second before I stumbled as I rushed toward him. My side hurt. He was my golden tiger to call, which meant I gained power through him and he through me, but there was a price. I actually glanced down to see if I was bleeding, but I wouldn't be. It would hurt like I was, but I wasn't actually cut; knowing that helped keep me moving forward, ignoring the pain.

Other guards had separated the two men by the time I got there. They had Thorn pressed to the floor with three guards on him. They weren't being gentle, and I was okay with that. Two more guards were holding Dev back, but the blade that was still stuck in his side helped him not fight that hard. It was stuck in almost to the hilt. It looked like Thorn had stabbed and tried to retract the blade, but couldn't get it out before the other guards swarmed him, or maybe the knife was stuck on a rib? I put a hand to my own side and thought, yeah, maybe. My side was a dull ache, a phantom pain of what was happening to Dev, but if the wound had been worse, so would my damage. The death of your animal to call could kill you, too, which made Thorn's behavior all the more careless.

Dr. Lillian came into the room with her own wererat bodyguard. Doctors were scarce in the lycanthrope community; the few we had were treated like gold. Dr. Lillian was still slender, with gray hair gone almost white. She looked like I thought fifty-plus should look, which meant she was actually much older. Shapeshifters aged more slowly than humans, and she matched her bodyguard as part of the wererats' rodere.

"What happened?" She looked at the two weretigers, and me holding my side. She came toward me first, but I motioned her to Dev. "He's the one who's hurt, not me."

"Why are you holding your side?"

"He's my golden tiger to call, and I was hooked up to him power-wise when it happened." I looked around the room and just said, "Jean-Claude, Nathaniel, Micah, are any of you feeling this?"

"I'm not," Micah said.

"I have shielded, *ma petite*, and am fine."

Nathaniel had a hand to his side. "It's a dull ache."

"Shit, that means I need to contact everyone else I'm tied to."

"I can answer, ow," Domino said as he came through the door. The black-and-white curls that had given him his name were mainly white, which meant that his last shift had been to the white side of his mixed heritage, and not the black.

Crispin, whose hair was only white curls, because he was pure white clan, came in with a hand to his side.

Echo jerked harder on Thorn's right arm. "If you kill a vampire's animal to call, you can kill them, did you forget that?"

"I wasn't trying to kill him."

Fortune pulled his other arm hard enough that he made a small pain sound. "Did you remember that hurting Dev would harm Anita?"

"Did you?" Echo jerked as if she meant to dislocate his shoulder.

"NO!" He said it through gritted teeth.

Lillian was kneeling by Dev now. "If you were human we'd be packing this so it wouldn't move and going to the hospital for a surgeon to help remove it, but it's not silver."

"See, I wasn't trying to kill him," Thorn said.

"Shut up," Fortune said.

"Brace yourself, Anita; I have to pull it out now."

"Give me a few seconds to warn everyone." I opened my shields a little more and let everyone connected to me know what was coming. Jade was crying in her room. I so did not need that right now, and I shielded hard from her. Everyone else got a glimpse and a warning; the "wound" hurt more with my shields down even a little. I put my shields hard in place like metal walls and said, "If Dev is ready, do it."

The guards helped brace Dev; Lillian put one hand on the hilt and the other against his side with her plastic gloves on, and pulled hard and quick.

Dev's breath came out in a sharp hiss, and he swayed a little, letting the other men keep him on his knees. I'd been safe behind my shields for the most part, but I held my hand out.

She looked at me. "You want the knife?"

"Yeah."

Dr. Lillian looked at me. "Why do you want it?"

"I'm going to give it back to Thorn."

"Don't do anything foolish."

"Just making a point," I said, and after a moment's hesitation she let me take the bloody knife from her hand.

I went to where Fortune and Echo still had Thorn on his knees with his arms damn near dislocated. At six feet plus he was tall enough, or I was short enough, that with him kneeling we had good eye contact. "Did you forget that stabbing Dev would hurt me, too?"

He hesitated, and the women made him hurt a little more, so he answered, "Yes."

"So you forgot that he was my animal to call, just having touched the power we share?"

He looked sullen. "I didn't think."

"That is part of your problem, Thorn, you don't think. You react, you let your temper best you, but you don't think. I'm going to make a point that I hope helps you think more clearly in the future before doing something stupid."

His eyes flicked to the blade in my hand.

"Nice knife, good balance," I said, as I tested the hilt in my hand.

"Thanks," he said, but he didn't sound certain now. Good.

I plunged the blade into his side; I didn't hit a rib, so it went in nice and fast, all the way to the hilt, the way he'd planned on hurting Dev. Echo and Fortune eased down on his arms so he could react to it. I got close to his surprised face and said, "If you ever forget again what is mine, and harm Dev, or any of my animals to call, outside a practice ring, I will give you your blade again, but it will go in a little higher and more to the center, are we clear on that?"

His voice came out between gritted teeth, breathy in a I-will-not-scream way. "Yes."

"Yes, what?" Echo said.

"Yes, ma'am."

"Try again," she said.

"Yes . . . my queen."

"That's better," Echo said.

I nodded. "Yeah, that's better." I pulled the knife out hard and fast. He whimpered for me.

I stared down at him with his blood staining the blade and mingling with Dev's. "There won't be a second warning, Thorn, do you understand that?"

He swallowed, nodded, stopped like it hurt, and finally said, "Yes, I understand."

"Take him out of my sight for a while, before I decide to give him his blade again."

They forced him to his feet and Echo said, "I like you."

I smiled and shook my head. "I don't dislike you, but I don't know if I like you yet."

She smiled at me. "Oh, now I know I like you."

"Aren't you going to let the doctor look at me?" Thorn asked.

"You'll heal," I said. "Get him out of here."

Fortune said, "As our queen wishes."

"Whatever she desires," Echo said.

I raised an eyebrow at her. "Violence do it for you, or was it the ruthlessness?"

"Both," she said, and gave me a look that I was more used to seeing on a man's face. Once it would have freaked me out, but standing there with the bloody knife in my hand I knew that a little girl-on-girl flirting was so not that big a deal. I cleaned the blade off on a clean part of Dev's shirt and offered him the blade hilt-first.

He looked at it and then up at me.

"Think of it as a present from your cousin Thorn."

"He won't like you giving me one of his favorite knives."

"I want him to see you carrying it. I want it to remind him that if he pulls this shit again I will end him now and forever."

Dev took the blade from me, nodding. "I'm healing already, Anita."

"You know how you growled at him, 'Mine'?"

"Yes."

I put my hand on the back of Dev's neck, just under the hair where the skin was so warm, and brought him down so our foreheads touched. "Mine."

He smiled then, and moved in for a kiss, which I gave him. "Yours," he said, as he pulled back.

"Damn straight."

22

ONCE A WEEK we tried to eat dinner like a family at the Circus of the Damned. The small table that Jean-Claude had put into Nathaniel's dream kitchen wasn't big enough for everyone. We'd tried to do it in the formal dining room that Jean-Claude kept for more serious occasions like visiting master vampires, but that was too far away from the kitchen for the cooks, so we turned one of the smaller bedrooms nearby into a bigger but still-cozy dining room. Tonight hadn't been planned for one of the meals, but Nathaniel had said, "We all need to give Dev energy to heal, and that takes fuel. Food is the easiest way to fuel up. Give us thirty minutes and it'll all be ready."

"It wasn't silver, he'll be healed in minutes," Doc Lillian said.

"Anita could heal me and give me extra energy besides," Dev said, his arms sliding a little more solidly around me, our bodies suddenly pressed tighter together. I was about to say, *You're hurt*, but others spoke for me.

"What would Asher say about that, *mon ami*?" Jean-Claude asked.

"I'm allowed to be food in emergencies."

"What would Kane say?" Nathaniel asked.

Dev scowled and rested his face against the top of my head.

I moved him enough so I could look up into his face. "Why does Kane have more say over you than Asher does?"

Dev sighed and hugged me tighter, not in a sexy way, but just holding on for comfort. "It's complicated," he said finally in a voice that let me know that *complicated* translated to *sad and frustrating*.

"Explain it to Anita while we get dinner ready," Nathaniel said.

Micah came to stand near us. "How long will it take to fix?"

"Thirty minutes tops; the chicken is already marinated and we're just steaming veggies."

"Please tell me there's a carb of some kind," Domino said.

Nicky answered, "No, if you want carbohydrates have them at lunch."

"It's not my fault that your metabolism can't digest potatoes," he said, frowning a little, but smiling to take the edge off it.

"Have potatoes at lunch," Crispin said. "Most of us have to take our clothes off onstage. No carbs at dinner."

"Nicky doesn't strip," Domino protested.

"Nathaniel does," Nicky said.

"What's that got to do with you?"

Nicky gave Domino a flat, unfriendly look.

"What?"

"I'm the main cook," Nathaniel said. "If you want different food, you plan the week's menu, do the grocery shopping, and prep the meals."

Domino held his hands up. "You win; I am so not that domestically talented. I can't even sous chef the way Nicky and Cynric can."

Micah slid his arm across my shoulders. Dev moved his arm enough so they could both touch me without touching each other. For some of the men it was a sign that they didn't touch other men, but for others it was a sign of respect. Since Dev was cheerfully bisexual, he moved because he knew Micah didn't touch other men casually, and Micah was their leader. If the leader wants to hug his fiancée, then you move so he can, even if you are one of her lovers. Poly isn't about being completely fair for most people. There are some who run it with a near perfect equality, but for most of us there are primary relationships, there are secondary, and even ones less serious than that. If we'd been touching

Dev and Asher came, I'd have made room for him, because Dev was one of his primary relationships, but he was a tertiary for me, at best.

"Before dinner, Anita, Jean-Claude, and I need to talk with some of the weretigers."

I glanced at him and so did Dev. "Did I do something wrong?" he asked.

Micah smiled. "No, Dev, you didn't do anything wrong, but you are included in the talk."

"Weretigers that are connected to us already, or new ones?" I asked.

"No new ones, not yet."

"You have but to ask, *mon chat*," Jean-Claude said.

Micah picked the tigers he wanted, and we all trusted him enough to believe he'd explain when we had some privacy. There was a time in my life when I wouldn't have trusted anyone that much, but Micah had earned it from me, from Jean-Claude, from all of us. The fact that no one argued or even questioned the request proved that. We just all trooped off to his office here in the underground. It was newer than even the dining room remodel, but it was the only room that had a table with enough chairs for everyone, besides the dining rooms. Before the office was put in, most group meetings had been in Jean-Claude's bedroom, and you sat either on the floor or on the bed once the two chairs by the fireplace were taken.

But now we all got to sit around the oval table in the conference room area off the office. It had a desk that Micah actually used sometimes, but I found him most often sitting at the far end of the big table with papers spread out in front of him, or with a bunch of other shapeshifters talking Coalition business. The desk was beautiful, but it was almost untouched. The table was the office for Micah.

Micah, Jean-Claude, and I ended up sitting at the far end of the oval with me in the middle so that I could lay a hand on Jean-Claude's thigh and hold Micah's hand. Jean-Claude's arm was across my shoulders so that his hand rested on the back of Micah's shoulders. Dev sat beside Micah, who he wasn't that close to, but tonight he seemed to huddle near him, not touching, because Micah didn't let just anyone touch him casually, unless they were part of our pard. Other flavors of animal had to earn the right to casual touching from Micah. Come to that, neither did Jean-Claude and I, but Dev was on my touching list. Domino and Crispin were on the side by Jean-Claude but had given themselves a seat between so they weren't crowding him. Dev was as close to Micah as he could get and not touch him. He kept rubbing his hands on the tabletop as if trying to memorize the grain of the wood with his fingertips. I didn't have to lower my metaphysical shields to know he was nervous. I didn't think it was the fight with Thorn, or even the injury; they'd been raised together. Think about the fights you used to have with your siblings, now what if you could heal almost any injury; yeah, that kind of vicious squabbling had been pretty normal for them growing up. Dev even had a scar on his back from a silver knife used in practice with Thorn years before we met them. So what was wrong? My bet was it was something to do with Asher, Kane, and Dev's dynamics, but matters of the heart were going to have to wait until later; right now it was metaphysics time.

"When Anita and I touched Dev together, you felt the power?" Micah asked.

Jean-Claude said, "*Oui*, it was like the first time you touched him together. I assume it isn't always like that between the three of you."

"I don't know," Micah said.

Jean-Claude frowned slightly. "How can you not know? If it happened every time you touched each other, I know you would have mentioned it to me. So it is a rare occurrence."

"This is only the second time it's happened," I said.

"Very rare then," he said.

Micah shook his head, his long ponytail catching slightly under Jean-Claude's arm. "This is only the second time that Anita and I have touched Dev."

Jean-Claude frowned a little more. "But I know Anita has had sex with Dev and you in the bed more than just that first night."

"I've touched Anita while Dev has touched her, but tonight was only the second time she and I have touched Dev; do you see the difference?"

Jean-Claude did the long blink, his face pleasant and unreadable; it was his version of blank cop face. Even his leg had gone very still under my hand, as if he were holding more than just his breath. Older vampires could almost suspend movement, as if all the "being alive" could just stop.

He blinked again, and it was as if someone had hit the on switch. He took a breath and said, "Are you saying that you have never, even accidentally, touched Dev at the same time he was touching Anita, even during sex?"

"Yes."

Jean-Claude looked at me; it was an eloquent look.

"Dev and I haven't had sex that often. Asher is too insecure when his male lovers want to bed women, you know that."

"He has been working that issue, but yes, he is more insecure around bisexual men. Heterosexuals he sees as a challenge to seduce, but with bisexuals he thinks he is simply not enough to keep them entertained."

"Which is just weird, because he likes women, too," I said.

"Emotional issues are seldom logical, *ma petite*."

"You know, you're all talking like Dev can't hear you, and he's right there," Crispin said. It made me look from the tall, slender dancer to Dev, whose hands were still trying to rub a hole through the tabletop.

"I'm sorry, Dev," I said.

"Thank you, Crispin," Micah said, "you're right."

Dev didn't look at anyone.

"Dev," I said, "what's wrong?"

He just shook his head.

"Kane has become even more possessive lately," Jean-Claude said.

I glanced at him. "He has already forbidden Asher any women but me, and even then only when we were with you, Richard, or Nathaniel. What other restrictions did he put in place?"

"Kane says that I don't meet any needs that he can't meet for Asher. Nathaniel and you meet his need to dominate in the bedroom and dungeon. Richard meets his need to be dominated in the dungeon." Dev looked up, and there was such raw pain on his face. "I know Kane tried to forbid Asher your bed, too, Jean-Claude."

"I did not tolerate it. Kane needed to remember his place."

Dev nodded a little too often and too quickly. "Yeah, you and Asher have been an item for a few hundred years, and you're the king, so Kane had to eat that jealousy, but I'm new and I'm no one's king."

"Are you saying that Asher has allowed Kane to cast you out as his lover?"

"Almost."

"What does 'almost' mean?" I asked.

"I'm getting less and less sex from Asher and every time we do, Kane throws a huge fit. I'm pretty sure that Asher loves me, but not enough to put up with the emotional . . ." Dev spread his big hands as if he couldn't find the words.

"Over the centuries it has been Asher who made the emotional cost too high with others for me. I did not always give in, because I found that there would always be more jealousy, but now it seems Asher has found his match in Kane."

"I was ready to marry Asher," Dev said.

I reached across Micah and patted Dev's hand. "I know, and I'm sorry he's being a shit."

"It's not him, it's Kane."

I took my hand back and didn't say anything, but I knew from experience with other people that no one can be a shit unless the other person tolerates it, so it was still Asher's responsibility to run his relationships better than this.

"Why didn't you tell me?" I asked.

"I thought we'd work it out, but Asher only loves one person enough to fight for them and that's Jean-Claude."

"And the fact that I do not want Asher to be my primary relationship hurts him," Jean-Claude said.

Dev nodded. "Yeah."

"Maybe it's time to let Asher find a territory where he can be Master of the City away from the rest of us," Micah said.

I felt Jean-Claude startle, which didn't happen often; he was too controlled for it. "We have had this discussion. Asher has won the li-bido, if not the heart, of Narcissus, who controls the St. Louis werehyenas. They have vowed to move with Asher if he goes, and the hyenas are a large part of our guards."

"Not as much as they were. Rafael, Richard, and I have slowly been working the rats, wolves, and other animal groups up to size and skill set. Give me a few weeks more and the werehyenas can do as they like."

Jean-Claude, Dev, and I stared at him. Crispin and Domino didn't. Only three of us at the table hadn't known this little plan. Domino traveled out of town as security for Micah, but I hadn't thought he was that close to Crispin, and that was interesting. Richard Zeeman, who was the local Ulfric, wolf king, was usually useless when it came to choosing new wolves for his pack who could actually help us fight better.

"Have you really been plotting to remove Asher from St. Louis, *mon chat*?"

"He's proved himself unstable on multiple occasions and used the threat of removing the hyenas from us to emotionally blackmail you and Anita. I thought it was a good idea to take away his leverage and make us strong enough to tell him to go to hell, if he tries it again."

"I didn't realize," I said.

He looked at me. "Realize what?"

"You really don't like Asher."

"Not particularly."

"I am sorry, *mon ami*, if I have not done more to foster better feelings between you and him."

"It's not you who needs to work harder at fostering good relations between Asher and me; that would be his responsibility."

"Is it totally lame to say that we missed Asher when he was gone for six months?" I asked.

Micah smiled. "Not lame, but we can find you and Nathaniel another dominant to play with; we can't afford to let Asher's issues rise and hurt us again."

"I agree with that last part, but he has been working his issues, or I thought he had." I glanced at Dev. I wasn't so sure now.

Micah said, "I know that Asher meets a lot of needs for people here, and he's happy up to a point here, but beyond that point he still feels jealous of you, and conflicted about Anita, and damn near predatory of any of the men in your life who don't want to sleep with him."

"Is he still pushing upon your boundaries, *mon chat*?"

Micah shrugged. "Nothing I can't handle, and it's not personal. Asher doesn't want me any more than he wants any attractive man, or maybe he wants me to want him, that seems to be the prime thing for Asher. He wants to be desired, and anyone he desires who doesn't return the favor hits his insecurities, especially if that someone is in your bed, or Anita's. He's liked me even less since he found out that Nathaniel and I are intimate, and it's not just the way Dev and I are with Anita."

"And what way is that?" Crispin asked. He leaned forward, his long arms clasped on the table in front of him. When I'd met him he'd seemed like just another handsome stripper that I'd managed to accidentally attract, but the press of intelligence in his blue tiger eyes, the demand in his face, the set of his shoulders, showed just how much more there was to him than the body that made it rain money onstage. Domino sitting beside him was shorter, looked a little stockier, but it was the extra muscle from working out with the other bodyguards; with his hair mostly white with only a black curl here and there, he and Crispin looked more alike than normal. You had to look past the tiger eyes the color of flames to see it, but it was there in the bone structure. I realized that I didn't see the two of them this close together that often. Most of the dancers didn't hang out with the guards, or hit the gym at the same time for the same kind of workouts. They weren't technically cousins, because Domino had been an orphan found and adopted by the white tiger clan, but centuries of inbreeding in the clans had left its mark on both of them.

Dev answered, "A lot of straight guys will share a woman with you, but they put rules in place about how much touching of each other you can do, and for Micah that's no touching. We use Anita like a bridge, or a shield between us."

"I'm not that into men, it's nothing personal."

Dev nodded again, then looked at Micah. "You've liked me less since you realized that Nathaniel and I would do things together that you won't do with him."

Micah's face darkened and I felt the first prickle of his beast, which meant what Dev had said was true and had pissed him off.

I stared at one of my other halves. How had I missed this whole thing? I had to have been in the bed when things were happening, because Dev and Micah were never in the same bed without me, but then I realized that Nathaniel mentioning Dev earlier as a potential shared husband might have had more behind it than just their shared bisexuality. Had he and Dev had more alone time than I knew?

"Okay, I'm just going to say it, I've missed something big. I'm sorry to everyone, but we need to step back and fill me in."

"We don't need to be here for this," Domino said, and stood up.

"But you do need to be here for the power question," Micah said. He turned to Dev. "Can we discuss the magic first, and then we can let Crispin and Domino out of the personal business."

Dev nodded.

Micah turned to the other tigers. "I want to see if the power jumps between Anita, Dev, and me again. If it does, then I'll have us try it with Crispin. If it happens between the three of us, we'll try with Domino, and I think that may be a big enough sampling that we'll just assume it would happen with all the tigers."

"What if it only happens with Dev?" Crispin asked.

"Then the two of you can go, and we'll discuss the metaphysics and the personal stuff in private."

The two of them exchanged a look, then looked back at Micah. "Metaphysics first and then we'll discuss the personal stuff and whether we want to leave Dev on his own."

Dev looked at them. "You don't have to stay for me."

"It's not for you," Crispin said, "it's for all of us. Anita was supposed to look at all the tigers tonight and here we are in an isolated group, caught up in some new magic. It keeps distracting us from what we say is our goal."

"And what goal is that?" I asked, and knew my voice wasn't entirely friendly.

Crispin gave me a look that wasn't entirely friendly either. "To make sure the Mother of All Darkness does not rise again. It should be everyone's goal, Anita, not just the clan tigers, and everyone should be dedicated to making certain the prophecy is fulfilled as completely as possible."

"We are," I said.

"You don't really believe you need to marry one of us to finish the prophecy, Anita. You've made that clear."

I sighed, and would have let go of Micah's hand, but he held on. Jean-Claude was just still under my hand so I stopped touching him. If he wanted to "go away" while he was still sitting beside me, fine.

"Jean-Claude and I are willing to let Anita add another man or woman to our commitment ceremony, and bring them into our bed. I think we're taking the prophecy pretty seriously," Micah said.

I looked at him. "You're the one who brought up the whole marrying-a-weretiger thing, not me."

"I think it's necessary, but am I thrilled with sharing you with another person, especially another man? Not entirely. I see it as necessary, and that's not the same thing as wanting it."

"I'm not going to be forced to marry anyone that I don't want to marry."

"See, none of you believe," Crispin said, voice low.

"We believe enough for Anita to interview more weretigers."

"Why don't you just marry Cynric? He's the one who's already in the house with you," Domino asked.

I looked down, fighting not to make eye contact, or to lower any shields between me and the tigers in the room. I didn't want to share my revelation with anyone, and definitely not with any other tigers besides Cynric, though I wasn't sure it was a really good idea to even tell him. I was still too confused about it myself.

"Cynric was happy to entertain the idea of another woman added to our household," Jean-Claude said in his most pleasant and emptiest voice.

Crispin shook his head. "But you didn't interview anyone, did you? You had a metaphysical crisis and it's all back-burner again."

"They couldn't have planned my fight with Thorn," Dev said.

"No, but there is always something that can be used as a legitimate excuse to postpone things that Anita, or Micah, or Jean-Claude doesn't want to address, and there always will be something."

Domino was looking uncomfortable, as if he wanted to push his chair farther away so it was clear that either he didn't agree with everything Crispin was saying, or he didn't want to get included if we got angry.

"It is true that there will always be a crisis to attend to," Jean-Claude said.

I frowned at him. "We don't do it on purpose."

"No, but you admit that there is always something, right?" Crispin asked.

Micah finally said, "I can't disagree."

"Good, then test the magic, or whatever it is with Dev, and if it works again try it with me; if it only works with Dev we'll see what comes next."

"We haven't agreed to you staying for the personal talk, but let's just do the power test and we'll go from there," Micah said.

"Just let me say that the next time you have serious reservations about sharing me with more people, don't be the one who brings the subject up," I said.

He let go of my hand, and I didn't try to keep holding on. "You don't like Envy well enough to be in the bed with her when she's with Jean-Claude, or Richard."

"What does that have to do with anything?"

"Just pointing out that I compromise a lot better with your male lovers than you do with the only other woman who's crossed the line to becoming a regular lover for any of us."

"Are you trying to pick a fight?" I asked.

He sighed and rubbed his hands over his face as if scrubbing something away. "I don't know, maybe."

"It is very rare for you not to be the diplomat, *mon chat*," Jean-Claude said.

"It's just Cynric is like my little brother. Nathaniel calls him a brother-husband and I understand that. There's no weirdness between Cynric and anyone else in our inner circle, but Dev is truly bisexual, as much as Nathaniel is, which means that there are expectations from him that there won't be from others."

"Bisexual and male doesn't mean I want to fuck you, Micah," Dev said, and he was finally getting angry, too.

"I didn't mean it that way."

"How did you mean it, then?" Dev's energy was starting to radiate out like a stove being slowly turned up.

"I'm as happy as I've ever been in my life, Dev. I don't want that screwed up because of some ancient prophecy, or anything else. I've got two people that I love and that love me; we all want to marry each other, and I'm being forced to include another person that we're not in love with, and it scares the shit out of me. What would you do if things were perfect between you, Asher, and Kane, but you were being forced to add a fourth person?"

Dev opened his mouth, closed it, and finally said, "I'd be pissed."

"Exactly," Micah said.

"But you're the one who brought it up earlier," I said.

"I did, because what if by refusing to risk screwing up my own happily-ever-after, I cause the Great Evil to rise again and destroy not only you, Nathaniel, and Jean-Claude, but everyone and everything? The destruction of civilization as we know it seems a high price to pay for not wanting to add another person to our commitment ceremony."

Crispin pointed a thumb in Micah's direction. "What he said."

Dev's energy had quieted. "I'm sorry, Micah, I didn't understand it like that. I think if I were in love I might let the whole world go to hell rather than risk my own happiness."

"I've seen you risk your life to save the day," I said.

Dev gave me a smile that managed to be more sad than anything else. "But that was before I saw Asher after months apart from him and realized just how much I loved him. It was before I thought I had a chance at what you, Micah, and Jean-Claude have. I was raised being told my life was at the disposal of the Master of Tigers once he, or she, appeared, but no one ever explained what to do about love. I mean, they covered lust, because if one of the vamps from Belle Morte's bloodline was our master, then sex would be a given, but love . . . No one ever talked to us about that."

Crispin said, "So you'd lay down your life, but not your heart, for Anita?"

Dev shrugged those big shoulders. "I'll do my duty, but if I had the level of commitment from Asher that Micah has from the people in his life, I'd make that my priority."

"Love can unman you," Jean-Claude said.

We all looked at him.

He gave that graceful almost-shrug that meant everything, nothing, or some emotion in between depending on his facial expression, or the timing. "I have loved people more than I loved my duty. It can be wonderful, and terrible."

"How is it terrible?" Crispin asked.

"Because, *mon ami*, sometimes if you do not do your duty, then a kingdom can be lost, and you must weigh your love, or even your lover, against the lives of many more. It is a terrible choice."

"That sounds like personal experience," I said.

He looked at me with a pleasant but unreadable face. The shielding between us was as tight as he could make it. Whatever memory was behind his words, he didn't want to share it. I had my own share of things that I'd rather not share, so I'd learned not to pry. Sometimes you really did want the sleeping dogs to keep napping, because once they woke up they tried to tear your throat out.

"Our choice isn't that hard today," Micah said. "Right now we just need to figure out if the power rush between Dev, Anita, and me works every time, or if it's a special-occasion rush."

"I've always admired how you try to keep everyone on track," Crispin said.

Micah nodded. "Thank you, but let's test Dev with us, and if that just works, we'll try it with one of you."

"It's a plan," Crispin said.

"Yes," Micah said, "it is."

23

JEAN-CLAUDE OBSERVED THAT the very first time we met Dev it had been the two of us and then Micah had joined us, so we tried it in that order again. Metaphysics wasn't very science-like sometimes, but now that we knew the phenomenon could be duplicated, we could still use the scientific method to learn more faster.

What I hadn't counted on was how neglected Dev was feeling and how much his skin hunger had grown. Newborns will die from lack of touch; it's one of the causes of failure to thrive. The elderly will also begin to decline faster if they don't have anyone to touch them. Patting someone's hand, or shoulder, a hug, all of it is necessary to be happy and healthy for most people. It doesn't have to have anything to do with sex; in fact, most of the touch that keeps us all going is as innocent as a newborn lamb frolicking on the spring grass, but Dev wasn't a lamb. I tended to think of him as not harmless exactly, but not predatory either, and suddenly staring up into his blue-gold eyes I saw that his energy was very solidly big bad wolf. There was nothing innocent or lamblike about the way his arms wrapped around me, or how his big hands dug fingers into my back, just enough to let me feel the strength in them. I was struck again by how big he was: tall, broad-shouldered, just *big*, as if he filled out every inch of his six-foot, three-inch frame. If he'd been willing to lift weights like Nicky did, he'd have been massive. I was sort of glad he didn't, as he pulled me close and I saw his eyes unveil themselves. I don't mean they changed to tiger eyes, his eyes were always that, but suddenly I could see the need in him. People say that sex is a want, not a need, but for some of us I'm not sure that's true.

Dev's hunger was naked in his eyes, and I suddenly felt small in his arms. As he leaned over to kiss me, fingers digging deeper into my back, the promise of strength and pain sped my pulse and caught my breath in my throat. How badly had Asher neglected him to fill the mild-mannered and typically gentle Dev with such fierce need?

His lips touched mine and it was as if he drew my golden tiger up through my body, as if that one kiss had reached down through my body and touched the deepest part of me. The gold spilled upward like a shining flame, and the rainbow of my other tigers followed that shining yellow: red tiger the color of flame itself, black like the coals at the heart of the fire, white where some metals will begin to melt into incandescent puddles, and blue where the flame burns hottest of all. All that color, all the power, all that heat spilled up through me and into Dev everywhere our skin touched. The kiss should have looked like a carnival fire eater trying to blow out a plume of colored flame, then being kissed at just the wrong moment, so that the fire poured into the mouth of his lover.

I don't know how much the rest of the men could see, but to our eyes it was like kissing in the middle of a burning color and power. It felt wonderful and frightening, like flame dancing across our skin, but not quite burning . . . not yet.

Then Micah's hand was on mine and the power spilled out through my skin and into him like a river seeking a new way to the sea. His leopard spilled up my arm and brought mine to life so that the calm darkness of it mixed with the tigers and suddenly the heat wasn't frightening. I knew that together we could tame it, control it, and with that thought all my beasts came to life in one woven knot of intermingled power. Lion came to join the tigers and leopards, and then wolf, and lastly hyena. It was the newest beast I carried; less than a year ago Ares had contaminated me with it while he died. He hadn't meant to share the disease that forced him out of the marines. He hadn't meant me to have to use the skills he'd taught me as a sniper to kill him before the madness drove him to harm civilians. Neither of us had meant a lot of things, but I carried a piece of his beast inside me and would until I died. I didn't need anything else to remember my friend but that hot, wild energy spilling up through my body and into the men who touched me.

"Anita smells like all her beasts at once," Crispin said, and just that let me know he was closer to us than he had been.

I tried to turn to see how close. Dev's big hand touched the side of my face so the energy kept flowing across our skin as we both broke from the kiss to look. Micah was only holding our hands, so he just had to turn and look. Crispin was on all fours on top of the conference table. He was sniffing the air, his hands still solidly on the wood, like a much smaller cat when it smells something interesting and wants to investigate without actually touching it first.

"Micah smells like all her beasts and more. Something more, that I don't understand. Domino, what do you smell?"

Domino spoke from behind me, and I turned in the circle of the men's hands, and the invisible rush of that flaming energy, to see him on all fours on the floor, leaning in toward us in an almost identical pose to Crispin.

"Their beasts, all their beasts."

"Does Micah smell like more than leopard to you?"

Domino leaned in closer to Micah's leg. "Yes."

Crispin leaned further, stretching that long torso out, until he could almost have licked Dev. The golden tiger growled softly at him. Crispin backed up a fraction. "Can you smell everything on Dev, too?"

Domino crawled around my legs so he could sniff closer to Dev. It should have looked awkward to see the guard, still carrying all his weapons, crawling on all fours, but he moved as if the tigers inside him knew exactly how to move this human shape so it was graceful even without paws. He sniffed loudly, drawing in the scent, and then reached out as if to caress the energy. Dev growled louder this time.

"Easy, big gold, I'm just trying to taste the energy." Domino raised those red and orange eyes to us. "Dev smells like all the beasts, too."

"That's not the way it's supposed to work," Crispin said.

"How is it supposed to work?" Jean-Claude asked. He was leaning against the wall closest to the three of us. His hands were behind him, so they were pinned between his body and the wall.

"Anita is a panwere, so she has other beasts, but it shouldn't transfer to anyone else," Crispin said.

"I think it's just the power of them, not the true beasts," Micah said. His voice was half breathy with that edge of growling undertone.

"What if it's not?" Domino asked, still on all fours at our feet.

The three of us didn't truly look at each other, but we shared what the look would have meant in an instant of emotion. The marks were open between us, not all the way, but we were already beginning to think as a unit—three people, one mind, one heart, if we weren't careful.

"Try to change," Domino said.

"What?" I said.

"One of you try to change shape into something you're not."

We all looked down into those startling fire-colored eyes, and then Micah said, "I like these clothes."

"I don't care about mine," Dev said.

"Then you change," Crispin said.

"While we're all still touching?" he asked.

"Yes," all the wereanimals said at once. Jean-Claude and I weren't sure, but we didn't say no.

"Okay," Dev said, "what should I be?"

"What do you want to be?" I asked.

He smiled; it was fierce, more a flash of teeth than a true smile. He knew exactly what he wanted to be.

24

I'D SEEN DEV shapeshift before, but only in a very special type of weapons practice. The fastest shape change often was the deciding factor in a fight between wereanimals, so our guards practiced that just like they did on the gun range, or hand to hand. So I'd seen Dev and all the guards shapeshift, but never while I was touching him. Never while Micah and I were sharing our beasts with each other, and the metaphysics between us all was wide open like a river flooding its banks.

The heat began in his hand, going from warm to hot as if he'd spiked a sudden deadly fever, and then the heat ran through his body so that it radiated even through his clothes as he wrapped himself around me and drew Micah closer by pulling on his hand. I felt Micah hesitate, and then his body relaxed in against me. He let go of some issue that was holding him back and just relaxed into me and Dev, because the other man was holding me so close that he couldn't really get nearer to me without getting closer to us both. I felt Dev's happiness spike, as if he appreciated Micah letting go; whether it was Micah's giving himself to the moment, or Dev's emotion, something spiked the power higher like gasoline thrown on a fire.

That invisible colored fire flared around us, so bright inside my head like a waking dream, but this dream had heat, and the solidness of the two men, so that it was an intermingling of reality and the images inside of my head.

"Do you see the colors?" I asked in a voice that was more breath than anything.

"Smell them," Micah whispered.

"Feel them," Dev said, and he reached a hand out, as if he expected to actually be able to touch the flames. The colors reacted to his hand, brightening as his fingers touched the energy and fading as he ran his hand further through the air.

"It's reacting to your touch," I said.

"Like I said, I can feel the different beasts."

"Pick one, *mon ami*, let me see your clothes vanish and you slip this mortal skin," Jean-Claude said, in a voice that caressed along my skin even with all the energy that was already there. I had a moment to realize that he was flirting with Dev, either to get him to hurry up and choose a form, or for the reason anyone flirts.

I felt Dev startle, his body reacting to Jean-Claude's voice more than Micah or I did, but then we spent more time with him and had built up our endurance. Dev had been Asher's boyfriend, so Jean-Claude had put him on the "do not touch" list. Maybe Dev wasn't the only one tired of Asher and Kane's tantrums.

"Choose," Micah said. "Choose, or I will."

Dev chose, or tried to, but he made one mistake. He tried to choose by simply letting his beast rise, except now he had nine animals trying to get out all at once. I'd learned they did not share well.

They spilled up into his body like a flood being forced into a narrow passage, except this flood had teeth and claws. Dev screamed and started to fall, the strength of his hands dragging at us, as we fought to keep our feet and tried to hold him up. I could feel the claws and teeth trying to fight through him, but I didn't feel the pain of it the way Dev obviously did.

I glanced at Micah. "Are you protecting us?"

"Yes, can you hold him by yourself?"

I wrapped my arms more firmly around the bigger man's waist and held on. I nodded, and Micah took me at my word like he always did. He stopped trying to hold Dev up, and I was suddenly holding up nearly twice my body weight of a supernaturally strong man whose body was bucking and writhing against itself. It was like holding a muscular bag of huge snakes. Micah put his hands on either side of Dev's face and made him look at him.

"Close it down, Dev, shove them all back just like you do with your tiger. Do it! Do it now!"

Dev screamed again, his eyes tightly closed, seeing nothing but the shapes inside him trying to get out. Micah pressed his hands so hard I could see his fingers imprinting on Dev's face. "Dev, look at me!" He shouted it.

The other man blinked at him. I held on, but I could feel something pushing against my chest where I was pressed tight against him, as if some huge thing were pushing against his stomach from the inside.

"Dev, it's just like your tiger. Control it!"

"Too many," Dev said, and screamed again.

Crispin said, "Stop this."

Dev rolled his eyes at the other weretiger. "No!" It came out as another scream, but Crispin backed up and left us to it.

"Dev," Micah said, "are you a golden tiger?"

"Yes." The word squeezed out between clenched teeth.

"Then do what the golden tigers are meant to do—conquer and rule!"

I felt Dev's body go still in my arms, as if the animals inside him heard the distant sound of hunting horns and froze. The next moment either they would fight harder, or they'd keep still, hoping the "hunt" would pass them by. I tightened my grip around his waist, one hand holding my other wrist, tightening my core, planting my feet. My only job was to keep him upright, that was it; Dev and Micah were doing the complicated part. I just had to hold on; I could do that.

Dev closed his eyes again, but I didn't think it was from pain, more to help him concentrate on things that could only be seen clearly inside his head. I'd noticed that outer vision could interfere with inner vision sometimes.

People talk about flexing muscles, but willpower is a muscle, too. I felt Dev gather himself, felt it in his body, as if he were tensing muscles to do something wholly physical, and then his power, his beast, everything that had first attracted me to him roared back at all the beasts. I had a moment to see the pale gold of his tiger with its white fangs wide and snarling. It tried to come forward and be him, but he pushed it back and reached out with will alone to pull something else out of the snarl of animals.

It was pale and golden, too, but not the yellow of his tiger, and there were no stripes on this furred body. Modern lions didn't have stripes. I wasn't sure if I heard Micah, or just his thoughts were loud in my head: "Lion, of course, it would be a lion." He was almost unhappy with the choice. I didn't have time to ask him why, because Dev's body began to shift. His human skin went from fever-warm to almost too hot to hold, and then all that smooth skin began to give way to fur. Thick, clear liquid ran hot as blood as his body re-formed itself. I was too close not to feel the bones migrate under his skin, the ligaments shift. I'd had lycanthropes shift on top of me before, but never when I was holding them as tight as I could. It was as if I could feel things move that I'd only heard, or guessed at, as his tall body remade itself in my arms. I closed my eyes as the hot liquid spilled over me, and his body grew taller than his human size. He was a big man, but he was a much bigger werelion.

I blinked my eyes clean of the liquid that I had all over me, but Dev rose above me with his fur dry except where it touched me. His thick mane was a pale yellow-blond, close to his own hair color, though I knew it didn't have to match anything on the human body of the shape-shifter. He blinked large orange-gold eyes at me from a face that was a graceful mix of human and cat.

He was so tall in this form that his head almost touched the ceiling, which meant he was over seven feet tall. Half-man form for most were-animals gained them between a few inches and over a foot in extra height when they were wolfmen, or lionmen, or whatever-men.

Like I'd said, Dev was a big guy, and the werelion was fucking massive.

"Holy shit," Domino said from somewhere behind us.

"This isn't possible," Crispin said.

I felt Micah draw himself in, a second before he ran with heat and power. His change was neater, cleaner, faster, but then he was one of the best at shifting from one form to another I'd ever seen. He stood over me, black-furred as usual, but taller than ever, and just as the spots of his leopard were visible when the light hit them just right, so now the stripes showed in the overhead light, and for the first time he gazed down at me with different eyes. Golden eyes with a line of red around the pupil like an echo of his own gold-green. He loomed over me, but nothing to equal the lionman. The two of them together seemed to fill the room, as if there weren't enough square footage for anyone or anything else. The table had been pushed back, the chairs lay on their sides, and I couldn't remember when it happened, or if we had done it, or the others had done it to save the furniture.

Dev's voice came out in a growling deep bass even deeper than his tiger form. "I thought you liked your clothes."

"I had to try," Micah growled back.

I started to step back from both of them, but they each grabbed one of my arms.

Micah said, "I don't know what happens if we stop touching each other."

I stayed put with their massive hands wrapped completely around my arms. Dev was almost able to wrap his fingers around my bicep twice. My bicep isn't that small; he was just that big.

Jean-Claude stepped around them, pressed to the wall to move around Dev's tawny side. "Impressive, *ma petite, mon chat, mon tigre*. Very impressive."

Dev shook that thick mane. "I'm not a tiger now."

"*Mon lionne*, then."

"Am I your lion, Jean-Claude?" The question seemed to mean more than it should have.

"All that is here is mine, Mephistopheles." Hearing him use Dev's full name was almost startling. I heard it so seldom that I sometimes forgot he had another name.

The big lion nodded, his shoulders pressed against the ceiling, back bowed for lack of space as he held my arm, and held hands with Micah. Their tawny and black fur looked like yin and yang curved around each other.

"You are the king, all that you desire is yours to take," he said, and again I knew there was more meaning there than I was certain of. I would ask Jean-Claude later.

"Fur is not to my liking, *mon lionne*."

"We can fix the fur part; the implications beyond that, we'll discuss," Micah said. "Feel what I'm about to do, Dev. You have the power to do the same, most of the clan tigers do."

"I'm looking."

"With more than your eyes?"

"Of course," Dev said, as if you always looked with more than your eyes.

The black fur seemed to shrink, as did his body, and his skin rose through it all like a figure trapped in melting ice that just rose to the surface as the spring thaw freed it. Micah stood there nude and beautiful, with his dark brown curls cascading around his shoulders. His hair tie had gone with the rest of his clothes that were scattered ripped around the room. He blinked his yellow-green eyes at me, and I was relieved; for just a moment I'd worried that he'd keep his tiger eyes.

"God, you make it look easy," Dev growled, and then I felt his body run with heat. The fur didn't retreat as effortlessly as it had for Micah, but it was cleaner and faster than any change I'd ever seen from Dev. He swayed on his human feet, because rapid shifting between forms takes energy. Micah and I both steadied the bigger man.

Dev looked at Jean-Claude. "No fur here."

"I see that," Jean-Claude said, trying for a neutral voice but not quite succeeding. The fact that he couldn't control his voice meant something about all of this had hit either an issue or a potential happy spot; whichever it was, it moved him.

"The first night I came here, you put me with Asher while you and Richard took Envy. She's already dumped him, and you're not happy with her."

"She does not share well enough."

"She's a beautiful woman."

"She is."

"Most men are grateful that anyone that beautiful is with them."

"Beautiful men can be the same way, *mon ami*."

"Envy's never been with anyone who thought they were the pretty one in the relationship."

Jean-Claude gave that Gallic shrug that could have meant he agreed, or not.

"It's the girl rule," I said. "Never date someone prettier than you are. I broke it so long ago, I don't worry about it."

Dev smiled, hands still gripping us as he swayed slightly again.

"Maybe you should sit down," Micah said.

Dev gave a small shake of his head. "Envy thinks she's more beautiful than you are, you know that, right?"

I nodded. "She's tall, leggy, blond, and blue-eyed; of course she does."

"And that doesn't bother you?"

"Women have been doing that math on me all my life, I'm used to it."

"Modern American women seem to believe that being tall and thin is beauty, but I have lived in centuries when that was not so."

"But when she enters a room, heads turn and follow all that height and blondness," I said. "I've never gotten that same treatment just walking through a crowd."

Dev grinned. "Only because you're so short we can't see you over the crowd."

I gave him the look the comment deserved, but truth was truth.

"In a crowd we're invisible," Micah said.

Dev laughed and then swayed again. Jean-Claude moved a chair up and we helped sit him down. "How do you do this without feeling tired afterward?" Dev asked.

"I do rapid change better than most."

"You do, but damn, I feel shaky."

"You need to refuel."

"You mean eat something."

Micah nodded.

"But you don't?"

"I should, but I don't have to."

Dev looked back up at Jean-Claude. "You're in love with Anita, so Envy let that go, but when she realized you see so many of the men as more attractive than she is, that's when she couldn't deal with it."

"Has she looked at the men in our group?" I asked.

Dev smiled. "She's not used to having to compete with men and women for someone's attention, Anita, no matter how pretty they are, because you don't just value the men for their beauty—well, except for Asher maybe. For the rest you prefer men who hit the gym, and the only woman in your life besides Envy hits the gym as hard as the men."

"I'll never muscle up like Richard, no matter how much I lift."

"But you've got more muscles than most women, and a hell of a lot more than Envy."

"Why is it that most of the golden tigers learned to be good in bed and with fighting, but Envy and a few other men, and women, didn't?"

"Even among our clan not everyone is great at athletics, so we let people play to their strengths. Adam is an amazing lawyer, but I wouldn't trust his fighting skills. For some of the females of our clan, the legend says a new Master of Tigers, not a new mistress. I think Envy believed that just being a beautiful woman would win her points with the new master."

"What if he'd been gay?" I asked.

"I'm not the only one of our males who thinks men are cool."

I nodded.

The power was beginning to fade; we just couldn't hold it.

"Whatever we're going to do with this power, we need to do it, Jean-Claude. I think Dev's being tired is helping it fade."

"I know what I wanted to do with it," Dev said, "but I don't think I'm up to what I wanted to do earlier." He gripped our arms tight and looked up at all three of us. "But I still want us to raise the power and have sex later; I haven't changed my mind."

"We'd have to negotiate what you mean by sex between the two of us," Micah said.

Dev nodded. "I know, but if I can bring this kind of power to the table I want to have a serious shot at being the tiger you commit to."

"I understand that."

Jean-Claude looked at Micah. "You made your vote very clear earlier, *mon chat*, and it was not for Mephistopheles."

"For this kind of power, my vote could change."

"Such a very practical cat."

Micah nodded. "Usually."

"I'm sleeping with all of you, so sex with all of us would work, but we're talking about a lot more than just sex."

"That is true, *ma petite*; are you saying you have reservations about him joining us?"

"Nothing personal to Dev, but Micah expressed serious reservations just a little bit ago. I don't understand why he changed his mind this quickly."

"Power," Micah said.

I looked into his face and saw only certainty. "The power changed your mind?"

"The next time an animal group calls us to help them solve a problem, I might be able to do rapid shifting between forms and not have to fight, or seduce, or anything but show them that I'm more than just leopard. That's rare. It might be enough of a show of strength that there wouldn't need to be anything else."

The Coalition only traveled into other people's territory when they were called in by either the police or the shapeshifters themselves. Sometimes Micah was able to negotiate a peace between everyone, but more often the lycanthropes would handle things in private away from human eyes, and that usually involved a fight. Sometimes sex, but most of the time blood, injury, or death had to happen before the problem was solved, like with the lion pride on the West Coast that thought it could take over the local cougar group. Their feeble excuse had been *They're mountain lions, and all lions belong to us.* Forget explaining the biology that made cougars much closer to leopards evolutionarily, because it would turn out to be a love affair gone horribly wrong between the dominant female of the cougars and the Rex of the pride. Micah risked his life with every fight, and risked the females thinking the political seduction was actual seduction. One group's queen had tried to make Micah her long-distance relationship and even made noises about threatening me. If a little sex would keep him from having to fight shapeshifters twice his size I'd have been okay with it, but after that incident he'd been more reluctant to use sex as a bargaining chip.

If just changing shape like this could stop the fighting and the need for seduction, then . . . "The fights have been more serious than you've let me know, haven't they?"

"You and I are the same size, Anita. Speed, surprise, and utter ruthlessness are our advantages, but my reputation as a fighter has gotten around. They know most of my tricks and they usually outweigh me by a body weight. That wouldn't be so bad, but they're as trained as I am, or more trained, in fighting. No one wins every fight, Anita."

"So far, you have."

"So far," he said.

We gave each other some very serious eye contact, and he let me feel what he hadn't before, that he'd begun to worry about the fights, the same way Rafael the rat king was worrying. He gently closed that line of reasoning down, so I couldn't read his thoughts anymore. If I'd tried that I'd have shut down all the power flowing through us, but Micah was able to shut down parts without shutting off the whole. Only Jean-Claude was better at it. "That was Rafael's secret; please don't bring it up unless he tells you."

I hesitated and then nodded. "Okay."

"I won't tell either," Dev said.

We looked at him and realized that he was sitting there quietly, and probably peeking inside every thought we shared. The fact that neither of us had thought about that meant either we were more power drunk than we thought, or the power liked Dev so much it was smooth and didn't alert us.

"What of Asher?" Jean-Claude asked.

"Are you king?" Dev asked.

Jean-Claude went very still for a moment as if his whole body held its breath, and then he said, "Yes."

"Then be king," Micah said.

"*Ma petite*," he said, looking at me.

"When we raise the power again, touch us and see what happens. See if you can control it. See if you can control us."

"How could any man resist such a delicious challenge?"

"Don't resist," Dev said.

He gazed down at the man. "You must be very angry with Asher to suggest such revenge."

"Can't I just want to sleep with you?"

"*Oui,* but there is no one you could sleep with that would hurt Asher more than me."

The power was fading fast, but the flash of anger in Dev gave it one last boost, so that we were bathed in that invisible fire again. "You and Micah get more power than ever before, and Asher suffers the way he's made both of us suffer. It's a win-win."

"You cannot win such games with Asher, *mon tigre*, I know this for a sad fact. You can either be with him and tolerate him playing such games, or walk away; there is no middle ground with him."

"Besides, revenge sex is always a bad idea," I said.

Dev looked at me and put some of that heat into his eyes, so I got not just the power but a wave of his physical need. It made both Micah and me gasp. "I'll make it good for both of you, I promise."

He turned and looked at Jean-Claude. "For all three of you."

"You know, we might already have the power without needing to cement it with sex," I said.

Dev's hands gripped us so hard, it was just this side of hurting. "No, no, I won't be just tolerated on the edges of someone's life. We try, really try, and then if Micah can't deal with me that's one thing, but I won't be cast out without really trying first."

"You have tried very hard with Asher and it has not worked, *mon ami*."

"That's because it's Asher; he's like a rigged game, you can't really win it, can you?"

Jean-Claude reached out and touched his face, gently; the power curled over his skin and through all four of us, so that it suddenly blazed brighter again and left us all crying out with the rush of it. Jean-Claude drew back with a shaky laugh, his eyes ablaze with his own power, so that they looked like a midnight sky set with blue fire.

Dev swayed, even sitting down, and let us go. The moment we stopped touching, the power began to seep away. "I need food and rest, but after that I want a real chance at making this work."

"It will give us time to tell our other lovers that there may be a change of . . . menu," Jean-Claude said, voice still holding that edge of laughter he got when he was a little power drunk.

"If this works I won't just be food," Dev said.

"What are you saying?" I asked.

He held up his left hand and wiggled his fingers at me. "I want you to put a ring on it."

It was Micah who said, "If this works, you'll get your ring."

I looked at one of the loves of my life, who I knew wasn't comfortable around large athletic men, at all, and knew in that moment that the Coalition visits out of town had been dangerous. Dangerous enough that he was willing to tie himself to someone he could never love, someone that he would have to share me, Jean-Claude, and even Nathaniel with, and I knew he didn't want to do that. I hugged him hard, as if I couldn't press enough of him against me to be sure he was safe. He was startled, and didn't seem to know what to do as he hugged me back.

"Don't die on me; whatever it takes, don't die on me."

His arms tightened around me, holding me as tight as I held him. "Whatever it takes," he said.

"Whatever it takes," I whispered back.

"If there is anything this side of heaven and hell that I can do to come back safe, I will always come back home to you, Anita."

Suddenly having to tell Asher that we were borrowing his lover, or how it might mess up our domestic arrangements, didn't seem important; we'd deal, because the thought of how close I must have come to losing the man in my arms scared me more than anything else. Sex was not a fate worse than death, because with life there was always hope. Hope that the big breakup wasn't permanent. Hope that the issues that drove you apart might bring you back together again. Hope that you'd see their smile again, even if they were with someone else. Only death was final, and without hope; short of that, there were options. I buried my face in the sweet scent of Micah's neck, and I wanted those options more than anything else in the world.

25

ABOUT THAT TIME we got the text that dinner was ready; Micah and Dev went off to find fresh clothes. Jean-Claude went to explain why I needed a shower and clean clothes more than the men. I was never sure why the shapeshifter form that came out of the goopy stuff was always dry and clean, but it was, so both of the men just needed to wash off a few bits that I'd gotten on them, but they were pretty much clean. I, on the other hand, was covered in rapidly drying goop from nearly head to toe. Even my hair was stiff with it. It wasn't the first time I'd been slimed head to toe by having a wereanimal beside me, but every time was a new experience in needing to scrape it off in the shower.

In fact, the men in my life had requested that I not use any of the showers in the main bedrooms, because the stuff clogged up the plumbing. The group showers were large enough to satisfy any gym, and had mainly been created for the guards so they could clean up after hitting our specialized gym area that could accommodate the extra strength and speed of a lycanthrope. If I stopped up a drain in there, there were a dozen more showers that still worked in the line—though the people in charge of maintenance had given us little plastic signs to hang on any shower that had been used for tough cleanups; that way they knew where the potential problem might be and didn't get surprised.

Domino tried to follow me as a bodyguard, but I'd finally convinced everyone that if I needed guards down here in our inner sanctum we had other problems, so I got to walk to the showers alone. It was a relief in a way. I loved the men in my life, but sometimes a little quiet and solitude wasn't a bad thing.

There were two guards outside the locker room area leading to the showers. I recognized one of them, but not the other. "Hey, Benito."

"Hey, Anita."

Benito was tall, dark, and dangerous-looking. He dressed in nice, tailored suits most of the time, and the body underneath was in good shape, but he never managed to make me think handsome—sinister maybe, but not handsome. His dark brown eyes smiled at me, though, and softened his face. He'd moved up the ranks until he was the main bodyguard for Rafael the rat king.

"I'm assuming that Rafael is in the showers if you're here," I said.

"Yeah, he said he didn't want to be disturbed."

I sort of motioned at the mess of my clothes and hair. "Any way to get an exception?"

"You, Jean-Claude, Micah, and Richard are the exceptions. Rafael says that we can't keep the kings, or queen, out of their own stuff."

"Nathaniel isn't on the list?" I said.

Benito grinned, flashing white, nearly perfect teeth. My dad paid good money for my half-sister to have that kind of smile. Benito's face was pockmarked and rough; it always made me wonder if he was just one of those people who had a naturally perfect smile. I never asked, because I couldn't figure out how to ask about the nice smile without insulting the rest of him.

"He's a prince, not a king; no insult meant."

"None taken, so I can go clean up?"

He motioned me through the open doorway. The other guard just watched me with eyes so brown they were nearly black, but he said nothing. If Benito said it was okay, then it was.

There were small dressing areas with curtains if I'd wanted to undress in absolute privacy, but the locker room was empty and no one was getting in the door that I wasn't already sleeping with thanks to Rafael's men, so I stripped off in front of the lockers. I put my weapons in a locker, but the clothes had to go on the floor and stay there. Whoever did the laundry for us had complained that the clear junk could ruin certain fabrics, so please put it in with the other body-fluid wash. I grabbed a towel from the shelf, and the conditioners that Jean-Claude had made me keep down here for my hair, and went into the shower area.

I heard the water running and knew it had to be Rafael. If he'd just been one of the guards I'd have avoided him and showered around the corner, but he was a great deal more than that. What was protocol if you happened to know a king was in the showers? Did you avoid him, acknowledge him, say hi? He wasn't my king, anyway, but he was my friend, and occasionally my food. Since the way I fed on him was through sex, it meant we were a little closer than typical friends. He was probably the closest thing I had to a true fuck buddy. You know, you're in town, they're in town, and you hook up. I hated the phrase, but for Rafael and me, it wasn't inaccurate.

I stood there for a minute in the showers debating, and then I heard a small sound. It was a pain sound. I'd seen Rafael after bad guys had flayed the skin from his back. He didn't make sounds like that for nothing. My hands were full of hair stuff, so I kept the extra-long towel over one shoulder, where it nearly dragged on the ground. I was mostly covered, and that would have to be good enough for whatever was happening. The small, involuntary noises stopped as I looked around the open shower area. He wasn't in sight, but I could hear a shower still running, so it had to be one of the three private stalls that had shower curtains. I admit that I used them a lot when other people were showering after workouts. Shapeshifters don't have a problem with nudity, but I wasn't the only woman who didn't want to strip down completely with the guys in the shower, so we had the stalls.

I debated on whether to ask if he was all right, but if he was having a moment in the showers, he was entitled. The guy rule was that even if you were crying, the other men ignored it unless you said something to draw attention to it, but quiet crying, especially when you'd tried to get privacy for it, meant you left it alone. Women usually want you to seek them out and ask what's wrong; men don't, as a general rule. There are men who want you to ask, and women who don't, but the rule was true for most people I knew, so I left Rafael to fight his private battle and turned on one of the showers in the middle of the room. I could see if he opened the curtain and wanted to share, but otherwise he had his privacy.

I admit that it was a quick shower for more than one reason, just in case Rafael did come out and want to talk. The second round of conditioner that Jean-Claude had started making me let set in was irritating, but I admitted that my hair looked and felt better since I'd been doing it. I hate when the prissy stuff works so well. It makes me suspect that there's more practical use to all the pampering than I ever wanted to admit.

I was finally clean and dry and had put in the five, yes five, leave-in products that Jean-Claude had given me to use. I still wasn't as good as he was at working it through, but it was a start.

In the silence Rafael made a sharp sound, as if moving had hurt.

I couldn't stand it. "Rafael, it's Anita."

"I know your scent," he said, in a voice that was almost normal, and didn't match the sound he'd just made.

"Is there anything I can do to help?"

"You can't fight my battles for me, Anita."

I was outside the stall he was in, watching the water splash underneath the curtain. "I know that; the rats don't allow their king to substitute the way some of the other animal groups allow."

"We all appreciate that you study each of our cultures," he said.

I leaned my shoulder against the cool tile. "Is there anything I can do to help you right now? Just say it, tell me, and I'll leave you to it."

He was quiet for so long that I started to move away. He called out, "Pull back the curtain if you want to see the wound, but there is nothing you can do to save me from my own weakness."

I didn't know what he meant by that, but I set down the conditioners and shampoo and pushed the curtain open. He was kneeling on the floor of the shower, his hands spread on the wall as if to hold himself upright. His shoulders still looked strong, but they were bowed, the top of his short, black hair resting against the tile. The back of his body was the dark, smooth, muscled line that I remembered, except for the wound on his back. I stepped into the stall and knelt behind him.

"It's a puncture wound, but it's not like any blade I've ever seen."

"Nor I," he said in a voice that held the same edge of pain I'd heard in the small noises he'd been making.

"I thought you weren't allowed weapons when you were fighting for kingship of the wererats."

"We aren't."

"So he cheated," I said.

"Yes."

"He's dead, then," I said.

He ran one hand through his short hair, slicking it back, as he turned to look at me. His face was dark with high, square cheekbones. He was a handsome man. His Mexican heritage was printed on his face the same way some Irish bloodlines are, though Rafael was as many generations away from Mexico as most Irish Americans were from Ireland. Sometimes DNA just survives to remind us who we are.

"Cheating means his execution was a given, yes."

"What did he hope to gain?" I asked.

"My death."

I looked into solid brown eyes, so dark they were almost as black as his eyes in rat form. I touched his wet hair. "He can't be king if he's dead," I said.

"I suspect he was a sacrifice for someone else who would have stepped forward if I had died there."

"I thought you couldn't be king unless you killed the old one first?"

"Normally, no, but there are provisions in our laws for kings who die in battles that are outside leadership challenges." His shoulders convulsed, his head pressing against the tile again.

"Why haven't you changed form and tried to heal?"

"I did."

I reached out to the wound in his midback but didn't touch it. "It's as big as the palm of my hand still."

"I do not believe the wound size has changed."

"It should have, even if it was silver. You're too powerful to still be this hurt."

"I was too powerful, but even kings age and grow weak eventually, Anita. It is usually age, not lack of fighting skill, that slows us enough to lose the crown. The king I defeated was white of hair in human and rat form."

"You aren't old, Rafael." There was something wrong with the wound. It didn't look right.

"Older than I look," he said.

"What made this wound?"

"It was a four-sided blade, very wide as it went toward the hilt."

"Sounds more like a spearhead of some kind than a knife," I said.

"It was unique."

I got up and pushed the curtain back further so I could get more light directly on the wound. "He shoved it in and twisted it, or something."

"He broke off part of it into the wound. Their healer had to fish it out after I left the challenge circle."

I thought of having something that big shoved into my back, and then the wrenching strength used to twist and break off the blade inside the wound. The flesh inside the wound looked . . . burned. "You should be in that nice hospital area the wererats staff for the local lycanthropes."

"I cannot afford to let the others know I am weakening, Anita. I killed the one who did this, but if people realize I can no longer heal better than this, then there will be another challenger next week, or next month, but they will come like vultures to a wounded animal."

"So you came here so none of your people would figure it out."

"You and your kings are my allies. My being weak is a bad thing for all of us, so you will keep my secret until we can find a new king who would not be a disaster in my place."

"If you mean set you up to be killed by someone you want to be the next rat king, you can just forget that. I'm not a big believer in suicide."

He grabbed my wrist. "Anita, don't you understand? I am the king not of just the local rodere, but all the rats across the country. The group here, alone, is large enough to challenge almost every other shapeshifter group."

I looked into his almost desperate eyes and said the only thing I could. "I understand that, but I won't let you sacrifice yourself until we've exhausted all the other options, Rafael."

He knelt straighter, rotating his back so he could look at me more straight on, and the movement made him double up in pain, almost taking us both to the floor with his grip on my wrist.

"I need more light. There's something wrong with this wound."

"Do what you must," he said. He'd let go of my wrist and was just on all fours, letting his head hang down like an exhausted horse. I got his arm across my shoulders, my other arm around his body, being careful not to touch the wound, and helped him to his feet. He usually stood so straight, so strong, but now he stumbled and I held most of his weight for a second; then he fought his feet back under him and helped me get him out into the better lighting of the main shower area.

I debated on whether to make him walk to the benches in the locker room or just let him slide to the floor here, because standing wasn't happening unaided, and he wanted as few people as possible to see how badly he was hurt. I finally put him near a wall so he could lean on it, but he was back on his knees where he started. He was kneeling in a bright pool of light, though, and that was what I needed.

I could see the initial thrust of the weapon in the outer part of the wound. The edges had started to heal, but it was silver and there was only so much even Rafael's body could do. That wasn't the part of the wound that looked odd to me. It was deeper into the meat of his body.

"As deep as this is, it should still be bleeding, but it's not."

"Have I healed it, then?"

"The outer edges of the wound, yes, I think so, or your body is trying to, but deeper in the wound track it's like the flesh is burned. I'm not even sure that's exactly the right word, but *burned* is the best I have to describe what I'm seeing. We need a doctor."

"No." His voice was very final as he said it. I'd been in enough meetings with the leaders of the lycanthrope community to know that when Rafael said no like that, it was a decision, not a suggestion.

"Fine, but can I bring Micah down here to give a second opinion?"

He leaned his forehead against the tile as if just staying on his knees was effort. "Yes, I trust him as I trust you."

I had to go to the locker room to get my phone and call Micah.

His greeting was, "Nathaniel says dinner is getting cold."

"I need you down in the group showers. One of the shapeshifters is hurt and the wound looks wrong."

"We have a doctor on call for that. Anita, what aren't you telling me?"

"It's Rafael and he doesn't want the doctor to see. He says he trusts you, me, Jean-Claude, Richard, and the other kings and allies, but no one else."

"I'll be right there," he said, and the earlier slight domestic chiding was gone. He was all business. One of the things I'd always valued about him was how he let all the small stuff fall away and just concentrated on the important things.

I stayed by Rafael. He started holding my hand, squeezing occasionally from the pain, and reminding me just how freakishly strong he was. "If I hurt you, you must say something."

"Trust me, I will."

He shuddered again, his upper body arching toward the floor. His head touched my thigh, and I stroked his wet hair. "Stay down, it's okay."

"You mean lay my head in your lap and you will pet me?"

"If that will help, yeah."

He let his forehead rest a little more solidly on my thigh, hesitated for another moment, and then eased onto his side, his head cradled on my thigh, one hand in mine. When he'd settled as much as he could, I touched his hair and stroked it back from his face again. When he didn't protest, I kept running my fingers through his damp hair while he lay in my lap, huddled around his pain, his hand squeezing periodically against mine, as the pain spiked.

"Thank you," he said, softly.

"For what?"

"I trust Micah, Jean-Claude, and even Richard, but I can't allow myself to be this weak with them."

I tried to make light of it. "Oh, I don't know, I think Jean-Claude would let you put your head in his lap."

"Don't do that," he said.

"Do what?"

He moved his head enough so he could look up at me. "Discount something that is important."

I didn't know what to say to that, and fought not to squirm. "You're my friend," I said, finally. It seemed the wrong word.

"Do you let all your friends put their heads in your lap when you're nude?"

I hadn't felt naked until he remarked on it. I fought off the automatic embarrassment and said, "It's against the shapeshifter code to remark on nudity if it's not meant sexually."

"That is true, but though we are not in love with each other, nor dating, what we have is more than just friendship, Anita."

I looked away from the demand in his eyes but forced myself to look back when I realized how much I didn't want to meet his eyes. No cowardice in anything, large or small, because if you start flinching in small things, it can spread to larger ones. I needed to be brave for my job, and just for myself.

I studied the face of this strong, brave, honorable man and laid my hand against the side of that face. "Yes, more than friends."

He smiled, and that alone made it worth saying.

I knew Micah was near before he came into the shower rooms, though I wasn't sure if I'd smelled him, sensed him, or heard him; I just knew before he walked in the room that it would be him.

He hurried toward us, still dressed, which seemed odd enough in the showers that I wanted either him to strip down, or us to magically have clothes. He knelt down beside Rafael, hand going to the side of the wound in his back. It was big enough that he didn't have to ask where, or what.

Micah made a small hissing sound under his breath like a cat when it's startled. "Tell me what happened, Rafael."

He did, with me helping to expand the bare-bones story he told. "The wound looks burned or something—I mean it's deep and not healing, but it's not bleeding either. It should be bleeding, right?"

"Did their healer pack the wound?"

"Initially to stop the bleeding, but you know we can't leave it full of bandages."

"Yes, our bodies can heal the dressing inside us," Micah said.

"Why isn't this healing?" I asked.

A shudder ran through Rafael that made him squeeze so hard on my hand it stole my breath away. "That was a bad one," I said.

"I did not mean to hurt you," he said.

"It's just the pain seems to be growing worse, and it should be getting better, right?" I looked up at Micah for reassurance, or an explanation.

"Yes, it should be," he said. He put his hands on either side of the wound and peered down at it like I had earlier. "Maybe the healer left silver in you. I would like to search the wound, but it's going to hurt."

"Do whatever is necessary," Rafael said. He took a firmer grip on my hand and closed his eyes. I kept stroking his hair as if that would make everything better, but sometimes it's not about logic, just comfort. What comforts you is like emotions; they may not make any sense at all, but they're still true.

I watched Micah slide his fingers into the wound, though I could tell what he was doing from Rafael's hand in mine. He was silent in his pain now, fighting not to show how much it hurt even in his body movements. He was being stronger and more stoic in front of Micah. It was as if all his reaction went directly into his hand, so that he whitened his fingers gripping so hard. I gritted my teeth and let him hold on.

"There's something in the wound," Micah said.

"Silver?" I asked.

He plunged his fingers almost out of sight into Rafael's back. The grip on my hand made me have to say, "Ease up, Rafael."

"I am sorry."

"It's okay, I'm glad to be here, but you're so strong, just don't want to break a bone."

"Forgive me."

Micah said, "Fuck!" He almost never cursed.

We both looked at him as he jerked his fingers out of the wound and showed us the tips of his fingers. There was whitish-gray liquid on them, and the skin was blistering. He stood and turned on the shower next to us, running it over his hand.

"What is it?" Rafael asked.

"I'm not sure," Micah said, "but it's in the wound. Whatever it is reacts almost like liquid silver; you're never going to heal with that in there. None of us could."

"I should know what that is," I said.

"What do you mean, should know?" Micah asked.

"I've seen it before; I didn't know it did this to lycanthropes, but . . ." I took a deep breath and tried to dredge up the memory. "Vampires, it was supposed to kill them if you injected it into the bloodstream."

"What was supposed to kill them?" Micah asked.

"Silver nitrate," I said.

"I thought that looked more silver."

I shook my head. "People think that, but the silver liquid that beads up is mercury; they use that in movies, but in real life silver nitrate isn't as silver as that, and it doesn't bead up like mercury either."

"Did it work on vampires?" he asked.

"It worked, but it wasn't quick enough for the older ones, and a vampire can do a lot of damage to you in its death throes."

"How did it get in my wound?"

"Maybe it was in the blade when he broke it open inside you," I said.

"The healer would have seen it," Micah said.

"Unless she put the silver nitrate in the wound when she was supposed to be putting dressing on it."

Micah knelt beside Rafael again. "Did it burn when she dressed the wound?"

"Yes, she said it was a coagulant and antiseptic. The bleeding did stop."

"Because she burned the wound closed," Micah said. He turned to me. "Help me turn him so the water will flush out the wound."

We got him on his knees. I knelt in front of him, letting him put his hands on my shoulders, and steadied him as Micah turned on the water. It hurt at first, but as the water flushed out the poison he began to relax. The water ran for a long time before Micah was satisfied.

"How does it feel now?" he asked.

"Better, much better," Rafael said.

"Are the burned edges in the wound healing?" I asked.

Micah knelt down and examined the other man's back. "No, it's reacting like a burn on us. The healing just stops."

"I can't keep an open wound in my back forever," Rafael said.

"You don't have to, but making it so you can heal it is going to hurt a lot," I said.

He looked at me from inches away because we were both still kneeling on the wet floor. "How will you cure me?"

"If you get a limb amputated and burned at the same time, what do you do as a shapeshifter?" I asked.

His dark eyes studied mine, and then I saw him understand. "How much and how deep is it burned?"

"A lot of the wound and as deep as it goes into your back," I said.

"You're talking about cutting off the burned area so his body can heal the new wounds, aren't you?" Micah said.

"Yeah," I said.

"That's going to hurt more than just a lot," he said.

"Yep, but now we can get the doctor on call to do it."

"No," Rafael said in that so-certain voice.

"Yes," I said.

"No," he said.

"This isn't weakness on your part; no lycanthrope could heal this, Rafael. If you'd been weaker it could have killed you, but you were just too strong for the bastards."

"Is the pain making me miss your point?"

"Maybe, but this was a deliberate plot to kill you; the challenger was only one of the conspirators. The healer was at least his partner in crime, if not part of a larger plot."

"Anita is right, Rafael; only someone as strong as you could have survived this attack. If your body hadn't healed fast enough to keep the silver nitrate from entering your bloodstream, you might never have made it here alive."

"The healer must die for this," he said, at last.

"Yes," Micah said, "but first we need to find out if she and your challenger were the only ones involved in the plot. If it's a larger problem we need to know that."

"Yes, yes, of course, I think the wound is clouding my thinking."

"Pain will do that," I said.

"Let's get your guards in here to help take you to the medical area. I'll alert the doctor on duty."

"I need to give orders to Benito about the healer, before the doctor begins cutting on me."

"Agreed," Micah and I said together.

"Will you both help me give the orders needed? I want to make certain she is alive long enough for questioning."

"We'll help you give clearheaded orders," I said.

"Thank you, both of you." He hugged me and held his other hand out to Micah, who took it. Sometimes I wasn't sure if the sex I had with Rafael was really what made us more than friends; maybe it was the shared mantle of responsibility instead? Something about having people trying to kill you, and knowing that the three of us were on the short list of those we could trust implicitly, was a pretty good bonding experience. Uneasy lies the head that wears the crown, and all that jazz.

26

MICAH AND I stayed with Rafael long enough to see him safely with the doctor in the medical area we'd put in under the Circus. We had too many injuries that we didn't want to explain to a normal hospital, like Rafael's stab wound. Dr. Lillian had even found a painkiller that would work, briefly, on shapeshifters so he didn't have to feel every cut as she sliced away the damaged tissue and let the blood flow. Once it was just fresh wounds he'd be able to heal himself, maybe slower than normal because of what caused the damage, but he'd heal.

But before he let Doc Lillian give him the painkiller, he talked to Micah, Benito, and me. He set in motion that the healer who had done this would be taken, questioned, and eventually killed. That last part wasn't stated, but it was a given. You try to assassinate the king, you die; period. Regicide is just one of those crimes that has to carry maximum punishment to discourage anyone else.

Micah went back to see if there was still food for dinner. I went to get clothes, because even though most of the lycanthropes would have walked around nude if we'd let them, I just felt better with clothes on if it was normal, everyday stuff. Naked was for sleeping and sex. Nathaniel texted me that he'd saved me food. I'd stopped off at the locker room to free my guns, because now that I had belt loops and pants I could load up again. My good gun belt was tacky with the clear stuff that I'd washed off myself. I'd planned on cleaning the leather after my shower, but the next emergency had distracted me. I was debating on cleaning it before I went to dinner, which would mean I was unarmed but would give the leather time to dry out, when my phone rang.

I might have ignored it, but the ring tone was work, as in raising the dead, not catching bad guys. "I'm not working tonight, what's up?"

"Anita, it's Manny."

That made me pay more attention. He wouldn't have called without a good reason. "What's wrong?"

"I'm on duty tonight, so I'm watching the GPS on the zombies we have out."

"Zombie babysitting, better you than me."

"The zombie you raised tonight isn't at any of the addresses on the list of clients."

"Where is it?"

"Denny's."

"Denny who?"

"The restaurant," he said.

"You mean the zombie is at Denny's restaurant?"

"That's where the ankle GPS says it is."

"Shit, they can't take him to a restaurant. It's illegal to have a zombie inside a place that does food service. Health services will close them down for an investigation if they find out."

"I know."

"Of course you know. I'll call the client. Maybe they got the munchies and the zombie is sitting in the parking lot."

"Didn't they request hours to question this zombie for historical battles, or something?"

"Yeah, they did."

"Most of the ones that ask for that don't go out for munchies," he said.

"You're right. I'll call them, let you know what they say."

"Can't wait to hear this one," Manny said.

"Clients are weird," I said.

"Amen," he said.

"Thanks, Manny, I'll call you back." I hung up and called Mr. Mac-Dougal. What the hell were they doing at Denny's with my zombie?

MacDougal answered on the third ring. "Ms. Blake, what can we do for you?"

"The GPS on the zombie says you're not at any of your home addresses."

"No, we went out for food."

"And took the zombie with you; is it sitting in the car?"

"No, he's right here."

"Inside the restaurant."

"Yes."

"You're not allowed to bring zombies inside restaurants, Mr. MacDougal."

"Whyever not?"

"It's a health ordinance, something about rotting corpses near food."

"But Thomas isn't like that."

"Yeah, I do good work. Why did you take him to a restaurant? If you're done questioning him, then I can put him back in his grave tonight."

"He was hungry."

"What? Who was hungry?"

"Thomas."

"Thomas is a zombie, they don't get hungry."

"Well, he's done a very good imitation of it."

"What?"

"He's enjoying his meal, quite a lot."

"Zombies don't eat," I said.

"Would you just like to speak to him directly?"

"What?"

"Thomas, it's Ms. Blake calling to check up on us."

A man's voice, cultured, with a slight southern echo in it, said, "Miss Blake, I am told that I owe my adventure on this side of the veil to you."

My mouth was suddenly dry. I had to swallow before I could say, "Mr. Warrington, I hear you're enjoying your meal. What did you order?"

"A breakfast skillet, they call it."

"Yeah, they can be tasty." My voice sounded normal, but my pulse was fighting to speed up.

"I like this Coca-Cola very much."

"Me, too," I said. "Can you put Mr. MacDougal back on the phone, please?"

"And the phones, they are amazing. Whoever thought that I could be talking into this little box and you hear me miles away. It is a marvel."

"Yes, it is, just need to speak with Mr. MacDougal for a minute."

MacDougal came back on the line. "Isn't he wonderful?"

"Yeah, he is. Finish your meal, have coffee, dessert, let him get the full ride."

"We intend to."

"Great, maybe you can take him to someplace a little higher end tomorrow."

"Denny's was all that was open this time of night, near my house."

"Totally understand. I'll see you soon."

"Good night, Ms. Blake. This experience has surpassed our wildest expectations."

"Customer satisfaction is always a priority," I said, and hung up. I called Manny back.

"What did the client say?"

I told him.

"Anita, zombies don't get hungry, and they are incapable of eating. They don't have a working digestive system."

"I know," I said.

"It's one of the clients having you on, Anita. You couldn't have talked to the zombie. They answer questions, but not like that."

"I've had a few that could," I said.

"You didn't tell me that."

"We haven't been working together much the last few years," I said.

"Have you ever had a zombie that did this?"

"If you mean eat a real meal like a live human being, never, but I've seen zombies that got hungry."

"You never told me that either."

"I don't mean go-to-Denny's hungry, Manny, I mean flesh-eating zombies. You know some of the cases I've had. I didn't raise them, but I got to clean up the mess afterward."

"Do you think he's a flesh eater?"

"I think he's eating a skillet breakfast at Denny's and enjoying his adventure this side of the veil; his words, not mine."

"Hell, Anita, that's wrong, that's so wrong. He should not be that aware."

"I know that, I so know that, Manny."

"Pick me up on the way. I gotta see this zombie for myself."

"The office is on the way, see you in about twenty minutes. Maybe sooner if I hit the lights and sirens."

"This isn't police business, Anita; isn't that against the rules?"

"No one knows how a flesh-eating zombie starts out, Manny. Just in case it starts with wanting a nice meal at a sit-down restaurant, let's get there sooner rather than later."

"You really afraid the zombie will start rampaging through Denny's?"

"Yeah, aren't you?"

"Yeah, I am," he said.

"See you in twenty, or sooner."

"Make it sooner," he said.

"Lights and sirens it is." I took the time to put all my weapons on and grab my vampire-hunting kit, because it had the really big guns and scary shit in it. I'd fought flesh-eating zombies before; they were as strong as a vampire but didn't feel pain, which made them a whole lot harder to stop. I prayed as I ran for the stairs, *Please God, don't let him turn on them. Please, don't let him hurt anyone.*

I was calling the zombie a him, not an it; that was not a good sign. All the flesh eaters I'd seen had been truly walking corpses and hadn't looked alive at all, but there was always a first for everything. I did not want the very first gentleman flesh eater. I really didn't.

I made the mistake of telling the truth when Nathaniel asked why I was running out with my whole kit over my shoulder. Everyone insisted I take guards as backup, just in case. I didn't have time to argue, so Nicky and Domino were with me as I hit the stairs. Nicky had called ahead so that bigger guns were waiting for them in the storage room up top. Again, I didn't argue, because if the worst happened we were running out of time, and we'd need the firepower.

Why not call other police to meet us there? Because maybe I'd just raised a zombie so alive that he could eat a meal and talk about his adventure, and the only thing scary about him was that he was too human. I preferred that to him turning into a ravaging cannibalistic killing machine, but him being that alive scared the hell out of me, too. It was just a different kind of scared.

Nicky asked to carry my vampire-hunting kit. "You'll be faster on the stairs without it."

Normally I would have argued and carried my own damn equipment, but since it weighed almost as much as I did, I gave it to Nicky. He threw it over his shoulder. I started running up the stairs, and then the men were up with me, and the three of us fucking ran.

27

I CALLED MANNY from the car, and he was waiting for us outside work. He wasn't much taller than me, a slender, dark figure with salt-and-pepper hair standing under the streetlight. It highlighted him like a spotlight, ruining his night vision and making him a great target if anyone was aiming for him. He'd been my teacher in the early days of vampire hunting, but he'd never really stopped being a stake-and-hammer man, and that was only good for daytime vamps dead in their coffins, or morgue kills where the vamps were chained down with holy items. Outside those two instances I preferred shotguns or assault rifles, though handguns would do in a pinch.

There were cars having issues with parking, or not parking, in front of us, so we got to wait while we looked at Manny. I didn't think he'd seen us yet. He was talking on his phone.

"This is the guy who taught you how to hunt vampires?" Domino asked from the backseat.

"Yeah."

"He taught you how to raise the dead," Nicky said from beside me. "Edward taught you how to hunt vampires."

"Actually, the second part was a learn-as-you-go program," I said. "If I hadn't been good enough to bother with when Edward met me, he'd have just killed me."

"Edward is like one of your best friends," Domino said.

"We weren't always friends."

"Why didn't he kill you then?" Nicky asked.

"I was useful, and he saw some of himself in me, I think."

The people who couldn't drive in front of us finally managed to have one car pull out and leave, so the other could park. Manny finally saw us, waving and giving a bright smile.

"He needs glasses," Nicky said.

"How do you know?"

"He's squinting a little, and he didn't see your car sooner, so his night vision is going."

"You think that's why he's standing in the light?" Domino asked.

"Maybe; tell him to get his eyes checked," Nicky said.

"I didn't know you cared about Manny," I said, as I pulled up to the curb.

"I don't, but you do," Nicky said, opening the door so Manny could ride shotgun. "If he has a car accident or gets himself killed on the job because he's too vain to get his eyes checked"—he got out, poking his head back in to finish what he was saying—"it would make you unhappy, and I want you happy." He held the door for Manny, then moved to the backseat to sit with Domino.

I waited for Manny to buckle up, then introduced him to Domino as I hit the gas. I tried to see the man beside me not as my mentor and teacher, but like Nicky and Domino were seeing him. I'd seen him weekly for years and hadn't noticed the eye issue, but now that they'd pointed it out I wondered how I'd missed it.

"What's wrong?" Manny asked; he knew me, too.

I shook my head. "When's the last time you had your eyes checked?"

"Why?"

"You didn't see us until we pulled into the light, but we were sitting there for a while waiting for the idiots to finish arguing over the parking space."

"I was talking to Tomas; he's got girl trouble and wanted his papa's advice." He grinned when he said it, and I knew he didn't want to talk about his eyes anymore.

"How old is Tomas now?"

"Thirteen."

"A little young for girl trouble, isn't he?"

Manny grinned again. "He is precocious."

I smiled and shook my head. "You mean he's cutting a swath through the little girls the way you did before you met Rosita."

He shrugged but looked pleased. I let it go for now, and just hit the lights and sirens; one problem at a time, or you get overwhelmed. I drove fast and had to keep slamming on my brakes, because St. Louis drivers were slow to get out of the way. I'd had out-of-town marshals complain about it, so it wasn't just me.

"Jesus, people," I said, as I sat behind a line of cars waiting for them to creep to the side of the road.

"The zombie is still at Denny's," Manny said.

"Yeah, but is he just eating dessert or the waitress?"

"How likely is it that he's really turned flesh eater?" Nicky asked.

"Not likely, but since we aren't entirely sure what makes a zombie turn flesh eater, forgive me if I worry."

"I'm not saying don't worry, or don't hurry, just trying to get a feel for what I don't understand."

I slammed on the brakes as a truck tried to get out of the way of the lights and sirens by pulling out directly in front of me. "Idiot!"

"You drive, I'll talk," Manny said, and glanced back at Nicky as he started to tell everything we knew about flesh-eating zombies, which wasn't actually very much. "The most common cause of a zombie turning flesh eater is a murder victim called from the grave."

"I know murder vics rise with only one purpose, to kill their murderer; that's why police can't just raise the dead and ask who killed them."

"You've been asking questions," Manny said.

"It's the only way to figure stuff out if I can't do it myself, and I can't raise the dead."

"I like this one," Manny said to me. He got a death grip on the oh-shit handle, but his voice never wavered as I careened around yet another car that wasn't getting out of the way.

"Me, too," I said, and then went back to concentrating the hell out of driving.

"Thanks," Nicky said automatically, but I knew his face would match the tone; he said thanks because he was supposed to, not because it mattered to him. "But are you saying that murder victims attack and eat people, or eat their murderer?"

"Most of the time, no," Manny said. "They just rise willing to hurt or kill anyone who gets between them and their murderer. Until they get their vengeance, they don't obey the animator who raised them, or any other magic, but if they can't find their killer right away sometimes they turn to flesh eating."

I roared through a red light, flinching, hoping the cars all obeyed my lights and not the traffic ones. We got through safely, but it always freaked me out to run a red light. "It's like they wake up more the longer they're out of the grave, and if they start to eat flesh they don't rot as quickly," I said, risking a glance in the rearview mirror, so I could see Nicky's serious face.

"So do all murder vics who don't get their killers turn flesh eater?"

"No," Manny said.

"This zombie isn't a murder victim, though, right?" Domino said.

"No, I made certain of that. He died in his bed of disease, not in battle."

"Do soldiers count themselves as murder vics?" Nicky asked.

"I've known it to happen," Manny said, "but usually not."

"Manny taught me to be uber-cautious about shit like that, though."

"The most common flesh eater is a zombie that was an animator, witch, or voodoo priest in life," Manny said.

"Like you and Anita," Nicky said.

"Yes," Manny said, "which is why we both have legal papers in place to be beheaded and cremated upon death."

"Scary stuff," Domino said.

I slowed down and turned off the sirens. We were close enough to the restaurant that I didn't want to spook the zombie. He was far too aware for comfort.

"So this zombie isn't a murder vic, or a witch, or anything, so why is Anita so worried he'll start eating people?" Domino asked.

"Because zombies don't eat anything. They don't need to eat, because they're dead, and there's no reason to put fuel in something that isn't burning fuel anymore," Manny said.

I said, "Any time a zombie has ever said it's hungry, to me it's hungry for the flesh of the living. I've never, ever heard of one wanting to go out for a nice breakfast of sausage and eggs."

"So you're afraid when he finishes his food, it won't satisfy him and he'll turn on the people in the restaurant," Nicky said.

"Yes." I turned off the swirling lights on my SUV as I spotted the big yellow Denny's sign.

"Exactly," Manny said.

"So neither of you has ever heard of a zombie eating anything but people?" Domino asked.

"Yep," I said.

"Yes," Manny said.

"Okay then," Domino said, "I understand the rush."

"Do we start out with the shotgun and rifles?" Nicky asked.

I slowed down, easing through the last bit of traffic as I made toward the restaurant. Once I turned off the lights I was just another car and all the traffic laws applied to me again. I'd had some of the other regular cops explain to me that once the lights and sirens were turned off on an unmarked car, the magic get-out-of-my-fucking-way card vanished. Some people seemed to go out of their way to block you once the light show was over. It was like they resented it or something. It was hard to slow down after driving like a bat out of hell, but I'd learned that the other plainclothes cops were right, and people would get in your way just like now. It made me want to scream at the cars, but an accident this close to the goal would slow me down more than a little bit of traffic.

"No, we go in with just the handguns and what we have on us. Let's see if I can persuade the zombie to walk out with us; less chance of any innocent bystanders getting hurt," I said.

"Doesn't the zombie have to obey you?" Domino asked.

"Normally, yes, but if he goes flesh eater he won't obey anyone. I can probably hold him with will and magic for a few minutes; if that happens, then go to the car and get the big guns while I try to control the zombie."

"Combined we might be able to control the zombie longer," Manny said.

"We've combined powers to raise more and bigger dead, true, but I'm not sure how to combine our talents without a blood binding."

"If we think the zombie is dangerous, cut my hand under the table, or behind our backs, cut yours, and hold on," Manny said.

"That quick, no words needed, no circle of power?"

"I'm betting we can do it without anything else, just the blood," he said.

I nodded. "Okay, but only if the zombie doesn't cooperate."

"Of course."

"Do you want one of the shotguns if we have to use them?" Nicky asked.

It took Manny a second to realize Nicky was talking to him. "No, I'm not a shooter."

"If we have to shoot, then Manny's part is over, and he takes cover."

"And when we come back inside with the big guns, how do we shoot the zombie? I know it's different than shooting people," Domino said.

"Shoot the legs first," Nicky said, "so he can't run; if you don't have a good leg target take the hands and mouth, those are his weapons. Take the hands and the mouth and he can't hurt anyone, then shoot his legs so he can't run, and we move up on him and shoot him to pieces."

Manny looked from Nicky to me.

"It's not his first rodeo," I said.

"I was on the trip to Colorado, too," Domino said.

"You weren't with us in the morgue," Nicky said.

"You weren't with me in the graveyard," I said.

"I was protecting Nathaniel, Micah, and his family like I was or- dered to," he said.

"That's true," I said, as I finally eased us into the parking lot. I so wished I could give tickets out to people who swarmed in front of me as soon as the lights and sirens stopped. It would have been childish, but satisfying. It looked like a normal late-night Denny's with a few people at booths and tables; a waitress carried a full tray like nothing was wrong. Great; if no one was running and screaming for help, then the zombie was behaving itself. Once they take a bite out of someone everyone panics; same thing if you shoot someone, violence makes people react like prey animals. You hurt one and the herd scatters to save itself. It was so hardwired into all of us; only training would stop the reaction.

"So why do I feel like I let you down that I don't know this stuff?"

"This ain't the time, kid," Nicky said.

"We're the same age," Domino said.

"Only in years," Nicky said.

I parked in the handicapped spot, because it was the only spot open near the door, but I said a small prayer that no one who really needed it would pull up. I'd learned long ago that there but for the grace of a few injuries go I, or something like that.

I turned and said to Domino, "Either get out of the car and follow our lead, or stay in the car and out of the way." It was harsh, but I didn't have time for hand holding, and the fact that Domino didn't know that was one of the reasons he wasn't my first choice for marshal work, or a lot of other things.

His face said he was angry, but in that moment I didn't care. Manny was out on his side of the car. I got out of my side. Domino got out, too. I guess he wasn't waiting in the car.

28

WE WALKED THROUGH the door with me in my official Windbreaker, the one that read *MARSHAL* in big letters. If we had to pull weapons I wanted the civilians to know we were the good guys and not robbing the place. The jacket was harder to miss than a badge at my waist. People would also assume that everyone with me was a marshal, too, so it was easier to explain why most of the people with me were armed.

I let Nicky get the door, but he didn't hold it for me; he went through first, and then I came through, catching the door behind him. He was still technically my bodyguard and he could also take more damage than I could and keep moving, so letting him go through first just made sense. Manny came behind me, and Domino brought up the rear.

The hostess hurried toward us, her face worried. We just so looked like trouble. "Is everything all right, officers?"

I smiled as bright as I would at any client, and said, "We're just looking for some friends, need to touch base." It was vague but gave her something normal to concentrate on.

She nodded as if it made perfect sense, one hand smoothing her long brown hair back behind her ear. "Who are you looking for?"

Nicky shook his head. He didn't see the zombie, or the clients. I couldn't remember if Denny's took reservations, but I said, "It's a large party under the name MacDougal, or Willis."

She relaxed. "Oh yes, they're in the back. We needed one of the big tables." She grabbed menus as if we were staying for food. I didn't tell her different; I've found that if you can let people do normal things they're more comfortable around the guns and badges. It didn't hurt to give her the illusion that everything was normal—maybe it was, except for the zombie. If the health department found out about it, they would close them down until they sterilized the whole place top to bottom.

We followed the hostess to the back room with its bigger tables. It used to be where they sent smokers, but once you couldn't smoke inside anymore it just became more table space. I saw Owen MacDougal first; even sitting down he was the biggest guy at the table. I looked around the table for the zombie and didn't see the black suit jacket, just polo shirts, T-shirts, and the women in some blouses. Ethel Willis, the cow lover from earlier, wasn't with the group. Maybe seeing the cow slaughtered had been too much for her?

MacDougal raised his hand in greeting at me, smiling, and only when the man beside him turned and looked at me did I realize that was the zombie. They'd let him change clothes. I hadn't recognized him in the Ramones T-shirt. My heart just stopped for a beat; the fear went through me in a rush that left my fingertips tingling.

I swallowed hard and whispered to Manny, "Pick out the zombie."

"What?"

"Pick out the zombie."

Manny looked at me, but when I nodded him toward the group, he looked that way. I walked around the table to take MacDougal's offered hand. He was terribly pleased with himself. "Ms. Blake, I didn't expect to see you again tonight, and not in full marshal gear." A tiny frown touched his face. "Is everything all right?"

I gave him the full client smile, the one that actually reaches my eyes. "I was out on other business when I got the call that you were out at a restaurant, not a place most clients take, um, mutual friends, so I thought we'd stop by, see how things were going, since we were in the area."

One of the women at the table said, "Everything is great." She smiled and laid a hand on the arm near her on the table.

The zombie smiled back at her, damn near as warmly.

My phone binged, and I checked it. Manny's text read, "I can't tell."

I smiled into the face of the man that I'd raised from the dead and wondered, could I have told if I hadn't known? Would I have picked him out of the smiling, laughing group? I tried to see them with clear eyes, but I couldn't. I looked into Thomas Warrington's happy, alive face, and fought to keep the horror off mine. What the hell had I done?

The woman who touched him had long brown hair tied back in a ponytail. Her face was young and pretty, eyes a solid brown, but they were all alight as she touched the dead man beside her. I was engaged to a vampire, who was I to bitch, but the sight of her hand on his arm chilled me. I wondered if that was how some people felt when they saw me holding hands with Jean-Claude. I hoped not, because I was truly horrified as the zombie put his hand over hers on the table. Fuck.

I moved around until I was next to MacDougal, so I could lean over and talk low. I kept smiling and being pleasant as I said, "It's illegal to bring a zombie into a restaurant."

MacDougal turned and looked at me, face shocked. "I must really protest the word being used for Tom."

I smiled harder. "I understand that he passes for human, which is really cool, but legally if the health department finds out that a zombie has been in a restaurant, then they have to close the place down."

"But surely not in this case."

"I know that he looks good enough to pass, but the law doesn't differentiate between a rotting corpse that could potentially carry disease and . . . Tom here."

MacDougal looked around the restaurant. "I didn't know."

"If I'd dreamt you'd take the zombie out for a meal, I'd have mentioned it."

The zombie said, "Miss Blake, can I thank you again for this unexpected reprieve?"

I looked into his face, the clear hazel of his eyes, brown and green all mixed together. His longish blond hair looked freshly washed and dried. Had he showered the grave dirt off himself? If so, he was holding up very well; most zombies begin to disintegrate if you add water. "*Reprieve* is an interesting word."

"The appropriate word, though, I think, Ms. Blake."

I studied his face, and finally just looked into those brown eyes with their edge of green. I tried to see beyond the color, the smile, the energy, and into his soul, if he had one.

Manny came up beside me. "Anita, introduce me."

I introduced him to the ones whose names I remembered. The others offered their names. I threw Warrington in the middle somewhere, and Manny never blinked at him. It was only when he shook his hand that I saw Manny's shoulders shift, ever so slightly. I doubted anyone else noticed it.

Justine was the name of the woman who was holding hands with Warrington. Manny raised an eyebrow at me, widening his eyes a bit at them. I gave a small nod, letting him know I'd seen it. We'd worked together for years, so that was enough. Again, I doubted anyone at the table saw what passed between us. Nicky was the only one who might have followed it all.

I hadn't bothered to introduce Nicky and Domino. First, because they hadn't asked, and second, because you didn't introduce security. You wanted them to be grim and unfriendly; if you gave them names it humanized them and took some of the threat factor away. They were just waiting to be sent to the car for more firepower, or to go outside with the zombie and us, and for that they didn't need to be anyone's friend.

"Mr. MacDougal, Mr. Warrington, could I speak with you outside for a minute?" I was still smiling as I asked.

MacDougal got up immediately, but Warrington didn't. He put a hand over Justine's hand where it rested on his arm. It was a possessive gesture, and I didn't like it one little bit. Had they already done more than hold hands? God, I hoped not. There was no way for this to end that wouldn't be bad.

"Mr. Warrington, come outside with us."

"I'm fine here, Ms. Blake, or should I say, Marshal Blake?"

"Either will do, Mr. Warrington, but we really do need a few minutes outside to talk in private."

MacDougal touched the other man's shoulder and said, "Come outside, Tom."

He looked from one to the other of us, and finally stood up. It didn't seem to be because he had to obey either of us, but then I hadn't given him a direct order. I felt Nicky shift at my back like a small mountain flexing its shoulders, probably to get rid of built-up tension.

Justine stood up, wrapping her fingers through the zombie's hand. "I'll go where Tom goes."

"I don't think that's necessary," I said.

She wrapped her hand around her other one so she had a two-handed grip. "I do."

Warrington didn't shake her off, just stepped away from the table with her still clinging to his hand. "I would like Justine to come with us, if she wishes to."

She smiled up at him with one of those beatific smiles that usually requires serious dating, or good sex, or at least years of semiserious flirting. "I wish to."

I hoped she just had a crush on him. If it was more, she was going to have a very bad time, because Warrington was going back in the ground tonight. Whatever was happening with this zombie, I had to pull the plug as soon as possible. His finding true lust didn't change that.

Most of the rest of the group wanted to come, too. "We don't need a crowd."

They protested.

"If you make me wave my badge around I'm going to be unhappy with you."

Warrington turned to them all and said, "There is no need to threaten my friends. We will go outside and speak with you in private." His calm voice did what my threats couldn't.

Domino led the way, checking and holding the door like Nicky had on the way inside. Nicky brought up the rear this time. Our client, the zombie, and his girlfriend walked ahead of me. The guy who had been recording things at the cemetery with his phone now had a small hand-held video recorder. His name was Bob, and he followed us in case we did something worth recording. I'd let Bob come along for two reasons. One, his recording everything so the rest of the historical group could see it later helped them be happier with us going outside without them. Two, I was going to have to confiscate everything he'd recorded. Proof that I could raise something this lifelike could not get out on the Inter-net. I'd had a government element interested in me for raising a certain dead world leader, and that zombie had been much less alive than this one. If they saw this one, I'd be lucky if they didn't show up before the night was over. Keeping Bob close to me seemed like the best way to ensure I could bully him out of the "evidence" later.

We stepped away from the doors to find a little privacy near some shrubs, close enough to the light to not be in the dark, but Nicky, Domino, and I didn't stand under the light. Manny kept to the light with MacDougal and Justine. Warrington kept her hand in his, but he moved toward the shadows, so that their arms were held wide between them, as she tried to keep standing in the light the way modern women are taught to in a parking lot, and he tried to stay more hidden. Maybe it was being a soldier in life, or maybe it was the instinct of the dead to hide from the light. Or maybe I was being too poetic; I was so far out of my comfort zone I didn't know anymore.

I told the zombie what I'd told MacDougal, that the restaurant would be closed down and fined if anyone found out he'd been inside. "But Miss Blake, surely such laws are meant for those poor creatures that look like rotting corpses."

"How do you know what other zombies look like?" I asked.

He flinched a little, as if the way I'd phrased it bothered him. Justine stepped closer to him. "My new friends showed me images on their handheld devices."

I looked at Justine and Warrington, and Bob the tech guy.

"One of us said he didn't look like a zombie and he wanted to know what we meant," Bob said, shrugging.

"But look at me, Miss Blake." The zombie held out his hand toward me. "I am not like those poor creatures."

"You are a very lifelike zombie, if I do say so myself."

He frowned. "If the pictures and movies online are what I am supposed to be, then I am something else, Miss Blake."

It was really hard to argue with him as he looked at me, his face alight with force and emotion.

"However lifelike you appear now," Manny said, "it won't last."

"What do you mean, it won't last?"

Manny gave the zombie his best I'm-sorry-you're-grieving face. "No matter how alive you look and feel right now, you will begin to . . . rot, just like the zombies you saw on the Internet."

"I don't believe that."

"Of course you don't," I said.

"It is still true," Manny said.

The zombie frowned, and squeezed Justine's hand. "No zombie we saw on the . . . computer looked like me."

"Anita is a very, very powerful necromancer. I don't believe that anyone else could have brought you back in this state of completeness."

"Completeness," the zombie said, "yes, that's a good word. I feel complete and whole, and quite myself. Why am I not simply alive, rather than dead?"

"You're undead," I said. "It's not the same thing."

"You are engaged to marry a vampire, Ms. Blake. Is he any more alive than I am?"

I frowned at MacDougal.

"He had questions for us about how he got here, Ms. Blake. The Internet was the easiest way to explain, and when your name is typed in, the engagement story is the first thing to come up in the feed."

I sighed. "Of course it is."

"I ask you again, why am I not as alive as this Jean-Claude you love?"

Staring up into his so-alive face, I didn't have a good answer. Saying *Because you're not* didn't sound good enough, as he stood there holding hands with Justine.

"Because Anita isn't Jesus," Manny said.

"I don't understand what you mean by invoking our Lord and Savior," Warrington said.

"Jesus brought the dead back to life, but we can only raise zombies," Manny said.

The zombie shook his head. "Blasphemy isn't going to convince me that I am not alive."

"Isn't it blasphemy to think that I can raise the dead just like Jesus?" I asked.

"Lazarus was dead only a few days. You've been dead a lot longer than that, Mr. Warrington. Do you truly believe that Anita can do what our Lord and Savior never dared?"

Warrington, I mean the zombie, didn't have a comeback for that, but he was thinking of one when a funny look came over his face. He went pale, and then a little green, and then he stumbled to the bushes and started throwing up. He fell to his hands and knees, still puking up all the food and drink he'd consumed. Justine held his hair back for him, which meant maybe it wasn't just lust. You usually have to love someone to do that.

"Should have started with something lighter, like broth," Nicky said.

"What?" I asked.

"His digestive system couldn't take the heavy food."

"That's like treating his being dead for hundreds of years like he had the flu, or something," Domino said.

Nicky shrugged as much as the development of his shoulders would let him. "Why not?"

I didn't know what to say, so I turned to MacDougal. "And if he'd started doing that inside the restaurant, that would have been bad."

He looked very serious, and a little pale. "I see your point."

"What's wrong with him?" Bob asked.

"He's been dead for a few centuries," I said.

The vomiting had slowed down, and was into that dry-heaving phase. Justine asked Bob to go get some napkins from inside.

Warrington muttered, "What's wrong with me?"

"You're dead," I said.

"What does that mean?"

"The dead can't eat solid food," Manny said.

"I don't feel dead."

"I know, and I'm sorry for that," I said.

He blinked up at me. "Why are you sorry? This is a gift."

"Because it will make other things harder."

Bob came back out with napkins and the zombie wiped his mouth clean. Justine wiped the sweat from his forehead. Zombies didn't sweat. "What other things?" she asked, staring at me.

I debated on what to say, and how to say it.

Manny helped me out. "You've just seen his body reacting to food, but without being able to consume something he will begin to rot, Justine."

She shook her head over and over as if denying it enough would make it untrue. Warrington stood up and swayed. She reached out to steady him, and MacDougal came closer in case he was needed. It wasn't just Justine who was bonding with the zombie. Apparently Warrington was a very likable guy. This all would have been so much easier if he'd been a mean bastard.

"Is that what happened to all the zombies you have raised, Ms. Blake?" Warrington turned his now-pale face to me as he asked.

"All the ones that I've seen aboveground long enough have rotted, Mr. Warrington. Not just my zombies, but everyone's. There is no known way to keep the body intact once we raise a zombie from the grave. I'm sorry."

"I will end like one of those poor souls we saw images of?"

I nodded. In my head I thought about the female zombies in the FBI videos. They never looked this alive, though the soul capture was a way of preserving the body. But since I didn't have Warrington's soul in a magical container somewhere, that wouldn't help him. That thought led to one other: If it wasn't his "soul" staring back at me from his eyes, then what was it? My magic animated him, but was that what filled him with personality? I'd expected him to be able to answer questions about historical events, but this level of aliveness . . . I'd never seen anything like it. The zombies that Dominga Salvador had shown me years ago had looked alive, but the shell had been the most lifelike thing about them. They had still been zombies, standing around waiting for her to order them to do something. None of them had this level of . . . personhood.

"I would not want . . . Justine to see me like that."

She clung to his hand with both of hers again. "No, Tom, no."

He put his big hand against the side of her face and gazed down into her eyes with a look as real as any I'd ever seen. Shit, he was in there, really, truly in there. What the fuck had I done?

"I would not want to see this look in your eyes turn to horror as I fell away, piece by piece."

"I would never look at you that way."

"I have seen friends turned into horrors just by battle injuries, so that their sweethearts could not bear to look upon them. I would not have my last glimpse of you on this side of the grave be you turning away from me like that. I would rather remember you gazing up at me as you are now."

Justine turned to me. "How long?"

"How long what?" I asked.

"How long would he look like this?"

"It varies."

"What does that mean, it varies? Hours, days, what?" She came to stand next to me, her body nearly vibrating with emotion.

"Tomorrow he'll probably be about the same, but the day after he won't be. Sometimes the mind goes before the body, and that's a mercy."

"What do you mean, that's a mercy?"

"I've seen zombies whose body went before the mind, so they were trapped in a rotting shell, but totally aware and in there. You don't want him to go through that, you really don't."

She gripped my arm, and normally I would have told her not to touch me, or jerked away, but there was too much emotion in her. I understood some of the pain and it made me let her hold on to my arm. I'd have liked to think this was just a crush mixed with lust, but whatever it seemed like to me, it was more than that to her.

"That's not true, you're just trying to scare me."

"I swear to you that I am not lying about this. I have seen zombies rot in a lot of different ways, and it's unpredictable. I can't guarantee how it will happen for him."

"Darling girl," Warrington said, "you can't want to watch the process regardless of how it happens, and I do not wish to be trapped in a decaying shell while my mind stays intact."

Her grip tightened, her eyes almost fever bright. "But he'll be like this . . . intact until tomorrow night when you planned to put him . . . back, right?"

"Probably," I said.

She turned back to him. "We have until tomorrow night. I'll call in sick to work."

I didn't know what to say to that, but Manny did. "No, Justine, he has to go back tonight."

"No!"

I decided for partial truth. "Are you hungry again, Mr. Warrington?"

He said, "No," and then stopped. A look I couldn't quite follow came over his face, and then he nodded. "I am. Ravenous."

I nodded. "I was afraid of that."

"Afraid of what?" Justine said. "Everyone gets hungry."

"People do, zombies don't."

Her face lit with a smile. "Then Tom isn't a zombie; see, I told you so."

"There's one kind of zombie that feeds, but cooked meat and coffee doesn't satisfy them."

"We should have done soup, or something, like the other man said. It was just too heavy a meal for him tonight," Justine said.

I shook my head. "There's only one kind of zombie that eats things."

"Tom's kind," she said, and went back to holding his hand.

"Flesh-eating zombies," Manny said.

"What are you talking about?" MacDougal asked.

"It's very rare, but an occasional zombie rises with a craving for human flesh," I said.

"That's ridiculous," MacDougal said, "movie nonsense."

"I wish it were, Mr. MacDougal, I truly do, but I've seen it. I've hunted them down after they started killing, and helped destroy them."

Justine clung to Tom. "You're just trying to scare us again. Everyone knows that's not true."

"Did you see the news reports from a few months ago out in Colorado?" I asked.

"That was a flesh-rotting illness, not real zombies," she said.

"There was a disease, but there were also real zombies involved. They were all flesh eaters."

"They were all just the walking dead; none of them were as alive as Tom."

She was actually right, but I needed to win this argument. "He didn't say he was hungry, he said he was ravenous."

"What?" she asked, as if the topic had changed too fast for her.

I looked up at the tall zombie. "Tell her how you feel. How hungry are you?"

He frowned at me, and seemed to think about it. "I feel empty, as if I'll never be full again. It's like this pit inside me needs filling, and . . ." He stared at me. "What is a flesh eater, Ms. Blake?"

"It's a rogue zombie that attacks and eats the flesh of the living."

His nice hazel eyes widened. "Are you saying that I could go mad and attack Justine, and my other friends?"

"There's enough left of you inside your head right now that you might attack strangers at first, people you don't have an emotional attachment to, but eventually you'd be a danger to everyone." In my head I thought, vampires and wereanimals will go after their nearest and dearest first, usually because of proximity, and some vampires are attracted to people they love when they first wake, thirsty for blood. I didn't add any of that, because it would just muddy the waters and I did not like how Warrington was describing his hunger. It sounded too close to bloodlust, or the flesh craving that new wereanimals get. It's a hunger that must, MUST, be satisfied.

"'Tom would never hurt me," Justine said, wrapping her arm around his waist. She fit under his arm the way so many men seem to prefer, though she was tall enough that her head still came up over his shoulder, which made her about five-eight. She was taller than I'd thought, or maybe she just seemed smaller; whichever, they fit together like a jigsaw puzzle when you find the corner pieces and can finally start making progress.

"Everyone thinks that about the people they love," I said. "Trust me, supernatural hungers don't care about emotions."

She hugged him tighter. "I don't believe that."

"Why is a vampire able to control his craving for blood enough to be a legal citizen, but zombies cannot?" Warrington asked.

"Zombies eat the flesh of living, screaming bodies. Vampires sip a little blood from two fang marks. They can't even drink enough blood at one sitting to kill a person. Zombies seem to consume more than a human stomach can hold at just one sitting, and before you ask, no one knows how that works. Zombies seem to have lost that part of us that lets us know we're full."

"Like that one genetic disorder?" Bob the camera guy asked.

I nodded. "Yeah, Prader-Willi syndrome. Zombies are eating the living, but same principle."

"How did you know about Prader-Willi syndrome?" MacDougal asked.

"I know things," Bob said.

MacDougal and even Justine looked at him.

He looked a little embarrassed and said, "*CSI* had an episode about it."

MacDougal nodded as if that he believed. "Is there no cure for this hunger?"

"For zombies, eating the flesh of the living cures it until the hunger hits again, but I don't think Warrington wants to start eating people."

"No, I do not. It is not a choice that any man should have to make."

Maybe it was just a longer way of saying no, but something in the phrasing made me look at him. He met my eyes, and when I said, "Can I have a few minutes in private, Mr. Warrington?" he nodded.

Justine had a death grip on his arm. "Whatever you have to say to Tom, you can say to me." She was pretty much repeating his own words from inside the restaurant back to me, but this time he patted her arm and said, "Miss Justine, there are some topics that aren't meant for a lady. Ms. Blake here has seen things that most grown men couldn't have handled from what I saw on the . . . Inter . . . web. I'd rather we just talk soldier to soldier for a few minutes."

She protested, but in the end she let him put her in the girl box, and we stepped away from the others. Nicky started to follow, and I shook my head. Manny gave me a look that offered to come with, but I shook my head at him, too. I was hoping that Warrington would be more honest with just me, and I needed honest right now.

I put him so his back was to the group so they couldn't see his face. I was sure I could control my expression, but if he looked stricken then

Justine would hound him for why he was emotional, and that wouldn't go well for either of them.

"It's just us, Mr. Warrington, so I'll ask the question and you'll be honest with me."

"I will do my best," he said, his slight southern drawl coming out under stress. The fact that this stressed him more than waking up as a zombie said something about the topic.

"Did you consume human flesh when you were alive?"

"We were trapped in the mountains by an early blizzard that blocked the pass, and then true winter fell upon us. I was young and inexperienced, and it was only after we were well and truly trapped that the senior officer admitted that we had started too late. He thought we could make it out before snow, but that once we were delayed we were there until they found us in the spring. We were able to trap and hunt meat for a time, and we had melted snow to drink, but in the end the animals fled the heights and it was just our small group up on the mountain."

I watched his face, though he'd looked away into the distance so he wouldn't have to see the look on mine. I gave him blank cop face, because I'd learned that people will tell you their horrors, but you can't be horrified by it. You have to be their blank witness, because what they fear most is that you will see them as monsters, or broken, if you know the deepest, darkest stuff in them. I tried to make sure that this man I'd called from the grave wouldn't feel more of a monster than I'd already made him.

He was quiet so long I had to prompt him. "What happened then, Mr. Warrington?"

"We ran out of food, and the snow was ceaseless. It was like being buried alive." He laughed then, but it had more bitterness in it than sweetness. "And then Charlie died. We put him out in the snow to preserve him, but some predator that we'd missed in our hunting found him, dug him up, and ate part of him." He looked at me then. "Have you ever been hungry, Ms. Blake?"

"If you mean starving, then no."

"That is a blessing for you, then."

"It is," I said.

"I'd known hunger as a child, but not like this. My stomach didn't hurt anymore, there was no ache of emptiness. It was almost peaceful. We were starting to sleep whenever we stopped moving; even talking became too much. We'd be talking to each other and suddenly drift off in midsentence. It was as if we were already partially dead and the sleep was merely a preview, but then we saw Charlie all torn up and . . ."

"You saw meat," I said.

He wiped a hand across his face, the broad shoulders rounding, and I realized he was crying softly, silently, so that he could only nod. He finally mumbled, "God forgive us. God forgive me."

I almost said what I was thinking, which was, *You've already died once; whatever God thought of your actions has already been decided*, but I didn't. I so did not want to have a discussion about theology with someone I was going to put back in his grave tonight, because if his soul was here in him, then had I just dragged him out of heaven, or rescued him from hell? Or, if you believe in reincarnation, how could I possibly have ripped him out of whatever body he was currently incarnated in? It was all beyond my pay grade as a Christian. I needed to sit down with my priest and see if he was open-minded enough to talk about it. Or someone's priest. There had to be some clergy somewhere that I could talk with about all this. I prayed that I'd find the right person to discuss things with, and added an extra prayer that I'd be able to do the right thing by the man, or zombie, standing in front of me.

He was looking at me now with tears still wet on his face. "Your silence speaks volumes, Ms. Blake. I understand your disgust with me."

"It's not that, Mr. Warrington; I'm just thinking about other things a little too hard."

"You do not have to save my feelings, Ms. Blake. I deserve whatever you think of me."

"It's not my job to judge your ethics, Mr. Warrington. I have too many skeletons in my own past to be high and mighty about anyone. I've never been that hungry in my life; who am I to judge you?"

"You are very understanding, Ms. Blake. I am most grateful."

I shrugged. "I do my best."

"I believe that you do."

I smiled. "You described yourself as ravenous right now, Mr. Warrington. How does that compare to the hunger you experienced in the mountains that awful winter?"

He thought seriously before answering, which I appreciated. "I feel empty. My stomach is beginning to hurt, with that ache you get when you've gone too long without eating. It's early stages, but I shouldn't be feeling this way with everything I ate tonight."

"You threw all of it up," I said.

He shook his head. "It's not the same thing as going hungry, Ms. Blake. My body should know it ate tonight, and it doesn't seem to have counted any of that good grub I just had."

"I'm afraid that there may only be one kind of food that fills the needs of your body now, Mr. Warrington."

"You mean human flesh," he said, voice serious and low.

I nodded. "I'm afraid so."

He frowned just enough to wrinkle the skin between his eyes. "Do you think it's because I ate it in life that I've risen like this?"

"Honestly, I'm not sure, but I think so."

He smiled at me, the tears still drying on his face. "Thank you for admitting that you don't know for certain. I do appreciate that level of honesty."

I shrugged again. "I think you deserve it."

"You feel guilty about me for some reason."

I nodded, not even arguing that he was right. "I think I shouldn't have slaughtered the cow to raise you. I think it helped boost my power too much and here you are so very . . . alive-ish."

"I feel alive."

"I know."

"If I had been able to keep my food down and eat like a man, would you still have to put me back in the ground?"

"I don't know; technically yes, but honestly, I don't know. It doesn't matter now."

"Because I can't eat food like a man and I'm still hungry, so very hungry."

I nodded. "Yeah."

"You have to put me back before I try to hurt anyone, Ms. Blake."

"Yeah, I do."

He nodded, then straightened his spine all the way up, so his posture was military straight. He tugged the T-shirt down as if it were a suit coat. "Do I need my old clothes before we do this?"

"Again, honestly I don't know."

"Better safe than sorry," he said.

"Yeah, let's get your clothes."

"They put them through a dry . . . cleaner."

"I'll have MacDougal call and see if we can pick them up."

"If they aren't ready to go?"

"One problem at a time."

"Very true, very true." He looked down, gave that little frown again, and then gave me very direct eye contact from those hazel eyes of his. "I never found the right girl when I was alive, but I believe Justine would be that girl. What does it mean that I had to die and come back to find someone that I loved?"

This question was soooo above my pay grade. "I don't know what to tell you, Mr. Warrington, except that we don't plan who we fall in love with, it just happens."

"Justine has spent her life studying the past. She feels more at home with it than current reality."

I nodded. "I figured something like that, and here you are a true blast from the past."

"Blast from the past?"

"It's a saying, just something old, like a song you haven't heard in a long time, or a trend in clothing."

"Ah," he said. "Well, then I am truly a blast from the past."

I smiled at him; I just couldn't help it. He seemed like a nice guy. I really didn't want to see what would happen when the hunger gnawing at his gut overrode all that niceness. "I can give you a few minutes with Justine."

"Would it be safe to have some true privacy with her?"

I debated and then went for truth. "I don't know; maybe. How much privacy were you wanting, and for how long?"

"I'd love to have all night, but you have to put me back in my grave before dawn."

I nodded. "I do."

"Would it be possible to have an hour?"

"I'm going to have to be blunt here, Mr. Warrington, and I'm sorry for that."

"You raised me from the grave, Ms. Blake; surely we can be blunt with each other."

"Are you just planning to talk for an hour, or have sex?"

He blushed. Zombies didn't blush. Fuck. "Well, that is indeed blunt, Ms. Blake. I think I am shocked."

"Sorry, but I feel responsible for you, and that means whatever you do with Justine is kinda my responsibility, too."

"Would it be so wrong?"

"I can't answer that, but I know that if a woman gets pregnant by a vampire over a hundred years old, then you can have birth defects, things wrong with the baby. So I'd need to know to keep an eye on Justine, if anything happened."

He nodded. "I could not leave her with child and me dead; it would ruin her."

I didn't bother explaining the change in morality, because it wasn't ruining her morally I was worried about. It was more the thought of the baby being part zombie. I couldn't even imagine what that would mean for the child, or Justine.

"Justine did mention there were ways to prevent such things."

"There are, but they aren't a hundred percent reliable."

"Blunt for blunt, Ms. Blake; do you have . . . intimate relations with your vampire fiancé?"

I nodded. "I do."

"Aren't you afraid of the very thing that you fear for my lady?"

"Yeah, but we take precautions and so far, so good."

"Then isn't it a choice for Justine and myself?"

I rubbed my temples. I was getting a headache. "I don't know, I just fucking don't know."

"There is no reason for such language from any woman," he said, and he was genuinely outraged. It made me laugh; I couldn't help it.

"I am sorry that I shocked you, and I will watch my language in the future, Mr. Warrington."

"I truly do not see the humor in a woman, a lady, using such language."

"I suppose you don't, but . . . I will refrain from using that word in front of you again."

"Or in front of Miss Justine."

"Of course not in front of her," I said, and managed to keep a straight face. I cussed like a sailor, but no need to tell the zombie that.

"I am asking you for time to be with the only woman I have ever loved."

"You just met her tonight."

"Have women ceased to believe in love at first sight?"

"I believe in lust at first sight, Mr. Warrington, but not love."

"You are very cynical for a woman. I suppose it is being a law officer that has done it."

"I was cynical before I put on a badge, but yeah, most police officers end up pretty cynical."

"It is a sad state of affairs if a beautiful woman doesn't believe in love at first sight."

"You're a romantic, Mr. Warrington."

"Most gentlemen are, Ms. Blake; we just hide it better than the gentler sex."

I wasn't sure women had ever truly been the gentler sex—it depended on how you defined *gentle*—but I didn't argue with him. I just wanted time to discuss the moral implications of Warrington and Justine with Manny before I said yes or no. It wasn't the romantic in me; it was the fucking guilt. I'd raised him from the grave and Justine was in love with him. There was no Hippocratic oath for animators, but it seemed like I'd broken some rule somewhere. I just wasn't sure what rule, or when it broke. It was just all so fucked up in ways that I'd never imagined. I called Manny over to me; Nicky and Domino trailed him and I didn't tell them to stay back. Warrington went to hold hands with Justine while I tried to decide what was the lesser evil. Or hell, if it was evil at all.

29

"YOU CAN'T REALLY be thinking this is a good idea," Domino said.

"I didn't say it was a good idea."

"Anita, you can't let the nice white-bread girl have sex with a zombie," Manny said.

"What does her ethnicity or lack thereof have to do with anything?" I asked.

"It's not her ethnicity, Anita, it's that she's never had a bad thing happen to her."

"You don't know that, she could have a tragic past."

"Look at her, Anita, she's nearly thirty and still shiny." All four of us turned and looked at Justine, like one of those movie takes where everyone looks and tries so hard not to look like they're looking that it's painful. She was gazing up at the zombie as if he were the most wonderful thing in the world, but that wasn't it. Her brown hair was straight and untouched by chemicals, skirt not too short or too long. Her blouse was long-sleeved with a little frilly collar; her shoes were sensible pumps. But it wasn't the clothes either. I'd known people who dressed like that who actually had had horribly tragic childhoods, or old romances that had needed police to save the day. I couldn't put my finger on it, or list the reasons, but Manny was right.

Justine looked at us and said, "What's wrong?"

"Nothing," I said, and we all looked away at once, which wasn't suspicious at all.

"See, white bread," Manny said.

"I get it, she still has that new-car smell," I said.

"Yes."

"How do people get that old and be that . . ." Nicky groped for a word.

"Untouched," I offered.

"Fresh," Manny said.

"Innocent," Domino said.

"Yeah, that."

"I don't know," Domino and I said together.

"Dominga Salvador's sister was like that," Manny said.

"Was, as in past tense?"

He nodded.

"What happened to her?" Domino asked.

"She fell in love with a man she thought was the moon and stars. We all liked him, too."

"Your voice has that bad sound to it."

He nodded again, face very solemn. "He ended up beating her; by the time Dominga got her away from him they had two boys. The oldest is just like him. There's something wrong with him."

"Has he hit any of his dates yet?" I asked.

"I lost touch once I left Dominga's circle, but her sister remarried a nice guy from all accounts."

"How do you know that there's something wrong with the boy then, if you lost contact?" I asked.

"I watched him from a baby, Anita; he's not right. He's never been right. That's not going to change. Men like that are attracted to girls like that."

"The crazy bitches are attracted to the male equivalent," Nicky said.

Manny and I nodded.

"Bad boys and girls either like the good boys and girls, or people as bad as they are," Domino said.

"Agreed; now what are we going to do about Justine and the love of her life?" I asked.

"Anita, he goes back in the grave tonight; you can't let this girl carry the memory of the one perfect night with her forever."

"She knows he goes back in the grave tonight, so it won't be perfect. It'll be sad and full of her knowing this is the only time they'll ever have together."

"It's like *Romeo and Juliet* stuff," Domino said.

"Girls like her eat that tragic shit up," Nicky said.

"Anita," Manny said, "someone like her could take the tragic romance of tonight and live on it forever."

"Is that bad?"

"No man will ever be able to live up to the romance of this, Anita. Either she'll never date again, or she'll compare every man to this, and every other man will lose."

"Why will they lose?"

"Because she'll build it up in her mind until it was the perfect sex, the perfect man, and if they had been born in the same century then they could have been perfectly happy."

"You sound like experience talking again," I said.

"I had a good friend in high school, Maria. She lost her first love in a car accident. She married and had children, but her husband is still fighting the ghost of that perfect love thirty years after they married, and thirty-two years after the boyfriend died. I knew Ricky, he was a good guy, but he wasn't all that Maria remembers. I've always felt sorry for Carlos, because he's still fighting the perfect boyfriend who will forever be young, handsome, and perfect."

"You have two stories that are perfect for this moment?" Domino said, and let the suspicion be thick in his voice.

"Hey, I'm in my fifties looking at sixty; you learn a thing or two just by surviving this long."

Domino smiled. "Okay, I get that."

"Some people are stupid and mean if they live to be seventy," Nicky said.

"Or a hundred and seventy," I said.

We all just nodded and agreed.

"But I'm not one of them, or I try not to be," Manny said, "and what happens tonight could mark this woman forever."

"You think I'm being stupid to not just say no."

"I think you're letting your guilt and fear override your common sense," Manny said.

"What he said," Domino said.

"And I think you need to let the woman decide for herself," Nicky said.

"You're a sociopath," Domino said. "You don't give a damn for her feelings, or how her life will turn out."

Nicky shrugged. "True, and not true."

"What's the not-true part?" Domino asked.

"I don't care for this particular girl's feelings, but she's older than any of us, except Manny."

"She's over thirty?" I asked.

"Thirty-four."

"You asked."

He nodded.

"So what's your point?" Domino asked.

"She's thirty-four, that makes her old enough to decide for herself. Fucking a zombie no matter how alive"—and he made little quote marks with his fingers—"wouldn't be my idea of fun, but what if she spends her life pining for the dead guy, so what? She'll have had one night of absolutely Shakespearian-level tragic love, which is more than most people ever have."

"That is both one of the most cynical things I've ever heard, and the most romantic," Domino said.

"It can't be both cynical and romantic," I said.

"Why not?" he asked.

"So, I'm a cynical romantic?" Nicky asked.

Domino seemed to think about it, and finally nodded. "Yeah."

Nicky grinned. "I like it."

I rolled eyes at both of them.

Manny looked thoughtful.

"What if you tell Justine everything you just told us, and Warrington, too?" I asked.

Manny raised his eyebrows. "Good idea, but she won't believe me. No one ever thinks they'll make the same mistakes everyone else does."

"All we can do is try."

"Besides, if she's a die-hard romantic she could build not having sex into this great love affair that never happened, and compare all the other guys she dates to that, and then the men really would be screwed, because the only thing harder to compete with than a tragic lost love is a tragic lost love that never actually happened. Fantasy is almost always better, to a certain kind of person, than the real thing."

We all looked at Nicky; even I was surprised. "Wow," Domino said, "that was like really smart."

"I thought sociopaths couldn't understand emotions," Manny said.

"Sociopaths spend their lives studying people, because we have to imitate things we don't understand, or feel, to blend in. It makes us some of the most observant people on the planet. We have to be or people figure out what we are, and I'm pretty sure centuries ago they killed us, or put us in charge of killing people."

Manny made a *hmm* face and said, "Okay, let's talk to Justine and Warrington."

"You know, you both call him by his name now," Nicky said.

Manny and I looked at each other. "Creepy, isn't it?" I said.

"Oh yes," he said, "very."

Manny and I went to give all the warnings to Justine and the zombie, knowing full well what she would decide. Sometimes you can't save people, and sometimes they don't want to be saved.

30

WE HADN'T COUNTED on Warrington's sense of honor. He didn't want to leave the only woman he had ever loved haunted like that. "Show her that I am a zombie," he said at last.

"What do you mean?" I asked.

"If I am truly what you say I am, then shouldn't you be able to order me to do things and I will have no choice but to obey?"

"You get that from the Internet, too?"

"Yes," he said, with no hint that he'd heard the sarcasm. I guess he hadn't been exposed to modern culture long enough to know that people could lie, and frequently did, on the Internet. Of course, in this case it wasn't a lie; fancy that.

There was a tiny part of me that wondered if Warrington really had to obey me like other zombies. I think part of me was beginning to think of him as a person, and not undead, or at least not a zombie. Sometimes doubt can undo your abilities. It's like if you don't believe you can, you can't, or something like that.

I pushed the unhelpful thought away, and just believed. I wasn't just an animator; I was a necromancer, which was a whole new level of power. I'd raised the zombie, which meant I could control it, period.

I closed my eyes and breathed in and out, slowly, letting the tension, the doubts, everything slide down into the ground, away from me. Grounding, Marianne, witch and my metaphysical teacher, called it. You could air, instead of ground, but that usually needed wind for me to do it. Ground and center, she had said over and over, until it was almost automatic for me.

When I opened my eyes I was calm again, and I could look at Warrington without the guilt and all the emotions getting in my way. He was warm to the touch now; so what? He could love again; so what? I looked at him not with my eyes, but with that part of the brain just behind them where you can see dreams. I didn't usually "see" auras around people, but I could "feel" energy around them. I brushed my abilities over the waiting group and found the humans warm; Nicky and Domino's energy was warmer still, and Manny's energy was cooler. An ability to work with the dead leaves its mark like a kiss from the grave on our energy signatures. I couldn't see my own the way I could see other people's—most practitioners couldn't, Marianne said—but she'd told me my energy could be very cool, like no other human she'd ever touched. I let my power trail over Warrington, and his energy was very different. It wasn't just a trace of the grave, but as if the lightbulb of his aura were going out, not like death, or not like he was injured and dying, but . . . He wasn't as alive as everyone else, because he was the undead. He was a zombie, just a zombie, a really good and high-functioning one, but still it was my power that animated him, not that more divine spark that filled the living.

It was impressive as hell, but in the end I could feel what he was, and it wasn't alive. I had no idea how I'd brought this much of his personality back, but it didn't matter in the end. He wanted me to prove to Justine that he wasn't alive; I could do that.

I used what Nicky had started calling my command voice and said, "Thomas Warrington, come to me!" I held out my hand.

Justine shivered and held on to his arm. "Don't do it, Tom, don't go."

He frowned at her and then at me. "I seem to have a choice, Miss Blake."

I shook my head. "If I'm nice about it, you have some choice, but I don't have to be nice."

"I don't understand what you mean by that, Miss Blake."

"I know you don't."

Justine wrapped herself around him, hugging him tight, making him look down at her. "She may have raised you from the grave, but something else happened when we kissed for the first time. You get warmer every time I touch you."

"Romantic wishful thinking, Justine," I said.

She turned and looked at me, eyes a little wild. "No, no, it's not. His skin gets warmer every time we kiss, or hold hands. I'm not making it up." She went up on tiptoe and offered her lips to him.

He hesitated, looking at me. I nodded, and only then did he bend down to her. I didn't think he was a zombie looking for permission, but just Warrington wondering if it was still all right, with my magic creeping over their skin, because I knew he felt it, and her reaction let me know that Justine was feeling some touch of it.

They kissed and I looked with power, not my eyes. Energy flared between them so that his glow went from a pale, almost invisible shine to a flare of scarlet. When they parted from the kiss his energy stayed brighter, and so did hers. It was as if she gained power from it, too, but then maybe we always do from love, or even lust. If we didn't gain shared energy it wouldn't be so addictive.

She turned to me. "See, see, he's more alive every time."

I couldn't even argue with her, because I'd seen it. "It doesn't matter," I said.

"We love each other! How can that not matter?" She walked toward me, and the moment she let go of his hand his energy faded again. Whatever was happening between them was temporary.

"Take his hand again," I said.

"What?" she asked.

"Take her hand in yours, Tom."

He reached out and did what I asked, but again I didn't think it was because he was obeying me; he wanted to touch her. His energy sparked again, not as much as it had when they kissed, but it was there. He was gaining something from her.

"Let go of her hand and shake hands with Mr. MacDougal."

He hesitated, but let Justine go and reached out to the other man. MacDougal hesitated, too, but shook hands with him. Warrington's energy brightened, not as much as it had with Justine, but it was there, a little boost. That was very interesting and totally shouldn't have been happening. Zombies didn't care if you touched them, but then normal zombies didn't care about anything; they just obeyed orders, or answered questions when asked. Whatever kind Warrington was, it was something different, maybe something new. I wondered if anyone else had raised a zombie that gained energy from human contact. I knew a few animators in the business that I trusted enough to ask, but that was for another night. Tonight had enough weird without borrowing.

"You can stop shaking hands; thank you both."

"See, see, you thanked them both, even you think Tom is a person."

I looked at the woman and understood some of the demand on her face, in the tension of her body, her hands caught somewhere between fists and claws ready to scratch. I wondered if she even knew that she was getting ready for a fight; probably not. Fight-or-flight can affect people oddly, if they're not used to the reaction.

"He is the most alive zombie I've ever raised," I said, but my voice was still calm and unemotional. It was a headspace similar to the one I'd used in college when I was getting my biology degree and doing my senior project. You record what your test subjects do; you don't anthropomorphize them. I was looking at them all with a dispassionate distance that was part of the scientific mind-set, and a little bit socio-pathic, but then what is either but a lack of emotional projection? One is so you can record events without editorializing, so the data is as pure as possible, and the other is so you stay sane while the bad things happen.

"He's a man, not a zombie!" she yelled at me.

We'd taken long enough that some of the other history lovers had come out to stand near MacDougal. "What's going on?" they asked. "Why is Justine upset?"

I could answer that last one, because I was about to be the villain in her tragic love affair. To be fair I was also the fairy godmother who had used magic to make her wish come true, but magic is like a gun some-times, neither good nor bad, but capable of doing both.

"Thomas Warrington, come to me," I said, and held out my hand again.

He started moving toward me immediately, but there was no tug along the line that bound us. I could feel my power in him, as if even if he tried to run away I'd still be able to track him without the GPS on his ankle.

Justine grabbed his arm. "No!"

Bob told the others, "Blake is going to put Tom back in the ground tonight."

One of the other women said, "We paid to have him until tomorrow night for questioning."

MacDougal said, "It's all right, Iris; Ms. Blake and I have discussed things and circumstances have changed."

"Is it because Justine and he are boning?" one of the younger guys asked. The rest of the group immediately turned on him with looks that said, *Way to overshare.*

One issue at a time. "Come to me." He did what I wanted and finally touched my hand. God, he was warm. Zombies weren't supposed to have body heat like this; they just weren't.

"You can't take him away, you can't!" Justine grabbed his other hand while I was still touching him. The energy spiked, but this time I wasn't just seeing it from a distance. It ran through me from the hand touching him, and thrilled through my body like a rush of electricity and power. It upped my energy just like it had Warrington's. I realized I could gain energy through him the way a vampire does from a human servant, or in my case a vampire servant to my necromancer. When the servant fed, you gained energy. It had begun as a way for vampires to travel long distances without having to take blood and be discovered on the ship, train, or however they were traveling. The servants ate, and that was enough energy to keep the vampires going until they could feed on blood.

Warrington looked at me and said, "What is that? What is happening?"

I didn't really want to explain out loud. I'd discuss it with Manny in private, but not here with strangers who were probably not going to like me very much by the end of the night. Justine swayed on her feet, and I realized that once I knew I could feed on her energy I'd opened the channel wider and was drinking her down faster through my zombie.

I let go of him, and Justine fainted. He had to catch her, or she'd have hit the parking lot hard. "What's wrong with her?" her friends asked.

Warrington looked at me as he held her in his arms like a child, or a romance heroine. "What have you done?"

"We. What have we done," I said.

"Did I help you hurt Justine?"

I nodded.

"How? What did you do to me? I would never deliberately hurt her."

"I believe that, Warrington, but you don't really get to choose."

MacDougal was beside them, touching Justine's cheek. "She's cold and clammy to the touch. She was fine a few minutes ago."

"Is it what happens if you sleep with a zombie?" Iris asked.

It was a good question, and in fact it was pretty clear that Justine had slept with one of my zombies, and recently, but out loud I said, "If I'd dreamt any of you would sleep with the zombie, I'd have warned you."

"Dear God," Warrington said, "what have I done?"

"So you've already had sex with her," I said.

He looked embarrassed, blushing again, while Justine kept looking pale and wan. "Yes, yes, God help me, I was weak, and now I have hurt the one person in this world I never wanted to harm. I thought I could be . . . modern, but lust is punished just as much here as it always was for the woman." He hugged her to him and said, "I am so sorry, Justine, so sorry."

"Will she be all right?" MacDougal asked.

"If he stops touching her, she should recover, but I'll want to check back with her in twenty-four hours just to make certain."

"Are you saying that his just touching her like that is hurting her more?" Iris asked.

"He's taking energy from her, that I know."

Warrington went down on his knees with Justine still clasped in his arms. He kissed her gently on the cheek, then slipped her into the arms of MacDougal and the woman, Iris. "Tell her I never meant to hurt her, and that I am more sorry than I know how to say."

"I will," MacDougal said.

"Time to go," I said.

Warrington stood up, glancing at the love of his life one more time, then turned and came to stand beside me. "Put me back where I belong, Ms. Blake, before I hurt someone else."

"That's the plan, Mr. Warrington, that's the plan."

The four, now five of us got into my SUV and left the history group clustered around Justine. If someone called 911, I wondered what they'd tell the ambulance was wrong with her. Zombie love? It made me smile, until I saw the grim look on the zombie's face. Did I tell him that it was my fault Justine had fainted? Was it? Or had he taken too much energy when they had sex? He and Justine had lied to me earlier when we talked about them having sex again tonight. Was it a lie by omission, or directly? I couldn't remember their exact words, but either way he'd known I'd be upset, or maybe he'd just tried to be a gentleman. They didn't kiss and tell.

"Justine should be fine, Warrington. She just needs time to rebuild her energy."

"Are you certain she will be all right?" he asked from the very backseat.

Was I? Manny answered for me. "She'll be fine, Warrington."

A tension went out of the zombie's face and shoulders. I exchanged a look with Manny in the front seat. He knew that neither of us was sure that Justine would be a hundred percent. We'd never had a client that boned one of our zombies before. It made me wonder about the men who were screwing the zombies on the Feds' sex tapes. Were the men feeling drained like Justine? Was the animator who raised them gaining energy from it? Maybe there was more than one reason for someone to turn zombies into sex slaves. Was it for power as well as profit? I didn't know, but I knew one thing: I needed to watch the videos again, but this time not as a cop, but as a necromancer. I needed to look at the images with power, not eyesight. I'd try to find out how much Manny had seen with his own power of what just happened. If he'd sensed enough, I'd ask the Feds if he could watch the tapes with me. It was either Manny or try to make friendly with fellow animator and U.S. Marshal Larry Kirkland. We'd started out friends—hell, I'd trained him as an animator and vampire hunter—but we weren't buddies anymore. He thought I was a monster who killed too many and too easily, and I thought he was weak and didn't kill easily enough to do our job. I wasn't the only marshal who thought that about Larry. He'd gotten a reputation for not being a shooter. It made other marshals with the Preternatural Branch not want to work with him. Every time someone requested me over him, he resented me more. But if I needed someone to watch the videos for raising magic, Larry was good. Truthfully if he went all out he could raise more zombies in a night than Manny could.

I still hoped the Feds would work with Manny, or let me show him the videos. The thought of watching sex videos this hardcore with Larry, who was a right-wing, squeaky-clean, vanilla kind of guy, was just . . . awkward.

31

BUT FIRST WE had a very special zombie to put back in his grave. I'd called MacDougal from the car and found that Warrington's clothes weren't going to be ready until tomorrow, something about the older fabrics and not knowing how to clean them safely. I asked Manny and he thought it should be fine to put him back in the new clothes.

"You don't think the clothes are like pieces of the body can be sometimes?" I asked out of earshot of the zombie in question.

He shook his head. "The missing pieces are only for raising a zombie, and only for low-level animators who need all the parts to raise a body. It's one of the reasons they can't raise older bodies, because too much has turned to dust. They need solid bits to work with; you never have."

"It never occurred to me: Do any animators need all the parts to put a zombie back in the grave?"

"I've known a few who couldn't lay the zombie to rest if a hand had rotted off and was lost, but I always wondered if it was really a problem, or if they just thought they needed all the parts."

"You mean they believed they couldn't do it without the missing part, so they couldn't?"

He nodded. "I've been called in on a few cases where the animators were powerful enough to do it, but they still couldn't."

"You think they psyched themselves out," I said.

"Yes."

"So, if I don't worry about the clothes, they aren't anything to worry about?"

"Exactly."

I frowned at his logic, but in the end I wanted Warrington below-ground enough to try. He stood on his grave in a T-shirt advertising music that he had probably never heard, and a pair of jeans that whoever had lent them to him would probably miss, but it wasn't my problem.

Traditional wisdom was that you needed salt, steel, and will. I'd learned that the most important part was sheer force of will, but tonight I went old-schoolish, because I wanted to be sure that this zombie went quietly back to rest.

The blood circle had darkened and was smudged in places. "The circle isn't intact anymore," Manny said.

I looked at the ground, and he was right. The blood circle was there, black in the grass, but it was seriously smudged in places, and nowhere near complete.

"I don't really need it to put him back; it's only in raising the zombie that the circle matters to me."

Manny raised eyebrows at me. The look was enough to let me know he did need the circle to lay his zombies back. I forgot sometimes how little we'd worked together over the last few years. Once he took himself out of the vampire execution side of things, he and I had very different dance cards for work.

"Maybe an intact circle for laying the zombie to rest is like the missing body part; you only think you need it," I said.

He grinned at me, smile bright in the darkness. "The student be-comes the teacher."

I smiled back and shrugged.

"What do you need, then?"

"I've done it with just will and word, but tonight—" I lifted a con-tainer of salt and the machete still sheathed out of the nice leather bag. Every time I used Jean-Claude's gift I knew it was just a matter of time before I got something bloody, or worse, on the nice leather, but I'd use it until I ruined it. Sometimes nice things don't last long, but they're pretty while they do.

"You don't need another sacrifice?"

I shook my head.

"I should shadow you one night when you're on the job. I think you've changed a lot of the rituals I taught you."

I shrugged again. "I've streamlined some."

"It's all right, Anita. I knew you were a more powerful animator than I was the first week I took you out with me."

I let him see that he'd surprised me. "You never told me that."

"I didn't want you to get a big head about it, or put too much pres-sure on yourself as a new animator. I knew you'd figure out just how powerful you were."

"It took me a while, but yeah, I guess I did."

Domino called out, "Anita, you might want to get over here."

The tone in his voice was enough to make us turn and look toward him, Nicky, and the zombie by the graveside. Warrington was still standing on the grave nice and passive, but something had spooked Domino, and Nicky was standing ready, like he expected to be using the handgun at his side.

I handed the machete and salt to Manny and reached into the back for the shotguns and the AR.

"Why are you getting the big guns?" Manny asked.

"Not sure, but I trust my guys." I put the AR in its tactical sling over one shoulder and carried a shotgun in each hand, and headed for them. Manny came behind with the salt and steel I'd need to lay the zombie, but right that moment the guns meant more to me.

I heard Warrington say, "I'm so hungry, so hungry."

I handed one shotgun to Domino, kept one for myself, and tossed the AR to Nicky. He caught it and stepped a little away from the grave. I'd have preferred him with me for the close-in work, but he was a better shot with the AR than Domino, and they could both handle shotguns just fine. Honestly, I might have been the best shot of the three of us with the AR, but I couldn't back off the grave and let them take the close-in part. It was my zombie, and I wouldn't let them take the bigger risk.

I snugged the shotgun to my shoulder and got a bead on one of the zombie's knees. Yeah, a head shot would take away his ability to tear with his teeth, but I'd had enough large men run into me and just the force of that could hurt; take out one leg and he'd have to crawl to reach us. Crawling gave you more time to pick your shots.

"How hungry are you, Mr. Warrington?" I asked, voice very, very calm, as if I weren't standing beside Domino with both of us pointing shotguns at him.

"Famished," he said.

"As hungry as you were in the mountains that winter?" I asked.

Domino didn't react to the question, which probably made no sense to him at all. He just kept his position and his aim, and did what I needed him to do. I didn't have to look behind us to know that Nicky was doing his part. I trusted him to have our backs, absolutely.

"Yes, and no," Warrington said. His face wasn't as human as it had been. The flesh seemed to be thinning down, so you could see the bones of his face, almost as if he were starving right in front of our eyes. His body was consuming its own flesh, so that the skeleton was beginning to show underneath the skin. I never seen anything like it, but then he'd been a surprise from the start.

"Explain what you mean, Warrington; how can it be yes and no?" I asked, and realized I'd taken my eyes off targeting his knee so I could see his face when he spoke. I went back to watching the target I'd chosen, but it was hard not to watch his face.

"I don't feel as hungry, but I'm looking at your two men here and I see them like I saw Charlie after he died."

"You see them as meat," I said, resettling the shotgun to aim at his face. I had to watch him talk; it was almost a compulsion. Those nice hazel eyes, grayed in the dark, were rolling in their sockets, because the flesh had receded enough that they weren't secure. What the hell was happening to him?

"Yes, they're meat, but I don't see you that way. Why do you still look like a woman that I should take care of and help out of carriages? The men are worse than any enemy on the battlefield to me now."

"You mean you hate them more?"

"No, but I don't see them as the same as me, as men. They're just something I want to tear into and devour. I've never even looked at a cow and thought these terrible things, and I do like a nice steak, but this is something far worse, Miss Blake, far more terrible than butchering a steer."

"I understand," I said, voice soft.

"Do you? Then please explain it to me, because I am mystified that I could look at another man and think such terrible thoughts, and be filled with such horrific longings." He looked at me with his eyes beginning to roll wildly in their sockets. He was having more trouble controlling the muscles that moved his eyes as the flesh that held them in place wore away.

"You're becoming a flesh-eating zombie, Mr. Warrington."

"I am so glad that you took me away from Justine before she saw me like this. Thank you for that, Miss Blake."

I was glad he hadn't been alone with her when the change came over him, because what I was seeing now would eventually tear her throat out while she screamed for help. I'd seen zombies do it before, just never talked to them while they lost their senses and became a ravening thing.

"Let me put you back in your grave, Mr. Warrington."

"Please do, Miss Blake, and hurry, before I give in to these terrible images in my mind."

Nicky asked, "Do you mean you have pictures in your head of what you want to do to us?"

"Yes."

"Are they your thoughts, or is someone putting them in your head?"

"I do not know, but even speaking with you now, it's as if my pork dinner were talking back. I'd think I was mad, but I still want to eat it."

"Eat me, you mean?" Nicky said.

"Yes, very much." The southern drawl was thicker with every word, as if by the time he rushed us, or we shot him, he'd sound like Scarlett O'Hara.

"Interesting, Nicky, but save it," I said.

"There won't be a later for asking him questions."

He was right, of course, but only a sociopath could have stood there this close, watching the process, and asked the questions that might help us understand what was happening. It was good that we had Nicky with us, because I was so spooked my mouth was dry.

"Manny," I said.

"I'm here," he said from behind us. He sounded a lot farther away than Nicky, but he was unarmed, so I was okay with that, but now I needed him.

"I need you to get some salt ready to throw and unsheathe the machete."

"Okay." I felt the machete's blade bare like a thrill of energy through me. I trusted that the salt was in his hand.

"Ready, Manny?"

"Ready," he said, and just from his voice I knew he was much closer to me, just behind me.

"With salt, steel, and power, I bind you to your grave."

Manny threw a handful of it in the zombie's general direction. I wasn't sure it actually hit him, but it touched the grave; I hoped that was enough. Manny started to come up beside me with the machete naked in his hand, but I told him, "Don't cross in front of the guns." He moved back without arguing.

"I still want to eat them," the zombie said, and now he looked like the corpse he was; the handsome man who had wooed Justine wasn't there anymore.

"No, you will not harm them."

"I want to obey you, Miss Blake, I truly do, but I'm so hungry, and they're so close."

"Do not move off your grave, Warrington."

"Again, I want to obey you, but only part of me does; the other half wants fresh, bloody meat between my teeth."

"I bind you to your grave, Thomas Warrington!" I let my voice fill with power so that it echoed through the trees around the grave.

He struggled to leave the grave, but it was as if some invisible force held his feet in place. His long arms lashed out trying to touch Domino, but he couldn't reach him without taking at least a few steps and I had bound him to his grave at last.

"Go back to sleep, Thomas Warrington; go back to your grave and walk no more!"

The ground underneath his feet began to flow like mud and thick water, sucking his legs down like movie quicksand. "No! I must feed! Don't put me back with this hunger in me, Ms. Blake! Please, don't put me back like this!" He screamed as the earth swallowed him up. The last thing I saw was his eyes, wide and terrified. That wasn't supposed to happen either.

Then the grave was smooth and hard as if the earth had never been disturbed; that was the only thing that was normal about what had just happened. "Fuck," I said, and that one word seemed to hold all the emotion that I hadn't let myself feel in the last few minutes.

"Anita, you have to get an order of exhumation," Manny said.

I turned and stared at him. "What?"

"You have to dig him up."

"We barely got him covered before he went berserk," Domino said. "Let him stay in there."

"He should have gone empty and quiet before the grave swallowed him. He was still struggling, Anita, he was still aware. You can't leave him down there awake and trapped."

"Maybe he's just dead, just bones and dust again," I said.

"Maybe, but if he's not, would you really be able to rest knowing he's down there forever trapped and starving?"

I closed my eyes and said a silent prayer for strength and patience, and just help. "Motherfucking son of a bitch." God is okay with me cussing; if He weren't He'd have stopped listening to me a long time ago.

"I know what you're feeling," Nicky said.

"Because you can feel it, too," I said.

"Yep."

"Then you know what I'm going to do."

"We have to dig him up."

"Unfortunately, yes."

"You mean like with shovels ourselves?" Domino said.

"No, legally we need an exhumation order now, and honestly I'd rather be using a backhoe than have anyone close to the coffin with a shovel."

"You just raised the man as a zombie; why not do it again?" Domino asked.

"Because then I won't know if he's alive or dead down there, and that's what I need to know."

"Okay, I get that, but how do we get an exhumation?"

"We need a judge," I said.

"What are you going to tell the judge?" Manny asked.

"I don't know."

"What do you mean, tell the judge?" Domino asked.

"We have to give a reason that we want the body exhumed," Manny said.

"I don't suppose you can tell the truth."

I just looked at Domino.

Nicky said it. "Do you really want Anita to tell a judge she raised a flesh-eating zombie and now she wants to make sure it's not trapped undead in its grave?"

"It wasn't technically a flesh eater. It just wanted to eat flesh," Domino said.

"Oh, that's much better," Nicky said.

"Enough," Manny said. "We need a judge and a favor."

"I know who to ask for a favor, and I'm hoping he knows a judge, because I don't know one who would sign off on this for me."

"I can't think of a lie that would work to get us an exhumation order for a grave this old," Manny said.

"Me, either." I rested the shotgun on my arm, dangerous end pointed at the ground, and got my phone out with my other hand. I couldn't leave Warrington down there undead, aware, struggling, starving, afraid for all eternity. There wasn't a sin bad enough to put someone through that kind of hell, and Warrington had seemed like a good man. He so didn't deserve this.

"Who are you going to call?" Nicky asked.

"Zerbrowski, he owes me. I just hope a judge owes him, or he knows someone else who owes him a favor who knows a judge." His number was in my favorites list. I let the phone dial it, and prayed that someone I knew, knew a judge.

32

"TELL ME AGAIN why I'm awake and in a cemetery at the ass end of night?" Zerbrowski asked, as he stood beside me in the dark listening to the backhoe drive closer through the headstones.

"Because you love me like a brother," I said.

"I never had a brother, and I like you better than I like my sisters, though if you tell either of them that I'll deny it."

It made me smile, which was probably why he'd said it; he was good that way.

Manny stepped closer to us as the backhoe got nearer and noisier, and said, "I'm afraid it's my fault, Sergeant Zerbrowski. Anita brought me in to consult, and I was the one who thought the zombie might be trapped down there."

"Explain how a zombie can be trapped in its grave again?" Zerbrowski asked.

I answered, "I told you that this zombie didn't go down like the others. Their eyes should be dead again, just corpses that lie down and wait for the grave to swallow them. This one was afraid and screaming. He went under the ground begging me to save him; I've never had a zombie do that."

Zerbrowski blinked at me behind the faint glint of his silver-framed glasses. "And you're afraid that this one is alive down there, but trapped."

"Not alive, but undead and aware and trapped."

He looked at Manny as if for confirmation, and the other man nodded.

"I'd hoped I'd dreamt that part of Anita's phone call," he said, shoving his hands deep into the pockets of his slacks. He'd apparently put them on over his pajamas, or at least he'd kept his pajama top on instead of getting a shirt, unless he had shirts with little trains all over them. I wouldn't put it past Zerbrowski, but I knew his wife, Katie, would have made sure the shirt "disappeared" out of his wardrobe. They'd been happily married for a couple of decades, but she lived in hope that she'd get his clothes down to things that would look good no matter what he grabbed. I was pretty sure it was a vain hope, but I'd seen the choo-choo pajamas before at late-night crime scenes. Though I guess technically this wasn't a crime scene.

"You know that just adding a tie to the train jammies doesn't fool anyone, right? We still know it's jammies."

He grinned. "Hey, I put on a tie and a suit jacket."

I shook my head at him.

Domino came up to us. "They're asking if they can move the headstone, or if that will mess up what you need to learn from the zombie?"

I shook my head. "They can move it. They just need to be careful not to damage it out of respect for the family, not out of worrying about the zombie."

"I'll tell them," he said, and hurried back through the tombstones toward the waiting men. He still had the shotgun over his shoulder, like I had mine in its tactical sling. Before we got the grave dug out, I'd be loading up on all my gear in the back of the truck, which would put up my customized AR and leave Nicky with the spare he'd grabbed at the Circus.

Zerbrowski said, "I thought zombies couldn't feel emotions."

"Normal ones can't," I said.

"But this one wasn't normal?"

"Not even close," I said.

"No," Manny said.

"Any idea what made it go wonky?"

"Actually, yeah, he'd eaten human flesh while he was alive."

Zerbrowski gave me wide eyes.

"Yeah, it was a first for me, too, but he got trapped up in the mountains during winter, a companion died, and they had enough meat to survive."

"And you think that's what made him go weird?"

"We both do," Manny said.

I nodded. "I'll write a paper about it for the academic publications, and just put the word out to add that to the list of things that put a big fat *do not raise this corpse* sign over a site."

The backhoe was at the graveside, so we moved farther back so we could hear ourselves talk.

"What else is on the list?" he asked.

Manny answered and I let him. "Anyone who was a priest or priestess in real life of any religion is a question mark, but if they were voodoo practitioners then you don't raise them from the dead, ever. Any psychic abilities, a witch, sorcerer, anyone who was involved in a supernatural event while alive is iffy and best avoided."

I was wondering where Nicky was with the extermination crew. They'd have flamethrowers and the protective suits that went with them; if Warrington came out of the grave still ravenous we'd need them. Nicky had gone up to the main road to lead the crew back to us. He had also made sure that all three of us ate a protein bar from the stash Nathaniel had started putting in my car. It wasn't dinner, but it helped to keep us from having the blood sugar crashes that could make me drain energy from the people I was connected to metaphysically. The grave diggers had already gotten lost and had to reload the backhoe back on their truck once and drive to the right location, which had taken time we didn't have. We had to dig the grave up before dawn or the zombie might be dead to the world because it was dawn, and we still wouldn't know what happened once darkness fell inside his coffin. *His*—there, I'd thought it again; even though he was a zombie, a flesh-craving zombie, there was enough mind left that he was still War-rington to me. He could still be down there thinking and feeling, and I had to know before I walked away tonight; I had to know.

I stared off into the darkness and wondered again where Nicky was, and . . . It was as if the energy had changed in the cemetery just since earlier tonight. It had that feeling that places get sometimes when peo-ple have been performing rites that can affect the sanctity of holy ground, or as if something metaphysical has happened between one visit and the next.

"Do you feel it, Manny?" I asked.

"Feel what?" he asked.

"The cemetery had better energy earlier tonight."

"I haven't been to this one before, but a lot of the older cemeteries feel like this, Anita."

"I swear it didn't earlier tonight."

"Or maybe you just feel guilty," he said.

"What do you mean, it feels different?" Zerbrowski asked.

"Sometimes older graveyards can sort of run out of holiness," I said.

"If they haven't had a new grave and funeral in a long time, it's as if the holy ground doesn't last," Manny said.

"So this is no longer holy ground?" Zerbrowski asked.

Manny made a waffling gesture with his hand.

"A priest can do one quick ceremony, basically walk the boundaries with holy water, or another funeral could fix it," I said.

"Ghouls can disrupt holy ground," Manny said.

I shook my head. "I think the holy wears off and then some of the bodies rise as ghouls."

"Wait, what?" Zerbrowski asked.

"Ghouls are the most mysterious undead, and there's a debate even among animators and witches whether ghouls move into a graveyard and somehow damage the sanctity of it, or if ghouls only crawl out of the graves once the holy ground is no longer holy."

"Sort of a 'which came first, the chicken or the egg' debate," Zerbrowski said.

"Exactly," I said.

"It's the one kind of undead I've never seen," he said.

Manny said, "They're harmless cowards. You say boo, and they hide."

I looked at him. "If you believe that, then you've only seen regular ghouls."

"Ah, I forgot, you've seen them when they turn predatory," he said.

"I'm sensing a split decision here," Zerbrowski said.

"Manny's right about most ghouls. They're just scavengers that build tunnels underneath the graves and come up underneath to feed, at first. In fact, the first thing that usually clues a caretaker in that there's an infestation is a few scattered bones, or a grave collapses into the tunnels."

"Or they dig too close to a gravestone and it falls over, or into the tunnels," Manny added.

"Yeah, and the main complaint is that people don't like the idea of their loved ones getting munched on in their graves."

Zerbrowski made a face. "I bet. Nothing like coming to put flowers on Grandma's grave and discovering she's been scattered all over the place like dog food."

I smiled and shook my head. "Yeah, something like that. They call in an exterminator team to fill the tunnels with fire during daylight, and whoosh, no more problem. Usually."

"What happens if it's not usual?" he asked.

"They're always faster, smarter, and less physically fragile than zombies. They don't rot. Bullets hurt them but don't stop them. I've heard of them getting hit by big trucks, so they can be killed if you can crush them thoroughly enough, but it's hard to accomplish without the truck. Set them on fire and they burn like vampires, which means really well."

"I've seen a couple of vamps afterward; they go up like kindling if you add an alcoholic drink to them for a starter fluid."

I agreed. "But it doesn't matter how hard they are to kill, most of the time. They seem to be afraid of people, just like Manny said."

"Drop the other shoe, Anita, I know there is one."

"Once they've cleaned out the bodies in the cemetery and don't have any food to scavenge, they can start being more active hunters," Manny said.

"Define *active*."

"If a drunk passes out, or someone injures himself and can't get away, then they'll become a danger," he said.

"I think they'll always take an injured or incapacitated person; anything that they feel isn't a threat to them is food," I said.

"There's nothing in the literature that says that," Manny said.

"I've been up against ghouls that were real active, Manny, and I just don't believe anything that's that good at killing and eating people doesn't do it when they get the chance."

"Those are aberrant cases, Anita."

"Yeah, but all it takes is one aberrant case to kill your ass."

"So animators can't control them like zombies; they're more like vampires."

"Yeah," I said. In my head I thought, I'd known one animator who could control them, but he'd been mostly dead himself, so I wasn't sure it counted.

"There are legends of those who had enough ability to control all undead, even vampires, but Anita is the closest we have to the necromancers of yore. If she can't control them, then they can't be controlled."

"You're such a brute," Zerbrowski said.

I shrugged.

"Wait, you said they're stronger than zombies, who are already stronger than us. Aren't there any undead that aren't stronger than humans?"

We both shook our heads. "Though they did some experiments on zombies, and it turns out they may not actually be stronger than people," I said.

"How so?"

"Zombies just have no stop on using all their strength at once. It's like how a baby will use everything it has to kick a blanket off, but as you get older you use the effort needed, not all your effort together. Until by the time you're grown up you sort of forget you have more strength available to you—until an emergency happens."

"Like grannies lifting cars off their grandkids," Zerbrowski offered.

"Yeah, like that."

"So if people knew how to automatically use all our strength, we could be lifting cars all the time?"

"That's one theory," I said.

"Remember before you try lifting a car that zombies will also tear their own arms off trying to lift something too heavy for them," Manny said.

"That's true. Zombies, just like babies, don't seem to understand that even if you can lift something, it doesn't mean your body can handle the load," I said.

"Hanging around you is like the Discovery Channel for monsters sometimes; I always learn something new."

The grave diggers had moved in with tools to help loosen the tombstone, but they were gesturing at the backhoe for some reason, even though they weren't ready for it yet. "What are they doing?" I asked.

"I think they're trying to use the backhoe to move the tombstone," Zerbrowski said.

"How can you possibly know that from here?"

"I speak guy hand gestures," he said with a completely deadpan face.

I might have argued with him, but Domino came back to report that was exactly what they were talking about doing. The tombstone was solid marble and taller than I was, so it was heavy and unwieldy. The two men they'd sent couldn't lift it by themselves.

"Can I offer that Nicky and I help them, or do you not want them to know that we're stronger than the average human?"

"Offer. We're running out of moonlight."

"Besides, they'll take one look at Mr. Muscles and totally believe he could lift it by himself," Zerbrowski said.

I gave him a look. "Mr. Muscles, really?"

He gave a head nod like he was pointing with it. "Look at that sil-houette and argue with me if you can."

I looked where he'd gestured, to find Nicky outlined by the moon-light and the floodlights that the diggers were setting up. Some trick of the light and shadow made his shoulders look even more massive than they already were, so he was proportioned like some cartoon strongman.

"Okay, I see your point."

"You know me, I try to make my irritating nicknames accurate." He smiled at me.

I rolled my eyes at him, and he grinned.

"You are incorrigible."

"It's one of his charms," Nicky said as he walked up to us, stepping out of the light show and into the darkness near us so his shoulders were just their normal impressive spread, not the caricature that had made Zerbrowski comment.

As if he'd read my mind, he said, "I still stand by the nickname."

"What nickname?" Nicky asked.

"Mr. Muscles," Zerbrowski said, grinning up at him.

Nicky frowned at him, just a little. "I've been called worse."

"You know you're no fun to tease, right?"

"People have mentioned it before," Nicky said, face totally serious. It had taken me a little while to realize that Nicky being very serious and pretending not to get Zerbrowski's jokes was actually his way of teasing the man back. The fact that Zerbrowski hadn't quite figured out that Nicky was teasing him was part of the joke. I'd never seen anyone else get the better of him when it came to that kind of teasing. That it was Nicky who had figured it out was interesting, and had totally sur-prised me. I sort of liked that he could surprise me that much.

He surprised me again by leaning over for a kiss. I didn't do that in front of the police much; it ruined my image as one of the guys. I de-bated on letting him know it wasn't okay, but it just seemed wrong to lean away from someone you were in love with, so I kissed him back.

"Well, la-di-da, does Count Dracula know?"

"And this is why I don't kiss my boyfriends in front of the other cops," I said, with my hand still on the swell of Nicky's arm.

"It's just Zerbrowski," Nicky said, "he doesn't count."

Zerbrowski stared up at him openmouthed for a second, then burst out laughing.

Nicky finally let himself smile at the other man, because just that one dry comment had ruined the deadpan joke. Zerbrowski knew he'd been had and was enjoying the hell out of it.

I asked Nicky if he thought he and Domino could help the grave diggers move the tombstone. He said, "Sure."

"You're a man of few words, Muscles, but I like you."

"I don't hate you either," Nicky said, and turned before Zerbrowski could see the smile that went with the words. That set Zerbrowski back on another laughing jag.

The extermination team came up in their shiny silver suits with their hoods under their arms. "Hey, Eddie, Susannah," I said.

Eddie asked, "What's so funny?"

For some reason that made Zerbrowski laugh even harder. "Ignore him," I said. "Thanks for coming down on short notice."

Eddie smiled. He was broader than when I'd met them six, seven years ago. He was also completely bald now, the gray butch cut gone. "Hey, it beats the heck out of hunting possible wererat infestations in the walls of some family's house in the city."

"You know that wererats are the size of large dogs and won't fit inside a normal wall, right?"

"I know that, and you know that, but the people who get all freaked out and call us for it don't."

"We try to tell them the truth, but they never believe us, and their money spends," Susannah said. She was Eddie's daughter and must have looked like her mom, because she was a little taller than me, still short, a little more muscled and less thin than when we'd met on her very first night on the job. She'd put on muscle so she could handle the equipment better, and because she'd asked me what I did to make the men respect me more. Easy answer is hit the gym and make sure you can handle yourself physically. Nothing screams weak like not being able to pull your weight on the job.

I smiled back. "I hear that."

Eddie excused himself to go talk to the grave diggers about what would need to happen if they had to use the flamethrowers. They used what amounted to napalm, so that it burned and kept burning. You really didn't want to take collateral damage.

Now that her dad was gone, Susannah's eyes flicked up Nicky in that long sweep that goes from the feet to the top of the head like you're wondering what the person would be like out of their clothes. She hadn't seen him bend down for the kiss or she wouldn't have done it. I'm not saying she wouldn't have speculated, but she would have been polite enough not to let me see her doing it. It's okay to look at someone's boyfriend and wonder; you just keep it to yourself and don't act on it, ever.

Once upon a time, I'd hidden how many men were in my life, partially out of embarrassment and a lack of comfort with my own lifestyle. The other part had been because cops treat women who sleep around differently than they treat those who don't—unfair, but true. But my hiding my love life too well had led to Detective Jessica Arnett having a serious crush on Nathaniel and feeling like I'd let her make a fool of herself over my boyfriend. I didn't work with Susannah all that often, but I still didn't want a repeat of the issue.

I took Nicky's hand and said, "Did Nicky introduce himself?"

She glanced down at the hand holding. "Got his name, and that he was with you, but not that he was 'with' you." She made little quotes around *with*.

"Just wanted to make sure you don't waste energy in Nicky's direction, that's all."

"Good to know." Then she frowned. "But I thought you were engaged to Jean-Claude?"

"I am."

She looked at Nicky and then back at me, raising both her eyebrows in a question.

"Jean-Claude knows all about Nicky."

"And he's okay with it?"

"Yep."

"Very understanding fiancé you have there," she said.

"I'm one of Jean-Claude's blood donors," Nicky said.

I fought to keep my face blank and pleasant, because he'd just lied. He had a very serious rule that he didn't donate body fluids to anyone. He fed the *ardeur* for me and only me, period. So why had he told Susannah otherwise?

"Ah," she said, and you could just see her interest fade. His being my lover hadn't really dimmed her speculation, but find out he gave blood to Jean-Claude and she was done. Again, why? I felt like I'd missed something important in the last few minutes, but I'd have to wait for alone time with Nicky to have him explain it to me. Weird having to have a sociopath explain social interaction, but I was lost and he wasn't. He'd gotten the results he wanted out of the exchange, and I had no idea why, or what, but the way he stood next to me, hand in mine, let me know that he was satisfied with what had just happened. Nice someone was.

I held his hand and smiled and vowed to ask him later.

Domino motioned from near the grave. Nicky kissed me and then went off to help move the grave marker.

"Thanks for letting me not waste my time, Anita; I appreciate it."

"Not a problem."

She smiled then. "But if you know anyone else who's built along the same lines and isn't involved, let me know."

"Aww, I'm not your type," Zerbrowski said, making a fake pouty face exaggerated enough to show in the dim light.

"Sorry, Sergeant, but I don't go for middle-age leches who are happily married."

"Ouch, it's the middle-aged comment that hurts; the rest of it is just true." He grinned at her.

"I'll keep my eyes peeled for anyone who looks like Nicky but isn't taken," I said.

"Thanks, you seem to have the best luck finding men who will commit and share. Most of us can't even find one who isn't a bastard."

"I've had some men who were pretty rotten to me, but usually it's as much me as them when it all goes to hell."

She gave me the look that other women had given me before when I opted out of doing the "all my exes suck and I have absolutely nothing to do with the fact that my love life sucks" thing. I'd found that most relationships worked because everyone worked at it; it was a group effort even if only two people were involved.

"Either you've never had anyone hurt you that badly, or you are a saint."

"Anita's had her share of bad ones," Zerbrowski said.

"She confides in you?"

He put his arm across my shoulders and did a brotherly hug. "We share all our girly secrets," he said.

Manny had to walk away trying to turn his laugh into a cough.

I realized that Zerbrowski was trying to help me out of another social minefield, which meant he didn't think I could get out on my own, which might be true. Also he didn't entirely like Susannah. That I hadn't known. I filed it under *I'll ask them later* and said, "All our girly secrets."

Susannah laughed. "I don't even believe you have girly secrets, Anita."

I shrugged, smiled, and bumped the fist that Zerbrowski offered. Then he looked past me and something made his eyes widen, made him look surprised. I pushed away from the hug, bringing the shotgun around, thinking I'd let myself get distracted from the business at hand, and . . . there wasn't anything to shoot. The ground was still untouched. They'd even turned off the backhoe so we could hear the distant sound of late-season crickets, so what had surprised my partner?

They'd managed to get the tall obelisk gravestone out of the ground where it had been placed centuries ago. I think the two grave diggers and my guys had been walking it back, but Nicky had gotten impatient. He had it in his arms like he was hugging it, except he had one hand clasped over the other wrist, which let me know it was even heavier than it looked. He'd taken off his jacket so that his weapons were visible, and so were the muscles in his arms as he walked away from the grave with the stone.

Susannah had turned and was watching, too. She didn't turn around until Nicky placed the stone on the ground, with Domino helping him steady it so it didn't fall over and break. She finally turned back to me and said, "Not human, I take it."

"Not exactly," I said.

She shook her head. "Someone who looks like your guy there, but human, please, if you're looking for me."

"Why does human matter?" I asked, not sure if I should be offended on Nicky's behalf, or not yet.

"Because if he can lift that, I do not want to be on the receiving end of him being pissed at me. I had one boyfriend in high school who hit me. He played football and was on the wrestling team. He was strong, but not that strong. I never want to be at the mercy of someone stronger than the jock who first broke my heart and my jaw."

"I'm sorry, Susannah, really sorry; that must have been awful." And just like that I had my lesson. I shouldn't assume that every woman a man bashes gave him a good reason to do it.

She nodded, and her face had too many emotions flying over it for me to read them. "It's not them turning furry once a month, Anita, or even the vampires living on blood, it's the superhuman strength that scares me. I can't deal with a boyfriend who could hurt me that badly."

"Men really can be bastards," Zerbrowski said, and this time he meant it.

"You've got a daughter, right?" she asked.

"Yeah."

"I don't want daughters, ever. I'd worry too much." She stopped as if she meant to say more but had thought better of it. She turned and just walked off toward the grave, her father, and the rest of the men.

"Well," Zerbrowski said.

"Yeah," I said. "I didn't know you didn't like her until tonight."

"I may have to take it back; she freaked out on one of the other cops, but he's a big guy and when he drinks he has a temper."

"You think he got out of hand?" I asked.

"Not like you mean, but I bet it wouldn't take much to spook her."

"I bet you're right."

"Damn, now I have to either ask him what happened, or defend her the next time he says what a bitch she is."

"You don't really have to do either," I said.

"Yeah, I do. If I help trash someone's reputation and then find out I'm wrong, I have to fix it if I can."

"There's a reason we're friends, Zerbrowski," I said, smiling at his uncharacteristically serious face.

"Thanks, but you'd do the same thing."

I thought about it, and nodded.

He smiled. "Yeah, there's a reason we're friends, I'm the only one who's been safe from your feminine wiles."

I shook my head and smiled back. "You're not my type, and I like your wife and kids."

"It's the middle-aged thing, isn't it?"

"Nope, it's the railroad-themed pajamas; I just could never lust after someone once I knew they like little choo-choos all over their jammies."

He grinned at me. "Katie likes them."

I gave him the rolled eyes he expected and said, "*So* didn't want to know that."

"Let's go help dig up your zombie."

The backhoe's engine started again, as if on cue. "Let's," I said, and we walked together through the soft dark. We'd never hold hands, or go shopping, or actually share confidences about our sex lives, and we might not be partners forever; he was dangerously close to getting promoted out of the field and onto a desk full time, but we'd always be the kind of friends that you can call up at two a.m. for a favor, whether it's an exhumation order or picking the kids up from school when emergencies happen. I'd only done that last thing once, but I'd been on the list of approved names that the school was allowed to give his kids to, in case of emergency. We were damn close to the "If I had a body and needed help getting rid of it, I'd call you" phone call, but honestly we could both probably handle that one on our own. Cops can make very good bad guys, and very good friends.

33

IF IT HAD been a modern grave we could have used the backhoe to remove most of the dirt, but older graves weren't always as deep as they should be, and Warrington had been buried before wooden coffins were put inside metal vaults. If we dug too deep, then we might crush the coffin and the body inside it. If Warrington was a flesh-eating zombie and came out trying to kill us, then that wouldn't be so bad, but if he was just a body then we'd have screwed up the exhumation. Judges tended to get cranky if you destroyed perfectly peaceable dead citizens who had once been taxpaying good guys. Before you ask, no, we couldn't have sworn ourselves to secrecy and not told anyone we goofed, because people will talk, especially when the story is this good. I mean, I was a necromancer, nicknamed behind my back the Zombie Queen. That I and a senior member of the Regional Preternatural Investigation Squad/Team totally destroyed a grave, because we thought there was a killer zombie in it, when it was just some poor body . . . See, it's too good not to share at the bar on a Saturday night, or the next time any of them work with other cops, so the backhoe got turned off and the shovels came out.

The men who'd come to dig the coffin out got into the open grave and started doing their job. They never questioned it, and I wondered why they didn't at least ask if it was dangerous. Then I realized they probably didn't exhume many bodies buried before metal vaults went around the coffin.

I went to the graveside and looked down at the two men. The tall blond was almost waist deep in the open grave; his shorter dark-haired partner was already up to his waist in it. "Can you get out of the grave for a minute?" I asked.

The blond looked up at me, but Dark Hair kept shoveling dirt. "We'll be down to the coffin in just a few minutes, Marshal."

"I believe you; that's why I'd like you to get out of the grave."

The moonlight showed his frown clearly. It was bright tonight for being only half full. "Honest, we'll be out of your way in just a few minutes if you let us do our job."

"Nicky, Domino, get them out of there."

Nicky didn't argue, or hesitate, just reached down and pulled Dark Hair up by a handful of his thick coveralls like you'd pick up a puppy by the loose skin at the back of its neck. "Hey," the man said as his feet dangled and he got set on solid ground.

Domino had reached toward the blond, but he scrambled out on his own. "What the hell was that?" he asked. His buddy had stumbled away from Nicky like he was afraid he'd do more than just pick him up.

"Did anyone tell you why we want to exhume this body?" I asked.

"Yeah," Blondie said. "You're checking to see if it's a killer zombie."

"That's right, which means it may come out of the grave trying to eat people."

"No worries, we'll get to the metal vault and it's all yours after that."

"Did you check the date on the tombstone before you moved it?"

They looked at each other, as if they were both going to ask, *Did you check?* Finally Blondie said, "It's old, so what?"

"Putting a coffin in a metal vault is a modern concept. Before that it was just wood boxes, and those rot right along with the body."

They exchanged another look between them. I watched them think it through and finally Dark Hair said, "Shit."

"Yeah," I said.

"They said something about it being a really old body, but that was all," Blondie said.

"They didn't explain the possible danger?" I asked.

They both shook their heads.

"You might want to discuss that with your boss later, or do your own research into burial practices through the ages. It might save your lives."

"Are you saying the zombie could be just a few feet down and . . ."

Blondie stopped and stared into the hole as if it suddenly had a sign above it that read, *Abandon all hope, ye who enter here.*

"It's possible," I said.

"They don't pay us enough to risk getting eaten alive," Blondie said.

"Fuck, no," Dark Hair said.

"You guys wait over there until it's time to put the dirt back in; we'll take it from here for a while."

They started to walk away with the shovels still in their hands.

"We'll need the shovels."

They looked at them as if they weren't sure they were willing to give them up. "If you break them, the cost comes out of our paycheck."

"We'll do our best not to break them," I said, and held out my hand.

Blondie started to hand me his shovel, but Nicky interceded and took it instead. "I'll dig for you."

Domino took the other shovel. "We're paid to do the heavy lifting, right?"

"You know my rule, I don't let anyone take chances I won't take myself."

"Yeah, and we love you for it," Domino said, "but you're the only one who can control the zombie. Nicky and I can dig."

"They're right, Anita," Manny said.

"I don't want them in harm's way either."

"One of us will dig, and the other one can cover with the rifle," Nicky said.

I thought about it and finally said, "Okay, Nicky covers with the AR, Domino digs."

"Why does he get to cover and I have to dig?"

"Because he's a better shot than you with a long gun," I said.

"He's not better than I am with a handgun."

"No, he's not, and if we empty all the rifles and go for handguns feel free to join, but since we're starting with the AR, he watches your back while you dig."

Domino didn't like it, but he couldn't argue with my reasoning, so he climbed into the grave and started digging with Nicky beside him, rifle pointed down at the dirt in case something tried to grab them. I got to stand beside the grave and watch the dirt for signs of wood, or pale flesh, or anything that wasn't dirt. I could have unleashed my necromancy and searched the ground for the body, but I was afraid that even that little bit of power might push the zombie awake, if it was dead to the world again. I was so far out of known territory that I was afraid to do much of anything but wait to see the body, or the zombie, or whatever Warrington was now. The fact that even I couldn't define what he was, or wasn't, bothered me a lot. I was a necromancer, the first true one in centuries; if I didn't know what was going on, then no one did. We were so screwed, because I had no one I could ask for advice, or help. I'd killed the last two necromancers that I'd met. They'd been trying to kill me first, so it was self-defense, but still it would have been nice to have someone to consult with—maybe I could ask some other animators and we could coffee-klatch? The trouble was, I knew that Manny knew less than I did about all this, and he'd trained me. That didn't make me hopeful about getting real advice from anyone else in the field. Yes, I was trying to think of anything but the fact that one man I was in love with, and another that I liked a lot, both of them my lovers, were in a grave digging up a flesh-eating zombie, and all I could do was watch and wait while they endangered themselves. I liked being in the front of the charge, not leading from the rear.

With the rifle tucked up tight against his shoulder and cheek, Nicky asked, "Do I shoot at the first movement, or wait to see what he does?"

It was a great question; my answer wasn't nearly as great. "I'm not sure."

"Better be sure soon," Domino said, as he stripped off his jacket and tossed it out of the grave. His guns were very stark against the whiteness of his T-shirt, even by the light of the moon.

He was right. It wasn't like me to waffle so much; I was usually yes or no. Manny touched my arm. "If he's still moving, they need to shoot him, Anita."

I nodded, but I didn't give the order.

"Why are you hesitating?" he asked.

"I think I feel guilty."

"Feel guilty, but do what is needed."

I nodded, and said, "If he grabs for either of you, shoot him."

"Thanks, Manny," Domino said as he went back to shoveling dirt onto the edge of the pile the backhoe had already made beside the grave.

"He heard that?" Manny asked.

"He can hear your heartbeat from feet away," I said.

"Yards away if it's beating hard," Domino said, without looking up or hesitating as he shoveled.

Manny gave me wide eyes, shrugged, and smiled. I almost asked him if he had any friends who were shapeshifters, but if he did they'd be very careful around him to appear as human as possible. If I told him that, he'd just be uncomfortable around them next time they socialized, so I let it go. A lot of friendships are based on partial truths and work for years.

"Do I stop when I reach the coffin?"

"The coffin may not be intact, so if you touch wood just stop and we'll reevaluate."

"How not intact?" Nicky asked, rifle still pointed very seriously down at the dirt.

"Maybe not there at all," Manny said.

"So I'll hit body before I hit wood?" Domino asked.

"Maybe," I said.

"A lot of maybes tonight," he said.

"I know."

He glanced up at me. "You're not even going to apologize for it?"

"No."

We had a moment of looking at each other. "You're the boss," he said, and went back to digging.

"Maybe more scraping the dirt than digging," Manny said, "so the body isn't damaged."

"If it's moving, I intend to damage it."

"A lot," Nicky said.

I wanted to tell them, *Don't.* This was my fault, somehow this was my fault, because I hadn't known Warrington had been a cannibal? That was ridiculous; there was no way for me to have known that. It was his deepest, darkest secret; he wouldn't have written it down where someone could find it, read it, know. I had done my due diligence. Both the research firm we used for searches and our office staff had found out everything they could on him and checked for the red flags that would have made me pass on the job. So why did I feel like I'd done something wrong?

Domino was scraping smaller scoops of dirt now, looking to see what he was hitting with the bladed edge of the shovel. Nicky was very seriously watching the ground underneath them for movement. Manny and I were here to help control the zombie if it woke ready to eat people. Susannah and Eddie were close by with hoods in place, so we could all scatter and they could fry the zombie. We had it covered, but I was supposed to be the big bad necromancer who knew everything there was to know about the undead. It had been a long time since I'd been caught this flat-footed by a zombie that I'd raised from the grave. I'd been surprised badly by other people's undead, but never by my own. Was it professional pride that was hurting? I didn't know. I just didn't know why this was hitting me so hard, but it was; it really was.

"Movement!" Nicky said, voice loud, but the rifle never wavered.

Domino sprang out of the grave like magic, one minute in the grave, the next not, as if he'd translocated, not just leapt up like the cat he could be. Nicky stayed on post in the grave. I moved up with the shotgun, trying to see what he had noticed. The dirt looked black and empty to me.

"Get out, I'll cover you," I said.

"Maybe it was a mole or something," Zerbrowski said, peering into the grave.

"Not unless it's bigger than any mole I ever saw," Nicky said.

"No self-respecting mole would stay around this much digging," I said. I had the shotgun tucked in tight to my shoulder, my cheek sighting down the barrel, while I looked for movement. "Get out of it, Nicky, that's an order."

He had to do what I told him to do as my Bride, though my own desire for him to be more independent had made it not as automatic as it had once been. He grabbed the edge of the grave and started to jump out when I saw the ground heave, a second before a hand grabbed his ankle.

"Shit," I said.

I couldn't fire that close to Nicky's leg without risking hitting him. He tried to leap out of the grave the way Domino had done, and if a human, or even another lycanthrope, had grabbed him he could have done it, but the dead hold on tighter than the living. Nicky made it to the edge of the grave and halfway onto the ground, where Domino grabbed him and helped pull him forward, but it didn't free him from the zombie's hand. It pulled the hand, the arm, and part of a T-shirted shoulder into sight, but the hand stayed tight to Nicky's ankle.

I had my finger on the trigger, half-pulled, when I heard something that made me hesitate. A voice calling, "Help me!"

Warrington was down there, alert, awake, and craving flesh. He was down there begging for help. Motherfucking son of a bitch.

34

"SHOOT IT!" DOMINO said.

"Shoot it!" Manny said.

Zerbrowski had his own gun out and pointed.

Domino was fighting to keep Nicky from being pulled back into the grave. Nicky's fingers were digging into the ground like he was trying to grow roots, which let me know the zombie was pulling hard.

"I won't let him hurt you, Nicky," I said.

"I trust you," he said.

"Anita, shoot the damned thing," Domino yelled.

I kept my eyes on the grave, the shotgun snugged up tight, ready to shoot. "Can you hear it, Manny?"

"Hear what?"

"The zombie."

"I can," Nicky said.

"So can I, so what, shoot it!" Domino said.

"Help Nicky pull the zombie up."

"What?" Domino asked.

Even Zerbrowski said, "Anita . . ."

"Can you hear him?"

"No."

"Trust me," I said.

"I do," Zerbrowski said, "you know that."

"Thank you. Nicky, can you help Warrington get his face above-ground?"

"If Domino helps steady me and the zombie keeps holding on, yes."

"He won't let go," I said.

"I'll help you hold on, but this is crazy," Domino said. He got an even better grip on Nicky. Manny was shaking his head, but he knelt down and helped hold Nicky, though I wasn't sure either of them needed the help. Zerbrowski stayed with his handgun pointed at the arm and the body underneath.

Susannah came up to the grave and was looking in at the zombie. "Anita, get your guy out of there and let us do our job."

"Not yet."

She took off the big silver helmet and said, "Anita, how can you endanger someone you're dating?"

"Back up, Susannah, give me room to work."

"Work how?"

"I don't have time to explain. Warrington, Mr. Warrington, can you hear me?"

The screaming just kept repeating, "Help me! Help!"

"We're coming, Warrington, we're coming."

The scream changed to, "Ms. Blake, Ms. Blake, help me!"

"Jesus," Domino said.

"What is it?" Manny asked.

"Bring him up a little, Nicky." I kept the shotgun on him. If he tried to bite Nicky I'd blow his head off, but I was hoping I wouldn't have to do that.

Nicky just flexed the leg that the zombie was holding on to, while his hands and one knee dug into the ground so hard that he started to make divots in the dry earth. Domino and Manny held on to him so he didn't topple back into the grave, which would have been really bad.

The zombie's hand stayed tight around Nicky's ankle, and then his head came up above the earth like a drowning swimmer pulled from the sea. He came up screaming, high and piteous, his words lost in the horror of it all, and then he started coughing.

"Warrington," I said, still aiming at the face.

He coughed harder.

"Bring him up a little higher, Nicky, not too much more yet."

Nicky crawled farther out of the grave with the other men holding on to him and brought the zombie up so that his upper chest was free, but the other arm was still trapped in the soft dirt. The zombie coughed harder, then started puking up dirt the way he'd thrown up food earlier.

"God help us, he was buried alive," one of the grave diggers said.

"Not exactly," I said.

"He was buried undead," Manny said, his face pale even by moon-light.

When enough dirt had come out, the zombie leaned against the side of the grave but still had Nicky's ankle in its grasp. I wasn't sure if War-rington even knew that he was still holding on to anything, or if he was like a drowning victim—once they have hold of anything they don't let go. It's how lifeguards get drowned every year trying to save people.

I wanted to help Warrington, but I wasn't letting him hurt Nicky, or anyone else, trying to save himself. I would help him if I could, but if I couldn't I'd let Susannah and her dad do their job. Once I had that decision dragged into the front of my head, I was calmer.

"Warrington, can you hear me?" I asked, still pointing the shotgun at his face.

He blinked up at me, but those fine hazel eyes were corpse's eyes now, half lost in their wasted sockets, color stolen by the moon. His face was waxy and skeletal; all the miraculous humanity had been lost, so that he was just another zombie except for his words.

"Ms. Blake, that is you, yes?"

"It is, Mr. Warrington."

"I can't seem to see as well as I usually do."

"Your eyes aren't working as well as they did."

"Is it from being buried?"

"Something like that," I said.

"Are you pointing a gun at me?"

"I am."

"Are you going to shoot me?"

"Are you going to keep holding on to my friend's ankle?"

"Is that what I'm holding on to? I can't seem to think clearly."

"Yes, it's Nicky's ankle that you're holding on to."

"The big gentleman with the odd haircut."

"Yes, that's Nicky."

"I can't seem to make my fingers work to let go."

"Give it a minute, and then try to let go; for now just rest a minute, Mr. Warrington."

"I thought you meant to leave me down there in hell. I know I deserve it, but I'm so glad you came to rescue me."

Rescue him. We hadn't come to rescue him; we'd come to try to find a way to kill him for good. He'd never be raised from the dead again; I'd make sure of that. "Manny and I were worried that you hadn't gone back to sleep and were trapped, so we came to get you out."

"Thank you, oh God, thank you." His fingers slowly unfolded and Nicky was able to pull himself completely out of the grave. He stood there tall and firm and looked at me. Of everyone at the graveside he felt most what I was feeling; nothing I could do would keep him out of my emotions. Domino and the rest I could shield against, but not Nicky; he knew.

I lowered the shotgun just a little and looked down at the talking corpse that was still trapped in the earth of his own grave. His body was decayed, so he looked like a regular zombie, but his mind was still awake and human. God help me.

"Jesus, Mary, and Joseph, Anita, what is going on?" Zerbrowski asked. He stared down at the zombie with the horror plain on his face, which you don't see from veteran cops much, not in public anyway. They save the horror for private moments, or getting drunk with friends.

"Please, help me out of this grave."

"Are you still craving human flesh, Mr. Warrington?"

He shook his corpse head. "No, no, I just want out of this place."

Manny came to stand beside me. "What are we going to do?"

"Damned if I know."

"Do we dig him out?" the short dark-haired grave digger asked.

"No, no one else goes in the grave," I said.

"Help me, Ms. Blake, help me."

"We're going to, Mr. Warrington, just as soon as we figure out how to do that without endangering anyone else."

"I'm not craving flesh anymore, Ms. Blake."

"You're too scared right now. No one craves food when they're this scared."

He raised his free hand and looked at it. The flesh had molded to it, so that it was just a skeleton hand with pale, waxy skin formed over it. "What's wrong with my hand? Why does it look like that?"

"Oh, God," I whispered.

"He doesn't know what he is," Zerbrowski said.

"He knows," I said.

"What's wrong with me, Ms. Blake? What's happening?"

"Do you remember why you wanted me to put you back in your grave?"

"No, I mean . . . I was craving human flesh. I was dangerous to others."

"Yes, potentially, and I told you that all zombies did one thing, do you remember what that was?"

He shook his head, then looked up at me, blinking those rotting eyes. "You said all zombies rot; no matter how lifelike I looked, I would rot."

"Yes."

"Is that what's happening to me?"

"I'm afraid so."

He started screaming then, over and over, just ragged screams, and struggling to free himself from the dirt of his grave. Manny touched my arm and motioned me to walk with him. I told Nicky and Domino that the zombie could free himself a little more, but if he tried to get out of the grave to shoot him.

Manny took me far enough away so we could hear over the zombie's screams. Zerbrowski came with us. "What the fuck, Anita? I mean, what the fuck is that thing?"

"It's a zombie," I said.

He shook his head. "I've seen zombies, and this isn't it. I mean, it looks like one, but they don't think, and they don't feel. One of the things that makes them so dangerous is that they don't feel when you're chopping them up, so the bits just keep crawling after you. This one, this one feels things."

"I know, Zerbrowski, I know. Don't you think I know?"

He nodded. "Of course, you do; I'm sorry, partner. This is why you wanted to exhume him."

"I couldn't leave him down there like this."

"No, God, no."

"Anita," Manny said.

I looked at him.

"How are we going to give him back to death?"

I thought it was an odd phrasing, but I didn't have a better one. "I don't know, Manny, there's no ceremony for this, not really."

"We could try a second animal sacrifice and blood circle and put him back with salt and steel."

"You're talking about the old-school way where we sew his mouth up with salt, aren't you?"

"We try modern first and if that doesn't work, we go old-school."

"You really want to try to hold him down while we sew his mouth shut, while he screams for help? Fuck no."

"I second that," Zerbrowski said. "No, we are not doing that."

"Do you have a suggestion, Sergeant, because if you do I am eager to hear it," Manny said.

Zerbrowski looked at him, then to me, and back to Manny. "I don't have suggestions, I'm just agreeing with Anita that we are not holding this . . . thing down and sewing its mouth shut in the hope that it will be dead for real then, because you aren't sure that will work either, are you?"

Manny sighed. "No, Sergeant, I'm not."

"What is wrong with this zombie, Anita? Why is it this alive?"

"It's not alive."

"Why is it this aware, then?"

"I told you, he was a cannibal in life."

"And that explains why he didn't die again when you put him in the grave tonight?"

"Maybe; it's all I got to explain it, so yeah, we'll go with that."

"Anita, you don't know, do you?"

"If you were your boss I'd deny it, but no, Zerbrowski, I don't know."

"Shit," he said.

"Yeah."

"Then we have no choice but to treat him like you would treat any rogue zombie, Anita," Manny said.

"What do you mean, Manny?"

"Shoot his head off and hopefully blow his brains out so he's not aware, and then let the fire team turn him to ashes."

"There's got to be another way, Manny."

"Legally, we can put the dirt back and just leave him as he is."

"No," I said.

"No," Zerbrowski said, "we can't do that."

"If we can't put him back with voodoo, then what choice do we have but to treat him as we would any rogue zombie?"

"Manny, there's got to be another way."

"I would be glad to hear it, Anita. I liked Warrington, he seemed a decent man, but what's in that grave is not him. It was never him."

"Then what was it, Manny? What the fuck did I raise from the grave tonight?"

"I don't know, but it's rotting like any zombie; you know that sometimes the mind is the last thing to go. It is the cruelest way for them to
rot, but it happens, we've both seen it before. This is no different."

"They don't have this much mind to begin with, Manny, and you
know it. Don't stand there and tell me it's not different this time."

He just looked at me.

"Manny, damn it."

"I'm sorry, Anita, truly, but we must do something before dawn. If
that happens first then he could fall back into death, but it might last
only until nightfall and then he would be trapped again, drowning in
the dirt of his own grave. Can you not feel how close dawn is, Anita?"

I had been feeling it, but finally acknowledged it. It was still as dark
as it had been all night, but there was a softness in the air, a breath of
dawn. All the animators I knew who had survived for any length of time
as vampire executioners had been able to feel the rise and setting of the
sun, even underground in the dark. We just knew, as if the sun traveled
not just across the sky but through our bodies.

Zerbrowski checked his iPhone in the dark. "We've got an hour
until dawn, though I never understand how both of you always know
that."

"It's a gift," I said, but I was already turning toward the grave. The
zombie had stopped screaming.

"When did he stop screaming?" Zerbrowski asked.

None of us could answer him. Into the strangely eerie silence came
not a sound, but a feeling, as if the air had changed. "What is that,
Manny?"

"I'm not sure."

We looked at each other and without a word started walking back
toward the grave. I pointed the shotgun skyward, but my hands were
now in position so the gun could be brought to bear immediately. I was
no longer holding it safely, but idly.

"What are you guys sensing that I'm not?" Zerbrowski asked.

"It's not vampires," I said softly.

"I would not know that for certain," Manny whispered.

"Trust me," I said.

"On this, I do."

"Is it more zombies?" Zerbrowski asked.

"It's too . . . active for that," Manny said, voice still soft, but there was no reason to whisper when we could hear everyone else ahead of us talking normally.

Nicky was motioning to the extermination team. He was wanting them closer in with everyone else. "I didn't think Mr. Muscles was sensitive to this stuff."

"He's not, but he felt me sense it."

Zerbrowski frowned at me. I had a moment of wondering just how much I'd told Zerbrowski about Nicky. Did he know absolutely that he was my Bride? No, I hadn't burdened my fellow cop with that knowledge. If the police understood just how connected I was to the "monsters" they'd be sure my loyalty was compromised. They already mistrusted me because I was with Jean-Claude and Micah. Zerbrowski didn't care, or I didn't think he would, but his bosses would, and I didn't want to put him in a position that could hurt his career.

"We're very in tune with each other," I said, and knew it sounded lame.

He gave me the look the weak comment deserved, but his gun was in his hand in a more serious way, just like my shotgun. He didn't know what was going on, but he was following my lead just like Nicky. I glanced at Manny.

"Are you armed at all?"

"You know I don't carry guns."

"Knife?"

"Pocket knife."

"Stay safe, stay behind us, or out of the way, or something."

"You'd send me to the car if you could."

"Yes, you're unarmed."

"This feels like a matter for magic, not mayhem, Anita, but because you carry a gun you think about shooting before you think about using your necromancy."

That made me hesitate and look at him. Was he right? Well, yeah, but most bad things weren't bulletproof, and a lot of them were necromancy-proof. I went with the sure winner in an emergency, but he was right about one thing: This was something that hit my power, and his.

Susannah and her father were beside the grave but still on the opposite side of it from the others. The grave diggers were already close to Domino and Nicky. Domino was staring out at the night, shotgun held pointed at the ground, but ready. Nicky was still trying to get the last two people with us around the grave so we'd all be on the same side of it.

I heard Eddie say, "Fire scares everything; bullets don't." Translation: He trusted their flamethrowers more than the guns.

Susannah said, "Dad, just do what they say."

I saw movement, but it was more an impression, and then something was leaping out of the darkness onto Eddie. I had a moment to see silver-gray skin, a humanoid face, and then I'd brought the shotgun up and knew that Nicky and Domino were doing the same.

Manny yelled, "Don't shoot!"

Domino yelled, "Anita!" I knew he was asking for orders. I had a heartbeat to decide whether we were shooting the ghoul, or I was using magic. It was one of those moments when being the cop, the psychic, and the person in charge crashed headlong into each other. I hesitated and knew that was the biggest mistake of all.

35

"MAGIC, ANITA," MANNY said.

Susannah was yelling, "Shoot it!"

Eddie was on the ground covering the back of his neck and head; he'd made his decision that he'd give the ghoul an arm to chew first. It was the right decision; I wasn't sure about mine.

"Give the word," Nicky said. I didn't have to look to know he was aiming at the ghoul's head just like I was from my angle.

The ghoul had flattened itself to Eddie's back, the darker gray of its skin looking less silver than usual against the shininess of his fire suit. It was mostly nude with only remnants of pants clinging to it like some comic book hero that had to get by the censors. Muscles corded in the back of its body as it pressed itself against Eddie and the tank of fuel on his back.

"Domino, stand down, no shotguns." I lowered mine to show I meant it.

The ghoul hissed at us, flashing red eyes that seemed to glow in the dark. It made a high chittering sound and was answered from farther back in the trees.

"There's more of them," Zerbrowski said.

"Ghouls always run in packs," I said.

"Nicky, do you see the problem?"

"Fuel," he said, voice tight and controlled.

"Do you have it?"

"No."

"What does he mean?" Zerbrowski asked.

"He doesn't have a shot without risking hitting the fuel on Eddie's back." If we'd had a clean shot, would I have tried Manny's suggestion? Probably not, but we didn't have a shot and this ghoul wasn't acting normal.

"They're cowards, they don't attack like this," I said, more to myself than anyone else.

"It hasn't attacked," Manny said.

"What do you call it then?" Zerbrowski asked. He still had his gun out, just pointed two-handed at the ground.

The ghoul hissed again, kneading long curved talons against Eddie's back. I knew there'd be matching talons on the bare feet. They might look like gray-colored people, but they had teeth and claws like your worst predator nightmare. It chittered again, and the others answered it from the woods. I caught pale glimpses of other figures, but they were staying back out of range. The only other time I'd seen ghouls this active and thinking, a murderous necromancer had been controlling them. It was the only time I'd ever known anyone to be able to control ghouls. They were the wild cards of the undead; no one knew why they rose from their graves, but they were scavengers, cowards, skulkers in the dark eating buried corpses and bones of the long dead if they couldn't get fresh.

"Eddie was right, they are afraid of fire," Manny said.

"Ghouls don't strategize, Manny."

"If we can't shoot it, try magic," he said.

"Do something fast," Domino said. "They're trying to surround us."

"If you see anyone in the woods that isn't ghoul, or us, shoot them."

"Why?" Domino asked.

"Because the last time I saw ghouls act like this, another necromancer was controlling them."

"Shoot the wizard first," Nicky said.

"Usually," I said.

I'd never tried to use my necromancy on ghouls. One, they were rare; two, they usually minded their own business and hid from people. You were only called in when they tunneled from an older cemetery into a new one where people got upset about their loved ones' bodies being eaten by them, or when a drunk passed out and got eaten by them, just like we'd told Zerbrowski earlier.

I didn't so much lower my shields as just let my necromancy go. It was like opening a fist that you've kept tightly closed; suddenly you can spread your fingers and let the tension go. My necromancy flowed out from me like a seeking wind. Once it hadn't been a real wind; that was just the closest analogy I'd had for it when I searched a cemetery for hot spots, ghosts, ghouls, and such, but it wasn't a metaphorical wind anymore, and hadn't been for years.

Manny shivered next to me. He said something in Spanish too fast for me to catch it all, but he called on God in there somewhere. I wasn't sure if he was asking for help, or afraid of what he was feeling; maybe I didn't want to know.

That seeking wind touched the grave and the zombie first. It curled around him, knew him, so that Warrington said, "God"; again I wasn't sure if it was a cry for help or I'd become his god. Again, I didn't want to know. My magic swirled out just a little farther and found the ghoul sitting on top of Eddie. It stopped snarling and looked at me. Ghouls' eyes were usually like looking into the eyes of wolves or other wild animals—no one home that we could understand or talk to—but there was more there in this look; not a lot more, but it wasn't just animal looking back at me. I knew then that it hadn't been accidental, him jumping on Eddie and compromising the fuel tank. That was a fuckton of reasoning for a ghoul.

I sent my power out wide and fast, searching for whoever was holding this one's leash. I touched the other ghouls and knew Domino was right; they were trying to outflank us, but like the one at the grave, when my power touched them their energy calmed. I felt them grow quiet under the touch of my necromancy. Whoever was controlling them either was backing off or didn't have that much control over them after all. Good, great, but I still wanted the necromancer. I sent my power out seeking him, or her. If she could do this, then I needed to find her and make it clear this shit didn't fly in my territory.

I sent the wind of my power out and out, then finally sought farther than the wind could reach, until Jean-Claude entered my mind and whispered, "*Ma petite*, is something wrong?"

"No," I whispered.

"What?" Zerbrowski asked.

"You fill the night with power like a seeking wind. What do you seek?"

I didn't try talking again; I just let him see my night, and know what had been happening. "*Ma petite*, my love, your night is one of wonder and torment."

"That's one way to put it," I said.

"Put what?" Zerbrowski asked.

"She's talking to her power," Manny said. I wondered if he understood what he meant by that. Did he know I was talking to Jean-Claude? I'd ask later; maybe.

"Oh, sorry," Zerbrowski said.

"Is there anything I can do to aid you, *ma petite*?"

"No . . . I don't think so."

"Then I will say only this: Your power is like a beacon tonight; it may draw things to you beyond the necromancer you seek."

"What do you mean?" I asked. I could see him sitting in the living room, curled up onto one corner of the living room couch. Someone was with him, a man's hand resting on his thigh. The size of the hand meant it wasn't Nathaniel or Micah; beyond that I wasn't sure. It didn't even have to be a lover; as the other vampires reminded him often, he was far too touchy-feely with his animals. Yeah, that would be the older vamps among the Harlequin that said it.

"Our lesser vampires may find your power irresistible, or even zombies that belong to others." He made a waffling motion with his hand. "You are heady stuff to the dead tonight, *ma petite*."

"I'll try to tone it down."

He smiled. A blond head came into view, moving so close to Jean-Claude's chest that I could see the hair as he moved upward. It was only as he turned his head to sniff along Jean-Claude's neck that I realized it was Dev.

He smiled and said, "Anita."

I was all necromancy tonight. I realized that it had closed certain doors inside me, and I wasn't feeling my connection to my wereanimals as strongly as normal. Sometimes it was hard to find the balance between all the power.

Dev lay back against Jean-Claude's shoulder and smiled up at my viewpoint as if he were smiling for a camera. He'd seen me inside his head like this before, and for some reason it was always an up view with me looking down, so that we always looked upward into each other's faces from a distance. There were moments when we could just look in and see what the other was doing, but for anything this interactive the viewpoint was always hovering. None of us knew exactly why it worked the way it did.

Dev's smile was content like a cat that's been into the cream. I had a moment to wonder what he and Jean-Claude had been doing to put that smugness on his face, but I knew that it wasn't sex. If they crossed that boundary there'd be discussion beforehand, at least on Jean-

Claude's part. I'd let Dev be his own person for most of our relation-ship, so I wasn't sure on his part. He might consider that Jean-Claude was the king, so . . . I shook the thoughts away. One issue at a time, damn it.

Jean-Claude either read my mind or knew me that well, because he said, "Mephistopheles and I have been talking about his new form and what it might mean for his power level."

"He seems pretty happy with himself."

"He is enjoying the thought of being closer to the seat of power."

It took me a moment to realize it was a double entendre. I trusted Jean-Claude to handle the other man and keep things from getting out of hand before we'd all discussed it among ourselves. An in-depth talk with Asher and Kane was so on the to-do list before we decided what to do with our golden tiger.

"I'll try not to attract too much undead attention; you guys be good."

Dev's smile broadened, and he leaned in against Jean-Claude in a very intimate way. "We'll be good."

I hoped he didn't think he was home free and on Jean-Claude's list of lovers just because of gaining more power. It was a mistake to under-estimate how carefully Jean-Claude orchestrated the people around him. He valued domestic happiness highly; even power wasn't always enough for him to upset personal issues. Some of the Harlequin saw that as a weakness, but when you can have several hundred years of companionship from someone, being happy with them should be im-portant. I'd actually begun to think that one of the reasons most of the older vamps I met were miserable bastards was that they spent too much time being all Machiavelli in their life, and not enough time being Cupid. It sounded stupid, but love isn't stupid; it's necessary for a happy life.

I shook my head and closed the link between us; anything else I said was just going to distract me more. I needed to find the necromancer who had loosed the ghouls from their cemetery. I was almost a hundred percent certain that they hadn't originated in this graveyard, though it would definitely need a priest to visit soon or they might spread here.

I knew how to search for the undead, or even vampires, but I'd never tried to search just for someone like me. I knew what vampire felt like to my power. I let it "taste" the zombie in its grave. Warrington felt it, because he said, "What would you have of me, Ms. Blake?"

"I'm trying to find other undead, but first I have to ignore your energy, so I won't keep picking up on zombies." He probably didn't understand most of what I'd said, but he replied with, "Let me but feed and I know I can help you."

"Feed how?" I asked.

"Flesh."

"You're craving flesh again?"

"So hungry," he said.

I still didn't know what to do with the zombie in the grave, and I didn't have time to figure it out right that minute. "I'll attend to you later, Warrington; right now I have other dead to visit."

"Free me and I will help you."

"Be quiet, you're distracting me." He stopped talking, either because he wanted to be helpful or because I'd given him a direct order and he couldn't disobey it. I hoped the latter, because that would mean he was closer to a normal zombie, and I needed some normal tonight.

I aimed my necromancy at the ghoul closest to me. He went very still, that stillness that zombies and vampires can have, as if the body stops. It's a cessation of movement that live beings can't do. We can hold our breath, but we can't stop our hearts from beating, or the blood from flowing through our veins. The undead can do exactly that.

The ghoul looked at me and gave me the stillness that only the dead can, and my power tasted him, and then spilled out into the night to taste his brethren. There were five of them. The typical size for a group was between three and six, though I'd seen much larger packs before, but that had been the one under control of the other necromancer. I took their being a standard-size group as a good sign, because either the other necromancer couldn't raise more, or it had been a normal pack that got taken over but not raised from the grave by the other necromancer. The first was impressive; the second would have been scary impressive.

I let my power taste all the graves, but in a cemetery this old there weren't many hot spots; more likely over newer graves if the soul hasn't gone on like normal, haunts that are more active hot spots, and then the very rare graveside ghost. Ghosts usually haunted places they'd lived, died, or enjoyed in life; most weren't that attached to their actual graves. There were no ghosts at all, no hot spots, and only two haunts. I didn't know what had tied the spirit to the graves, but it was wearing away like a string rubbing against a sharp rock; eventually the connection would break and the remnant of soul would join the rest of itself on the other side. Just getting a priest down here to reconsecrate the ground might free them both. Older graveyards like this one were usually quiet places, downright peaceful by my standards.

I knew the feel of all the dead and undead near me, so I set my necromancy searching for something that wasn't a vampire, or a zombie, or a ghoul, or a ghost, or a haunt, or a hot spot, but was still of the dead. Manny flared next to me, his own power showing up now that I'd narrowed my search. That was a good sign; if I could sense Manny this strongly, then I'd be able to find someone powerful enough to control ghouls. They couldn't hide from me now.

I aimed and searched for someone like me. I found others, but they were known powers: my coworkers at Animators Inc. and fellow U.S. Marshal Larry Kirkland. I'd combined my power with theirs back in the nights when I needed more help to raise multiple, older zombies. Manny had been the one who taught me I could act as a focus for other animators' power. As I tasted the other animators' magic I realized that combining all of us hadn't been that different from bringing together all the different types of wereanimals, or even the vampire marks with Jean-Claude and the rest. It was all about combining power so you'd be able to do more together than apart, except the vampire version was permanent and the other wasn't, but I still recognized their magic from miles away.

I reached past the familiar energies and searched for someone I didn't know and had never worked with, but there was nothing. Nothing close enough to be controlling the ghouls around us in the dark. That needed proximity to work, just like controlling zombies.

"There's no one close," I said softly, my voice distant with power.

My phone rang, sharp and jarring, so I lost some of the thread of what I was doing. It's easier to do magic while shooting a gun than answering a phone, or so I've found. I fumbled it out to turn the sound off, but recognized the number, so I took it.

"Larry," I said.

"What the fuck are you playing at, Anita?" In person he looked like a grown-up Howdy Doody complete with orange-red hair, freckles, and a boyish face that still got him carded, though the fact that he was about my height probably didn't help.

"Well, hello to you, too," I said.

"Your power is all over me and you think I'm being rude?"

"Manny and I are in a cemetery with predatory ghouls; forgive me if my trying to control the situation got my psychic cooties on you."

"Tell me where you are. Police can be there in minutes, and I'll—"

"It's okay, I think, Larry. Manny urged me to handle it with magic, not guns, and I'm trying."

"What kind of magic could save you from ghouls once they've gone predatory?"

"I'll explain later, but I can't do metaphysics while I'm on the phone."

"You're using your necromancy?" He made it a question.

"Trying to."

"If the two of you need backup, call."

"I will, thanks, Larry." I hung up. It was the friendliest conversation I'd had with him in months. He and I had come to a parting of the ways over our views on vampires and the fact that I was a shooter and he wasn't, and the other marshals respected my kill count over his moral high ground.

The ghoul was still pressed to Eddie's back, but it wasn't snarling at us. "I can't find another necromancer anywhere in the city, or the miles beyond."

"But you were able to touch Larry enough for him to call?" Manny made it a question.

"Apparently, so if I did touch someone with our psychic gift they'd know it when I did." I stared at the ghoul, and a quick thought let me feel the others still out in the darkness.

"We need to get him off my dad," Susannah said in a voice that was squeezed down into a tight, frightened sound.

"I know."

"Ask him to get off the man," Manny said.

"What?" I asked.

"Ask him, or tell him to move."

"So, what, we move him away from Eddie, so we can shoot him?"

"No need to shoot him if he does what you tell him to do, Anita."

I looked at Manny. "I can't control ghouls, especially wild ones that my necromancy didn't do anything to bring to life."

"If it were anyone else but you, I'd agree, but if any animator I know can do this, it's you."

"Manny . . ."

"Try, Anita," Nicky said.

I glanced at him.

"Please, Anita, at least try before that thing hurts my dad."

I sighed, and looked at the ghoul. It was watching me, not in a hostile way, not even in a neutral way. There was a demand in its large reddish eyes, not the kind of demand human eyes give you, but closer to the way a really active dog will look at its owner, as if thinking, *You're going to do something interesting now, right? We're going to do something now, right?* And even that wasn't exactly it, but it was the closest thing I'd ever seen to the look in the ghoul's face.

"You"—I pointed at the ghoul—"move off the man."

It blinked, looked at me for a second.

"Move, now," I said.

The ghoul blinked one more time and then crawled off the man he'd pinned to the ground. He kept his eyes on Nicky, Domino, and Susannah while he did it, but he moved. I think we all held our breath. The ghoul sat beside Eddie, but he wasn't on top of him anymore.

"Tell him to move farther away from Eddie," Manny said.

"Move farther away from the man," I said.

The ghoul looked at me.

"Try it simpler," Nicky said.

"Like you'd talk to a dog," Zerbrowski said.

I looked at him.

He shrugged.

If the ghoul were a dog, what would I say? How would I order it to get away from Eddie? I'd say, *Get away from the man.* I tried it. "Get away from the man."

It looked at me, puzzled, but it moved a few more inches away from Eddie.

"Call him to you, Anita," Manny said.

"He's not really a dog, Manny."

"Just try."

My heart was beating a little fast; it wouldn't work, it couldn't work. "Come to me," I said.

It looked at me sort of sideways, suspicious, but it came to me slowly, each movement stiff and reluctant like a half-feral dog. It wants to be petted and loved, but it's learned humans are bastards and more likely to hurt than help. The ghoul moved in that awkward, nearly four-legged gait they had sometimes, as if the legs didn't quite hold them upright, so they had to use their arms more like an ape. He, or it, sat a few feet away from me, out of reach, but closer to me than to Eddie, which is what we wanted.

Eddie got up slowly, and when he stood up, Susannah started to run to him, but Manny said, "Don't run; that attracts ghouls and can trigger their chase reflex."

"He's right," I said, softly, still keeping my gaze on the ghoul in front of me.

Susannah went slowly to meet her father around the far side of the grave. They hugged hard. One win for the good guys.

I went back to staring at the ghoul, and he stared back. He was less than eight feet from me. If he tried to jump me I'd never get any of the guns up in time to defend myself. Minimum safe distance for drawing, aiming, and firing a gun is twenty-one feet; anything closer and a human being can close the distance faster than you can draw a weapon.

All the people who complain about cops shooting someone from a distance don't understand how fast people can move, and how long it takes to draw, aim, and fire. The ghoul would be faster than a human. Eight feet between us was like giving him a free try at me, or at Zerbrowski or Manny, who were clustered around me.

"What now?" I asked.

"I'm not sure," Manny said.

Nicky was moving slowly toward us. Domino started to follow, but Nicky shook his head. The ghoul noticed Nicky and shifted uneasily, making a low anxious sound in its throat. "Hold up, Nicky."

"Why isn't he afraid of me? I've got a gun," Zerbrowski said.

"I don't know, maybe Nicky looks like more of a threat."

"I think he can smell what I am," Nicky said, keeping his voice low and as nonthreatening as he could.

"He's more afraid of shapeshifters than humans; interesting," I said.

"Don't go all Mr. Spock on us, Anita. This isn't interesting, it's dangerous," Zerbrowski said.

"It's both," I said.

"Add scary to that, and you're about right," Domino said, still at the graveside. He was watching out into the trees, trying to keep attention on the other ghouls, and trusting that Nicky would handle the one closest to me. He was right; there were four of them still out there, and they might not be as obedient as this one.

"Okay, but now what do I do with it?"

"Dawn is less than half an hour away, Anita. The ghouls will run for cover as the light comes," Manny said.

"I don't believe they came from this cemetery; if we let them tunnel in here to hide from the sunlight, they'll start feeding on the bodies buried here. They need to go back where they came from."

"And where is that?" Manny asked.

I looked at the ghoul. "Maybe he'll play Lassie for me," I said.

"What does that even mean?" Zerbrowski asked; he sounded nervous. I guess we all were, but he usually hid it better.

"Show us where your cemetery is," I said. The ghoul blinked at me.

"Too complex," Nicky said.

"If you say *Is Timmy down the well*, I'm going to punch you later, just so you know," Zerbrowski said.

"Go back to your own cemetery."

It made a sound low in its throat, halfway between a growl and a purr. I didn't understand the sound.

I repeated my order.

It made the sound again, but this time it went up and down the scale, and there was more trill to it. There was an answering noise from the dark here, there, over there, so that the whole pack made the noise back and forth at each other.

"What are they doing?" Susannah asked.

"It doesn't sound threatening," I said, but knew I sounded less than absolutely certain, because I wasn't certain. I was so far outside my comfort zone that I just didn't know. Ghouls didn't act like this, and they sure as hell didn't obey me. I'd been chased through my share of graveyards by the damn things. They were animalistic scavengers that would turn into opportunistic predators if they found something wounded enough. I'd heard them growl, howl, chitter, scream, but never this up-and-down, half-questioning noise.

"Not to complicate things," Zerbrowski said, "but won't the zombie have an issue with sunlight, too?"

"Shit," I said.

"Will it burn in sunlight like a vampire?" Nicky asked.

"No," I said, "but zombies hide from the light."

"Why?" he asked.

"Some of them fall into a vampire-like torpor once the sun rises. Flesh eaters are smart enough to find cover before dawn sometimes."

"Will this one die at dawn like a vampire?" Zerbrowski asked.

"I don't know."

"You're saying that a lot tonight," he said.

"I've noticed."

"Order them to go back to their cemetery again, Anita."

"I tried, Manny."

"Make it more of an order," he suggested.

I looked at the ghoul in front of me and said, "I order you to go back to the cemetery you crawled out of tonight."

"Think dog, not person, Anita," Nicky said.

"How would you word it?"

He was quiet for a minute, and I almost said, *See, not so easy*, but he said, "Do they burn in daylight like a vampire?"

"No, but they hide from daylight, so it doesn't feel good. They can come out at dusk before it's truly dark; most vampires can't."

"If dawn comes and they aren't near their tunnels, what do they do?" he asked.

"Take shelter until dark."

"Look around, Anita, where can they hide? It's going to be light soon."

I looked for a shed, or a mausoleum, and found a tomb that rose above the others in the distance. I motioned toward it. "They might be able to hide in there."

"Are they strong enough to break into it?"

"Oh, yeah."

The ghoul looked at me, his crimson eyes doing that flat shine again as if reflecting light I couldn't see. It made a different noise higher in its throat and started backing away. I had a sense of movement out among the graves, and knew it was the other ghouls.

"What are they doing?" Domino asked.

The one in front of me got very low to the ground and sort of groveled, and then it began to crawl backward away from us. It kept looking at Nicky and then Domino and the two exterminators in their fire suits, as it tried to keep all the dangers in sight. It stopped and groveled again, but that was always aimed at me.

"The others are at the mausoleum," Nicky said.

I glanced up and could see the others like gray shadows skulking around the huge stone. The ghoul in front of me made an abrupt, sharp almost-growl that made the hair at the back of my neck stand up, and then he turned and crept out among the tombstones, using them for cover the way a lion used the long grass.

"Don't shoot it," I said.

"No, we'll burn them out once daylight comes," Susannah said.

"No," I said.

She looked at me. "Yes, we will."

"You're not paid for ghoul extermination tonight."

"You're protecting them."

Manny said, "Contact the company that runs the graveyard, and then they'll pay you to do it."

"Is that what you meant, Anita?"

"Why do it for free if you can do it for money?"

Her body language was all relief as she let go of the serious mad-on she'd been about to aim at me. Her father added, "I like the way you think, Anita; business first."

"If I took it personally every time a monster pissed me off, I couldn't do my job."

"I guess not," Susannah said.

Zerbrowski gave me a look, and then Manny. Both of them were wondering if I'd meant business, or if I just hadn't wanted them fried in front of me. Since I wasn't sure, I didn't try to enlighten them. You can't share the light if you're still in the dark yourself, and I was stumbling around in the pitch black, wondering why the hell a ghoul pack had come to visit me tonight. The ghoul had taken my orders, which wasn't possible, but it had happened, so it was possible. *Impossible*: I was beginning to think it didn't mean what I thought it meant.

36

FALSE DAWN CAME, making the darkness lighter, but it wasn't truly daylight. Vampires would still have time to run for cover before they started to burn. The ghouls had broken into the crypt and were crawling inside like rats in a hidey-hole. That left just one undead to deal with, and I turned back to the open grave.

The zombie had managed to free itself to its waist in the dirt and was still wiggling more of itself free. Domino was keeping an eye on it the way Nicky and I had told him to. If I gave the word, or the zombie tried to get out of the grave, he'd shoot it. I didn't want to shoot it, but I didn't know what else to do with it either.

"Ms. Blake," it said, "please, I just want out of this awful place." His face looked more cadaverous with the growing light, so that no matter how cultured his language was he still looked like a rotting corpse.

"Are you still craving flesh?"

He stopped trying to get his legs free and seemed to think about my question. "Yes, yes, I am."

"Do you feel as empty as you did in the mountains when the snow trapped you?"

"I don't understand what that means."

"Do you remember your name?"

"Tom."

"Tom what?"

"I don't know." He'd gone back to trying to free his legs; he was only caught below the knees now.

"Do you know what Tom is short for?"

"Thomas."

"Thomas, what's your last name?"

It blinked eyes up at me that were still hazel, but watching the balls roll in the nearly exposed sockets meant that they weren't lovely hazel eyes anymore. There was so little flesh on the face that I couldn't read his expressions anymore.

"Thomas Warrington," I said.

"Is that me?"

"Yes."

"I should know my own name, shouldn't I?"

"Yes, Mr. Warrington, you should."

"Why does it sound strange, as if it's not me at all?"

"Dawn is coming," I said.

"I don't understand."

I didn't know if he had forgotten what dawn meant, or if he didn't understand that the sun coming up was a potentially bad thing for a zombie. Hell, maybe he didn't even know that last part. Most people didn't understand that zombies preferred darkness, and some couldn't move around in daylight at all. I was pretty sure Warrington would still be moving, but his mind was going as the light grew, and that wasn't going to be a good thing for any of us.

I motioned to Susannah and her father to suit up. They didn't question me, just pulled their hoods up over their heads. They were out of sight of the zombie. What was left of Warrington might not understand what their suiting up meant, but I didn't want him to be frightened in his last few minutes of conscious thought, because that was what he seemed to be losing. When the sun came up, I was pretty sure he'd be the walking dead inside and out. Once he was that, he wouldn't be able to be afraid. I was going to wait for it.

"He'll stop moving and just fall down like a broken doll when the sun rises," the tall blond grave digger said from the edge of the grave as he gazed down at the zombie.

"Not always," I said.

"Anita's zombies don't die at dawn," Manny said.

"Yours don't either," I said.

He grinned at me; the white in his hair seemed to glow in the growing light. It was a nice effect. "I do all right for an old man."

I shook my head. "Don't old-man me, Manny, you can still raise more zombies per night than anyone at Animators Inc. except Larry and me."

He shrugged and didn't try to hide the pleased look on his face.

"Anita," Domino said, and he was pointing the shotgun down into the grave now.

The zombie was almost free, and he was fighting harder, not like a person struggles, but more like that mindless give-it-your-all that real zombies have.

"Thomas Warrington, are you in there?" I asked.

"Hungry," he said in a voice that didn't sound like Warrington at all.

"Mr. Warrington, can you hear me?"

"Hungry," it said.

"It's almost free, Anita," Domino said.

"I order you to stop struggling," I said.

It didn't stop; in fact, it struggled harder. It was making a high-pitched hissing noise and staring at Domino as if the gun didn't exist. About every other sound or so, it was still saying, "Hungry."

"If it gets free, I'm shooting it," Domino said.

"Agreed," I said.

Nicky was beside me now. He had the AR snugged to his shoulder. "Let us shoot it."

"When the sun rises."

"Anita," Domino said.

The zombie freed one leg, only a bit of its foot still caught in the dry dirt. "Hungry . . . hungry . . . hungry." It said it like a mantra, as if that were all that was left in his brain.

"Susannah, Eddie, get ready."

"Just give the word, Anita," she said.

"Wait for it," I said, and raised the shotgun to my shoulder. I sighted at the zombie's face as it gazed up at Domino as if it had picked its target. They could be single-minded sometimes. "I've got the head," I said, voice even.

"Leg," Nicky called.

"Arm," Domino said. He probably didn't have a clear shot at much of anything else; I probably should have let him have the head. I might even have said that, but then two things happened at once; the sun rose like a ball of fire above the trees and the zombie freed itself.

It grabbed the edge of the grave to scramble out. Nicky's rifle sounded first and the zombie stumbled, one leg taken out at the knee, but it still held to the edge and was still trying to get out. I pulled the trigger and the shotgun rocked in my hands, putting a lot of energy into my shoulder where I held the butt. The top of the zombie's head exploded into blood, brains, and bits. It pulled itself up on the lip of the grave. Domino fired and one arm vanished at around the elbow, so that the zombie started to slide back into the grave. I fired at the head again and took the rest of it. If it had been a vampire it would have lain down and known it was dead, but it was a zombie, and headless it kept fighting to get out of its grave.

Nicky had moved around so he could shoot the other leg that was helping to push the body up and out. It fell a little into the grave then, only one hand holding on, and then Domino shot that hand into bits and the zombie fell back into the hole.

"Burn it!" I yelled, and stepped back from the grave. Nicky followed my lead, but Domino was still beside the hole. He fired again.

"Domino, get back!" I yelled that, too.

He glanced up, as if he hadn't realized we'd moved back. Maybe he hadn't heard over the guns. He moved back to stand with us, as we gave the grave over to something more cleansing than bullets.

The flamethrowers whooshed to life and filled the grave as if we were trying to set fire to hell. The heat drove us back; without the protective suits, human flesh would burn as quick as anything else. The sun was chasing back all the shadows, but under the tall trees it was still dusk, the fire rolling back out of the grave setting the last shadows of night dancing around us. Then something appeared at the lip of the grave; it was covered in flames, but it still moved. It took a moment for my eyes to see that it was using the stumps of its shattered arms like blades driven into the ground, almost like belaying pins as if the grave were just a mountain to scale. Nicky shot it in the upper chest with the AR a second before I shot it and the chest exploded into flame and burning bits. It fell back into the grave, and they kept pouring fire into the hole.

Sunlight patterned through the leaves above us and the fire stopped, as if the coming of the day had made that impossible, too. Susannah came over, dragging the hood of her suit off. Her face was dewed with sweat. It's hot working that close to hell.

"It'll burn for a while longer, but it's done."

Now that they weren't actively burning it I could smell the burning meat. Burning person may smell like cooking meat, but zombies don't. They always just smell burned and acrid. I fought an urge to cover my nose and breathe shallow.

"Burn it to ashes and bones," I said; my voice was empty and sounded unmoved by any of it.

"This is usually good enough," Susannah said, wiping sweat from her forehead.

"This isn't a usual kind of zombie. I need as close to ashes as you can get it."

"You're going to treat it like a vampire, aren't you?"

"Yeah," I said.

"We won't be able to get much ash, but we can give you burned bones. It's going to stink if you put it in your car to transport it."

"I've got containers in the car."

"Okay, I'll tell Dad. I'm not sure we brought enough fuel with us to do what you're asking. It takes a lot of heat to turn a body into ash and bone."

"Zombies are like vampires; they burn better than human bodies."

She nodded, shrugged, and then shook her head. "Okay, like I said, let me see if we have enough with us to get the job done." She went to talk to Eddie and see if they had the supplies they needed.

Manny came up as she left. "What are you going to do with the ashes?"

"There's a stream just down the slope," I said.

"It's a tiny stream; you can't put much into it, or some hiker will find human remains and call the police. They get upset about wasted man-hours," he said.

"I know. I'll be careful, but a little in the stream here, and a little bit more dumped into the river on the way home."

"Different bodies of running water," he said, studying my face.

"Yep."

"You want to make sure that no one else can raise this one as a zombie again."

"Oh, yeah."

"It's not a vampire, Anita. It's just a zombie. We've never taken these kind of precautions for one of them."

"Have you ever seen a zombie act like Warrington did?" I asked.

"No."

"Anything close to this kind of behavior?"

"I've never even read about a zombie like him in back issues of *The Animator*." That was the professional publication for us zombic raisers.

"And I've never seen anything like it in any of the preternatural biology write-ups either."

"That's probably not a good thing," he said.

"Agreed."

Susannah came back over. They had to get a second tank from their truck, and the body was still big enough to look like a body, but they were able to scrape some ash and bone fragments into the two small screwtop containers I gave them. The containers were in my vampire-executing kit in case I needed to spread vamp ashes; like Manny said, we'd never done it with zombie ashes before, but hey, there's always a first time.

Zerbrowski joined Manny and me and said, "I've never known you to treat a zombie like a vamp, Anita."

"Cautious in my old age, I guess."

He raised an eyebrow at me. "If you're old, then I must be ancient."

"And I should be dead," Manny said.

Nicky and Domino joined us; they had been having a little heart-to-heart of their own. I didn't know what it was about, but Domino wasn't happy. I'd ask later, or they could tell me later; right that minute

I didn't have anything left to play emotional caretaker for anyone else. I was having my own issues about Warrington, and the ghouls, and what the fuck was going on with my necromancy. And I was tired of the weretigers in my life pouting about shit; what was it with all of them and all the fucking angst? The voice in my head that tried to be more reasonable than my temper, or my personal intimacy issues, said I had more weretigers in my life than any other kind of shapeshifter and maybe it wasn't the tiger part that made them pouty; maybe it was just the sheer number of them. On one hand that was a positive thought, it wasn't just because they were tigers, but on the other hand it put me right back into thinking there were too many people in my life who looked to me for most of their emotional support. Always nice when the reasonable part of me manages to be both helpful and unhelpful in one fell swoop.

I explained what I was going to do with the jar in my hand, because bodyguards tend to get cranky if you just walk off without them.

"I'll go with," Domino said.

Nicky just came at our back without asking. I didn't mind; if I hadn't wanted to keep one hand free for my gun and had a container of zombie ashes in the other, I'd have taken his hand in mine. A little comfort would have been a good thing. At least I had the shotgun back behind my shoulder on the tactical sling, so it didn't take up another hand. Nicky and Domino had done the same thing with their long guns.

"Be careful going under trees with the tac slings, they can get caught," I said. Honestly, I was saying it more for Domino than Nicky. I knew my Bride could handle himself in actual woods. He'd proven that in Colorado, not that long ago.

"If that was for my benefit, just say so," Domino said.

"Fine, city boy, be careful under the trees near the stream."

"I've been camping before, Anita."

"Where at?"

"Near Vegas," he said.

"So desert?"

"Yeah, why does that matter?"

"I don't see many trees in the desert, so my caution stands."

"You won't give an inch, will you?"

I frowned at him. "I don't know what's got your panties in a twist, Domino, but I don't have the energy to deal with it right now."

"You never do," he said.

I sighed, and turned to Manny and Zerbrowski. "Can you give me and the guys a few minutes?"

"Of course," Manny said, and walked away.

Zerbrowski looked at me and then at both of the men. "I was going to make a smart-ass comment, but I can barely have a serious relationship with one person; I don't know how the hell you're doing it with this many." He tipped an imaginary hat and started to walk away.

"She's not," Domino said.

Zerbrowski stopped, looked at him, and then looked at me.

"It's not serious with all of us, Sergeant, or not equally serious; trust me."

"Go, just go," I said.

For maybe the first time ever, Zerbrowski just walked away from a barrel full of snarky comments instead of shooting the fish. I really appreciated it. When the three of us were alone I turned to Domino and said, "What the hell was that about? This is work for me, and I don't bring personal stuff to work."

"Nicky may be able to separate out work from personal like that, and maybe you can, too, but I'm not that good at compartmentalizing."

"Fine, I'm getting that, so what the fuck has got you so upset that you're sharing personal details with Zerbrowski?"

"Oh, hell, I don't know."

"That is not an answer," I said, glaring up at him.

"Well, it's the only answer I have, right now."

"It's not Anita and the relationship stuff you're upset about," Nicky said.

"You can say that because you have the kind of relationship the rest of us want and don't have with her."

"I can say that because I smelled how scared you were with the zombie tonight."

"We were all scared," I said.

"He was more scared than he should have been."

"She left me beside the grave like bait, not you," Domino said, pointing a finger at Nicky's chest.

"I didn't leave you as bait, Domino. It just happened to be where you were standing. I put myself at the edge of the grave at the end, too, and Nicky."

"But it was me that thing was staring at and saying *Hungry*, over and over again." His eyes were a little wide and his breathing was speeding up just talking about it.

"I didn't know the zombie would fixate on anyone. I didn't put you in harm's way on purpose."

"I wish I believed that."

"What does that even mean? I don't endanger any of you on purpose."

"We're her bodyguards; it's our job to put ourselves in danger," Nicky said.

"You stay out of it, lion."

"I'll stay out of it when you stop whining," he said.

Domino went very still, but it wasn't the stillness of the dead; it was more the quiet before the storm when the world holds its breath, just before all hell breaks loose. His arm was a blur, so fast I couldn't follow it, and only knew it impacted because Nicky rocked back a half-step. But the next blow landed on the arm Nicky raised to guard his face, and then he hit back. Domino blocked one fist, but the second got through his guard, taking him in the ribs. Domino flinched a little to that side and when Nicky feinted with his right for the ribs again he blocked, but Nicky's left hit him in the mouth and rocked him back. It rattled him, but he was able to keep moving. He backed up and avoided the next three blows altogether, but the knee that Nicky threw connected with Domino's hip, which doubled him a little, so the next knee was all ribs. I thought I heard something break, which meant I was probably too close, but they were so fast it was like there wasn't time to move. Domino tried to cover his face and ribs, so Nicky kicked him on the thighs, hips, and shins with legs, feet, and knees, over and over again in a blur of movement. Domino blocked some of it, but more and more of it was getting through his guard, so the barrage of knees, shins, and feet was punishing. Domino got in one more hit at Nicky's midsection, but he batted it away and the whole right side of Domino's face was open. Nicky closed with a hard left hook and then followed with a right uppercut that rolled Domino's eyes back and made him drop his hands enough for another left hook. Nicky used the momentum of the hook to send him spinning through with a kick to the side of Domino's face, and it was over.

Domino fell to the ground heavy. I knew by how he fell that he was completely out, even before I knelt beside him and checked for a pulse. It was there and a tightness in my gut went away; as long as everyone lived, it was all just good, painful fun.

"He's not dead," Nicky said; his voice was only slightly breathy, as if the fight had been a good warm-up. He was still in a fighting stance, slightly up on the balls of his feet, arms still half-raised as if Domino was going to get up again, or as if there might be someone else to fight.

Zerbrowski, Manny, and the grave diggers were all standing at a little distance, as if they'd run toward us to stop the fight but it was over before they could get here. It had been like most fights, over incredibly quickly. It probably hadn't lasted more than two, three minutes tops. It just seemed much longer when you were in it.

"Shit, he's fast," the tall blond grave digger said into the sudden quiet.

"Anita, do we need an ambulance?" Zerbrowski asked.

"No, I don't think so."

"This guy so needs an ambulance," the short, dark-haired grave digger said.

I couldn't really blame him for saying it. The lower half of Domino's face was covered in blood, his skin was pale, and there were cuts on the side of his face higher up. He lay utterly still as if he'd never wake up, and if he'd been human he might not have, but he wasn't human. One rattling breath came, and then he tried to sit up, but that seemed to hurt too much, so he fell back to the ground coughing blood, or maybe it was coming out of his broken nose, it was hard to tell. I helped him sit up enough so he didn't choke on his own blood.

Susannah was near enough now that she could comment. "That was brutal."

"He's not dead. If I'd been brutal, he would be," Nicky said; he was easing out of the fighting stance, but it was as if once put on alert he was having trouble letting it go.

Domino coughed more blood up and there was no way not to get some of it on me. Susannah came to kneel beside me, to help. "He's a lycanthrope," I said.

"I don't have any cuts for the blood to get into." She started trying to help hold pressure on his nose, but that made it harder for him to breathe. It was still a point for her that she was willing to touch a shape-shifter that was bleeding; a lot of humans wouldn't have.

"Don't press on the nose, you'll make it harder for him to breathe," Nicky said.

"Like you give a damn," she said, glaring up at Nicky, but she stopped trying to press so hard on Domino's face.

"Is this where you call me a brute and feel sorry for him?"

"You are a brute and a bully! It was vicious!" she said, and sounded totally indignant.

Nicky looked at me. "How about you, Anita? You think I'm a brute and a bully? That I'm vicious?"

"I think we just saw a serious cultural misunderstanding."

"What?" Susannah asked.

"They aren't the same kind of wereanimal. Domino comes from a culture where a fight like that would go so far and then stop; Nicky's culture finishes every fight pretty much like that." I didn't want to say what kind of animal each of them was, because it was like telling people what gun you carried; if they got spooked or wanted to make trouble for you, they could give details that made their bullshit seem more real to the police. I didn't think Susannah would do that, but it was just a rule when dealing with this many outsiders. I didn't know the grave diggers at all.

"You're not making any sense," she said.

"Can you sit up?" I asked Domino. He nodded, still coughing or wheezing out blood. Susannah came behind him and let him rest against her shiny fire suit. I wondered if it was dry clean only, or if the blood would even be able to soak in. One arm of my jacket and the side of my hip and thigh were bright with his blood. I tipped my dry cleaner generously and often.

"He threw the first punch," I said.

"But he didn't have to beat him senseless!" Susannah said as she cradled Domino.

"Well, that is true," I said.

"Yeah, that is true," Nicky said. He was standing more normally now, most of the tension of the fight drained away.

I stood in front of him, gazing at the tiny spot of blood on the corner of his mouth. "Did he actually make contact, or is that his blood spattered on your face?"

He licked the corner of his mouth. "Mine."

I smiled. "Once he drew blood it was all over."

Nicky made a little hands-out gesture, as if to say, *Of course*.

"You broke my damn ribs," Domino said in a voice thick with blood and the damage to his nose.

"The way you're coughing blood, one of them might have nicked your lung," Nicky said, but he didn't sound sorry.

"Does he need an ambulance?" I asked.

"A doctor, but not an ambulance, unless he wants to pussy out and says differently."

"Fuck you," Domino said; he coughed more blood, then bent over something that hurt.

"No ambulance, I guess," I said.

"He needs a hospital," Susannah said, "and you should be in handcuffs." She looked at Zerbrowski. He spread his hands wide and said, "Just because he lost the fight doesn't mean he didn't throw the first blow and start the fight."

"That's insane," she said.

"No, it's just the truth," I said.

"You're not going to call me a bully?" he asked.

"No." In my head, I thought, *A lion maybe*, and to the uninitiated that amounted to the same thing. Werehyenas would fuck you up quicker, cripple you, so the fight could end sooner, but werelions would kill you quicker, and they were more likely to start the testosterone throw-down among themselves. When dealing with other wereanimals they tried to tone it down. Our old lion pride hadn't worked that way, and it was only when talking with Micah about other prides having issues across the country that I'd learned some of the cultural divide. I'd also seen it when Nicky fought anyone. He didn't start fights, because he knew I wouldn't approve, but he sure as hell finished them.

"Are you going to be mad at me?" he asked.

I thought about it and shook my head. "No."

He smiled. "Does this mean the winner gets the girl?"

"Don't push it."

He smiled wider, which made him touch the cut in the corner of his mouth with his tongue again, more exploring to see how deep it was, which meant the wide smile had hurt, at least a little.

"I've still got to dump the ashes in the stream, and then we can get Domino to medical."

"I can put the ashes in the water," Manny said. "You take care of your boy."

I shook my head. "I'll finish my job, and we'll stop on the way home to dump more in the river, because I'm still working."

"You can't mean to make him wait to get medical attention while you do all that," Susannah said, holding Domino a little close and protectively.

"If he wants you to drive him to a hospital, or to the Circus of the Damned, that's fine with me."

"He beats me to shit, and you reward him," he said, and he was coughing a little less.

I went to one knee beside him. "Nicky didn't start this fight; you did. You drew first blood, and you did it while you were supposed to be on duty as my bodyguard, so you didn't just take your attention away from guarding me, you took Nicky's away from the job. If something bad had happened while the two of you were fighting, I'd have had to deal with it, with no help from either of you, because you let something spook you tonight. You let yourself lose sight of the job."

"Heaven help anything that comes between you and your job," he said.

"I'm done, you're done, we're done."

His eyes got worried then. "What do you mean?"

"I think I was pretty clear, Domino." I stood up.

"Anita, don't do this."

"You're the one complaining that I'm not as serious with you as I am with Nicky, that I don't have enough time and attention for you; well, you're right. There are too many of you and not enough of me, so if you don't like the way I run our relationship, then let's be done. Now you're free to find someone else who would think you're the victim here, and not that you just picked a fight that you were too fucking weak to win."

"I lose one fight and I'm weak."

"You knew better than to pick a fight with Nicky. You train with him, Domino. You've seen him spar. Hell, you've sparred with him. You knew what would happen the moment you threw the first punch, and if you didn't that makes you weak *and* stupid."

"Anita, how can you say that?" Susannah asked, and she seemed genuinely outraged, but I was done discussing it.

I started walking toward the slope that I knew would eventually lead me to the stream. Nicky fell into step beside me. "In case you need bodyguarding between here and there," he said, voice almost neutral.

I smiled and transferred the jar of zombie ash to my right hand, and offered him my left to hold. "What if we have to go for our guns?" he asked.

"I'll risk it."

"As your bodyguard I should refuse."

"It's up to you," I said.

He smiled and took my hand. His knuckles were skinned and bleeding a little. It probably would have bothered Susannah, but it didn't bother me. We walked through the graveyard, me covered in Domino's blood, Nicky skinned up from hitting him, and I was okay with that. I felt relieved to be done with Domino; one tiger down, a few more to go.

37

DOMINO WAS TRYING to get out of his clothes when we came back from the stream. Susannah seemed confused as he asked for help out of the straps of his holsters and his shirt. She looked up at me. "He's delirious."

"No, he just doesn't want to ruin his leather holsters when he shifts," I said. I squeezed Nicky's hand, knelt in the grass beside them, and started helping him take off the holsters that held both his handguns and the extra ammo clips.

Susannah was still half-cradling him as I started helping him slip his bloody shirt off. He flinched, and it was obviously hurting a lot. Nicky loomed over us. "Shirt's ruined anyway, just let it shred."

"Get away from him!" Susannah said.

"No, he's right. I can lose the shirt," Domino said in that stuffy voice you get when your nose is well and truly fucked up.

"Lose it, how?" she asked.

I helped him pull his shirt back down, trying not to hurt his ribs. "He's going to shapeshift and that will help heal some of the damage."

"Shift into what?" she asked, but she let him lean back without any sign of flinching.

"Pants aren't bloody," I said. "You like them enough to save them?"

"I'll do tiger, not half, pants . . ." He swallowed hard, as if something hurt when he talked. He coughed again, spat more blood, and curled his shoulders down like he was wanting to cradle an injury in his torso.

Nicky finished for him. "If he shifts into his full tiger form the pants may not rip; we'll just have to help him out of them once he changes."

"You're not touching him," Susannah said.

"You think we're enemies now, don't you?"

"You beat him senseless, so yes." She seemed outraged that he'd even mention it.

"We enemies now, Domino?" he asked.

"No, help me out of these pants, I'm not sure I can control what form I take, just got these tac pants."

Nicky took a knee on the other side of Domino. Susannah put an arm around Domino's shoulder and leaned them both back away from him. Domino made a pain sound, because bending that way obviously hurt.

"Don't touch him!"

"You're hurting me," Domino managed to say.

"You're bending him the wrong way," I said.

Susannah said, "How can you be so calm?"

I wasn't sure if she was talking to Domino or me, but I answered. "Because it's over."

"He's still bleeding and hurt; it's not over."

"The fight is," Nicky said, and reached for Domino's belt.

"What are you doing?" She sounded outraged, but she didn't bend him away from Nicky this time.

"He asked Nicky to help get his pants off, remember?" I said.

Nicky unbuckled the other man's pants with the same sure, deft movements he used when he got me undressed. I wore almost the exact same kind of belt these days; it was sturdy enough to hold up to gun holsters without buckling or getting too damaged, too fast.

It was when Nicky started easing Domino's pants down from his waist that she said, "How can you let him touch you like that?"

"It's going to take Anita and Nicky to get my pants off with minimum pain," Domino said.

I joined Nicky in helping to work the pants down around Domino's hips. I got to see that he'd worn black underwear today, a Brazilian, or Rio cut, so that it was high on the sides. I knew he was wearing it for Jade. It was one of the few strong preferences she'd expressed for men to wear around her.

"He tried to kill you!" Susannah said.

"If he'd meant to kill me, he would have," Domino said. He made a face as we got his pants down to midhip, and he tried to raise himself up to help us. He started coughing again, and a fresh gout of blood came up very bright red in the morning light.

"If that's your lung, then we need to get you to a hospital, or you could die."

When Domino could speak without coughing blood he wiped his mouth with the back of his hand and said, "I'll heal, and Nicky knows it."

"I don't understand any of this," she said.

"You seem nice, but no, you don't understand."

"Then explain it to me, because this makes no sense."

Domino looked at her, and it was as if she hadn't really seen the yellow and red fire color of his eyes, and maybe she hadn't in the dark. She stared at his eyes and whispered, "Oh, my God, your eyes."

"Beautiful, aren't they?" I said.

She just stared into the fire of his eyes, like a mouse hypnotized by a snake.

Domino said, "You think I'm nice, because Nicky is less nice, but I was raised to be muscle for an old-school mobster; that is not a nice business. It is not gentle, or kind, and for me to stand as a guard beside the boss, neither was I. Nicky is a better bad guy than I am, but that doesn't make me a good guy, or not the kind of good guy you think I am."

"I don't understand any of this."

He turned and looked at me. "I think Susannah needs to go somewhere else."

I nodded. "Eddie, can you take Susannah to the truck? Domino would like a little privacy for his clothes coming off."

Domino looked at me. He knew, and I knew, that he didn't give a damn if she saw him naked. He just didn't want someone who was this much of an outsider making him feel like a freak, or maybe just continuously pointing out how very alien we all were from the "ordinary" folks.

Eddie came and helped his daughter stand up, which meant Domino had to support all his weight, using one hand and leaning to the side. He couldn't hide the fact that it hurt, and that he'd rather have it hurt that much than take the comfort of a pretty woman said just how much her attitude had bothered him. It's one thing to know you're a freak; it's another to have people's attitudes drive it home with an axe.

Zerbrowski said, "You need any help, just yell," and then he went to join the others, who had taken my request for privacy to undress Domino very seriously. The three of us were alone in the filtered sunlight playing through the trees.

We eased Domino's pants down his ass; the black undies stayed put. They were stretched a little tight across the front, but not as tight as they could get.

"Susannah is cute," he said.

"I guess she is," I said.

"You want to save the underwear?" Nicky asked.

"Yeah."

I reached back to one side of his body, Nicky echoed me, and we eased the underwear down, baring his ass, but that wasn't the tricky bit. Tricky was easing it off the front of him with him partially erect. Normally, it wouldn't have bothered me that much, but we had just broken up; it seemed weird to be undressing him after having THE fight, like it was a breach of some breakup law somewhere. A last chance at sex I understood, but just undressing him seemed odd.

"Could I date her?" He asked it about the time the underwear spilled off him and he was just there, embarrassingly prominent, but still beautiful. There was no one in my bed who didn't make me pause for at least a second and go, *Pretty*. Of course, Domino wasn't in my bed anymore, so . . . fuck it, I went back to helping Nicky get him out of his clothes.

"Sure, though I think your last speech to her may have queered the deal."

"Would it bother you if I dated her?"

"You mean because she's almost a friend, or because you're with another woman, besides me and Jade?"

"The last part," he said, as we eased his pants down his legs. He was taking more weight on one of his arms than the other. I didn't think his hands were hurt; it was more that one side of his ribs hurt more than the other.

I thought about it and then said the truth. "No, it wouldn't bother me."

"Thanks, that's what I needed to know."

"Remember, Domino, it doesn't bother her when Jean-Claude is with Envy, either," Nicky said.

I frowned at him. "You're not helping."

"It's just that your being okay with your men being with other women, or other men, doesn't prove you don't care."

I looked at him and let him feel that I wasn't happy with him. I was rid of one person in my bed; I did not want to make this fight up. I wanted to be done with someone, and the moment I thought it, I said, "Shit."

"See?" Nicky said.

"Fuck you," I said.

"Later," he said.

"Arrogant."

He smiled. "I didn't say tonight, I said later. A few days from now is still later."

I didn't know what to say to that, so I didn't try. I could be taught.

"I feel like I just missed a whole conversation," Domino said.

"Nicky reminded me that I'm a little overwhelmed personally right now, and feeling pressured by all the tigers and your prophecy."

"Sorry," he said.

"You don't have to apologize for that, Domino. I'm not sure anyone owes me an apology for it, but when we broke up I felt relieved."

He looked sad, even through the pain. It made me touch his bare thigh and say, "I thought, one tiger down, a few more to go. That's not a good enough reason to dump someone."

"So are we broken up, or not? I'm confused."

"You aren't the only one who's confused," I said.

Nicky started unlacing one of Domino's boots, and I did the other.

He was right; we couldn't finish taking off his pants with the boots still on him. Shoes were always the sticking point when you stripped in real life; the trick was to take the shoes off early in the process if you're wearing real pants. Most professional strippers wear pants meant to rip away with Velcro and be put back together for next time. In movies, it's all distraction and stopping the scene a dozen times to change the clothes, so that some scenes it's like five different outfits that look like a single strip scene; it's all illusion. In real life, take the shoes off first.

"What does that mean?" he asked.

Nicky surprised me by answering, "It means that Anita can't be your girlfriend; there isn't enough time or energy for anyone to be a girl-friend to this many people, but she still needs to feed the *ardeur* and Jean-Claude still needs to feed on blood."

"Neither you nor I let the vampires feed on us."

"I'm going to try it with Jean-Claude."

We both looked at Nicky. "You were very clear on not being food for the vamps," I said.

He nodded as we got the last of Domino's clothes off him. He leaned on the grass, totally nude and a little less excited to be there, but then it had been painful and Domino didn't mix pain with sex.

"I've decided to try it," Nicky said.

"Why?" I asked.

"Because you are going to have to cut your list down, especially if you add another tiger. Keeping lovers who will also feed Jean-Claude is practical, and you can be surprisingly practical in this area."

I was in love with this man, and he thought I might jettison him because I was overwhelmed. I wasn't sure what that said about me; for Nicky it was just part of being a sociopath. If you're not meeting enough needs, why do I need you?

"I don't think I can be with Jean-Claude like that. I've seen him take blood and it's too close to sex," Domino said.

"True, but Jean-Claude respects limits."

"Why not get rid of people that she only sees every once in a while, like Rafael, or the swan king?"

"They're too powerful as allies, and the feeding of the *ardeur* is part of what keeps them our allies, and it is an amazing power feed when she takes either of them," Nicky said.

"Yeah," Domino said, buck naked on the grass, "it's a rush, like a drug rush."

Nicky nodded.

"We undressed you so you could change form, not so you could discuss my feeding schedule."

"If Jade liked you better, would you be okay with just her?" Nicky asked.

He nodded, winced, got very still, and said, "I would love her if she'd let me, but she's so afraid of men, it makes me one of the bad guys to her, just because I'm attracted to her."

"She's a mess," I said.

"That's not fair," he said, and motioned at me, as if he meant to point, but the moment he did fresh blood spilled out of his mouth, and he began to gasp, as if he couldn't breathe.

"Your lung just collapsed," Nicky said.

"Shapeshift," I said.

Domino collapsed slowly to his side, his breathing so harsh it hurt to hear it. His skin was already darkening around the edges as he fought to breathe.

"Why doesn't he change?" I asked.

"I don't know."

"He'll pass out and then he'll change, right?"

He shook his head. "No, if he passes out he could die."

"What?"

"Vampires don't need to breathe; we do."

"Fuck!" I touched his face and the moment skin touched skin I couldn't breathe. My chest was on fire, and there was one sharp point that just fucking hurt. I was on the ground still touching him; our eyes locked. I stared into those orange and yellow eyes and thought, *We're dying*.

38

NICKY JERKED MY hand off Domino, and I could breathe again. It still hurt, but it was distant, dull, aching, as if my chest were sore from a days-old beating. Nicky pulled me into his lap and I lay there watching Domino writhe, gasping for air. He reached out to me, and Nicky grabbed my hand, kept me from touching again.

"Change form, Domino," Nicky said.

Jean-Claude's voice was loud in my head as he said, "*Ma petite*, what is happening?"

I didn't bother talking, just let him "see" what I was seeing. "Shield from him, Anita." He almost never used my real name. "Shield, or he will drag you down with him. I will shield as many of the others as I can."

And he was gone, doing what he'd urged me to do, shielding hard and complete like the walls of a castle newly made, perfect and unassailable. My shields hadn't had six hundred years of practice, and they weren't as perfect as his; I could still feel Domino through my shields, and it was hard to ignore him while he was right in front of me dying. I could feel Nathaniel and Damian the strongest, because they were the first animal to call I'd ever found and my vampire servant. Damian was supposed to be to me what I was to Jean-Claude. I felt the others I was tied to, but Jean-Claude had done his best to shield them from me. I felt them all offering their energy down the leash that held them to me, but there was other power even closer. I looked up at Nicky while he held me. I'd accidentally drained him to death once, and I wasn't joking about the "death" part. The doctor had to restart his heart twice, and no one had been nearly this badly hurt. If he'd been my lion to call I would have been able to feel him giving up his energy, but he was my

Bride, which meant the energy flow was one way, and much more sub-tle. I had to fight through the aches, the fear, worries, all of it, to find a quiet place in my head where I could feel the flow from him to me.

It was there flowing from his skin to mine. I pushed myself out of his lap to fall on the grass and crawl away from his reaching hands. "NO!"

I lay there between the two men, one trying to drain my life away and the other willing to give his. I turned on my side and told Domino, "Change, damn you!"

He stared at me, eyes wide, face starting to change colors the way you do when you're choking. I knew it hurt as much to breathe as it sounded, as he lay on the ground and gasped his life away.

I knew how to call someone's beast. Richard had taught me, and as if thinking about him was enough I smelled forest, thick with ever-greens that didn't grow anywhere near this cemetery. I heard Richard whisper in my head, "Anita."

"Help me bring his beast." I said my part out loud, because it was too hard to think inside my head, in that moment. I expected him to argue with me, because we always argued, but he didn't. I don't know if Jean-Claude had contacted him, or if he saw what was happening, but he just reached down that long metaphysical line and poured the warmth of his energy into me. I smelled the musk of wolf, and saw him, the morning sunlight shining through his shoulder-length brown waves with lines of gold and red, all framing that permanently tanned face with its almost heartbreakingly handsome lines. The moment I met his brown eyes they changed to wolf amber and the rush of energy danced along my skin in a warm surge of power. I rolled over and pressed my hand to Domino's shoulder. This time he didn't drag me down into his pain; I shoved power into him, and didn't care that it wasn't gentle, we were out of time for gentle. I slammed it into him the way you'd hit someone's heart with electricity and adrenaline to restart it.

Domino's body reacted as if I'd hit him with real electricity, spine bowing, limbs straining, blood pouring out of his mouth as the ribs ripped through more of his lungs, and then his pale skin rippled like silk over water one moment, and then the next his body exploded in a wave of hot liquid that poured over me, so that I was blind until I used my other hand to wipe my eyes.

A white tiger lay on its side, black stripes crisp and clean in the light, like it had been newly made right this moment. It lay dry and somehow unreal in the middle of the wet grass. It was a white tiger twice the size of a natural one, which made it the size of a horse. I didn't see my lovers in their pure animal form much; sometimes I forgot just how massive they were in this form.

I felt that warm pulse of energy again, and the scent of wolf and evergreen was strong. Richard thought at me, "Is Domino okay?"

I looked at that huge, furred side and waited for it to breathe. I didn't realize that I was holding my own breath waiting for it until the tiger breathed, and I let my own out, and had to take another quick breath to sort of catch up.

Nicky took its pulse inside the leg, near the armpit, the way you do on dogs. He nodded. "He's unconscious, but pulse is good."

"Thank you, Richard, thank you so much."

"I'm glad I could help. Domino is a nice guy. I'll look forward to hearing how he got hurt tonight after the meeting."

"What meeting?"

"Rafael and Micah called a meeting of the local leaders. I'll be over after my last class."

"I didn't know."

"Busy day," he said.

"Yeah."

"I've got to run, hitting the gym before my first class."

"Thank you again, Richard."

He smiled and it was a good smile, if not quite the one that used to melt me into my socks and out of my clothes. "You'd have figured it out."

"But maybe not in time."

"This is part of what the triumvirate is supposed to be for, Anita. I'm sorry that I didn't understand that for so long."

I heard someone say, "Oh my God, it's beautiful."

"Company," I said, "gotta go."

"Tonight," he said.

"Tonight," I said, and cut the connection at the same time he did, so it was almost disorienting. It felt odd to be on the grass, covered in wereanimal goop again, and not standing in Richard's driveway—though I was left wondering about tonight, and exactly what he might expect. We hadn't seen each other much lately. Which probably meant he was dating someone seriously, and I had plenty to keep me busy.

Susannah was standing gazing down at the gigantic tiger with a look of awe on her face. She started to drop to her knees and reach out, but Nicky interfered. "Not a good idea; when he wakes up he may not know where he is for a few seconds. You don't want to startle him."

She looked at Nicky, blinking, uncomprehending.

I said, "Think of him as a combat vet; they don't startle awake well."

She nodded, looking serious, because I knew that one of her ex-boyfriends had let his post-traumatic stress disorder ruin their relationship and his life. I'd heard too much about that failed relationship, too, come to think of it. There was a reason that Susannah and I had never gotten together for drinks and girl talk; I didn't want to know more about her love life than I already did.

"That is a damn big cat," Zerbrowski said.

I nodded. Nicky offered me a hand up and I took it, though I was shaking gunk off my hands and scraping it off my clothes again. Jesus, I was going to need another shower. Nicky was almost untouched except for the knee of one pant leg where he'd knelt to check Domino's pulse.

"How come you're clean and I'm covered in it?"

"I was almost two feet farther away," he said.

"Far enough, I guess," I said as I flung the goopy stuff from my hand onto the grass.

Zerbrowski was grinning at me.

"Oh, just say it, before you bust trying to keep it in," I said.

"This has got to be a fetish, it's like clear bukkake."

I gave him a dirty look. "It's thicker, lasts longer, and doesn't break down as quickly." I scraped more of it off my arms and onto the grass.

"Wow," he said, still grinning so hard it looked like he'd hurt himself.

"Do you need help getting him into your SUV?" Manny asked, gazing down at the tiger.

The air flexed, almost like heat over a summer highway, and then the enormous tiger seemed to shrink in upon itself, and Domino's human body appeared like an insect melting out of an ice cube, until the only thing left was him.

"Wow," Susannah said, and she wasn't remarking on the stuff I was scraping off my face. She was looking down at the still-unconscious Domino almost the same way she'd looked at his beast, like it was one of the most beautiful things she'd ever seen, except this time there was good old-fashioned lust mixed in with the nature-admiring awe.

It was a bad sign that he'd shifted back so quickly and been unconscious through both changes; it meant he was very hurt. Nicky and I exchanged a look between us. We were the only ones standing there who knew it was a bad sign. But two of the people with us knew my face well enough to know it was bad.

"He going to be all right?" Zerbrowski asked.

Manny just studied my face and Nicky's.

I nodded. "Eventually."

"He's easier to carry like this," Nicky said, as he knelt down and picked up the unconscious man. Domino's long legs trailed over his arms, but the rest of him was tucked in close to Nicky's chest, the way you'd carry a child.

"You really are as strong as you look," Susannah said.

"Stronger," he said, and turned to me. "We ready to go?"

I nodded. "Yeah, I'm past ready to get out of this cemetery."

Manny helped me pack my bag up and carried it for me so I wouldn't get gunk all over the nice leather. I carried two of the long guns, and Zerbrowski carried the second shotgun. Eddie told me that he had a call in to the company that ran this and several other cemeteries in the area.

"Hopefully we'll get a contract for the ghouls, before nightfall," he said.

I nodded. "Yeah, we can hope."

Susannah kept looking at Domino, still very nude in Nicky's arms. She'd catch herself staring and then look away, but her gaze kept going back to him. It was a nice sight, but it was still a little rude. I started to tell her to keep her eyes in her head, but then I remembered Domino asking if I'd be all right if he dated Susannah, so I kept my mouth shut. If they dated, she'd be doing more than just looking at him nude. It wasn't my business, really, honestly, it wasn't, so why did her staring at him like it was a peep show bother me so much? That was the question, wasn't it? Damn.

39

THE THREE OF us that were conscious put on sunglasses against all the morning sunlight. I called Special Agent Manning from the car; let's hear it for Bluetooth actually working. "You want to watch the videos using your ability with the dead, is that what you said?" she asked.

"Yes."

"Didn't you use your expertise with the dead the first time?"

"My expertise, but not my ability."

"Explain the difference to me."

"I looked at the videos like a cop who can raise the dead. Now, I want to watch them with my psychic ability actually active, to see if I can pick up any clues I couldn't see with just my eyes; does that make sense?"

"Actually, yes."

"I'd like to include a second animator for this second viewing, Manny Rodriguez."

"He's the animator who trained you originally; we're familiar with him." She said it like the words meant more, like she'd checked into him in a more than typical way. I let it go with him sitting in the car with me, since I hadn't mentioned that I was making the call on the Bluetooth so that everyone in the car could hear it. I would ask later, though.

"Can he be my second set of eyes on the viewing?"

"No, Marshal Blake, he can't be."

"If I asked why not, would you answer me?"

"You know that he was an intimate of Dominga Salvador, whom you've described as one of the most evil people you've ever met."

It was hard not to look at Manny, but I managed. "I'm aware of Manny's past."

"Then you can understand why we don't want him involved on this case."

"Once a bad guy, always a bad guy, huh?"

"In my experience, Marshal Blake, yes."

I patted Manny's shoulder as I drove, just to let him know I didn't agree. "We don't have time to argue about it, Agent Manning, so I'll just go it alone, psychically speaking, through the videos again."

"You can have another psychic with you, Blake, just not Rodriguez."

"There's no one else at Animators Inc. that I'd want to share the duties with," I said.

"How about Kirkland?"

"Like I said, no one at Animators Inc."

"He's full time with us and the Marshals Service now, so he doesn't work there anymore," she said; the tone in her voice was trying to get me to share information, though I couldn't have explained how: I think she'd just been on the job so long that everything was a potential inter-rogation. I wondered if she'd ever had teenage kids; they must have loved it, in that I-hate-you kind of way.

"Larry and I have a fundamental difference of methodology," I said.

"What does that mean?"

"He thinks I'm a cold-blooded, murdering sociopath, and I think he's a weak-willed rule lover who flinches at the hard shit."

She laughed, which was interesting since I hadn't meant to be funny.

"You and he do seem to have a very different approach to your jobs, that much is true."

"I think what I said was more accurate, but have it your way."

"Is he powerful enough psychically to help you spot things on the videos?"

I thought about it, and I tried to be fair. "Is he powerful enough? Yes. Is he willing to embrace his gifts enough to see everything he can? I don't know."

"You think he doesn't embrace his gifts with the dead fully?"

"I just said that, so yeah."

"We at the bureau have found Kirkland to be fully integrated with his abilities."

"Fully integrated? I've never heard that phrase used like that before."

"Bureau-speak, you know how it is." She made light of it, but her voice gave something away; I wasn't sure exactly what that something was, but she was hiding something, or maybe wished she hadn't given me the phrase.

"Yeah, I know how it is," I said, when of course what I really meant was, *You know you overshared, I know you overshared, and you're hoping I missed it, but you know I didn't. You're hoping I won't try to chase down what it means, but we both know I will.*

"I'll see if Agent Kirkland is available later today to help you view the videos."

"I'd really rather not watch them with him," I said.

"Why, Blake? And it needs to be a good work reason, not a personal one."

"One, I'm not convinced he's fully integrated with his powers, so I don't know that he'll really be helpful to me. Two, he's very conservative, and I really don't want to watch sex tapes with someone who thinks I'm sleeping with the enemy."

"Come again, Blake? I don't understand."

"Agent Kirkland has an issue with me cohabiting with the monsters, Agent Manning."

"Has he said as much?"

"He sees vampires as walking corpses, so yeah, he's pretty creeped out that I'm boning one or two of them."

"Do you really think he'll let his personal opinion interfere with his job on this case?"

"Maybe, or maybe I just don't want another lecture about how I'm evil and going to hell."

"Did he truly say that to you in those words?" Now she sounded serious.

"Not in those exact words—oh, well, he's called me evil, but he didn't tell me I was going to hell; it's just sort of implied."

"I've found Kirkland to be absolutely professional, very by-the-book."

"Yeah, if you haven't noticed I'm not really a by-the-book kind of gal."

She laughed again. Glad I could amuse someone today. "Well, your record does certainly speak to a level of rule breaking that I could see Kirkland disapproving of in a partner."

"God, you do good polite-speak, Manning."

The laughter died off in her voice. "I do more paperwork than you do, I have to be more polite."

"True, and how did Larry keep his marshal's badge while he went full time for you guys?"

"We made a special arrangement between the agencies so he could carry both badges."

"Isn't that a conflict of interest, a man can't serve two masters and all that?"

"It is a level of interagency cooperation that I've never seen before," she said.

"I know he needed to stay part of the Preternatural Branch so he could keep being a legal executioner. We have some serious loopholes when it comes to violence and killing that straight FBI or even the main-branch Marshals Service doesn't have. You wanted an FBI pet, but you wanted him to be able to kill like an executioner. Larry isn't a shooter, Manning; I hope you guys didn't bring him in thinking otherwise."

"Kirkland gets the job done."

"Out in the field, I doubt that."

"And if you weren't such a fucking wild card you might have been the first agent with dual badges, but it's not just Kirkland who mistrusts your allegiances, Marshal." She was back to serious, bordering on unfriendly.

"I was told a long time ago that the Feds decided they couldn't control me, so they didn't want me in their sandbox."

"Told by whom?" she asked.

"I think I can find fresh clues using my powers if I watch those awful videos again, Manning."

"Name a time."

"I have to clean up from the zombie-raising side of my job, but then I'm at your disposal."

Nicky said from the backseat, "You have to eat and feed before you go back out. Nathaniel and Micah texted me to remind you."

I flinched, waiting for Manning to ask, *Who is that?* but she didn't. Let's hear it for technology actually being aimed at just the driver. I knew it was designed so soccer moms and dads could talk hands-free while kids were screaming in the car, but hey, it was good for my job, too.

"I have to clean up and get food. My sweeties have been complaining I forget to eat when I'm on a case and it makes me . . . grumpy."

She made a sound that was almost a snort. "Well, eat before you watch the videos, because you know you won't want to eat afterward."

"Yeah, not so much," I said.

"I'm going to try to get Kirkland in on this round of video watching, Blake, just so you know."

"I figured you were."

"Will you watch the videos with him?"

"Will you sit in with us and make sure we don't fight?"

"Like you're teenagers that need a referee?" she asked.

"No, more like we're those two officers that haven't thrown a punch at each other yet, but it's coming. Think of it as the grown-up version of the teenage thing."

"I'm not sure I call that grown-up behavior."

"Call it what you like, but I'm requesting that you don't leave Larry and me alone with the videos, because it will not go well."

"If you were one of our agents, admitting that you couldn't work professionally with another agent would be a tick against you in my report."

"Well, isn't it just peachy that I'm not one of your agents, Special Agent Manning," I said, and I knew the smile that went with the words was my unpleasant one, the one that was more snarl than happy smile. I didn't care, and she couldn't see it anyway.

"And this is exactly why the bureau doesn't want you to come play with us, Blake."

"I'm never going to be team player enough for the FBI; you know it, I know it, we all know it. Now, can we move on, and will you give Larry and me a supervising agent or someone so we don't kill each other, metaphorically speaking?"

"Yes, Blake, I'll make sure you have a supervising agent to babysit the two of you while you look for clues."

"Great, thanks, let me know when Larry is free to watch the horror show. Wait, I thought you said he had seen the videos and told you to show them to me, that I'd see more than he had?"

"He's seen some of the videos," she said, and her voice had that I'm-hiding-something tone again.

"He stopped near the beginning of them, didn't he?"

"He said that he didn't have your level of expertise and that you would be able to help us more."

"Son of a bitch," I said.

"Blake, there's no call for profanity."

"The hell there isn't; he didn't want to watch the videos all the way through, because he didn't want to see the nightmares on them, but he's fine with me seeing the whole fucking mess."

"You are better with the dead than Kirkland, aren't you?"

"Yes."

"Then he was right."

"He was right, but not for the reason he said."

"I don't understand, Blake."

"Nothing, just fuck it. I'm going home to clean up and eat; let me know when Kirkland's schedule opens up."

"I will, and Blake, I don't know what personal beef you have with Kirkland, but don't let it hurt the investigation."

"I won't if Larry won't," I said, and it sounded childish even to me.

"I really expected better of you, Blake. We need to stop these men before they pick a new victim."

"We need to free the victims they have already, Manning, I know that. Trust me, I'm motivated to stop this shit."

"Okay, that's what I needed to hear, Blake. I'll text you later with times."

"Thanks, Manning. See you later."

"Not if I can help it; I do not need to sit through those images again, but you'll have your agent to babysit and take notes." And she hung up. You'd almost think she didn't enjoy talking to me, or something.

40

MANNY THANKED ME for trying to include him in the investigation. "*De nada*, Manny, you'd be a lot more help than Larry will."

"You know that I did things when I was with Dominga that I would undo if I could."

"I know."

"I'm just glad that Rosita found me and made me leave all that behind before the Señora talked me into having a child with her."

"What?" I asked, and glanced away from the road long enough to stare at him.

"Red light, Anita," Nicky said.

I had to brake hard not to run the light. "Okay, explain that last comment, Manny."

"The Señora wanted us to have a child together; she hoped it would be even more powerful than we were, or than she was; she made no bones about the fact that I was strong, but not as strong as she. One of the reasons you intrigued her was that she sensed a power that could rival hers."

"Yeah, she made it clear that her interest in me was strictly magical, in that 'join me in my evil plot to take over the world' kind of way."

"She didn't want to take over the world, Anita. She just wanted your help to find ways to make a profit from raising zombies. She enjoyed that people were afraid of her, but she was a very practical woman, the Señora, and she thought you could help her find new ways to expand the business."

"Like sex slave zombies; I remember, Manny." I shuddered, which made passing cars in traffic a little challenging, but I managed.

"She saw you as a way to forge a dynasty of undead."

"What does that even mean?" I asked.

"She wanted you to have a baby with her nephew."

"The one you described as not right?"

"No, not Artie, his brother, Max. He was always a polite boy, good student, a gentleman to his brother's bad boy."

"Artie and Max; Arturo and what?"

"Maximiliano."

"That's a new one to me."

"You have the Latino genetics, but not the culture. It's actually a fairly popular name right now."

"How about Arturo?"

"Not so much," he said, smiling.

"So if I had agreed to work with her she'd have tried to set me up with her nephew?"

"Almost certainly."

I shook my head. "It's just weird to think that she wanted me to breed with her family."

"Why is it weird?" Nicky asked.

I glanced in the rearview mirror. "It just is."

"It's how we breed a good working horse, or hunting dog."

"I'm not a horse, or a dog," I said.

"Yeah, but it's still the same principle, Anita. Most of the horses that have won the Triple Crown are from bloodlines that have other champions in their pedigree. We don't like to admit that people are just smart animals, but you see the star athlete marry the athletic cheerleader or gymnast, and most of their kids are great at sports, because it's in their genes. Why can't necromancy be the same?"

"I didn't say it couldn't work, Nicky, I said it was creepy."

"You said it was weird that she wanted you to breed with her family, but it's actually really logical if you want to get some uber-necromancer out of it."

I glanced back at the next light and found his face calm, peaceful, because it was all about logic. I'm not saying all sociopaths are logical, but not having to deal with many emotions seemed to help Nicky be very clear about things that bothered me more.

"I wonder if having a vampire father would help your child be a more powerful necromancer?" Manny asked.

"Don't you start," I said.

"I think it'll be about Jean-Claude's original human genetics, so it shouldn't matter to Anita's magic," Nicky said.

"I'm not planning to have a baby with Jean-Claude, we're just getting married."

"You don't want children, ever?" Nicky asked.

"No," I said.

"I know you think it wouldn't work with your job."

"It wouldn't," I said.

"But you're actually not having sex with anyone who's psychically gifted. We're all just vamps, or shapeshifters, but the preternatural stuff isn't native gifts; it's add-on parts."

"Why are we having this discussion again?" I asked.

"Because I said Dominga wanted you to breed with her nephew."

I glared at Manny. "All right, I know what started it, but I'm just saying, I'm done with this conversation."

"Tell me to stop talking about it, and I have to do what you say," Nicky said.

I glared at him in the rearview mirror. He knew that I didn't like telling him not to talk about things, because once I did he actually couldn't bring the topic back up unless I told him it was okay, and I kept forgetting what I'd told him to drop as a topic. Nathaniel and Cynric had actually come to me with a list of things that Nicky couldn't discuss with me, because of offhand comments during everyday conversations. Do you know how many times a person tells someone to drop something, or don't talk about it anymore? A lot, right? Now imagine that the person you said that to could never, ever bring the topic up again. I'd started being very careful about using certain phrases around Nicky.

"Damn you, you know I won't."

He smiled at me, so pleased with himself that I could see his eyes crinkle even around the sunglasses and the long triangular fall of his hair. "Your dad is blue-eyed and blond, right?"

"Yeah." I said it all suspicious-like.

"Then you carry the gene for both, so if you pick someone who's blond and blue-eyed on both sides of their family you might end up with a baby that is, too."

"You volunteering?"

He shook his head. "My mother is a diagnosed psychopath, and I'm a diagnosed sociopath; I don't think my genetics is what you want to mix with yours. I'm just saying, you could pick and choose some of it, because of how many men you have in your life; that's all."

"I'm sorry," I said.

"Why, because you agree that babies would be a bad idea with me, or that my family tree is such shit?"

"That your mother was an evil bitch, I think."

He smiled. "It's a shame that Jean-Claude doesn't have parents to be your in-laws."

The change of topics was too fast for me. "What? Why?"

"You'd be a blunt hell on wheels as a daughter-in-law."

Manny gave a loud, surprised laugh. "Oh my God, she would be! She so would be!"

"Micah's parents like me," I said.

Nicky and Manny were laughing so hard I don't think they heard me. Nicky finally managed to say, "Yeah, but you did save his father's life, and the whole damn city, maybe the country, from being overrun by killer zombies."

"Oh," Manny said, "no other daughter-in-law, or son-in-law for that matter, can ever compete with that. 'What does your wife do? Oh, she saved the world from murderous zombies; what does your spouse do?'" They started laughing again, and I just gave up and let them have it. Ending the night with laughter was better than the alternatives. Domino was still passed out in the very back of the SUV. The doctor on call would meet us at the Circus of the Damned. I let the men laugh at my expense, because laughter was so much better than tears.

41

WE GOT TO the Circus of the Damned with the light still soft and yellow, letting you know from the color and feel of it just how early it was. We'd caught the beginnings of rush hour traffic after we dropped Manny at his car in front of Animators Inc. and headed north on 270, but you could make it from Olive/270 to the Circus in record time this early. The air was still soft, and the white yellow that lets you know that kids aren't in class yet, and people are still rushing for coffee and breakfast but not quite at their desks. I used to hate this time of day, because it meant I'd worked far too many hours the night before and it made me grumpy, but when death had come so close the light was a victory. We'd survived the night. After a night when I wasn't sure everyone would survive, morning did not suck, and dawn was a blessing.

I carried my equipment bag. We divided up the long guns on their tactical slings, and Nicky carried Domino in his arms as if the man weighed nothing. I could have carried him over my shoulder in some kind of fireman's carry, but division of labor meant it made more sense for the biggest guy to carry the second-biggest guy.

I had a key to the back door of the Circus, but I didn't have to use it today. The door opened and a medical team dressed in street clothes came to swarm around Nicky. They checked Domino, but they didn't immediately take the unconscious man from his arms. I'd learned that doctors are very hesitant to move people until they know that moving them won't make things worse. They were dressed in street clothes because we just assumed we were under surveillance from somebody; whether it was a rival group, cops, or government, it was just better to be cautious. Having a full medical team come swarming out might start to look even more suspicious than carrying an unconscious nude man inside. We could at least explain that part as a lycanthrope doing the typical pass-out when they first hit human form after hours of being furry. Most of the people in my inner circle didn't pass out like that, but strangely, Domino did, which meant he was less powerful than most of my inner circle; maybe that was why he'd almost died from the beating.

Guards I knew took my bags, and I let them. Once I wouldn't have let anyone carry my bags, but I'd learned they weren't doing it because they thought I was weak, but as a sign of respect. The boss doesn't carry shit.

Lisandro and another guard I didn't recognize came out the door in the distance, as we all moved across the parking lot. The new guard was taller than Lisandro by inches, which made him at least six-three or six-four. Lisandro's hair was black, but the new guy's hair was that deep black that had blue highlights in it as the morning sun hit them. The hair had fallen forward, hiding his face, and then I couldn't see either of them past the herd of taller people around me; when the view cleared I saw the black-and-silver T-shirt that I'd picked out for him, the black jeans that fit his hips nicely and clung to his thighs and all that long leg, until the slight flare at the bottom that gave room to go over the black-and-silver tooled cowboy boots that he'd just gotten. I felt silly not realizing it was Cynric from the moment I saw him. I just almost never saw him from a distance except on the football field, or the track, and this was different.

Seeing him all rock-star casual for school made me wonder who he was dressing to impress. Technically he could date other people, in fact I was encouraging it, but wondering who he was dressing up for caused a slight flare of jealousy, which was totally ridiculous. He was only nineteen, twelve years younger than me, and I was always trying to get him to meet a nice girl his own age, or to admit he felt neglected being just another man in my life, but seeing him like this, noticing just how tall, how filled out he was from lifting weights and team practice . . . he looked older than nineteen. Maybe it was the height?

He looked up, and the moment he saw me his face lit up in that way you only look at someone that you love. He didn't look much like the kid I'd met in Vegas. The issue was still there, big and ugly and therapy-worthy, but the issue wasn't Cynric. The issue was what had been done to both of us against our will. We were both survivors—no, we'd done more than just survive what Marmee Noir had done to us; we had thrived. Some tightness in my chest eased, and I smiled at him. Maybe it wasn't as good a smile as he gave me, but I would work on that. However we got together, the thought of him dressing up to catch the eye of another woman bothered me, in a way that Domino having full-blown sex with someone else didn't.

My head and my issues had made me doubt, but it was as if admitting the issues out loud had freed me to look at them and begin to work through them. I was happy to see him, so happy it surprised me. Whatever he saw on my face made him look even happier as he hurried toward me.

"Go give Sin his good-morning kiss," Nicky said.

I hesitated.

"Docs are here, I got Domino. Go."

I touched his arm, not sure I could get through everyone else for a kiss, and went to one of the other men in my life. I started to hug him, but remembered that I was still covered in drying weretiger goop in time to save his outfit. The kiss turned awkward as I stopped him from hugging me. He looked hurt for a second, then touched my shoulder and said, "What did you do in the cemetery tonight? What's in your hair?" He laughed and shook his head.

"Long story, but you look too nice to ruin the outfit by smearing this stuff all over you."

He looked out and saw Domino. "I felt some of it, before Jean-Claude shielded us all. Is Domino going to be all right?"

"I think so, but I keep forgetting that he's weaker than some of you, so he doesn't heal as well as you, or Nicky."

"Or most of us," he said, and looked worried.

I traced my relatively clean hand down the front of his shirt, where it covered a very nice chest. "What are you all dressed up for?"

"I knew you'd forget, and that's okay, but today they're handing out the senior awards at school. Family is welcome to come watch and there's snacks afterward."

"I did totally forget, but I thought our deal was that I didn't come on parent days, since that's not what I am to you."

"I'm asking Nathaniel to come as my brother, Nicky too, and Micah, but you"—and he touched my face, tilting it up toward him—"you I want to come as my girlfriend."

I got all flustered again. All my new resolutions to not blame my fellow survivor for the evil machinations of the Mother of All Darkness fled, and left me panicking again. "I'm not sure that's a good idea. In fact, I'm sure it's not."

He touched my face again, which made me stop talking, probably for the best. "I know you have issues with me being a senior in high school, and the age difference, but I'm nineteen, legally an adult. We live together, we're lovers; if that doesn't make you at least my girl-friend, I don't know what does."

"I don't know what to say to that."

He smiled, a little less happy, but still a smile. "Say you'll be there wearing some fabulous dress so that all the other guys will be insanely envious that I have you in my life."

"I don't know."

"Anita." He said it the way Micah said it sometimes, or Nathaniel, like *You can do better than this*. Since when had Cynric been able to do that tone?

"What time today?" I asked finally. It didn't hurt to get the time. He told me.

"I have to go back to work with the FBI."

His eyes got that cautious look that I'd taught him as I pulled away again and again. I grabbed his hand. "Don't look like that; I don't mean to be a pain in the ass."

"Then stop being one," he said, and he sounded so reasonable.

"It's not that simple," I said.

"Anita, I've been a good sport about not being the tiger that you put a ring on for the commitment ceremony, haven't I?"

He had; he really had. "I'm sorry," I said.

"Don't apologize, just bring us home a cute girl tiger to share and all is forgiven." He grinned at me and waggled his eyebrows.

It made me smile. "I can't promise a girl, but I can promise to look for one."

"That's all we're asking."

I looked up at him and said what I was thinking. "When did you grow up and how did I not notice?"

"You've been too busy trying to shove me in the kid box to let me grow out of it," he said, voice soft.

"That's fair," I said.

"I don't care if you're fair, Anita, just say you'll let Nathaniel help you dress and you'll be with me today."

"I'll try."

"Try to get away from the FBI in time for it, or try to be comfortable enough to take my hand in front of everyone at school?"

I thought about it, and tried to tell the sinking feeling in my gut to stop it. "How about both?"

He smiled. "Both is good." He leaned down and I went up on careful tiptoes, balancing with my hands on his chest so I didn't fall against him and ruin his shirt. We couldn't touch like normal, but this kiss wasn't awkward. He whispered, voice low and deep, "I wish I could stay and help you clean up in the shower."

It tightened things low in my body and made me stumble back to stand flat-footed. The fact that he could have that effect on me still bothered me, but not as much. I mumbled, "Me, too," but couldn't quite look at him as I said it.

He laughed, and it was a very masculine laugh. "Later tonight, I'll help you get all messy again; Nathaniel and I have been working on something."

"Working on what?" I asked, suddenly suspicious.

"You'll see, and you'll like it, I promise; I mean I think you'll like it." He looked like he was thinking too hard, then laughed more at himself than me, I think. "I've got to run or I'm going to be late for class." He gave me one more quick kiss and headed for his car. It was a brand-new Corvette Stingray, a deep, rich blue that was somewhere between the color of his eyes and Jean-Claude's. It had been an early graduation present from Jean-Claude. He slipped into the car like he'd been built to match it, sleek, pretty, and purringly muscular. It was a pretty car, and he looked great in it, and drove it well after a few lessons at using a stick. I still thought it was a ridiculous present for high school graduation and set the bar too high. I mean, what the hell were the rest of us going to get him for graduation? Technically, the car was from a bunch of us, but Cynric wasn't stupid. The sleek sports car had Jean-Claude's taste written all over it. Micah and I would both have picked something far more practical. Nathaniel loved the car.

Nicky came to stand beside me. "First, I'm glad that you're working your issues with Sin."

I turned and looked at him. "What's that supposed to mean?"

"You know exactly what I mean," he said, and gave me a look out of his one blue eye that said, clearly, I did know what he meant, and I did.

I shrugged and looked away.

"Second, I'm sorry about Domino. I didn't mean to kill him."

"You didn't," I said, looking at him.

"I almost did, and it would have been an accident; if I kill people, it should be on purpose."

I studied his profile, because he was the one looking away now. "So, you're not apologizing for almost killing him, really; you're apologizing for accidentally almost killing him."

"Yes."

"Because if you kill anyone it should be on purpose, is that it?"

"Yes," he said.

I laughed, started to hug him, and settled for patting his arm. "That is one of the weirdest apologies I've ever had, but I'll take it; thank you."

He nodded. "You're welcome."

My phone gave Micah's text tone, which was how I knew to look at it. The little word balloon read, "Can you meet me down in Rafael's room in medical?"

I texted back with one finger, much slower than Nicky, Nathaniel, or Cynric. "Is Rafael all right? Is he worse? Not healing?" I sent the message and realized it was awkward as hell, but hey, at least I texted instead of just calling back. It was a start.

"He's healing, but not healed. Won't be healed by tonight's meeting."

I started to text back and finally just called. "Micah, I tried texting, I did, but I'd still rather hear your voice."

He laughed. "I don't mind, I'd rather hear your voice, too."

I smiled and said, "Good, now what's up, short, dark, and handsome?"

He gave another chuckle, and then said, "Well short, pale, and beautiful, I'd rather discuss it in person."

"Okay, that sounds serious."

"It is, but not in the way you think."

"Okay, mysterious then."

"Oh, hell," he said.

"Now I *am* worried, you almost never curse."

"Rafael is healing, but not as fast as we'd hoped when we scheduled the big meeting for tonight."

"Everyone here in St. Louis is friendly, so it shouldn't be a big deal," I said.

"We're including people via Skype that aren't so friendly, including the rat group that was behind the assassination attempt."

"He needs to appear strong in front of them, not weak," I said.

"Exactly."

"Okay."

"Rafael needs a little help to make that happen tonight."

"To appear strong, you mean?"

"Yes."

"We're here to help him."

"It's more your help he needs right now, Anita."

"Define *help*."

"He needs to be healed more by tonight, if possible."

"Agreed."

"Will you help me heal him?"

"Sure, how do I help you do that?"

"I can call flesh like I did for you the first time we met, and you've healed using more than one method."

"I thought calling flesh only worked on wereleopards for you."

"I've managed to use it on werelions out of town."

"You never mentioned that." I could feel that first spurt of resentment, or anger. His reaction to Dev's power-up with us had let me know just how much danger he'd been putting himself in to help out-of-town animal groups, or consolidate our power base with them.

"I think we both keep a lot of our out-of-town work private from each other, Anita." And just like that I had to swallow whatever pissiness I'd planned on dishing out, because he was absolutely right. I did a lot of dangerous stuff on vampire hunts, and rogue lycanthrope hunts for that matter, though my out-of-town work was usually vamps. I'd woken up in the hospital more than once far from home and the people I loved.

"You're really good at that," I said.

"Good at what?"

"If I said *You know what*, would that be too passive aggressive?"

He gave a small laugh. "Oh, Anita, there's usually nothing passive about your aggression."

I debated on whether to be grumpy and then finally had to smile and shake my head. "Fair enough."

"I feel awkward asking you to have what may end up as sex with Rafael, after I made a big deal out of not wanting to share you with more men."

"Unless it's for a good cause, and then you see sex as just another tool in our arsenal, whether it's you having sex with other people, or me."

"That sounds cold-blooded."

"A little, but you and I both decided a long time ago that sex isn't a fate worse than death."

"True, but it still makes me feel inconsistent and I hate that."

"You are one of the most consistent people I've ever met, Micah."

"Thank you."

"And you still adapt to change, or let your plan adapt to battle conditions, better than almost anyone I know."

"So I'm both consistent and adaptable?"

"You are very leopard. Did you know that motion-sensor cameras have caught them living in major cities in India and no one knew they were there until the images showed up?"

"I didn't."

"The smallest of the big cats is also the most adaptable, and the one most likely to turn the tables and hunt the hunter, back in the day."

"I did know that part. Are you delaying coming down here?" he asked.

"Not on purpose."

"What does that mean?"

"Rafael is pretty private about sex; I think he'll be cool if we can do something short of healing with sex, but once a line is crossed I think it will bother him. And does he know that calling flesh for you is done by biting and licking the wound?"

"I've explained the mechanics."

"If you say so."

"I feel the doubt in your words."

"I know how you told him, Micah. It was very clinical, very business, but I've been on the receiving end of you calling flesh and it wasn't business once your mouth was on my arm."

"You were my Nimir-Ra, Anita; the connection was there from the beginning. It made things very different between us."

"So you're saying that when you've called flesh on other people, it's not been sexual at all?"

He was quiet on his end of the phone.

"Micah," I said.

"You've made your point, but I'm not attracted to Rafael in that way, so I think I'll be fine."

"But he's one of my regular lovers, so I do have that kind of connection to him. I'm just concerned that might change how your healing works if we're double-teaming him."

Nicky came back the few steps of privacy he'd given us. "I heard that last part, and I agree with Anita. You should warn Rafael of the possibilities."

I started to ask Micah if he'd heard him, but he said, "Once Anita is down here, then we'll explain it more completely to him."

"Unless Rafael is well enough to get naked in the shower, I'm going to have to clean up before I join you."

"Blood might not be a problem."

"Some blood, but mostly shifter goop."

"Again," he said.

I told him some details about what had happened with Domino in the cemetery. "So Richard helped you, that's good."

"It surprised the hell out of me," I said.

"Richard has been working with the other leaders in town in a very real way, Anita."

"Let's hear it for good therapy," I said.

"He has mentioned that, even encouraged other leaders to try it."

"He's like a born-again, you want to evangelize for what saved you," I said.

"Something like that, but whatever the cause, he has really stepped up to his responsibilities as Ulfric of the wolves, and the other third of Jean-Claude's triumvirate of power. That he helped you with Domino proves that he's working his issues about the metaphysics, too, and that is very good news.

"Clean up and join us, Anita."

"Did you remember that Cynric has his senior thingie today?"

"It's on my calendar, and you've got the same app on your phone. It's on the group to-do list for today."

"I don't know how to use the app yet." It sounded whiny even to me.

"Pretend it's a weapon, you'll figure it out."

"Guns are simple; technology is hard."

"I love you, please hurry."

"I love you, too."

"I love you more."

"I love you mostest," I said; we hung up, and Nicky walked me in and down to the showers with the waiting guards carrying my equipment bags. Nicky was the local Rex, which meant when there was other muscle around he didn't carry shit either.

42

I PUT MOST of my equipment away and was down to minimum dangerous toys when I headed to the group shower area for the second time in less than twenty-four hours. I'd sent Nicky to bed, because one of us needed to get some sleep before we went to Cynric's senior awards banquet today, and it wasn't going to be me or Micah. It was as I headed down the hallway after kissing Nicky good-bye that I heard the rumble of male voices—a lot of male voices.

I'd totally forgotten that now was one of the busiest times for the showers, because it was either people who came in early to make sure they got the required gym workout done before work, or those who finished their shift and then headed to the gym before bed. I'd done it both ways. Honestly I preferred to work out in the early or late afternoon and then head in to work, but some weeks I just struggled to get the exercise in like most people did. The difference was, if I wasn't in good shape I might lose the next fight with the bad guys, or not be able to outrun them or chase them down; either way exercise wasn't a luxury for me, it was a serious necessity.

Hearing all those voices, feeling the energy of them even from a distance, made me slow down. I so did not want to deal with having to either walk through the group shower and all the naked men to one of the covered shower stalls, or throw the boss card down and make them all get out and wait while I showered. Either way it was awkward. I almost turned back for the room I shared with Micah and Nathaniel when we slept at the Circus, but two things stopped me. One, Nathaniel was probably asleep and I'd wake him. Two, I was being all cowardly about the group showers and I hated being that uncomfortable about anything. I'd found it was just better to face it head-on and keep going. It wasn't a perfect plan, but it worked for me—most of the time.

I walked up to see a laughing group of guards, most with their hair still damp from the shower, walking toward me. The laughter faded a little around the edges, as they all tried to do their own version of greeting one of their bosses. Two nodded, one said, "Ma'am," and one gave a very crisp salute. It wasn't the first time one of the fresh-from-the-military guys had done that. I'd been told the rules. I did not salute back; if I'd been a superior officer then it would have been my call whether to return the salute anyway, but since I'd never served in the military for real, my saluting could be seen as a sign of disrespect.

I nodded back. If I could remember names I used them with the nod, though honestly we had so many new guys coming in to use the gym that I didn't know all the names anymore. Now that I knew that Micah and the other leaders were trying to recruit enough "soldiers" to replace all the werehyenas if we needed to, I understood why there were so many new faces. Most of the new guys must have liked a morning workout, because the amount of noise from inside the showers was a lot.

I stood just outside the door, steeling myself to go into the shared locker room where we could put our weapons and some people undressed. If we'd known we were going to have more female guards we might have built two locker rooms, but no one thought of it when the plans were laid out, or maybe lycanthropes just didn't sweat nudity, even in the shower, so maybe it was just me feeling all squirmy awkward about it? Either way, I wished for a girls' locker room as I hesitated at the open doorway; I wished really, really hard. But like all the female sportscasters who'd been told, sure you can have all the chances to interview the players that the male sportscasters have, but you still have to go into the shower and see the people you're trying to interview possibly naked—there really is no such thing as equality, just different levels of inequality, and how hard are you willing to fight for it all? Fuck.

Did I yell out "girl in the locker room" the way they did in some of the professional sports locker rooms? I realized I would have been a lot more comfortable if someone inside there were a lover of mine, but knowing they were men I'd never seen nude, or had no "right" to see nude, made me more embarrassed. I'm not saying that made sense; I'm just saying that's how I felt.

Someone walked around the open doorway so fast, they ran right into me and sent me stumbling backward. I barely kept my feet. It was one of the new female guards from L.A. She was a little taller than me, and built like a feminine square with shoulders broad enough to make most men very proud. Sheer greater mass had almost set me on my ass.

"Oh, I'm . . . so sorry." She blushed scarlet even through the darkness of her skin, which was a nice solid brown, as if she'd tan incredibly dark given a chance.

"It's okay," I said.

She reached out to touch my arm as if to reassure herself I was okay, then dropped her hand as if she didn't know what to do with it. "I didn't see you. I mean, I wasn't noticing. I mean . . ."

I laughed. "It's okay, Pepita, right?"

She nodded. "Yes, I'm Pepita, but they call me Peppy."

"Which do you prefer?" I asked.

She looked confused for a second, and then said, "Peppy, I am so not a little anything." And she spread her hands wide to sort of take in the thickness of her body.

"Don't apologize for not being little; you'll be able to lift weights that I can't even imagine lifting."

She looked pleased and ran a finger through her short, black hair, tucking it behind one ear where it didn't stay. Either she had only cut it short recently, or it was a very old habit from years of having much longer hair. Some habitual gestures stay on for years after the reason for them is long past.

She was still dressed in baggy gym shorts and an oversized men's T-shirt, as if she wanted to hide her body even while she worked out, or maybe it was just comfortable and I was projecting.

"You just finish working out?" I asked.

She nodded, smiled. "Yes."

"But you didn't shower yet."

The smile faded. "No," and she looked down, not meeting my brown eyes with her own anymore.

"Too many men, and not enough privacy for you in there?"

Her eyes darted up to me and then she looked at the floor again. "I know we're all shapeshifters and nudity is okay, but . . ."

"You're still the only girl with a bunch of guys, most of whom are cute and very in shape, and you're all expected to pretend you don't notice each other."

She looked at me. "Yeah, we didn't do this kind of big group thing at home. Claudia told me that she did it and so could I."

"Is she in there now?" I asked.

Pepita, I mean Peppy, shook her head.

"When did Claudia tell you that?"

"When she showed us around the gym area. We asked where the girls' locker room was and she told us that we were going to be professional about this, just like we were about any other part of our job."

"That sounds like Claudia," I said.

"I know she's right, but . . ." She looked at the ground again.

"Honestly, I don't like coming down here when there are this many of the guys either."

She looked up at me, hopeful and suspicious all at once. "Really, or are you just trying to make me feel less like a pussy?"

"I swear that this is a little too much testosterone in one place, at one time, even for me."

She grinned suddenly and it made her look even younger than I knew she was, but it was also a good smile. She was suddenly pretty, and not just muscle that happened to be a girl.

"We'll go in together; that way at least neither of us will be the only girl."

The grin turned to relief. "Thank you, Señora Blake, thank you so much."

"Anita, call me Anita."

She nodded, smiling. "Okay, Anita, thank you."

"Don't thank me yet, we still have to brave the locker room and run the gauntlet of naked guys to get to the covered shower stalls."

She laughed then. "If you can do it, I can do it."

"Then let's do it," I said.

We walked into the locker room together, and because Peppy needed me to be brave, it was easier to do it. Yay for easier.

43

THE ROOM WAS so full of men in various states of undress that we had to thread our way through them like a maze of naked guys. It might have been erotic, but they were also joking and doing that rough talk that passes for sweet nothings between guy friends. I kept my head down and studied the tile floor like we were going to be graded later.

"Fuck, Ricky, your dick is going to fall off if you keep using it that much." I couldn't tell who said it, but the Ricky in question was beside us as I pushed my way between them to one of the weapons lockers, because he answered.

"Hey, can I help it if the ladies can't get enough of this?" and he gyrated his hips, making his junk swing. I did my very best to ignore it, but since it was damn near hitting my elbow, it was harder to ignore than it might have been.

I willed myself not to blush and opened the locker.

"Jesus, Ricky, stop shaking your junk at the new girls," a third voice called out. I realized that with my head down, my hair plastered to my head from the drying goop, and me wearing the black on black that was damn near the guards' uniform, they'd mistaken me for one of the new female guards from L.A. Perfect.

"Hey, she's not complaining, are you, baby?" Ricky said, and he actually leaned his shoulder against the closed lockers, arms crossed, in that popular-jock kind of way. They start doing it in high school, or earlier, but I'd never had anyone do it while they were naked. Life is just full of new experiences.

I froze with the door open on the locker, and looked up. I had to look way up, because Ricky was over a foot taller than me. I finally met the handsome, arrogant face, his shoulder still leaning against the lockers, arms crossed over the muscular chest, so high school jock. His eyes were big and brown with thick eyelashes, and the nearly perfect arch of black eyebrows that women want but never seem to have naturally. His hair was a brown so dark that calling it light black seemed more accurate. He'd already blow-dried his hair back in feathering on the sides as if the 1980s had never died, but hey, maybe it was coming back in style.

I glared into those big brown eyes. My glare is pretty good; I've had really bad people flinch at the sight of it. Ricky was unimpressed; in fact, he grinned at me. He didn't recognize me. Maybe we needed an introduction to the new troops; I'd suggest it to Claudia later.

"First, don't call me baby."

"Anything you say, darling," he said, still grinning.

"Second, leave the 'darlings' to Bobby Lee, he's southern and I can't seem to break him of it."

"Okay, sugar britches," he said, still so pleased with himself. But the other men had started to go quiet; not all of them, but it was spreading through them. Someone had recognized me and shared with the class.

I smiled and knew it was the unpleasant one, the one I couldn't seem to keep off my face when I was unhappy with someone. Ricky just saw a smile, because he started to lean down toward me.

"You're not very bright, are you?" I asked.

He stopped leaning down and had a moment of puzzlement, but

then the grin came back and he was all arrogant recovery. "Oh, sugar britches, I'm smart enough to rock your world."

I laughed then; I couldn't help it. "Jesus, please tell me that line never works for you."

He was back to softly puzzled, and his eyes were finally showing that he knew something was wrong, but not what, yet.

"God, I hope you shoot better than you think," I said, as I unbuckled my belt so I could begin to unthread all the holsters.

"Well, sugar britches, I think well enough that you're starting to take off your clothes."

"Before I decide to nickname you, dumbass, let's have a quiz."

"No need to be mean, sugar britches."

I held up my Browning BDM. "What's this?"

He smirked. "A gun."

"What kind of gun?"

"A nine-millimeter."

"More specific," I said.

"I don't have to play 'what the fuck is this' with you," he said, finally not happy with himself, because he didn't recognize the Browning. A lot of the newer guards didn't.

"Too hard for you? Let's try something easier." I took out my backup gun, the Sig Sauer P238.

He frowned at me and turned to his locker. He got his underwear on, a pair of black fitted briefs. The underwear wasn't bad.

"Come on, just the make, not even the model; you can do it, Ricky-boy."

"Fuck you," he said, wiggling into a pair of tight jeans, but hey, I wore my jeans tight, too.

"What, if it's not a Glock you don't know what the fuck it is?" I asked.

"Fuck you."

"Dumbass it is," I said, putting the Sig in with the Browning.

He turned and glared down at me, trying to use his height to intimidate. The first trickle of energy eased out from him, his beast peeking out with his anger.

I sniffed the air near his chest, invading his personal space, but he didn't tease me about it now. He'd decided not to like me. I was okay with that.

He smelled like wolf, but out loud I said, "You smell like puppy."

He leaned over me again, but this time it was supposed to be menacing, not seductive. It managed to be neither. "Werewolf, I'm a werewolf."

"Great, since you obviously don't know guns, let's try something that werewolves are supposed to be really good at. What am I?"

He drew back from me, forgetting he was trying to loom menacingly. "What?"

"I could smell that you were a puppy; tell me what I am."

"I'm not a puppy, I'm a wolf," he said between gritted teeth.

"Prove it, what am I?"

"I don't have to prove anything to you, chickie." He pulled his T-shirt on without spreading the neck open, so his carefully styled hair was mussed. He was mad.

"I'll make it easy for you." I raised my arm up toward his face.

He turned away and tried to ignore me.

"So much for the famous nose of the werewolves; I guess that reputation is all talk, too," I said, and unthreaded the extra magazine holders from my belt and laid the extra ammo in with the guns.

"What's that supposed to mean, *too*? You don't know me, or my reputation."

"You are an arrogant, bragging blowhard, who refused to take the sniff challenge. What kind of weak-ass wereanimal can't tell another person's flavor of beast by scent?"

"Wolf!" He snarled it into my face.

I laughed at him as the energy prickled along my skin. My wolf stood up, shaking her pale fur inside me. "A big bad wolf would know what I am; you don't, so you aren't a big bad wolf."

"You're a rat like all the other short Hispanic chickies from L.A."

I gave the unpleasant smile again. "Since *chickie* can be slang for *prostitute*, don't ever call any of the female guards that again."

"Or what? What will you do if I call you all chickie?"

"You didn't really listen to what I said, did you, puppy?"

"Don't call me that." He snarled it in my face, and it got him close enough to smell me. He stopped and the anger began to fade a little. "The gunk is tigers, more than one kind, but you"—he sniffed along my hair and face—"you smell like wolf, but you can't be."

"Why can't I be?" I asked.

"I've been here almost two months, and I've never seen you at any of the get-togethers."

"My schedule's a little full, makes it hard to be everywhere."

The room had gone quiet a while ago, but Ricky hadn't noticed. His powers of observation sucked. I hoped he fought well, because if he didn't he was just good-looking muscle that at best was cannon fodder, and at worst was going to get someone else hurt, because he wouldn't be up to the job. Had Richard picked him? If so, I was going to ask Rafael if he could help the wolves pick their new recruits from now on, because this one looked good, but he wasn't.

Micah reached out to me, just a barest brush of energy, and my leopard raised its head and sniffed the air. "Now you smell like leopard, but that's not possible," Ricky said.

"What's not possible, puppy?"

"Stop calling me that!" His anger was so ready to spill up and over him, and his wolf came right with it.

"Make me, puppy," I said.

"What?"

"Ricky . . ." someone said, taking pity on him at last.

"Make me stop calling you puppy; prove to me that you're the big bad wolf."

"Bitch!"

"Sticks and stones, puppy, sticks and stones."

"What are you fucking talking about?"

I moved closer to him, drawn by the heat of his anger and the musk of his wolf, but it was the anger I wanted. I was hungry, and his anger sat on my tongue bittersweet like super-dark chocolate; it's sweet, but there's that undertone of bitterness that can become its own addiction.

"Here puppy, puppy, puppy," I whispered from inches away. I was too close for him to swing at me, sex close. He was so angry it was like a fire that I could warm my hands over, such rage, just because I'd pricked his ego. I was provoking him, because I needed to feed and I had other options besides sex now.

I caught movement, as some of the others, including Peppy, started to move forward to intercede as the big man menaced me. I said, "Everyone back off, this is just puppy and me, isn't it, puppy?"

He yelled, "STOP CALLING ME THAT!" And he moved, too fast for even me to follow. His hands were around my upper arms, picking me up, feet dangling, as he slammed me against the lockers. But I was ready for it, and my head didn't slam back into them, which would have stunned me, and my back had had worse done to it. I wrapped as much of my small hands around his arms as I could, but it wasn't to keep him from slamming me again; it was to get skin-to-skin contact. The moment I touched him, I fed. All that anger, all that rage, that red haze that could have pounded me against the lockers until I broke, was mine to drink down from his skin to mine.

He looked confused, and then he began to collapse as his knees buckled. I was set back on my feet as he sat down heavily on the benches in front of the lockers. His hands dropped to his lap, as if he had lost strength in his arms. His face was soft and confused. The heat of his wolf was gone, siphoned away with his anger. Oh, he was still a were-wolf, but he wouldn't be able to shapeshift until he recovered a little more of himself; until then it was almost like being human. Some of the guards I did trust had been working with me in private, discovering the limits of this new ability to feed on anger by touching someone. I could drain from a distance, too, but it wasn't as powerful or as satisfying a feeding.

"What did . . . what did you . . . do to me?" he asked, and he couldn't quite make his eyes focus on me, or much of anything.

I felt so much better. "I fed on your anger."

"What . . . are you?"

"Wrong question, Ricky," I said.

"What?" He was still fighting to focus his eyes, his hands limp at his sides.

"It's not what am I. It's who am I?"

"I don't understand."

"I'm Anita Blake."

"Oh, fuck," he said, softly, trying hard to look at me without his gaze wandering to the side.

"You're lucky, I've gotten better at eating anger; when I first started doing it I took people's memories, so it was like being rolled by a real vampire, but you remember everything that just happened, don't you, puppy?"

"Don't . . . call me that." He managed to focus his eyes.

"Then prove to me that you're more wolf than puppy. The next time I ask you what make and model a gun is, I'll expect you to know. Don't ever wave your junk in the face of any of the female guards again, unless you know, absolutely know, they want you to do it. Don't ever call any of your fellow guards chickie, or whore, ever again. Just because a woman thinks you're a horse's ass doesn't mean she's a whore; it just means she sees through your bullshit."

"I didn't know who you were," he said, but the anger was already back.

"Anger, back so soon, puppy, maybe I'll just make you my bitch for feeding on rage."

His eyes showed fear for a minute; that scared him.

"Oh, you don't like that idea at all, do you?"

"No," he said, and there was a little bit of snarl to the word.

"Then learn your guns, respect your fellow guards regardless of gender, and don't be a sleazebag about the women you're fucking."

"Anything else . . . ma'am?"

"Yeah, be careful who you piss off here; not everyone is as nice as I am."

That made his eyes widen and that flash of fear return. He buried it under the anger again, but it was in there, behind the bravado and the macho posturing.

I shut my locker, gathered up a towel, and headed into the showers. The men cleared the way for me with silence, or "Ma'am." There were other men, nude or in towels, in the doorway to the showers; apparently we'd had more of an audience than I'd realized. That was okay; I didn't have a problem with all the men now, nude or clothed. I'd been scary and that was what they'd remember, not that I was small and a woman. Peppy followed behind me, smiling. Girls rule; boys drool.

44

I HADN'T REALIZED just how much stuff had dried in my hair until I tried to get it out. I was still peeling it out of my curls when Peppy told me she'd wait for me. "If you're done, go ahead, and tell Micah that I'm running late, trying to get cleaned up."

"Having trouble getting it out of your hair?" she asked.

"Yeah, how'd you know?"

"You had so much in your hair that it looked straight and paler. Long hair is a pain in the ass when it's got that much in it."

"Micah's in medical talking to Rafael."

"He's with our king?" she asked.

"Yeah, is that a problem?"

"No, no, just . . . I'll get Micah the message."

"Thanks," and I went back to literally scraping with my fingernails down the length of my hair, before shampoo did me any good. It had just made the stuff sort of gelatinous before, so I'd scrape it off and try again. Maybe I'd start packing some of those plastic hair coverings like they wear to crime scenes. It had to be an improvement over this.

When my hair was finally clean I wrapped the oversized towel around me; since it was meant to cover men that were closer to seven feet tall and four times as broad as I was, I was covered from under my arms to my ankles and had enough material to wrap around me tight and secure. I gathered up all the hair stuff to put back where I kept it and stepped out. I knew just from the noise level that the shower was a lot emptier than it had been when I went into it. What I didn't know was that Kane, Asher's new lover and Dev's nemesis, was in the showers near the door to the locker room.

Kane stood with his back to the room. He had serious tan lines low on his hips and in a narrow line across the tight roundness of his ass. The contrast between his skin tones let me know that he tanned darker than Micah did, or his base skin color was paler than Micah's, so the contrast was greater.

"Are you staring at my ass?" he asked.

I looked up and saw he was looking over his shoulder at me. He was almost bald, but it wasn't because he'd lost all his hair; it was because he cut it down to black fuzz. The way his hair looked shaved down that short made me almost certain that if he grew it out it would be curly. He had two deep areas on either side of his head where his hair had receded from a sharp widow's peak, which again raised the question of baldness, or fashion choice. The lack of hair bared the bone structure of his face and let you know he was handsome, bordering on pretty, especially for a six-footer.

"Yeah, I guess I was." I kept walking, which actually brought me closer to him, but if I kept moving maybe I wouldn't get caught in our usual snark-tastic repartee.

"Like what you see?"

"I was actually wondering if you tanned darker than Micah, or if your natural skin color was paler, and that's why your tan lines are more pronounced."

"What, you don't like tan lines?"

"I think I'm neutral about tan lines."

Some of the guards close to us were rushing their showers. They darted covert glances from me to Kane. They shouldn't have been looking at him like that; he wasn't their king, or a prince, or whatever. He was just the lover of one of our shared lovers, but there it was; they were treating him like he had enough power to make them afraid, or at least enough that they didn't want to get caught in the middle of us. Asher was technically Jean-Claude's second-in-command if you were counting vampires, but honestly as Micah and I had taken on more responsibilities Asher's role had gotten smaller, partly because his emotions got in his way, a lot, and partly because Asher had spent over six months exiled to another city. By the time he came back we'd divided up a lot of the daily upkeep without him. So why were the guards looking at Kane like getting on his shit list could ruin their day?

Kane turned around in the shower, so I could see that the tan lines went all the way around. It was a nice view, but the sourness that always seemed to roll off him ruined any momentary attractiveness. Asher had finally found someone who was more cranky than he was, and dealing with Asher was hard enough; Kane just seemed like too much work for too little payback to me.

He ran his hands down his body to cup himself, massaging a little so I could see he had room to grow. I raised an eyebrow and started walking. I was done here.

"Does it bother you to know you can see, but not touch?" he asked, with that edge of meanness his voice so often held.

That made me stop and look back at him. "Excuse me?"

He was working himself up with his hands in the spray of the shower, almost like he was masturbating. "There's finally a man in town that you want, but who doesn't want you; how does it feel, Anita?"

I laughed; I couldn't help it. It was the wrong thing to do if I'd wanted to de-escalate; most men don't like being laughed at when they're naked and turgid, but Kane had no sense of humor about it. His face went from sexy pouting to scowling at me.

"You think you can lead everyone around with your pussy; well, here's one man who doesn't give a damn about it. If it's not a cock, I don't care."

"Trust me, Kane, you're not on my hit list either."

Two of the guards turned off their showers and hurried past me through the door into the locker room. They smelled scared, and they shouldn't have been. Kane wasn't good enough to be one of our guards, which meant they could have taken him in a fair fight, so why that cold sense of panic?

"But you like dick."

"I like dick when it's attached to the right person. Since you make such a big deal of being monogamous for Asher, I'd think you, of all people, would understand that."

Two more guards got out of the showers and fled, and that was the right word. They sensed a fight that no matter which way it went gave them something to lose. They shouldn't have felt that way, which meant I had missed something important between our bodyguards and Kane, but what was it?

"Asher said you liked men."

"I do, but not all men, and I have a couple of female lovers now, so I'm exploring my options sans dick." I smiled when I said the last, because it was just such a weird conversation to be having, especially with Kane. It was probably the longest one-on-one conversation we'd ever had.

"I've got to go meet Micah; enjoy your shower." I was actually at the door this time when he said something that stopped me.

"How many lycanthropes did you fuck last night to cover yourself in that much of us?"

I frowned at him. "Not that it's any of your business, but I had to call Domino's beast to save his life. Forcing the change like that can be violent and messy."

"Nice story, but if that were true then you wouldn't have had sperm mixed with Domino's juices so that the guards didn't recognize you."

"I know stories grow in the retelling, but I was only in the shower for an hour, that's damn quick embellishing."

"You're denying it?"

"Yeah, though frankly if I wanted to bring in all my wereanimal lovers and have a bukkake festival, what difference would it make to you, Kane?"

"Your level of debauchery keeps surprising me, Anita, that's all."

"You're the one who was playing with himself in the shower, trying to get me to watch the show, so tell me again which of us is debauched?"

His anger flared like a hot wind, the edge of his beast riding with it. It was a lot of heat, far more power than the last time I'd been near him when he'd been pissy. "You've had a power jump, Kane. How?"

"Guess," he said, and he was far too pleased with himself, so whatever had happened, he didn't think I'd like it.

"I don't know, and I really do have to meet Micah before I go meet with the FBI, so I really don't have time to play twenty questions."

"Let's play *Jeopardy* instead," he said.

"What are you talking about, Kane?"

"Categories are vampires, lycanthropes, and love; pick one."

I narrowed my eyes at him, but said, "I'm not playing games with you, Kane; tell me, or don't."

"You're no fun."

"Not for you, no, and I really don't have time for this shit today." I went into the locker room. There was no one else in there, but the towels were scattered everywhere. There was even a pair of jogging shoes left forlornly on their sides as if people had left too quick to double-check their gear. Why would everyone run like that? What the hell was going on? Why was Kane so smug? Shit, I needed to know. I almost went back into the showers, but Kane saved me the trouble. He came out soaking wet, as if he hadn't even bothered with a towel.

"What is one of the most sacred things a vampire can do for a shapeshifter?" he asked.

"I don't know," I said.

"Oh come on, what's the phrase for a lycanthrope attached to a vampire?"

"Pet?"

He frowned at me.

"Just tell me, Kane, the foreplay is getting freaking tedious."

"What is something that a vampire does for love and power?"

I was frowning, too, now. "Makes someone a human servant."

"And if they're not human to begin with?"

I looked into those dark eyes of his, the smug look on his handsome face. "Oh shit, Asher made you his hyena to call."

"Ding-ding-ding, you win!"

"Fuck, Kane, Narcissus has been after Asher to make him his hyena to call for almost two years. You're not even one of the most powerful hyenas in your group. You've gained a hell of a lot of power, but Asher hasn't gained nearly as much from you."

"He loves me."

"Yeah, so freaking what? Narcissus could kill you and him for this."

"He wouldn't dare harm me now, because that could kill Asher, and everyone knows that Jean-Claude would kill to protect his vampire lover."

"Why was everyone scared of you in the showers just now?"

I didn't think he could look any more pleased with himself, but I was wrong. He positively glowed with self-congratulations. "I'm working out with the guards now."

"You started working out with the guards when you saw how much Asher appreciated all the muscles and gym work."

"I have muscles, and every hyena works out, or you don't survive unscarred."

"Yeah, yeah, you and the werelions are all macho and shit, but you've never worked out to the level we hold our guards to; you still don't."

The anger was back, full and rich and . . . more. In fact, the anger had a familiar flavor to it. I laughed.

"What's so funny?"

"Did Asher tell you that when you bind yourself to a vampire, you and he exchange some personality, or quirk?"

He frowned, water still beading down his face. "What are you talking about?"

"You taste of some of Asher's anger added to your own, which means he got something of yours, too. I can't wait to find out what, since you are such a shit."

Anger went to rage, his hands in fists at his side. My weapons were still in the locker, and it was just the two of us. He wasn't as well trained, but he had me in reach, size, strength, and speed, and he had some training. I didn't want this to get out of hand, or did I?

"Why were the other guards that practiced with you this morning afraid of you?"

"For the same reason that Narcissus won't hurt me, because that would piss off King Jean-Claude."

"Why would you getting your ass handed to you in practice piss off Jean-Claude?"

"Because if you hurt me, it could hurt Asher, and Jean-Claude doesn't let anyone hurt his golden-haired vampire boy." There was anger when he said it, fueled by a very serious case of green-eyed jealousy.

I realized that with a little bit of prodding, I could make more food for myself. One thing I'd noticed is that anger never seemed to be "full." Lust could be satisfied, at least temporarily, but my ability to absorb anger didn't act like a full stomach, or a content libido. I could always be angry. "No matter what you do, or how much Asher says he loves you, you'll always know that the man he wants most in his arms and in his coffin isn't you."

"Asher loves me."

"Oh yeah, he loves you enough to be incredibly stupid."

"Don't say that."

"Narcissus is free to discipline his hyenas in the way that works for him. We don't dictate that."

"Because hyena isn't one of Jean-Claude's beasts to call, but they answer to Asher, to my master."

"Up to a point, yeah, but this . . . Narcissus will make an exception for this."

"You're just jealous."

"Of what, of you? Of you and Asher? I'm still having sex and bondage with Asher, because you're vanilla. You're a fucking freak emotionally, but in the bedroom you're the gay male equivalent of missionary position with the lights off."

"Asher didn't say that about me."

"If you weren't too tame in bed for him, Kane, he wouldn't still be fucking me and Nathaniel, and Jean-Claude."

"Shut up," and his voice held an edge of growl. His beast was thick in his anger, as if they were even more entwined than before.

"If you didn't bore Asher out of his mind in the bedroom, he wouldn't still be letting Richard chain him up and press his body against his; you know Asher would let Richard fuck him in a heartbeat."

"That's not true!"

I let him see my version of a pleased, unpleasant smile, and said, "It is, you know it is."

He screamed and tried to hit me, but I moved just enough for him to smash his hand into the lockers behind me, and I touched his bare chest. I fed on his anger, the way I'd fed on Ricky earlier.

Kane dropped to the floor, and I rode him down, keeping my hands on him, draining all that delicious rage. I fed until I felt my eyes go all vampire, and I knew when I looked down at him he saw them like cognac diamonds with the sun shining through them, as if brown could be the color of fire.

I felt Asher down that long cord that bound them together now, more surely than the wedding ring he'd denied Kane, and far more permanent. But Asher was still hours dead and couldn't give extra power to his beast to call, so I could feel the tie between them, but the vampire couldn't help him.

I took my hands back from Kane, forced myself to stop feeding from him, so he could look up at me and still hear and understand what I was about to say to him. I could have fed him into unconsciousness and he'd have woken not even remembering why he was so tired.

"If I find out you hurt one of the guards, because you made them afraid to hurt you first, I will make certain that you step into the practice ring with them again, and they get to kick your ass. Narcissus is going to want you and Asher dead for this amazing insult to him. He is the Oba of your entire clan, one of the most powerful groups in this territory, and you just superseded him as Asher's beast to call. He will not forgive, hell, in hyena society, he *can't* forgive and forget this, because it would make him appear so fucking weak that his own people will turn on him. You and Asher have left Narcissus with no choice but to punish you. If Asher had told him first, discussed it with him, but he didn't, did he? Just like he didn't mention it to Jean-Claude first."

Kane managed to say, "No."

"No, what, Kane? No, he didn't discuss it with Jean-Claude first? No, you didn't talk to your Oba first? *No, no, no* isn't going to save you from whatever Narcissus is going to do to you."

"Jean-Claude . . . will save . . . Asher." He couldn't quite make his eyes focus, as if he were struggling to stay conscious; maybe I'd taken a little too much energy from him?

"No, Kane, not this time. I won't let Jean-Claude endanger us all because Asher lets his fucking heart overrule his head again and again." My towel was loose; I didn't try to keep myself covered but took the towel off and sat across his waist as naked as he was. The only thing that made it not a preamble to sex was that I was a few inches too high.

I put my glowing eyes just above his, and he still couldn't move enough to do anything to stop me. "I haven't made anyone my hyena to call yet, Kane, did you remember that? One of the things I learned from the Mother of All Darkness was how to break the bonds between vampires and their servants. I could just take you from Asher, bind you to me, and thanks to the *ardeur* I would be your exception, Kane. You'd fuck me, because you'd crave me like a drug."

"No . . . lies."

"Oh, I'm not lying. Why tell a lie when the truth is so much more terrible?"

"Bitch."

"Oh, Kane, you can do better than that."

"He'll never . . . top you . . . again if you hurt me."

"Narcissus is going to kill Asher if he can, so he won't be topping, or fucking, anyone."

"He loves Asher."

"You know, I think he does, but Asher never loves the people who love him the most; he always chases the ones who don't want him, haven't you figured that out yet?"

"He loves me enough to . . . do this."

I nodded. "Yes, he does, because in you he's finally found someone more problematic, more jealous, more of a shit, than he is—it's only taken him six, seven hundred years to find someone who exemplifies his own worst traits. He'll keep you close, Kane, I don't know why, but he sees something in you he wants."

Kane swallowed, and his eyes were able to look at mine again. I got up still nude and left him lying on the floor with my towel curled up beside him. "You and Asher deserve each other, Kane, you really do."

"Thank you," he said.

"It wasn't a compliment," I said. I got my weapons out of the locker and since I'd totally forgotten fresh clothes I carried all of them, mostly in one arm, because the other hand was for my Browning BDM naked in my hand. I left Kane lying on the floor to recover, or pass out. I didn't shoot him, not even to wound. And people say I have no sense of humor.

45

I LEFT THE showers nearly vibrating with energy, but the combination of being buck naked and juggling all my holsters, guns, knives, and ammo pouches because they had nothing to attach to was just awkward, and then I started seeing the early-morning shift of the guards coming and going. Have you ever tried nodding good morning to people while naked and holding a small arsenal of weapons? It was a first for me, too, and I didn't care for it. Though they were almost all lycanthropes, which means technically they don't give a damn about nudity, they kept doing the little eye flicks. It may have been the guns and stuff, but I was self-conscious enough to want to start snarling, *What are you looking at?*

I didn't, but I know I was scowling with every morning greeting after a while. I felt squirmingly awkward, like one of those nightmares where you have to give a major speech and you've forgotten your clothes. Apparently embarrassment can tone down vampire powers; who knew?

I was relieved to finally get to the little locker area near medical. One, it was in a small cave-y alcove so I had a moment of privacy. Two, I could finally empty my hands into the locker, lock it, and keep the key, though I didn't have any pockets to put it in. I debated long and hard on whether to keep the smaller Sig Sauer with me, but again I had no way to carry it. I was surrounded by guards, our bodyguards; they were armed and paid to keep us all safe, so why did it bug me so much to shut the locker with all my guns inside it? Now I really did feel naked.

I finally gave in, reopened the locker, got out the Sig still in its holster, and just carried it all in my left hand. With my left hand, since I was right-handed, because if I really had to use it, I'd hold the holster with my left and draw the gun with my right. My left hand would do what the belt normally did: hold the holster tight so the Sig could come out with one hard, smooth pull. Maybe I was being paranoid keeping a gun with me, but hey, I left both of the Sig's spare magazines in the locker. See, not paranoid, just cautious, and if you think otherwise you haven't had enough people shoot at you.

Benito was standing just around the corner from the locker area. He wasn't exactly at the head of the medical area, but just inside it, so he wasn't easily visible but could just step out and surprise them like he had tried to do with me.

"You saw me?"

"Felt you," I said, and that was the closest I could come to explaining how I had known someone was in the shadows there. Then Bram stepped out of the shadows, and I knew it hadn't been Benito the were-rat that I'd sensed; it had been the wereleopard. I was better at sensing all the wereanimals that were my flavor to call. Bram was Micah's main bodyguard. He was a few inches taller than Benito, but they were both built lean and I knew Bram was wicked fast. Benito didn't practice with us, because he wasn't one of our guards; he was all for Rafael. Bram's hair was cut very short on the sides, but with a little more left on top to style as he let go of the military haircut he'd come to us with; he was darker than Benito, and it wasn't just tan. He still looked unfinished to me without Ares standing at his side; they'd partnered each other as guards and as friends. Ares had been the blond physical counterpoint to Bram's oh-so-brunette. Ares was dead, and Bram was like a shadow with no light to balance him, or maybe that was just my guilt talking, since I'd been the one who had to kill him. A vampire had bespelled Ares and suddenly all that military skill and werehyena strength was turned against us. It was one thing to not be able to save someone, but to have to pull the trigger on them, that was something that stayed with you.

Benito grinned, eyes shining with some suppressed mirth.

"Leave it alone, Benito," Bram said.

It took me a second to realize that the wererat guard's eyes were looking lower than my face. I guess the fact that it took me even a few seconds to remember I was nude meant I was getting more comfortable with it than I'd thought.

"Your eyes better stay on my face, Benito, because one rule across all wereanimal cultures is that if someone is just nude and not trying to be sexy you're supposed to ignore it."

"My apologies, Anita," and he tried to keep his eyes on my face, but it was as if my breasts had a gravitational pull that he just couldn't resist. I refused to cover up, because he was the one being rude; I wouldn't let him embarrass me, damn it.

"I've never seen you on the practice mat, or in the gym working out, but I'd really credited you with more control than this," I said.

He looked at my face then, frowning. "What do you mean?"

"It's been my experience that a man who can't control himself in one way has poor control in others."

The frown turned to a scowl, but he was giving me great eye contact now. "My control is excellent, or I would not be trusted to guard our king."

"Good to know, and the eye contact is appreciated."

A look went through his eyes that I couldn't decipher, and then he smiled. "Very well done." He gave a few soft claps. "You manipulated me beautifully," and something about the way he said it was still not as friendly as normal.

"I just got you to behave professionally, that's all."

He scowled again.

Bram said, "Micah and Rafael are in room three."

"Thanks," I said, and moved past them, though admittedly I walked on the far side of the hallway so that Bram was between me and Benito. I didn't think he'd hurt me, but there was something odd about the last few minutes of interaction with him, and until I understood it I'd err on the side of caution.

I had a moment of hesitation just outside the door to the room, because again I suddenly felt very naked. Maybe it was the weirdness with Benito, but I suddenly felt awkward again. Micah wasn't the problem; if he saw me nude and it made him think sex, and I wasn't rushing for work, then I was all for it. The problem was Rafael. Even though we were friends with benefits, showing up without clothes seemed a little abrupt for him and me. He was actually quite fond of silky lingerie with robes. The first time we'd had sex had been very slam, bam, thank you, ma'am, but either because of how he'd behaved the first time, or because it was his natural bent, there was always a bit of talking and just awkwardness as if he was never quite sure how to transition from *good evening* to *hey, baby*.

Me walking in naked would definitely not be the style to which Rafael and I had become accustomed. I started to wonder about looking for a robe, or something, or texting Micah . . . and I realized that I'd left my phone in the locker with the weaponry. Sigh.

The door opened and Micah was there. His eyes went a little wide as he saw me, and then he smiled. It was a good smile, and the look in his eyes said plainly that he appreciated the possibilities of the view.

"The shower took longer than I'd planned, and I didn't want to wake anyone in the bedrooms to get clothes."

He grinned at my obvious discomfort. "It's okay, Anita, you just surprised me, that's all. You usually don't like walking through the Circus without clothes."

"Yeah, way too many new guards to say good morning to for my comfort," I said, frowning.

He reached out to take my left hand like normal and found it full of gun. He switched to my right hand without missing a beat. "You don't have to explain, or apologize."

"It's just a little . . . brazen for me."

"Brazen?" Rafael said from inside the room, and followed it with a laugh.

"Laughing about this will not make me more comfortable, Rafael," I said.

"Then I am no gentleman to increase your discomfort; please come inside. We can give you one of the extra sheets, if you truly wish to cover yourself." See, very formal most of the time.

Micah led me into the dimly lit room. The lights were very low, because shapeshifters could be light sensitive when they were doing major healing. I didn't hide behind him, but I did sort of make certain I wasn't revealed completely in a sort of "ta-da" moment. I was engaged to Micah and had been having sex with Rafael for a year; I had no idea why I was this uncomfortable, but I let myself feel what I was feeling. Ignoring emotions doesn't make them go away; I'd learned that the hard way.

Rafael lay on his stomach, the sheets neatly folded where the body curved down into the ass, leaving the long expanse of his upper back bare. If he had been one of my main lovers it would have been inviting, but he and I weren't dating. He would never be my boyfriend, or anything I had a word for; we came together so I could feed the *ardeur* and he could gain a closer tie to the throne. It was like solving political problems by fucking, which on one hand sounded wrong, and on the other hand almost seemed a better system than normal politics.

"You are thinking very serious thoughts, Anita," he said; his eyes were so dark that only the glitter of them catching the light let me know for sure he was looking at me.

"Would you understand if I said politics makes strange bedfellows?"

He laughed then, hard enough that he winced, hands digging into the covers, as he fought not to writhe in pain, which apparently would hurt more. Seeing him in that much pain took away my discomfort and replaced it with worry.

I went forward, still holding Micah's hand. "I thought you'd be more healed by now."

"So did I," he said, in his deep voice, but there was more of an accent than normal, which meant either he was trying to play to his ethnicity, or he was stressed. He didn't have to play the big bad Mexican boss for us, so stress it was.

I knelt down beside the bed and had to let go of Micah's hand to lay my hand on Rafael's arm. I still had the Sig in my left, though I was beginning to wonder what I was going to do with it, when I needed both my hands. "The doctors cleaned the wound out, right?"

"Yes."

Micah answered before I could ask the next question. "They don't know why he's not healing faster."

I looked up at Micah, then back to Rafael. "I see why you wanted me to come down and try healing with the *ardeur* now."

"Rafael would also be more comfortable with my healing gifts with you here," Micah said. Since his ability to call flesh, as the wereleopards call it, only worked if he licked and bit the healing into the flesh, I could sort of understand that.

I smiled and patted Rafael's arm. "It's a little too much like foreplay for comfort, isn't it?"

He laughed again, but more carefully than he had before, so that he didn't move his body as much. "Especially midback from behind."

"It could be worse," I said.

"How?" he asked.

"It could be your, um, very lower back," I said, smiling.

He grinned then, a bright flash of teeth in the room's gloom. "That is true, much more problematic."

"Okay, I'll hold Rafael's hand while you try to heal him, but can you heal a wound this deep?"

"I'm not sure, but if I can't it's your turn to try to heal him with the *ardeur*, or the wolves' munin."

"Sexual either way," I said.

He nodded. "We're both aware of that."

"Remember, Anita, I knew Raina when she was alive. I saw her use her healing gift on the werewolves, and it was very sexual. You carry her munin, her memory, inside you, which means it's still her healing gift."

"And you know how the *ardeur* works for me, better than most," I said.

He smiled. "I do."

"Almost all my power is either sex or death."

"It is an interesting paradox that you represent fertility and death," Rafael said.

"She raises the dead, so it's giving life, not taking it," Micah said.

Rafael seemed to think about it. "Interesting, and true."

"For now, just stay where you are beside the bed and hold his hand while I call flesh," Micah said.

"Have you ever tried to use your hands instead of your mouth?" Rafael asked, which to me said that Micah's method of healing was bothering him even more than I'd thought.

"I have, and it doesn't work."

"I've seen films of humans who could heal with their hands, I think it's called the laying on of hands," I said.

"But leopards don't have hands, and this seems to be a gift from the beast side, not the human," Micah said.

"I wonder if there are any leopards alive today that can heal like this?" I asked.

"That would imply that animals can do magic," Micah said.

"Why not?" I asked.

He shook his head.

"It's just psychic ability, Micah, and they've proven that some animals have forms of telepathy, and certainly empathy, why not more?"

"I don't know, maybe, but right now I only have one way to try to heal Rafael."

"I would request that Anita sit on the bed and allow me to rest my head in her lap, rather than just kneel by the bed."

I agreed without thinking through the whole I-was-totally-nude part. What would have been just a friendly gesture with clothes on, as I held his hand and cradled his head, was suddenly much more intimate. He was already my friend with benefits, so why did it bother me? I have no idea; if you figure it out, let me know.

46

I LAID MY gun, still safely in its holster, on the tiny bedside table, and sat on the bed so my lap could be Rafael's pillow. Since he had to be on his stomach, again it was more intimate than if he'd been able to lie on his back, but I'd agreed and it wasn't like he hadn't been in my lap before. I bucked up and tried to act like a grown-up and not an embarrassed teenager, and stroked Rafael's black hair with one hand and let him hold tight to my other hand. I felt Micah call his healing in a rush of heat that traveled along Rafael's body and into me, so that the rat king's body was like a conduit between two points of electricity, or wood between two fires. Micah bent down, and I had a ringside seat to see him place his lips against Rafael's bare back. Micah was totally dressed in T-shirt and jeans, but even with him dressed there was still something sensual watching him put his mouth on the other man's skin. Micah's hair was back in a braid, so I had a perfect view of his lips caressing the skin, the muscles of his jaw flexing as he began to work his tongue along the wound.

Rafael was fine until he felt tongue and then he flinched, hand gripping tighter in mine. I didn't think it was just Micah French-kissing the wound that bothered the rat king, but the push of energy that went with it. That warm, probing energy pulsed through my body so that I had to catch my breath. I knew it was stronger for Rafael, because the rush of it was being focused directly on his body. Sometimes what freaks us out most aren't the things that feel bad, but the things that feel good.

Rafael's head moved against my thigh and I couldn't tell if it was a pain movement or a cuddle one. I petted his hair, playing with the shortness of it. It was grown out just enough that there was the promise of waves in it, but I knew he would be trimming it soon, and it would go back to being neat and straight and controlled. Control was very important to Rafael.

His body spasmed against the bed, his free hand convulsing in the bottom sheet, his other hand in mine, and then energy rode down his skin and over me. It caught my breath in my chest and tightened my body in a line that went all the way through me. Rafael's head rose off my lap, eyes wide enough to show white edges. His breath came out in a sharp sound that shook at the end. We had a moment of our eyes meeting and a shared knowledge of just how good this was feeling.

I bent over and kissed him. His lips were soft, mouth open with another sigh. A rush of energy took us while we kissed. It rode through Rafael and into me, as if his mouth were a sweet tunnel spilling into mine. I made eager noises, half-muffled against his lips, and slid my body underneath his, so that my hips were under his chest before we had to break the kiss, because we didn't quite bend that way.

I ended with my hips trapped underneath his chest; my knees were up on either side of his body, angling my groin up against his stomach as if I were already prepping for lower things. His face was pressed against my breasts; one hand was behind my body holding me against him, the other pressed to the bed as if he, too, had started that next movement so lower body parts could touch. I looked down his body at Micah.

His mouth was buried tight against Rafael, his throat working convulsively as he swallowed. I had a moment to think he was drinking blood from the wound, because that was what it meant when I saw Jean-Claude or Asher swallow like that. Then his gaze rolled up to meet mine, and those leopard eyes stared at me over Rafael's body. Usually even though the eyes were cat, it was still Micah looking out of them, but in that moment it was leopard that gazed up at me over Rafael's body, with its human mouth pressed against bleeding flesh . . . meat; it was meat. In that second I knew that the friendship, the alliance between us and the rats, how much we liked and respected Rafael, all the hopes for the future, even the reason we were trying to heal him before tonight's meeting, all of it meant nothing to the eyes looking up at me. Those eyes thought only one thing about our friend stretched between us—food.

It thrilled through me from toes to fingertips in a rush of fear, because I was too close to those eyes, that thought, but with that thrill came another one that turned what could have been terror into a different need. A need so strong that it tightened things low in my body and tore an eager moan from my throat.

It helped fill the eyes with a thought that wasn't all leopard, but it was just as predatory. Rafael reacted to my reaction with his hand pressing tight against my back; his mouth spilled over my breast, hot and eager to suck. I held Micah's gaze while the other man reacted to us, and now the thought of "food" included Rafael's hand holding my breast so he could get a better angle to lick and suck. I hadn't fed the *ardeur* in over twelve hours, and the man playing with my breasts was such good food. Rafael brought another eager sound, made my hips rub upward against his body, so that he caressed parts that his hands hadn't touched yet. Micah's gaze stayed locked on mine the whole time. Rafael was luckier than he knew in that moment that Micah wasn't into men, because predatory could mean so much more than just meat.

Rafael's mouth at my breast tried to flutter my eyes shut, but I fought to keep Micah's gaze. He lifted his mouth away from the wound enough so his tongue could lick the edges of it, while he stared at me. My pulse quickened. I felt the energy begin to build as he licked the edges, and then worked slowly lower, his tongue going in and out of the wound in fast quick movements as if he were licking entirely different things. It made me press my groin harder against Rafael's body, grinding myself on his stomach. It wouldn't bring me, but it helped me climb the edge we were beginning to ride.

The healing energy built and built, and then Micah thrust his tongue and magic deep into the other man's body. It thrust through Rafael and into me like a sword thrust so that it was almost too much, almost pain, and then it burst in a warm rush across my body, making me scream in pleasure. I fought not to close my eyes, but to hold Micah's gaze, the leopard's gaze, because they were flipping back and forth—sex, meat, sex, meat—as I bucked underneath Rafael's body.

Rafael pulled my body underneath his. I was suddenly trapped beneath his chest, Micah lost from view. I might have protested, but he pulled me just that bit lower and I felt him hard and eager a second before he started pushing himself inside me. I was wet, but tight, and the angle wasn't quite right. He was making low, eager noises as he rose enough to scoot me that last fraction into place and could finally push himself inside me. I felt the energy from Micah building again, as Rafael forgot he was hurt and started working himself in and out of my body. He rose enough so he could look down at me as he fucked me. I could glimpse Micah's legs on one side of him, as one arm slid around Rafael's waist, holding on, pressing his mouth tighter against him. Rafael raised his upper body higher but kept his groin pressed tight to mine. I had a moment of meeting the dark glitter of his eyes, and then Micah thrust into the wound, and it all happened at once. The magic and Rafael's body brought me screaming, while his body thrust so long and so hard inside me that it brought me again, screaming and writhing underneath him, nails racking down his ribs. He cried out, body convulsing, thrusting again, as Micah rode his back, arms locked around his waist, holding Rafael's body tight against his mouth and the power that poured out of him.

Rafael and I cried out together as Micah's power poured through us, until he drew back and let Rafael fall to the bed, collapsing half on top of me, our bodies still locked together. Micah's face appeared over Rafael's body and the eyes were leopard eyes again. My pulse was a trapped thing in my throat, as he gazed down at me while I was trapped under the bigger man's body.

A growl trickled out from between those human lips, but the eyes . . . there was nothing human in the eyes. Micah's body was still there, but his beast was driving the bus.

He climbed over Rafael's back, adding his weight, so that I was even more trapped under their combined weight. He leaned down toward my face, a continuous growl vibrating out from between those lips that I'd kissed a thousand times, but in that moment I wasn't sure whether he was going to kiss me or eat me.

47

HE KISSED ME, thrusting his tongue and the last of the magic into my mouth, so that I screamed another orgasm into his mouth. Rafael cried out again, and this time it was more pain than pleasure, I think, but Micah's hand grabbed my face, spilled into my hair, pulling me up so he could kiss me harder. It was rougher than he usually liked, but it wasn't really his human half biting and kissing at my mouth. It was as if his leopard were still trying to eat my lips, but he kept fighting it into a rough, insanely eager kiss.

Micah slid off the bed but kept kissing me. He pulled me out from underneath Rafael and spilled us both to the floor. He was on top trying to thrust himself inside me, but he was still wearing clothes, so all he could do was rub that hard bulge tight against me. It made me cry out, but it made him growl louder and hiss in frustration like a cat. I pulled on his T-shirt, trying to remind him that it needed to come off. It brought more of Micah back into his face again, so that he went up on his knees, pulling his T-shirt off in one smooth motion. I sat up and undid his belt. He let me unzip his pants, but then his hands were there sliding them down his slender hips. I got a glimpse of his underwear as he pulled his pants down to his thighs, but the rest of the show distracted me. Micah was always large, longer and thicker, but now he was pressed up high and tight against the front of his body. I reached out to touch him, but his hand grabbed my wrist. I looked up to find his eyes doing that back-and-forth again. I wasn't sure if it was the leopard or the man that pressed me to the floor and pushed himself inside me, and I didn't care.

Just feeling him push his way inside me made me cry out. I was writhing and making small eager whimpering sounds before he got himself as tight inside me as he could go. There were inches left outside my body, but we'd learned that I wasn't deep enough to hold all of him. He was growling and making frustrated noises as he fought to get enough room to thrust the way he wanted to. He pulled himself out of me, flipped me over onto my stomach on the floor, and was on top of me before I could decide if it was a good idea.

He pushed inside me and pulled my hips up so that I was on all fours for him as he began to push himself in and out, in and out. I felt that warm pressure begin to build deep in my body where he was rubbing himself over and over inside me. I did what I usually did, and said, "I'm close."

The only answer I got was a deep, rumbling growl that almost didn't sound like Micah in any form. I looked back over my shoulder, trying to see him, and found that his chartreuse eyes were gone, and I was looking into the fire-colored eyes of the black tiger he'd turned into only once before. I had a second to wonder if it was like any new beast form, harder to control at the beginning, and what that might mean if he shifted now, and then he picked up his rhythm so it was fast, and faster, thrusting all that hard, eager thickness deep within my body, so that he brought me screaming, but he didn't stop. He pounded himself into me while I screamed orgasm after orgasm. I wasn't sure if I let the *ardeur* go or if it rose on its own, as if the orgasm had made me lose control of more than just my pleasure. Always before Micah could keep me from feeding on him until he orgasmed—that brought all his barriers down—but when I reached out to feed this time he was just there, ready, eager to give it up, to give it all up. I had a second to feel how tired he was and how much he needed to let it go, and then the *ardeur* spilled up and over, and through us both. Micah thrust inside me and we both screamed our pleasure, as I drank him down everywhere his skin touched mine. His scream went from human to leopard, as his body gave one last thrust. I felt him go inside me, and we cried out together, but this time his scream was a lower, deeper, bass sound that I'd never heard from him. I felt the rush of heat just before his body shifted and then liquid hot as blood ran down the back of my body, but only where he touched me, so much neater than Domino had been.

The new form was like a reset and he was suddenly hard and impossibly big inside me. It was still black furred arms that reached for my shoulder, but the arms, like other parts of his body, seemed bigger. Claws dug in to hold me in place as he thrust one last time, so deep inside me that it was just this side of too much, just this side of pain, but it was the kind of pain you'd sell your soul for just one more time.

Blood began to ooze down my shoulder as the claws tightened and his body convulsed inside mine. He gave another coughing scream, and I knew before I looked back over my shoulder that it would be the tiger with fire-colored eyes that was pouring himself thick and hot inside me.

48

I HEARD THE door open behind us but couldn't see anything but the change of light behind the tigerman's body. I called out, "It's Micah, he's all right, I'm safe." I trusted Micah, I did, I did, damn it.

"Holy shit!" A man's voice from the door.

The tiger snarled over its shoulder, its claws digging in a little more, so that blood trickled faster from the points of its claws in my skin.

Rafael spoke from the bed. "Do not startle him."

"Us, startle him?" I could see Benito now as he moved farther into the room so he could see me around the tiger's body, so if he had to shoot the bullet wouldn't go through the weretiger and into me.

"It's Micah, he has two forms now," Bram said; I knew his voice without seeing him.

"That's not possible," Benito said.

Rafael said, "I saw him change form; it is Micah. I don't know how it is possible, but it is him."

I looked at the floor, where my blood was starting to form tiny drop patterns. "Micah . . ." But the growl came again, and this time he leaned over me, nuzzling me, pressing his face into my hair, until I could feel the hard push of his muzzle against the back of my neck. Male cats often bite the back of their mate's neck during sex, but if what I was feeling bit the back of my human neck I was gone, or crippled for life, unless I could heal it.

Bram stepped wide around us, hands held out so that his gun was pointed at the ceiling. "Micah, Nimir-Raj, can you hear me? I am one of your leopards."

His breath was hot as he huffed into my hair, but he wasn't just getting my scent; I was getting his and my black tiger snarled inside me, awake and pissed. We didn't like the claws in our shoulder, not one bit.

"Run, get Jade, bring her here, now!" Bram said. I heard someone running away, and Benito was still in the room, so there were more guards in the hallway.

"Micah," Rafael said, "say something, let us know you understand us and that you are not going to hurt Anita."

The tiger leaned back from my hair. I felt a tension ease from the muscles in his arms, and the claws in my shoulder eased. "I'm here. I'm here," he said in a voice that was lower and deeper, coming from the chest of the tiger, bigger than even his leopardman form could boast.

Benito spoke, "My king, move to me, you do not need to be here."

"Is that right, Micah, are you a danger to us?"

"I am aware, but I am having some issues regaining full control," the tigerman said; for some reason I couldn't think of him as Micah the way I did his panther form.

"What kind of issues?" Benito asked.

"Do not shoot him, Benito," Rafael said.

"The room is too small, and you are too close, my king."

"Anita, call your leopard, remind him who he is," Bram said, and he knelt, very slowly, down beside us as the tiger turned and snarled at him.

"I'm sorry," Micah said. "I don't like how many people are in the room, or the guns."

Bram kept his hands up, gun pointed skyward, but he was less than three feet from us; he might not get the gun down, pointed, and fired this close before the weretiger was on him. He wasn't just risking his life; he was offering it.

I wanted to say, *Bram, don't*, but my own tiger chose that moment to start running up that long corridor inside me. She was coming to take care of us, to give us claws and fangs to fight back. The spatter pattern on the floor was growing more decorative, and the trickles down my arm had finally met the spatter so it was beginning to pool. I was hurt, bleeding. It made it hard to argue with the tiger as she raced to help.

"My black tiger is coming, Micah."

The weretiger snuffled my neck again, but it wasn't a growl he breathed out against my spine this time. It was almost a . . . purr. "She smells good to this body."

"She won't be good if you bring her; she's pissed that we're hurt."

He bent over me, and it was as if he hadn't realized what he'd done until that moment. "Oh, Anita, I'm so sorry, I've never hurt you like this before."

"You might dismount before her tiger forces the issue, my friend," Rafael said.

"Please, Micah, she's close, and she's not listening to me."

He started to pull out of me, moving his hips back, but his body still mostly inside me. I saw my tiger leap like a piece of darkness made furred and muscled, snarling, and she crashed into me. It was like getting hit by a freight train, except my body was the tracks and the train and the prison she was trying to break. The impact drove me upward, shoving me into the weretiger on top of me, sending us both careening across the room and into the wall. His body took the impact or I'd have broken something.

My human body was stunned, breathless, smashed against the furred body behind me, but the tigress could move. She sprang to her feet, but something about my being stunned let her stand in my human body, so that we were suddenly in the hallway facing back toward the doorway, snarling, crouched on the balls of my feet and fingertips, as if I couldn't remember if I was four- or two-legged.

The weretiger that was Micah spilled through the doorway on all fours, the massive humanoid upper body hunched as it looked at me with eyes like fire. I screamed at it, and it was a tiger's scream that felt like it tore my throat just to make the noise, but it was as if the tigress had figured out how to drive and I couldn't get back behind the wheel. All I could do was watch as she launched us at the black figure in the doorway.

Bram was there to block my arm, to stand between me and my prey. I tried to slash his face, but the claws I could "see" in my head passed through him as if they weren't there. I tried to throw a left hook, but my shoulder wasn't working right, and Bram just pushed my arm down and moved into me, forcing me back not with blows, but just his size. He was taller than me and he shouldn't have been. My tiger was bigger than that; it was . . . wrong.

My tiger snarled and it came out of my mouth, but it hurt as if my throat couldn't, or shouldn't, make the sound. I dropped to my knees and could see Micah past Bram's legs. He was still in tiger form, but he reached out for me with a clawed hand still stained with my blood. "I'm sorry."

He collapsed slowly to the floor, hand still reaching for me. I started to crawl toward him, but Bram knelt down and stopped me. "I don't know if he's himself yet."

I understood the words, and my inner tiger agreed he was too dangerous to approach, but me, myself, I wanted to touch him. The black tigerman looked at me, and then from one blink to another his eyes changed from orange and yellow to Micah's chartreuse leopard eyes. He slid to his side and looked at me as the black fur began to slide away and his human body melted upward through the black-on-black stripes.

I went to him when he was back to being my Micah, and no one stopped me as I knelt by him. He put his hand in mine and looked up at me. "I love you, Anita."

"I love you more," I said.

"I love you most," he said. His eyes started closing, eyelids fluttering as he fought it. His eyes closed; his hand went limp in mine as he passed out.

I kissed his cheek and whispered, "I love you mostest."

49

THEY PUT ME in the room next door to Rafael while they looked at my shoulder. Adding insult to injury, Rafael wasn't healed. Once the endorphins from the sex, the magic, and then the emergency with Micah had passed, his back had started to hurt again.

Dr. Lillian looked at my shoulder, shaking her head. "I spend far too much time patching you up, Anita."

"Some of the other guards get hurt more than I do."

She frowned at me. "They're guards, you are not. It's their job to risk injury, not yours."

"Patch me up, doc, I need to meet the FBI."

"You need to rest and heal," she said.

"No time, gotta catch the bad guys."

She gave me a flat look out of her pale eyes. "The tough-guy act is getting old, Anita."

"It's not an act," I said.

She sighed. "Fair enough, you are as tough as you think you are, but you are not as indestructible as you act."

"This was not my fault," I said.

"Was it Micah's fault?"

I looked down and thought about it. "I don't think so, he only got this new form earlier today. I think he was able to control his leopard when we had sex, but the tiger was newer. I think it surprised him when I fed the *ardeur*."

"Don't feed the *ardeur* on him again until he's had tiger for at least a month, Anita. He had enough control to only puncture you; if he had clawed you . . ." She shook her head, looking way too serious for comfort.

"I know it would have been worse," I said.

"I heard he was sniffing your neck; if he'd bitten you there . . ."

"Stop, just stop, okay; I was scared enough while it was happening."

She looked at me. "You never admit you're afraid."

"Well, it's been a hard day, and I have to be well enough to meet with the FBI when they let me know the meeting is on."

"What could be important enough to push yourself this hard?"

"I can't tell you about an ongoing investigation, but it is one of the worst things I've ever seen, doc. If I can stop it before they take one more victim, then it's worth pushing myself."

"Some of the things you've seen are terrible, Anita, really terrible."

"Yes, they are," I said.

She nodded. "Do you really think that your being there will make that much difference?"

"Yes."

She sighed. "All right, I'll bandage you, and put your arm in a sling, but what you really need is to lie in this bed with some of your animals to call and let their warmth and energy help you heal faster."

"That'd be great, doc, but the FBI could call anytime, and I'm supposed to go to something for Cynric this afternoon."

"He's old enough to understand that you're hurt, Anita."

I shook my head.

"If he doesn't understand, put me on the phone and I'll explain it, but once you finish with the FBI, then you must rest. Can you at least call the agents you'll be meeting with and see if you have time for a quick nap, or some solid food?"

It sounded reasonable, so I called Special Agent Manning. "We're waiting on one of our agents to get into town."

"Marshal Kirkland is in town already," I said.

"We've got another specialist coming in to help review the videos."

"How long until he arrives?" I asked.

"She, but maybe three hours at the outside, probably more like two."

"Jesus, Manning, they could be picking a new victim right now."

"They're zombies, technically they aren't victims."

"You know that to capture their souls like this they have to be there ready at the time of their deaths. They may not be leaving that to chance; they may be killing these girls."

"I know, Blake, I know that, but we've been ordered to wait for the last agent to arrive, and I have to listen to my superiors more than you do."

"Fine, fine, I'm too tired to argue." I was tired, suddenly and completely exhausted.

"How much sleep did you get last night?" she asked.

"None."

She made an exasperated noise. "Then go to bed, take a nap. You won't be any good to anyone if you're too tired to focus."

"That's what my doctor said."

"Doctor? Are you hurt?"

"Long story; I'll get some sleep while we wait for the new guy, girl, whatever."

"You do that; I'll call when she gets into town. Now get some sleep while you can."

I fought the urge to say, *You're not the boss of me*, because sleep sounded amazing. I hung up and said to Dr. Lillian, "You're in luck, I get to take a nap."

She smiled and then went back to tut-tutting at me. "This is going to need stitches unless you get some help to heal it while you sleep."

"I'll find people to sleep between."

"Not Micah, and he's tucked into bed with Nathaniel, so not him either."

"You're ruining all my fun, doc."

"I can stitch you up, and we'll see how much fun that is."

"Point taken; fine, who else is one of my flavors of lycanthropy and available for sleeping in one of the bigger beds?"

"Hold this dressing on your shoulder while I check." I did what she told me to do, because if everything went well I'd heal and not need stitches. I hated stitches, especially now that painkillers were almost useless for me. Getting sewn up when you couldn't have anything to dull the pain sucked, a lot. I promised myself I wouldn't complain no matter who the doc found for me to bunk with if they could help me heal faster.

50

I LIED; I did complain. Graham, one of our local werewolves and guards, offered to share his bed with me and Clay, his good friend and fellow wolf and guard, but Meng Die was already in the bed. Yes, she was dead to the world and the men wouldn't make me sleep next to her cooling body, but I didn't trust her not to do something unfortunate if she woke before I did. She'd already hinted that she was willing to fuck me. I did not want to wake up with her trying to make that happen. I did not fuck people I hated, or who hated me. It was a rule, because a girl's gotta draw the line somewhere.

Next offer was two of the wereleopards, Elizabeth and Caleb, who had been a couple, though not exclusive, for a while now. I'd once shot Elizabeth full of non-silver bullets, so she'd healed, and she'd feared me after that, but it didn't make us buddies. She was the only one of the local wereleopards who had pushed me that far after I'd taken over their pard. Caleb would have been a bad guy if he'd had the balls to be truly evil; instead he was just sour, and cruel when he could get away with it. It was a shame, because he was cute in a Goth-boy, I've-pierced-too-many-things way, but his attitude stole all his attractiveness. I was glad they were dating each other; it saved anyone else from having to date either of them. They both went under the same rule as Meng Die. I wasn't falling asleep in a bed with people who hated me.

"It doesn't have to be matching animals, doc, they just have to match my internal beasts."

"True, but we've discovered that matching wereanimals from the same group that you are already connected with speeds your healing even more, and with such limited time before you have to go back to the police, it makes sense to use our resources efficiently."

I sighed. "Fine, and you're right, who else is available?"

Magda, the werelion who had been beating the shit out of Kelly, and the other Harlequin lion, Giacomo, were the next ones Doc Lillian offered as a possibility.

"No."

"Anita, you are going to use up all your sleeping time being picky. I'm not asking you to have sex with any of these people, just sleep between them and let the group energy help you heal."

"Falling asleep between two people takes a lot more trust for me than fucking them," I said.

She frowned at me. "Anita, we are running out of people who match your animals. We have far more wererats on duty right now, but we are not your animal to call, so we can't help you heal."

"Is that why Micah and I couldn't heal Rafael?"

She nodded. "I'd hoped that Micah's abilities might stretch to more wereanimals, but you seem to only be able to heal people you have some metaphysical tie to, so even if you could call rats, I'm not sure you could have healed Rafael, or any of us."

"I'm sorry, Lillian, I honestly am not trying to be difficult."

"Well, if this is you not trying, I can't wait for more effort on your part," she said, voice dry and unhappy.

I couldn't tell if she'd made a joke or was genuinely upset with me. "Are we really down to the bottom of the barrel on choices?"

"I would recommend not saying it that way to Magda, but yes."

"I'll compromise, then; one of the Harlequin, but not two."

"I can wake Nicky for you."

"No, let him sleep. If I'm too hurt to go to Cynric's school thing, then I want him and Nathaniel to be able to go."

"Very few of the werelions bunk here, Anita." Then I watched a thought cross her face. "How about Travis, he's spending the week here so he can do fight training."

"Travis is my size, and more bookworm than gym rat; he's never going to be that good," I said.

"Bookworm doesn't mean you can't be a great warrior," she said.

"No, but your heart has to be in both your books and the practice field. Travis practices fighting because he knows he has to in order to survive in lion society, but his heart isn't in it."

She smiled. "That may well be true, but he seems to be thriving under Nicky's leadership."

I didn't tell her that the only reason Travis was still alive was that Nicky protected him and made it clear that all challenges to Travis were met with a double team of both men. Why did Nicky do it? Travis knew that being smart and being gentle were his strengths, neither of which did him much good with the werelions. He'd come to me, asked me to help him talk to Nicky about an idea he'd had. Real male lions, and some lionesses, worked in groups. There were prides in the wild that were ruled not by one male, but coalitions of two to six. Some were brothers, or cousins, but genetic testing had revealed that a lot of them were just battle buddies that had met along the nomadic wanderings that young males are forced to do when their fathers kick them out of the home territory when they get old enough to challenge their dad and uncles. Almost anything that the natural version of the animal did was fair game to be part of the wereanimal's culture.

Travis proposed that he and Nicky do that; when we'd asked what Nicky got out of it, okay Nicky asked, but Travis had said this: "Nicky feels emotions through you, but on his own he's pretty much a sociopath, which means he's not understanding the emotional dynamics of the pride, and especially with the lionesses he needs that. I'll explain the emotional stuff in private to him, and do any research he needs on wereanimal culture, or anything else he needs."

Nicky had said, "The research is pretty useless, but I know I'm missing stuff in the pride dynamics. Is it that obvious that I'm not getting the emotional stuff?"

"My emotional intelligence is really high."

"What does that mean, emotional intelligence?" Nicky asked.

"It means he's as smart about emotions as he is about book stuff," I said.

"Like Anita's social/communication intelligence is really high when she doesn't get in her own way, and your physical intelligence is amazing. There's a lot of ways to be smart; the kind that gets you straight A's in school is only one way."

Nicky had agreed to try it for a month as an experiment, and then made it permanent. Travis helped make Nicky a better Rex, and understanding the emotional stuff helped head off problems before they snowballed into fights. It was like being the kind of bouncer who knew when to step in, before something got out of hand, rather than the kind who had to wait for the fists to fly to know how to fix the problem. Preventive maintenance wasn't just for your car.

Nicky had insisted that the first time off Travis had, he had to come and spend it training to fight here with our guards, because Nicky couldn't be with Travis all the time. Also, Nicky had confided in me that Travis sucked at fighting, like seriously sucked. I'd actually forgotten that last night was the start of a long weekend of training for our scholarly lion.

I said yes to Travis and Magda for bunkmates. Travis I liked as a friend, and a chance to talk to Magda about her treatment of Kelly would be a good thing. I wouldn't bring up the topic, but I needed a better feel for Magda if I was going to understand why she was challenging Kelly to a fight that would gain her nothing in the pride except a token title of head lioness. Maybe that was enough for her to do it; if it was, then I didn't know how to stop it, but I was hoping for more of a clue. If I had a chance to talk with Travis alone, I'd ask him for his take on Magda. But I was suddenly exhausted, as if everything were catching up with me all at once.

I'd rinsed off wereanimal goop again, and blood, in the shower. Doc Lillian had to bandage me again, because I couldn't keep the dressing clean. She'd been quite cranky about it, as if I'd done it on purpose. I sat on the edge of the bed with bandages running across the top of my left shoulder and a little down my arm. I still had the towel from the shower wrapped around me. I couldn't decide if I just didn't want to walk back through the underground naked again, or if I'd simply been so tired I forgot to take it off. At least my hair hadn't gotten messy, so it wasn't wet this time. It would make sleeping on a pillow more comfortable and I wouldn't wake up with my hair dried in odd positions like some curly Rorschach test.

I heard voices and knew someone was talking their way past the two guards outside my door. Bram had tattled on me to Fredo, so now I had bodyguards everywhere I went, at least for today. There was a soft knock, and that alone let me know it wasn't Magda. She knocked like a cop with a knock-and-announce warrant—loud, authoritative, and about to knock your door down. This was a knock you could say no to, and they'd just go away. It had to be Travis.

I said, "Come in."

Travis peeked around the door. His short curls looked dark brown, instead of their usual brownish blond. It also looked like his hair had grown out a little, and it was only when he'd walked into the room and shut the door behind him that I realized his hair was wet, which made it darker and, with the curls relaxed, longer. My hair wet and heavy was nearly four inches longer in back. He was also wearing nothing but a towel around him, just like me. In fact, the towel covered him from armpit to nearly ankle like it did for me, because we were almost the same height. The extra-big towels were like dresses on both of us, but on Claudia they barely covered the essentials.

"Sorry you're hurt," he said.

"Me, too. Sorry I'm interrupting your fight training."

He smiled then. "I'm not, I hate it."

"You're starting to show some muscle definition," I said, starting to motion at his arms, but having to stop in midmotion because I'd forgotten and tried to raise my left arm.

"Yeah, and if the women I wanted to date were into that sort of thing it'd be great, but they're more impressed that I can recite Shakespearian sonnets by memory in their ear."

I gave him a look. "Tell me you're joking."

"Haven't you ever dated someone who was into literature?"

"I thought I had, but maybe I'm wrong, because I think if I'd tried to whisper sonnets for pillow talk they'd have giggled at me."

"You have to know your audience," he said. "Mine likes poetry."

"I didn't say I disliked poetry, just not that fond of the sonnets."

"You don't like Shakespeare?" He pretended to be offended, hand to his chest as if I'd wounded him.

"I prefer the tragedies," I said.

He smiled again. "Of course you do, but I don't think whispering Lady Macbeth's soliloquy would get me laid."

It was my turn to grin. "I don't know, depends on the girl."

"You?"

"No," I said, still smiling, and it was good to be smiling. It helped chase back the tiredness.

He came and sat on the bed beside me, careful to sit on the side that wasn't bandaged. "You look beat, Anita."

"Good to know I feel as bad as I look, or look as bad as I feel, or something like that."

"I didn't mean you look bad, you always look good."

I looked at him. "Now, that is totally not true."

He smiled, frowned, and finally said, "Is this one of those girl moments that I can't win? So if I agree with you, are you going to accuse me of not thinking you're beautiful, and if I disagree with you, are you going to tell me I'm lying?"

I laughed; I couldn't help it. "If you were a boyfriend, or lover, maybe, but no, I'm not going to go all girl-logic weird on you."

"Whew," he said, and pretended to wipe sweat off his brow.

"Am I this tired, or are you funnier than normal, and happier than normal?"

"The second is definitely true," he said.

"Happier even with the extra gym work?"

He nodded. "I had to shower before I came in here, because I was all sweaty from lifting weights and getting my ass kicked."

"I know you're getting intensive training these next four days, so who's doing your one-on-one fight drills?"

"Fredo."

"He's good hand-to-hand, but he's even better with knives."

"So I've noticed. He says I'm better with blades than my hands. I can't tell if it's a compliment, or his way of saying I'm so bad with my fists that I need a knife to win a fight."

"If Fredo compliments anything you do with a knife in your hand, it's a good thing. He's the main blade instructor for the guards, and he's wicked good at it. I bloodied him once in a practice match. Impressed the hell out of the other guys."

His pale brown eyes went very wide and made him look even younger. He was actually twenty-five, but he looked closer to eighteen; with his eyes wide and his curls all wet and careless he could have passed for seventeen easy.

"You touched Fredo in a knife match, wow, that is impressive. He's so fast."

"Rats and leopards seem to have an edge in speed. Lions have more muscle."

"Not this lion," he said.

"I was going to ask you something if we were alone."

"You don't remember what it was?"

I shook my head.

He hugged me, careful of my shoulder. "You have had a rough day."

"Oh, Magda, what's your take on her? Why is she beating up on Kelly?"

"She wants to be the official first lioness of our pride."

"Nicky has already turned her down for sex, and I'm his Regina, so she can't be that. First lioness in our local pride is a pretty hollow title, actually."

"It is," he agreed.

"So why is Magda pushing this?"

"I'm not sure, but I know she's not going to stop."

"Why not, if it gains her nothing?"

"I didn't say it gained her nothing, I just agreed that being first lioness is an empty title."

"Okay, what does it gain her to fight Kelly?"

"I don't know, but I know she sees some goal. The Harlequin are very goal driven whether they're the vampire masters"—he made finger quotes around the word *masters*—"or the wereanimal companion."

I might have asked more, but there was a very purposeful knock at the door. I hadn't heard any conversation first; either I'd been too busy talking to hear it, or Magda had just come up and glared at the door guards until they let her knock.

"Come in," I said.

Magda didn't peer around the door; she just walked in like she owned the room. She was tall for a woman, five-ten, which meant she'd have towered over people back in the day. Her hair was blond, cut so it fell below her ears but never touched her shoulders. The hair was blunt cut, which would have worked with straight hair, but she had waves to hers, so it was just messy like someone had started to style and cut her hair but stopped partway. Her vampire master had absolutely straight hair, as black as hers was yellow. Her eyes were blue-gray, changeable as the sky. They looked bluer now, because she was wearing blue satin pajamas. It had never occurred to me that Magda would own jammies, let alone pastel blue ones, and satin, just not what I'd pictured. Even dressed in something soft she filled the room not with height, but with attitude. She turned those human eyes on us, but it was like her lion was the one seeing out, and the lion thought everything it surveyed belonged to it. Not all the Harlequin were like that, but she was; even the male lion Giacomo didn't have that air of command to him. It was like a constant slap in the face of any alpha around her, as if she knew she was the strongest, fastest, bestest in the room, unless you could persuade her you were better, but until then . . . it was her room. Magda made me tired, even when I wasn't. She was like a constant pissing contest waiting to happen. Part of that was a lion thing, but she had more than her share of it.

I was already remembering why I didn't spend much time with her and she hadn't been here five minutes yet. How was I ever going to sleep with her on the other side of me? It must have shown on my face, or maybe my scent changed; whatever the cause, Magda picked it up.

"You are not pleased with something I've done, and I've done nothing yet, not even spoken."

"Your energy is sort of . . . loud," I said.

Travis was sitting straighter beside me, not hugging anymore. He was tense; the question was, why?

"I don't know what you mean by that," she said.

"I know," I said.

Travis was watching her less like another lion and more like a gazelle. No wonder he had problems with the other lions, and no wonder Magda did, too. They just had opposite problems.

"Okay, I need to sleep and the two of you need to work together to make that possible," I said.

"We will sleep on either side of you and our lions will mingle with yours and help heal you," Magda said.

"Yes, but not if your energy makes me feel like I have to prove I'm dominant to you all over again."

A frown appeared between her yellow eyebrows. You didn't see a lot of natural yellow eyebrows, not even on blondes. It softened her eyes even more, I think, or maybe black eyebrows would have given them more color; who knew?

"I have done nothing to challenge you, Anita. I acknowledge you as Regina to our Rex, and have never said otherwise."

"You offered to sleep with Nicky," I said.

"It's customary when entering a new pride to offer yourself to the Rex."

Travis finally said, "No, it's not."

She narrowed her eyes at him, and they were suddenly gray as rain clouds. "It was once," she said, voice growing lower, as if the next sound she made would be a growl.

"That was then, this is now," I said.

She turned that unfriendly gaze to me. "I am more aware than you will ever be that this is a future unforeseen and very unlike the past I knew."

"I'm not going to apologize for killing the Mother of All Darkness, Magda."

She looked genuinely puzzled. "I would not expect it; you do not apologize for conquering an enemy."

"All right, I'm not going to apologize that my victory cost you a way of life; how's that?"

"Again, I would not expect you to do any such thing. You do not apologize for winning a war."

"You should Google the Vietnam War and see how people can apologize for a war, though I guess we didn't win that one."

"I don't understand."

"Anita is referring to more recent American history, and Vietnamese history. I guess the French and Russians were involved, as well."

"I will look it up on the Internet," she said, and walked farther into the room.

Travis tensed. I turned to him. "If she needs to tone down the big bad energy, you need to man up and stop giving off prey energy."

His pale brown eyes darkened while I looked into them. He wasn't changing into his lion; he was angry, and it turned his eyes darker. I thought the anger was a good sign; it meant there was more fight in him than he was showing.

"I'm trying, don't you think I'm trying?" he said, and his voice was a little deeper, too.

"Just because he is a werelion doesn't mean he is not a lamb, Anita."

"I am not a lamb," Travis said, voice lower still, so that it sounded like he needed a wider chest to make that bass.

Magda ignored him, talking directly to me as if he didn't exist. "You cannot make a lamb into a wolf, Anita. Even if he has the skills to fight, he does not have the will to win."

I actually feared she was right, but I hoped she was wrong.

Travis's anger came off him like heat, and his beast rose with it. My skin prickled with the nearness of it. I looked at him and found dark orange lion eyes looking out of his face.

"Do you have such poor control of your beast, boy?"

The boy stood up, and I did not want to see her beat the shit out of him in front of me, nor did I want to get hurt again today trying to stop it.

"This is not restful," I said.

Travis startled. Magda looked at me.

"I have a limited amount of time to sleep before the FBI calls and I have to leave for work. I haven't slept in about twenty-four hours, so if you guys are going to fight, take it outside and I'll find some other bunkmates."

Magda dropped to one knee but kept her eyes on Travis the way you do in martial arts when you bow before a match. You bow, but your gaze stays on your opponent; otherwise he could kick your ass while you're not looking. The fact that Magda accorded Travis even that much attention either was a good sign for him, or meant that she was just always that cautious.

Travis knelt, too, though he got tangled in his towel, so it wasn't as smooth, but he did it. "I'm sorry, Anita."

"Forgive me, my dark queen," Magda said.

"First, don't call me dark queen. I'll forgive you both if you just stop squabbling and climb into bed, so I can sleep. You guys were not my first choice as a bed duo, and unless you shape up really quickly, you're going to be off my list of ever bunking over with me, for any reason."

Magda bowed her head, her eyes on me, but I knew somehow that she was still very aware of Travis. She was just that cautious; she didn't see him as a real threat. "I am ashamed that I put my own petty grievances ahead of your comfort, my queen."

"Me, too, Anita, I'm sorry."

"Fine, I'll accept the apologies on the understanding that we sleep now, quietly, with no more bickering." I lay down and slipped under the covers, hoping that would speed things along. I couldn't lie on my left side, so I had to lie with my back to the door. I couldn't do it. I sat up in the bed, and tried to think if either of the other two rooms had a bed that was oriented the other way. I didn't think so.

"Allow me to lie in front of you so that I block anyone who might come through the door to harm you," Magda said, and slipped her blue pajama top over her head to expose a pale but very fit upper body with high, full breasts, and just below those very nice breasts was a scar that traced below them like an angry red scythe, with a straight line running down from one end of the crescent to vanish below her waistband, as if someone had cut a proverbial death scythe on her body. The fact that it was red meant it was recent, and since she should have been able to heal almost anything, it shouldn't have been there. She could have had it as an old white scar, but not fresh. Muscles moved in her arms, chest, and stomach as she moved toward the bed. Her body was lean and athletic the way that J.J.'s was, though genetics had let her keep more breast, but other than that she reminded me of the ballet dancer who I enjoyed so much.

"You get front," Travis said, "because if it's a real fight all I can do right now is help delay them while you keep Anita safe." He let the towel fall to the floor and climbed onto the bed, totally unbothered by the fact that he was now nude as he clambered over my legs to get to the wall side of the bed.

"The fact that you understand your limitations is the beginning of wisdom," Magda said, as she slid out of her pajama bottoms. She was even leaner below, as if whatever trick of genetics had let her keep more breast hadn't left room for much of a swell of hips, so they were very narrow, and her legs very long. She even moved more like a man than most women I knew, though I'd seen female martial artists who could take the sway out of their hips when they were fighting, or getting ready to fight. I wondered if it was her natural walk or just centuries of practice. I wondered how she'd gotten the big scar, and when.

I finally settled on my right side, snuggling up against Travis, with Magda wrapped around me from behind. Her arms were so long that she was really wrapped around both of us. Neither she nor Travis seemed to have any problem with her arm going across him and using his body to pull me tighter into the curve of hers. I had a moment of discomfort when her breasts pressed around my shoulders. I'd never slept this close to another woman with that much breast. I wasn't sure why it bothered me, but it did. If I could have slept on my other shoulder, I could have gone to sleep, and by the time I had to deal with someone else's breasts I'd have had hours of getting used to it before I noticed. Now, I was noticing.

"You are tense," she said.

"I don't like my back to the door," and that was part of it.

"If we get up I will remake the bed in moments and you can face the other way."

I felt stupid for not thinking of it, but that was what we did. Travis helped her remake the bed with the covers tucked under the opposite side and the pillows moved down. The bed had no footboard or headboard, so it worked fine. This time Travis cuddled me from behind and I was way more comfortable feeling his guy parts against my ass than I had been with Magda's breasts. I know, it's weird, but it was still how I felt.

I wrapped my arm around her waist, and because of the height difference my face was about midback to her once our hips were spooning as solidly as I was with Travis. He threw his arm across mine so he snuggled Magda, too. Again, neither one complained.

I thought it wouldn't work, that I'd lie awake and be all weird because I'd never slept with either of them before, but exhaustion makes strange bedfellows. I fell asleep to the sound of Travis's soft breathing, and I knew he was asleep. Magda wasn't, though her body was still and comfortable as if she were pretending to sleep, or just letting me sleep. Somehow I knew she'd stay awake, or at least alert. I might not like her, and she couldn't stop someone from coming through the door, that was the job of the guards outside, but I was betting good money that nothing would get to me until she had given her life to try and prevent it. You don't have to like someone to know that they'll lay down their life for you. You don't even have to like someone to do it for them. You just know what your duty is, and how much you're willing to sacrifice to do that duty. Magda had already lost one queen on her watch; I was betting my life she wouldn't want to lose another one.

I slept, and I dreamt of a gray sky with golden clouds that looked like puffy lions, and bears, and all sorts of animals. The sky turned blue, the sun was warm, and there was the sound of an ocean on a beach just out of sight, over the hill. I walked toward that sound all night but could never find the sea.

51

THERE WAS MUSIC playing; it climbed into my dream and pulled me out. I came to with a vague memory of water and a boat, and zombies juggling kittens that slashed and clawed through the air. I woke, but snuggled down between the two men and tried to ignore the music. The music finally stopped, and I started to drift back to sleep, so warm in the darkened room. I snuggled against the man in front of me, putting my face against his bare back, and didn't know the smell of his skin.

My eyes opened, my body tensed, and I tried not to panic. I'd been asleep long enough that Magda and Travis had had to go do something else. I'd been through this before when I was injured, or exhausted, and slept so long that I needed shift changes for my bed buddies, but logic had nothing to do with it. The warm press of the two men, sandwiching me in the dim room, in the nest of sheets and bodies that had been so comforting a second before, now felt like I was trapped and couldn't move.

The music sounded again, and I realized it was my phone ringing. I didn't remember bringing my phone with me, so someone had put my stuff in here for me. People were taking care of me, so why was my stomach tight and all I wanted to do was fight my way free of covers and bodies and grab the phone? I started trying to sit up and realized I was lying on my left arm, which meant I was at least partially healed. I was also trapped under the covers because they were tangled around me and the men somehow.

The man in front propped up on his elbow and reached a long arm out from the bed. He was very dark-skinned, black in the room, though I wasn't sure if that was true color or just the very dim lighting. He came back with my phone in hand, and I still didn't recognize the short,

almost shaved black hair and long, very tall body. I could feel that the
man behind me was shorter and more delicate than the one in front of
me, but I hadn't even bothered to look. I knew by just lying there that
it wasn't anyone I was that familiar with . . . no one I had slept and
woken up with.

I took the phone and finally recognized the glimpse of face of the
tall man. It was Seamus, werehyena to call for the Harlequin Jane. I hit
the button and said, "Yes, I'm here."

"You sound like you were asleep, Blake," Special Agent Manning
said.

I snuggled back down on my left side, burying my face against Seamus's back. The smaller man in back snuggled in against me, too. I
stopped worrying that I didn't know who it was and just let it feel comforting. "I had to work all night, so yeah I was asleep, sorry."

"You raised the dead all night?"

"Something like that, yeah. What's up?"

"You do remember that you requested to view the videos again?"

"Yeah, I remember."

"By the time you get dressed and down here we should be ready for
you."

"Ready for me? I just walk in and your partner does his computer
magic and we watch the videos; just this time I use my psychic abilities
to look for clues."

"The home office wanted another pair of eyes to help you look for
clues."

"What does that mean?"

"We're flying another agent in to view the videos with you and
Marshal Kirkland, remember?"

I'd forgotten all of it; it made my shoulders tighten and took some
of the comfy out of my nest of bodies and covers. "Fine, I know not to
argue with the home office."

"Can the sarcasm, Blake; just because you ride around like the Lone
fucking Ranger doesn't mean the rest of us don't have superiors riding
our ass. Working with you makes all the upper-management types nervous. I wonder why that would be?"

"I think that was sarcasm."

"I think you're right." She sounded unhappy, and I didn't think it was just at me.

"I know the upper muckety-mucks don't like me at the bureau. They think I'm a pain in the ass and don't follow orders well."

"Prove them wrong," she said.

"I can't, because I'm a pain in the ass, and I don't follow orders well." She gave a small laugh then, and finally said, "Shit."

"What'd I do now?" I asked.

"Not you, the plane is delayed. Take your time, Blake, you've got two extra hours before the bird lands and we get our extra agent on the ground."

"Good to know, maybe I can eat something."

"You know what's on the videos; like I said last time, eating first would probably be a good idea." She hung up without saying good-bye.

52

THE MAN BEHIND me snuggled down so that his nose was buried against my back, but I knew from where the rest of his body was that it wasn't because he was that much shorter than me. He was just burying himself under the covers.

"Are the FBI always so abrupt on the phone?" the man asked.

I froze, because I did know that voice.

"Now you're all tense, Anita, why would that be?"

I turned over and actually had to pull the sheet up and off him to see Narcissus's face. He was smiling up at me, but it didn't reach his eyes. They were dark and glittering. He was holding a tight rein on it, but he was angry. I couldn't blame him after what Asher and Kane had done, but I also couldn't figure out what he was doing bunking over at the Circus. He rarely, if ever, left his club and home, Narcissus in Chains.

He rose on one elbow, still smiling at me. His short black hair was tousled from sleep, but I could admit that the slender triangular face was pretty. Remnants of black eyeliner had smeared around his large, brown eyes, as if he'd been crying, though I knew it was just from sleeping with eyeliner and mascara still on. Maybe he never took his eye makeup off, but I was betting he'd rushed to be here. He usually slept the day away and worked nights, just like me.

"You look like you've seen a ghost, dearie," he said, and there was a bitterness in his words to match the harshness in his eyes.

I swallowed hard, and finally managed to say, "I just didn't expect you to be here, Narcissus. The Oba of the hyena clan doesn't make house calls."

"We're supposed to work together, aren't we?" He scooted higher up in the bed, so that we were both lying there propped up on our elbows, and looking into each other's faces from inches away. It was too intimate for me with him, so I started to sit up.

He grabbed my arm, not hard, it didn't hurt, but I didn't like it. "If I say don't touch me, then you say, but I touched so much more of you while we slept. That about how it's going to go?"

He smiled, but again his eyes stayed glitteringly cold, or hot, but it was anger-hot, not sex, not anything positive. His hand on my arm was gentle, as if I could have jerked away easily. I didn't try, because if he fought me for it . . . it wasn't worth it, yet. Just by his being here I knew that Jean-Claude had done his best to fix the mess that Asher had made of things with the local hyenas. I was pretty sure that Narcissus helping to heal me like this was part of some compromise that kept Narcissus from declaring war, or demanding Asher's head on a pike, or just killing Kane—who was just one of his lower-level hyenas, and that meant in hyena society he lived or died at the whim of his king, his Oba, Narcissus.

"Yes, that's about how it would go," he said.

"Let's skip it, then," I said.

He smiled. "Let's."

"I have to get dressed and go play cops and robbers."

"Leave us, Seamus," he said.

Seamus got out of bed. I turned so I could see him; he was well over six feet so I didn't have to turn my head that much. "I'm not sure us alone is a good idea."

Seamus hesitated, standing there looking down at both of us.

Heat and energy rose off Narcissus, as if I'd opened the door of an oven set to broil. I looked down at his hand and it almost burned against my skin. God, he was so powerful. I'd known that, felt it before, but not in a long time, and not like this.

"Either I am your king, or I am not!" He spat the words out. "If I am not, then stay, but if I am—get the fuck out of here!"

Seamus dropped to one knee, head bowed, but eyes up the way Magda had been earlier. "You are my king."

"But that bitch vampire, Jane, calls to the hyenas, all of them, like some fucking siren." His hand was tighter on my arm now. His beast rose like nearly visible flame around him. It called to the newest beast inside me. I'd been so careful to stay away from the hyenas up to now, so careful. Most of my animals to call had all been accidental, whoever was nearest me at the time that I had some major power-up metaphysically. I hadn't wanted to tie myself to any more people, and Jean-Claude had urged me to think carefully before I chose someone for political and personal reasons, since the animals to call could become part of our poly group.

Narcissus looked at me, a low animal noise sliding out of his thin, well-shaped mouth. He usually wore lipstick to make his lips fuller and pouty. Now they were just pink and I could trace the line of them. I realized two things: First, someone had turned on the light in the room so I could see the paleness of his skin, the deep brown of his eyes, and the pink of his natural lip color; second, I'd tried to move my hand to touch his mouth and trace the line of it.

He still had my arm, so I couldn't reach him, but my hand was raised trying to touch his face. We looked at each other.

"Get out," Narcissus said, and neither of us looked as Seamus went for the door, but someone else was in the room now. I could feel them, and Narcissus just had to raise his gaze and see them.

"All of you, get out!"

"I am not one of your hyenas, and you don't sign my paycheck." It was Dino. If I hadn't been inches from the most powerful wereanimal in the room, I'd have turned and looked for the big guy. I wondered how Seamus had even moved past him with both of them being so big, like two trucks getting stuck in a tunnel.

I almost smiled at my own joke, but staring into Narcissus's face, feeling his hand grip my arm ever tighter, I didn't think he'd get the joke. I was having trouble breathing this close to all that energy. He was heat, and sun, and . . . I smelled that dry grass, burned under the sun that I smelled when my lion came to me. I smelled the native land, or territory, of my beasts; I knew that, and I knew that hyenas and lions shared the same landscape, but it jarred me to smell the same land. It called my lion awake, as if the hyena smelled like home.

Narcissus jerked me those last few inches closer, so that he snarled in my face. "It's not your lion I've come to see."

I felt Dino loom up above the bed, before Narcissus's gaze rolled upward. "Be very careful what you do next, rat." His voice was low, growling, but very calm, each word enunciated carefully. I knew why he was controlling his voice so tightly, because if he lost control of even that much he wasn't sure what else he'd lose control of. I'd had moments like that, usually when I had a gun pointed at someone.

"Back off, Dino," I said, keeping my voice low and even. I stared into Narcissus's eyes from inches away, bathing in the heat of his beast, his grip almost painful on my arm. He wanted to lash out at someone, so badly.

"I don't think that's a good idea, Anita."

"I didn't ask your opinion; I gave you an order," I said, looking only at Narcissus. My hyena was awake and looked at him but didn't try to come closer. She was much more cautious than most of my beasts when they smelled a potential mate.

"Anita . . ."

"Get out, Dino. Send someone in here who won't make things worse."

Narcissus looked at the big man. "You heard your mistress, and she does sign your paycheck." His words were calmer, some of the horrible tension easing.

In my head I thought, well technically I didn't sign the paychecks, but I decided not to quibble since things were improving. Dino did what we told him to do, and we were suddenly alone just inches from each other, naked, with his power spreading over me like a warm bath that was just this side of too hot.

"Thank you for helping to heal me," I said, voice still low and calm, as if I were afraid of spooking him.

He frowned, his eyes losing some of that angry edge. "You're welcome, but aren't you going to ask why Jean-Claude sent me in to sleep with you?" His voice was growing calmer, and his energy was easing down, more like a bath you'd enjoy relaxing in, and not one that would boil your flesh from your bones. He had so much power to offer, which was why he was Oba of the clan, and why the other leaders tolerated his ultimatums. They all respected power.

"To help heal me," I said, almost whispering.

"I am tired of games, Anita. Do you know what has happened, or don't you?"

"Do you mean the dickwad stupidity that Asher pulled with Kane?"

He gave the tiniest smile. "*Dickwad*, I haven't heard that since junior high."

"Would you prefer jackass, idiot, fucking bastard, asshole? Stop me when I get to an insult you like, I've got a million of them."

He smiled a little more. "Well, I do like assholes."

That made me smile. "So I'm told."

The energy eased down a little bit more, and he stopped squeezing my arm so tight. "I have called Asher every name I can think of today."

"How'd he take that?"

"I don't know, I haven't seen him yet."

"You mean you've cursed him in absentia?" I asked.

He smiled. "I like that, yes, I've cursed him in absentia. I was afraid of what I'd do to him if I saw him." He let go of my arm and just lay down on his side of the bed. I did the same so we lay on our sides, facing each other, but not touching.

"I told Kane you'd want to kill them both."

"I heard you spoke with him." He laughed, but it left his eyes bleak and starting to fill with anger again. "I heard you fed on him and left him on the floor to twitch, after threatening to make him your hyena to call and break his tie with Asher forever."

"I was pretty angry myself when he told me what they'd done."

"Would you really tie yourself to Kane for all eternity?"

"Nah, I don't do stupid, and he had to be stupid to not understand what it could mean for him to be Asher's animal to call."

"I am within my rights to kill him." His face was calm when he said it, his eyes looking down the bed as if he were thinking.

"If you'd seen him, or Asher, when you first found out, you might have."

He looked at me then, the anger flaring back. "His life is mine if I so will it."

"It is, but part of the reason you're in here with me is that you didn't kill him, or Asher."

He laughed then, a real laugh, and hugged me. "He is so stupid; how can I love someone who is this fucking stupid?"

I hugged him back and answered with my face in the bend of his neck. "I don't know, but Jean-Claude loves him, too, and so do I, or so did I."

He drew back enough to look into my face. "You don't love Asher anymore?"

"I don't think I do anymore."

"Teach me how to stop loving him."

"He's teaching you, just like he taught me, and Nathaniel. We love how he tops us in the bedroom and dungeon, but . . ."

Narcissus shivered happily. "He does have a talent for sex and pain." His eyes were a little unfocused when he said it, and that reaction was one of the reasons he put up with Asher.

"But," I said, "he's also teaching all of us that he values other people more than us, and after a while if you have any self-respect you finally get tired of the shit and start to move on."

"You have more people to move on with," he said.

"You slept with, or topped, almost all your werehyenas—once. You had built yourself a harem of hundreds."

"That was before Chimera took us over and I learned the difference between muscle men and real fighters. I fixed it by finding other men who were the real deal so that no one could ever hurt us like that again." His eyes looked haunted, and angry, and things I couldn't understand. He'd been captured and used as a hostage to get the rest of the werehyenas to do what Chimera wanted. I still remembered the torture room where he'd hung some of the werehyenas after he cut limbs off them, because they'd grow a new one eventually, so he'd made a forest of them to hang from the ceiling of the room. I'd hidden in the dark among the bleeding and the few that hadn't survived the torture.

Narcissus touched my face, brought me out of my memories and looking at him again. "I don't think I ever thanked you for killing him and saving my hyenas from that evil piece of shit."

I smiled, but I knew my eyes were still as haunted as his. I took his hand from my face and held it over the covers like we were five and one of us had had a bad dream. "It was my pleasure to put him out of his misery."

"You know that I enjoyed what he did to me at first."

"I know you are a serious pain slut."

He grinned. "Yes, yes I am." His eyes went bleak again. "He didn't like how much pain I could enjoy, because that meant he wasn't really hurting me. He wanted to hurt me, wanted to find things that even I didn't enjoy. He was an almost pure sadist; causing pain was his aphrodisiac. Until Chimera I thought I enjoyed causing pain, but I have limits that I don't want to cross outside of fantasy. I don't want to destroy my lovers until they are useless and broken, but that was exactly what Chimera wanted."

I squeezed his hand. "But he didn't break you; you're still here, still Oba of the clan, and he's dead."

He smiled, but his eyes stayed sad. "He didn't break me, but he put a few new cracks in where I thought I was safe."

"I'm sorry, Narcissus."

"What are you sorry about?"

"That I didn't kill him sooner."

He smiled. "I am grateful, but not grateful enough to let this insult go."

"You can't let it go; it makes you look weak in front of your hyenas."

"You understand," he said, studying my face.

"Hyenas and lions are both very much about the strongest, most powerful wins, more even than most wereanimal groups."

"Yes," he said, softly, but not like it made him happy.

I looked at this delicate-seeming man and knew there was more to him physically than I had ever seen, because he had fought his way to the top of one of the most violent animal groups. Hyena society wasn't for sissies, but that was exactly what Narcissus was; he was as likely to wear a nice evening dress to his club as a well-tailored suit. He usually wore more eye makeup than I did, and he was cheerfully gay, but he was still Oba, still king. It had hurt my head a little the first time I'd met him.

"I demanded Asher's head, and when Jean-Claude said no, I said I'd kill Kane and if the death of Asher's animal to call killed him, too, so be it."

"Jean-Claude talked you out of it."

"He did, now ask me how, or rather what he said to me that made me willing to spare the two idiots."

"I think I can ballpark it. He offered you a closer connection to the throne."

"Yes." He looked surprised. "I didn't expect you to be this calm about it."

I frowned a little. "Okay, I thought you sleeping in here was part of it, I mean literally closer to me, to him, but now I think you should just tell me. I feel like I'm missing something."

"You have no hyena to call, yet. There is no more fitting match for a queen than a king."

I frowned harder. "Last I talked to you, you told me to stay away from your hyenas because I'm a girl and hyenas are instinctively matriarchal. You were worried I'd take over your clan."

"I've had to let women in just to keep all the new straights happy." He rolled his eyes.

"So you've got women in the clan now, but you're still king."

"I'm not just king, I'm truly queen, and apparently I'm girl enough for everyone's inner beast."

Narcissus looked like a man, but apparently he had girl parts, too. In fact, both functioned well enough that he'd gotten pregnant from Chimera raping him. He'd lost the baby and I couldn't say I was sorry for that; Chimera did not need to breed more monsters like him, and Narcissus hadn't seemed the most stable cookie in the box, but I knew that Narcissus had wanted the baby.

"So, since you're woman enough, you've decided I'm not such a threat?"

"That, and Seamus's mistress Jane."

"You described her as a siren to Seamus just now."

"She seeks to possess my clan and add to her power base, Anita. She claims that she wishes to give Jean-Claude a hyena vampire that is truly loyal to him and the power structure, unlike Asher, who uses us like a threat. Do what I want, or I'll take the werehyenas to another territory and leave you with too few guards to protect your territory."

I watched his face as I asked the next thing. "I heard you were encouraging Asher to use your clan to overthrow Jean-Claude and take over."

He gave a little shrug. "I thought about it, but Asher is too weak to take Jean-Claude's place, even with me at his side."

"You can't fix stupid," I said.

He looked startled, like he didn't understand what I meant.

"I mean Asher. You can't fix how stupid he is about politics and power. He lets his heart overrule everything else, like this bonehead move with Kane."

"It's not his heart that overrules his head, Anita, it's his dick."

"You don't think he loves Kane?"

"I don't know if he truly loves anyone, except Jean-Claude, and since he can't have him he tries to find other people to fill that hole in his heart."

"He and Jean-Claude are lovers," I said.

"But Jean-Claude still loves you more than he loves Asher, and that's one thing our golden-haired vampire can't abide, to be second."

"He's not that ambitious," I said.

"Oh, he doesn't have to be first place in anything that matters, but he's like some women I've known who had to be the prettiest girl in any room, or men who have to be the best man at any party, or meeting. It's the same deal, except Asher wants to be first in everyone's libido and heart, but his heart belongs to only one man."

I squeezed his hand. "I'm sorry he's such a turkey."

"But such a beautiful turkey," Narcissus said.

I sighed. "He is, unfortunately. We wouldn't put up with half this shit if he wasn't so pretty."

"And so good in bed," he said.

"And in the dungeon," I said.

We sighed together.

"Can't live with him, can't live without him," I said.

"And can't kill him," Narcissus said.

We sighed again.

"I was so mad this morning that I was going to come in here and demand shit from you, but you've been too nice and I know Asher has hurt you, too." He held my hand in both of his, looked me in the face, so sincerely, and said, "Would you consider me for your hyena to call, Anita?"

He made it sound like a proposal, so I treated it as seriously. "Well, one little problem: You don't like girls, and I am one."

"If you weren't part of Belle Morte's line of vampires and all sexy-pants, that wouldn't be an issue, you know. Most vampires choose their animal to call for power, not sexual compatibility."

"I know, but no matter how hard I try, things just go all lust, love, and domestic bliss, so you not liking girls is a problem for both of us."

"If it's a deal breaker I'd be willing to try."

I must have looked shocked, because he laughed and patted my hand. "Oh, the look on your face." He lay back and just laughed.

I lay there and let him, because I wasn't sure what to say.

He finally slowed down enough to say, "If you were a man, we could have such fun."

"But I'm not a man," I said.

He looked at me, face still shining with the laughing fit. "I hear your pussy is almost as tight as an asshole; it might work."

I gave him a very unfriendly look and sat up, the sheet held in front of my breasts, though since he didn't care about breasts, I guess it was really for my benefit. "Jean-Claude did not say that."

"No, he didn't." He was serious again.

"If Asher . . ."

"As amusing as it would be to let you be that angry at his vampire ass, no, it wasn't him either."

I frowned. "There aren't that many people who would know and would comment; in fact, none of them would talk to you like that about me."

"One of them did, I swear. I talked to him after Jean-Claude offered the idea of being your hyena to call, so I wouldn't kill Asher, or start a war over the insult."

"Did you actually threaten to go to war with the rest of the were-animals and vampires in St. Louis over this?"

He actually looked embarrassed, which wasn't something I ever thought to see from him. "I might have said that."

"So you called someone who likes boys, but has been with me, so you could ask what? Pointers? Opinions?"

"Something like that, yes."

I frowned. Who the hell had it been? "This is going to bug me until you tell me who it was."

"I'll tell you under one condition."

I frowned at him. "What?"

"That you don't hurt him for it. I wanted someone who's primarily into men to give as honest an opinion of you as possible, because you're right, I'm not a fan of women. I honestly think girl parts are just unappealing."

"I like boy stuff better, too, so I can't really fault you, but I also don't know how to be with a man who finds my genitalia unappealing."

"Fair," he said.

"So who talked?" I asked.

"Byron."

I frowned. Byron had been fifteen when he died, so he was caught forever in that first blush of high school when the guys fill out and muscles seem to happen. He was forever unfinished, never to find out what he'd look like at twenty. "Byron? We only had sex once. It was an emergency feed for the *ardeur*."

"Yes, but he actually came inside you, and he's only done that with three women, ever, counting you."

"Hmm . . . I didn't know that."

"It's a huge compliment, Anita."

I frowned harder; I had a headache starting right between my eyes. "Okay, I guess I can see that as a compliment."

"The *ardeur* is the other thing that might make us work together. You unleash it on me and I think even I will find you irresistible."

"Unappealing lady parts and all?" I asked, giving him a look and raising an eyebrow.

"Don't give me that look; I think we need to be absolutely honest with each other, or this will not work."

"I don't think it'll work now."

"I understand that, but if we aren't honest it will surely fail."

I looked down at him, so serious in the bed, with his eyeliner decoratively smeared, and his hair looking almost artful in its messiness. He was one of those people who wake up looking good; I was so not one of those people.

"One other thing that you need to know before you give your answer," he said.

"What?" I asked.

"You know, they used to call intersexed people like me a hermaphrodite."

I nodded.

"I have functioning boy parts and girl parts."

"Yes."

"Knowing is one thing, actually seeing and touching is another. I've had people be intrigued and then get grossed out, or scared, so you should see everything before you decide."

I looked down at his body where it was covered with the sheet. I hadn't felt nervous about it until he announced the possibilities; now suddenly I wasn't sure I wanted to see the whole show. "You know, I wasn't weirded out by the idea of seeing you nude until you said that."

He studied my face, his own expression cynical. "Really, I find that hard to believe; most people are either intrigued or horrified by my . . . uniqueness."

"I honestly hadn't spent a whole lot of time thinking about what your plumbing might look like, sorry."

"I thought that was part of your issue with me."

I shook my head. "My issue with you was that when I met you, you managed to let my words and your club rules hurt people I loved and cared about."

"I am sorry for that, by the way. I honestly didn't understand what they were doing to them, especially Nathaniel. I would never have let them leave the swords in long enough for his body to heal around them."

I could still remember that moment when I'd finally gotten a good look at what Chimera's men had done to Nathaniel. The anger came back to me, so that my hands made fists before I could stop them. "It was your club, your rules, Narcissus, and you had a werehyena in the room, reporting to you."

"Your eyes are almost black with anger, just remembering that moment."

I gave him the full weight of that darkened gaze. My hyena rose in the dark center of me and looked up with golden brown eyes; again she wasn't behaving like most of my beasts around another of her kind. She seemed reluctant to approach him, but why?

"I thought my man was reporting accurately to me that night, Anita, but I swear to you, he was not."

"I believe you taunted me with comments about it being my fault for ordering you to order them to stop what they were doing and wait for me."

"I did not know what they had done. I would swear on my honor, but my reputation says I have none."

"And that would be another reason you and I aren't buddies."

"And you have a reputation for being a ruthless murdering bitch, which I didn't see as a problem, but you were a woman and metaphysically powerful. I did not want you near my hyenas."

"You thought I'd take them over," I said.

"Yes."

"If I feed the *ardeur* on you, I'll feed off every werehyena that is tied to you metaphysically. Are you sure you really want to do that?"

"No, but I've seen you with Rafael's wererats. They feel more and more loyalty to you, but they still feel more to him. You have not stolen them away from him. You work with him, and he grows in power because of it."

"Rat isn't one of my inner beasts; hyena is."

"You think that will make a difference?" he asked.

"I'm saying it might. I just don't know for sure, and I don't want you to pop this cork and then find out the champagne costs you more than you'd planned on paying."

He smiled up at me. "I like the metaphor, but I don't really like champagne, or dry wine. I like sweet things, not bitter."

"I don't like dry wine or champagne either. Hell, I don't really like most wine. I drink it because Jean-Claude can taste it through me, and he misses good wine."

"So you blamed me for Chimera making Nathaniel suffer."

I nodded.

"And I avoided you, because I feared you'd do what the Harlequin bitch is trying to do."

"I didn't know that Jane was giving you a problem. You should have come to us and said something."

"Come to you and Jean-Claude and admit I wasn't king enough to handle one master vampire that could call hyena? No, so no. Kings do not go before kings from a position of weakness, Anita, not if they want to remain king."

"Then don't let Asher's stupidity make you do something you'll regret," I said.

"I'm not here out of a position of weakness, Anita. I'm here because the wolves and the leopards, and the lions, and the rats, and all of you motherfuckers haven't yet got enough new soldiers to be certain of defeating me."

I fought to keep my face blank but knew my pulse rate and breathing had probably betrayed me to him.

"Did you all think I would be oblivious to what you were doing, or why?" He sat up and snarled in my face, "I am Oba of my clan! I am not so besotted with Asher that I have ceased to watch all the rest of you bastards." His hyena flowed over him like heat and spilled over my skin. The power of it caught my breath.

He leaned in closer. "Tell me honestly, Anita, if you felt this much power from anyone else, wouldn't you have been in their bed by now?"

"You in my bed, maybe, but you like boys, and I'm not one."

"The *ardeur* can take a person's preference away and just make them want you, or Jean-Claude. You know that."

"Yeah, but if you use it to force someone to have sex with someone they don't want to have sex with, then it's rape, and neither of us is into that."

The heat of his beast was just gone, like a candle blown out. He lay back on the bed in the nest of sheets and just stared at me. He looked astonished. "You believe that; you really do."

"Yes, I really do. Why does that surprise you this much?"

"Asher has told me what Jean-Claude and he did at Belle Morte's court. Rape was one of her things, and Asher misses some of it."

"Jean-Claude doesn't," I said.

"He tells me that."

"Ask him, you're powerful enough, you'll be able to tell if he's lying." We looked at each other and there was just no sexual tension between us. I said, out loud, "This, this is why I never hunted you up for sex."

He frowned. "What is this?" He made a vague hand gesture.

"Neither of us is really attracted to the other. We are so not each other's type."

The look on his face was beyond cynicism, beyond jaded. He still looked young and just-woke-up handsome, but he also looked world weary, as if he'd seen everything, done everything, and I was being naïve.

"Anita, oh, Anita, you make me feel old."

"I'm either older than you or about the same age."

"In years, maybe, but in experience . . ." He just shook his head.

"I've probably seen as much bad stuff as you have. I'm a cop, re-member."

"But somehow emotionally you aren't like most of them. There is a freshness to how you view love and sex that is quite . . ." He sighed, shook his head, and finally said, "Sobering, as if there's no way to play with you. You taste of commitment and promises you intend to keep."

I shrugged. "I try to keep my promises. I think everyone should."

He smiled, but it left his eyes cynical and guarded. "I am a lying bastard if it suits my goals."

"Don't lie to me, or Jean-Claude, or anyone I care about."

"And if I do?"

I just looked at him.

"That look, so absolutely serious."

"Serious as a heart attack," I said.

He smiled, blinking so that I couldn't see what he was thinking. His brown eyes smiled up at me when he opened them, matching the smile. "Are you ready to play 'you show me yours, and I'll show you mine'?"

I don't know what I would have said, because the door opened and Jean-Claude came through the door wearing a blue robe, almost as dark a blue as his eyes. "*Ma petite*, Narcissus, I see that you haven't come to blows yet; that is better than I had feared."

"Oh, I don't enjoy hitting girls, but boys, I'm always up for hitting bad little boys," he said, rolling over on his back and looking more lascivious than he had the whole time we'd been alone. "Do you want to be my bad little boy again, Jean-Claude?"

"Cut the shit, Narcissus," I said. "You were actually behaving like a reasonable human being until Jean-Claude stepped into the room. Don't go back to being all creepy-sexy."

He aimed that sexy, predatory smile at me. "You think I'm sexy? Really?" He writhed under the covers, stretching his body like a cat, except cats weren't self-aware. Cats weren't trying to draw your gaze to their groin, wiggling their hips as if they should have been onstage at Guilty Pleasures.

"I've never said you did not move well, Narcissus," Jean-Claude said as he came to take my hand and look down at the man in the bed.

"And yet you don't want to play with me anymore," Narcissus said, pretending to pout.

"I do not enjoy your idea of play, Narcissus."

"You got here just in time for a little 'show me yours and I'll show you mine,'" Narcissus said. "Of course, you've seen mine, and I've seen yours. It's only Anita and I who need a show-and-tell, isn't it, *ma petite*?"

"Never, ever, call me that again. Only Jean-Claude gets to call me that."

"Oooh, we get pet names special just to us; I like it."

I sighed. "There was someone in this bed I could actually talk to, and then Jean-Claude comes into the room and you go back to being a caricature, hiding behind the flirting and the irritating shit. Why?"

"Why what?" he asked, but he stopped wriggling under the covers and looked at me.

"Why do you put on a show when he comes into the room?"

He blinked and I knew now that meant he was hiding whatever was in his eyes. "I don't know what you mean, darling."

I let it go, because either he didn't want to address it, or even he didn't know why he acted weird around Jean-Claude. "Fine, just get this over with, I have to go meet the FBI soon. And don't call me darling."

Narcissus looked up at me, but his eyes slid to one side and looked at Jean-Claude as he said, "But if it's a show you want, pumpkin, I can give you a show."

"Don't call me pumpkin."

"Well, if you insist, snickerdoodle."

I put my head against Jean-Claude's shoulder. The robe was satin, which meant it was soft and cuddly, and he was in the robe, which made it even cuddlier. He wrapped his arms around me, and I sank in against his body, letting him hold me, letting go of all of it for a minute.

"I hate you both, just a little, right now."

We broke apart enough to look at him, but stayed in each other's arms. "Why do you hate us, *mon ami*?"

"I thought I had someone to hold me, and I woke up this morning to find that it had all been a lie. I'm going to hate any happy lovers for a while."

"We all woke to find one of our lovers had betrayed our trust," Jean-Claude said.

"But you have other lovers, Jean-Claude; I do not."

"Bullshit," I said. "You are not monogamous any more than we are."

"True, I have other lovers, and other play partners, but none of them are putting a ring on my finger. Asher was going to do that."

We both stared at him. "He promised to marry you?" I asked.

He stared up at us with those big brown eyes, with the black tears of his smeared eyeliner framing them. The white sheets had swirled around his upper body like rumpled wings fallen to earth. If angels could have mornings after full of regret, they might look like that.

Of course, angels probably didn't cry black tears; that would probably be the other guys, if either angels or demons cried physical tears. If the real angel I'd seen cried anything, it would have been tears of fire. I guess the demon might have cried physical tears, but I'd been too busy quoting Bible verses at him to ask.

"Oh, *mon ami*, I am so sorry."

"Don't pity me, Jean-Claude, help me make him sorry."

"What would you have of us?"

"You talked me out of killing either of them. I wouldn't miss Kane."

"But Asher would not let his death stand, and we would miss him," Jean-Claude said.

"Eventually," Narcissus said.

Jean-Claude wisely let that go. "You do not wish to tie yourself to us for the sake of revenge, Narcissus."

"I would tie myself to you, Jean-Claude, but you don't want to play 'tie me up, tie me down' anymore."

"Not with you, no."

Narcissus looked at me. "Asher says you like rough trade, snicker-doodle, do you want to come play?"

"Don't call me that, and I've heard your idea of rough trade and I don't play that rough."

"Asher says you do, snookums."

I just looked at him, all irritating and disheveled in the bed. "Don't call me that, either. I'm pretty sure you and I wouldn't match any better in the dungeon than we do in the bedroom."

"Maybe, or maybe we could both learn a few new tricks, cupcake." He sounded tired as he said it, so the teasing was softened.

If you can't beat 'em, join 'em. "Okay, angel, show me a new trick."

"Am I your angel?"

"A fallen one, maybe," I said.

He smiled, sudden and happy. "Say it."

"Say what?" I asked.

"Your nickname for me."

"Angel?" I made it a question.

"Not quite," he said, moving around in the covers so that they started sliding below his waist.

"*Ma petite*, think upon the last few minutes and you will know what he wants you to call him."

I thought, and was about to ask for more of a clue, when I got it, or thought I got it. "Fallen angel, you're my fallen angel."

"I like it," he said, and used one hand to jerk the covers off him and out of my hands, so that both of us were suddenly exposed. Narcissus lay back smirking, revealed in all his glory, fallen or otherwise.

53

JUST LYING THERE on the bed, legs together, he didn't look that different from most men. If I'd seen him nude in the locker room, I'd have just kept walking past him, but I wasn't supposed to keep moving past; I was supposed to do a hell of a lot more than just look at him. It was a little like going into the produce section and fondling the fruit and veggies; was it ripe, would it be sweet, was it too soft, too ripe, firm enough, but not too firm? Except this veg was looking back at me with serious attitude.

"Well?" he said, and that one word was so defiant that it instantly made me want to snap back.

Jean-Claude touched my shoulder. "Do not let his defiance bring your own, *ma petite*."

I looked at him, sighed, and turned back to Narcissus. He was almost glaring at me now. I wasn't sure if it was Jean-Claude's thought or mine, but I realized that the other man was so sure I'd reject him that he was trying to give me a reason to do it that wouldn't be about his physicality. It was like someone who is so used to being made fun of that they say the mean things first, try to make it their joke, so the bullies don't get a chance to cut them up. It works, in a way, but it means the person saying the words internalizes the message more, because they're the ones saying *stupid, clumsy, fat, ugly*—whatever the bullies might say.

I counted to ten and spoke, looking into those angry eyes. "You don't look that different from most guys."

He gave a bitter laugh. "Lying bitch, you're staring at my face so hard, just so you don't have to see it!"

"Look, angel cakes," I said, almost snarling back at him, "I'm giving you eye contact, because when I'm naked in a bed for the first time with someone I like them to talk to my face, not my body parts. I get sort of pissy at anyone who talks to my breasts. I'd probably hit them in the face if they talked to my groin instead of my face."

He watched my face, eyes glitteringly angry, but his face relaxed a little.

"Now, if you want me to just talk into your penis like a fucking microphone, ya gotta tell a girl, because that's a request I haven't had before."

He smiled as if I'd surprised him, and he hadn't expected to be amused. "Not one of my kinks, cupcake, but if you like eye contact when we talk, that's cool."

"Good, because I do."

"*Ma petite* is almost aggressive in her eye contact."

Narcissus looked up at Jean-Claude. "It's a dominance thing, I get that. If I look away then she wins, like a blinking contest."

"I was raised that you look someone in the face when you talk to them. It's just polite," I said. I crossed my arms under my breasts, because without something to hold them out of the way, crossing my arms over them was too awkward.

He smiled again. "I'll bet whoever taught you that is aggressive."

I tried to think if Grandmother Blake was aggressive, and finally said, "Unpleasant, but I'd have to think on aggressive."

He smiled more, and turned to Jean-Claude. "Does she always do that?"

"Do what?" I asked.

"You listened to me, thought about what I'd said, and actually answered the question."

I frowned. "Wasn't I supposed to?"

He looked at Jean-Claude. "Is she always so . . . earnest?" he asked.

"I am not earnest."

"Actually, *ma petite*, I think it is a very good word for you, but you will have to leave soon for your work, and earnestness takes time."

Narcissus said, "I will respect that we sprang this on you today,

Anita, but never tell me again that I look like all other men. A lie that big . . . just don't, okay, just don't."

I nodded. "I honestly was expecting more visual difference, so I didn't lie."

"I have only one ball, and it's more to the side than below, and my penis is lower on the body than any man you've ever been with, and between my legs is an opening like yours."

"Well, that is different."

"Different, she says. The only reason I still have a dick and an opening is that my penis was large enough that the doctors and my father didn't want to cut it off at birth and make me a girl, and my mom got pissed that they were going to sew up my vagina, so they waited to decide what to do. They were stubborn enough to get an intersexed baby out of the hospital with no surgeries thirty years ago, unheard of. They listed me as a boy, raised me as a boy."

"Was that what you wanted to be raised as?" I asked.

He nodded. "Yes, I was a boy, a gay boy, and I grew into being a gay man, who occasionally cross-dresses, and I like lovers who pay attention to all my parts, but yes, I feel and think male. I'm just gay and male, but I think I'd have been that no matter what my junk looked like."

"We're talking this to death instead of getting up close and personal, because you don't want me, because I'm a woman, and you don't do women. You and I were getting along better before Jean-Claude came into the room, because once you saw him you knew what you wanted and it's not me."

"But he can't make me his hyena to call, and you can."

"Yeah, but I'm not sure that's a good enough reason to tie ourselves together for all eternity, when we don't really like each other. I've done the whole hate-you-love-you-lust-you with Richard, and you and I wouldn't even have the lust going for us."

"The *ardeur* would force it upon you both, *ma petite*."

I looked at Jean-Claude. "I don't want it forced anymore. I don't want to tie myself to someone else that I know isn't a good match for me, and watch the *ardeur* change them into something that fits, or make me fit them more."

"Do you believe that is what is happening?" he asked.

"Maybe. I know that Micah and I become more perfectly matched; Nathaniel, too. I think the magic is changing all of us."

"Couples do that on their own, Anita," Narcissus said.

"I've never had a long-term relationship, outside of Jean-Claude and everyone in my life now."

Narcissus propped himself up on his elbow and looked at me. "Really, Jean-Claude is your first serious guy?"

"Him and Richard, yeah. Before them it was like six months and then broken up."

He looked at me, face serious, showing me the mind that had built his group into one to be reckoned with; he was a lot smarter and wiser than he let on most of the time. "You did jump into the deep end of the dating pool, cupcake."

"Whatever, we're here now, and you and I don't like each other that much. We might be work friends, and that would be it."

"Yes, but I'm willing to let the *ardeur* take away all my doubts for a chance to be tied to the throne, because that's what Jean-Claude offered if I spared Kane's life and didn't risk killing Asher when his hyena to call died."

I shook my head. "You aren't going to kill Kane," I said.

"Why not?" He lay back on the bed, smiling like a cat who'd gotten into the cream.

"If Jean-Claude were just the local Master of the City, and I were just his human servant, then yeah, we'd have to do something to placate you, but Jean-Claude is king of all the vampires in this country. He's the first king of America, and I'm not just his human servant, I'm a necromancer and I'm the Executioner. That nickname was earned from the vampires long before I got a badge and became a marshal."

"What has any of that to do with me and my small army of hyenas?"

"You don't get to come in here and blackmail our asses into an alliance that gains you a hell of a lot more than it gains us. If we put the word out that I'm looking to tie us to a really powerful hyena, there are cities in this country where the hyenas are the major animal power. They're bigger and have a hell of a lot more foot soldiers than you do."

"But they're not here, I am."

"Jean-Claude is king of all of it, from sea to shining sea, which means he could just negotiate them coming here and slaughtering you all, or we could just give you the choice of getting the fuck out of our immediate area, because you are a disruptive influence on the peace and power base we have built."

"And what of your precious Asher?" he asked, and there was no teasing now.

"His death won't hurt our power base; in fact, he's a deficit, not an asset, politically."

"So I can kill him, just like that."

"No," Jean-Claude said finally, "no, you cannot."

I looked at him. "Jean-Claude, we are not going to tie ourselves to Narcissus just because Asher is being a shit again."

"We will not watch him be killed."

"No, but we don't have to bargain like we are still just squabbling over the local territory. Narcissus is powerful here, but outside of here he's nothing. Rafael, even the swan king, they have ties across the country, people across the country to feed on—they are truly fellow kings. Narcissus is not."

"I will kill Kane," he said, still lying there, but now it wasn't sexy, or flirty. He was very serious, eyes watching me carefully.

"And that may kill Asher," I said.

"I will not . . ." Jean-Claude started to say.

I touched his lips with my fingers. "You cannot sell us down the river for Asher's mistake. I love the little shit, too, but that he made Kane his hyena to call without consulting you first says that he has no respect for you as his ruler. He counted on your love and mine, and even Narcissus's love, to keep him and Kane safe."

He took my hand in his, and let me see the pain in his eyes. "I know you are right, *ma petite*, but I cannot stand by and watch him die, not if I can save him."

I took his hand in both of mine. "Jean-Claude, you did your best for him when the Church took him."

"Not enough, my best was not enough." His eyes held the loss of Julianna, their shared love, who had been burned at the stake as a witch, while the Church fathers tried to burn the devil out of Asher with holy water and had scarred one of the most beautiful men that may have ever lived. He was still beautiful, but sometimes he couldn't see that.

"You bargained your freedom to Belle Morte for a hundred years so she would save Asher's life. A hundred years of pain and torment, and being her bitch, it's enough."

"She tormented Asher, as well."

"Yes, because she tortures everyone around her in one way or another, it's one of her things, but you cannot let the guilt of something that happened hundreds of years ago ruin the empire you are building now."

"Are you telling me to choose power over love? Power and politics over Asher?"

"No, not if it was that clear-cut, but Asher counted on you doing exactly that. He counted on us all valuing him above anything else, and that's not cool."

"There is a reason that master vampires are either killed or forced to leave and find another territory by most Masters of the City," Jean-Claude said.

"Yeah, because they're an arrogant pain in the ass if you don't."

He almost smiled. "Asher has been that for a very long time."

I looked down at Narcissus, still holding Jean-Claude's hands. "You're angry, you're hurt, and you have every right to be, but you also saw this in all its political ramifications as a way to solidify your place as top animal group here in St. Louis."

He gave a little shrug. "If we can get a little revenge and solidify my power base, why not?"

I turned back to Jean-Claude. "Even brokenhearted he's thinking better politically than you are."

"I know about your little plan to get enough soldiers in the other animal groups so that I won't be a power here anymore."

Jean-Claude looked at me.

"He stated it up front before you came into the room."

"I'm a king, did you not think I'd know?"

"You're Oba, not king; there is no king as a title among the hyenas, because they prefer queens."

He growled at me.

"You can be a power here, Narcissus," Jean-Claude said, "but you cannot keep using your greater numbers to threaten us. Anita is right, I was thinking like a Master of the City, and I am more than that now."

I said, "Threatening to take all your hyenas and go to another city would have gutted our guards once, but I think you've waited too long, Narcissus. I think we have the numbers to be just fine without your hyenas."

"I'd noticed how few of my men were on your guard duty lately, but that doesn't mean there aren't enough of us to start a war here with all of you. That wouldn't play well in the news, would it? The vampire king of America losing control of his city would undermine a lot of things."

"No, Narcissus," Jean-Claude said, "for if you declare war on the rest of the city I will simply turn you in to the human authorities. I will make it clear that you are the rogue, and that most of your people are innocent. The human authorities will kill you before they allow you to engulf our city in a shapeshifter war."

"You have no proof that I've said any such thing."

"Have you forgotten what my day job is?" I asked.

I watched his face, and he had.

"Don't let the fact that you woke up naked in a bed with me make you forget what I am, Narcissus."

"You're Jean-Claude's human servant, his pet necromancer." But I watched his eyes as he said it, and he had remembered.

"I am a U.S. Marshal and a legal executioner of all the bad little vampires and shapeshifters. All I have to do is tell them I heard these threats and I think it's credible. To save the city from a bloodbath, they will put out a warrant of execution so fast it'll make your head swim."

"My hyenas will fight to save me."

"Your hyenas follow you, but most do not love you or feel the loyalty that Rafael's rats feel for him," Jean-Claude said.

"And I've talked to them, Narcissus," I said. "They aren't so happy with you as leader."

"I know, you've become all buddy-buddy with them in the gym." He made it sound disdainful, as if he couldn't be bothered.

"And you're more a yoga kind of guy, I get that, but I talk to them and to the other guards, and they talk to me," I said.

He gave me unfriendly eyes, arms crossed over his chest, and I realized that one side of his chest had a little more breast than the other, as if he were almost an A-cup on one side. "Are you looking at my boobie?"

"Sorry, guess I was," and I went back to giving him eye contact.

"I know the people I brought in after Chimera aren't my kind of people for the most part. They do seem more your type of he-man." The disdain dripped from his voice.

"I've seen the kind of man you usually date, Narcissus; you like muscles more than I do. Asher is your exception, not your rule."

"Do you even have a point to make, cupcake?"

"Yeah, angel cakes, I do. The men left over from the slaughter that Chimera did, well, they think you let your lust lead you astray with him. That's how he got into your inner sanctum and captured you all, because you, like Asher, will let your dick override your brain if the sex is good enough."

"Your Ulfric let his sense of fair play hurt his wolf pack much more than my little peccadilloes."

"Richard undercuts himself as Ulfric pretty constantly, but he's never fucked up as badly as you did with Chimera," I said.

"Chimera loved me at first, thought I was the answer to his dreams, because he could fuck me like a woman and still get boy parts to fuck, too."

"I know part of his personality was deeply conflicted about being gay," I said.

"He wasn't gay, he was bisexual, but he was from a generation that thought you had to choose. He was less gay than I was, and liked women a hell of a lot more."

"Yeah, I think he offered to rape me in front of Micah, while Micah died from being gutted."

"It was the rape and gutting part that got his rocks off more." Narcissus was quieter as he said that.

"What do you mean?"

"He didn't do straight sex of any kind. I thought I wasn't vanilla, but he was farther out than even I wanted to swim."

"He was a serial killer, Narcissus; you're not. That puts him in a category not just of rough sex, but death sex. It's beyond even risk-aware kink."

"When he found out I was pregnant he was happy, and then he decided if I were a woman then he could marry me and we could be happy, it would fix everything. He was going to cut off all the boy parts and just leave the hole, and then you rode to the rescue and killed him for me."

I looked at him and all the pain, raw in his face and in the way he held himself on the bed, pale and vulnerable. I touched his shoulder, and he smiled at me, sadly.

"Oh, that was well done, *mon ami*, that was very well done," Jean-Claude said.

It startled me, and Narcissus and I both looked at him uncomprehending.

"You were making a point, before Narcissus distracted you with his painful story." He raised a hand as if to stop both of us from saying anything. "I know you are telling the truth, Narcissus. Chimera was an awful man and deserved death, but you trotted out your story at just the right time to distract *ma petite*. You counted on her sympathy so she would not say what needs saying."

"I don't know what you're talking about."

"You do not like her, or me, really. We are not your friends, and yet you confide in us these painful truths from your capture. You do very little that is not thought out, except for letting your lust override your head, but you do not feel that much attraction to either of us. You liked having me as your victim, but our idea of sex outside of that does not match."

"I don't like girls."

"You also prefer to give rather than receive with men, and I am the same, so who would top whom?"

"You received plenty from me when Nikolaos gave you to me."

"Yes, the old Master of the City gave me to you to seal her bargain with your hyenas. She also saw it as a punishment for me. She gave me to you with no hope of a safeword. You are not the serial killer that Chimera was, but you are a true sadist and you enjoy doing things to people that you know they don't want you to do."

"I don't usually get to play with men as dominant as you. It was a treat." He licked his lower lip as he said it, as if he could still taste some of the treat.

"And I was about to tie *ma petite* and myself to you for eternity. I let my fear for Asher's safety blind me, but no longer. *Ma petite* has thrown the logic on it all, and like cold water it wakes me with a shock from this mistake."

"So I'm a mistake, am I?"

"No, I have been saved from that particular mistake." He kissed my forehead. "Thank you, my queen."

I wasn't sure about the queen part, but out loud I said, "We take turns being smart for each other; I think it's part of the job description of being a couple."

"You think you've tamed me, just like that?" Narcissus said.

"I'm sorry Chimera hurt you. I'm sorry you lost the baby, because I know you wanted to keep it. I'm sorry you were hurt, and I'm sorry that Asher has hurt you more, but one thing police work has taught me is that everyone has a sad story, but they'll still shoot you, or stab you, or tear your throat out with their teeth. The fact that they were abused, or abandoned, or even tortured doesn't make them one bit less dangerous. Social workers and therapists get to worry about the sad backgrounds; if I worry about shit like that I can't do my job."

"I'm not one of your bad guys, cupcake."

"The hell you're not; you come in here threatening to kill one of your own people because your lover chose him over you. If you were all human, that would be first-degree homicide. You threaten to kill Asher so that Jean-Claude will agree to you becoming my hyena to call; it's like threatening to kill someone unless a woman agrees to marry you. Again, that's a crime; marriage under duress isn't legal, and threatening to kill people, well, the cops frown on that, too. Then you threaten to pull out all of your hyenas and go to another city, knowing that we didn't have enough muscle to protect the city from other preternatural baddies without your guys, unless we play with you. That may not be illegal, but it's still not honorable. But wait, there's more, you threaten to use all the soldiers at your beck and call to declare a preternatural war of a scale that hasn't been seen in this country since the 1800s. Dozens, maybe hundreds, would die, and threatening shit like that is what makes gang task forces bust your gang up and take the leader off to jail."

"And you threaten to lie to your superiors and get a warrant of execution for me, which is also murder."

"I'm not going to lie, Narcissus, I'm going to tell the truth. You are threatening exactly that."

"You going to tell them we were naked in bed together when I told you?"

I laughed then, and he didn't like that one bit. "If you think sleeping with you could hurt my reputation with the other cops, think again. They already disapprove of me sleeping with all the vamps and shapeshifters. Hell, some people want me to give up my badge because I'm about to marry Jean-Claude and it's a conflict of interest."

"So I'm a bad guy."

"Yeah, you are."

He sat up. "I will kill Kane."

"Asher survived the death of his human servant hundreds of years ago, when he was a lot less powerful than he is now; we'll take our chances."

"You don't believe I'll kill Kane."

"I believe that if you kill Kane because your lover prefers him to you, the rest of your hyenas will see that as yet another strike against you as their Oba. How many strikes you think you got left before they decide they need a new leader?"

"No one under my command would do that unless they knew they had powerful friends backing their play," he said.

I smiled at him. "I'm just so darn friendly," I said.

"Bitch."

"Asshole."

He glared at me, and I smiled back.

"Go, Narcissus, just go, before I think better of it and have guards escort you to a room without a view," Jean-Claude said.

"You wouldn't dare."

"I am king!" he yelled, eyes suddenly blazing with vampire fire as if the midnight sky could burn. "Guards!"

Dino and Seamus came through the door first, but there were others behind them.

I said, "Seamus, go, this is not your fight."

"No," Narcissus said, "stay with me, Seamus, they mean to imprison your king."

The big black man just looked at him. "My mistress has woken for the day here in the underground. I feel your call to me, Oba, but my mistress protects me from having to answer."

"Six of you, that are not hyena, escort Narcissus to one of the rooms reserved for when we have a new shapeshifter who is not trustworthy on their first full moon," Jean-Claude said.

"You would not dare," Narcissus said.

"You keep saying that, but I do not think it means what you think it means," I said.

He growled at me.

I blew him a kiss.

"Take him," Jean-Claude said.

"What do I tell the other werehyenas when they ask why we have done this?" Seamus asked.

"Tell them that Narcissus threatened us, and even the Oba of the werehyenas does not get to do that with impunity," Jean-Claude said, but not like he was happy about it.

They surrounded him and escorted him out. He didn't try to resist. "Some of the other shapeshifter groups in other cities are afraid of you, Jean-Claude. They fear that Rafael is just your puppet, and that you mean to take them all over through Micah and his Coalition. When they find out that you have imprisoned a leader of a group you do not favor, they will be more convinced than ever of your intentions."

"Get out of my sight, Narcissus, before I decide to do more than just imprison you."

He left without another word. I think he saw on Jean-Claude's face what might happen if he kept pushing. When we were alone again, I hugged him. "Is he right? Will this help fuel the same people that tried to assassinate Rafael?"

"Most likely," he said, as he rested his cheek on the top of my head.

"I didn't think that part through."

"You were right in your thinking, up to a point, and beyond that it is my job to think. You made me remember I am king and not just Asher's lover."

"I'm his lover, too."

"But you are more ruthless than I am, *ma petite*, far more ruthless."

"I thought you'd gained my ruthlessness through the vampire marks like I'd gained the *ardeur*."

"More ruthless, *oui*, but where Asher is concerned I am weak."

"Don't be weak while I'm with the FBI, okay?"

"I promise to make no decisions about Asher and the mess he has made without consulting you and Micah."

"Good," I said, and leaned up for a kiss.

He kissed me back, and then said, "You need solid food, before you go."

"I'll grab another protein bar, but I've lost too much time for a meal."

"Water and a bar, but you must promise to at least go through a drive-up and eat real food after this meeting."

"Promise," I said.

We kissed; I got dressed, checked that Micah was recovering from too many rapid shapeshifts in one day, and went back to work. Normally police work was a nice change from furry and vamp politics, but today work was voodoo and zombie sex slaves. I'd have rather kept doing the preternatural politics; at least that I understood. It was not a good sign that I didn't understand what was happening with the zombies and even my own powers. I still didn't know what had gone wrong with the zombie Thomas Warrington, not for sure. I'd stop using cows as my blood sacrifice, but beyond that I just wasn't sure what to do. I wasn't used to saying that about zombies. I drove to meet the FBI with a sinking feeling. I was their expert, and their expert didn't know shit.

54

IT WAS DÉJÀ vu back in the office with Special Agents Manning and Brent. He had the computer all set up and ready to go; we were just waiting on the rest of our little party. "I'm sorry Zerbrowski can't make it, he's a hoot," Brent said.

"Hoot?" I said, and smiled.

"Don't mind him, he likes to remind me that he's from the backwoods and I'm a city girl," Manning said. She'd gone from black pants, jacket, and a white button-up to navy blue pants, jacket, and a pale blue button-up—a daring use of color for FBI. Brent was still in brown on brown. Either it was the same suit, or he had bought them in bulk. He also still looked like he should be back at college trying to decide if he really wanted to be an FBI agent or pursue that computer career.

"Yeah, Zerbrowski is a hoot, but his kids had a dance recital tonight. He's damn near a psychic null, so no reason for him to watch me use my mumbo-jumbo on the videos when he won't be able to sense anything."

"I've got a little girl, too," Brent said. "I like the idea of Zerbrowski with two of them."

"He's got a boy and a girl; both of them are in dance," I said.

Manning said, "I'm surprised you called your psychic gift mumbo-jumbo; most practitioners take offense at the term."

"I've been in the business working with police longer than most of the practitioners. I've had my abilities called a hell of a lot worse than mumbo-jumbo."

"It's true that Captain Storr was one of the first to see a use for psychics with nonstandard abilities."

"Yeah, we were sort of a pilot program."

"The great experiment, that's what one of the instructors at Quantico called Storr's use of you in investigations," Brent said.

I frowned at him. "Hmm, okay, yeah, I guess so. Who are we waiting on again?"

"Why, do you have to meet Jean-Claude later?"

"Not exactly, more an ongoing attempt to have a life and a career."

She gave me a tired smile. "I understand that. When my kids were teenagers I'd be away so long that they looked like strangers to me. When did you get to be four inches taller, that kind of thing."

"I can't imagine trying to do this with kids," I said.

"I was lucky, my husband worked from home part time and was Mr. Mom full time."

"My wife and I are still at that fighting-about-whose-career-comes-first point." Brent frowned. "I'm sorry, that was oversharing."

"Did you sleep at all last night?" Manning asked him.

"I don't . . . maybe two hours."

Manning turned to me. "He was working long distance with our tech crew trying to trace the origin of the videos. Some of the items in the room make them believe it's still being filmed here in the United States, if we could just figure out where."

"I think it's here, too, and I don't have anything but a gut feeling to go on," I said.

"Or maybe we all hope it's here, because that makes them easier to find," Manning said.

"And catch," I said.

She smiled, but she looked tired, too.

"Why didn't you sleep?" I asked.

"Going over all the files we have on this, so I'd be fresh to look at the films with you today."

"I was out doing zombie stuff all night. I managed to grab a few hours this afternoon, but I guess we're all behind the sleep curve," I said.

There was a brief knock at the door. Manning said, "Come in."

A woman came through the door, smiling. She looked so young she could have been one of Cynric's classmates, except for the FBI suit skirt that no self-respecting teenager would have worn unless forced. She was wearing a round Peter Pan collar and a little chain with a heart on it; I hadn't seen either since college, and the blouse had been on a student teacher. Straight brown hair was fastened back behind her ears with a barrette. She wore no makeup except for light pink lip gloss and was still delicately pretty with a dusting of freckles across her cheeks and the bridge of her nose. Her eyes were big and pale brown like Bambi's. Maybe it was the eyes that made her look so young?

"This is Agent Teresa Gillingham, Marshal Blake," Manning said.

I got to my feet and held out a hand to Agent Gillingham's offered one. The moment we shook hands I knew she was another practitioner, which was politically-correct-speak for psychic. I didn't know what flavor she was, but whatever she was it tingled all the way up my arm.

She withdrew her hand with a little laugh. "Wow, they told me you were psychically hot, but that was something."

"Agent Gillingham," Manning said with reproach plain in her voice.

"I know we were supposed to hide what I was, so Marshal Blake would be more likely to use her gifts without hiding from the FBI psychic, but she knew I was another psychic the moment we shook hands, didn't you, Marshal?"

"Yeah, your energy's pretty obvious, too."

"What kind am I?" she asked.

"I don't know."

"You're not even going to try to guess?"

"No."

She looked at me a little like Manning had; maybe it was FBI training? "You're no fun, not to even try."

"You're not the first agent to tell me that."

"About guessing their psychic ability?" she asked, frowning slightly.

"No, about not being any fun."

"Oh, I bet you're lots of fun away from work," she said, smiling and raising an eyebrow at me.

I was suddenly wondering if she was flirting with me. I wasn't very good at subtle, and maybe she was just being friendly.

"We're all more fun away from work," Brent said, and he definitely didn't mean anything by it, so I let it go. Maybe I was starting to look for people flirting with me, or expecting it; weird. There was a time in my life when I was pretty oblivious to all of it.

Agent Gillingham said, "Special Agent Kirkland is right behind me; he had to take a phone call."

I didn't even try to hide my unhappy about that bit of news. "That makes you unhappy; why?" Gillingham said.

"You don't have to be psychic to know that," I said.

"It was in my report," Manning said.

"I meant I wasn't trying to hide my feelings," I said.

"There's not hiding your feelings and then there's being obvious about it," Gillingham said. She looked hard at me and I felt a brush of something. She was probing me.

"Keep your powers to yourself, Agent."

She actually blushed a little.

"What do you mean, Blake?" Manning asked.

"Did Gillingham just try to peek?" Brent asked.

"Yeah, she tried to peek," I said.

"I didn't feel anything," Manning said.

"Me, either, which meant it was really subtle," Brent said, smiling and friendly, but there was something in his eyes that was thinking too hard. I realized that he was a little bit psychically gifted, at least enough to usually pick up active psychic probing, but he hadn't sensed what the other agent had done.

"It was," I said. I looked at Gillingham.

"I'm sorry, Marshal."

"Sorry for trying to sneak a peek inside when you know full well that's considered rude among practitioners, or just sorry you got caught?"

"Both," she said, and her lips smiled when she said it, but her eyes stayed serious and thoughtful.

"If instructors told you I was hot psychically, then you should know I'd sense it."

"They said you were powerful, but like a bull in a china shop."

"I smash things, is that it?"

"Sometimes, but it's more you are so powerful psychically that you just bull your way through everything, so subtle energies are lost to you because you give off so much of your own energy it makes you blind to other practitioners."

"Once, maybe, but not much gets by me anymore."

"You're even more powerful than I was told. Being around you is like standing next to power lines just humming through the air."

"Most psychics don't describe me that way."

"How do they describe you?" she asked.

"Scary."

She laughed, and I wasn't sure if it was humor or nerves. I might even have asked, but the door opened behind her, and it was my fellow marshal and unhappy coworker.

"Hi, Larry," I said.

"Anita," he said. He closed the door behind him. He didn't shake hands with Gillingham, just nodded at her.

"I see you've met Agent Gillingham before," I said.

"Did she try to probe your thoughts yet?"

"Yeah."

He looked at Gillingham. "I told you not to do it, didn't I?"

She looked embarrassed again. "I was very low-key about it. I thought her own power would hide it."

"You thought your little knock-knock would be lost in the loudness of her own energy, is that it?"

Gillingham nodded.

"What did I tell you?"

"Not to try," she said.

"Why?"

"Because Marshal Blake is better at being a practitioner than the instructors at Quantico seem to think."

"Remember, I sat through those same classes, Teresa. Their information is several years out of date about Anita, and I suspect several other major powers in the states."

"Not the world?" Manning asked.

"Interpol seems to keep better track of their psychics and whether they upgrade their skills," he said.

"Why do you think that is?" Manning asked.

"They've had practitioners on their force longer than we have, for one thing."

I said, "And they keep files on psychics in case they get powerful enough for Interpol to feel they represent a danger to the public, because they have to have enough proof in their files to get their version of a warrant of execution for the witch."

"Witch is a religion, not a psychic talent," Gillingham said.

"In the United States," I said.

She frowned and looked at Larry, as if for confirmation. I wondered if he'd been one of her mentors, or even a teacher. "Anita's right; in parts of Europe you're a practitioner, or a psychic, until you get powerful enough for the government to see you as a danger and then they label you a witch. It's still legal to kill witches in parts of Europe."

"I thought witch meant what a rogue vampire or lycanthrope is here, that they've killed people," Gillingham said.

Larry and I both shook our heads. "They just have to prove that the practitioner is sufficiently dangerous," Larry said, "but they don't actually have to have hurt anyone yet, in some parts of Europe. It's even worse in parts of South America and Africa."

"That's not how the books explain the European system," she said.

He smiled, but it was a cynical smile. "Yeah, it made my little trip to Europe interesting."

"I didn't know you were in Europe," I said.

"Let's say it made me appreciate my own country more, and be a little less judgmental."

"You hit the psychic radar pretty hot yourself, Larry," I said.

"So I was told in several countries that I won't be traveling to again. They accused me of being a necromancer, and that particular talent is an automatic death sentence in several countries, especially in Eastern Europe."

"Former Soviet bloc countries don't allow necromancers," I said.

"I didn't think I qualified as one, but they thought differently."

"Oh, Larry, I'm sorry," I said, and meant it.

He smiled. "Yeah, I wasn't quite chased out of the country with pitchforks and torches, but I think if I hadn't been FBI it would have been even more dangerous; as it is I've been marked as a person non-desirable in several countries."

"Why were you traveling in Europe?" I asked.

"Looking for more animators and necromancers."

"Anyone with gifts like ours hides there," I said.

"They hide, or they're dead," he said.

"Why were you looking for necromancers?" I asked.

He shook his head. "I can't tell you, Anita, you don't have my clearance level, I'm sorry."

"You sound like you mean that," I said.

"I do."

We had a moment of looking at each other, and he suddenly put his hand out. I hesitated and then took it. We shook, and I saw something in his eyes that I hadn't seen in years: sympathy toward me. He'd been hating on me so long that I'd started to hate him back.

"I am truly sorry, Anita." I was pretty sure he wasn't talking about Europe.

"I'm glad. I'm still sorry it was scary over in Europe for you," I said.

"Me, too. I had no idea the level of hate people have over there for our talents."

"They've had more large-scale undead incidents over the centuries there than we have here, I think."

"I got a little taste of people not trusting me just because I was too good with the dead. I didn't like it much," he said.

"I understand that," I said.

"Truce," he said.

I nodded. "Truce."

We still weren't back to being friends, and he hadn't asked for that. He knew he'd done too much damage for that, but it was a start. I sat down to watch the videos with Larry beside me, and for the first time in years, I was glad he was there.

55

THERE WAS ONLY one extra person in the room for this viewing, but the room seemed way more crowded. Maybe it was Larry going pale beside me and saying out loud, "They told me what I'd be seeing, but words can't prepare you for it, can they?"

We'd all agreed that no, words didn't do the horror of the actual visuals justice.

I lowered my psychic shields as the blond zombie was told to walk to the bed. I looked at the man in the corner who was giving her orders. All I could see was a shoulder or arm in a long-sleeved shirt, and that was only every once in a while. He obviously didn't want to be on film, so why stand where he was even a little visible?

I felt something brush against me. I looked at my arm to see if an insect had gotten into the room, but there was nothing on my arm. I put it down to lack of sleep and went back to watching the blond zombie. Something brushed against my leg, as if there were a cat in the room, and I knew that wasn't true. I stopped trying to "see" what was on the screen, and turned my attention to the here and now in the room.

Larry beside me was like an orange/yellow energy that I could see from the corner of my eyes, but he was just sitting there looking pale and watching the film.

The invisible something brushed my leg again. I'd never experienced anything like it before; it was almost like a ghost, but I knew that wasn't it. I knew what ghosts felt like. I looked slightly back and found Agent Gillingham like a pale yellow/white light. I turned back to the videos, in time to see the man's arm so that his hand showed. Why wasn't he more hidden? Was he the animator who had raised the zombie? I tried to see if I could see a connection between them that wouldn't show to my physical eyes. I wasn't sure I'd be able to see it, even if it was there, but if he was the one who had raised them, then we were looking for someone who could raise the dead and who would be willing to do something this monstrous. Contrary to movies and TV, most animators and voodoo priests are nice law-abiding people, so this kind of shit would narrow the field. The voodoo priest and priestess I knew would help find this guy, if I could prove to their satisfaction it was him standing there, and not just the client he gave the zombie to.

Something brushed my shoulder. I thought it was my own hair, until I went to move it and realized it wasn't. I looked around the room without moving my head, letting my own power search outward, and I kept it aimed at Gillingham. She was the only other psychic in the room; if it wasn't her doing something I'd search farther out, but I'd learned that you start with the obvious and then try weirder stuff.

I couldn't get a good read on what was onscreen, because whatever was trying to get my attention was dividing my focus too much. Two things happened at once, that soft brush at my shoulder, and again I might have thought it was my own hair, but I knew the difference now. It wasn't me, and Gillingham's energy sort of pulsed a soft red.

"Pause the videos, please," I said.

Brent did what I asked without questioning it. The zombie's face was caught in a scream like a clip from a horror film. Shit.

Manning asked, "Is something wrong, Blake?"

"Yeah." I turned and looked at Gillingham. "What are you doing?"

She smiled that innocent smile that went with the big eyes and freckles, the Peter Pan collar and all the rest. She'd dressed to look inoffensive, harmless, but it was just camouflage for something else.

"I'm sitting here," she said, voice mild.

"Cut the crap, Gillingham, I saw you."

"Saw her do what?" Brent asked.

"She's touching me psychically. I don't know why, but it's distracting me from actually being able to aim my gifts at the screen."

"I don't know what you're talking about," she said.

"You're trying to do something to me and my shields are noticing it, blocking you, so your gift translates it to something normal, is that it? A bug on your skin, a cat rubbing against your legs, hair brushing against your arm, some sensation that grabs a person's attention, so they think that was it, and don't notice you."

She smiled some more.

"Agent Gillingham," Manning said, "are you messing with Marshal Blake?"

"I don't know what you mean, 'messing with,'" and she made little quote marks with her fingers.

Larry said, "Teresa, you think you're good, but what you are is powerful. Good would be if you could peek inside people's shields without announcing yourself."

"How did you know it was me?" she asked me.

"Why should I tell you?"

"Because I'm trying to get better and the only way to do that is feedback."

"Are you telling me we waited for your plane for hours, and you're just here to practice your psychic snooping skills, and not to help on this actual case?" I could feel the anger start bubbling up.

"It was your suggestion that you wanted to look at the videos using your necromancy that had them send me. They wanted me to observe you working, and get a feel for your talent when it's not being used to actively raise the dead."

"I don't care about that. What I care about is, did you actually come here and aren't planning to help solve this case?"

"I'm here to help, of course."

"How?"

"What?"

"How can you help?"

"We've discovered that some psychics can use their talent via electronics to a surprising degree. If you can do that, then we want to have you involved in the live event from these perpetrators."

"What do you mean, live event?"

"I can answer that one," Brent said.

"Then answer it," I said, and my voice was still not friendly at all.

"They started out just advertising zombie sex tapes, but then they asked their customer base what they wanted to see."

"You've seen the tapes that have more storyline to them," Manning said.

"Storyline, what storyline?"

"The ones where the younger man seemed to be afraid, and it was made to appear as if he were being raped by the zombie."

"That was toward the end, right?" I asked.

"Yes."

"I'm afraid by the time we got there I was sort of glazed over with too much horror porn, but I remember it vaguely."

"It is hard to watch this stuff and keep a fresh eye," Manning agreed.

"That's why we watch it over and over," Brent said, and he looked tired at the thought, "so we can be as sure as possible that we don't miss something that might help."

"They've grown more sophisticated in story, and more ambitious on the kink," Manning said.

"Don't call this kinky; it's an insult to everyone who lives an alternative lifestyle," I said.

"Like yourself?" Gillingham said.

"I didn't mean to insult you, Marshal," Manning said. She gave Gillingham a dirty look.

"What I do, or don't do, in my private life is none of your business, Agent."

"Yes, of course, I'm sorry."

"I can't tell if you're this stupid, or if it's all an act so no one sees you coming psychically," I said.

"It's both," Larry said. "She is a disaster socially sometimes, but they dressed her so she'd look like this."

"Like the favorite second-grade teacher that we never had," I said.

"Or Sunday school teacher, yeah," he said.

"Tell them it's too much. They'd do better if she was just dressed like a normal American woman of her age and socioeconomic level," I said.

"Duly noted, I'll let them know."

"Did you know that's why she was here?" I asked.

"No, I just know she can follow psychic ability like a dog on a scent. I honestly thought she was here to help us aim our talents at the bad guy on the videos."

"It only works if the feed is live," Gillingham said. "I mean, I might be able to get impressions, but to follow it back to the bad guy it has to be currently happening."

"Have you tried to follow this bastard before?"

"Yes, and it didn't work."

"Why not?"

"We're not sure, but higher-ups think maybe it's just too different from most psychic ability."

"What does that mean, too different?" I asked.

"It's like I don't understand the necromancy enough to trace it."

"Or he's better at detecting you, like Anita," Larry said.

"He doesn't feel as powerful over the computer as she does sitting here," Gillingham said.

"It's not as strong over the computer sometimes," Brent said.

"You pick it up, too?" I asked.

He nodded. "I'm not nearly as gifted as the three of you, but I actually seem to get more via electronics. One of our instructors says that he's found other computer techs who actually have more talent to feel things over the computer than in real life. They don't even have a name for it yet, but apparently it's a talent just like the others."

"That might explain why so many techies spend all their time on-line; they get addicted to feeling the buzz," I said.

"We think so," Brent said, smiling as if I'd said a smart thing. It just seemed logical to me.

"So what's a live feed?" I asked.

"It's real time," Brent said, "and in this case the customers can call in and suggest what they want the zombie to do. Depending on what they want, they pay more money to get their idea onscreen."

I blinked at him. "Okay, ick, but okay."

"The more odd your request, the more they charge you, and if it damages the zombie they charge a lot more."

"Damage the zombie, I don't remember them doing that."

"There's been a new film. It was never live to the general customers, but only put online once the customer who requested it saw it live." Brent's face was a little gray around the edges.

"I don't like the look on your face right now. How much worse could it be than what we've seen?" I asked.

"Technically even though they look alive, they're zombies, so it's not murder, and it's not convictable for the customers really. Now that the word has gotten out about how lifelike the zombies are, the films are attracting people who usually haunt more serial killer sites. By that I don't mean real serial killer videos, but people pretending to film things that you could only do once in real life. Pretend torture and snuff films, and some real torture with willing victims."

"Real torture, or real BDSM?" I asked.

"BDSM for the most part. I'm told other divisions have traced people who were torturing people for viewers online, and shut them down, but for the most part it's all consensual and no one gets hurt more than they've bargained for," Brent said.

"Technically, the only way we got these films to be investigated this seriously was to raise the question of, if the soul is in the body, then is it a zombie, or is it a person?"

"You got to investigate this by raising a spiritual debate at the FBI?" I asked.

She made a little shrug and wobbled her head at the same time. "Yes, no, sort of, but once a voodoo priest told us that they had to be capturing the soul at the moment of death, then we treated it like any other serial killer case with magic added."

I looked at Gillingham. "So, if I can trace this via a live feed, then what do we gain? I mean, it's not like I'll be able to trace it back to an address. At best I'll get a taste for his power."

"Would you know the feel of his talent again if you felt it?" she asked.

"If I got a good enough feel for it, yeah."

"It might not work in court, but it could help us narrow it down once we have some suspects," she said.

"Okay, when's the next live event?"

"They only announce it close to the actual event."

"So what, you keep me on speed dial, and then what?"

"We have someone undercover as a customer. You'll be in the room while he types at them."

"Is this a group live event, or one of the special customer things?"

"It's group, but if this doesn't get us the information we need, then we're trying to find something for our undercover agent to request that is different enough that they think it would work as a film."

"Do we want to know what this new video is?" Larry asked.

"Do you think what you've seen so far is awful?" Manning asked.

"Yes."

"Then you probably don't want to see the next one, because you've got about another three hours of watching the milder stuff," she said.

"If I think I'm going to throw up, I'll just leave, and come back," he said.

"I thought I was the one that threw up at crime scenes," I said, trying to lighten things up.

"I never saw you do that, but this . . . I don't think it's the sex, I think it's the terror in their eyes. This is just so wrong, no, so evil."

"I'm not sure the FBI lets us use the word *evil* in official reports, because it's hard to prove something, or someone, is evil in court," Manning said.

Brent added, "But what they're doing is evil."

We all just nodded, even Gillingham. "If you can stop messing with me long enough I might be able to tell you if this guy is the animator who raised the zombies, or just a client of the animator."

"I promise to behave until you tell me you've got all the information you can this afternoon."

"Okay, then let's watch this shit and try to find a clue."

Brent hit the pause button and made it go again. The zombie's scream cut through the quiet of the room. "Why is she screaming in this one, but not the others?" Larry asked.

"She's tied up," I said, "so she could struggle, or scream."

"So they ordered her to lie down, let herself be tied up, and then removed the orders, and just let her be afraid like anyone," Larry said.

"We think so," Manning said.

We went back to watching the films, and I cracked my shields again, enough to try to sense something from the videos. I looked at the films not with my eyes, but with that part of me that could see the colors of Larry and Gillingham's auras out of the corner of my eyes. The man in the corner ordered the zombie to go down on the man on the bed, and there was a flash of something. I so wouldn't have wanted that rotted mouth on my junk, but it wasn't my kink. Either the man was a good actor, which I doubted, or it felt good. It was hard to concentrate on seeing with the corner of my eye when what my main vision was showing me was so damn disturbing. When the white stuff spilled out through a rotted hole in her cheek, Larry got up and went for the door. Leaving sounded really good, but I stayed and tried to learn something useful. But I had trouble concentrating on the man in the corner and his possible tie to the zombie, because what he was ordering the zombie to do was just so terrible and sad.

I finally got close to the screen and put my hand over the man's image. It was all I could think of to help me concentrate more on him and less on what was happening to the zombie. I felt a little silly with my hand over the screen, but when he gave an order I felt the pulse of it in my hand. I did it a few more times with different zombies, but it was there with all of them.

I had Larry try, but he couldn't sense anything through the screen. Teresa Gillingham tried, too, but she could only feel the barest energy from all of it. "It's like static to me."

"I'm eighty percent sure, maybe ninety, that this guy is the actual animator."

"Why not a hundred percent?" Manning asked.

"Because I've never tried to sense this kind of thing through a computer video, so I'm not going to say a hundred percent until we catch this guy and he really is the animator."

Manning nodded. "Okay, we'll never be able to use it in court anyway."

"We want you there for the live feed," Brent said.

"Do we, Gillingham? I mean, did I pass your little psychic test?"

She smiled and nodded, looking fresh and happy, as if she hadn't been watching the same films. Larry had come back in, looking green around the edges. Gillingham might look like a lamb, but there was something a lot scarier in there, or at least a lot stronger than she looked.

"Now what?" I asked.

"Now we wait," Brent said.

"Is there anything else we can do?" I asked.

"We have a file of stills for the man in the corner."

"Anything useful?" I asked.

"He has a tattoo on his left lower arm. It shows in two videos where his sleeves are uncuffed and rolled back enough for us to glimpse it."

"What is it a tattoo of?" I asked.

"Bring up the pictures, Brent. Maybe you can tell us."

Brent did his magic with the keyboard and two images showed side by side. It was faded and that bluish ink that some tattoos seem to fade into after a few years. We had one image of a smeared circle and another with a line through the circle. Larry and I both turned our heads trying to decipher it.

"I have no idea what that is," Larry said, at last.

"Me, either."

"There's a birthmark with a mole near it on one of the main leading men in the films, but other than that, no distinguishing marks," Manning said.

"That's not a lot to go on," I said.

"The corner man is dark complected. He could be Hispanic," Manning said.

"Or Greek, or southern Italian, or part Indian of either ethnic group," Brent said.

"The report is as helpful as they can make it from the information we have," she said. She seemed to feel like she needed to defend the FBI to us, or maybe she wasn't happy with them either.

"It looks like I'm going to be here until after the live feed, at least," Gillingham said. "So what do you do for fun in this town?" She gave me a look out of those brown eyes that didn't match the conservative clothes at all.

"I go home to spend time with my fiancé," I said.

Her lower lip did a slight pout that I was betting would have been more pronounced if she hadn't been surrounded by other FBI agents.

"And boyfriends," I said.

She raised eyebrows at me. "Fiancé, boyfriends, and girlfriend, if the rumors are true?" She smiled.

"Yeah, the rumors are true," I said.

Her smile brightened. "Sounds like fun."

I laughed. "I'm going home now; everybody be good while I'm gone."

Manning was watching me and Gillingham with narrowed eyes as I went for the door. Larry was telling her how great the St. Louis Zoo was, and the Arch was a great view. I agreed about the zoo, but I was pretty sure that wasn't the kind of wildlife Gillingham was wanting to see. I kept walking and didn't look back. I had all the fun I could stand, and then some, waiting for me at the Circus of the Damned.

56

I DROVE BACK home in the dark. All the little vampires were awake and starting their night. The Circus of the Damned had been just one more huge warehouse in the district when Jean-Claude had found it for the then Master of St. Louis, but the idea behind making it a permanent "traveling carnival" and one-ring circus catering to vampires, wereanimals, and other preternatural acts and businesses had been all his idea. There was a line stretching in front of the Circus past all the brightly colored posters announcing the acts and wonders inside, and down around the edge of the warehouse. It was Friday night; the weekend was always big. There were jugglers and street magicians entertaining the line to help the crowd pass the time. I caught a family with two small kids laughing at a clown, and a magician giving a paper flower to the female half of a couple as I drove past. There were also a few of our guards hovering around, just in case, though I doubted many of the laughing crowd noticed them. Our security measures weren't just for us, but for our customers. After all, nothing chases away your customers like getting mugged in line. This had been a bad section of town before the Circus moved in and brought in money, which attracted other businesses. The area had been gentrified not because of some government interference, but by good old-fashioned capitalism, which was one of Jean-Claude's favorite things.

I drove around to the employee parking lot in back and found it packed. We even had a roped-off section for valet parking, which meant our valet lot had filled up and they were moving cars back here. That didn't happen all the time, so it was a busy night indeed.

There was a man pacing in front of the back door; I thought at first it was more security, but as I parked in one of the reserved spots near the door I realized it was Cynric. His shoulders were hunched with tension, movements jerky with anger. Crap. My stomach sank to my knees, then tightened like an aching fist. I did not want to have a fight about my not being able to make the senior awards ceremony.

By the time I got out of my car I was ready to have a fight. If he couldn't understand that my job had to come before a lot of things, then he wasn't the right person for my life. I'd been hurt so badly that if I'd been just vanilla human I'd probably have needed surgery to fix some tendons or lose the use of my left arm. That was what had cost me the time to go to his school thing, and why the hell was he wanting our first public outing as a couple to be a school thing anyway? It was guaranteed to hit every issue I had.

He stopped pacing as he watched me walk toward him, and when I was close enough he said, "Good, you're as pissed at Asher as I am."

I actually said, "If you can't understand . . ." Lucky for both of us I stopped there and did an almost painful reverse in my head. "I'm sorry, what did you say?"

"You've got a serious mad on, and I just thought it was about Asher. Was I wrong?" He looked at me more closely. "Did I do something wrong?"

I laughed, smiled, and said, "No, no, it's just been . . . a day."

He offered his hand and I took it. His hands had gotten even larger since he moved to St. Louis, or maybe I just hadn't let myself see the spread of his fingers that did such a great job of holding and throwing a football. He drew me in for a kiss, and I went up on tiptoe to meet him partway, and let his lips touch mine. The kiss was gentle, his arms felt good, but the tension I'd seen when I drove up was still under there thrumming away.

I opened my eyes after the kiss, his arms still around me, and asked, "What has Asher done now?" I sounded more tired than mad.

"Nothing, Jean-Claude and the others are talking to him now." That sullen look that had almost gone away crossed his handsome face and made him look younger, and not in a good way.

"Then what's wrong?" I asked.

"He sent me out of the room."

"Jean-Claude?"

"Yeah, he ordered me out of the room while they talk to Asher."

"The last time Asher had a fit . . ." I started to say.

"I know, I know, he hit me once and I was down for the count."

I hugged him tighter around the waist. "He could have broken your neck, and that can work the same as decapitation, so dead."

"Jean-Claude reminded me, and Asher stood there smirking with Kane right beside him, holding his hand." He looked down at me, face so earnest, and I realized that it was a good word for him, too. "You know how hard I've been working out in fight practice."

I hugged him and rested my chin on his chest, so I gazed up the line of his body as he looked down at me. "I know you have."

"Jean-Claude doesn't work out with us, he doesn't know how much better I am now." It was the complaint of a child wanting to be a man, no, wanting to be treated like a man. I'd spent years having the other cops treat me like the "girl" until I proved myself; even now I still had to convince officers who hadn't worked with me before that I wasn't just a zombie-raising slut fucking her way to power through the pre-ternatural community. You think I'm being harsh? I wish. I stared up at Cynric. I could feel the extra muscle that gym work and fight practice had given him. Genetics had put him over six feet tall; in the boots he was wearing he was two inches taller than that, so that my chin rested at his diaphragm. I'd held enough men in my arms to understand the potential in his body not just for sex, but for violence, and that last included protecting himself. People treat learning to fight as if it's all about hurting people, but a lot of it is about making sure no one can hurt you, or those you love.

"Cynric," I said.

"Anita, please, tonight of all nights, call me by my name."

I took in a deep breath and said, "Sin."

He smiled, bright and happy. "Thank you, I know you don't like it."

"At least you started spelling it S-i-n, and not C-y-n."

He laughed. "No one could spell it or pronounce it the other way. I got tired of being called Cyndi, or Kenny."

"Well, Sin, let's go inside and see how Asher and Jean-Claude are holding up."

His eyes went a little wide. "Jean-Claude was very adamant about it. He even offered to have me escorted out by the guards."

"Well, you weren't the only one who got hurt last time Asher threw a hissy fit. Remember, he bit my mouth so badly that I'd have needed stitches if I'd been human. Hell, I might have needed plastic surgery or lived with permanent scars on my lips."

He touched my cheek, then traced his fingers delicately across my lower lip. It brought my breath in a sigh. He caressed his finger over my mouth again, then said, "Later I want to do that again, but push my fingers and other things between your lips."

I shivered at the thought of it, which made him laugh, pleased with himself, but he'd earned it. He was as good as his promises in the bedroom.

"Now stop that, or we'll both get too distracted to go in and talk to Asher."

The laughter faded around the edges, leaving his eyes angry again. "I really hate Kane. I don't like Asher sometimes, but Kane is just . . ."

"Irritating as hell," I finished for him.

"Yes."

"I know, but you be careful as hell around both Asher and Kane. He doesn't practice as hard as the rest of our guards, but he's still been doing this longer than you have. If you get hurt I will never forgive myself, or you. But you have a right to be in on the group discussions, and you're right, Jean-Claude hasn't seen you in fight practice."

"Kane has."

"Then be extra careful of him, because he knows how you move." I stepped away and offered him my left hand, and we went for the door. Cynric, I mean Sin, came with me smiling, happy to be included. I hoped he would be as happy afterward.

57

OF COURSE, IT wasn't that easy to get to Jean-Claude and the rest, because they were in the underground. The miles of stairs stretching downward meant there was no way to walk and be that quick. My phone buzzed at me. I fumbled it out of my pocket and saw a text from Nathaniel. "Jean-Claude is backing down. Need you."

Micah texted while I was still reading the first text. His text was shorter. "ETA?"

I showed Sin the texts. "Estimated time of arrival, what do you think?" I asked.

"At my speed, less than five minutes."

"You have to stay with me, not ahead of me," I said.

He grinned. "Well, then what's your mile time?"

"On stairs?" I said.

He nodded, still grinning.

"Shit, it's less than two miles." I texted both of the men back using a group message, and typed, "On stairs, less than 10 ETA."

"It'll be a lot less," Sin said.

I put the phone back in my pocket and started down the stairs. I was a little afraid of trying my top speed on the stone steps, but the guys needed me now. Jean-Claude had only two weaknesses: me and Asher. I said a little prayer and let myself run, really run, down the steps. I was glad I'd worn jogging shoes to work today. Sin stayed with me in his less-stair-friendly boots. He could have gotten there sooner, but he stayed with me like I'd told him to; it helped me move faster knowing that I was slowing him down, and that Nathaniel and Micah needed me with them. I prayed that Jean-Claude wouldn't do anything too stupid before I got there, and I ran.

58

I GOT TO the bottom of the steps in a rushed breathlessness that left me stumbling. Sin caught me, or I might have fallen. I was breathing too hard to speak, my heart in my throat like a drum. Sin was looking down at me with a huge grin on his face, deep blue eyes sparkling happily. "You did good!" he said, voice excited, but completely even.

I wanted to ask how much faster he could have run it on his own but didn't have the air to waste on it. There were two guards on the door, which wasn't typical. One was new, but the other one was Clay, tall, blond, athletic-looking, but he'd been taken off security at Guilty Pleasures for letting underage people slip past him because one of the ladies was flirting with him and vouched for her friend. Not my favorite guard. But he led the rush toward me, asking, "What's wrong?"

Sin answered, because I still didn't have enough air to speak. "Micah wants Anita at the meeting."

"So do I," Clay said. The other guard just watched everything quietly, dark eyes taking in details. I saw him clock all my weapons, or most of them. He'd have had to pat me down to find some of them.

"How bad is it?" I managed to gasp.

"Bad enough." He touched his earpiece, which they didn't always wear, and said, "It's Anita."

The big door swung open, and I could hear raised voices before I saw that it was Dino at the door. "Glad you're here, Anita, but he can't come into the meeting. Jean-Claude's orders." He motioned at Sin.

Micah's voice: "Anita is on her way, Jean-Claude. I'd rather wait for her before any decisions are made."

"Why are you even here, king of cats?" Asher asked. "You're not in my bed, or Jean-Claude's."

"I am in Jean-Claude's bed a lot more than you are."

"You little bitch," Asher said.

I told Dino that Sin was with me, and he accepted it, because I think he was more worried about the meeting than obeying Jean-Claude's orders. I touched the drapes that were the walls to the living room, but Sin's long arm reached over me and held it for me. He stayed behind me, but he held the "door." I was okay with that.

I entered the room with "I think I'm the bitch here" to find that Micah and Nathaniel were sitting in the love seat by the door with Nicky, Dev, Bram, and Domino behind them as guards. I was glad to see Domino well enough to be back on duty. Nicky and Nathaniel were still in the suits they'd worn to Sin's awards ceremony.

"Well, you're certainly everyone's pussy," Kane said, from the big white couch across the room, with Asher at his side. The vampire's hair fell in glittering gold waves past his shoulders, and I mean gold, not yellow. I'd never seen hair that looked metallic, but his was; some mix of blond and brown had made magic, and then those eyes—a pale, icy blue so pure in color that it was a pale match to Jean-Claude's darkest of blues. Belle Morte, their originator, had collected beautiful blue-eyed men, and these two had been two of her greatest finds. Asher had spilled that shining hair over half his face to hide the burn scars, so that he peered out at us like some sort of feral angel, showing only the perfect half of his face to the room—the face that looked down from the painting above the fireplace where his perfect profile had made Belle commission him painted as Cupid to Jean-Claude's Psyche in the same picture. The painter had taken some liberties, as they do, but they really were that heartrendingly beautiful, or could be.

I looked around the room and nodded. "I am actually sleeping with almost everyone in this room, but I don't think my pussy belongs to everyone here; I see it more as, all the cocks belong to me."

"Slut," he said.

"Who's your daddy, Kane?" I asked.

"What? Asher is."

I shook my head. "Not in the locker room earlier today he wasn't."

He actually started to get up, but Asher pulled him back down and cuddled him closer to his side; he'd already put him on the far side against the couch arm so he wasn't in touching distance of Richard and Jean-Claude. I hadn't expected to see Richard here, especially not with his arm around Jean-Claude's shoulders. He'd put his arm across the back of the couch, but not actually around the other man's shoulders, especially not without me sitting with them. They looked as they usually did, like they didn't match: Jean-Claude in one of his white shirts with all the lace at the sleeves and collar and going down the V to midchest, black leather pants that looked like someone had sewn him into them with the stitching on the sides of his long legs, and a pair of boots that only went to his knees, conservative for his footwear. Richard in blue jeans and a plain white T-shirt that made his spring tan look even darker, with nice brown leather hiking boots that had begun to soften because he actually hiked in them. Jean-Claude's black curls that fell almost to his waist, Richard's shoulder-length brown waves. Jean-Claude's almost androgynous beauty, Richard's face so very masculine in its handsomeness. Richard was only an inch taller, but with the swell of his muscled arm across Jean-Claude's shoulders it made the other man seem fragile, though I knew he wasn't. Richard was one of those big men who doesn't look that big most of the time, until he does.

Richard's main bodyguards were Shang-Da, the only six-foot-five Chinese man I'd ever met, and Jamil, who was darkly African American with cornrow hair to his waist. One was dressed in a black suit tailored big to hide the weapons I knew he was carrying, and the other was dressed in a white suit, red shirt, and tie to match the red beads in his hair. Jamil was the only man I'd ever known who could really pull off a white suit and not look silly. He made it look just right.

Sin took my hand and said, "I think I missed something, but it sounds good."

"I told you to stay away, Sin," Jean-Claude said.

"He's earned the right to be here, Jean-Claude."

"She defies you at every turn, Jean-Claude." Kane again.

"Even your young prince obeys her over you, *mon amour*," Asher said.

"The guards were all talking about how Anita handed you your ass in the locker room," Nicky said. "They found you flopping around on the floor. You couldn't even stand up."

Richard laughed, and once he did the guards joined him in a round of very masculine laughter. Micah joined them; only Nathaniel and Jean-Claude stayed somber. Nathaniel was watching Asher with a very solemn look as he sat holding hands with Micah. Jean-Claude's hand was playing with the lace on his shirt, which was something he did to calm himself, or when he was trying to calm himself. Richard had his other hand pinned against his thigh. I wasn't sure if they were holding hands, or if Richard had just pinned Jean-Claude's hand so it wouldn't keep petting his thigh, which was another nervous thing he did. It was usually my thigh, or Asher's, or occasionally Micah's.

"Did you hit him that hard?" Sin asked.

"I didn't hit him."

"She ate his anger," Nicky said. "I hear that leaves you pretty messed up afterward, Kane." He stared at Kane; it was a speculative look, somewhere between sizing someone up on the practice mat and watching someone you were thinking about fucking, or maybe just about tearing their throat out and eating them. It was an incredibly predatory look, the kind a serial killer might give his victims, all violence, sex, and cannibalistic speculation.

"Not as messed up as being her fucking Bride makes you." Kane said it with an unpleasant smile.

Nicky smiled back, but it was a pleased smile, an anticipatory smile.

Kane's smile wilted around the edges. He knew something was wrong, but not quite what. He might have been intelligent, I'd give Asher the benefit of the doubt that he didn't fuck stupid, but one thing was for sure; Kane was not wise.

"I say again, why are you even here, Micah?" Of course, Asher wasn't the wisest cookie in the jar either.

"I'm here because I have a relationship with more people in this room than you do, and I represent the interests of all the shapeshifters in Jean-Claude's immediate territory and beyond."

"Tell that to Narcissus, whom you have imprisoned," Asher said.

"He wanted to kill you both, when he learned what you had done."

Jean-Claude's voice was as empty as his face, as if he couldn't bear to show any emotion.

"I know you bargained for our lives, *mon amour*, and I am grateful," Asher said.

"Then act like you're grateful," Micah said.

"Was it you who made Jean-Claude deny me my own bodyguards, as due me?"

"Due you? Nothing is due you, Asher."

"I am a master vampire and my animal to call is the most powerful shapeshifter group in this city." His eyes flared to icy blue fire for a second, then calmed.

"Was," I said, "your animal to call *was* the most powerful shapeshifter group in the city. Past tense." I wanted to sit down, but I didn't want to sit that close to Kane, or Asher, and I sure as hell didn't want to take Sin closer. I could sit beside Nathaniel and Micah, but if I did then it might bother Jean-Claude, and Kane would certainly remark on it; that would not go well.

"I know you've been plotting behind my king's back," Kane said.

"It was Narcissus who tried to persuade Asher to overthrow Jean-Claude and take over the city," I said.

Kane frowned. "No, that's not true. He lied to you about my Oba." He pointed at Micah, rather dramatically I thought.

I looked at Asher. "He doesn't know, does he?"

Kane looked at Asher. "What don't I know?"

"Narcissus did try urging me to help him in a bit of kingmaking, but I refused like a loyal second-in-command should." Asher gave a little bow toward Jean-Claude, but sitting on the couch made it a halfhearted gesture at best.

"Yes, Asher, technically you are still my *témoin*, my second-in-command."

"Jean-Claude, what do you mean, technically?" He reached out as if to bridge the space before him and touch the other man.

Richard drew Jean-Claude in tighter against him and moved his other hand so that it was free, leaving room to wonder what he'd do if Asher tried to touch Jean-Claude. It was the kind of thing you do when someone is touching your girlfriend too much in a bar, and Richard gave him the challenging look that went with it. It was a way of saying, *Mine, stop touching it*, without having to say anything. Unless the other man was drunk, they usually backed off, and Asher wasn't drunk.

It startled him enough that he moved his head and let the hair spill back from all of his face so he could look at Richard and Jean-Claude together. The scars on his face were white and didn't cover much of the right cheek at all; the full, kissable mouth was untouched, as if even his torturers hadn't been able to bear the thought of ruining that pout.

I knew what Asher was wondering: Had Richard and Jean-Claude crossed those last inches and become lovers for real? I was betting good money they hadn't, but part of the BDSM relationship that Asher had with Richard was that the Ulfric liked figuring out what the vampire wanted most, and denying him that. Richard's body was one denial, but to imply that Jean-Claude was getting what Asher wanted but had never had, that was sadistic denial and domination of Asher's very thoughts and emotions. It was brilliant, because it would freaking torment Asher. One thing I think we all agreed on was that he'd earned some torment.

Jean-Claude settled more securely in the circle of Richard's arms and gave Asher a look that was all cat that ate the canary. That alone let me know just how angry Jean-Claude was with him, because Asher's jealousy was legendary and this was guaranteed to raise it, but there comes a point where you just want to hurt the other person, logic and common sense be damned.

Sin's hand tensed in mine. He knew this was a bad idea, too, but we weren't the ones pulling the green-eyed monster's tail.

Jean-Claude said, "You didn't consult me at all before you made Kane your hyena to call. What kind of *témoin* enrages the leader of one of the largest animal groups in the city without telling his master first?"

"One that doesn't give a damn about his master, or his territory," Richard said, and turned more toward the other men, ostensibly so they could look at each other while they talked more easily, but it also meant that Jean-Claude was now leaning his back completely against the other man; with a little encouragement he was lounging against

Richard, who put both those strong arms around the other man. Jean-Claude wrapped his own hands around those muscled arms. It was a display of familiarity that I'd never seen from them. It would have been more exciting in so many ways if I hadn't seen the cruelty in both their eyes. I wasn't sure I'd ever seen both of them this angry with Asher at the same time. I guess we were all that angry with him, though strangely their anger was helping me let go of some of my own. I was usually the hothead, but if they got pissy, someone needed to remain calm.

"I did not mean to cause such disarray," Asher said, and used his hair to hide the scars again, so that he was all golden hair and angelic face peeking out. The pale blue shirt made his eyes seem even bluer, like a startling sky that could look back at you. The shirt left a small V of his chest bare, and was bigger than it needed to be so the color complemented, but the size left him looking lost in it, like he'd borrowed the shirt, though I knew better. The black vinyl pants with their slashes of matching blue, on the other hand, were like all good vinyl and looked like a second skin. The black boots barely came over his ankles so they left his long legs looking even longer. The shirt looked careless, almost sloppy, but I knew how hard it was to get into vinyl; he hadn't done that casually. He'd been Jean-Claude's lover for hundreds of years, which meant he knew what the other man liked to see him in, and though it didn't make sense to me, Jean-Claude watched him in the clothes. He held on to his anger, but even wrapped in Richard's arms he watched Asher in that way he did sometimes—hell, the way I did, and Nathaniel did sometimes, and the way Dev almost always watched him.

I squeezed Sin's hand and told him, "Sit with Micah and Nathaniel."

He kissed me, light and chaste, and did what I asked. I went to Jean-Claude, which meant going to Richard, too, but the days when I went to him for anything but occasional rough sex were long past. He was still handsome, and great in bed, but that wasn't enough to get me past the temper tantrums. Asher and he had taken turns making Jean-Claude and me miserable.

I ended up having to sit in front of Jean-Claude so that the three of us were sitting spooned in each other's laps on one end of the couch. Jean-Claude wrapped his arms around me and I put my hands around his arms like he'd been sitting with Richard before I sat down. Then Richard's long, tanned arms came around on either side of us and held us, and his legs settled more firmly on either side of us. It was another reminder of just what a big guy he was, in every way. He'd sacrificed some of his weight-lifting time to hit fight practice more seriously. I'd seen what the length of his arms and legs could do when he sparred; now they made a nest for the two of us. There'd been a time when I'd have given almost anything for this closeness to be as real as what we were advertising, but my reality was sitting on the other side of the room.

"Anita didn't mean that Narcissus has lost power, Asher, she meant that you had," Richard said.

"I don't understand what you mean; nothing has changed for me. I can still call and command the hyenas."

"If you had made Narcissus your animal to call, then you could have commanded the werehyenas, but now you have Kane, just Kane," Richard said.

"You underestimate my abilities with my animal to call, Richard. Because Jean-Claude is so gentle with you and your wolves, you think that is the only choice."

"Narcissus didn't want to fight your control of him before, Asher, so you thought you were more powerful with your animal to call than Jean-Claude, because I was able to fight his control, but Narcissus couldn't. He'll want to fight now."

"He can try to fight me, but I am still his master."

"No," Jean-Claude said, "no, you are not. Do you not understand yet that if Narcissus fights you he can keep most of his people free of your call? He is more powerful than he has let you see; like a woman who hides how strong she is so as to stroke her man's ego, so Narcissus has been with you."

Asher shook his head.

"Did you, do you still think that you can have control of Narcissus against his full will?" Micah asked.

"He will fight you, *mon ami*, and he is more powerful than Richard, because he is not conflicted about his ties to his group, or his own leadership; he revels in it. He will keep you out of himself and thus out of everyone else. One on one, you may be able to force your will on them, but as a group you must go through the head to gain the body, and you have insulted and discarded the head. You have forced me to lock him up. Do you think he will forget, or forgive that?"

"I am sorry, Jean-Claude, truly sorry if my decision made things difficult."

"Difficult?" I said. "He bargained my body and my hyena to call to Narcissus, so he wouldn't kill Kane, at least Kane. He wanted to kill both of you."

Jean-Claude hugged me tighter, either willing me to be nicer or for comfort. I could have opened my shields and known what he was feeling, but not if he wanted to keep me out, and I was betting that he didn't want me in his head that far right now. Some things need to be private, and how he actually felt about Asher was probably one of them. Richard was stroking a hand over each of our arms, soothing us both, I think.

"If you had made him your beast, he wouldn't be imprisoned," Asher said.

"The werehyenas are almost not the largest group in St. Louis anymore," Micah said, "but combine the rats, wolves, leopards, and lions, and they aren't even close to having the most soldiers."

"It is unnatural for different kinds of wereanimal to work together like this," Kane said.

"You say that as if there's anything natural about us in the first place," Micah said.

"One last time, why the fuck are you here for this talk, cat?" Asher said, and almost snarled it at him, flashing fangs, which he almost never did.

"He's my other fiancé, and one of the two men who may be joining me in a commitment ceremony with Jean-Claude."

"You're marrying Jean-Claude."

"Yes, but hadn't you heard that we were doing a group commitment ceremony, too?"

"I heard rumors of it, but I did not credit it." He looked at us sitting all cozy on our end of the couch. "Now it would seem you would need to add the Ulfric, if you are truly doing a second ceremony."

"Why don't you believe that we are going to do a group commitment ceremony?" Micah asked.

"I would have believed it of the three here on the couch with me, once. I would believe it of you, Nathaniel, and Anita. But I do not believe that you and Jean-Claude would tie yourselves together, and I know you and Richard loathe each other."

"You know that old saying, the enemy of my enemy is my friend?" Richard asked.

"Fighting beside someone you hate is one thing, my top. Sharing a bed with them is very different. You loathe Micah, and Nathaniel, so I do not fear you joining them."

"You are quite right, *mon ami,*" Jean-Claude said, and even using the 'my friend' as opposed to his usual nicknames was calculated to make Asher insecure. "We cannot include Richard in the ceremony, because he does not get along with enough of us, that is true. But Micah, Nathaniel, Anita, and I are going to join with others in a commitment ceremony. I had advocated for you to be included in it, but you just couldn't leave well enough alone. You had to alienate, or anger, too many of them."

"You are not allowed to touch Micah; how can you commit to something so empty? Even Nathaniel is only food for you. Nathaniel is my lover, my submissive, but only food to you, Jean-Claude. You do not marry your food."

"Who I marry, who I commit to, who Anita makes her animal to call, who feeds us, who fucks us, none of that is your concern anymore. As you did not see fit to ask my opinion, I shall no longer ask yours."

"Jean-Claude . . ."

"No, Asher, no, it is enough."

"Why is the girl always what drives a wedge between you and Asher?" Kane asked.

Jean-Claude sat up, abruptly, and though we were still touching each other it wasn't cuddly anymore. "It's not Anita, it's not the girl, that drives a wedge between Asher and me, it's Asher! It's always Asher that drives the wedge home again and again into a piece of wood until it breaks apart, so he pushes at me and the love we have for him." He lay back against Richard again, taking me back into a suddenly strained cuddle. "You consulted none of us before you took Kane as your animal. Narcissus almost killed him and you. I would have bargained for him to be Anita's hyena to call, and catapulted him back to an even higher perch in our power structure and tied her forever to someone she loathes."

Jean-Claude stood, not fighting free of us, but needing to stand, so we let him. I was suddenly left with only Richard to cuddle and it felt awkward, but my moving away now would undercut the show the two men had put on, so I let him hold me against his body while we watched Jean-Claude pace in front of us.

"Richard has been your dominant for over a year. You top Anita and you like being with them both very much. Nathaniel has been your submissive for almost two years, along with Anita as your bottom, and both are your lovers. You have told me how much this means to you, and yet you talked to none of us before you mortally insulted Narcissus and threw all our careful plans to ruin!"

"I am sorry, Jean-Claude. I am sorry to all of you; I do not regret making Kane my animal to call, but I regret not discussing it with all of you first."

"I would have urged you to make Narcissus your *moitié bête*, your animal half. You could have married Kane, but to share power it needed to be Narcissus; do you not see that?" He was almost pleading with Asher, wanting him to at least understand what he had done wrong.

"Marriages can end. Asher wanted to show me he loved me forever and meant it," Kane said, cuddling into all that golden hair while his gaze stayed on Jean-Claude the whole time. It was a defiant, or maybe triumphant, look.

"Oh, my God," I said. "You let Kane manipulate you into this, didn't you? It's his attempt to isolate you from all your other lovers, and it's a damn good attempt."

Asher looked at me, letting me see all that beauty like a weapon aimed straight for my heart, or at least my libido.

"Kane isn't that smart." Nathaniel said it. We all looked at him, because it was snarky for him, more like me.

Kane started to stand up, but again Asher held him in place on the couch. I think at least the vampire had realized that they were in hostile territory with us tonight, and none of us liked Kane.

"Nathaniel is right, that's far too devious for Kane," Micah said.

Asher pointed a finger at him. "The others are in our beds, or guarding our safety, but you are nothing to Jean-Claude, or to me."

"I was the one who talked Jean-Claude into not allowing you any hyena guards," Richard said, "not Micah."

"I do not believe it," Asher said.

"You are not a king. You are not even a master of your own territory. You do less and less business as Anita and Micah take on more responsibilities, especially Micah. He has become Jean-Claude's right hand, which I should have been, or you, but we both failed him, and Micah didn't. Because Jean-Claude loves you, because so many of us are intimate with you, that makes you think you have more power than you do, Asher. I wasn't here the last time you tried to throw the hyenas in everyone's face, but people ended up injured. People could have died, so we treated you like what you are, a master vampire who is fourth in command in a territory. That earns you nothing, nothing! No guards, no honors; nothing. You used hyenas to hurt Anita, Sin, and Nicky last time, so you get nothing."

Richard was still holding me, but the tension of his emotions sang through his body, so it wasn't exactly restful. I was petting my hands down his arms, trying to soothe him a little, because it was either that or I had to get up off this couch.

"You almost had a kingdom in your hands," Micah said, "but without Narcissus the only thing you have in your hands is the hand you're holding now. You have Kane, and that's all."

"That is a great deal," Asher said, and kissed the man he loved to prove that point.

"If you're talking love, then I'll take your word for it that Kane is worth that to you, but if you're talking power, then he is weak, Asher, you know that."

"You know nothing, cat, nothing about me, or Kane, or Jean-Claude."

"Why do you keep picking on Micah?" I asked.

"He doesn't like Micah, because Micah doesn't find him attractive, at all, and Asher can't stand that," Dev said. He was looking across the room at his lover, the only person he'd ever proposed marriage to, as if he'd never seen him before. People say liquor makes everyone pretty, but sobering up is a bitch—well, being in love makes people beautiful, and falling out of love makes you see the truth. It may set you free, but it's going to fuck you up before it does.

"You are not a part of this, Dev," Kane said.

Asher ignored Dev. "I do not like Micah because he keeps you at arm's length, Jean-Claude. I know how it ate at me to see you closer to others, before you recommitted to me as your lover. I dislike Micah because he offers such pain to someone I love."

"Micah is the only one who doesn't want you, Asher, and that eats at you," Dev said.

Nicky raised his hand. "I'm not attracted to Asher either, just saying."

"Me, either," Domino said.

"Asher doesn't care about either of you, not seriously. He'd fuck you once if he thought he could seduce you. He has a real thing about being a straight guy's first, or even only, male lover. That totally does it for him," Dev said.

"So not happening," Domino said.

"He wouldn't be my first," Nicky said.

That got everyone's attention. "You told me you didn't like guys," Dev said.

"I don't, but the bitch who raised me made me sort of anti-girls for a few years. If I were a little less of a raging heterosexual, and had a different therapist, I'd probably still be hooking up with guys."

"I guess I'm just not pretty enough," Dev said. "You shut me down in the shower with Anita pretty fast."

"The only thing I looked for in a guy when I was a teenager was good hygiene, good at giving blow jobs, and a willingness to take anal sex."

"Hey, I'm all of those things," and Dev pretended to pout at him.

Nicky smiled, shook his head hard enough for the triangular fall of hair to swing, and said, "If I were still into guys, I'd totally do you."

Dev grinned at him.

"Empty words, Rex, because you know you'll never have to do it," Kane said.

"You know that I don't like you, right, Kane?" Nicky said.

"You don't like Dev any more than you like me."

"I like Dev a hell of a lot more than I like you."

"But not enough to fuck him, even naked in the shower with him."

"You and I were naked in the showers, and I didn't want to fuck you," I said.

"I don't do girls."

"And I don't do stupid, so we're both safe."

Kane stood up. Asher tried to pull him back, but this time he stood his ground and kept his feet. I stood up. Richard didn't try to hold me on the couch. I stood there facing Kane. He had his hands in fists. Mine were loose, cupped, and waiting for me to decide whether I was fighting.

"I already proved that I can beat you, Kane. Do you really want an audience for it this time?"

"You cheated in the locker room."

"You're almost a foot taller than me, with an arm and leg reach that's almost twice mine, you're a man, and you're a werehyena; there is no such thing as a fair fight between us."

"So you admit you cheated."

"Talk like that is for amateurs, Kane."

"I am not an amateur," he said.

"Okay," I said, and half-turned away from him, so that I could plant my foot, turn my shoulder, make a fist, cock my arm, and turn back around with everything I had, so that my whole body acted like a spring to power the punch into his solar plexus. He doubled over, unable to breathe for a second, and his face was low enough for me to put a knee into it, so I did. In rapid succession, holding the back of his head so I could drive my knee into his face with all the force I had, four times. I backed up from him, giving him room in case he recovered enough to try to grab me. I did not want those long arms and stronger body grap-pling with me.

If he'd been human the fight might have been over, but he wasn't human. He came at me with a roaring growl that danced over my skin in goose bumps, but he gave me time to get set for a kick. I still had my hands up guarding my face, elbows tucked in over as much of my torso as I could cover, but I didn't plan on him getting that close. He was so angry that he just forgot all his training and simply ran at me. I kicked him in the solar plexus, which stopped him. He fought not to double over as much and guarded his face better than last time, so I didn't go for his head. I kicked him in the side of the knee, and he fell to the floor with a scream. He didn't try to get up, just stayed on his hands and one knee, the other leg held out to the side the way a dog will when it's hurt.

"You broke my leg."

"It's not broken. I didn't even hear that meaty pop, so I didn't even dislocate it. One shape-change and you'll be good as new."

"You bitch, you sucker-punched me, you cheated again."

"And that's why you're an amateur," I said.

"What the fuck does that mean?"

"Did you expect rules? A referee or a judge to step in and give a list of the do's and don'ts for the fight?"

He just glared at me, and said, "Bitch."

I smiled and said, "Pussy."

Heat poured off him, and his brown eyes turned paler, golden brown—hyena brown. The Browning was just in my hand; muscle memory took over before I could even decide. I was already aiming at his head, right above his eyes. It was my best kill shot from the angle I had.

"Don't shift, Kane, not here, not now," I said; my voice was low and careful, because my finger was already on the trigger. No matter what gun you have, once your finger crosses that point, you treat all guns as if they have hair triggers, and be damned sure that if you pull, you want whatever you're aiming at dead.

The heat spread through the room like someone had left the tap open on a really hot bath, and we were about to drown in it. "Silver bullets, Kane, you won't heal a head shot."

There was movement to my left. "No one move," I said.

"Anita," Asher said, "please," and I felt him coming closer.

"Freeze where you are, Asher, or I swear to God I will shoot Kane and then turn on you."

"Ma petite . . ."

"No, Jean-Claude, not this time. If Kane shifts I will shoot him. If Asher interferes, I will shoot him. That is the difference between amateurs and professionals. Amateurs whine about rules, fairness, and plead for mercy. Professionals know that there is only one rule—survival—violence is not fair, and there is no mercy."

"Anita," Nicky said, "if you kill Kane, fine, kill Asher, I'm fine with that, too, but you won't be."

I kept staring at Kane's forehead, and that spot where the bullet would go. I'd shot people up close like this before. I knew the mechanics of it, and exactly what would happen. It was just a different face staring back at me.

"Ma petite . . ."

"Don't." That was Micah. "Let Nicky talk to her." Hearing Micah's voice helped me listen better to something outside the calm in my head. I felt nothing, staring down the barrel of my gun at Kane; nothing.

"You're not alone out in the field, Anita," Nicky said. "We got this regardless of what Kane does. You don't have to kill him. If you wanted to kill him, I'd be okay with that, you know that."

I whispered, "I know."

"But I can feel what you're feeling, and you don't want to kill him. You've just gone quiet in your head, but your emotions are waiting outside that quiet. You don't want the emotional fallout if you killed Asher, Anita. I think he's a manipulative shit, but you love him, and Jean-Claude loves him more."

"So not worth it," I said, each word enunciated carefully between almost gritted teeth. I wasn't really looking at Kane anymore, just at that point on his head where the bullet would go if I finished this.

"No, he's not," Nicky said, voice soft, and closer to me, but his closeness didn't make me want to turn the gun on him and protect myself. Asher I didn't trust not to do something stupid, but Nicky—he wouldn't be stupid. He might be violent, but it would be on purpose, with a better reason than not thinking things through.

I drew back from the empty quiet in my head, and the pinpoint concentration that had narrowed down to the aim of my gun and my target, and realized that the energy that had been rolling off Kane was gone. I blinked and saw his brown eyes staring up at me. He'd pushed his beast back in its box. He was still holding his damaged leg, but he was trying to be as still as the injury would let him be, as if he were afraid to move too much, afraid of what I'd do if he did.

"Good," I said, softly, "very good."

"What's good?" Nicky asked.

I eased my finger off the trigger and raised the gun toward the ceiling. I kept looking at Kane's face, though. "Did you see your death in my face, Kane?"

"I thought you were going to kill me."

"So did I," I said. I put the Browning back in its holster at my side. I felt light and empty, not bad, but it was odd. I didn't usually get to this point and not shoot someone. I felt weird, as if the process were incomplete. I'd tried to explain to friends the difference between what I did and what other cops did, and that was it. Most cops go whole careers and never draw their gun, or if they do, they still think more about saving lives than taking them, but I didn't. When I drew my gun I almost always got to use it, and using it, for me, meant someone was dead. Legally, lawfully, no review board, no questions asked—dead. I was the Executioner long before I was Jean-Claude's *ma petite*.

"Get him out of my sight. Let him heal, but I don't need to see him do it."

More guards came through the drapes, as if they'd been waiting for some signal that they could enter without spooking me into shooting Kane. They got their hands under his arms and helped him to his feet. He couldn't stand, so in the end they formed a cradle with their arms and two of them carried him out of sight—toward medical, I guess. I honestly didn't care, as long as it was away from me.

I turned toward Asher, looked into that beautiful face, remembered the feel of his kiss, his body, his strength. "I don't know what is broken inside you, but if you don't work the issue it's going to get you, or Kane, or both of you, killed."

"You will kill us?"

"No, not if you don't make me, but someone will. Narcissus would have if he'd seen you before Jean-Claude talked him down. You're away from Belle's court for the first time in a century, and it's like you think none of us will hurt you." I stepped up close enough that the oversized blue shirt brushed against me. It was too close, if I really thought he'd hurt me. I stared up at him, tried to see some comprehension in that gorgeous face, but he was hiding his emotions too hard, and it was like staring at a work of art. You could admire its beauty, but you couldn't talk to it.

He started to put his arm around me; I thought he was going to kiss me, but I put my hand on his chest and stepped back out of arm's reach. "The last time you kissed me during one of these little disagreements you damn near ate my lips off my face."

"I am sorrier than I know how to express for that, Anita."

"You're sorry now, but in the heat of the moment you don't think. Because we're not cruel like Belle Morte you think we're weak, but never mistake kindness for weakness, Asher. It's not the same thing."

"I understand," he said.

"Do you? Do you really? Because I don't think you do. I don't know how to teach you this lesson without really hurting you. Is that what it takes to get you to behave like a thinking person? Do you only respond to cruelty?"

"No, no, that will not be necessary," he said, voice as empty as he could make it.

"Look around you, Asher; we aren't vampires that are bored with centuries of life so that we play at cruel games like children pulling the wings off flies. How Belle did her power plays was professional, but how she ran her court was indulgent amateur shit. I have enough memories to know that she wasted so many people, so much potential that could have helped her, and helped people around her. Jean-Claude regrets that waste and works to make his court different, better. Is there any regret in you, Asher?"

"Yes, of course, I regret some of what I've done over the centuries, we all do, even Belle."

"She regrets losing your and Jean-Claude's adoration, I've felt that when she tried to invade my head, but the only other thing she seems to regret is when things don't go her way. Still, she's far more practical than you are."

"She is also more cruel."

"Yeah, she is, but she never lets indulging her cruelty get in the way of business, and you let everything get in your way. If you had made Narcissus your animal to call you could have really brought something to the table, powerwise, but instead you threw it away on a whim to please your lover, and never gave a thought to what might happen afterward. It's like you're stuck at about fifteen and think nothing bad will happen to you."

"I have had bad things happen, Anita."

"I know, which makes your behavior all the more confusing to me."

"*Ma petite* . . ." Jean-Claude came to us, but I put a hand up to stop him from coming closer.

"No, I'm pissed at you, too."

"Why?" He looked genuinely surprised.

"Where were your bodyguards? Everyone else had guards with them, but not you. You are the motherfucking king of America, and you know that he's dangerous when he's like this. You should have had personal protection with you."

"He was not allowed guards . . ."

"Stop talking," I said.

He gave me narrow eyes.

"Be angry with me, that's fine, but you have to start treating Asher like he is, not like you want him to be. He is childlike, in that throwing-temper-tantrums way. He breaks things and regrets it afterward, but the damage is done. I don't want you to be part of that damage one day, Jean-Claude."

"I would like to say that I would never hurt Jean-Claude, but Anita is too right. I do not think when I am in certain . . . moods. I don't know why I do such things."

"Then talk to that therapist we found for you, and figure it out, before you force me to kill you. Nicky's right, Asher, it would kill something in me to do it, and Jean-Claude would never forgive me, but mark me on this, Asher."

I went to him and touched his face, made sure he was looking down at me with all that golden hair and those eyes, that kissable mouth. I stared up into all that beauty and I said the truth. "Mark me on this, Asher, if you ever do anything that damages Jean-Claude's power structure, or Micah's work with the Coalition, without consulting them first, then you will be punished, and if you won't take good treatment, I'll find someone to give you bad treatment. If the only way you learn is by having the lesson carved into your skin, or painted in blood, or echoed in screams of pain . . . we can do that."

"That will not be necessary," he said quietly, and very slowly, very carefully, as if waiting for me to protest, he put his hand over mine where I touched his face.

"I hope not, because if pain doesn't work, the only thing left is death. Do you understand that?" I spoke slowly, as carefully as his hand had touched mine.

"I do now," he said.

"Good, good. Kane's afraid of me now and that will help, but you aren't afraid of me. I can't make you afraid of me without damaging our relationship more than you already have today."

"I am sorry, Anita, truly. May I kiss you?"

"No, I don't want your touch to make me forget this moment, and I don't want you to think a little sex and bondage will fix it all, because it won't. We may get back to that, but that doesn't make all this okay, it just means I'll have decided it's not a deal killer."

"Are you . . . would you refuse me?"

"Right now the thought of letting you tie Nathaniel and me down, and being at your mercies, and trusting that you'd honor our safewords, just doesn't seem like a good bet."

"And for that, I am even more sorry. I value you both, I love you both."

"Then act like it, Asher, because right now I'm not feeling very valued, or loved." I took my hand away from his face, his touch, and stepped back.

Nathaniel came to me looking handsome in a black suit tailored to his body like a European glove, lavender shirt and a black tie with tiny purple fleur-de-lis. It made his skin look darker, his auburn hair tucked back in a long braid redder, his eyes almost purple, though maybe that was him being angry. He took my hand in his and said, "I hope you can earn back our trust, because I'll miss your body if you don't." Not *I'll miss you*, but *I'll miss your body*. I thought that was interesting phrasing; apparently so did Asher.

"My body, but not me; then I have been a bad dominant to you, for you should love me as I love you, my flower-eyed boy." He touched Nathaniel's face, but all he got was a very cold look from that handsome face.

"You've been so into Kane that the rest of us haven't really counted for much," Nathaniel said.

Asher let his untouched hand fall back to his side. "I did not realize that I had neglected all of you."

I said, "You and I pretty much just have bondage sex with Nathaniel, and sometimes without him, but I'm just your bottom, not your submissive. Submissive needs more caretaking."

"I will do better by all of you, I swear it." He looked at Jean-Claude and Richard standing off to one side.

"Does Dev count in all that?" Nathaniel asked.

Asher looked past us to the guards still waiting at the edges. Dev had stayed with them, not moving forward even as far as Nicky had. I wondered if he'd stayed back because he'd been ordered to, or because he didn't trust himself not to hurt Kane, or Asher. It would have been the perfect excuse.

Asher looked at Dev, and it was . . . *dismissive* was the only word I had for it. It must have cut Dev to the heart. "I am committed to Kane now. I will be keeping the relationships that give me things he cannot, but what Dev and I have is too . . . standard. I could not come up with a need he met that Kane, Jean-Claude, you, and Nathaniel did not."

My chest ached just hearing him dismiss Dev's love like that. I realized I was feeling some of the bleedover of emotion from my golden tiger. He was hurting too badly to be able to shield himself off completely, and in that moment I didn't want him to. What good is being able to sense someone else's emotions if you can't help them cope with them sometimes?

"God, Asher, aren't anyone's feelings real to you but your own?" Sin said it from the far side of the room, where other guards had forced him back from the potential danger. He practiced fighting, but he wasn't a guard, and when the emergency happened they'd treated him like what he was, a guardee.

Sin went to Dev and hugged him. He was almost as tall as the six-foot-three guard, but there was still something very young in his wanting to hug and make it all better. Dev startled and tried to stay in stoic bodyguard mode, and then he hugged Sin back, blond head bowing to mingle with the dark blue. They broke apart and it was Sin who had tears trailing down his face, as if he were crying tears Dev couldn't, or wouldn't, shed.

Micah went to him next and offered his hand, and then did that one-armed guy hug, which was a little awkward since Dev was about a foot taller, but I heard Micah say, "You deserve someone who treats you better than this, Dev."

Nicky hugged him next, and then ended with his hand on the back of Dev's neck, underneath his longish blond hair. Nicky kept his hand on the man's neck, so they touched foreheads, faces apart enough that I could see Nicky's lips move as he said something—I couldn't hear what he said, but whatever it was it made Dev smile.

Domino hugged him, too, and just said, "Dude, I'm sorry."

Dev said, "Thanks, brother."

Nathaniel hugged Micah, and said something so quietly that like with Nicky I could only see his lips moving, but heard nothing. Micah nodded, then motioned me over. I went to them, taking his hand. We put our heads together and Micah said, "Nathaniel wants permission to be with Dev as friends with benefits."

"I thought the two of them had been talking about that, but I thought you were against it," I said.

"Was I jealous at first, yes, but I can't, or don't want to do certain things with Nathaniel. I've learned that I don't know how I feel about some things until we try, but I promise not to be mad at Dev for the one night even if I can't deal with more."

Nathaniel looked at me. "Are you okay with it?"

"I think so, I mean I'm already able to have sex with both of you, and I know how much you miss certain guy-on-guy sex from being in the bedroom with you and Asher, so if Micah is okay with it, then I don't see a problem. Should we ask Jean-Claude?"

"None of us are sleeping with him but you," Micah said, "and you already have his okay for sex with Dev."

"Dev may be negotiating with Jean-Claude for something," I said.

Micah sighed. "We're going to have to ask, then."

"Another spontaneous romantic moment spoiled by poly negotiations," I said.

"Better than not talking about it and having it all blow up in our faces," Micah said.

Nathaniel nodded. We asked Jean-Claude and Dev to join us by the fireplace, and we asked. Yeah, at first it's totally awkward to ask such blunt questions, but it's pretty much the only way to run a poly group, especially one with so many moving parts. Asher had just demonstrated what happens when you don't talk to the people in your lives, so fuck that, let's talk. So we did.

We ended with Jean-Claude turning to Dev and giving a gentle but thorough kiss. He turned to Asher and said, "A male lover who does not wish bondage, but is in my bed in every other way, is a precious gift to me. One I would not throw so lightly away."

"As I have done, you mean?"

"I do not understand your infatuation with Kane, but love is like that, is it not?"

"The five of you have consulted each other, but Richard and I are left out of the requests and permissions."

"Don't drag me into this, Asher," Richard said from where he'd sat back down on the couch.

"But do we not have rights, as well?"

"I wouldn't start complaining that you haven't been consulted about changes in your BDSM and poly, after the lack of communication you've given all of us," he said.

"I will endeavor to do better in the future."

"Well, it's hard to do worse," I said.

"You will take Dev in to punish me?"

"Oh, for the love of God, Asher," Micah said, "not everything is about you. Jean-Claude and Nathaniel miss having a male lover who does the whole ball of wax, and is separate from their BDSM relationships, and thanks to you Dev is looking for new relationships. Dev and Nathaniel will be friends with benefits. Jean-Claude and Dev will be lovers and he'll become a regular blood donor. Everyone gets something they're missing."

"And you, Richard, are you so logical about Dev being added?"

"Fine. I'm about as far into being what Jean-Claude needs as I'm comfortable with, which isn't close to enough. If Dev can meet those needs that I won't, great, as long as I'm not expected to share the bed, or Jean-Claude and Anita, with Dev as a group thing. You, Jean-Claude, and Anita is about as much guy-guy as I want to deal with. Nathaniel and I are nothing to each other except that we share you, Anita, and Jean-Claude sometimes, so what he does is really no business of mine. I see everyone about once a month, maybe twice, and that's it, so it really is up to them as long as our relationships remain as they are."

"So logical. I am afraid my heart is not so easily reasoned with."

"Why does it bother you that we are picking up what you discarded?" Nathaniel asked.

"Dev means nothing to me."

"Thanks, Asher, thanks for that," Dev said.

"I know how to make you happier," Nathaniel said.

Dev looked sad, but said, "How?"

"Brace, literally."

Dev looked puzzled, but I saw him set his body as if he were about to lift something, or do something physically. Nathaniel threw his arms around the taller man's shoulders and jumped up, wrapping his legs around Dev's waist, and kissed him. Dev seemed startled, but then relaxed into it, his hand coming up to cup the back of Nathaniel's head, and then playing his hand along the braid of hair, the other arm around his waist helping hold him in place, though I was pretty sure Nathaniel didn't need the help.

I watched them kiss long and deep, more and more body English in it, and my body clenched so tight that I had to catch myself against the fireplace. Everyone had their kinks and I loved watching my male lovers together; I just did.

"I wish I found that as exciting as you do," Micah said, hugging me.

"Me, too," I said.

Nathaniel broke from the kiss to say, "Me, three."

"I don't," Dev said, "because then Nathaniel wouldn't need me."

"Micah's too well endowed for giving anal, so you'd still have your uses," Nathaniel said, smiling inches from Dev's face.

Dev looked like something hurt, but I don't think it hurt. I think he'd just had a reaction similar to the one that had made me grab the fireplace. "Do you just like receiving?"

"I like giving, too."

"Hard limit either way with me," Micah said, "sorry."

"Me, too," I said, and hugged him.

The two vampires and Richard stayed very quiet. Once upon a time I'd have asked why, but I'd learned that while ignorance may not be bliss, sometimes you really don't need to know.

Dev helped Nathaniel stand again, and Nathaniel gave me that smile, the one that let me know that whatever he was about to say was going to either be wonderful, or make me cringe that he'd said it in front of this many other people.

"I love that you enjoy watching me have sex with other people."

"I like watching my lovers with other lovers, as long as I get to do more than watch eventually."

"Oh, why didn't you say so?" Dev said, and he held out his hand to me, smiling.

Micah kissed me on the cheek. "Go on."

I went to the other men and let Dev and Nathaniel draw me in between them. Nathaniel picked me up around the waist and lifted me so I could kiss Dev, while he nuzzled his face across my breasts, still covered by all my clothes, but it was still almost too much for this much crowd.

"Is there a way for a straight guy to get in here somewhere?" Sin asked.

"If we had another girl or two, we'd have a hell of a daisy chain going," Dev said.

There was movement among the guards. I turned, still held between Dev and Nathaniel, to find three of the Harlequin guards dropping to one knee near us. Echo bowed her short black hair, Fortune with her short blue curls beside her. They didn't surprise me, because they'd shown up to the tiger get-together as lovers earlier, but Magda the werelion took a knee, too. That, I hadn't seen coming.

Echo spoke, "If it meets with your approval, mistress, we would gladly try to help fill out your chain of daisies." She raised her face so I got the full force of those deep blue eyes framed by all that pale skin and black hair. Her face was a delicate oval, and she wasn't much bigger than me, but something about her coloring evoked Jean-Claude; it was probably just the hair-eyes-skin combo, but still . . . it wasn't a bad thing.

"I don't know what to say, I mean, gentlemen?"

"None of us are going to say anything until you do," Micah said. The other men nodded.

I sighed. I was the girl and the one most likely to not want more women. I had Nathaniel and Dev put me down, so I was at least standing on something solid.

Domino stepped forward and said, "Sorry, but do you need to talk to Jade about adding more women?"

"I told her weeks ago that I was looking for women who liked both men and women, that it didn't work for me to be with someone who dislikes men." I had; I just hadn't expected to have so many potential choices this soon.

Fortune looked up at me with a smile almost visible on her broad mouth. Her blue-on-blue eyes were shining as if she knew a joke that I didn't. Echo watched me out of those dark blue eyes. I looked at Magda with her thick blond hair cut just above her shoulders. She so needed a new hairdresser, but if we took her into our bed then Jean-Claude would help her, like he'd helped me. She stared up at me with those gray-blue eyes. They were almost completely gray against the unrelieved black of the guard's typical clothes.

"Okay, with Echo and Fortune I guess we can do what I did when the tigers first came to town."

"Kiss them," Dev said.

"Unless you have a better idea," I said.

He shook his head.

"Magda, before we even get that far, I need to know why the hell you're beating up Kelly, when it gains you nothing."

"I have stopped challenging her. She can retain her place in the pride."

I frowned, and asked, "Why the change of heart?"

"I was doing it in hopes that she would ask you to intervene."

"You wanted me to do what? Punish you, fight you, what?"

"Pay attention to me; I had done my job flawlessly, worked at practice to the best of my ability, but you had not noticed."

"I noticed, you're great in the gym."

"I could not tell that you had noticed."

"Sorry, I should have given you an 'atta girl.' Next time you need something from me, just ask, don't beat the shit out of anyone trying to get my attention, okay?"

"Once I was able to sleep beside you and help heal you, then I knew you had noticed me."

I didn't know what to say; she seemed to think I'd requested her to sleep with me, and not that Lillian had just offered her name out of a hat, so to speak. Kelly was safe and that's what counted. I turned to Nicky. "You okay with this? You're Rex."

"I'm not sleeping with her, so her sex life is her business."

"Okay, cool." I turned back to Magda and the others. I motioned them to stand and then had the weird moment of having three women in front of me and having to decide how to decide if I wanted to include them not just with me, but with the other men in my life. Weird did not cover it, and only one of them was a tiger, so it didn't even help much with the whole commitment thing.

I turned to Jean-Claude. "Some help here."

"What would you have of me, *ma petite*?"

"I think they need to kiss everybody, not just me, to see if there's a spark, because I do not want to have another woman in my life who doesn't work with the men in my life."

"But you must kiss them first, because I do not want another woman in my life who doesn't want to sleep with you. Envy was enough of a lesson."

"Okay." I turned to the women and thought, *where to start*?

"We could do it by height," Fortune said, smiling, "shortest to tallest, or the reverse."

"I know you're kidding, but I don't have a better idea." I moved down to Echo, who was only a couple of inches taller than me. I stared in her face and again there was that jolt of recognition, as if I should know her face from somewhere, but it was more one of those memories that makes me think that past-life memories aren't just silliness.

I moved in closer to her and felt incredibly awkward. I touched her face and moved in for a kiss. She moved toward me, and our lips touched. It was a soft brush of lips, and I thought what I usually thought about kissing women, what small mouths they had. I drew back from her, not sure what to think. It wasn't a bad kiss, but I'd learned I was a lot pickier about women than I was about men when it came to sex.

"Fortune next," Echo said.

I moved a step over. Fortune was at least five-eight, so I stepped into her like I did for Nathaniel. She put her arms around me, and it seemed natural to do the same, as she bent down and I went up on tiptoe to meet her kiss. Our lips touched, a soft kiss like Echo had done, but then Fortune pressed her mouth against mine harder, more insistent, and I responded to it, so that our hands dug into each other's backs, lips and finally tongues exploring, so that when we parted Fortune laughed, excited and nervous.

I was a little breathless, but smiling. "That worked," I said.

"May I try again, after Magda?" Echo asked.

"Sure," I said, and stepped down to the last woman. She was taller, at least five-ten; in the boots she was wearing she had to be six feet. I looked up at her, one hand on my hip.

"You don't like tall women?" she asked.

"I haven't been with enough women to say I have preferences yet, but I think I like shorter. I don't know."

She dropped to her knees so she was gazing up at me, her head at chest height. "Is this better?"

"Yes, actually." I stepped to her, and my arms went around her shoulders easily, like I knew what I was doing, and hers went around my waist. She raised her face up to me, as I lowered mine and her mouth met mine. It was a teasing kiss at first, lips touching and gliding away, as if we were both playing hard to get, and then she slid her hand through my hair and pulled just a little. It made me catch my breath, and she used that little *O* of surprise to slip her tongue inside, and she kissed me eagerly, biting lightly at my lips, and I melted into her kiss the way I would have with any man. We parted with her eyes bled to lion amber, and me smiling a little dazedly.

"I think we have a winner," someone said; I wasn't sure who.

"There's no winner, no losers," I said. "We share well, remember."

Echo came to me. "May I?"

I nodded, and this time she wrapped herself around like she wanted to be there, so that I could feel our breasts pushing against each other, as she kissed me eagerly, hungrily, my tongue running lightly between the delicate points of her fangs. The smaller mouth made French kissing between them more of a challenge. I found myself wondering what her breasts looked like out of the shirt, and just like that I realized I wanted to know. I had a moment to wonder how much of this was bleed-over from the men, but I didn't care. It worked for me, too.

The three of them went to the men to see if it worked for more than just me. Fortune kissed Sin like she was going to climb into him through the kiss. Micah looked just right kissing Echo, because the height matched better. Magda took a knee before Jean-Claude first. He drew her to her feet and they kissed. He had to caution her that she was going to cut her mouth on his fangs if she wasn't careful, but he didn't look unhappy. Fortune left Sin breathless and looking dazed, and went to Dev. There was a lot of laughing in their kissing, but it worked. Echo turned from Micah to Nathaniel and kissed him, but ended by licking the side of his neck until he shivered for her. Magda and Micah weren't sure about each other. She wasn't as sure about Nathaniel. Jean-Claude and Echo were strangely careful of each other, but Fortune went to him smiling and that worked better. Magda and Dev kissed like they were fighting to see who was going to be on top, but it seemed to work for both of them. Fortune seemed to like everyone, and everyone liked her.

Richard never offered to join in, and neither Jean-Claude nor I called him over. He wasn't here enough to be a part of this, and apparently he agreed. It was good to agree. The rest of us were starting to negotiate a time to negotiate for what we might be doing with each other in the bedroom, when my phone rang.

It was Special Agent Brent. "Live event scheduled in one hour; we need you here before that."

"I'm on my way." I hung up and turned to all of my lovers and potential lovers. "I am sorrier than I can say that I have to go, but I have to go."

"You are a police officer, your duty must come first," Magda said.

"We understand duty," Echo said.

"We understand duty all to hell and back," Fortune said.

I realized that they'd all served the Mother of All Darkness as bodyguards, spies, and assassins for hundreds or even thousands of years. I guess that was about as much duty as anyone could ask of a person.

"I guess you do," I said.

"Go, *ma petite*, we will discuss, but await your input for any decisions." I kissed him good-bye, then kissed all my other men good-bye, including Richard.

"Don't I get a good-bye kiss?" Asher asked.

"No," I said.

"Ever again?" he asked, and looked sad, though I knew most of it was like pretend pouting.

"Don't push me tonight, Asher; even you aren't beautiful enough for the shit you pulled today."

He started to protest, and I just held up a hand and said, "Enough."

I wasn't sure what to do with the three women, so I said, "Whether we do good-bye kisses or not, we'll discuss."

"Looking forward to it," Fortune said.

"As am I," Magda said.

Echo blew me a kiss.

And I left to watch a live online zombie sex show, and try to catch the evil bastard that was making it possible. It had been a full day, and the night was shaping up to be the same. Of course, except for the addition of extra women, how was this night any different from so many others?

59

THEY PUT US in one of the conference rooms; I guess Dolph needed his office back. It also gave Brent room to put up what looked like a huge-ass flat-screen TV, but was actually a new monitor, so we didn't have to crowd around the screen of his portable computer. Honestly, I'd have been okay with the smaller monitor. I really didn't need to see the glint of terror in the zombie's eyes quite that clearly, thanks. I think Manning and Gillingham agreed with me.

Unlike most of the films, these cam shows started with an image of the as-yet empty room. It didn't fill the screen like I'd thought it would though, because there was a sidebar of chat. Brent's undercover name was one of thirty screen names that were chatting with the computer tech, and with the other customers. They were giving requests for what they wanted the zombie to do, or to be done to the zombie, and then the monitor name typed, "We have enough requests—let's bring on our star attraction."

A man's voice said, "Open the door and walk into the room." The room's only door opened. It was the blond zombie that had starred in the first film. She was still only as rotted as we'd seen her last, the once beautiful face made partially cadaverous, but they'd changed her funeral clothes to a red nightie and matching stiletto sandals. The zombie did exactly what she was told, taking the first step into the room and stopping. "Close the door behind you, and walk farther into the room." She closed the door and took one extra step. The zombie had to obey him, but there was a mind in there with the soul, so she was making it as defiant as the magic would allow. I cheered the effort, even as it made her more real. It was going to be harder to pretend she was just a zombie, and not a person, and that was going to make watching this worse. Distance, emotional distance, or we were all going to have nightmares.

His next order was, "Walk to the bed," so she had to go all the way in the room now. We couldn't see her eyes, barely any of her face now, because her hair had spilled forward enough to obscure even her profile.

"Turn around and sit on the side of the bed," the man said. He had to be back in the same corner as in the earlier films, but none of him was visible now. He was just a voice.

"Ready when you are, Anita," Brent said.

I'd been briefed; all I had to do was use my necromancy on the zombie on the screen, and on her handler in the corner. I was sure he had a tie to the zombie from the older videos; we were here tonight to see if I could sense more from something happening in real time. It had sounded like a good idea, but suddenly seeing the zombie like this . . . It made her more real, and even more of a victim. Shit.

I'd lowered my shields to try to search the older videos, but this was supposed to be just my necromancy. I opened that part of myself like unclenching a fist, but instead of sending it into a grave, or a cemetery, I aimed it at the zombie I saw on the screen. I don't know what I expected, but nothing happened. It was like my necromancy didn't know where to go, or how to get there.

Gillingham shivered, rubbing her hands up and down her arms, as if she was cold. "Your power is amazing, but it's like it's just filling the room higher and higher, as if we'll all drown in it when you finally fill the room."

"Interesting, I've described really strong lycanthrope energy like that."

"Really?" she said, and started to ask me questions.

"Focus, ladies, you can compare psychic notes later," Manning said.

Gillingham looked embarrassed, but I was at a loss.

"I don't know how to direct my power at the zombie there," I said, pointing.

"Well, she's not really there," Brent said. "She's miles away. Maybe hundreds of miles away."

"So how do I tell my necromancy where to go?" I asked.

"Try touching the screen," Brent said. "That helps some people."

It was worth a try, so I stepped up and touched the screen, over the zombie. I closed my eyes and sent my necromancy through my fingers into the zombie on the screen the same way I'd send my power into the ground to explore a grave, or search a cemetery, or sense for vampires. All the dead belonged to me, all of them, all of them, all of them, even the zombie on the screen, even hundreds of miles away. It was just another zombie. I opened my eyes and found myself staring into the zombie's face from inches away. One eye was still blue, while the other was gray and shriveled along with that side of her face, but it wasn't the rot that made her eyes mesmerizing. It was the terror in them, the helpless fucking terror in them.

I touched those eyes and wanted to help her. I wanted to find her and help her. What he'd done was wrong, it was just wrong, and I wanted to fix it, to fix her, to save her. I prayed, "God help me find her. Help me save her from this."

Her eyes went wide, and I felt the shock of connection. I had her. I could feel it like a thread of power from me to her, because it was her, and to think anything else was lying to myself.

"What did you do just now, Anita?" Brent asked.

"I can feel the zombie, I have her."

"I can feel you through the keyboard and all over my stuff now. Shit. The technician just typed, 'Who are you?' I think he means you."

The man in the corner who was just a voice said, "Lie down on the bed."

"He's typing, 'Who are you?' over and over between taking customer chat," Brent said.

The man who was going to be the zombie's co-star walked into frame. He was young and in great shape, down to washboard abs, which takes a hell of a lot of gym time and nutrition work to get and maintain. If the face matched the body, he could have been a movie star, but he was wearing one of those black leather hoods that covers the whole face except for the mouth. Even the eye-holes had mesh over them so the color and shape of his eyes were lost.

"Shit," I said.

"What is it?" Manning said.

"She's afraid."

"It shows in her eyes," Manning agreed.

I shook my head.

"Can you feel her fear?" Gillingham asked.

I nodded, but it was more than that. I could . . . hear her. "She's praying. She's praying for help. She's praying to be saved."

"You're not a telepath," Gillingham said. "How do you know that?"

"I'm not hearing what she's thinking, I think I'm hearing her prayer, literally hearing her prayer."

"Interesting," Gillingham said.

"We're losing people in the chat and we haven't even started the sex yet. They don't drop out this early, not in numbers like this," Brent said.

"What's happening then?" Manning asked.

"We started at thirty, and now we're down to twenty . . . nineteen."

Gillingham said, "The guy who was monitoring all of it on their end keeps typing *Who are you? Who the hell are you? Why are you here?*"

"I think he's typing for the guy in the corner."

"*Who the hell are you?* he's typing now," Gillingham said.

I could have moved my gaze by inches and read the screen, but I didn't want to look away from her eyes. I could feel her. I didn't want to lose that.

"Uh-oh," Brent said.

"What's uh-oh mean in this context?" Manning asked.

"I just got a private message from the monitor. They're telling me to drop out, they'll refund my money and give me a credit for another session, just drop out now."

"Then just drop out," Manning said.

"If we drop out, Anita's energy stops and my cover is blown, but if we don't drop out, then eventually everyone else will. . . ."

"And my energy will still be coming through so your cover is blown anyway," I said.

"Yes."

"Damned if we do, damned if we don't," Manning said.

"Unfortunately," Brent said, hesitating over the keyboard.

"Then answer his question," Gillingham said.

"What question?" Brent asked.

"Tell him who is here."

"The FBI?" Brent asked.

"Anita Blake, that's the energy he's picking up that's making him frantic."

"You okay with being outed to this nut job?" Brent asked.

"Nut job? Really?" I asked.

"I'll give you the standard vocabulary that'll go in my report later, right now decide whether you want this man, these people to know who you are."

Manning said, "Once they know who you are, then they can find you, Blake. You're all over the news right now."

"Let them find me, that means we have a better chance of catching them."

"Are you sure?" Manning asked.

"We have to decide soon, he's gone past me in the queue. If everyone else drops out first, then we've lost him."

"A bold front is our only chance," Gillingham said.

"Do it," I said.

"Bold it is," Brent said, and typed on the keyboard. In between the repeated "*Who is this?*" he answered, "*Anita Blake, who is this?*"

"Private message again: *What do you want?*"

"Is it too bold to say, your head on a pike?" I asked, still looking into the zombie's eyes.

"That's a little aggressive. The longer we keep him on, the better chance we have of our techs tracing this to its source."

"You mean where they're filming?" I asked.

"If we're lucky, very lucky, yes."

"He's asking the question again, what do you want?"

"Type: *You know what I want.*"

"Really?" Brent said.

"Just type it," Manning said.

I heard the keys click. "Sent," Brent said.

"*No, I don't,* he says."

"Liar, tell him liar," I said.

Brent typed it.

"*We're not breaking any laws with the videos,* he says," Brent read.

"Tell him, not with the videos, but where are you getting your zombies?"

"He says, *We have someone raise them for us.*"

I put my other hand on the corner of the film where he had to be sitting, and I flexed the connection to the zombie and there it was, a line of power flaring so bright. "Tell him, he's lying, he raised the zombie."

"*We'll kill whoever told you,* he typed."

"Anita, try and make the zombie do something that he's not ordering," Gillingham said.

"I can't do that to someone else's zombie, and I sure as hell can't do it over a computer like this."

"Stop saying *can't* and try, damn it. Don't you understand, if he thinks someone ratted them out, they'll start killing people that they suspect."

"Fine, type: Then kill yourself, because your power called to me. You told me you existed."

"Repeat it slower," Brent said.

I repeated it.

It was so long before he replied I thought we'd lost him, but he sent back, "*I thought I could hide.*"

"Tell him, a power as great as his shines out. It attracts the dead and those who work with the dead."

"That's bullshit, right?" Manning asked.

"Yeah, if I hadn't seen the videos I wouldn't have known he existed, but he doesn't know that."

"*I've felt your power, too, Anita*, he says."

"More bullshit," Manning said.

"Maybe not," Gillingham said. "Anita shines bright even to me, but to someone who raises the dead she might come up on their radar."

"It doesn't matter if it's true or not, I just want him to stay on the line so they can trace him," I said.

"*You're trying to keep us on the line so you can trace us*, he says," Brent read.

"Make the zombie do something, Anita," Gillingham said.

"That may make him hang up," I said.

"He's going to hang up soon anyway."

"*I don't believe you felt my energy, Anita. Who told you?*"

"Make the zombie move, Anita."

I said it out loud as I thought it at her, "Walk toward the door."

She swayed.

I repeated it. "Please God, let her hear me."

She took a step toward the door. The man's voice said, "Stop moving."

"Walk," I said, and willed her to do it.

She took another step.

"Stop!" He yelled it, and she obeyed.

To Brent I said, "Type, 'Your power called to me. Did you really think you could do this and I wouldn't know?'"

He typed and read the response, "*How are you doing that? How are you giving it orders?*"

I thought, and prayed, "Talk to me, I'll hear you."

The zombie said, "Ruthie, my name is Ruthie Sylvester."

"Shut up!" he screamed.

"Help me! Oh, God, help me!" she yelled.

"Come on, tell us where you are," Brent whispered.

"Give us a clue," I said.

"Illinois, he took me in Chicago."

He screamed, "Shut up!" To the actor who was standing there waiting for direction, someone offscreen said, "Hit her."

He hit her hard enough that she fell to the floor, but she kept talking. "Melvin's Diner, Trust Bank, Lucky Lady strip club."

The man in the corner rushed out into camera view. Short black hair, trimmed neat, and a hooded sweatshirt with a design on it. He grabbed the zombie's arm and the moment he touched her she stopped talking. I could still feel her energy and his now, but I couldn't hear her in my head. His touching her had put her back under his control. Damn it.

He kept his face turned away, but he spoke to me, not to the zombie when he said, "Anita, I've wanted to meet you."

"Type: We should have coffee sometime and talk."

A voice off camera read back my words to him. He laughed. "A coffee date with Anita Blake, my mother would be so happy."

The screen went blank. I couldn't feel the zombie anymore except as a vague sensation. "I'll know that zombie again when I get close enough to it, but I can't hear her now."

"They cut the feed," Brent said. "They're gone."

"What was all that the zombie was saying?" Gillingham asked.

"Clues," Manning said.

"She was trying to tell us things she'd heard or seen, to help us locate her, I think," Brent said. He typed in what we could remember, and then went back over the screen capture of the video for any place in Illinois that had a Trust Bank, Melvin's Diner, and a Lucky Lady strip club.

"Trust Bank is a Midwest chain, that's not helpful. There are about twenty Melvin's or Mel's Diners across the country, but there's only one Lucky Lady strip club. Holy shit! We may know what city they're in!"

I prayed that he was right, and that we found them soon, and I said thank you, because when God lets you hear the prayers of the dead, well, He's pulling out some serious stops for you. I was grateful. I'd be even more grateful when we found Ruthie Sylvester and set her soul free, set all the souls free that we'd seen imprisoned on the videos. Then I wanted the animator, or voodoo priest, or whatever the fuck he called himself punished to the full extent the law allowed. If we could prove that he'd killed any of the girls so he could trap their souls at the moment of death, then it was an automatic death sentence, because it would fall under the magical malfeasance acts. If someone killed with magic or for magical purposes, they were treated like rogue vampires or shapeshifters. It was the only time a warrant of execution could be issued specifically for a live human being. I hoped we proved it. I didn't have to be the one to pull the trigger on him, but for this, he needed killing. I'd have apologized to God about that whole vengeful thing, but I'd read the Old Testament; I was pretty sure He'd be okay if we helped Him out with that whole "Vengeance is mine saith the Lord," just this once. I felt that little pulse that I got sometimes when I prayed; it usually meant that I'd get what I asked for, or at least He was listening. Holy Wrath of God, Batman, your ass was going to be ours soon, you soul-trapping son of a bitch.

60

THREE DAYS LATER I was standing in the room where they'd filmed the videos. It was really half a room, with the other half set up with a box of props and even a makeup area, as if the zombies, or their customers, really cared that much. I stood looking down at the bed that had been the main prop for all that horror and thought aloud, "Where are you, you son of a bitch?" Apparently, I said it out loud.

"Did you say something, Marshal?" Gillingham was sitting at the mirrored makeup area in her Windbreaker with FBI emblazoned on it, but then I was in my U.S. Marshal's version of the same. We were both wearing our body armor, which was standard for most fieldwork.

"Sorry, talking more to myself, just wondering where the hell our bad guy is."

"We caught a lot of bad guys," she said, and turned around to face me. She looked more herself somehow in the dark pants and boots than she had in the costume conservative skirt outfit. The only thing still the same was the upper layer of her hair being held back by a barrette, and the lack of makeup, but that part was pretty standard for most female operatives in the field.

"We caught a lot of the guys helping make the videos, but they swear they didn't know if he trapped the soul at the moment of death, which means they didn't think they were doing anything illegal."

"If they didn't know the zombies might be murder victims then they weren't."

"See, that's the thing, regular zombies always kill their murderer. They are unreasoning, almost unstoppable killing machines until they strangle or tear apart the person who murdered them, but these were as pliable as a normal zombie."

"And you have no idea why," she said.

"No, not really. It's almost as if the soul going into them so soon after death prevented the normal homicidal fixation to kick in."

"More's the pity," she said.

"Yeah, that would have been a short, unpleasant career for him. Instead he's still out there somewhere able to start all this over, or worse."

"How worse?"

"He could make the perfect sex slave if he knows how to give control over to a customer the way Dominga Salvador did. Hell, I know how to bind a zombie to a client so they can control it for a day or two. With the soul intact and never coming out, the zombie might be able to pass for human indefinitely."

"Do you honestly believe that no one would notice it was the undead?"

I thought about Thomas Warrington. "If you could keep the mind and body from ever rotting, and retain the personality, hell, Teresa, the zombie itself might not know it was dead."

"But it would never age, eventually someone would notice that," she said.

"That could take decades," I said.

"Mother of God." She whispered it and crossed herself. Funny what habits stay with us in times of stress.

The FBI hostage rescue unit, HRU, had been the ones that raided the place once everyone figured out where it was, because they were closer, and though in the movies it would have been just our little band of agents and psychics, in real life you didn't make potential hostages wait eight hours for rescue, or give the bad guys an eight-hour head start on destroying evidence and fleeing the country. So Manning, Brent, Gillingham, Larry, and I had come late to the party.

They'd found the zombies, including Ruthie Sylvester, in the basement, lying in a heap like someone had swept the garbage up in the center of the room, except this center had been an altar. I'd only seen pictures of the zombies piled up, but they'd left the broken shards of pottery and glass scattered around the bodies, and the chalk drawings that covered the floor and the walls were still there, so that there was only a narrow walkway through it all. The drawings were verve symbols meant to draw and keep power in a place. It was the inner sanctum of a voodoo priest, or priestess, and it was damn near identical to the setup that Dominga Salvador had had almost seven years ago in her basement in St. Louis. She had had extra rooms off of her altar room though, and they had contained more of her creations. She'd learned how to take dead flesh and melt it together like wet clay and make monsters. She'd used human and animal zombie remains so it had been particularly horror-show worthy. The practitioner in New Mexico who could do it had used only human parts, so his haunted me more, but I was still glad that the new guy couldn't do it.

They'd brought in a voodoo expert, who was still here when we arrived. I'd asked him if the basement setup had to be that way, or was there room for variation. He said there was room for variation, but he wasn't a follower of voodoo, only an academic, so I didn't trust him to have real world knowledge, because he didn't.

I'd ask Manny when I got back home. He'd know. I couldn't use anything he gave me in court, but the information might help me figure out if having the verve downstairs so close to the same arrangement as Dominga's was part of how this awful spell was done. Did that mean they had to kill the girls in that room and capture their souls right there? If it did, then the guys in custody were lying, because you'd notice if living girls went downstairs, but zombies came back up. Or was everything below so he could make the bottles that captured the soul? If that was true, then the other men and one woman we had in custody might honestly not have realized they were part of a murder conspiracy. I just didn't know enough, and the FBI expert wasn't sure enough to testify in court, so unless we could prove they knew, they actually hadn't broken any laws. We might have to let them go. I didn't want to do that. Hell, he wasn't even sure you had to capture the soul at the instant of death. But did we really believe that they'd just waited for the right type of natural death to occur so they'd get a nice-looking corpse? No, but we couldn't prove they hadn't done just that. Damn it!

"Why don't any of the files on Dominga Salvador show the verve like we have here?" Gillingham asked.

"I told you, she had to literally whitewash everything and destroy her creations when she realized she was going to be raided by the cops."

"So we only have your word for it looking identical to this."

"Yeah, as your boss keeps pointing out."

"I'm sorry for that. Jarvis is usually really excited about meeting new psychic talents."

"I think he likes meeting new bright and shiny straight-out-of-the-academy talent, because you're still willing to drink the FBI-flavored Kool-Aid. I'm a little past waving the company flag and saying, go, team."

"I think I've been insulted," she said, but smiled to take the sting out of it.

"It's not your fault that Jarvis recruited you for his pet program when you were young and impressionable. I remember being a rookie and thinking I could save the world."

"You don't believe you can save the world anymore, Anita?"

"No, Teresa, I don't. Some nights just saving myself takes everything I got."

The door opened and Very Special Agent Jarvis walked through. He was tall, athletically thin, with dark hair cut short and neatly, with eyes that seemed to see everything and approve of maybe half of it; the rest he distrusted completely. I fell into the half of the world he distrusted.

"When are you going home, Marshal Blake?"

"When I feel that I've got no more to contribute here, Special Agent Jarvis."

His face made that little moue like he'd tasted something sour. "I think you've given us all the information that you have to offer."

"Doesn't it bother you that he's still out there?"

"Of course."

"Then why do you keep trying to give me the bum's rush, when I'm probably the best you have at dealing with the undead, which is his specialty?"

"I have one of the most powerful touch clairvoyants to come down the pike in a decade, all she has to do is find something he's touched."

"Touched often," I said.

He nodded. "I grant you that."

"He took everything, Jarvis. Beck can't find any common item that belonged to our missing man," Gillingham said.

"I can't believe we don't even have a name," I said.

"Sir, he's just sir," Gillingham said.

"It's like he treated them all as if he were their dominant and they were all submissive to him. He was on a serious power trip."

"No one will argue with that," Jarvis said.

"Wait, did you say your clairvoyant is trying to find common items to touch?"

"Yes."

"What about the zombies he made?"

"We tried that, but she got the impressions from the bodies themselves. Their lives, not his."

"Beck was hysterical for hours after that," Gillingham added.

"No need to overshare, Agent," Jarvis said.

"Sorry, sir."

"Damn it, we can't lose him like this."

"They say he took one zombie with him, the most lifelike. He only let her do two films with actors, and he never took her soul out and let her rot. She was special to him, they all agree on that," Gillingham said.

"Do we have the videos of her?" I asked.

"Yes, they weren't put out online, but they have them."

"Do we have a still frame for a picture?" I asked.

"Yes."

"If she was special to him, maybe he knew her when she was alive?"

"We do know our job, Marshal."

"Sorry, I'm just brainstorming."

"Well, we don't really need your brainstorming, we're pretty good at it ourselves here at the FBI."

"Why don't you like me, Jarvis?"

He looked startled. "I don't dislike you, Blake."

"I didn't ask that, I asked why don't you like me?"

"I heard you were direct."

"Yeah, now are you going to answer the question?"

"You are uncontrollable. Your powers seem to have grown exponentially and no one knows what the limit of that power is, or if you have limits to your necromancy. You have your uses for helping the common good and keeping the peace, but your gift has been misused for centuries. Necromancers always seem to be creating armies of the undead and trying to conquer countries."

"Actually, everyone says that, but I can't find a single historical account of it really happening; can you?"

He was caught off guard for a moment, but he recovered his surety and his prejudice rapidly. "I don't have to debate with you, Marshal. You can go home and leave things in our capable hands."

"You mean in the hands of people you can control, with talents that don't scare you."

"The man we're chasing, this Sir, is a necromancer like you. Will you argue that he's not evil?"

"He's evil, but he's not necessarily a necromancer. He could just be a powerful voodoo practitioner. I hesitate to call him a priest, because that implies followers and I think he's solitary."

"His powers are still over the dead and he has abused them."

"I don't abuse my powers."

"You raise historical figures for academics to question. You raise families' lost ones so they can cry at the grave and ask forgiveness. You raise people from the dead over disputed wills and grand jury testimony. You disturb the dead for money, Marshal Blake; I think that is an abuse of power."

"So you think the touch clairvoyants working in the major museums worldwide to help with antiquities are abusing their power?"

"No, that is a good career path for the talent."

"So it's just the ability to work with the dead that you don't like."

"I have yet to meet anyone who deals in your brand of psychic gifts who isn't mad, or a charlatan that can barely call a shambling corpse from the grave."

"If they can call the dead they're not a charlatan, they just aren't powerful," I said.

"Be that as it may, I haven't found the more powerful animators to be cooperative in the way that makes a team player."

I laughed. "Well, we are a solitary bunch, I'll grant you that, but part of that is that people don't like you when you can raise the dead. They're afraid of you, and after a while you just want to be left alone rather than having people making the sign against evil behind your back, or to your face."

"You're saying I'm prejudiced?"

"Yes, I am."

"Perhaps, but what you did in Colorado just months ago . . . Blake, you did raise an army of the undead. You raised every corpse in the ground in the Boulder area, and found some dead hikers we didn't even know how to find. They dropped dead in their tracks when you made the magic go away at the end. The local PD closed three missing person cases that way."

"I'm glad I could give the family closure," I said.

"We've managed to keep it quiet that it was all you, but people put pictures of the shambling dead, hundreds of them, up on YouTube. The government told everyone that was part of the disease that was rotting people, but you know and I know it was you, all you."

"Actually it wasn't all me, it was another ancient vampire who had talent with the dead."

"That's another thing I don't like about necromancers: You can kill them, but that doesn't always stop them."

"Treat necromancers like master vampires, Jarvis. Take the head and heart, burn all of it, and scatter the ashes in three different bodies of water."

"Are you really saying that's what you want done at your death?"

"It's in my will, so yeah," I said.

He studied me for a minute. "You're afraid you'll come back."

"Yeah, I am."

"You're marrying a vampire, why don't you want to come back?"

"Because the only necromancers I've seen come back aren't vampires, they're just super-killing zombies, and I don't want that."

"You know you're a monster, don't you?" he said.

Gillingham said, "Agent Jarvis!" like he'd shocked her.

"I'm outta here. At least in St. Louis they're more open-minded than this."

"I'm open-minded, Blake, I just think you're dangerous, more dangerous than anyone knows. Maybe more dangerous than you know."

I shook my head, and said, "Bye, Teresa, I hope you don't drink too much of this man's Kool-Aid."

She made a point of shaking my hand; good for her. I hunted up Manning and Brent to say good-bye and good luck. They did show me good still-frame pictures of the one zombie that "Sir" took with him.

She was dark complected, maybe Hispanic, maybe Greek, or southern Italian like our missing bad guy. She was pretty, with long dark hair and brown eyes that were terrified in every picture.

I said good-bye to all the agents in sight that I wanted to talk to. Larry was staying on with the rest of the Kool-Aid squad, but he apologized for Jarvis and seemed to mean it. I wished them all happy hunting and left for the airport. It was time for me to go home.

61

I'D LEFT MY SUV at airport parking, because I hadn't had any idea how long I'd be out of state. The men in my life had tried picking me up from the airport for a while, but it only worked if I had a set schedule. Crime-fighting was hard to schedule, but I didn't mind as I drove home from the airport in the soft spring dark, or was that early-summer dark? May was one of those months that could be either in St. Louis, late-summer cool or almost midsummer hot. The calendar could say summer started at some arbitrary astronomical event, but the weather really got the last vote.

My phone rang and the Bluetooth headset actually worked again; I don't know why that kept surprising me. "Hello, Blake here."

"Anita, it's Manny."

"Hey, what's up?"

"I hate to ask, but Connie and Tomas went to pick up her dress and Tomas's tuxedo from the bridal shop, and now Connie's car won't start. I've asked everybody I can think of to go get them."

"They can't call AAA?" I asked.

"Tomas has to be on a bus for State tonight."

There was a time in my life when I wouldn't have understood how important that was, but that was before Sin got into sports, and I learned that colleges started scouting as early as junior high. "Okay, tell me where they are and I'll make sure Tomas is on the bus."

"Oh, Anita, you saved my life. Seriously, Rosita will kill me; I wasn't supposed to work tonight."

"I take it Bert persuaded you otherwise."

"I have one kid in college and a big wedding to pay for; Bert didn't have to persuade very hard. But I am covered in animal blood, and if I get any of it on the wedding clothes at this late date Rosita and Connie will both kill me."

I laughed. "Where are the bride-to-be and Tomas?"

He gave me the address for Pearls of Happiness Bridal. I made him repeat the name, hoping I'd misheard.

"I know the area, they've got an old cemetery near there. I'll make sure the clothes arrive unstained."

"Thank you, Anita, I owe you."

"You do, but Rosita is going to give me all sorts of wedding info about caterers and things, so maybe it will all even out."

"Rosita and I married in her mother's backyard, but for our eldest daughter's wedding it had to be the big deal."

"Rosita seems happier than I've ever heard her."

"She's talking about starting a wedding coordinator business, can you believe it, my Rosita?"

"Tomas is thirteen; she's probably seeing her days as a stay-at-home mom ending."

"But a new business beginning just as I'm thinking of retiring?"

"I didn't know you were thinking of retiring, Manny."

"Rosita and I had always planned for it when I was sixty, less than five years away."

"Maybe she'll go to work and you can be a stay-at-home dad for Tomas's high school years."

"Bite your tongue," he said, "and thank you for the rescue."

"No problem, Manny." We hung up and I headed for the bridal shop. I was probably going to have to start thinking about dresses myself soon. God, I hated to shop, and I shuddered at the thought of what kind of dress Jean-Claude would prefer for me. I really hoped he was joking about having crowns made for our wedding, but I was pretty sure he was serious.

I did a group text at a long light, letting them know I was on the ground, and had to rescue Manny's kids, and that I loved them. I got love back from everyone but Jean-Claude, and he might already be onstage at Guilty Pleasures. He was just announcing acts, not actually dancing tonight, but he still turned his phone off so it wouldn't disturb the atmosphere he was creating for the customers, and yes, that last was his phrasing, not mine.

The last time I'd seen Connie and Tomas had been the company picnic for Animators Inc. last year. Manny had warned me that his son had grown four inches since then, so I was prepared to not recognize Tomas, but Connie was twenty-five. I knew what she looked like, but I couldn't remember what kind of car she drove. Damn, I should have asked.

I called Manny back, and asked. "Silver Chevy Sonic, and I'll send you both their cell phone numbers just in case. I'm about to have to turn my phone off for the ceremony."

"It's okay, Manny, I got this." He thanked me again, and we hung up.

I had no idea what a Chevy Sonic looked like, but rather than ask, when I stopped at a red light, I Googled the car and there were all sorts of pictures of it. It was a smallish, midsize car and sort of roundish. I was not one of those cops that could rattle off car makes and models, or give a great description of a car from a crime scene. If there was an animal involved, that I could describe like gangbusters, but cars puzzled me.

Connie's car was in the parking lot. She'd even parked under a light, and close to the bridal shop, whose bright windows were advertising prom dresses more than anything else. I guess it was that time of year. It was brightly lit and neither of Manny's kids were in sight.

I parked beside the car, got out, and peeked inside it. There was a large garment bag on a hanger laid carefully on the backseat. I guess Connie hadn't wanted to risk wrinkling her wedding dress. I didn't blame her. There were two small garment bags hanging up. One was probably Tomas's tux. No idea what the other smaller bag was, some mysterious wedding thing that I'd probably be learning about soon enough.

Maybe they'd gone back into Pearls of Happiness, though I hated the name enough to never go near it. But if there wasn't a Combat Bride shop I'd probably go someplace equally saccharine. They had just gone back in to call AAA, though they both had cell phones. I took a deep breath, let it out slow, and tried to tell the tight feeling in my gut that they'd just gone back inside the shop for some reason. Being a cop of any flavor tended to make you paranoid. The paranoia wasn't always right.

I went to the bridal shop, telling myself that they'd be there. Maybe they had to use the bathroom? It didn't have to be something bad. I just needed to tell the cop part of me to lighten up. It was so bright inside the shop that it almost hurt after being out in the dark parking lot.

A woman in a nice but conservative black dress hurried forward, smiling. "Hello, I'm Anne, welcome to Pearls of Happiness, we're here for all your bridal needs, how may I help you tonight?"

I wondered if I'd looked young enough, would the slogan have been "for all your prom needs"? "Hi, Anne, I'm looking for Connie and Tomas Rodriguez; her car broke down and they called me to help out."

"Oh, yes, Connie did come in and say something like that. She was going to wait for a friend, and her brother had some kind of important sports thing at school."

I forced myself to smile wider. "Yes, Tomas is going to State. In fact, I need to get him to his bus ASAP, so if you could just tell them I'm here."

She frowned and looked flustered. "They went back out to get the bridal gown; Connie didn't want to leave it in the car, you know how brides are."

I didn't actually, but I nodded and smiled, and said, "The dress is in the car still, but Connie and Tomas aren't in the parking lot."

"They're probably sitting in the car," she said.

"I checked the car, that's how I know her dress is on the backseat and two other garment bags are hanging up."

"And they're not in the car?" she asked.

I took a deep calming breath. "No, Anne, they're not, and they're not in here?"

"No, and"—she looked up at a wall clock—"oh my, they went out to get the dress half an hour ago. You're sure they aren't out there somewhere?"

"I'm sure they're out there somewhere, Anne, because they're not in here, but they aren't in the parking lot." I resisted the urge to ask why she hadn't checked on them. She was a civilian, a soft, fluffy, easily flustered civilian, and it wasn't her job to serve and protect, or even to not be a fucking useless . . . It was my nerves talking. I would have been totally useless at her job here with all the sequined dresses and demanding brides; we all have our strengths. I told myself that as I dialed Connie's cell phone.

I prayed, "Please let them have called a friend, her fiancé, anything. Let me have made this trip for nothing, just as long as they're all right."

Connie's phone went to voice mail. I didn't leave a message. I hung up and called Tomas. "Come on, come on, pick up, pick up."

Anne the saleslady had picked up my anxiety by now and was hovering worriedly around me. I walked away farther into the shop for some privacy and because my nerves were enough without hers. The one thing I didn't like about the headset was that ambient noise could make it harder to hear.

I left a message this time. "Tomas, this is Anita Blake. I'm here to see you get to the bus for State. Where are you and Connie?"

I called Connie's phone back. Voice mail again, damn it. "Connie, this is Anita Blake, Manny sent me to get you guys. I'm at the bridal shop, where are you?"

I didn't want to call Manny yet. There could be logical, safe explanations, but part of me knew that if Connie was so worried about her wedding dress that she didn't want it left in the car for a few minutes, she would not have walked off and left it in the car like this. My Spidey-sense had been tingling since I found the empty car. Sometimes it's not paranoia; it's just the truth.

My phone rang; it was Connie's number. I hit the button on the earpiece. "Connie, where are you guys?"

"I'm sorry, Anita, Consuela can't come to the phone right now." It was a man's voice. It seemed familiar.

"Why can't Connie come to the phone?" I asked.

"She's a little tied up, or should I say duct-taped."

"Where's Tomas?"

"He's nearby, but I wanted to talk to my sister alone." I could hear that he was in a car, driving. They weren't that far yet. Maybe.

"Sister. Manny and Rosita only have one son."

"That's right, Manny and Rosita only have one son, and two beautiful daughters," he said.

I didn't like the way he emphasized *beautiful*, but I also knew the phrasing about Manny and Rosita was important to him. I just didn't know why. He hadn't told me not to contact the police. Thanks to being on the headset I could text and he wouldn't hear anything, like the text alert noise, not if I turned off my sounds. I knew how to do that, yay! I texted Zerbrowski while I kept trying to think of ways to keep the familiar voice talking. As long as he was talking he couldn't hurt them, or that's what I told myself.

The text to Zerbrowski was simple: "Manny's daughter & son kidnapped. I'm talking on phone with the kidnapper."

"So how can you be their brother, if they only have three kids?" I asked.

"Half-brother," he said.

Zerbrowski texted back: "where are you?"

I got the address from Anne the saleslady.

He texted that a car was on its way to my location now.

I texted back: "I don't know if lights & sirens will spook him, or help?"

"I'll make it a silent run," he texted.

I trusted his judgment. I went back to talking to the nut job on the phone, and suddenly I knew the voice. Brent had called him a nut job just three days ago during the live feed. My pulse was in my throat, and I had to breathe carefully for it not to show in my voice. "So you're Manny's son from a different mother."

"Yes, did he tell you about me?"

I debated on what to say, and finally chose truth; I didn't always lie well enough. "No, but I know he was wild when he was young, and Rosita never sowed any wild oats."

"She looks so dull and ordinary. How could he have chosen her over the Señora?"

"Señora?" I made it a question.

"The Señora—don't you know who I am, Anita? Don't you know who my mama was?"

I had one of those moments when things click into place. "Oh holy shit, Dominga Salvador doesn't have two nephews, she has a nephew and a son. That's why you called yourself sir, like Señora."

He laughed. "Very good. Yes, I felt like an outsider all my life. My brother, mother, and father all seemed so ordinary. I got straight A's, excelled at track, got a scholarship to college, and my brother just failed over and over. I was never like my family, and then I found out why. My mother wasn't my mother, my father not my father, my brother only my cousin. It was a revelation, Anita, a revelation that changed my life."

"It's always good to figure out where you belong," I said, because I couldn't think of what to say.

A uniformed officer was coming through the door of the bridal shop. I had my badge visible. I texted, "I'm on phone with kidnapper. Trying to keep him talking." and showed it to the officer.

He nodded, and used a notepad that Anne brought him to write, "More units en route."

More cops were coming. I just had to figure out a way to get information out of the kidnapper that would help us locate them. "My mother was dead, but my father wasn't. He had a nice family; they looked happy."

I didn't like him using the past tense. "You came to St. Louis and found Manny, and have been watching him."

"I saw his daughters and son; by rights they should have been my siblings. I could have been their older brother. I could have helped them, and my papa could have taught me how to raise the dead, but instead he taught you. He taught you everything he was supposed to teach me."

"It was a job; I've taught new animators, too."

"No!" He shouted it. "Don't belittle what my father taught you."

"I'm not belittling it, just saying that Manny and I are work friends. He doesn't think of me as another daughter."

"But he taught you, and my mother saw the greatness in you, Anita. I found people who would talk to me about the Señora. They said she wanted you to meet me. Said we'd have powerful babies together."

"Manny told me that, just like Dominga wanted to have a baby with him, because it would be powerful."

"And I am powerful."

"Dominga didn't tell Manny she got pregnant."

"You don't know that."

"I do, because I know Manny; if he'd known he had a son he'd have tried to be in your life in some way."

"He didn't want me."

"I swear to you that Manny would have loved you if he had known." In my head I thought about him describing one of the nephews as just wrong from the beginning, and then I realized the nephew who was "wrong" wasn't the one Dominga had wanted me to breed with; it was the good nephew.

"He rejected his true power when he left the Señora, and me with it."

"He described you as a polite, good boy, Max."

"He mentioned me?"

"Yeah, that the other nephew Artie was a screw-up, but you were great."

"Arturo fails at everything, he has no ambition."

"You have plenty of ambition, don't you, Max?"

"I do, but I go by my full name, Anita. If my father really talked of me, then tell me my real name."

"Maximiliano," I said.

He laughed again, but it held a brittle edge to it now, as if the sound could break like glass if you hit it too hard. It was the kind of laugh that would eventually start gibbering in corners. I wanted Connie and Tomas away from him before that happened.

"Yes, yes, I am Maximiliano."

I wanted to ask him what happened with college, and that scholarship? I wanted to know how the good boy, Max, got to be the monster who tortured souls, but I wanted him to keep talking. There were more police now. Anne had pointed out Connie's car. They'd be looking for clues, and someone in a suit had written on the notepad, "Try to find out where he's taking them."

I wrote back, "How?"

He made some suggestions and I tried. "So where are you, Connie, and Tomas going tonight?"

"Why, so the police can find them in time?"

I did not like his "find them in time" at all. "I can't meet you for that coffee date if I don't know where you are."

He was quiet for a few breaths. I thought I heard someone else make a noise. It was all I could do not to ask if it was Connie, but I didn't want him to know I could hear anything over the phone. I was afraid he'd hang up.

The detective in the suit wrote, "Do not agree to meet with him!"

I turned away from him. If he'd give me a location I could find him and find the kids. Manny's kids. Connie was almost my age, but she was still his kid.

The detective grabbed my arm and waved the note in my face. I jerked free of his hand and waved my badge back at him. "You said it yourself, Maximiliano; the Señora, your mother, wanted you and me to hook up. I've seen your zombies, they're amazing. We could do amazing, scary stuff together."

"I'm not crazy, or stupid, Anita." He sounded angry now.

"I know that."

"No, you don't. You think I'm crazy like my real mama."

"I thought she was evil, more than crazy," I said.

He laughed then. "That was honest."

"Meet with me, Maximiliano, and I will be so honest it'll blow you away."

"Oh, we're here," he said. The engine on the car turned off. I heard the door open on his car, and I think I heard him step on gravel. I know I heard someone trying to scream through a gag. It sounded like a woman. "You can both scream for me, Consuela. She was my fiancée once, but she left me. Now she's mine forever."

Connie was doing her best to scream through whatever was on her mouth, duct tape he'd said. Whatever she was seeing was scaring the hell out of her.

"I've got to go, Anita, my sister is being difficult, but before the sun comes up she'll be easy, because she'll do exactly what I tell her to do. Thanks to you I lost a lot of money, but Consuela will be perfect for a client who wanted his own slave. He doesn't even have to be here for the ceremony, he just needs to hold the bottle that contains her soul, like a magic ring for a genie."

My mouth was dry, but I said, "How did you get around the fact that murdered zombies attack their murderers?"

"The soul, Anita, the personality; people are so conflicted about violence. Pure zombies aren't conflicted at all, but add the soul back in and they're just as fucked up as the rest of us. I'm going to sell my sister to a very rich man as his slave forever. I don't know if I'll just kill my brother, or cripple him. Either way, my father will never forget me again."

"Maximiliano, don't do this, don't hurt them."

"Would you let me fuck you to save them, Anita?"

"Sure," I said.

He laughed again, and I heard Connie making helpless noises through the gag. It sounded like he was dragging her over gravel and then weeds, or something. "I've got to go, Anita, I have people to kill, souls to steal. You know I haven't found a buyer for a teenage boy, but I'm betting that one that was completely obedient to the customer's every whim, well, the right person would pay handsomely for that, don't you think, Anita?"

"I'm not joking, Maximiliano. Let's hook up. Let's fuck, just like your mother wanted."

"Rumor says you killed the Señora, is that true, Anita?"

"Never believe the rumors," I said.

"Oh, I hope they are true, because if they are then I'll give you a chance to see which of us is more powerful."

"More powerful how? How do we prove that?"

"First, find me before I finish the ceremony and there's no sister left to save, though maybe I'll fuck her first, before I kill her; that would give you more time to find me."

I fought the urge to threaten him, and tried for calm. "This is your last chance to do what the Señora wanted you to do, Maximiliano."

"I saw the videos from Colorado, Anita. More than giving my mama powerful grandchildren, I want to see which of us is the better necromancer."

"Fine, let's go, let's do it, just tell me where you are."

"Think about what I want, Anita, and you'll know there are only a limited number of places I could have driven in this amount of time that will give us the arena to test ourselves."

"I don't know what you mean."

"If you don't figure it out, then I kill them, sell at least her, and leave town a very rich man. I'll set up shop in a country that is a little friendlier to me and doesn't have extradition with America."

"Maximiliano, tell me how you do it. How do you capture the soul?"

"Come and watch," and then he said something harsh in Spanish. "The boy has undone his bonds and found the trunk release. Stupid boy." The gunshot was so loud I was deaf in one ear for a minute.

"Fuck, what did you do?"

"He ran, what else could I do, Anita?"

Connie was screaming as loud and long as she could through the gag. He wasn't worried about the noise; fuck!

"If Tomas dies, you die. If you touch Connie, I will cut your dick off and gag you with it."

"Oh, sticks and stones, Anita, sticks and stones."

"Tell me where you are, you son of a bitch, and I'll prove to you that I never make an idle threat."

"Find me, and then we'll see who raises what." The phone went dead.

I screamed my rage loud and wordless. If he'd been in front of me in that moment I'd have killed him, cops or no cops.

62

I HAD TO call Manny and tell him about Connie and Tomas. I started with just them being hostages, without going into details. I figured him knowing he had a long-lost son with Dominga Salvador could wait until his kids were safe, or until I saw him in person. Some things you don't want to try to explain over the phone.

"I need you to talk to the phone company and waive your rights to the phone records, so we don't have to get a warrant for them to use Tomas's phone's GPS to locate him and Connie."

"We're still paying for Connie's phone, too. Does that help?"

"Shit yes, I know he has her phone, because I was talking on it." I turned to Sergeant Hudson, who wasn't much bigger than I was, with a neat dark mustache to match the hair hidden under his helmet. He was the smallest man on his unit now, but they all still acted as if he were about eight feet tall and would hurt them if they fucked up. Hudson and I weren't buddies, but we respected each other, and I'll take respect over being liked any day of the week. He let me train with his team once a month to keep me from screwing up too badly. That he let me near his men at all was the compliment. He talked to all his guys like that.

"Manny, the father, is paying for his daughter's phone; if he waives his rights we don't need a warrant for the GPS records."

"Great, did you hear that?" He spoke into a phone that he'd been using to try to get the GPS location for either of the kids' phones. They wanted to help, but legally we needed a warrant . . . but Manny could waive his rights since it was his account and not Connie's.

It took us holding the phones next to each other and Manny giving some account information, but it was done. Hudson listened to his end of the phone for a few seconds. "They'll call us back in ten minutes tops with the phone's location."

"Perfect," I said, "now just one more warrant in hand and we're good to go."

"Anita, what's happening?" Manny asked on my phone. I told him.

"While we wait for the GPS I need to ask your voodoo expertise."

"I can't think, Anita."

"How complicated would the spell be to capture a soul? I mean, how long would it take?"

"I only know the theory of the spell; I had left her long before she came up with that piece of evil."

"I know, but you know way more voodoo than I do, Manny. I need to know a time frame, and I need to know it now."

"What aren't you telling me, Anita?"

"Dominga's nephew Max is the bad guy. He's taken over where Dominga left off on the zombie slaves."

"Why did he take Connie and Tomas?"

"I think Tomas was incidental, wrong place, wrong time."

"Oh God, oh God, you think he's going to do that to Connie."

"He's threatening it."

"Why? Why after all this time?"

"How much time do we have to find her? I need you to think, Manny."

"My kids are missing."

"And the more information we have, the better the odds for bringing them back safe and sound."

"All right, all right, if he has to make a container to house the soul, it will take weeks."

"Assume he has a container."

"He'll have to draw symbols, verve, and if he's a true believer he'll have to persuade the loa to ride him, or to ride the victim."

"I don't think he's a true believer," I said.

"An hour, maybe. You say he had verve all over his altar area like Dominga did."

"Yes," I said.

"He'll be careful to draw the verve then, because Dominga believed very much that the symbols helped call power and protect her. If he draws all the symbology, then at least an hour, maybe a little more. Does that help?"

"Yes, it does."

"I'm on my way to the bridal shop now."

"Go to Rosita, stay with her."

"No."

"All right, but I may roll out before you get here if we have a target."

"Save my kids, Anita."

"I'll do my best."

"I know you will."

What else was there to say? We hung up.

63

THE GPS ON Connie's phone and Tomas's phone led us to the same cemetery. I expected that, but what I didn't expect was that GPS knew which crypt the phones were in. That didn't guarantee that they were still with their phones, but it was our best bet. If they weren't with their phones we had to search two acres of graveyard, including about twenty crypts, one at a time, like making entry on a block of apartments. So we assumed they were in the crypt with their phones; it gave us a place to start, and a plan. The "we" wasn't Zerbrowski and RPIT; it was our local SWAT. A lot of preternatural branch marshals had been forced on SWAT across the country for no-announce warrants, which all warrants of execution were, but a few of us had proven ourselves enough to be invited to train with them, and were allowed to go out with the team. Most of the marshals who had been invited to play with SWAT hadn't been able to keep the training up. It wasn't the weapons practice—that was the easy part—it was the physical prerequisites, and gym time, that most of them failed. Honestly, if I hadn't been more than human I might not have made all of them either.

"This will be my first assault on a crypt," Killian said, smiling and tense in the dark as we stood behind the Lenco Bear Cat. They could call it an armored rescue vehicle if they wanted to, but it always looked big, black, slightly sinister, and very military. It could take heavy rifle fire and protect the men inside it, or even hiding behind it.

"If this is your first crypt, you haven't been hanging around with me enough," I said.

"Yeah, Blake takes you to the best places," Hill said.

In the movies you can always see everyone's face on SWAT, but in reality the helmets and gear hide nearly everything. I knew Killian was blond and pale Irish, and that Hill was dark and middle-of-America-not-from-anywhere ethnic, but all I could tell suited up in the spring dark was that Killian was a few inches taller than me, and Hill was much taller. Most of the men standing in the dark with us were taller than average, and then you had Saville, who even towered over these guys. He was darkly African American, but again I only knew that because I knew him. We were all generic in our SWAT gear, except for height and size.

"Will the ram work on a crypt door?" Saville asked. If we'd been doing a normal entry he'd have been using the ram to bust in the door.

"I'm not sure," I said.

Hermes said, "We brought stuff that will help us knock louder if we need to." He was tall, dark, and I guess handsome under all the gear. His wife thought so. I knew that from the time she made a point of meeting me, after I helped save his life but broke his leg in the process.

"We have about five minutes to figure out which dynamic entry we're making," Montague—Monty—said.

Another thing they get wrong in most movies is how much time you wait before you rush in. And you don't really "rush" in; you go in with a plan. Our plan was up on the tallest hill they could find with Sergeant Hudson and Sutton, their sniper. They were going to use the tech on Sutton's gear to see what they thought of the door. There were maps of the cemetery, but not specifics of the crypts and what their doors were constructed of; the way we got to "knock" and enter depended on the kind of door. It might be better to use small explosives on the lock than to blow the door open, because the stone construction of the crypt meant we couldn't see inside with infrared, so we didn't know where the hostages were standing. It would suck to blow a hole in Manny's kids because they were on top of the door we blew. We were waiting for more intel, as in intelligence, so we could go in smart. Slow is steady. Steady is smooth. Smooth is fast. Fast is deadly. I knew it was true, but if I hadn't had the rest of the team to keep me steady, I might have rushed in, because it was Connie and Tomas. I'd known them since Connie was Tomas's age and he was a toddler. I didn't want to go back to Manny with anything other than a win on this one.

"If Blake were the size of Saville the ram would work," Monty said. He was the same size and build as Hermes, so only Hermes's slightly broader shoulders let you know who was who, unless you saw the nameplate, or knew how they carried their gear. I knew, because I'd been training with them at least once a month for a year. They'd seen what my more than human speed and strength could do on the tests they had to pass to keep their place on the team.

"I've known a few guys Saville's size that are even faster and stronger than I am."

"Lycanthropes?" Hermes asked.

"Yeah," I said.

"I'd like to see what one of your guys would do on the obstacle course," he said.

"And the weight room," Saville said.

I grinned. "You'd need specialty bars in the weight room for them to max out."

"You mean like the bars made for power lifters, so they don't bend the steel?" Jung asked.

"Something like that."

Jung was still the only green-eyed Asian American that I'd ever met, but now I knew that he was a Korean/Chinese/Dutch American whose grandparents had met during the Korean War, and his mother had married a Chinese American man whose family had been in the country generations longer.

The radios in our ears came to life, and it was Hudson. "Crypt door just opened, but one of the hostages is tied up in it."

I touched my mic. "Say again."

"Strung up in the doorway," Hudson said.

"Shit," I whispered, but it carried over the earpieces.

"We need a new entry plan," Hill said.

"Sutton and I will regroup."

"Can't kick, ram, or explode a hostage to get inside," Jung said.

"Which hostage?" I asked.

"Woman."

My stomach tightened at the thought of Connie strung up in the doorway of the crypt like an animal for slaughter. "Any sign of other hostages?" I asked.

"Negative," Hudson said.

Sutton said, "Sorry, Blake."

"Don't be sorry yet, Sutton. We get them out, no sorry needed."

"I hear that."

"We'll get them out," Killian said.

"Cheerful is good," Hermes said, "but we have to get past the door to get them out."

"We have to get through one hostage to get inside," Saville said.

"We don't go through Connie," I said.

"Hostage, just hostage. Names cloud the issue, you know that," Monty said.

I wanted to protest, but . . . "Fine, we don't go through the hostage like she's a fucking door."

"We do what works best to save the most lives," Hill said.

I shook my head. "Not good enough."

"It's all we got, Blake," Saville said.

"Define 'go through the hostage,'" I said, and glared at Saville.

"You're too close to this," Hill said.

"I know."

"Don't let your emotions compromise the rest of us," Monty said.

I nodded. "I won't get you guys hurt trying to save them."

"It's our job to risk ourselves to save the hostages," Jung said.

"Monty knows what I mean."

"We need an idea for entry," Hill said.

"I need to see it," I said.

"See what?"

"The door, Connie, I mean the hostage."

"Seeing it won't make it easier," Saville said.

"I need to see how she's tied up in the doorway, Saville." I hit the button on my throat mic. "Sutton, is it just her hands tied, or hands and feet?"

"Wrists tied over her head to something inside the room."

"Is she in the doorway, or just inside the door?"

"Inside, but she still blocks the entrance."

"I need to see," I said, and pushed away from the side of the truck.

Several of them pushed away to stand around me. It was Hill who said, "You wait for Hudson and Sutton to regroup."

"I am, I just want Sutton and his high-tech gadgets to help me see into the crypt."

"We can't see through solid stone, not even with infrared," Jung said.

"Connie, the hostage, is five-nine, but she's slender like her dad. Her body may block us from rushing through the entrance, but we should be able to see around her with infrared and night vision."

Hill asked on his radio, "Sarge, could you see into the crypt?"

"Not from the top of the hill."

"Find Sutton and me someplace low, so we can look past the hostage's legs."

"What have you got in mind?" Hermes asked.

"Let Sutton and me see into the room, place the hostages. You guys find cover that allows you to get close enough."

"Close enough for what?"

"Dynamic entry."

"You got mad at me for saying we go through the hostage," Saville said.

"I didn't get mad, I got scared for her, but me afraid doesn't help."

"And so just like that you're not afraid anymore?" he asked.

"Hostage needs me to think more than she needs me to feel, right now." The hard, cold pit of my stomach didn't believe me, but my head was trying, and that was all I could do.

I heard Sutton and Hudson before they stepped into view. I watched the other guys and no one looked toward the small sounds of them moving in the grass, a pants leg brushing something taller and more dried than the spring grass, their boots swooshing through. If Nicky or any of the other lycanthropes had been with me, they'd have heard it even sooner than I had, but for once our prey wasn't someone who had super-hearing, or sense of smell, or vision, or anything. He could raise the dead and capture souls. Neither of those would help him see, smell, or hear us moving around in the dark.

The two of them looked at us, and Hudson said, "Tell me."

I told him. It wasn't a great plan. It wasn't a perfect plan. But sometimes you don't need perfect, just good enough. Good enough for everyone to survive. Well, everyone but Maximiliano. Him, he could die; it would save me having to execute him later.

64

SUTTON AND I managed to find a place out among the graves as directly in line with the doorway as possible and still keep hidden. Being on the ground meant we had to be closer to the target than if we'd been up on the hill. Higher up almost always gave you a better unobstructed view, but this once we were hoping lower down was better. We snugged down on top of one of the graves with its tombstone at our feet, and another taller one of a different grave to one side of Sutton and his M24. We'd had trouble finding a space between the graves where Sutton could stretch out flat on his stomach. He was so damn tall, and just a very big guy; he almost didn't fit between the older graves. I had no trouble finding room to lie flat on the cool ground, with its early-season grass and wildflowers here and there. Sutton used the edge of the gravestone to steady his rifle so he could see past the figure hanging in the doorway. I tried very hard to think of it as just a hostage, but seeing the tall, slender woman hanging by her wrists in the doorway, her dark hair spilling down her back while she struggled and pulled at the ropes, hurt me in ways I had no words for.

"Talk to us, Sutton," I whispered.

"Tall figure standing near middle of room; second figure lying down on stone structure in center of room, seems to be struggling, maybe tied down; third figure slumped in far right corner, no movement."

My gut tightened again at that slumped third hostage with no movement. Was it Tomas? Were we going to be too late for Manny's son? I pushed the thought away, because it didn't help anything right now. Tomas and Connie and even Max's fiancée needed me thinking, planning, helping to get them out. I held on to the thought that they needed me to do my job. They needed me to help SWAT do theirs. It was true, and I'd keep on doing all that, until we either saved them . . . until we saved them.

"Do you have a shot at the standing figure?" I asked. Was I a hundred percent sure that one was our bad guy? No, but it was my best guess, and sometimes that's all you got.

"Negative."

"Shit," I said, softly. I prayed that they would be okay. I prayed that this would work and no one else would get hurt, not because prayer was the only thing I could do, but because prayer never hurts, and if you can get God to help, why not?

I saw the other team members moving up through the graves on the side of the crypt. It was good to be hunting a human for once, because he wouldn't be better than the men with me. If you had to go into danger with just humans, these were good men. Maximiliano was not a good man, not in any way. Was that judgmental of me? Yes, and I was okay with that.

I felt magic on the air, a rush against my skin. "He's casting," I said.

"Casting what?" Sutton asked.

"Magic."

"Talk to me, Blake," Hudson whispered.

I heard screaming, muffled through a gag, but it carried on the soft night air surprisingly well. The woman in the doorway started screaming, too, and struggling harder, so that she spun her body around, and I could see her face for the first time.

"It's not Connie," I said.

"What?" Sutton asked.

"It's not Connie Rodriguez."

"Who is it then?"

"I think it's the zombie from some of the films."

"Doesn't look like a zombie," Sutton said, eye still snugged to his eyepiece.

I used his extra eyepiece to look closer at the struggling woman in the doorway. "It's the zombie. I saw her on film."

The magic tightened around me, so that it was hard to breathe past it, as if the air were getting heavier. "The spell, whatever it is, is almost complete, and when he finishes he will kill her."

Connie and the zombie were both screaming, because one was alive and wanted to stay that way, and the other one didn't know she was already dead.

"Knife, he's got a knife," Sutton said into his mic.

The other men were still doing the plan, working their way carefully up through the graves, because if the bad guy knew they were coming he could shoot them all before our team made entry.

"He's going to kill the hostage," I said.

Hudson said, "Sutton, do you have a shot?"

"Negative."

"Shoot through the zombie. Greenlight his ass," I said.

"I can't shoot through a hostage."

"Zombies aren't hostages."

"Sutton, Blake—give me eyes," Hudson said.

"Zombie," I said.

"Hostage," Sutton said.

The women were screaming. The magic was squeezing the world down; something big was coming. I didn't know if it was the loa coming to ride Max, or something else, and I didn't care; as long as I shot him before he finished, it didn't matter.

I moved to the other side of the tombstone from Sutton and used the stone to steady my rifle. I hit my throat mic and said, "I have the shot. Repeat, I have the shot."

"He's going to kill her," Sutton said. He still had a shot, because he could still see past the zombie's struggles to what the perp was doing.

"Greenlight, repeat, greenlight," Hudson said.

I used the skills that Ares had taught me, the ones that had let me shoot him from the doors of a still-moving helicopter and do the last thing he ever asked of me, to kill him before he hurt someone. I knew the woman hanging there was a zombie; she was just like Thomas Warrington. It only looked alive. I prayed with the breath I drew in to steady myself, "Let me be right," and I squeezed the trigger from that well of silence where I went when I shot, where there was nothing but the gun, my hands, my body, the target. It became not a person, but just the place you needed your bullet to go. Especially from these distances you don't think you're going to kill them, or shoot them; you think only be still, don't breathe, control your pulse. Even your heart slows, as you pull the trigger, and let it happen. The hardest things to overcome are, don't flinch, don't pull, don't anticipate that a small explosion is going to go off in your hands, because that's what it is really; just be in that moment when the world narrows down to the dot of your laser sight going on the woman's dress, but the target is behind her with its arm upraised and what you think is a knife coming down . . . and . . . the recoil of the rifle rocked against the snug of my shoulder, the firmness of my hands.

The body in the doorway moved, the target on the other side fell out of sight, the magic paused, like a giant had taken a breath. "Target down," Sutton said.

I saw the other team members enter the building. They didn't use flashbangs as planned, because they didn't need to; the target was down, no need to stun the hostages. Sutton and I put our rifles to our shoulders and moved at that jog-trot that was still strangely smooth. I fell in beside him and just to one side, so that we stacked, even though it was just the two of us, and we went to join our team.

Gunfire ahead of us; there was still something to shoot in the crypt, or to shoot back. We ran like we'd been taught, not as fast as we could have run, but as fast as training had taught us we could keep our rifles to our shoulders, ready to aim, and keep moving.

65

THEY WERE DRAGGING Max out in cuffs. He was leaving a trail of blood. The moment they put him on the grass it started to pool underneath him. I knew one hole was mine, but he was bleeding in places I hadn't shot him. The hostage from the doorway was on the grass with Saville, but there was no blood pooling under her. Max looked like so much bloody meat; she looked like an anatomy illustration, clean and bloodless. The dead don't bleed like the living.

I heard Connie screaming, "Tomas! Tomas!"

My stomach tightened and fell into my feet. Please, God. Sutton was stopped at the door to the crypt, too big to get through the other men, but I was smaller, and fuck protocol, I had to see why Connie was screaming her brother's name.

I yelled, "Make a hole!" and pushed between the men without waiting. They didn't so much make a hole, as I could fit through where the bigger guys couldn't. Sometimes small isn't a bad thing.

Connie was kneeling over Tomas's body in the corner, where it had been motionless through the scope. They were trying to pull her off him, so they could do what they could until the ambulance got here. I could hear sirens coming closer. Tomas was pale, eyes closed, face slack. His face looked more like the pictures I'd seen of Manny from high school than the last time I'd seen the kid. His upper body fell boneless against the stone floor as they pulled Connie off him.

I heard Hudson say, "Let us help him, Ms. Rodriguez."

I yelled, "Connie, Connie, it's Anita!" I took off the helmet and pulled the balaclava off so she could see my face.

She turned and looked up at me. "Anita! Oh God, Anita!" She got to her feet then and did what the men hadn't been able to force her to do, gave them room to do their best for Tomas.

Hudson motioned, and I did what he wanted, taking her outside so there'd be more room to work, and so if he died she wouldn't have to see it happen. Please, God, let me have saved them in time.

Of course, outside had other problems. The zombie I'd shot was shrieking. She seemed upset at the huge gaping hole in her side. There wasn't much blood, so her shattered ribs were very white in the dark, and her lungs were still moving in her exposed chest.

Connie yelled, "Estrella!"

I turned her away from the two team guys trying to figure out what to do for a wound that big that really wasn't bleeding much, and a victim with a hole in her that should have been fatal, or at least made struggling and screaming not possible. They'd hunted enough vampires with me that they knew she wasn't human now, but she still seemed like an attractive young woman who just wasn't quite human. If she'd been a vampire they'd have done first aid, so they were trying.

Turning Connie away from the zombie meant she could see Max where he lay bleeding out on the grass with Hill and Montague standing over him. Connie ran at him, yelling profanities that I was betting Rosita didn't know she knew. I couldn't blame Connie, but I caught her arm anyway and tried to turn her away. She fought me the way she'd fought the men in the crypt, and for someone without training she was pretty good. Maybe I'd give her some self-defense pointers after we all survived the night. I finally picked her up around the waist, having to bow my back a little, because she was inches taller than me.

She was screaming wordlessly, in between threatening to kill Max, and she was seriously trying to get away and get to him. I wasn't a hundred percent sure she wouldn't try to kill him when she got there, so I held on. It would be a bitch to save her life and have her spend the rest of it in prison for being the one that struck the final blow on Max's ass. At least she didn't kick.

The ambulance came down the gravel road in full lights and sirens. The paramedics spilled out and started to go for Max, but the guys waved them off and pointed to the crypt. I thought the paramedics might argue, but in the end they went in to see what SWAT wanted them to triage first. It actually wasn't a good sign that they brought Tomas out first on the gurney, with all the damage visible on the grass out front. It meant he was hurt enough that they chose him over Max, who was lying in a pool of blood almost bigger than his body, and a "woman" whose side was blown open.

I put Connie down and let her run to Tomas. They didn't argue with her getting in the ambulance with the one paramedic and the stretcher, though there'd be precious little room for her in the back. I was left to call Manny and tell him what hospital they were headed to, and then the ambulance was off in a spill of gravel, lights decorating the night, sirens leaving the night quieter than it actually was just by getting farther away.

Manny thanked me, and it was all I could do not to say, don't thank me yet, thank me after your son wakes up, but I knew better than that. I took his gratitude and turned back to the two problems lying on the grass among the graves—Max and the zombie. Connie had said her name was Estrella. It was Spanish for star. Jesus.

She was still screaming, and I guess I couldn't blame her. We'd need to find the jar, or whatever had been used to hold her soul, but if it was in her body now, would destroying the bottle free her soul? Would she end up like Warrington, put back in the ground, but alive and aware down there? I didn't know. I just didn't know enough about what he'd done to her, but I knew how to find out.

I walked toward Max where he lay in a dark pool of his own blood. If he could still talk, he'd tell me everything I wanted to know, because a warrant of execution meant I could kill him any way I wanted to do it. If I chose carefully, it could hurt a lot before that last moment. People tell you all sorts of things if you scare them enough, and pain scares most people.

Sutton was in front of me like a black wall, because I was staring at about his upper stomach. Why were so many men on special teams, police or military, so damn big? "Hudson called an ambulance, Blake."

"She's a zombie and he's a dead man walking," I said.

"You don't have a warrant of execution, Blake."

I stopped trying to walk around him. I couldn't remember the last time I'd shot someone and hadn't had a warrant for their death. It meant that I had almost carte blanche on what I did to him, or how I did it.

"We need him to tell us how to set her soul free before the ambulance gets here, Sutton. He's bleeding out, scared, and in pain; this is our best chance to get him to tell me how to free her so she won't be scared anymore."

"I couldn't have taken the shot tonight, Blake. I couldn't have shot her."

"I knew she was already dead, Sutton. I'd seen her picture as a zombie, you hadn't."

"He was going to put that knife in Connie Rodriguez's heart and I would have hesitated, because I didn't want to shoot a zombie."

"Lucky you had me to take the shot," I said.

"Hudson greenlighted you, but you still didn't have a warrant of execution. You'll be seeing Internal Affairs on this one, Blake, and you won't have the warrant to keep them off your back."

"Whoever shot him inside the crypt will be seeing them, too. What's good for the gander is good for the goose. Are you delaying me from questioning Max over there for a reason?"

"You can't lay a hand on him, not a fingertip, nothing. You've never had to do this without the warrant absolving you of damn everything. I need you to remember that before we walk over there."

I took in a deep breath, let it out slow, and nodded. "Thanks for the reminder, Sutton."

"You took the shot I couldn't. Next time you tell me someone is already dead, I'll believe you."

"If we get this son of a bitch off the streets, we may not have to debate zombies again." To myself, I thought, unless it's one of my zombies, but if it's one of mine, then I'll take care of it myself. I really hoped I never raised another one as "real" as Warrington. No more cows as blood sacrifices.

We went to stand with Montague and Hill over the handcuffed bad guy. I stayed up on my tac boots and didn't kneel down in the blood, but I stood in the pool of it so I could be sure Max could see my face. He was lying on his stomach and in obvious pain, so he might not be tracking well.

"Hello, Max, nice to meet face-to-face, isn't it?" I smiled when I said it.

He looked at me, and the hatred on his face . . . if he could have done instant magic something very bad would have happened to me right then. But he couldn't, and vaguely I realized there'd been verve drawn in chalk all over the inside of the crypt. I just hadn't realized I'd seen it, until that moment. I'd been too focused on Manny's family to worry about details.

"Anita Blake, at least you didn't get to shoot me yourself."

I smiled wider. "The first bullet was mine, Max."

"Liar, their sniper took me."

"The sniper didn't believe that Estrella was a zombie, they wouldn't take the shot. You almost got to kill Manny's daughter, your half-sister, but I stopped you."

"He'll still lose a son tonight."

"Tomas is on his way to a hospital. He'll be fine." No, I didn't know that was true yet, but I hoped it was, and it would upset Max. I wanted him upset. "Now, if you mean Manny will lose you tonight, I'm all for that."

"They called an ambulance, because you missed your shot."

"She didn't miss her shot," Sutton said from where he towered over us.

Max craned his neck to look at him. It looked awkward and painful for him; good. "She took you through the side, under the arm, your heart should be gone."

"She missed."

"Blake didn't miss, and neither did I," Hudson said coming up behind us. "He was trying to bring his gun up and shoot the boy when we got inside the crypt. His one arm isn't working too good, or he'd have done it. I shot him twice in the chest so I didn't risk hitting the boy. I wonder what would happen if he got shot in the head?"

"You don't have a warrant of execution, so you've lost your chance to shoot me in the head."

"Oh, Max, you should know that when it comes to people using magic to kill people, I'll get another chance at blowing your head off. But if you tell us how to free Estrella's soul, to give her peace, maybe they won't give me a warrant for you. Judges still don't like putting out execution warrants on humans."

"I want her afraid. I want her to know what is happening to her."

"She doesn't believe she's a zombie, Max. She doesn't really know what's happening to her, does she?"

"Maximiliano," he said.

"What?" Hudson asked.

"My name is Maximiliano." He wasn't having any trouble breathing, though he had three bullet holes in his chest.

"Okay, Maximiliano, I'll play," I said. "How do we free her soul?"

"You'll never find what contains her soul, and even if you do, you won't know how to free her."

"Tell me."

"No."

"We can just sit here and watch you bleed out," I said. Actually, technically, police weren't allowed to do that. They could triage the victims over the perpetrators, but they had to give medical aid where needed. Ironically, if the first bullet killed the bad guy, then it was done, but if you just wounded him you could go from trying to kill him, to having to try to save his life. Sometimes the rules for regular cops were just too confusing for me.

"I'll still be alive when the ambulance gets here," he said.

I hunkered in a little closer to him, my boots in his blood. The last time I'd seen another animator that could heal like a zombie, or a vampire, he'd had a spell helping him. "What have you done to yourself, Maximiliano? Am I going to find a gris-gris on you somewhere?"

His eyes widened just a touch, his shoulders reacting to it.

"What's a gris-gris?" Hudson asked.

"It'll be something he wears, so probably a bracelet, or armband. It'll never come off, because it needs to touch his skin at all times to work, doesn't it, Maximiliano?"

He was watching me now, and not nearly as happy with himself.

"It's a spell, and it's what let him take three bullets to the chest and keep on ticking. But they'll cut your clothes and jewelry off at the emergency room, so they can treat your wounds. What happens when they cut the gris-gris off, Max?"

"Maximiliano, and you will stop them from cutting it off of me, because you know it is keeping me alive. It would be the same as shooting me in the head now that I am handcuffed and no longer a danger to anyone."

He was right, unfortunately, but I still didn't hear the second ambulance so we had time to play with him. If I played well enough maybe he'd help us stop the zombie that was sobbing behind us.

I drew one of the smaller silver-edged blades from a wrist sheath.

"What are you going to do, Blake?" Hudson asked.

"Search him for magic. If he has a gris-gris to help heal himself, he could have other things on him that could harm us."

"We patted him down," Hill said.

"Magic can hide better than a gun," I said. I moved closer to him, and he started struggling so that Hill and Montague had to kneel down and hold him for me. Sutton finally knelt on his legs, because Max didn't want me near him with the knife. There had to be more than just the gris-gris for him to be this upset, or there had to be something about the gris-gris that he didn't want me to see. Either way, I was going to search him for dangerous magical objects, and I was going to make it thorough.

"Hold him still, boys, I wouldn't want to cut him by accident." I started at the shoulder of his shirt, along the seam. I wanted his sleeves off first. I kept my blades sharp; it didn't take much to slice through the seams and start peeling down the cloth to expose the smooth skin of his arms. He kept trying to move, but he had three large men sitting on him who knew how to subdue and hold someone. His right arm was clean, no jewelry at all.

I duck walked to his left side and he tried to struggle harder. They leaned on him more, forcing his face down into the pool of his own blood. He was afraid now. Why? I couldn't cut it off him now that we all knew it was helping keep him alive; he was right about that. It would take weeks or longer of court hearings to get permission to take the gris-gris off him, and by that time his body would have healed enough that he might not die when it was removed, unfortunately. But he knew that, so why was he afraid? Was there something else on him that he didn't want us to see?

I peeled his left sleeve down and there it was on his upper arm, snugged in tight so it dimpled his flesh. "That's a gris-gris. They don't have to be armbands. A lot of them are small bags on a cord, but for magic that keeps you this alive when you're this hurt, you'll want it attached to you."

I put up my knife and started to fish for the small flashlight I kept in one of the many pockets on the tac pants. Most of them held extra ammo, but not all of them. Hudson figured out what I was doing and hunkered down beside me with his own flashlight.

It was a band made of black hair woven together. I looked at his short black hair. It wasn't long enough to do this. Then the light picked up a strand of blond hair, and paler brown, and another shade of brown, and another blond. I touched Hudson's wrist and used it to move the light. There was hair to match every zombie I'd seen on the videos.

"You son of a bitch," I said.

"What is it, Blake?" Sutton asked.

"The smaller pieces of hair woven around the main band match all the zombies on the sex tapes. DNA will double-check that it belongs to all his victims, but the main hair is going to be Estrella's, isn't it, you fucking son of a bitch?"

He was quiet now.

"Not so chatty now, are you, Max?"

"I am Maximiliano," he said, though his voice was strained, because Hill was forcing his face down into the grass and blood.

"I don't care if you're Mother Teresa, you are going to die for this."

"I took hair from them, that doesn't prove I killed anyone."

"The hair doesn't, but a few voodoo expert witnesses, and all the practitioners of your faith will tell the truth, Max. They won't want to be anywhere near this kind of soul debt to the loa, or whatever else you invoked to do this piece of evil shit."

"Tell us what you see, Blake," Hudson said.

"He didn't tell us we wouldn't find the bottle that held Estrella's soul. He said I'd never find what contains her soul, and if I did, I wouldn't know how to free her."

"What's the significance?" Hill asked.

"Yeah, I don't understand," Montague said.

"He's the bottle."

"What?" Montague asked.

"He's tied Estrella's soul to that gris-gris and him."

"That's not possible," Maximiliano said. "Everyone will tell you it's not possible."

"They will, but you figured it out anyway, didn't you, you evil piece of shit?"

"You'll never prove it, and you'll never get anyone to be able to explain the spell to a jury, or a judge."

"We'll find someone," Hudson said.

"It's an original spell," I said. "Like his mother before him, he's real creative when it comes to evil."

He gave a small smile. Hill pressed a knee harder into his shoulders, leaning more into the neck and head to grind him into the bloody grass. "Don't smile," Hudson said.

"He's used soul magic, which isn't even supposed to work, to trap Estrella and use her soul, her being a zombie, to give him some of the same ability to take damage, but he'll heal, unlike her."

"You mean she's stuck like that, with a hole in her side?" Sutton asked.

"Zombies can't heal injuries, so if we can't free her soul, yeah."

Max smiled again. Hill ground more weight into holding him down. Max finally made a noise that sounded like pain, so he could still feel it; good.

He spoke between gritted teeth. "I did not expect someone to shoot a hole in her."

"You shouldn't have used her as a shield then," I said.

I could hear sirens now; the ambulance was on its way.

"What can we do for her then?" Hill asked.

"I hope that sunup steals her mind away, and she's only afraid at night."

"Her soul doesn't vanish with the sunrise," he said, voice still strained.

All the men leaned harder on him, grinding him into the ground and making him bleed faster, but it wouldn't kill him. Until we either removed the gris-gris, or found a way to destroy Estrella's zombie, he might not be able to die. Why is it that the really evil bastards are so fucking afraid of death? Cowards, such cowards.

It was two ambulances, and we had to let the paramedics take him, and her, though once they found out she was a zombie they seemed at a loss. One EMT asked me, "Can we sedate a zombie? Can we make her comfortable?"

"I don't know."

Then I realized that I'd been stupid, so caught up in the monstrous parts of what talent with the dead could do that I'd forgotten there might be better uses for my gifts. I went over to the zombie where she was strapped to the gurney, still whimpering and saying it hurt. I doubted it really hurt, but it could have been like phantom limb pain in an amputee. Some of them can feel pain in their missing parts for years afterward. Estrella expected the wound to hurt, so it did, and it certainly was scaring the hell out of her. If I'd known I couldn't free her soul tonight, I'd have still shot through her to save Connie, but I would have regretted it beforehand a bit more.

She looked up at me with wide, dark eyes. I took her hand in mine and aimed my necromancy at her. I thought, *Be calm, don't be afraid*. I whispered it to her, and watched her face lose some of the terror, felt her body relax.

Max yelled, "What are you doing, Anita?"

I ignored him, but Estrella jumped, flinching and whimpering. She knew his voice all right, and it meant bad things. "He can't hurt you anymore, Estrella. You're safe." That was both true and a lie, but it filled her eyes with calm again. It helped her relax.

"She's mine! Her soul is mine! Mine!"

I smiled down at the pretty face, the calm zombie that didn't know it was dead. She smiled back. "You're safe. Calm."

"I'm safe, calm," she repeated.

I patted her hand and put it on top of the blanket they'd strapped over her, as they moved her toward the ambulance. I went to talk to Max before they loaded him. We were going to accompany that ambulance, because when Hudson had asked me if Max might be able to use his magic to escape from the ambulance, or hospital, I honestly couldn't say yes or no. He'd already done a piece of magic that should have been impossible, so all bets were off.

"What did you do to her?" he asked, straining against the straps that held him down and the handcuffs on both wrists.

"I helped her be less afraid."

"I want her afraid. I want her to remember that she only has herself to blame for this."

"Why, because she dumped your ass? Stalker much, Max?"

"Maximiliano, and she's mine, Anita, mine! You keep your magic off of her!"

"She listens to me, to my necromancy, when you've got a piece of her soul trapped in you, and you still can't keep me from controlling her."

"I stopped you over the computer."

"Yeah, because you could touch the zombie and I couldn't, but now I can touch her and you can't. I'm betting I can control her, even if you don't want me to. I'll keep her calm and unafraid while we get a judge to sign off on removing the gris-gris so we can free her soul, because trafficking in human parts, even souls, is a felony. Did you know that?"

"How do you prove I have her soul?"

"I don't have to, someone tried to sell their soul on eBay a few years back and a judge ruled that a soul is the same as any human organ. It's a felony to sell pieces of ourselves."

"Fine, take it, it still won't prove that I did anything to earn an execution, and by the time you get through all the hearings to remove the gris-gris I'll have healed. It will be years in court before you can prove anything. Magic is so hard to explain to a jury, and I'll get to tell them what a bastard my father is, and how he abandoned me. His wife isn't going to like knowing that he had a bastard child with Dominga Salvador."

Max was right about that.

"Juries love videos, Maximiliano. The sex slavery angle will make them hate you. By the time they see it all, they will be thinking there but for the grace of God go I, or my sister, my daughter, my wife, my child. They'll put the needle in your arm themselves by the time we're done with you."

"A good lawyer will make sure those videos never see a jury, Anita. They are too prejudicial, and would bias the jury against me. If convicted it would be magical malfeasance, which means my execution would be swift. They won't take the chance of getting the verdict overthrown after I'm dead—that doesn't look good on a judge's record."

"What was your major in college again, Maximiliano?"

"Prelaw."

"Of course it was." I smiled at him.

He didn't like the smile.

"But, Max, all I have to do is get a court order to remove all dangerous magical items from you. I can honestly say that I don't know exactly what the gris-gris does. I mean, after all I don't do voodoo, not really. If we cut it off tonight, I think three bullets in the chest will be enough that natural causes will do it for us."

"You'll never get a judge to sign off while I'm this hurt."

I leaned in and spoke low. "You're probably right, but I'm going to try anyway."

He smiled, smug and safe behind magic too complicated to explain to most judges and nothing quite hard enough to be called evidence. He should have been safe as they bundled him up into the ambulance and we got in the Bear Cat and followed him. I didn't want him safe. I didn't want Estrella to be trapped in her ruined body for weeks while we fought this out in court.

I found Manny and his whole family in the waiting room outside surgery. I was still dressed for SWAT, so it took Mercedes a second to recognize me. She looked like a slightly younger version of Connie. She got up and came to me, hugging me. "Thank you for rescuing them!"

Then Rosita was there, all five-ten of her with her wide shoulders and nearly square shape. Her hair was back in a bun at the nape of her neck, so she could still undo her hair and let Manny brush it out at night. It was one of the things they'd done since they married in their teens. She'd probably have been embarrassed that I knew that, but I liked knowing it. It was sweet to know they still loved each other like that, after so many years. Connie hugged me and started to cry, which she hadn't done at the cemetery. Manny hugged me last.

"How's Tomas?" I asked.

He took me off to one side of the room away from the women in his life. "He'll live, but they aren't sure how hurt he is, and after the . . . man shot him he stomped his leg, broke it badly."

I thought about Tomas being fast enough to make State, and good enough to be scouted for high schools in the area, and even some colleges. He could run like the wind, Manny had said. I was sad I hadn't gone to one of the track meets now. "Max needs to die, Manny."

A look as bleak as any I'd ever seen filled his eyes. "Didn't he kill those girls and raise them as zombies? That will earn him a warrant of execution."

"We can't prove he killed them, not easily."

"He will be a danger to my family and to you while he is alive."

"I know, and if he could die we'd have taken care of it tonight."

"What do you mean, if he could die?"

I weighed the rules against sharing ongoing investigations against getting Manny's voodoo expertise, and you know what I decided. He was my friend, and this man had already traumatized Manny's family. I told him what I knew.

"So he has to kill the women and take their souls, and their hair represents that, or is it just their deaths that feed the magic?" Manny asked.

"I don't know, you're better at voodoo than I am, you tell me."

"There is always one thing you must never do, or it breaks the magic of a gris-gris like this," he said.

"I know. The last time I encountered a gris-gris like this, one kind of blood fed it, and another kind of blood broke the spell. There was no blood on this one, only the hair woven around a leather band."

"Women's hair?"

"Yes."

"And he was going to use a knife on Connie, but he never used the blade on Tomas."

"Yeah." I frowned at him, not following his logic, but letting him think it out.

"I wonder if a man's hair would be enough to break the spell?"

"I don't understand."

"Wrap a man's hair around the band, not a woman's, or maybe just something that has a man's DNA on it."

"Maybe, but if we know that would break the spell and potentially kill him, we still can't do it legally. It would be the same as putting a bullet in his head tonight."

"I suppose so, but for later, once it's removed from him, you still have to break the spell to free the last zombie."

"Okay, so boy parts, like boy cooties," I said, smiling.

He didn't smile back. "They don't know if Tomas will ever walk right again, let alone run."

"I'm so sorry, Manny."

He nodded, looking as grim as I'd ever seen him. "You brought my children home alive. Connie will still be getting married and Tomas will be in the wedding even if we have to push him down the aisle in a wheelchair. We are all alive, Anita, thanks to you." He grasped my hand in his and then hugged me again. I hugged him back, and then the surgeon was there to tell them some good news. The bullet had been an abdominal wound, so he'd lost a lot of blood internally, but he was going to make it. The orthopedic surgeon thought he'd be able to set Tomas's leg, and with a lot of physical therapy and rehab he'd be able to walk. He was young and in good shape; there was even hope that he'd run again.

There was a lot of crying and hugging again, and I got to leave them on a good note. I visited Estrella's room then, and she was calm, peaceful, but still trapped aware. Maximiliano so needed to die for what he'd done to her, not to mention everything else.

"I'm not afraid anymore," the zombie told me. "Thank you."

"*De nada*," I said, and though it's Spanish for "you're welcome," it literally means, "of nothing." This time it was how I felt. I couldn't free her soul. I couldn't make her forget everything. I couldn't put her peacefully in her grave. All I could do was keep her calm and unafraid while we fought in court to free her from Max's slavery.

Her eyes grew wide, and she reached out. I took her hand without thinking, and I felt her "die." One minute she was in there and the next she was gone. What the hell?

My phone rang, and made me jump. "Blake here," I said.

"Where are you?" It was Hudson.

"In the zombie's room, Estrella's room. She just went . . . dead. She's gone. I don't know what happened."

"I just got a call from the hospital, Maximiliano is dead. He died of his wounds."

"He couldn't die of his wounds," I said.

"I know."

"Shit, I'll check it out."

"Make sure you have witnesses when you're with the body, Blake. You have a personal connection, don't give them room to blame you for this."

"I haven't done a damn thing."

"Just be cautious, that's all I'm saying."

"Fine, I'll keep a nurse or someone with me."

"Make sure you do." He hung up, and I went in search of our dead bad guy.

There was a nurse and a doctor with me. "One minute he was fine," Nurse O'Reily said. "I stepped out of the room for just a minute and then his monitors sounded and he was dead."

I put on a pair of surgical gloves. "I got a call that he'd died of his wounds, is that true?"

"He took three large-caliber rounds to the chest cavity, so yes, I'd say it's a safe bet that they'll list cause of death as gunshot," Dr. Pendleton said, frowning at me.

"I need to check one thing on him."

"What?" Pendleton asked.

"Magic," I said, and used my gloved hands to slip the sleeve of his hospital gown away from his left upper arm. I expected the gris-gris to be gone, but it was still there. Estrella's thick black hair was still woven tight around his arm. The colored hairs of his other victims were still there, too.

"It looks fine," I said.

"I read the notes, and you thought that was helping him heal the bullet wounds."

"Yes," I said.

"The notes said it wasn't to be removed under any circumstances, and none of us even touched it," Nurse O'Reily said.

"You'd have to cut it off, and it's whole," I said.

"Did it just stop working for him?" she asked.

"I honestly don't know, I'm not an expert on this type of charm."

"I always hate the paperwork when magic gets in my hospital," the doctor said.

"Magic complicates everything," the nurse said.

"It can," I said. I stripped off my gloves and started to put them in the wastebasket, and there on the floor was a longish white and gray hair. It was curly, and I was betting if I touched it, the texture would be coarse, because Manny's hair was coarse, and white and gray.

"Motherfucker," I whispered.

"Did you say something, Marshal?" the doctor asked.

I shook my head. "No, just muttering to myself." I left the room. I did not try to pick up the hair. Maybe it wasn't Manny's. I mean, there were lots of other people whose dark hair was going gray and white. It didn't have to be his, but he was the one who had said that maybe a man's hair would undo the magic. Had he come down here? I didn't know, and as I walked down the hospital corridor I decided I wasn't going to ask him. Estrella was free. Max couldn't hurt anyone else, ever again. Manny and his family, and me and mine, were safe from him, too. He wouldn't be sending killer zombies after me the way his mother had. Maximiliano was not a loss to humanity; in fact we might be a few points ahead with him dead. So why did it bother me that Manny might have crept down here and done it? Did he look down at his grown son and wonder about what might have been, if he'd known and been a father to this one, too? Or had he only seen the man who tried to kill two of his children, and may have crippled one?

Epilogue

BY THE TIME of Connie's wedding Tomas was on crutches, and able to walk himself down the aisle to stand with his new brother-in-law. Tomas spent most of the reception in the wheelchair Connie bullied him into, but everyone was alive and there for the wedding. That counted; that counted for a lot. No one came knocking on Manny's door to ask about Maximiliano's death. "It's magic; who knows why it stops working?" seemed to be the general consensus.

But since he died of complications from the bullet wounds I finally got a full-blown Internal Affairs review just like Sergeant Hudson, who had been the other shooter. I'm barred from working with SWAT here in St. Louis until I get cleared. I think if Estrella the zombie had been "alive" to talk to they would have been more upset with me, but zombies have no rights under the law, so she couldn't even be counted against me—legally. I'd seen these two IA detectives before and they weren't fans of my working with SWAT. It's made me value my fringe status with regular police procedures even more. Let's hear it for orders of execution and being fucking assassins with badges. It makes shooting people amazingly simpler.

I've started using smaller blood sacrifices for raising zombies, so I haven't gotten another one like Thomas Warrington, which is great. But even without a large blood sacrifice my zombies are getting better, more "alive." Until Warrington, and the zombies that Max made, I wasn't worried about my zombies being so good, but now I'm beginning to wonder what's happening with my powers. How lifelike are my zombies going to get? I don't have an answer, but I'm beginning to think I'm going to need one someday.

Asher is still on our shit list. Even Jean-Claude has abandoned his bed for a few weeks, so Asher is getting all the couple time with Kane that he wanted, or that Kane wanted. The werehyena is happy to be monogamous, but it's obvious this wasn't what Asher had in mind. He's chasing everyone he took for granted, even Dev, who I think is enjoying turning him down.

Dev is getting along well with everyone else in our group. In fact one of his serious pluses is how easygoing he is compared to Asher. Dev is still wanting to be the tiger we put a ring on, but we're seeing how the domestic bliss goes before committing. We're being cautious about adding the three women, as well, mainly because the first woman who ever entered my life, Jade, is throwing a fit. She is incredibly hurt and Domino is asking me to consider her feelings. I'm giving her feelings a little time, but not much longer. She's requested a chance to meet the other women and try to understand why I think they're a better idea than she is, and the fact that she doesn't understand why I want women who like men, too, proves one of Jade's great weaknesses. Anyone who's been around me intimately, even briefly, knows I'm probably never going to be a woman just for other women. As Fortune said one night at dinner, "You like dick too much to give it up."

The fact that Fortune, Echo, and Magda could all understand that without sleeping with any of us, and Jade can't after over two years of being in my bed, says a lot about why Jade isn't making much progress in therapy. You have to be honest in therapy, with your counselor and with yourself. I know Jade isn't being honest with herself, which probably means her therapist isn't faring much better.

So, we still have no tiger for the commitment ceremony, though I've accepted that Cynric, Sin, is part of our domestic arrangement. Jean-Claude sees him more as a beloved nephew so he doesn't want to "marry" him in a group, which is fair, so unless Dev works out we are back to not knowing who to choose. I think we're all still hoping that Fortune may help in that area, but Jade stands in the way of that happy experiment. I'm about ready to throw both Domino and Jade off my dating list, because honestly they're both too high maintenance for too little return for me. I'd pretty much broken up with Domino as anything but food anyway. Jade may not even be food for the *ardeur* if she keeps hitting all the wrong relationship buttons with me. Hell, if she could only see that I hit the wrong buttons for her, too. Whatever love means to both of us, it's not the same thing, and I don't think that's fixable. I think it just is.

Narcissus is back with his hyenas for now, but he's screwed the pooch with most of them, and there is talk of a palace coup. Jean-Claude has let it be known that we won't interfere in the power shakeup, if it goes that way. Narcissus is trying to win back his people's loyalty, because he finally understands that a king without followers is not a king.

Dev is still able to transform into a lion and his golden tiger. Micah is still black tiger and leopard. I know now that Micah needs that extra power display to help him avoid the worst of the out-of-town battles. I worry about him more now. He seems able to call flesh and heal tigers, as well as leopards, now. It doesn't seem to matter what kind of tiger it is, so we're all wondering if more new tiger forms will come. Since clan tiger is a "born" type of lycanthrope and not a contagious form, it's raised a lot of metaphysical questions. So far we have more questions than answers, but the weretigers are researching that prophecy of theirs for clues.

Dev has joined Nicky with the werelions and he's formed a very friendly coalition with him and Travis. Dev is perfectly willing for Travis to continue to be the emotionally intelligent one of the three of them; as he said, "If I was brilliant with interpersonal stuff I wouldn't have loved Asher." He might have a point.

We're still working on the wedding band designs for Jean-Claude and me, but we've moved on to wedding dresses and bridesmaid dresses, and tuxes for the men. How many people are standing up with us? Asher was going to be Jean-Claude's best man, but now he's got to earn that privilege back. Jean-Claude wants a spectacular designer wedding dress for me. I just want one I can actually dance in at the reception without being a hazard to the other dancers. I am not doing a hoop skirt.

The designs for the crowns are actually coming along faster than the rings. I tried to protest them again, but Jean-Claude said, "You are queen to my king."

"I thought I was your general."

"That, too, and if you wish I can have a uniform tailored for you and you can play general to my oh-so-grateful nobleman."

I told him I didn't need a uniform, but thanks.

"I've never had a woman in uniform before," he said, and I watched the thought fill his eyes. Why do I think that when I get measurements for the wedding gown, there'll be plans for some uniforms, too? I don't really mind; after all, he dresses up for me.

Now you can buy any of these bestselling books
by Laurell K. Hamilton from your bookshop
or *direct from her publisher*.

FREE P&P AND UK DELIVERY
(Overseas and Ireland £3.50 per book)

Guilty Pleasures
The Laughing Corpse
Circus of the Damned
The Lunatic Cafe
Bloody Bones
The Killing Dance
Burnt Offerings
Blue Moon
Obsidian Butterfly
Narcissus in Chains
Cerulean Sins
Incubus Dreams
Micah *and* Strange Candy
Danse Macabre
The Harlequin
Blood Noir
Skin Trade
Bullet
Hit List
Kiss the Dead
Affliction
Jason
Dead Ice

TO ORDER SIMPLY CALL THIS NUMBER

01235 400 414

or visit our website: www.headline.co.uk
Prices and availability subject to change without notice.